THE AFFAIRS OF CHIP HARRISON
LAWRENCE BLOCK

Lawrence Block

The Affairs of Chip Harrison

NO EXIT PRESS

This edition published in 2001 by No Exit Press
18 Coleswood Rd, Harpenden, Herts. AL5 1EQ

www.noexit.co.uk

A CIP catalogue record for this book is
available from the British Library.

ISBN 1 8 4243 03 78

2 4 6 8 9 7 5 3 1

Book design and typography by Digital Typesetting
Printed by Omnia Books, Glasgow.

The Affairs of Chip Harrison

Contents

No Score

Chapter One

"I SHOULDN'T EVEN BE HERE," SHE SAID.

"Oh, you should," I said. I looked at her, and I got this very sudden, very tight feeling in my throat, as though I had done a very ungood job of swallowing something large. I swallowed again, and the tight feeling moved downward through my chest and stomach and down to the very pit of my stomach, where it settled and put down roots and applied for citizenship papers.

Now, you really must be cool, I told myself. Because she's here and so are you, and if you just Stay Cool and Play Your Cards Right everything will work out.

But the trouble with telling yourself things, I've discovered, is that the part of you that's being told is always dimly aware that the other part, the part that's doing the telling, is trying to *con* you, for Pete's sake. I mean, it's like staging a wrestling match between your two hands or trying to commit suicide by holding your breath. (If you try that, you eventually pass out and start right in breathing again. So I understand. I experimented once when I was about thirteen, but I got to thinking that maybe this was just a big story and you really could kill yourself that way if you were very strong-willed. And I decided that I was a pretty strong-willed person and was thus running a real risk, so what I did was go into this fake swoon and collapse gracefully on my bedroom rug. I was in my bedroom at the time, and all alone, so you might wonder why I didn't just start breathing more or less naturally instead of putting on an act. That would be a tough one to answer actually, but anyway none of this has very much to do with what was going on between me and Francine.)

What was going on between me and Francine was that we were in my room, not the bedroom where I held my breath and swooned but the room I was renting now, which was in an attic upstairs over a barbershop. Francine thought she shouldn't even be here, and I thought she should.

And I had this lump, or tightness really, in the pit of my stomach. Or, not to mince words, in my, well, groin.

"I should go home now," she said.

"You just got here."

"As soon as I finish this cigarette."

She took a puff on her cigarette and just let the smoke find its own way out of her mouth. She sat there on my bed with one hand on her lap and the other behind her on the bed and she let the smoke trickle out from between her lips, which were parted just enough to let this happen. The general effect was as though something was burning inside her. I could believe this.

I was on the bed next to her. That sounds sexier than it was. Because we were both sitting side by side on the edge of the bed, and we might as well have been sitting side by side on a bench, watching a basketball game, for Pete's sake. All it really was was uncomfortable.

Come on, I told myself. (Remember what I said about telling yourself things, about all the good it does.) Come on, *do* something. At least say something. Be masculine. Take the initiative. Act.

"You're beautiful," I said.

"Oh, come on."

"No, I really mean it. You are."

"Oh, sure," she said, but there was something going on in her eyes and around her mouth. She fluffed her hair with one hand. Her hair was the soft reddish brown of oak leaves just before they fall off the tree. I reached to touch her hair and she shook her head and I took my hand away. I did touch her hair more or less in passing. It was as soft as it looked.

She drew on the cigarette and let the smoke find its way to the ceiling again.

"That's easy to say, Chip," she said.

"No, I mean it."

"I'm sure you tell every girl."

"Well, how do you mean it?"

"Huh?"

She turned a little toward me, crossed one leg over the other (or perhaps it was the other way around). "Why do you say I'm beautiful?" she demanded. "I mean, what about me is that way?"

"Oh, well—"

"Just for the sake of conversation."

I gave a quick nod then, a reflexive gesture indicating that I had Gotten The Message. I remember reading somewhere that beautiful women are inclined to be very narcissistic, meaning that they are in love with themselves, and that the best way to have success with them is to let them know that you think they're every bit as great as they think they are. I read this in a book that told how to succeed with women, and that even gave little poetic lines to say to them at tender moments, but I had never bothered to commit any of the lines to memory because they struck me as fairly corny. Besides, it seemed to me that if the author was really such an expert at making out with women he would be too busy doing just that to waste his time writing books. Like the books that tell you how to make money at the racetrack, or how to turn a shoestring into a million dollars. If anybody could do those things, why bother writing a book? Why not just go ahead and do it?

"Your eyes," I said. Another book had suggested that every woman thinks her eyes are beautiful. "Brown eyes flecked with green, and so large, and so deep."

"Deep?"

"You think about things, Francine. You have deep and profound thoughts."

"That's very true."

"And it shows in your eyes."

"Honestly?"

"Honestly."

"So you like my eyes," she said, prompting.

And smiled a smile to let me know I was on the right track.

"And you have beautiful hands," I said.

"Do you think so?"

I reached out, trying not to let my own hand tremble, and I took hold of hers. She didn't draw away. This wasn't a pass, after all. It was part of the project of cataloguing Francine's charms. She made things easier by transferring her cigarette to her other hand, and I moved closer on the bed until I could feel the warmth of her body next to mine. We weren't exactly touching, but I could feel the warmth of her body.

I held her hand and told her how beautiful it was. As a matter of fact, it was a very fine hand, with just the right softness to it. The fingers were long and sensitive. There was just the finest tracing of soft downy hair on the back of the hand. And it had none of the faults that so many hands will have. It wasn't cold, it wasn't sweaty, it wasn't clammy. Of course, I didn't put things that way. I firmly believe in stressing the positive side of things. For the same reason I didn't mention the hand's one flaw, which was the nicotine stain between the first two fingers. I suppose I wouldn't have minded this if I smoked myself, but I didn't. I think it's a bad habit and I don't see any point in having bad habits. As a matter of fact, I do have one bad habit myself, but that stuff about it making you insane or blind is really a lot of nonsense, and anyway I've been doing my best to keep it to a rock-bottom minimum. And, of course, I intend to give it up as soon as I have a satisfactory substitute for it, which is what bringing Francine to my room was all about, actually, although from the way she had been acting you would have thought it was the furthest thing from her mind.

"And your hair," I said, reaching out to touch it. "And your tiny feminine feet, and your shapely legs—"

I went on like this. It was really pretty disgusting, when you come right down to it, but at the same time you have to realize that everything I said was the truth. Francine was so beautiful it could make your heart stop to look at her. A soft, beautiful, innocent face, and these gentle shoulders and slender arms, and her breasts—I still get weak in the knees just *thinking* about her breasts. You would think that breasts like those would be more at home on a heavier girl, but when your eyes moved down from those breasts (if in fact they did; mine often didn't, remaining there like two bees at two blossoms), you saw that the waist was very slim, and the hips just wide enough to be interesting, and the buttocks nicely rounded, and the legs as if they had stepped out of stocking ads. I could go on this way, but what's the point? Even if I pasted a photo of her right here, it wouldn't do it right, because all of us see things differently. So do this: Imagine an absolutely perfect girl (except for a nicotine stain between the first two fingers of the right hand, and a half-inch-long crescent-shaped scar on the inside of the left thigh) and you've imagined Francine.

I went on telling her this, leaving out those two flaws (only the first of which I knew about then) and wording my praise so that I came off more like an artist and less like a total sex maniac, and all the while I kept looking at her eyes, and the weirdest thing happened. She began to get hypnotized.

I don't know what else you could call it. She was nodding encouragingly in time to the rhythm of my words, and every now and then she would chime in with *Do you really think so*? or *Do you honestly mean it*? or just a little *Yes* and *Uh-huh* and *Oh* sounds and grunts, and it was as if she was completely caught up in the sound of my voice telling her how perfect she was. I was pressing her hand as I talked and she was giving me little rhythmic squeezes in return.

You've got her, I thought. Now hurry, before the spell wears off.

But I guess I was afraid to blow it. Things were going so well, see, and I didn't want to jeopardize my position. Because it seemed as though I had been waiting forever for this to happen, and if it didn't happen soon I didn't know

15

what I would do, except maybe go completely out of my head.

So I went on talking while the cigarette burned unattended between the fingers of her left hand—I was holding the right hand all the while. And very smoothly I went on talking and reached across and plucked the cigarette away and flipped it into the sink on the other side of the room. It was an easy shot because the other side of the room wasn't all that far away, the room being on the small side, but even so the whole maneuver was one of my smoother plays.

It encouraged me, and then, too, I realized that soon I was going to run out of parts of Francine to praise. So I got an arm around her and tipped up her face and kissed her.

At first it was like kissing—well, I was going to say a warm corpse, but that's really pretty revolting and it wasn't like that at all. Let's say it was like kissing someone who was asleep.

But then she started to wake up.

She kissed back, sort of tentatively, and I held her a little closer and kissed her a little more heavily, and she opened up like a flower. Her arms went around me and held me and her breasts pressed up against my chest and she sighed beautifully and her lips parted. There was a brief hissing sound as some drops from the leaky faucet put out her cigarette butt, and as the hissing died I let my tongue slip ever so gingerly past her lips and into the rich dark cave of her mouth.

She tasted of honey and tobacco and musk. She made the kiss a very urgent and hungry sort of experience, putting her own mouth into it and clutching my shoulders fiercely with her little hands.

First base, I thought.

I told myself to forget about the different bases, because that sort of thinking can be a trap. I had been to first base before, though not with Francine. I had been to second base a few times, and even to third base.

But, as you must have figured out by now, I had never been to home plate.

All right. Let's come right down and say it, let's put it down in black and white. I was a virgin.

What a stupid word.

I mean, it's a *girl's* word, right? Virgin, for Pete's sake. You really can't come up with a more feminine word than virgin. You hear a word like that and you picture a girl with flowers in her hair, wearing something with ruffles. But I don't know of any other word for it, so that one will have to do. I, Chip Harrison, was a seventeen-year-old virgin. I wasn't going to be seventeen forever. (Although there were times when it seemed that way.) And I wasn't going to be a virgin forever, either, if I could help it. (Although there were times, damn it, when it didn't seem as though I could help it.)

As a matter of fact, it sort of seemed to me that the two things, age and sex, were connected in some heavy way. That if I scored (which is to say got to home plate, which is to say stopped being a virgin) before I turned eighteen, then I won. Whereas if I didn't, I lost.

But the point of all this is that the business with the bases can be a snare and a delusion; or at least I have found this to be so, because they give you the feeling that you are making progress with the girl, in that each time you are with her you get a little closer to the goal line (wrong sport, sorry about that) and thus it seems to follow that sooner or later you will score. This is not necessarily true. And, in fact, it seems that the more you get into this kind of pattern with a girl, the better she gets at getting you to stop somewhere along the way. It isn't that you keep getting closer but that you keep not getting where you wanted to go, and all of this is not only frustrating (very) but it leaves her knowing that she can control you, and this is not a Good Thing in any sense.

Not that I am the World's Foremost Authority on all this. To be honest, some of this I got from the books on how to succeed with women, and some is just speculation on my part. But what it all boils down to is that the best way to do something is to do it, and the best way to Go All The Way with a girl is to just go ahead and do it. Not in stages but all at once.

Especially because, in this particular instance, I was not going to get another chance at Francine. Because she was two years older than I was, and practically engaged to some college jerk, and so it had been a case of wild luck that I had gotten her to my room at all. So the chances were very good that I would never see her again, which was too bad, but which was something I could live with If Only. If only I hit the first pitch completely out of the park and ran around the bases and crossed the plate before Francine realized what had happened. So we held the kiss, and she clung to me as tightly as her sweater clung to her, and my tongue went spelunking in her mouth, and her tongue met it and got acquainted with it. We kissed for a long time. Then we came up for air and looked deep into each other's eyes, and when her eyes went slightly glassy I kissed her again, and it was the same, only better.

When we broke this time she said, "Oh, Chip—"

"Francine—"

"I must go."

"Francine—"

"Please, I can't—"

"You're so beautiful," I said, desperately.

"Oh, Chip."

"I love to kiss you."

"Oh."

"So beautiful. A goddess."

"Oh, my God—"

I drew her to me. She resisted, but not in any really meaningful way. She sort of stiffened, and I drew her close and got my mouth fastened to hers again, and then she got into the spirit of things again, as if the token show of resistance made it all right for her to surrender now. And in the course of drawing her close, somehow or other my hand managed to get on top of her breast.

Around first base and streaking for second.

Getting the sweater off was an absolute stone bitch. It really was. I guess because there is no entirely natural way to pull a tight yellow sweater over a girl's head. You can't just make believe it's happening by itself. It's possible to sort of slide into a kiss, or let your hands accidentally settle on the more interesting parts of a girl, but sweater removal is just too damned obvious. Even if you're both all in favor of it, it's hard to pretend you don't know what's going on. Or coming off, I suppose.

I got the sweater out of the waistband of her skirt without too much trouble. But then I started to work one hand up under the front of the sweater, and she broke the kiss and put her hand on mine, and pushed.

"Please, Chip."

"Francine, you're so beautiful."

"Chip, I don't want you to do that."

"I think you have the most beautiful breasts in the world."

"I don't—you do?"

"Yes."

"You're just saying that. Chip—"

A kiss, but not a very successful one.

"You have a great line, Chip. My goodness, what a line you have."

"It's not a line."

"Oh, your hands just won't behave. Please don't do that."

"Francine, I want to look at you."

"Oh, come off it. I know what you want."

"I have to see you."

"Sure, you just have to see me."

"Your breasts are beautiful, Francine."

"You shouldn't talk like that. I hardly know you. I mean, after all—"

"Beautiful."

19

"Oh."

"Beautiful."

"If I thought I could trust you—"

"You can trust me, Francine."

"I mean if it wasn't so utterly physical—"

"You know it's more than that, Francine."

"I mean—"

"Francine—"

"Oh," she said, finally, and shrugged me away, and just as I was about to reach for her again and start the whole process over, she gave a little sigh and pulled the sweater up over her head. There was a moment when the yellow sweater covered her head completely while leaving her chest uncovered (except for the bra, of course) and that image imprinted itself on my memory. There was something really appropriate about it, the whole image of Francine with the best part of her right out in the open and her stupid mouth covered up. If I were an artist I would paint that scene. I think if it was painted right you could look at it and know everything you would ever need to know about Francine.

But she was only like this for a second, and then the sweater was off and the arms were extended and the lips parted and the eyes glazed, and it was at that very moment that I knew for certain that I could forget about bases and goal lines and all, that I could stop crawling around inside my own head and giving myself halftime pep talks, because it was all set and all arranged and all decided and it was all in the bag and Chip Harrison was going to stop being a virgin and start being a man.

I kissed her.

And we stretched out on the bed together.

Her skin was so soft. It's unbelievable how soft girls are. I got my hands around her and unhooked her bra, and although I am not the deftest person on earth it went well enough, and I eased it off over her shoulders and bared her breasts. And just as I was doing this our eyes caught, and I looked at her eyes and her mouth, the whole expression on her face, and she was pleased and amused and calm, and her eyes said that she knew what was happening and liked what was happening and that everything would work out just fine.

She was so beautiful.

I got completely involved in those breasts. I couldn't stop touching and kissing them. It wasn't a question of trying to do one thing and then another, of trying to get further and further with her, because it had already been established that we were going to do the whole thing and all that mattered now was to do it as well as possible. So instead of trying to put something over on her, I was trying to excite her as much as possible and to do things that I enjoyed, and it sure worked.

"Oh, Chip. That feels so nice—"

Her skin tasted of sugar and spice and secret girls smells. I liked her breasts like a little kid with an ice-cream cone, wanting to take a big bite but wanting to make it last as long as I could. I nibbled and gobbled and she made these wonderful heavy breathing sounds and started squirming on the bed underneath me.

"Take off your shirt, Chip. I want to feel you against me."

When I take off my shirt, you don't get reminded at once of Greek sculpture. I'm not a ninety-seven-pound weakling, but I'm not exactly Charles Atlas either. I'm sort of bony and undernourished in appearance. But I took the shirt off, and when I glanced at Francine's eyes, she didn't seem that disappointed with what I was unveiling. As a matter of fact, she looked hungry.

"Oh, Chip—"

I kissed her, and our tongues renewed their old friendship, and our chests pressed together. Mine got the better of the deal. Her nipples were as hard as little rosebuds and I brushed my upper body back and forth over them and she moaned and wiggled in response.

After a long time of kissing and touching and feeling,

after I had told her how beautiful her breasts were and how delicious her flesh tasted and felt, and after she had told me how wonderful I made her feel and how sweet I was and how much she cared for me, after all of that, she lay down and closed her eyes and raised her hips a little so that I could take her skirt off. It wasn't hard at all. I just opened the button and unzipped the zipper and pulled the skirt down and off—it was a green plaid skirt, for those of you who don't have color sets. And then it was off, and she was lying there in her panties, and I discovered the half-inch crescent-shaped scar on the inside of her thigh, and I didn't think of it as a fault at all. In fact, I didn't think that Francine had any faults. Only good points, and an abundance of them.

I ran my hands over her legs. Until that moment I don't think I ever realized just how important legs are. Girls' legs, I mean. How important it is that they be great-looking. I had always paid a lot of attention to faces and breasts and behinds, and I knew the difference between great-looking legs and lousy-looking legs, but I was never that excited about legs.

You live and you learn. Francine had great-looking legs, and all spread out like that, naked except for the panties, I was really able to see the whole girl. As an entity, I mean. And I realized the importance of the legs.

(I don't know if this is coming through very well. Call it an intuitive flash, a sudden burst of insight, which after all is how most great discoveries come about. The major breakthroughs never occur because someone sat down and thought things out. They come in flashes. Newton and the apple, for instance. Paul on the road to Damascus. Archimedes in the bathtub. Chip Harrison in bed with Francine.)

"Chip?"

Her eyes were closed, and if there was any expression on her face, I couldn't read it. She seemed very calm, completely relaxed, but I could see she was trembling inside.

"You can take them off."

I put my hands on her shoulders. I ran them very slowly down over her breasts and stomach and grazed her panties and went on all the way down those legs to her feet.

"My panties. You can take them off."

"Yes."

"You can...do anything."

"Yes."

"Anything you want to."

Her voice was different than it had ever been before, older and younger, both at once. Softer, mostly. And as if for the first time, I was hearing Francine speak without any phoniness in the way. I wanted to say something but I couldn't. My throat was blocked, knotted up.

I took off her pants. I took off her wispy nylon pants and squeezed them in a ball and held on to them with both hands. I wanted to nail them to the wall over the bed as a trophy. I wanted to sleep with them under my pillow. I wanted to chew them up and swallow them.

"Chip—"

I put the panties aside. I put my hands on her thighs and she opened them, parted her thighs, and I looked at her.

I could smell her.

I put out a hand, touched her. She was moist. I put my finger into her just a little ways and I felt her. She was all wet and hot and sticky.

And it came to me, all at once, that this was not just a dumb girl with a great body that I was going to ball. It came to me that she was far more than this. It came to me, as I crouched over her with my finger inside her, that I loved this girl. And that she was what I had been looking for, a beautiful, passionate woman whom I could love and honor and cherish forever.

But first, by God, I was going to ball her.

I played with her with both hands. I played with her, absolutely delighted with the way she was built and the way she felt and the effect it was all having on her. And she lay there, hips rolling so nicely, so sweetly, so gracefully, and she kept her eyes closed and her hands at her sides, and the words flowed in a stream.

"Oh Chip, it's so good, it's so good, I like it, I love it, it's so good. I'm so hot, I like it, I love it, Chip, it's so good—"

I fingered her with one hand and attacked my own clothes with the other. To do this properly probably takes great skill and coordination, like rubbing your tummy while you pat your head. I tugged on my belt to unhook it and I pulled so hard I very nearly strangled myself at the waist. But I did get my pants down, and wriggled until they were off, and my shorts as well. I had kicked off my shoes some time ago. I never did get my socks off. I might have taken the trouble, but while I was getting the shorts off my other hand slipped a little, and without really planning it that way I discovered Francine's clitoris.

(I hadn't planned on mentioning that. After all, it's pretty clinical, and maybe not in the best of taste to come right out and talk about something like a clitoris. Not that there's anything wrong with a clitoris, for Pete's sake. But that there might be something wrong with mentioning it. But the thing of it is, I had known about this part of a girl from my reading, and knew of the great importance of it, but had somehow not gotten around to looking for it, being so preoccupied with other goodies. But now just by accident I had found it, and a good thing it was.)

"Oh, wow! Oh, God, yes! Oh, Jesus Christ, do it! Oh, do it forever!"

I got on top of her. I kept touching her, and I got on top of her, and I thought that this was it, this was really it. I was still seventeen and in a second I would stop being a virgin, which was a damned good thing, because if you were old enough to fight for your country you were certainly old enough to have sex, and with a sexual revolution going on, the idea of an eighteen-year-old male virgin was pretty ridiculous, and here I was, getting ready not to be one anymore, and here Francine was, all wet and open and ready, and I loved her, by God, and I would love her forever, and wasn't I the lucky son of a gun?

I said, "I love you, Francine."

"Do it!"

"I love you."

"God, God, stick it in!"

And it occurred to me, albeit briefly, that this might be a kind of graphic thing for a girl to say, and maybe not in the best of taste, but then I decided that it was all to the good, that Francine was, after all, carried away in the throes of passion, and that it was a fine sign that a girl like Francine, so demure on the outside, could be so carried away by passion, and then I stopped thinking entirely, and readied myself for the move that would change my life once and forever, and stabbed blindly ahead, and missed, and took aim again, and—

And paused, because it seemed that a herd of elephants was stampeding up the staircase and down the hall, and voices were shouting, and Francine was roaring at me, begging me to do it, to stick it in, and I lay there, paralyzed, and the door to my room exploded inward, and a man the size of a mountain charged inside. He had a hand the size of a leg of lamb, and in that hand he had a gun the size of a cannon.

"You son of a bitch!" he bellowed.

And pointed the gun at me, and pulled the trigger.

Chapter Two

I SUPPOSE YOU'RE WONDERING JUST WHO I am, anyway, and how I got myself into this particular mess. At least I *hope* you're wondering something along those lines, because if you're not, it means that you aren't interested, which in turn would mean that I have failed to hook your interest and rivet your attention in the preceding pages. And if I fail to get high marks in hooking and riveting, I probably won't be able to sell this book when I'm done writing it, and then I don't know what I'll do. For the past two weeks I've been living in a room about the size of a midget's foot-locker and eating Maine sardines and stale bread. The sardines are seventeen cents a can and the bread is free, but even if they were both free they would not be all that much of a bargain, because a sardine sandwich, even when you haven't had one in a while, is not exactly a dish to set before a king, and when the sardines are the cheapest ones available and the bread is stale and the menu never changes, well, I'm not fussy about food, but I can think of things I'd rather have.

I'm sorry. I'm getting completely off the track. The point is that the last chapter was supposed to hook and rivet you. And now that I've got your attention (if I haven't lost it already by wandering off the subject), I really ought to tell you who I am and how all this happened.

My name is Chip Harrison. It wasn't always, although I was always called Chip, as what you might call a nickname, because when I was a little tyke my first word was something that sounded like *Tsib*. (God only knows what I was trying to say. *Mama*, probably.) Anyway, *Tsib* wasn't anybody's idea of a terrific name for a kid, but *Chip* was pretty good, as in *Chip Off The Old Block*. So I got called that a lot.

Then in late 1963 I started getting called that exclusively, and my actual name began not being entered on school records and things like that. Because my name, you see, was a combination of family names. Leigh, which was my mother's maiden name, and Harvey, which was my father's mother's maiden name. So that my name started out as Leigh Harvey Harrison, and ever since late 1963 people named Leigh Harvey Anything have been very willing to be called something else.

"The sheerest coincidence," my father told my mother. "The sheerest possible coincidence. But when there are enough people in the world, coincidences have to happen now and again. I went to school with a Jewish lad named Adolph Gittler. His parents named him this in all innocence, you know, never dreaming—well, the point is clear. The boy changed his name to Arnold Gidding. Didn't do him all that much good. The teachers called him Arnold, but we all called him Adolph. Or Der Fuehrer. Or Sieg Heil."

"Boys are so cruel," my mother said.

"Leigh Harvey," my father said. "A perfectly sound name turned frightful overnight. We'll change it to Chip. That's what everyone calls him anyway. Chances are no one really knows his full name. When he gets older, why, if he wants something more distinguished, he can select it himself."

If I ever do, I suppose I will.

I wasted all of yesterday writing out the story of my childhood, and where I was born and where we lived while I was growing up and the schools I went to and things like that, and I used up a whole lot of time and paper, and I just got through tearing it all up. Because in the first place I can't imagine anyone being very interested in all of that, since there was nothing the least bit unusual or attention-grabbing about it. And in the second place I'm not one of these people who can practically remember emerging from the womb. I have partial recall, and it's vague at best.

So why don't I just say that I came of rich but dishonest parents, and went to a couple of different private boarding schools, until that one jarring day when my father shot my mother in the back of the head and shot himself in the front of the head and made me, in the wink of an eye, an orphan.

I was playing basketball when I learned this. I'm fairly tall, which always leads people to think that I ought to be good at basketball, until they come to the realization that my lack of coordination offsets my height, since I'm not Gulliver or anything, just fairly tall for my age. This particular coach hadn't caught on yet, it being my first year at this particular prep school, so I was out there on the court missing layups and muffing rebounds when some kid came down with a note asking me to report to the Head's office.

The Head—he was always called this, and while this is true of a lot of headmasters, it really fit in his case, because he had a head the approximate size of a basketball, perched on a skinny neck above an insignificant body, the head itself as hairy as a doorknob, with vague indentations and protrusions here and there to indicate eyes and nose and mouth and all that. Anyway, the Head did a lot of pacing around his office that day, and told me what had happened, more or less, and then went on to tell me more or less why my father had done this unprecedented thing.

What it amounted to, without the hemming and hawing that the Head put in, was that Chip Harrison's parents had spent their lives as con men (well, con man and con wife) and had made a good if shaky living for many years, working one swindle or another, and had been in the process recently of pulling off a remarkable stock swindle, until suddenly the roof had fallen in, leaving my unpoor but unhonest parents *(a)* stone broke and *(b)* jailable. Evidently my father decided that there was No Way Out, whereupon he did what he did.

I can't understand why. I mean, it seems to me that there must have been something he could have done. Gone to Brazil or joined the Foreign Legion or something. But I guess he just had the feeling that all the walls and the ceiling were coming in on him, and it seemed simpler to go bang bang and end it.

"I never knew him," I said, dazed. "I was never around much, and then when I wasn't at some school or other, well, I was usually off at summer camp, or else I was with them and we were traveling. They always seemed to be moving to one place or another."

"One step ahead of the law," the Head said darkly.

"Uh, I suppose. I guess I never really knew what he did for a living. When kids would ask, I would say he was in investments. I thought he probably was, but I didn't have any clear idea of how."

"Rather shady investments," said the Head.

"I don't suppose I thought about it too much. I took it for granted, ever since I was old enough to think about it, because little kids don't think about the subject, or at least I didn't until recently—"

"Would you like a glass of water, Harrison?"

"I don't think so. What I mean is, I took it for granted we were rich. We always had everything, and then being at schools like this one, I just thought we were rich."

"Ah, yes, errmphhh," the Head said. "That does, errmphhh, bring up a painful subject, Harrison."

"It does?"

It did. The subject was money, and the pain lay in the fact that I didn't have any. I wasn't just an orphan. I was a penniless orphan, a seventeen-year-old Oliver Twist. If my parents had seemed to be rich, they had managed this illusion by spending every ill-gotten penny as soon as they ill-got their hands on it. And over the past months they had been spending a great deal of money that they didn't have yet, all of this snowballing up to the point when everything went blooey, so that not only did I have an inheritance of absolutely nothing coming to me, but I was in hock to the Upper Valley Preparatory Academy for a couple thousand dollars' worth of tuition and room and board.

29

Lawrence Block

"I'm sure you understand the problem, Harrison," the Head said. The light glinted off the shiny top of the Head's head. He picked up one object after another from his desktop—a pipe, a pipe cleaner, a pencil, an ashtray, a file folder; you name it. He played with each of these things, and he watched himself do this, and I watched him, and it went on like this for a while.

Then he told me I would have to make arrangements, find relatives who would take me in and help me carve out a fresh start in life for myself. Perhaps, he suggested, someone might come to my financial assistance. I told him that as far as I knew, I didn't have any relatives. He acknowledged that he had rather thought this might be the case.

"I really don't know what I'll do after graduation," I said. "I guess college is out, at least for the time being, not that any of them have been in what you might call a rush to accept me, but—"

I got a look at his face and it put me off-stride. I let the sentence die and waited.

"I'm afraid you don't entirely understand," he said. "I don't see how we could conscientiously let you remain here until graduation, Harrison. You see—"

"But it's February."

"Yes."

"Almost March."

"Errmphhh."

"I mean, this is my last semester before graduation. I would be graduating in June."

"Actually, you owe us tuition, room, and board since September, Harrison."

"I'll pay sooner or later. I'd go to work after graduation and I could pay—"

He was shaking his head, which in his case called for more than the usual amount of effort. I watched him do this. I felt, oh, very strange. Weird. I mean, thinking about all of this now, in what you might call historical

30

perspective, I get all sorts of vibrations that I didn't get then. Like what an utter shit, pardon the expression, the Head was. And like that.

But at the time, I was having my whole little world turned not only upside down but inside out, and I was like numb. I didn't know how I felt about any of this because I didn't feel. I couldn't. There was no time to react because everything was too busy going on.

The Head stopped shaking and spoke again. "No, no, no," it—*he*—said. "No, I think not. No, I'm afraid we'll simply have to write off the money, chalk it up to experience. If there were mitigating circumstances, but no, no, no, I don't think so. Your grades are not bad, but neither are they exceptionally good. Coach Lipscot tells me your performance on the basketball court is generally disappointing. And, of course, the social stigma, you must understand. Murder and suicide and confidence swindling, no, no, no, I think not, Harrison, I think not."

I was shaking when I left his office. I don't think I was ticked off or scared or any particular thing, but I was shaking. Everything happening at once. I went back to the dorm. My roommate was lying in his bunk, reading a sex magazine, and when I walked in he went through his little act of trying to pretend that *(a)* he was only interested from the standpoint of a future psychologist and *(b)* he had been holding the magazine in both hands. I don't suppose the guy beat off more than average. It was his attitude that bothered me. (As a matter of fact, an obnoxious attitude in this area isn't exactly rare. Either they're like Haskell, going to great lengths to pretend that they don't even have genitals, let alone touch them, or else they go to the other extreme and want to talk about it, or discuss methods, or do it right out in the open. Or worse. Either way I find it pretty disgusting. I think it should be a private thing, like religion or squeezing blackheads.)

Anyway, the sight of old Haskell draping the sex book

to hide his erection was enough to turn me off to the idea of talking with him, which hadn't been that outstanding an idea to begin with, I don't guess. He started babbling about something or other, and I wondered what he would say if I told him everything, and I decided it wasn't worth finding out. I turned away from him and went over to my dresser and started pulling out drawers. I thought I was trying to decide what to take and what to leave, but I guess I was looking for something without knowing what it was, something that would make everything go together in some, oh, meaningful way. If anything like that existed, it certainly wasn't in my drawers or closet. As a matter of fact, the more I looked the more I realized that there was nothing around that I particularly wanted to see again. It was just too much trouble to decide which stuff to put in a suitcase and which stuff to leave behind. It was easier to leave everything.

It was especially easy to leave old Haskell. I didn't even say goodbye. I mean, why do it? I thought about borrowing a few bucks from him—he always had plenty of money; everybody at Upper Valley always had money. The Head would just shake himself and say that he had expected me to borrow money before I left, and like father like son, and all of that.

So I didn't. Not from Haskell and not from anybody else, and the crazy thing is that if I had just gone and told people what was happening, not even getting specific about it but just that I was broke and with nowhere to turn and all, I could have collected a bundle. Not by borrowing, but as outright gifts, or on a pay-me-when-you-can basis. Because while the guys at Upper Valley were something less than princes, they were not a bad bunch. And if I was not Mr. Popularity, I wasn't anybody they despised, either. They were okay, and I got along with everybody. And, more than anything else, see, these guys were all at Upper Valley for a reason. They were all there because (a) they had money and (b) there was something less than wonderful about them, or else they would have gone to a better school. Either they were slow learners or marginal alcoholics or their family background had a bad smell to it or something of the sort. They had plenty of money and they knew how important money was and just what the limits to it were, and all of this added up to a gentle and wry kind of sympathy and all.

So they might even have taken up a collection for me, and it might even have come to enough so that I could have stayed at that crappy school until I graduated from it. At least it would have been enough to let me leave the school on a bus or train or something.

But I was, well, proud. And in no mood to explain anything to anybody, or take anything from anybody. In fact I couldn't even talk to anybody, although I had this need. I actually spent close to two hours just walking around the campus, trying to think who I could talk to. I couldn't work up any enthusiasm for talking to any of the guys or any of the teachers. I would have little conversations with some of them in my own mind, and it helped me get some of my own thoughts straightened out, but each time I came to the decision that I would just as soon talk to these people in my mind and not in the flesh. And I certainly didn't want to talk to the basketball coach. I did have an imaginary conversation with him. It didn't get too far, but it featured him explaining to me how, if I only drove more fiercely on those lay-ups and worked harder for those rebounds, if I could only be counted on to drop a sufficient percentage of foul shots, then my academic career might still be promising. "You've got the height and the reach, Chip, kid," he said, in the privacy of my mind. "Not enough to interest the college scouts. A year or two and the rest of them'll catch up with you. But on a prep school level— well, you had your chance, boy. This was the place for you and I gave you every opportunity, but you just didn't give me everything, boy; you just let me and the team down. A winner never quits, Chip, kid, and a quitter never wins."

I sat under a tree and looked through my wallet. I had a snapshot of my folks, and another more formal picture of my mother. I looked at these for a little while. I also had seven one-dollar bills in the bill compartment of the wallet, and forty-six cents in the change compartment. In the secret compartment I had a folded twenty-dollar bill and a lubricated Trojan with a receptacle tip. The two were related; I had planned, at some unspecified future date, to hitchhike to the city fifty miles away where, it was said, prostitutes plied their hoary trade. The twenty-dollar bill was to hire one, and the Trojan was to make sure that any scars left by the experience would be psychological in type. And the secret compartment, by the way, was not all that much of a secret. I had been carrying that stupid rubber for so long that you could see its elliptical outline through the wallet.

(I guess it worked, though. Not the secret compartment. The Trojan. In all the time I had it there, I never once caught a disease.)

I got up from under the tree and put the wallet back in my pocket. I had $27.46 and an old rubber. I had no place to go to and no one to turn to and I couldn't even stay where I was.

I went back to my room. Haskell, thank God, was not there. I think he was probably having dinner. It was about that time, and I could have gone over and had something myself, but I didn't even consider it. I got under the shower and washed myself a few times, and I got dressed in all clean clothes, and I brushed my teeth and combed my hair and made polishing motions at my shoes. I put things like my comb and toothbrush and a bar of soap in my pockets. I thought about packing a change of socks and underwear, but I didn't. I wanted to have my hands free. The phrase *walking away empty-handed* came to me, and it seemed proper to do this, and in a literal sense.

On the highway, neatly groomed and clean cut, I stood with my thumb in the air. A few cars came and went, as cars will do, and then a big Lincoln slowed down, and I got that good expectant feeling, and I straightened up a little and put a fresh, boyish smile on my face.

The car slowed a little more, and the driver looked at me, and stepped down hard on the gas pedal and roared off into the distance.

All I could think of was a joke. You probably know it. I guess it's the oldest joke in the world.

There was this guy who joined the paratroops, and after all the training it was time for him to make his first actual jump from a plane. Not off one of the towers but out of an actual plane in flight. And the flight instructor or jump instructor or whatever they call it, the guy in charge, went through the procedure with him. "When you jump, you count to ten. Then you pull the ripcord to open the chute. In the event that the chute does not open, pull the emergency cord to open the parachute. The chute will open and you will coast gently down to the ground. There a truck will pick you up and take you back to the base."

So the guy jumped, and he pulled the ripcord, and nothing happened, and he pulled the other cord, and nothing happened. And he said to himself, "I'll bet that fucking truck won't be there either."

Oldest joke in the world.

And I just fell out. I broke up completely. I rolled around at the side of the road, laughing harder than I ever laughed in my life. "That fucking truck," I said, and roared with laughter. "That fucking truck."

I never did cry. I don't know why, but I never did. And if I didn't that day, I don't suppose I ever will.

The car that picked me up, long after the laughter was over and done with, was a big Pontiac convertible with deep vinyl seats and power everything. The driver was about forty or forty-five, very pale and indoors-looking. He said he was a salesman and that he sold industrial bathroom fixtures. My first reaction was to wonder what an industrial bathroom was, and after I figured it out without asking

35

him, I got a mental picture of an endless row of urinals stretching as far as the eye could see, with an endless row of workers in denim overalls, stepping up to the urinals, setting down their lunchboxes, and urinating industriously.

And it struck me that I had done this myself maybe a million times, except for the lunchbox and the overalls but in all those times it hadn't occurred to me that there were people who made a living going around selling urinals, or that other people made their living buying them. I had just never really given much thought to the way people made their livings. But now, as an orphan with twenty-seven dollars and change, the whole subject of work seemed more significant.

I found about a thousand questions to ask him. About the different models of industrial bathroom fixtures, and the colors they came in, and how you got into that kind of business, and, oh, everything that came to me. Now and then I would see him giving me funny little looks, as if he maybe thought I was putting him on by pretending to be interested in such a ridiculous subject. But I guess it was easier for him to believe that I was interested than to accept the fact that his work was all that boring, so he told me a lot more about his field than anyone in or out of it would really care to know. And he got a kick out of it, I guess, maybe because no one else thought he was so interesting. His wife, he told me at one point, didn't give a whoop in hell about his life's work. In fact, he said, she seemed ashamed of it, as though there was something dirty about sinks and toilets and urinals, when, in point of fact, the world would be infinitely filthier without them.

I wasn't faking a thing. I was really interested at the time. Honestly.

He picked me up in western Pennsylvania, where the school was. We took the Pennsylvania Turnpike west. It turned into the Ohio Turnpike, and we went about halfway through Ohio before he had to turn off. He left me on the pike. I had said I was going to Chicago, and while I didn't have a great reason to go there, I was stuck with the story.

Before he left me off, he stopped for gas and bought me a meal at the restaurant. He went to the john, and when he got back to the table, he was all excited and took me back to the john to show me all the plumbing fixtures and explain various things about them. We got some very funny looks from the others, let me tell you.

Through Ohio and Indiana and Illinois I talked to a lot of different people and had a total of six more rides. The conversations were something like the one I'd had with the salesman. I won't bore you with what the various drivers did for a living or where they picked me up and dropped me off, or the makes of the cars and appearance of the drivers. To tell you the truth, I don't remember it all that clearly. They tend to run together in my mind. Anyway, none of it was that sensational.

I got to Chicago a little before noon. My last driver dropped me north of town near the lake, and I spent almost an hour trying to hitch a ride back toward the center of the city. I suppose it must have been a whole lot less than an hour. In that wind, though, it seemed like forever. Finally a cop car came along and a uniformed cop stuck his head out and said something about hitchhiking. I didn't catch the words, but it didn't take an IQ up around the genius level to get the message, which was that hitchhiking was frowned upon. If he hadn't told me this, I might still be there, frozen solid, with my thumb out.

Now, though, it occurred to me to take a bus, which cost me a quarter and which was the first expenditure I'd had since I left school.

Sitting on that bus, all I could think of was the damned quarter. I mean, after all, I had gone something like twelve hundred miles and eaten three times and all I was out so far was a quarter. You'd think I would be thrilled, for Pete's sake. But I kept thinking that my $27.46 was now down to $27.21. And that I could afford to take the bus a hundred and eight more times, and then I'd have twenty-one cents left, which would buy me two cups of coffee and a gumball. The point being that I had no money coming in, so *any* going out was something to worry about.

I kept planning to ask the driver to let me out when we got to the center of town, but I couldn't think of a way to do this without sounding like a hopeless hick, and for some stupid reason I didn't want to. So I just kept looking around and waiting. I had been to Chicago before with my parents but couldn't remember much about it. Except that we went shopping at Marshall Field's and stayed, I think, at the Palmer House—though when I went to take a look at it, I didn't notice anything familiar about it. I guess I must have been eight or ten at the time.

Anyway, I recognized the Loop when we first hit it, and when we got to State Street, I remembered that it was the main drag, or else I just recognized it from the song. The street signs have *State Street* and under it *That Great Street*. When I noticed this I was tremendously pleased. A point of recognition, as if the street sign was some old school buddy or something. Later, after I had walked all over the damned street, I began to realize how incredibly simple it was of them to put something like that on the dippy street signs. If everybody who goes to Chicago could just see one of those signs once, that would be fine. But to just have them there always, so that even the people who live there have to look at them—I got off the bus at State Street and started walking around. I mostly stayed right there on *That Great Street* because it was a nice familiar name and if I left it I was afraid I might never find it again. I walked up and down and looked in store windows at things I didn't need and couldn't buy anyway. I kept seeing things that for no reason at all I suddenly wanted. A combination nail clipper and pocket knife, for example, which I needed like the Venus de Milo needs gloves. And although a guy had bought me breakfast just a couple of hours before, I kept getting these dumb yens for food. I couldn't pass any place that sold anything edible without starting to drool. I stood in front of a restaurant where the cheapest dish on the menu was over four dollars, and I actually stood there reading the whole menu as if I could go in there and dive into a steak. I mean, even if I was fool enough to waste the money, I wasn't dressed for the place.

Eventually I got annoyed and bought a candy bar just to kill my appetite. They had the nerve to charge six cents for a stinking nickel candy bar.

$27.15.

Two hours later I was stretched out on a bed in a room in the Eagle Hotel (*$3.50 a night*), reading the want-ad section of the *Chicago Tribune* (*free, out of a trash can*). I used a yellow chewed-up pencil stub (*found at the curb*) to mark the ads that looked promising.

There were jobs all over the place. Just looking at those listings, you wouldn't believe there was anyone in the country who wasn't working. The only problem was that none of the advertisers wanted to hire a seventeen-year-old kid with three-and-a-half years of high school, no experience whatsoever, and not an awful lot of ability, either.

Not that they seemed to care too much about ability. The main thing seemed to be experience. I would say that ninety-eight ads out of a hundred wanted to hire people with experience, and what they were really hot to hire was someone who was already doing a much more important job at higher pay in the same field. I didn't blame them, but how could anybody get experience if you had to have it to get a job?

Another thing you had to have was an education. Judging by the ads, if the job was one where you might come up once a week against a two-syllable word, they wouldn't touch you unless you had a college degree, and they wouldn't be happy about it unless you had a masters. For less intellectual jobs, like picking ticks off horses, they were willing to settle for you if you had a high school diploma.

It was very goddamned discouraging, let me tell you. I folded the paper and put it down and sat up on the bed— $3.50 a night doesn't buy you much of a bed, incidentally— and said, aloud, "I'll bet that fucking truck won't be there, either."

This time it didn't break me up in the slightest. I went back to the paper and kept finding the two percent of the ads that I almost qualified for. Things like passing out handbills on the street, sweeping the floor in a grocery store, jobs that were either temporary or part-time and that didn't pay all that well anyway.

When I was done, I stretched out on the bed and closed my eyes. The hotel must have been made out of secondhand egg cartons. You could hear absolutely everything. Whenever a toilet flushed anywhere in the building, it was like being next to Niagara Falls. Sometimes I could hear conversations, either two people talking together just low enough so that I could make out every fifth word, or else some drunk shouting at the top of his lungs. I don't know which was worse.

But lying there I realized what I was going to do.

I was going to Succeed.

Of course you can't just succeed. You have to succeed at something, and I wasn't quite sure what that something might be yet. But the impression I got from the men I hitchhiked with was that one job wasn't all that different from any other. Once you got past the slave level and actually got somewhere in business, the idea was to take something and sell it to someone else. And it didn't really make very much difference whether the thing you were selling was advertising space or snake oil or industrial bathroom fixtures. The object, whatever it was, was to wind up with more money than you started out with.

I sat up in bed. I thought of my father and mother, and the life they had led, and where it in turn had led them. I would arrange my life differently. I would be honest and hard-working and stable. I would take as my own personal day-to-day objective the same goal that made all those hitchhikers the same—to finish each day with more money than I'd started the day with. If I had to pass out handbills or sweep floors or pick ticks off horses, I would do it for the time being, and I would make damn well sure that each day's work brought me at least as much as I needed for my meals and rent.

And meanwhile I would find some job that had some kind of real Opportunity For Advancement. That was a phrase that appeared in a great many ads, and they couldn't all be playing games. I'd find a job with an Opportunity For Advancement, and I would work long hours and apply myself and go to night school to get that high school diploma and then go on to take night courses at college and put myself through college, and work my way up the corporate ladder in the good old American way, using hard work and pluck and luck and good old common sense and elbow grease to make my way to the top.

And there would be women every step of the way.

My brain spun at the thought. Of course there would be women, I realized. The cheap-but-vital women in whose rough arms I would learn the rudiments of love. The secretaries and career girls with whom I would share idle moments of brief but intense pleasure. And, when I found her, the Right Girl who would share my hopes and dreams, and with whom I would climb the long ladder rung by rung and hand in hand, until together we would enjoy the fruits of success crowned by True Love.

I thought of the joys of True Love, and glowed at the thought. And then I thought of the Untrue Love that would come first, with the career girls and secretaries and cheap-but-vital women, and I began to be moved by these thoughts. The thoughts became quite vivid, as a matter of fact, and quite moving.

But then someone in a room down the hall was seized

by a coughing and spitting fit, and that ruined the mood completely.

I burrowed under the covers. A cockroach scuttled out from beneath the radiator, which had begun clanking. It seemed to be giving off a whole lot more noise than heat. The radiator, that is. Not the cockroach. Well, maybe the cockroach too, for all I knew. Or cared.

I settled my head on the pillow, such as it was. If there were more than thirty-five feathers in that pillow, they must have been very small ones. The man with tuberculosis (my diagnosis) did his number again.

I fell asleep. Which should give you an idea how tired I was.

THE MAN WAS MOSTLY SHOULDERS. He wasn't really big, I was taller than he was, but he had these wide shoulders and no neck at all, and he was wearing a sinister short-brimmed hat and a black suit, and he looked like a Chicago gangster. Maybe he was nothing more desperate than a Chicago mutual funds salesman, but I don't really think so. I think he was a Chicago gangster. If not, he's in the wrong line of work.

In which case I know exactly how he feels.

He came toward me, and I picked up the rhythm of his walk and got my timing into gear. When he was just the right distance away, I took the pasteboard slip from the top of the stack and thrust it at him. If it had been a knife, and a couple of inches longer, it would have pierced his left lung.

But it was just a piece of paper and it never touched him. And amazingly enough he never touched it, either. He just kept right on walking and went past me as if I were invisible. I turned to look after him.

"Stay awake, Chip!"

I spun around. Gregor clicked the shutter, and I opened my hand and let the piece of pasteboard float to the ground. My gangster friend had missed his golden opportunity, all spelled out in smudged black letters on a yellow card, and saying:

> ### HELLO THERE!
> Your candid photo has just been taken by Gregor the Pavement Photographer! Your picture will be ready within twenty-four hours! Bring or mail this card with the some of one ($1.00) dollar to Gregor the Pavement Photographer, 1104 Halstead! Find out

>   what you look like to others! See
>   yourself as the world sees you!

It was a pretty tacky little slinger, no question about it. And even if you dropped the excess exclamation points and spelled sum right and printed the message in unsmudged ink on a less gaudy stock, it would still be nothing that most people would want to carry with them forever. That few of them were so moved was readily seen by a glance at the pavement to my rear, where any number of the yellow cards presently reposed.

In plain English, there were little yellow slingers all over the place, some of them crumpled, others just plain dropped. Most people dropped them without even finding out what they were, but almost all of them did take the cards when I shoved them at them. The gangster was rare. The average person has trouble not taking anything you hand him. It's a reflex, I suppose. I don't know whether the gangster had lousy reflexes or tremendous cool, or whether he was so tied up in his own little world that he hadn't even seen me. Nor did I have time to worry about this, because I had to pass the next card to the next person, who would in due course add it to Chicago's littering problem.

The gangster came by around a quarter after four, and there wasn't another memorable person for the rest of the day. This was my sixth day working for Gregor, and by now a person had to be pretty remarkable in order for me to take any real notice of him. Every day I would see tens of thousands of people, and I would poke yellow slips at thousands of them. At first it was such a constant parade of new faces and bodies that I started getting a headache from it. But then it straightened out and smoothed out and the pedestrians lost their individuality. They were just part of the crowd, and I found myself tuning them out the way you tune out anything that's always there. I no longer really noticed the traffic noises, and I no longer smelled the smell of State Street, and in the same kind of way I no longer noticed the swarm of people. Every once in a while one of them would manage to be more than just another shadow in the crowd. The gangster type, and an occasional cripple, and particularly attractive girls, for example.

A few minutes after six, Gregor said, "Oh, the hell with it, keed, let's call it a day." He folded up his tripod and put his camera in the case. We walked to 1104 Halstead Street, where Co-op Photography was located. Co-op Photography was a name to put on the door, actually. Inside the door there was a large room jammed with desks and three smaller rooms, two of them darkrooms and one of them a slapdash studio with lights and a couple of backdrops. For ten dollars a month Gregor got the use of a desk, two hours a day of darkroom time, and use of the studio by arrangement. There was also a switchboard and a girl who functioned as a sort of collective receptionist, but it cost an extra five dollars a month to receive calls there, and Gregor figured it wasn't worth it. So we walked past the girl without asking if anyone had called, and Gregor put some things in the desk and took some other things out of it, one of them being a bottle of peach-flavored brandy.

"Jesus sonofabitching Christ," he said, reflectively. Gregor was a short dark mixture of various Balkan strains that didn't go together all that well. His eyes were sunken and his cheeks hollow. He had the heaviest beard of anyone I ever met. When he swore I always had the feeling I was hearing wrong, because he never sounded mad or aggravated or anything. He would say various obscene things in the tone of voice you would use to say, "I'm going down to the store for a new tube of toothpaste" or "I wonder how the White Sox did today." It took a whole lot of getting used to.

He uncapped the bottle and took a drink and asked me if I wanted one. I said it sounded like a good idea. He gave me the bottle and I took a drink. The first time he had done this I wanted to wipe the neck of the bottle or something, but then I decided that anybody who stood out in the middle of State Street all day the way I had done was already exposed to every germ known to modern man, and besides there was something vaguely insulting about insinuating that Gregor was diseased or something.

I don't know what good peach-flavored brandy tastes like, or even if there is any such thing, for Pete's sake. This was very cheap stuff. If you've never had it, you've got the right idea. I think you could duplicate the taste by mixing equal parts of the sweet syrup from canned peaches and Zippo lighter fluid, but if you mixed it that way it would probably cost you more than Gregor paid for it.

He took another drink himself and put the cap on the bottle and the bottle in the drawer. Another photographer, an old man who wore suspenders all the time, believe it or not, came over and asked how it had gone.

"How should it go?" Gregor demanded. "You take the pictures and you see what happens." He pawed through a handful of letters on the desktop, held one of them to the light, and squinted suspiciously at it. "So either there's a dollar in it or there isn't," he said thoughtfully. "And what difference does it make?"

You may have gathered that he didn't have the greatest money-making operation in the world. Good gathering. Gregor, from what I had seen, was a pretty fair photographer, but one look around that office told you that pretty fair photographers were in less demand than, say, pretty fair aerospace engineers. (Whatever they are: I don't understand the term, but the *Tribune*'s classified pages are filled with people who want to hire them.)

Gregor's business was straightforward enough. He stood there on State Street, taking pictures of people walking by, and as they passed I gave them a numbered slip, and theoretically they sent in the slip with a dollar, and theoretically the number on the slip enabled Gregor to find the right negative and print it and send the print to the customer.

"I don't always get the right picture to the right person,"

he had confided once. "Especially before I started using a kid, I would do the shooting and the card-passing all by myself, and I would get the numbers a little off-synch, and then I'd get some jerk writing in from Denver to tell me that he got the wrong picture, and I should either send him the right one or send his dollar back. So how am I supposed to straighten it out? Some of the jerks write back three, four times for a lousy dollar. Think how many times I must make a mistake and they don't write at all. Sometimes I wonder if anybody ever gets the right picture. But what do they want it for in the first place, huh, keed? Answer me that. I have this way of making a buck and I am damned if I can tell you why anybody at all ever sends for the Jesus sonofabitching Christ photographs."

Tonight his mood was less reflective. He seemed annoyed at the volume of late mail, and he cursed pleasantly as he slit the flaps of the envelopes and shook out the dollar bills. There were a couple of checks, and one clown had sent a dollar in stamps, and another hadn't enclosed any payment at all.

He put away the orders he would fill tomorrow and added the money to his wallet. "The one with the stamps," he said, "should sit on a hot stove waiting for his picture to come, the son of a bitch. Let's see, keed, eleven-thirty to five-thirty is six hours at a buck and a half is what? Nine bucks?"

"Eleven to six. Seven hours."

"Ten bucks?"

"Ten-fifty."

He counted out ten singles. He didn't have any change, he said. I had change, I said. So he discovered two quarters in his pocket and gave them to me.

"You're the only one making any money," he told me. "Don't spend it all on the same girl, huh?"

I laughed politely and counted the bills again, and counted the money in my wallet. "Hey, that's great," I said.

"You're in Rockefeller's class now?"

47

"Not quite, but at least I can pay my rent by the end of the week."

"Whattaya been doing?"

"Paying a day at a time. It's three-fifty a day, but the weekly rate is only twenty-one bucks, so I'll be getting one day a week free."

"Jesus. You're paying twenty-one bucks a week for a place to sleep?"

"That's right."

"Keed, that's *wrong*. Where you staying, the Ritz?"

"As a matter of fact it's a real dump. But at the price—"

"You're paying way too much, Chip."

"It's the cheapest hotel in Chicago. Or at least in the downtown area. I looked all over."

"Hotels!" He waved a great sigh and shook his head. "Hotels are for a night, two nights, a weekend maybe. Hotels aren't to live. Who the hell can afford it? Twenty-one bucks a week and you don't even get any meals or anything, is that right? Son of a bitch, you know what I pay? Eighty-five a month, and that's two rooms and a kitchen and a bathroom. You got a private bath in that hotel of yours?"

"No."

"I pay the same as you for Aileen and myself, an apartment instead of a room. That's what it costs you to live in that hotel of yours." He scratched his head. "Tell you the truth, I don't see how you can live. What did I pay you today, eleven dollars?"

"Ten and a half."

"Whatever it was. So three and a half from that for the room leaves seven, and figure a buck and a half each for breakfast and lunch is three from seven leaves four, and a decent dinner if you eat it out has to cost you two and a half bucks at the bottom, leaves you what? A dollar and a half? You can just about go to the movies." He shook his head again. "On top of which there's no work when it rains and no work when I got a big darkroom schedule. I don't know what I've paid you altogether over the past couple of weeks, but it can't come to all that much."

It didn't. I had worked six days out of the past nine, and my total earnings were $57.75. But then my expenses weren't as high as he had figured them. My breakfast was seventy cents and my dinner ranged from a dollar to a dollar-eighty. My lunch was generally a candy bar, and I had found a place where they only charged a nickel for a nickel bar. And sometimes I had a cup of coffee next door to the hotel before I went to sleep.

So actually I was saving money. I had hit Chicago two weeks before with $27.46 in my pocket, and I had earned $57.75 from Gregor and another twenty dollars and change on other jobs I had picked up a day at a time, and my current balance stood at just over $36.

At this rate, though, it was going to take me an awfully long time to become what you would call wealthy. Also I was due for some capital expenditures, if you want to call it that. Like washing my underwear and socks at night meant I had to put it on slightly damp in the mornings, which wasn't all that much fun. And it might be nice having another pair of pants and another shirt, not to mention the fact that the State Street sidewalks were having a bad effect on my shoes.

"Chip keed, I got an idea."

I looked at him.

"Suppose you could pay the same twenty-one bucks a week, or for the sake of convenience call it twenty, meaning you're saving a dollar right off the top, and you get a place to sleep and it's a clean place and all, and you share the bathroom with two people instead of three hundred, and on top of everything else, you get home-cooked breakfasts and dinners included. How's that sound?"

"Where is the place? Madrid?"

"Right here in beautiful Chicago. Just three blocks from here." One of the sunken eyes closed very slowly in what I had grown to recognize as a wink. "C'mon, keed, let's get our asses in gear. I gotta tell Aileen she's running a boardinghouse."

I was a little uncertain about this. I mean, it sounded great, and if anything it sounded too great. The only question was whether I wanted to get that tied up with Gregor. My job was doing menial labor for a failure, and that didn't quite fit in with my goal of a position with Opportunity For Advancement. Not that I figured Gregor would want to evict me if I went to work for somebody else. I was bright enough to realize that my room and board would just about pay the rent on his place, and I'm sure I wasn't the first of us to come to this realization. But I didn't know whether I wanted to be around him off the job as well as on it, and I didn't know if I wanted to be what amounted to a part of his family, sharing two rooms and a bath with him and Aileen.

Then I met Aileen.

I moved in that night. There wasn't all that much involved in moving in, since I didn't even have to go back to the hotel. The nice thing about not owning anything is that you don't have to go back for it. So when I say that I moved in, all it really amounts to is that I went to Gregor's apartment and met Aileen and had dinner and stayed the night.

It was a million miles away from the Eagle Hotel, believe me. Dinner was spaghetti and meatballs, and while it didn't fit the homemade label Gregor had hung on it—the spaghetti was out of a box and the sauce out of a can—it was still far better than the blue-plate special in a diner on Madison. And afterward we sat around in the living room and watched television and talked a little, and before they turned in Aileen made some more coffee (instant coffee) and brought out some A & P-brand jelly doughnuts, and afterward she gave me a sheet and a pillow and a pillowcase and they went to their room and left me the couch.

I wasted a lot of time and mental energy trying to figure out how to turn that couch into a bed. It wasn't designed to make the switch. It was just a couch, and by the time I figured this out for myself I was tired enough to sleep standing up in a closet.

I spread the sheet on the couch and got undressed and rolled up in the sheet. I wondered if I ought to buy a pair of pajamas or something. Then I wondered about Aileen, and if maybe she would come out and kiss me good-night or something.

She was pretty spectacular. Longish light blond hair and oval cat's eyes and high Slavic cheekbones and a full wet red mouth. She had the most goddamned suggestive mouth I have ever seen in my life. Her body reinforced the Lustful Peasant image in a big way. Large heavy pointed breasts, a hint of a belly, wide hips, large rounded bottom, big well-muscled thighs. The dress she wore was supposed to be a shapeless style. Only when she wore it, it took on a shape. It was really something amazing to watch her walk around in that thing, with all that flesh making interesting movements against the cloth of the dress.

I kept thinking about her, and imagining things. She was about the most sexual person I had ever met in my life. She just exuded this constant aura. It wasn't that she put out feelers or gave the impression that she was hot for me or anything, but even if she decked herself out in a nun's habit and cut her hair in a crew cut it would still be hard to spend ten seconds with her without imagining what she was like in bed.

I imagined she was fantastic. I imagined that she would make love like crazy, and that she would take a man and screw him absolutely blind (I now knew why Gregor's eyes seemed to be falling back into his head) and then, when she was done with you and you were deliciously half dead, she would wrap you up in her arms and legs and breasts and keep you warm as toast all through the night.

I kept on with this imagining, and you know how it is, what with one thing leading to another, well. There was a point when I realized that no one was going to break the mood by doing something creative with the plumbing, and I also realized that she was going to change my sheet in the morning, and maybe you can think of more embarrassing things to have happen, and maybe I can now, but I certainly couldn't then, and didn't even want to try.

The next afternoon I bought myself a second pair of socks.

"Now was I right or was I right?" Gregor said every now and then. "Here you're saving all kinds of money and living like a human being. Was I right?"

He was right, all right. Each morning I got up bright and early and had a glass of unfrozen orange juice and a cup of instant coffee and a bowl of cornflakes or rice toasties or something like that. There was one of those undairy creamers to put on the cereal. The list of ingredients sounded like the secret formula for the hydrogen bomb, for Pete's sake. Well, there's nothing like home cooking.

Then, about five days out of eight, I would go to work for Gregor, putting in an average of six hours' work. When he had some developing and printing to do, I generally kept him company in the darkroom. He wanted to charge me for photography lessons. I got out of that one by offering to help him in the darkroom for a dollar an hour instead of a dollar and a half. We compromised; he didn't charge me, and he didn't pay me. It was fairly interesting, and I learned what the different chemicals were and what they did. I also learned that one place I didn't want to spend the rest of my life was in a darkroom.

On my days off, I sometimes picked up day work handing out passes for television shows or going door to door in some place like Oak Park, taking sample bars of a combination soap and cleansing cream (*Neither soap nor cleansing cream, but new improved Urglegurgleblech*) and rubber-banding them to people's doorknobs. It's against the law to put anything that's not mail into a mailbox, and they wouldn't fit under the door the way handbills do, so you had to loop them on the door knob, which was very time consuming.

I took a few home for Aileen. You were expected to—what the hell, a sample was so people could sample it, no? But I didn't do what I really wanted to do, which was to stuff the whole batch of them down a sewer and go to the movies. For one thing, I had come to see that a man gets ahead in this world by doing his job to the best of his ability and playing fair with his employers. For another thing, a kid from Missouri dumped his soap and the crew chief caught him and beat the living shit out of him.

The rest of the time, when I wasn't working or helping in the darkroom, I divided between the apartment and the rest of Chicago. I would go out at night with no particular goal in mind, maybe stopping at the library for a while and then roaming around the city. The idea of meeting a girl of some sort or another was always in my mind, but then it always had been, and it had never done me any particular good before, and it didn't now, either. Most of the time, as a matter of fact, I never even saw a girl, or if I did she was with somebody.

There are supposed to be slightly more women than men in the country, but if you've ever wandered around a big city after dark you couldn't help becoming convinced that there are maybe twenty or thirty men on the open market for every woman. I don't know where the girls go at night, or what they do, but they aren't where the men are.

Once, in a sort of middle-class hippie place on Rush Street, I seemed to be doing pretty well with this girl with long hair and sunglasses. She was from some college. I told her I was a dropout, which wasn't all a lie. We were getting along fairly well, but then her date came back and that was the end of that. And another time a woman got interested in me at a diner. I was having coffee to keep warm and she was having coffee to sober up, I suppose, but it wasn't working. She had a puffy look, as if someone had taken a bicycle pump and put a little air in all the cells of her body. At first I thought she was about thirty-five, and the closer I looked the older she got. It was like watching the ageing process through the modern miracle of time-lapse photography, as they say in the commercials.

We went and sat together in a booth in the back, and she kept breathing on me and dropping single entendres. She put her hand on my leg. Then she put her hand a little higher and gave me a friendly squeeze. By this time she looked about a hundred and eight and I got this all-embracing wave of nausea. I said I had to go to the toilet. I was half afraid she would follow me. I wouldn't really put it past her. I went to the john, and then I went to the back entrance and slipped out, leaving her to pay for my coffee and find some other boy to molest. I went out of my way to avoid that particular diner ever after.

And you know something, by the time I was a couple of blocks away from that woman, I called myself every name I could think of. I mean I really felt stupid. Obviously she was nothing spectacular, but the thing of it was that she was *there*, for Pete's sake, and she was *willing*. And it wasn't exactly as though I had to beat women off with a club. I was, let's face it, a very horny kid with a desperate desire to stop being a there's-that-dumb-word-again virgin. She could at least have served that purpose. I didn't have to love her to ball her. I didn't even have to like her.

That was as close as I came to scoring in the streets of Chicago, that and a couple of others and come-hither glances from faggots, with one of them going so far as to make a tentative grab for me while I was making use of an industrial bathroom fixture. I told them all no, and they all took no for an answer. I guess nobody found me exactly irresistible.

You might think, after all that, that I would have spent all my time around the apartment. I did spend a lot of it there, as a matter of fact, but what drove me out of there from time to time was the fact that Aileen was driving me right out of my mind.

It wasn't just what she looked like, which I told you about. It wasn't just that their bedroom door was not very substantial, and that I could hear them whenever they made love, which they did almost every night. (If they hadn't, I would have worried about Gregor. Really.) And it wasn't just that she was so sane and healthy about her physical self that she was completely casual about walking around half-naked in front of me, giving me groin-grabbing glimpses of one part of her after another until I literally ached.

It was that, on top of all of this, I was really digging her and Gregor as human beings. And it was a strange relationship, see, because I really didn't know what sort of relationship it was supposed to be. They were both a lot older than me. I think Gregor was in his forties, and I suppose she must have been close to thirty. So some of the time they were something like replacement parents, and since they had come into my life so shortly after my own parents left it, this did seem a logical role for them to play.

But I had never felt about my own mother as I felt constantly about Aileen. (Or if I did, I wasn't aware of it, and I'd just as soon not find out about it now, either, Dr. F.) If Aileen was my mother, then I was King Whatsisname with the broken ankles. And proud of it.

They were also like an older brother and older sister, and they were also like my boss and his wife, and they were also like my landlady and her husband, and, oh, it was too involved to keep straight. So the outcome was that I felt very comfortable and secure hanging around the apartment, reading a book or watching television or playing knock rummy with Gregor or helping Aileen with the dishes. I felt very comfortable almost all of the time, and then all at once, I would just have to get out of there before I started running around on all fours and chewing at the carpet.

I mean linoleum.

It was on a Friday night when Gregor got a phone call and said he had to go out. The first time this sort of thing had happened I got very ginchy about being left alone with Aileen, very hopeful and very anxious both at once, but nothing happened then, and after that I got accustomed to it and thought nothing of it. If anything, I found it very relaxing to be alone with her. I could talk to her when there were just the two of us in a way I couldn't with Gregor around. About my folks, for instance, and what I wanted out of life, and various heavy things it would have embarrassed me to talk about in front of Gregor. Aileen hardly ever said much, but she had a way of listening that went down very smoothly.

Gregor went out around eight-thirty, and Aileen and I talked and watched television for about an hour and a half. Then he came back looking happy.

"We're in business," he told her. "Mark can use as much as five hundred or a thou's worth of the right stuff." He turned to me. "A photography assignment, keed. You thought I made the whole nut snapping dummies in the street, didn't you? But sometimes something good comes up." To Aileen he said, "I've got the studio from now until four in the morning if I want it."

"You want to go there?"

"Right. And use the darkroom right there, and deliver the goods in the morning. And have the money in my pocket before that kike changes his sonofabitching mind. You want to get ready, keed?"

"Me?"

"He means me," Aileen said.

"My prize model."

I said, "No kidding? You do the modeling?"

"That's how I found her, keed. My best and sweetest model. You ever look at the fashion magazines? *Vogue, Harper's Bazaar*—"

"Greg, put a sock in it, damn it."

He smiled at her. "Sure, they're all dying to give her a spread, aren't they, keed? And she'd give them a spread in return."

"Greg, in one minute you can go take pictures of soup cans."

"Just kidding."

"I mean with photographic artistry like yours, Greg, the subject's not really important, is it? You could go take artsy-craftsy shots of sewer gratings and the museums would stand in line for them."

"Baby, all I said—"

"I mean let's keep track of just who we all are, why don't we?"

This went on awhile. I had the feeling that I'd walked in on the last reel of a movie that only made sense if you'd seen the first part. I was still thinking it over while Gregor packed his gear and Aileen went off to change her clothes and make herself up. When they were ready, Greg started picking up his equipment, and I offered to help him carry it.

He said, "Well, sure, I suppose—" and she cut in to suggest that I come along and watch a photographic session.

"You futz around in the darkroom all the time, you might as well get acquainted with all sides of the photography business. Isn't that right, Greg?"

"You really think so?"

"Why not?"

"Well, it's fine with me, keed."

"It's certainly fine with me."

"If you say so."

"Because this would be a dumb time for modesty, I certainly think."

"If you say so."

"And Chip's practically one of the family, aren't you, honey?"

I listened to all of this without saying anything. I suppose you figured it out a long time ago, but then you're sitting down somewhere reading it all at once, while I was living it a little at a time. I knew there was a lot going on that I wasn't getting, but that was as far as I could go with it. I was lost, and waiting for someone to find me.

So we walked the couple of blocks to the office suite. It was empty except for a little guy at one of the desks who was catching up with his bookkeeping. He looked up when we came in and then looked down again. We ignored him and went into the studio. Gregor locked the door.

He set up his equipment and arranged various lights and things, explaining it all to me as he did it. I didn't catch much of what he was saying because I was too busy trying to figure out what I was missing.

Then he was ready, and Aileen gave an odd little smile and got up on top of this dark green velvet couch. She gave a tug and lifted her dress up over her head and tossed it across the room out of camera range.

There was nothing under it but Aileen.

Oh, I thought. Nude pictures. Cheesecake, so to speak. Now I understood.

But not entirely.

"It's a mutual thing we've got going." Aileen said, spreading her legs. "It's actually a beautiful relationship, Chip. See, Greg takes my picture, and in return I take his."

I looked at Greg. He was buried under the black cloth and looked as though he was part of the camera apparatus. I looked at Aileen again. She had her hands between her legs, one on each side of what I was looking at.

"Only I have a built-in camera," she was saying, "and I don't have to futz around with floodlights or exposure settings. I just take aim and snap away. Say cheese, Greg."

Greg didn't say anything. I suppose he was still under the hood.

58

I wasn't looking at him, actually.

My mouth was as dry as a sand sandwich and I had this weird chilly sweat all over my hands and feet and under my arms. And I couldn't quite catch my breath, and I couldn't stop shaking all over, and I couldn't take my eyes off the most fantastic thing I had ever seen in my life.

The shutter worked.

"Click!" Aileen said.

Chapter Four

FOR A LITTLE OVER AN HOUR I STOOD there with my eyes falling out of my head while Gregor took filthy pictures of his wife. After her opening round of flashy repartee, Aileen didn't have anything to say. Gregor stayed under the black cloth, and stayed quiet. And believe me, I didn't say one word. A lot of things came to mind, I'll admit, but I kept them to myself.

One idea that I couldn't get out of my head was that this was all a dream, and if that was so, I had to be very careful not to do anything to wake myself up before the dream turned wet. Because dream or no, I was in what you might term a state of advanced physical excitement.

It was really fantastic.

I don't know if I can clue you in as to just what it was like in that little room. (Which is probably a pretty dumb thing for me to say, for Pete's sake, because I'm supposed to be writing this, and if I can't handle it, that means I'm wasting both our time, and that it's going to be a long siege of Maine sardines and day-old bread.) Seriously, I could try to put down all the poses Aileen struck and to say which ones made me the horniest and all, and if I did this, well, you might begin to get your own idea of what it was like in there, but I'm not all that certain it would add up to anything.

Well, just as an idea of the whole approach the two of them had, this was how Gregor used up one particular roll of film. He did several rolls of individual series work, which came to an even dozen pictures, which would eventually get wrapped up and sold together, and which would tell some vague sort of a story.

This particular one was the banana series, and it started off with a muffled voice from under the black cloth saying, "The banana, keed." At which point Aileen got off the couch, went to Gregor's bag of tricks, found a pair of ripe bananas, and got back on the couch.

I remember seeing those pictures, the banana set, after they were developed and printed. And if you hit them in order and were in the frame of mind to believe them, it really looked as though old Aileen was getting her cookies that way. It was pretty realistic.

Only an hour or so had passed when Gregor came up for air. His forehead was dripping with sweat. I guess it was pretty hot under the black cloth. It wasn't all that cool anywhere else in the room, either.

"Wraps it up," he said. He dug his cigarettes out of his shirt pocket, lit one for himself, and offered the pack to me. I shook my head. Some people are just physically incapable of believing that some other people don't smoke. He tossed the pack and the matches to Aileen and she lit up and tossed them back. It was all very casual, almost athletic, with all of this underhand lobbing of cigarette packs and matchbooks. You could almost forget that Aileen was stark naked, and that she had spent the past hour holding her labia open and sucking on her own nipples and sticking bananas up herself. (I don't know if I ought to be quite that graphic about it, but that was what she was doing, and I think it would be worse to try being coy about it, for Pete's sake. I mean, if you're going to come right out and say that a woman posed for a batch of dirty pictures while you stood there watching, you might as well call a spade a spade, right?)

Aileen blew out a cloud of smoke. She said, "Is that all you want to shoot?"

"I think so, yeah."

"I thought you were going to take some pornographic ones."

I didn't do an enormous double take on that line. I just thought I was hearing wrong.

But he said, "Hard-core? No, the sonofabitching timer is on the fritz. I don't know what's the matter with it. Less than two years old and it just went. Nothing works anymore and nobody gives a damn. The whole civilization is coming apart at the seams."

I must have looked puzzled. Aileen said, "It's a timer on the shutter. He sets up the shot and then he has fifteen seconds to get in the picture with me."

"Twelve seconds," Gregor said.

She ignored the correction. "That way we can do the more interesting things, Chip. What you could call hard-core pornography."

I nodded.

"What we shot now tonight is called soft-core."

"What's the difference?"

"Redeeming social importance," Gregor said.

"Huh?"

"That's what the Supreme Court calls it. You know, that you can argue it's a work of art and not a hundred percent obscene. If you actually show people fucking, then it's considered a hundred percent obscene."

"In hard-core pornography," Aileen said, "the man's core is hard."

"That's an old gag," Gregor said.

"Professional humor," she said.

"But the point is that the timer is on the bum." He sucked on his cigarette and clucked his tongue pensively. "I'll tell you something, you wouldn't believe what a short time twelve seconds is until you tried to set up a shot and then get in it yourself. You know the worst part?"

"What?" I managed to ask.

"Staying up. You know, erect." His eyes dropped to his trouser front, and mine fought the impulse to follow. "When you set up with the camera and all, you know, your whole concentration is on technical matters. You don't even think sex. You might have trouble believing this, but when I'm taking these pictures, there's no difference in my mind whether I'm taking a picture of Aileen playing with herself or of the Chicago skyline. It's all the same as far as I'm concerned."

He was right. I had trouble believing this. I had seen the Chicago skyline, and I had seen Aileen playing with herself, and there was no chance I would ever get the two of them mixed up in my mind.

"So I set up a shot," he went on, "and then I have to turn on the excitement so that I'll get erect, and then rush rush rush to get into the right position before the sonofabitching shutter goes bang. It's the most nerve-racking thing going. And the thing is, the way I like to work, you know, is to shoot as much film as fast as I can, just one picture after the other. Just keep watching through the viewer and click them off whenever the pose is right. And the same way, Aileen likes to get into the spirit of a sequence and let it build the right way."

"To a climax," she said, with a wink.

"Yeah, to a climax," he said winklessly. "It's the same as whatchamacallit, method acting. Living the part. Look, you don't know the business, but I can tell you that if you looked at a set of the keed's photos and a set of the average model, there would be all the difference in the world." I had no trouble believing this. "The average girl, she'll put on this sonofabitching mechanical smile that looks painted on her face, or maybe she'll pout a little, and there's nothing the least bit natural about it. Aileen, she's something else. Sometimes I think she has, you know, a climax. Just going through the poses."

"Sometimes," she said, "she does."

"But without the timer," he said, and then he dropped his jaw a few inches and actually snapped his fingers. "Hey," he said, as an imaginary lightbulb formed over his head. "Now why the hell didn't I think of that before?"

"Of what?"

He pointed at me. "You," he said. "You could take the pictures. You want to be a photographer, you got to start sooner or later."

While I was busy not saying anything, Aileen said, "I've got a better idea. Chip's a smart kid, but he doesn't know anything about photography. You can't expect him to have your touch with a camera."

"Well, that's true," Gregor said.

"And anyway, I think the world's getting tired of the same old pictures of you and me, honey. But suppose you take the pictures and Chip and I star in them?"

They had done this before, Aileen assured me. Twice, as a matter of fact, with a fellow who neither of them really knew very well, as another matter of fact. And it was really perfectly legitimate as far as she was concerned, because after all it wasn't really sexual. Which was to say that they really didn't do anything. They would just set up a shot and Gregor would shoot it and then they would swing into another position.

The other fellow never actually got inside of her, Gregor explained. And that, he said, was an absolute requirement as far as he was concerned. Because while he and Aileen might have a more liberal attitude in certain respects than the average married couple, in other respects they were what you might call old-fashioned, and one of the respects in which they were old-fashioned was that neither of them believed in having sex outside of marriage. He was absolutely faithful to Aileen, and she in turn was a hundred percent faithful to him, and that was the way it had to be.

The two of them took turns explaining these things and filling me in on the fine points of pornographic photography, and let me tell you, it was the weirdest conversation ever. I wasn't tongue tied all the way through it, but I think I might as well have been. I would ask various dumb questions and they would chime in with the answers. Wouldn't Gregor be upset just seeing me in these various poses with Aileen?

"No, keed, because I know it doesn't mean anything and nothing's really happening."

Wouldn't Aileen be embarrassed by doing that sort of thing in front of her husband?

"Embarrassed, Chip? I've got a huge streak of exhibitionism in me. You must have figured that out for yourself. If anything, I got a kind of a kick out of you watching just now, during the soft-core shots. And you know, honey, I like you, and Greg likes you, and if anything I think it would be kind of, you know, fun."

Fun.

"We got time," Gregor said. "We got all night here and in one of the darkrooms, and we can probably use both darkrooms if it comes to that because I don't think the other one is booked at this hour. There would be a lot more dough if I had hard stuff for Mark. If you wanted to do it, well, I suppose I could pay you, and I don't mean any of that buck-and-a-half-an-hour crap. I could afford, oh, what the hell, let's say twenty bucks."

"Greg, honey, how on earth can you be so damn cheap?" She turned to me and grinned conspiratorially. "He'll pay you fifty dollars, Chip. How does that sound?"

After a few seconds passed, I realized we were all waiting for me to come up with an answer. "It sounds fine," I squeaked. If my voice had been any higher they would have thought I wasn't old enough for the job.

"Well, that's fine," Gregor said. "Fifty dollars—well, sure, I suppose so. The only question, and I guess nobody but you knows the answer, keed, if you know it yourself, is whether or not you'll be able to perform. Most of the time you can fake it, you know, but some of the shots have to show you—"

"With a hard core," Aileen put in. She rolled her eyes in exasperation. "Gawd," she said. "Of all the stupid questions to ask him. He's had the hardest core in America for the past hour and a half, haven't you, honey? So I don't think he's going to have troubles now."

We got things off to a sensational start by having Aileen put on her dress and shoes. And oddly enough the sight of her with clothes on really got to me. I'm not being sarcastic.

I had just about gotten to the point where I was used to her being naked, and now that she had the dress on again I was taking it back off again mentally and remembering what she looked like without it and getting hornier than ever at the memory.

She sat down and patted the couch next to her, and I sat, and she looked at me and gave me a grin as big as O'Hare Airport. I don't know if I can explain it, but when she grinned that way I knew that things were going to be all right, that this was my mother-sister-friend-landlady-sweetheart Aileen, and that we were going to have a little innocent fun together without anybody getting messed up. You may have trouble figuring out how she packed all that into a three-second grin, but it was all there and I read it loud and clear.

"Now the whole thing is to get into the part," she said. "You tell yourself that you and I are crazy about each other and that I'm very desirable and we're alone together and we're going to make love. Don't even think about the camera for now. It's just a little clicking noise; it's nothing to think about. And don't worry about striking poses, or what angles Greg's shooting from. Just get into the spirit of the thing and we'll wind up with some decent shots."

I thought, *Decent*? And then she puckered up invitingly, and I leaned forward, not too sure what came first, and we actually kissed.

That's an understatement. We went right off the bat into a deep soul kiss, and not because it was my idea. I was too dumb to think of it, but before I could think of anything at all, her tongue was halfway down my throat and her breasts were pressing against me.

Click!

We held the kiss, and she shifted a little and took my hand and put it on the front of her dress, over her breast. I gave a gentle squeeze and felt the nipple stiffen.

Click!

She wriggled her hips invitingly. I put my hand under

her dress and touched the inside of her thigh. She felt like—
I was going to say silk, but it was more like warm glass,
except even smoother somehow. I felt the play of muscles
in her leg. Her kissing got greedier. She was sucking on my
tongue as if she wanted to swallow it.

Click!

If this was method acting, I know why they use it. Maybe
she liked to think we were just going through the motions,
and maybe Gregor liked to think it, but if they really
believed it they were both fruity as a nutcake because Aileen
was hot enough to burn. I let my hand move higher, and
my mind filled up with what I had seen earlier, those pink
thighs and that puff of curly blond hair and all, and I
touched her and she was all warm and wet, and—

Click!

Jesus Christ.

Click!

I let her take the lead. It seemed only natural, since she was
the experienced one in every sense. Besides, I never wanted
to move out of one pose in order to get into another. But
she gave a reluctant sigh and steered us to the next bend in
the river, which consisted of her opening the dress to the
waist and letting me amuse myself with her breasts.

Click!

By handling them.

Click!

And kissing them.

Click!

And so on.

Click!

I'm putting all the clicks in to give you an idea of what
Gregor was doing, but don't get the impression that I was
always aware of the camera. Some of the time it was as
though it wasn't there at all and the whole sex thing
between me and Aileen was entirely real. Then that
sensation would fade, and I would be so completely aware

of the camera that I almost couldn't stand it. Then the clicks would seem loud enough to break glass, and I would start feeling like a machine making love to another machine. But this never lasted long enough to let me cool down, and each time I got into the mood completely again I would just be that much hotter than I was before.

It didn't take long for both of us to get out of our clothes. Aileen had already been giving my groin some gentle feels now and then, so exposing myself was no big deal to me, and as for Gregor, I wasn't very keenly aware of him just then.

Click!

I did have a second or so of concern after I got out of my shorts when I saw that she was looking at me. I guess every man who ever lived must have done a certain amount of worrying about his equipment at one time or another. And while I don't think I was more hung up on the subject than most, there were times when I wondered whether it was too small, or funny looking, or ugly, or I don't know what. Since I had no way of knowing how you could tell a pretty one from an ugly one, or how much was enough, there was no real way to avoid these worries completely.

So I had that flash of anxiety. But the next second Aileen's eyes went from the area in question to my eyes, and she gave that grin again, the same as before, and her lips parted just wide enough to admit her tongue, and she ran her tongue hungrily around her lips, and got the most beautifully lustful look in her eyes—

Click!

I hadn't felt so proud since I got my first quarter from the tooth fairy.

She touched me a little, and I'm sure the shutter went on clicking, but I didn't hear it. Then she got up on the couch and stretched out on her back with her knees bent. She motioned me on top, and we touched bodies from chest to groin, and my thing proved it had a mind of its own by going straight for her thing. I no sooner touched her than she gave a quick twitch of her hips and got out of the way.

"Easy," she murmured. "Remember the rules, Chip. The sign on the door says *Private*, remember? *Admission Restricted To Authorized Personnel.*"

I wanted to cry with disappointment. I had begun to think, somewhere along the line, that all of that business about not going all the way had been, well, something we would conveniently forget when the time came. I had put it in the same bag with her statement that none of this was really sexual.

I thought about just going ahead and doing it. I could always pretend it was an accident, I thought. Just put it where it belonged and keep it there long enough to finish, and even if she thought it was rape, she wouldn't be likely to go running through the streets shouting for a cop. And if she and Gregor got mad, well, the hell with them. Whatever happened, I would at least have done the one thing on earth I really wanted to do.

Lots of luck. I gave a well-intentioned thrust, and the shutter clicked behind me, and Aileen got out of the way with no trouble at all.

"*Naughty,*" she whispered. "*Bad boy.*"

I guess I could never make it as a rapist.

At this point it really did become pretty artificial and mechanical and phony. We stopped pretending and just went through the motions as quickly and effortlessly as possible, and it made for a lot less nervousness for both of us (and maybe for all three of us, because I don't think Gregor was happy seeing his faithful wife an inch away from technical infidelity). So what we did was just get quickly into a position, take shots of it from two different angles, and then get into another position. I had done a lot of extracurricular reading over the years—I suppose that's pretty obvious, for Pete's sake—but even with all the times I went through the *Kama Sutra* and the *Ananga Ranga* and *Eros And Capricorn* and *The Perverted Village* I had never quite realized how many different positions there are to not quite have sexual intercourse in.

Click!

Click!

Clickety clickety click!

By the time Gregor suggested we all stop for a cigarette break, I had reached a stage where I was just as glad to relax for a while. Not that I was relaxed in any meaningful sense of the word. I mean, face it, this wasn't a relaxing way to spend the evening. It just plain wasn't.

"Got some great shots," he said through a cloud of blue-gray smoke. "You want to know something, keed, you're a natural born actor. And how about the wife, huh? One great little actress."

He turned the key in the lock, peeked out. "Nobody home," he said. "Hang on a minute."

While he was gone I whispered to Aileen that I was going out of my mind.

"Poor baby," she said.

"I mean I don't think I can walk."

"You forgot the rules for a minute there, Chip. I've never done it with anyone but Greg. Not since I met him, and it's been almost six years now. You have to understand."

"I suppose so."

"You know, you're very nice-looking."

"Oh, come off it."

"You mean you don't know it yourself? You're a good-looking guy, and you've got a dreamy body."

"Cut it out. My bones stick out, for Pete's sake."

"I like the way you look."

"I mean—"

"I think we'll look good together."

She was beginning to get to me all over again. I started to say something, God knows what, but then Gregor came back in with his bottle of shifty peach-flavored brandy. I had the most unbelievable urge to take the bottle and shove it up his ass. I had the feeling that if I could just get him out of the picture, him and his goddamned camera, I could spend the rest of my life balling Aileen, and I couldn't think of any way I'd rather spend it.

He was saying that he thought we were all entitled to a drink. He tended to think of alcohol as a reward. I didn't know if I could hack the taste of that crud just then.

Aileen said, "Honey, I think just a short one, unless you're out of film."

"There's plenty," he said. "Why?"

"I thought like one more roll, that's all. I didn't do anything oral."

"I didn't know you were going to do that," he said warily. "I didn't even think of it."

"Well, it would be a case of faking it, really."

"I suppose," he said. "Son of a bitch, if they don't go for that stuff. You sure you want to?"

"Oh, I don't mind."

I went over and sat on the couch while he took a quick pull on the brandy bottle and then disappeared beneath the black cloth and went to work loading the camera with a fresh roll. Aileen finished her cigarette and came over and sat down next to me.

I reached for her.

"Not just yet," Gregor called out cheerfully. "I'll be set in a sec, keed."

"Aileen," I whispered, "you'll drive me up the walls."

"Poor baby."

"Look, I—"

She ran her tongue over her lips. This was a little trick of hers that didn't exactly leave me cold when she did it first thing in the morning over instant coffee and cold cornflakes. Now it was absolutely criminal.

"You'll like this," she said.

"Ready to roll," Gregor said.

"God in Heaven," I said.

"Lie down, baby." Her mouth was inches from my ear, blowing into it as she whispered. "Poor baby has had a mean night, huh? Mama will fix." Her hand moved over my chest and belly. My stomach contracted violently. "Ticklish," she murmured, blowing into my ear some more. The hand went on its merry way and grabbed. "Got small again," she said. "But Mama's gonna fix that, too."

Click!

I really felt like a baby, too. I lay there like a lump and felt so small and weak and helpless and so goddamned young I wanted to curl up and die. She kissed me on the mouth, and then on the throat, and then her mouth moved downward so that her long blond hair brushed over my face and chest and stomach.

Click!

I had my eyes closed, and my body was sort of stretched out the way you do when you float on your back in a swimming pool. I had that same kind of buoyant feeling, too.

She kissed it, and her hands did things, and the camera made stupid clicking noises, and the hard core was harder than ever. I could feel the blood in my head and I thought I was going to have a brain hemorrhage and die.

She did a million teasing things with her mouth. But there wasn't any contact to speak of.

Just her warm breath.

Click!

Breathing in and out, in and out.

Moistly.

Oh God, I thought, oh God, don't stop, for Christ's sake don't stop, whatever you do, don't stop, just another minute, just another second, God, don't stop—

Click!

And she stopped.

Since then I must have tried a thousand times to figure out why she bothered getting started if she wasn't going to finish it. I mean, face it, it's not as though she was some drippy virgin who didn't realize that a man had to finish what he started or get horribly frustrated. Everybody knows this; anybody old enough to read Ann Landers' column can figure it out. And Aileen was a long ways from a virgin. She may not have slept with anybody but Gregor since they were married, but I'm sure she must have had a few hundred men before he came around.

So she obviously knew what she was doing, but then why do it? She wasn't a cruel person. She was nice, really, and she seemed to like me.

I mean, I could understand why she felt compelled to perform the act without any actual contact. That is, I could understand it about as well as I could understand why it was all right for us to pet like crazy but not all right for me to get into her. Which is to say that I didn't understand and it didn't make any sense but at least I knew the basic rules of the game.

But if she was going to leave me high and dry, why start anything in the first place? What was the point? Gregor had been ready to pack up and go. So had I. And she hadn't wanted to have anything done to her. I was just supposed to lie there and leave everything to her, and I did, and it hadn't ended quite the way I had hoped.

I lay there like an overwound watch, going pingpingping inside and staying drawn hellishly tight. I couldn't talk or think or breathe or see. I didn't know where she was, but I knew where she belonged. In Hell, with a hot poker rammed up her behind.

And then I heard her voice, talking, not to me, but beyond me, to Gregor:

"Honey, baby, I have to give him some relief. He's a kid, you know, and I guess it was all too much for him. The excitement. Being with me, and in front of the camera and all, and going through the motions, and the different positions, and then this last thing. I think it stopped being just an act for him, and he got very excited, and if you look at him now, you can see how tense he is."

"I have to do something."

"Well, I don't—"

"I wouldn't be unfaithful."

"Because I wouldn't like that, keed."

"And I wouldn't do it."

"I should hope not. I should just sonofabitching hope you wouldn't."

Her hand on my leg.

"But this would be just like a massage. I knew a girl who was a nurse in a hospital—"

"That's the best place to be a nurse."

"—and she told me how they used to give the patients rubdowns all the time, and if they got excited they would give that a rubdown, too, and that isn't wrong, do you think?"

"I suppose not."

Her hand gripped me.

"Of course it isn't," she said, her voice softer than ever now, and now she was talking less to him than to me, and her words moved in a jerky rhythm as her soft sure hand moved up and down, up and down, pumping up and down.

"Of course...it isn't...wrong...baby baby...it's all right...all right..."

Not like this, I thought. Not with your hand, and not in the middle of the air, not like this.

"It's all *right*...it's all *right*...it's all *right*...it's all *right*..."

Oh, yeah, I thought. Okay. Sure, sure, oh.

"It's all *RIGHT!*"

It was all right, all right.

Chapter Five

THE NEXT DAY GREGOR DIDN'T BOTHER doing his sidewalk photographer number. He went off to see Mark Somebody to turn a suitcase full of dirty pictures into as much money as possible.

"Soon as I get back, keed," he said, "you get your twenty-five smackers."

"Fifty," I reminded him.

"Oh, sure. My mistake."

"Sure."

As soon as he was out the door, I went into the kitchen and cornered Aileen. She asked me how come I wasn't working that morning. I said that a photographer's assistant didn't have much to do when the photographer wasn't on the job. There wasn't much point in me handing out the little yellow cards if there was nobody on hand to take the pictures.

"I meant one of your other jobs," she said.

"Well, I didn't think I'd bother today. I earned fifty bucks last night."

"You make sure Greg gives you the whole fifty, Chip. Sometimes he tries to chisel people."

"He already tried."

"Well, you get the whole fifty. You worked for it."

"Yeah."

I wanted to reach for her but I didn't quite know how to go about it. You can't imagine how goddamned awkward the whole thing was. I mean, here we had gotten in this wild tangle the night before, with results that I told you about in probably too much detail already, so we won't go into that all over again, and now here it was morning and she was in the kitchen, wearing an apron and rinsing out coffee cups, and her whole attitude left me feeling that last night had never happened, that it was another dream of mine and when I woke up I would have a damp sticky sock in the bed with me. I mean, I knew it wasn't a dream, but it might as well have been.

"Chip?"

"What?"

"Are you angry with me?"

I looked at her. "Why should I be?"

"Because I teased you last night."

"Well, I knew what I was getting into."

"What you weren't getting into, you mean."

"Well."

"You're not angry?"

"No."

"I'm glad." She grinned quickly. "Because I like you a lot, Chip."

This time I did reach for her, and she moved her head aside, and I missed. I suppose practically any woman can make practically any man feel like an idiot, but it seemed to me that either she was particularly good at it or that I was particularly inept.

She said, "Last night was business, Chip."

"Yeah, sure."

"I'm not going to say I didn't enjoy it."

"You enjoyed it, huh?"

"Why, of course I did. I don't think there's anything wrong with enjoying your work, do you?"

"I guess not."

"I should certainly hope not." She put the dish towel on the drainboard and walked past me to the living room. There wasn't an abundance of room in the kitchen, and she managed to brush against me pretty good on the way, giving me the full treatment with that round rear end of hers. She got to me, all right. I suppose I'm pretty easy to get to, generally speaking, but old Aileen had a real knack for it as far as I was concerned.

I followed her into the living room. She went around straightening things up and emptying ashtrays, talking as she went. "There's nothing wrong with enjoying any kind of work," she went on. "I wouldn't pose for those pictures if I didn't get a certain amount of kick out of it. I like to think of all those people looking at pictures of me and getting excited. Sometimes I stop and think that there are men all over the country looking at naked pictures of me and playing with themselves. Having sex with me in their minds. And couples looking at different pictures of me, either alone or with someone, and getting so hot and bothered that they want to make love. When I think about that sort of thing I get a very strange feeling."

"Sure," I said.

She put an ashtray back on a tabletop and turned to look at me. "Just think of all the people who will look at those pictures of the two of us," she said.

"Yeah."

"Do you like the idea?"

"I don't know. I got bothered by that before. I mean, I thought somebody might recognize me, but then I thought that I didn't have anybody to care one way or the other. If some jerk I went to some school with saw it, well, what do I care? You know, let him envy me, let him eat his heart out. If I had any family it might be different, I guess."

"Poor baby. All alone in the world."

"Don't call me that."

"I called you that last night."

"I know."

She crossed to the television set, switched it on, and collapsed neatly on the couch. My couch. She patted the cushion next to her, and I remembered how she had given the same invitational pat to the green couch in the studio last night. I felt lightheaded and shaky.

I pretended not to notice the invitation. "I think I'll have another cup of coffee," I told her. "You want one?"

"I'll make them."

"No, stay there," I said. "I, uh, I need the exercise."

She was still sitting in the same spot when I brought

back the two cups of coffee. She said, "You know, Chip, that was fun last night."

"Here's your coffee."

"For you, too." She put the cup down next to mine on the coffee table. "We could have a lot of fun, you know. There are lots of times like this morning when Gregor is out and I'm home all alone. If you didn't try to force things, we could have a real good time."

"What kind of a real good time?"

"Like last night. Except without anybody watching or snapping pictures."

"And without finishing what we started."

She raised her eyebrows. "You finished, didn't you? I spent half an hour wiping the floor. If that wasn't what you would call finishing—"

"You know what I mean."

She put her hand on my cheek. "Didn't you get your kicks last night, baby?"

"I wanted to do it the right way."

"There's no right way, honey. Sex may be a game but there's no yo-yo keeping score. Whatever turns you on, that's the right way."

"I never got laid in my life, Aileen."

I turned away as I said this. I felt excited and happy and miserable all at the same time, and all tied in knots. She had my hand in both of hers and was petting it.

"I know that, Chip."

"It's pretty obvious, huh?"

"Well, reading between the lines of what you said. It's a big thing for you, huh? Being all hung up about being a virgin."

I nodded.

"Being a virgin, you know, it's something everybody is and something everybody gets over sooner or later. Even I was a virgin once. You may find that hard to believe—"

"Cut it out, will you?"

"Hey." I turned and looked at her. She gave me the wise

grin, and some of the tension went out of me. "Now listen a minute, baby," she said. "We can have a little fun, if you want, or we can just let it stay nice and loose between us, if you'd rather have it that way, but one thing not to do is be so serious about everything, because that's nothing but a big bringdown."

I nodded again. "But why can't we—"

"Because we can't. Because that's where I draw the line. That's for Greg and nobody else. Look, if all you want to do is stick it in, you can go out and find a pro. You're getting fifty dollars from Greg. You're a rich man. If you want to just get on top of some syphilitic pig and get rid of your precious cherry, all you have to do—"

"You know what I want."

"Uh-huh, baby, but I also know what I want. And that's some nice tender sweetness from my baby, and you don't have to worry, I won't tease, I won't leave you frustrated. You'll come, honey, and so will I, and it'll be very nice, just leave everything to me."

"I don't know what to say."

"What's to say?" She laughed deep in her throat. "Come here," she said. "Do something brilliant, like kissing me."

Do you have any idea how many ways there are to do it without really doing it?

Neither did I.

There's just no end to the possibilities. There were just three rules to the game—or one rule, actually, that closed three doors to me. What it boiled down to, really, was that I couldn't enter her. (With what she still liked to call my hard core, that is. Other things, yes.) I guess there's precedent for this. In the legal definitions of rape and sodomy and other nice things like that, the dividing line is that same line Aileen used. Penetration. If you don't get in, the argument goes, then you haven't really Done Anything Wrong.

We didn't Do Anything Wrong.

But we did just about everything else.

You know something? I've thought about it, and I've come to the conclusion that if only I hadn't been a virgin at the time, I would have been the happiest man on earth. Because from a physical standpoint there was nothing frustrating about the relationship we had. I was getting there, and not in the therapeutic massage way I had made it in the photo studio, either. We weren't playing that little game at all. It had been strictly for Gregor's benefit, and now that we were on our own, we didn't try to hide the fact that the name of the game was Getting Kicks.

Sometimes we spent five or six hours in a row on that couch, and by the time we stopped I had made it so many times that I didn't have the strength to lift a finger, let alone my unhard core. So in simple terms of the amount of sex I was getting I was in the class of a man on a honeymoon with a nymphomaniac, for Pete's sake.

So in that sense it was really great. The more I got the more I wanted, and the more I wanted the more I got, and it looked as though it could just go on that way forever and it would keep getting better all the time.

Here's a comparison that you might want to pass up if you're very heavy on religion. Not to offend anybody, but I think it fits. It was like being Adam and Eve in the Garden of Eden, with Paradise there, just everything you could want all spread out for you, except for these two trees that you couldn't go near. You could eat anything else in the world but the fruit of the Tree of Life and the Tree of Knowledge, so naturally what did you want? Right the first time. Well, so did I. The fruit was a cherry instead of an apple, and I wanted to get rid of it, not take a bite out of it, but otherwise it added up to about the same thing.

(Incidentally, suppose Adam and Eve ate from the Tree of Life instead of the Tree of Knowledge. Or from both of them. They'd still be alive, and the earth would be up to its neck in people. That doesn't have anything to do with anything else, but it's been bothering me ever since I was a little kid so I thought I would put it in. I'm supposed to be writing this straightforward, keeping to the subject and everything, but I was also told that the book ought to let the reader know how I feel about things and the kind of person I am, and frankly I think if I have to just tell everything absolutely cold and straight without putting down other things that come into my head while I'm sitting here, then the book might as well have been written by a machine. When I read a book, I like to have the feeling that a real human being actually sat down and wrote it, and that reading it will let me know something about him. Some books give you the feeling that the sheets of paper came out of the paper mill with the words already on them, for Pete's sake. Untouched by human hands, like the plastic food in turnpike restaurants.)

Well, to get back to what I was saying, if you're still with me, I sort of wish I could have rearranged my schedule so that I could have met Aileen five years later in life. That would have been perfect, I think. By then I would be twenty-two and years past being a virgin, but still young enough so that she would be the older woman showing me new ways to be the happiest kid on the block.

As it was, maybe I should have gone out and spent my fifty dollars (Gregor paid off in full, although he did make a half-hearted effort to make me settle for forty) on some professional prostitute. If I just could have crossed that barrier I would have stopped brooding about it. Or maybe I wouldn't. I guess not, really. I guess it would be impossible for anyone in his right or wrong mind not to want to ball that woman in every way there was.

I got to Chicago in late February, I was at the Eagle Hotel for about two weeks, I moved in with Gregor and Aileen about three weeks before we had the picture-taking session, and it was Memorial Day weekend when I got out of there. I just worked it all out with paper and pencil to save you the trouble, assuming you're interested, and the way I figure it there was a stretch of about six weeks between the night we took the pictures and the morning I left Chicago.

When I think back on it, sometimes it seems as though it couldn't possibly have been that long, and other times it seems as though it must have been closer to six months. They were six fantastic weeks no matter how you look at it. In all that time we never once crossed any of the cruddy lines she had drawn, and Gregor never got any idea of what was going on, and I don't think we once went as much as thirty hours in a row without having a shot at it. It wasn't always a five-hour stretch on the couch (although that happened plenty of the time) and sometimes it was just a fast fingering at the kitchen sink or a quick hand job at the breakfast table. But it was as steady as a pension from the Federal Government.

I remember one night when she slipped out of the bedroom after Gregor had zonked out. She did this quite a few times, and since she and Gregor generally knocked one off before going to sleep, the goods I was getting weren't exactly untouched by human hands. Sloppy seconds, I think they call it. (Not really sloppy, because she would wash up first, but even so it used to bother me. At first, that is. You might be amazed the way a person can get used to things, and can stop being bothered by things that used to bother him.)

This one particular night a couple of winks and hand signals during the late movie had given me the message that I could expect company. So I was waiting for her from the minute she and Gregor closed their bedroom door, and the sound of their bedsprings was background music while I thought of all the things I wanted to do to Aileen. I was developing a pretty wicked imagination along those lines.

Then the door finally opened, and she tiptoed across to the bathroom, and I heard water running. And then she tiptoed some more, from the bathroom across the floor to the couch.

I pretended to be sleeping. We both knew it was a pretty transparent act, but she liked to find ways to wake me up. She kept finding ways, and they always worked. I'll bet she could do the Indian rope trick just by touching the rope with those hands of hers.

Well, not to go off on tangents, I woke up, and she got on the couch with me, and we did things. Between her thighs, or under her arm, or in her hands, or between her breasts, or in the cleft of her buttocks, or—well, you name it. We made it, and I stretched out, and she curled up in my arms, and I felt like the King of the World.

"Oh, baby," she said. "You're so good for me."

I said, "Purr." Or something along those lines.

"You know what? I feel like a girl."

"You sure do."

"I'm serious."

I ran a hand over her. "You feel like a girl, all right. I'm glad, too, you know. I don't think I'd get as much of a kick out of all of this if you felt like a boy. I like these, see, and this, and—"

And a little later, when we came up for a breath of fresh air:

"Hey, I meant it before, clown. You make me feel like a girl again."

"You're not so old."

"Thanks a bunch."

"You're not that much older than I am, for Pete's sake. You do this mother bit all the time, but you're not exactly in the category of an antique."

"Keep saying it, baby."

"How old are you, anyway?"

"A hundred and ten."

"Shit."

Lawrence Block

"You know why you make me feel so young? Hey, that's a song. No, it's because of what we do. Necking and petting and fooling around like a couple of kids. It takes me back to when I was, you know, younger. And a virgin."

"I didn't know you ever were."

"Don't be a sharp-tongued son of a bitch, Chip. Your boyish charm is your biggest asset. Don't piss it away."

"I'll bear that in mind."

"Please do." She put her hand between my legs and gave me a reassuring pat. "Yeah, I was a virgin once upon a time. Isn't that remarkable? And when I'm with you I'm a virgin all over again, and the whole sex business is, I don't know, cleaner and hungrier and hornier and everything rolled into one. It takes me back, it really does."

"Being in bed with me."

"Uh-huh."

"Sort of like hearing an old song on the radio that was popular when you were a kid. An oldie but goodie."

I couldn't see her face in the dark, but I guess she raised her eyebrows at that one. She had that tone in her voice, saying, "You making fun of me, Chip?"

"I think you were, at least a little, maybe. Yeah, like hearing an old song, in a kind of way. The way a song or anything like that makes you feel the way you used to. Sometimes I'll walk outside during the late summer when there's a wet wind blowing off the lake, on like a really warm lazy night, and I'll walk around the block or something and the air will be the way it is in Florida. Just the right temperature and humidity, I suppose. What's the word? Sultry? But before this can even go through my mind, I'll get this feeling of being seventeen years old again, because I spent a summer in Florida when I was seventeen."

"You were in Florida? I thought you were always in Chicago."

84

"Oh, I would travel from time to time."

"What were you doing in Florida?"

"Fucking."

"That was a straight question."

"Well, it was a straight answer, honey bunch."

"At seventeen? I guess I'm retarded."

"Worry about it, why don't you?"

"I do, I do. When did you start?"

"Huh?"

"When did you start making love?"

"What are you, Mr. District Attorney? I never started. I'm a virgin, baby doll. Handle me with care." And, huskily, "If we keep on talking we'll wake Greg, and he might take a dim view of this. So let's not talk anymore. Why don't I just lie here and you can lick different parts of me and see whether or not I like it? Sort of what you might call a scientific experiment."

(I was just thinking, looking at the last part, that I'll bet it's word for word the way that conversation actually went. Obviously, since I'm putting all of this on paper after it happened, I'm just getting the dialogue as close as possible to the way it happened. I didn't wander through life with a tape recorder hanging around my neck, and I'm not the total recall type. I'm not absolutely convinced *anybody* is, and there are times when I think people who pretend to be are full of crap. But this one conversation stuck in my mind very vividly. I can hear her speaking the words even now, as if I were playing myself a record of the conversation.

(I guess that's because I thought about it so many times since then. And it struck me, and strikes me now, that it was a strange combination of games that Aileen was playing. First there was the bit about feeling like a girl, a virgin. And at the same time she kept coming on with the older-but-wiser routine and a heavy dose of the mother image. I couldn't understand how she could be a virgin and a mother at the same time. As far as I know, that only happened once.)

* * *

During the six weeks of trading orgasms with Aileen, her genius of a husband never suspected a thing. I'm just about a hundred percent certain of that. I went on working with him, and I saw him at meals and during the evening, and neither of us acted any differently toward one another than we did before. I had thought for a while that I would be eaten up with guilt over what I was doing with Aileen. No such thing. It may be that I'm just not the type for guilt, that I'm of such low moral character that I can live under a man's roof and take his money and share his bread and not feel bad about taking his beloved wife to bed. I think, though, that there's more to it than that.

After all, I wasn't doing a thing to Aileen behind his back that I hadn't done to her right in front of him, with his approval. (Well, that's pushing it, I guess; we did enlarge our bag of tricks, after all, and we went at them with a hell of a lot more enthusiasm. But you get the idea.) And she was still being faithful to him as far as their joint idea of fidelity was concerned. And, more than anything else, I knew damned well that I wasn't taking anything away from Gregor. Just by listening to the creak of his bedsprings I could tell he was getting all the use he wanted out of Aileen.

I was like a conscientious kid with the family car. I never used it when the old man wanted it, and I always brought it home in as good condition as I took it out, with gas in the tank and air in the tires.

I suppose it must go without saying that I stopped picking up odd jobs on the days when Gregor didn't need me. When it came to a choice between slipping cents-off coupons under doors or slipping fingers into Aileen, it was the world's easiest decision for me to make.

I also stopped helping out in the darkroom. I think Gregor was surprised, but I let him get the impression that I was losing interest in photography as a lifetime career. Since he didn't pay me for help, he couldn't really bitch about it very strenuously.

I had never gotten around to finding out about getting my diploma by going to night school, and of course I couldn't really do anything about it at that time of the year, it being the middle of the term, but I had planned to find out what I had to find out and write away to Upper Valley for transcripts of my record so that I could start taking courses during the summer session. I didn't bother doing any of this, and when I thought about night school at all, I more or less thought in terms of starting in the fall instead of rushing things.

And I stopped going to the library as often as I had, and I stopped wandering around Chicago looking for women, and what it came down to, really, is that if I wasn't working or sleeping or sitting around with Gregor and Aileen, then I was in bed with her. Those were just about the only four choices during that period of time.

I spent some money on clothes, and I bought things like new shoelaces and a nail file and stuff like that, but even without working the other jobs I was saving money. I would earn between forty and fifty a week helping Gregor, and my room and board cost me twenty, and I still didn't eat lunch, and it wasn't at all hard to save fifteen or twenty dollars out of each week's earnings, especially because I never left the house unless I had to. There was really no way for me to spend money, so I saved it.

This meant that by the end of May I had almost two hundred dollars, including the fifty for the modeling session. And because the money was accumulating with no strain at all I had the feeling that I was really getting somewhere and really making the kind of progress I had sworn I would make that first night at the Eagle Hotel.

When I think back on it now I wonder if maybe all of that sex was rotting my brain, because if there was one thing I wasn't doing, it was getting ahead in the world. Not in any way at all. I mean, a good long look at the pattern my life had taken would make Horatio Alger throw up.

Instead of a job with a future, I was, let's face it, working as sidekick to the world's most pathetic photographer. That's what he was, really. Taking candid pictures of morons on State Street and every few months making a big score by selling dirty pictures of his wife. And the dumbest part of it was that he worked harder for less money than if he'd been swinging a pick on a road gang, for Pete's sake. He took risks and put in long hours on his feet and just took nickels and dimes out of the street photography business. The dirty pictures made his real income, and he would have to space out the cash over a period of several months until Mark called him up and asked for more.

Now and then I wondered why he didn't go into the dirty picture business in a bigger way, hiring a variety of models and finding a way to distribute the pictures and making some real money. Not that I think being a pornographer is the best way to sail through life, but if you're going to be one anyway, why not be a successful one? It seems to me that if a girl is going to be a whore, she might as well be an expensive one. Right? So if Gregor had been the Kingpin of Filth in Chicago, or if he at least *tried* to be the Kingpin, I would have respected him. Or if he was a complete bum who just tried to coast along on the least possible amount of work, that would have at least made sense. But he wasn't lazy and he wasn't ambitious either, and this was the guy I was working for, this was the man teaching me his trade.

I mean, how stupid can you be?

I had wanted to save money, and I was saving it, but I was making, say, fifty dollars a week and saving twenty, and at the rate I was going, in twenty years I would still be making fifty a week and still saving twenty, and if you save twenty dollars a week, it will take you approximately a thousand years of steady work to save a million dollars.

(This is figured without what the savings-bank ads call The Miracle Of Compound Interest. According to them, if you put your money in a savings account you can't help winding up rich. I remember seeing a billboard telling what Washington's silver dollar would be worth today if he had put it in the bank. The figure was something ridiculously high, so I got a book from the library on coin collecting to find out what the same dollar would have been worth if Washington had *kept* it, and it turned out he would have been better off. But for all the good it did Washington he was even better off throwing it across the river. Or in it. So much for The Miracle Of Compound Interest.)

The thing is, I wasn't making real progress, and I wasn't looking for a real opportunity. And it was the same with my sex life, if you stopped to think about it, which most of the time I didn't. Because while I was having all this pleasure I was still as much a virgin as ever, and I wasn't coming any closer to not being a virgin. In fact I was actually locking myself out of any chance of losing my virginity, the same way I was keeping myself from any chance of getting a job with a future. See, I was getting satisfied with what I had with Aileen, and in the same way I was getting satisfied with that stupid job and everything else.

That was one thing about the kids in the Horatio Alger books. They were never satisfied. No matter how well things started shaping up, they had the decency to go on wanting more and more and more. So they kept pushing, and whenever opportunity knocked they ran to the door and answered it. If opportunity knocked on my door I never would have heard it because I would have been too busy putting blurry yellow cards in people's hands or putting my own blurry little hands on Aileen.

Not that I had these thoughts all the time. That was the worst of it—that I didn't. That I was content with the way things were going. Take a man who is content with what he does and the way he lives and what have you got?

A happy man, obviously.

But that's not exactly right, either, because I wasn't really contented, because I didn't have what I wanted. I was settling for less, that's what I was doing. I was having little off-in-left-field climaxes with Aileen when what I really wanted to do was slide into home plate. I was getting by in a dumb job when I really wanted to get ahead. And no matter how comfortable that couch was when Aileen was on it with me, and no matter how often that happened, sooner or later I would have to be bothered by the way things were going.

On Memorial Day, a veteran sold me a poppy. He stuck that poppy into my hand just as neatly as I had learned to stick the yellow cards into the jerks' hands, and I took it like any other jerk, only I couldn't just drop it on the ground and keep walking. Or maybe I could have done this, but then he would have been within his rights if he brained me with his crutch. I gave him a quarter and he said something about the Last Of The Big Spenders. I stuck the stupid poppy in my buttonhole. That way at least I didn't have to buy another one.

But when I walked another block, it hit me that I was more a cripple than the guy who sold me the poppy. I don't know how I made the connection. It came in one quick flash and once I had it I couldn't let go of it. I kept seeing myself with a leg missing, lurching through life like that.

And I couldn't stick around with an image like that in my mind.

I waited until the weekend was over. The Sunday paper was filled with want ads, and I bought it and sat in a diner and went through it, and I found what I wanted. It wasn't a job with a future, either, but it was one that would take me out of Chicago, and I had enough sense to know that I couldn't stay in Chicago if I wanted to get out of the tender trap I was in. I had to travel, and then I could concentrate on Getting Ahead and all the rest of it.

Monday was a work day, but I took a long lunch hour, and during that lunch hour I went over and applied for the job. And got it. (No big deal—you had to have two heads or something for them to turn you down. They were easier to get into than the Army. More later.)

And Monday night, after old Gregor went night-night, I did everything possible to score with Aileen. I tried to break those silly rules of hers and get something straight between us once and for all, and as usual it didn't work. I had more or less fixed up a game in my mind, making a bargain with myself that if I laid her I would stay in Chicago but if I didn't I would go. I gave it the old Upper Valley try and when it didn't work I took Aileen's motherly advice to behave myself and be a good boy and make sweet love with her. I got on top of her and rubbed the two of us together in a way we had both grown to enjoy no end. I made sweet love all over her stomach and she danced off to wash away the sweet love I had made, and she pecked my cheek and told me I was her sweet baby and to sleep tight, and she went into her bedroom and got back in bed with the State Street Shutterbug.

I got dressed in the dark and put my extra clothes and stuff in a paper bag. I thought about leaving a note, but I couldn't think of anything that wasn't either hopelessly corny or slightly nasty, and I didn't want to be either. I told myself I would write her a letter someday. You can tell yourself things like that as often as you want and it doesn't cost you a thing.

I sat up all night in different crummy diners, drinking

so much coffee that I kept shaking and peeing and shaking and peeing. I was downtown in plenty of time to catch my ride in the morning, and when our car left the city limits of Chicago it wasn't even noon yet.

So that was three months, and my $27.46 had turned into $191.80, which is better than it could have done through The Miracle Of Compound Interest. And I had spent more time on third base than Ron Santo.

That toddling town.

Chapter Six

WHEN I RANG THE DOORBELL, THE CHIMES played the first two bars of a hymn. I couldn't tell you which one. I stood there patiently, wanting to ring it again but holding off, and eventually I heard the pitter-patter of little old feet. I timed myself so that I was whipping off my little blue-visored cap just as she was opening the door.

She wasn't the girl of my dreams. When you are young enough and horny enough (like me, Chip Harrison, for instance) you can't even open a Coke bottle without hoping there will be a beautiful girl in it. And on this job I kept waiting for the time one of the doors would be opened by a Neglected Young Housewife, or a Wanton Suburban College Girl Home From School, or an Off-Duty Whore.

And instead the doors kept being opened by women who stopped thinking about sex the day Hayes beat Tilden.

This one must have gone to school with Tilden's grandmother, from the looks of her. She was a tiny wrinkled little lady with bright eyes the color of frostbitten lips. Her face cracked into a smile.

She looked up at me and said, "Yes, young man? You've come for the bake sale donation, haven't you?"

I said I was afraid I hadn't, and I went into a little explanation of who I was and why I had turned up on her doorstep. While I talked I held my cap in both hands and squeezed it in and out of shape. I didn't do this because I was nervous. That's just the way it was supposed to look, because according to old Flickinger the more nervous and earnest you seemed the more trustworthy you were, at least as far as old ladies were concerned.

It was hard to look nervous without doing the little bit of business with the cap, because I actually delivered my set piece without even paying attention to what I was saying. I might as well have been a record player. While my mouth got all the words out, my mind thought about how little this woman had in common with the girl of my dreams, and that I might have guessed as much, because nymphomaniacs don't go out of their way to have chimes that play hymns—at least most of them don't—and while I didn't recognize that tune, it certainly wasn't "Roll Me Over in the Clover."

"—free Inspection with no obligation whatsoever," I finished up, and gave my cap a final twist, and hung my head just the littlest bit, because you couldn't go overboard and look too pathetic or you got tons of warm milk and cookies shoved down your throat.

"*Rowrbazzle*," she said.

That seemed like a funny thing for anybody to say, let alone Tilden's grandmother here, but then of course I saw that she wasn't the one who said it. It was her cat. He was standing next to her, and he was as big for a cat as she was small for an old lady. He was built like a Siamese, with a blackish-brown coat and horrible yellow eyes. I always liked cats, but then they had always said sensible things like *Meow*. This was the first one that had ever said anything like *Rowrbazzle* within my hearing and I wasn't sure just how I felt about it. It put me off stride a little, if you really want to know.

"Now just one moment, young man," she said.

The woman this time.

"You wait right here, and I won't be a minute. You wait now."

I waited. So did the cat. Now would have been a good time for me to step inside and let the screen door close behind me, which was the recommended procedure at this stage of the game. Whoever had worked up the recommended procedure had never met a cat that said *Rowrbazzle*. I stayed where I was, and old Rowrbazzle stayed where he was, and the screen door was the Demilitarized Zone.

Then the old lady came back, and I slapped my smile back in place and whipped off my cap again, and then I noticed what she had in both her little liver-spotted hands.

What she had was an old dueling pistol that was almost as big as her dippy old cat. Her hands were shaking, and the pistol was bobbing up and down like a red red robin, and it was pointing at me, and it looked as though it might go off at any moment.

I said, "Hey! Hey, hang on a minute!"

"This weapon is loaded and primed, young man."

"I believe it."

"And let me assure you that it works perfectly well. It is old, but age is not always detrimental. This pistol is in full possession of its faculties."

I was sure it was. I was perfectly willing to believe that it was still every bit as good as it was the day Aaron Burr shot Alexander Hamilton with it.

"You don't understand," I said.

"You will leave this block of houses at once, young man. You will leave directly. The people on this block are all good Christians."

"You don't under—"

"Except for the young woman in Number One-twenty-one," she said her voice quavering. "She is a Methodist, and I believe her husband is a wine drinker or worse. You may stop there if you wish. I would not advise it. Last September a boy a bit older than you examined that young woman's furnace and took it all apart and refused to repair it unless he was paid. I doubt she'd let you into her house after an experience of that sort, but you may try if you wish. I've enough on my mind without protecting Methodists, and them wine drinkers in the bargain. Not that I know for a fact that she drinks with him, but they flock together, you know. And I thought you had come about the bake sale. You have an innocent face in sheep's clothing. Read the Book of Ezekiel."

"*Rowrbazzle.*"

"Calvin dislikes you, young man. Our animals can sense things which we can only discover through reasoning. I am going to count ten, and if you are not off my property by the time I reach ten, I will shoot you. I do not hold with violence, but the Lord protects those who look to their own protection. Read the third chapter of the Second Samuel. One. Two. Three. Four—"

I scrambled down the porch steps and between two rows of private hedge to the street, expecting a musket ball to come tearing into me at any moment. The only reason it didn't was that I was well out of the way before her tinny old voice got to ten. Otherwise she would have shot me. No question about it, she would have blown my goddamned head off without thinking twice about it. If Calvin said *Rowrbazzle* to you, you just didn't stand a chance around there.

I passed up all the houses on that block. Even the lady in Number 121, the Methodist. I didn't care if she was a Sun Worshipper. I wasn't taking any chances.

Around the corner I almost collided with Jimmy Joe. He started to tell me he had just written out an order, but I cut in and told him about Calvin and *Rowrbazzle* and Grandma Tilden. "Oh, that's nothing," he said airily. "I've had more guns pointed at me than fingers. They never shoot."

"This one would have."

"Ninety-nine times out of a hundred the guns aren't even loaded. These people keep unloaded guns around just to put guys like you and me uptight. And the average person, especially a lady, they couldn't hit a barn from inside of it."

"This gun was loaded, and she would have shot, and she wouldn't have missed."

"Yeah, sure. Prove it."

"Okay," I said. I was still having trouble catching my breath. "Okay, smart ass. You go up on the porch and give her a pitch and see if she shoots you or not. I'll bet you ten bucks you get shot."

"It's a sucker bet for you. If she shoots me, how do you collect?"

"I'll take my chances."

He laughed. When he did this, it always reminded me of a big old boxer who belonged to one of the masters at a school I went to in Connecticut. That dog barked just about like that. "Forget it," Jimmy Joe said. "The important question is did she call the cops."

"I don't think she would. Never even threatened to. She's the vigilante type."

"That's all to the good."

"But I'm not supposed to go on that block because of all the God-fearing Christians. And one Methodist."

"Methodists are Christians."

"You want to go tell her? If Flick wants me I'll be working the next block over."

"They're all new houses."

"How's the one after that?"

"Better."

"Then that's where I'll be. Luck."

"Up yours," he agreed. "And watch out for the Christians."

"Right, and you watch out for the Lions."

I didn't meet any more old ladies with dueling pistols that afternoon, or any cats named Calvin with weird vocabularies. I did meet a whole lot of people who had no trouble closing the door in the middle of my pitch.

I had always thought that was about the most aggravating thing that could happen to someone working door to door, getting a door slammed in your face. It can be sort of jarring the first couple dozen times it happens, but I'll tell you something, once you get used to it you learn to welcome it. Not that you set out looking to get doors closed on you, but if you're going to strike out anyway, which is going to happen ninety-nine times out of a hundred to the greatest salesman who ever lived, you might as well strike out as soon as possible.

The less time you waste on the stiffs, the more calls you

can make in a given period of time. And the more calls you make, the more sales you make, and that's gospel. Old Flickinger says he'd rather have a chimpanzee who makes a hundred calls a day than a genius who makes fifty. Good old Flick.

"I been on the road for thirty years and more, kid, and if I learned one thing it's you don't lose money by ringing doorbells. And if there's one word of advice I can give you it's never get into any woman's pants without she signs on the dotted line. Once you got the order written it's another story. With the sale made you can afford half an hour in the kip, even an hour if you like the broad's style. But without you get the order there's no percentage. You just waste time you can't afford, and then all she wants to do is get you out of there without she buys anything, or else she keeps you around and gives you coffee and dangles it in front of you that maybe she'll buy, and you wind up going another round in the kip, and you waste the whole fucking afternoon without you get any order at all. Now maybe you'll give her a kiss or a feel to set up a sale, on the lines of what you might call a free sample, but that's all. If there's one word of advice I can give you that's it."

Good old Flick. The first time I heard that little speech I saw myself giving in gracefully to one woman after the next, and doing so well in bed with them that I got order after order, and—Well, there's no big suspense to keep up, since Francine wasn't in the picture yet and you know I was still as pure as Ivory Soap when I met her, so let's just say that it wasn't like that at all in the door-to-door game, at least not for me, and while Flick's advice might have been sound, I wasn't getting a chance to put it into practice.

As I said, I got doors closed in my face, and I also got the usual percentage of dimwits who felt sorry enough for me to let me give them the whole speech, but who didn't feel sorry enough for me to let me sell them anything. And then just before it was time to quit I hooked a gray-haired lady who lived all alone in a Victorian house that must have had a hundred rooms in it. She had a cat, but it said what any normal cat says. She said its name was Featherfoot, and that it was a boy but she had had it fixed. She said it so daintily that I almost asked what had been wrong with it. She also had had it declawed so it wouldn't ruin the furniture. She might have gone all the way and had it stuffed so that it wouldn't go to the bathroom and to cut down on the cost of feeding it. If I ever have a cat, which I probably won't, since it's hard enough to keep myself in sardines, let alone two of us, I would let it keep its claws and its balls intact. I mean, if you don't want the complete animal, I don't think you should have any of it. I mean, how would you like it if you were a cat and they did *that* to you?

That's getting off the subject, but so did this old lady. She went on and on about one thing or another. She had lost her husband a year ago, she told me. I was sort of listening to every third word out of her mouth, so I thought at first that she must have lost him in one of the hundred rooms in that old barn. But of course she meant he was dead. I hate people who don't like to say certain words, so they say that the cat is fixed when they mean castrated, or that their husband is lost when they mean he's dead as a doornail.

She kept on talking, and I went around the house on a tour of inspection, and she droned on about how much trouble there was in keeping up a house when you were a woman all alone in the world. I knew I had her then. I worked my way around the back of the house until I found a spot where there were traces of sawdust on the concrete, and I whipped out my magnifying glass and made clucking noises.

"Oh, dear," she said. "Oh, land's sake."

I pointed to the sawdust. "See that?" I said.

She saw it and started apologizing for never having noticed it before. I developed a sudden thirst and asked her if she thought I might be able to have a glass of water.

When she came back with the water, I showed her a test tube half full of the little rascals. She almost spilled the water.

"Oh, dear. And you captured all of them while I was in the house?"

"That's right. There are some of the ones I missed. See, there they go."

She looked, *tsstssing* unhappily as the little devils scurried madly over the clapboard siding. That was always the real convincer. Even the most gullible person could look at the ones in the test tube and still figure his house was safe. There was always the hope in their minds that I had picked up the last of them. And the suspicious ones might point out that I could have brought the test tube along with me. But when they saw those termites actually burrowing into their own house it got them where they lived. No joke, it really did.

We went in the house and I filled out the service agreement and got her to sign it. She didn't even ask what the job was going to cost until after I had the agreement folded and tucked away. I said that the price would depend upon the extent of infestation, and that our costs were nominal, and that all our work was guaranteed. This didn't answer her question but she didn't ask again, so I guess she thought she was satisfied.

Before I could get out of there she asked to see the termites again. I gave her the tube. "Nasty nasty vicious things," she said, with all the hate in the world in her voice. And wouldn't you know that she insisted on taking the tube outside and spilling the devils out onto the sidewalk and then divebombing the living shit out of them with a can of spray insect killer. "Die die die," she said, and the poor little critters curled up and did just that.

It was a nuisance, but no real harm done. Flickinger had a five-gallon pickle jug swarming with the little bastards, and it wasn't that much trouble to get a tubeful of them. A pain in the neck, that's all.

* * *

That night I sat around the motel after I refilled the test tube. Jimmy Joe and Keegan were at a movie I hadn't wanted to see. Lester went off without saying where, probably to look for queers at the bus station. He liked girls and his suitcase was half full of pictures of naked women, but queers were always easier to find, even in the fifth largest city in Indiana, which is where we happened to be just then. You could jump off the top of the tallest building in the fifth largest city in Indiana without doing much more than spraining your ankle, but for our crew this was considered a pretty big city. We worked towns you honestly wouldn't believe. We went all through Illinois and Indiana, and sometimes the towns were so small that Lester had to find himself the one queer in the town, or what you might call the town's faggot in residence. But he always seemed to connect.

The reason I could tolerate old Lester was that he had a reasonable attitude about what he did. He didn't run on and on about it and he didn't bug you with a lot of details you'd be a lot happier not knowing, but at the same time he wasn't one of those nerds who did it on the sly, like my old roommate Haskell who tried to pretend his cock and his hand had never even been introduced to one another, for Pete's sake. If you asked him a question he'd answer it, but if you left it alone he'd keep quiet. This made him relatively easy to take.

As far as Lester was concerned there was nothing revolting about going with a queer. The only thing shameful about it was that it would be a lot better and more satisfying with a girl. But he didn't figure it made him queer to be with a queer. Not that Lester is the first person on earth to ever come up with this line of thought. But it seems to me, if you happen to care, that when two men had sex together they were both queer and it didn't make a hell of a difference which one was down on his knees. It wasn't as though Lester was just phoning in his part of the deal. But

101

whether you wanted to consider him queer or not (and if you did it wasn't a good idea to tell him about it), I got along fine with him.

See, that's one of the fringe benefits of selling termite extermination service door to door. You become very tolerant of people.

Anyhow, I was less interested in accompanying Lester to the bus station than in seeing the movie with Keegan and Jimmy Joe. There was one other member of the crew, a recently divorced ex-Marine named Solly, who was inclined to have much better luck with women than the rest of us. He was having some of that luck right now in his motel room. And Flickinger, the crew leader, was doing what he always did after sunset. What he did involved a bottle and a glass. He never minded company, but if you were going to sit with him he expected you to drink with him, and even without trying to match him shot for shot I was in big trouble, because if I took a short drink for every three long ones of his I would still be drunk in an hour and sick for the next day and a half. One drink of Gregor's lousy brandy was all right, but I wasn't ready to handle anything like a whole night of serious drinking.

Besides, as I discovered the second of the two times I had kept Flick company, he never remembered in the morning just what he had said the night before. He never said anything particularly weird either of the times I was with him, and he behaved the same as he did when he was cold sober—he never took a drink before the sun went down, or passed one up after it did—but the thing of it was that he wouldn't know one night that he had told you certain stories on an earlier night, and anecdotes that are fairly lively the first time around get a little stale the second time.

And if you tried to tell Flick that you'd heard such and such a story before, he argued with you.

So I didn't go to Flick's room, and of course I didn't go to Solly's room, and the other three guys were out somewhere, and I didn't have anything to read, and Flick owned the only car and had let Jimmy Joe and Keegan borrow it, which didn't really enter into it since I couldn't drive anyway.

Well, I mean I know how, but they get agitated if they catch you driving without a license, and I never got one.

So there was nothing to do and no place to go, and that gave this particular evening a whole lot in common with most of the evenings I'd spent since I left Chicago.

Unless you happened to work on one of those traveling sales crews, you probably don't know what they're like. I didn't have the faintest idea myself until I was actually hired and on the job. The arrangement was simple enough. The crew consisted of five guys anywhere from eighteen on up (well, I lied) and a crew leader. You would be assigned a certain territory, which in our case was eastern Illinois and western Indiana, and within that territory you would go wherever the crew boss decided and stay as long as it was worthwhile. The crew leader took care of all your regular expenses—hotel, meals, car expenses, and so on— and got reimbursed by the company.

For every sale you made, the salesman got twenty-five dollars and the crew leader got fifteen. The crew leader did his own selling too and got to keep the whole forty bucks on his own sales. (Flick's percentage was officially a secret, but it was one of the first things he told you when he sat drinking with you.)

The point is that if you made a sale you wound up with twenty-five bucks free and clear, since you didn't have any living expenses at all. If you sold one lousy exterminating job a day, you could salt away better than five hundred dollars a month. And on the other hand if you had a terrible day or a terrible week or even a terrible month, you never had to worry about missing meals or being locked out of your room, because your basic expenses were always taken care of.

I just read through that last paragraph, and it sounds as good now as it did when I first heard it. Because I haven't mentioned the one thing they didn't stress, either.

Which is that you go out as a crew for a three-month tour, and you don't collect nickel number one until you finish the tour. It wasn't hard to figure out why they did it this way. See, the system was based on the idea of five men and a crew boss, which was the best size group from an economic standpoint. And if two or three of those men decided to call it quits while the crew was working off in East Crayfish or Fort Dingbat, the whole crew stopped being a profitable deal for the company. But if a guy had to go back at the end of the hitch to collect his money, that tended to discourage him from quitting. . .

Of course you would still be entitled to your pay whether you quit or not. But being entitled didn't mean anybody was going to hand the money to you.

Or, in Flick's words, "Any of youse quits without the three months are up, you just kissed your dough goodbye. And if I ever catches youse again, you can kiss your ass goodbye, too, because I'll kick it clear to Wausau County for you."

I don't know where the hell Wausau County is. According to Keegan, who had been working what he called the Bug Game on and off for almost five years, there was another reason why they didn't pay you until your shift was done. They had to confirm the signatures. Otherwise the salesmen could just write up a couple of phony orders every day, knock down a couple of hundred dollars a week, and spend all their time watching television.

"And there are some that would do just that," he told me, with a wink. "You wouldn't believe it in a fine upstanding business like this one, Chip my lad, but there are hordes of dishonest people in this world."

I believed it.

Not that I had ever had any grave doubts on that score. But in the time I spent showing poor widow ladies my little plastic tube full of termites, I learned more about how people could be crooked without going to jail than I ever knew existed. One thing that I couldn't get out of my head was that my parents must have been real hard-core criminals. Up until then I always figured that they couldn't have been so bad if they went all their lives without getting sent to jail, but now I saw that I had been looking at it the wrong way around. If they had actually gotten themselves to a point where it looked as though they just might have to go to jail, then they were obviously a pretty criminal pair, old Mom and Dad, because you can be crooked enough to pull corks out of wine bottles with your toes and never see a cop except to say hello to, or fix a traffic ticket.

I already knew that nobody seemed to pay any attention to the law, or at least not in the way the law had in mind. In Chicago, for instance, you couldn't do commercial street photography, and even if you did you couldn't pass out handbills that way, because that constitutes an invitation to litter and means you're creating a nuisance. All of which meant that Gregor gave the patrolman on his beat ten dollars a week and never heard any more about it.

(I had always known things like this went on, but I thought, you know, that it was strictly Big Time Criminals who got involved in them. Not some plodding clod like Gregor, for Pete's sake.

And I knew some cops took graft, and how it's a big temptation and all, but to take ten dollars? A rotten ten dollars from a simp like Gregor?)

Well, this happens in more places than Chicago.

In every city or town our crew went to, there was a man Flickinger called the Fixer. The Fixer might be somebody in the police department or Sheriff's office, or it might be a politician, or it might be some lawyer or businessman who was in good with the local government. And whoever the particular fixer might be, Flick would tell him he was bringing in a door-to-door crew and he wanted to have all the red tape handled in advance, like the permits or licenses or whatever was needed, and without the bother of filling out a lot of forms. And then Flick would slip the Fixer an envelope, and the Fixer would talk to whoever had to be talked to, and he'd keep part of what was in the envelope and pass on the rest, and none of us would have to worry about any aggravation from the police. And I don't mean just that they wouldn't give us a hard time about not having licenses. Besides that, there was always the fact that a certain number of non-customers would call the cops and complain about us for one reason or another. But the word would be out, and when those calls came in the cop who answered the phone would say *Yeah* and *Sure, ma'am* and listen while all the information came over the wire and into his ear, but he wouldn't bother writing any of it down, and we would never even hear about it, unless maybe someone would call Flick privately and ask him to for Christ's sake ask his boys to be a little more diplomatic in their dealings with the natives.

Don't ask how much was in the envelope. One of the reasons Flick got that fifteen dollars a sale extra was that he knew what it would take to fix each particular fixer.

I went out into the hall and got a Coke out of the machine. I was leaning against the wall drinking it when Solly came out of his room with a plastic pitcher. He carried it to the ice machine and filled it up.

I said, "Heavy night?"

"All she wants to do is drink and screw, I wouldn't mind, only she drinks better'n she screws."

"Did you ask her if she's got a friend?"

"If she had a friend, I'd take the friend and boot this one out on her hinder. She's a pig. You, Chip, you got the right idea."

"I do?"

"Goddamn right."

He seemed to be more than a little looped. I said, "What's the right idea? Coca-Cola?"

"Not Coca-fuckin'-Cola. It's bad for your teeth, you know that?"

"Not if you use a regular bottle opener."

"Huh?" He blinked. "Smart ass. But you got the right idea. The girls I see you out with."

"Oh."

"Whattaya mean, *oh*?" Solly became very forceful when he drank. Not belligerent or nasty, just emphatic. "Decent girls, pretty girls. And I never see you with the same girl twice. Smart. The right idea."

He weaved away and plunged back to his room and woman while I tried to think of an answer.

Not that it was worth the trouble. The girls he had seen me out with were nice decent girls, all right. And pretty girls. And I guess I was getting a little better at knowing what to say to them and how to make time with them, because these weren't girls that anybody introduced me to, and they weren't girls who went out looking to get picked up. They were ordinary run-of-the-mill nice small-town girls that I would meet during the job or at a restaurant and that I would take to a movie and out for coffee or something like that.

If you can convince someone to sign a piece of paper agreeing to let Dynamic Termite Extermination, Inc. rid his house of termites and dendivorous vermin (that's what it said on the paper they signed, and you can look it up in your Funk and Wagnall's) for whatever fee DTE, Inc. wanted to charge, if you can do all that, you really ought to be able to convince some small-town girl to go to a movie with you.

But not to anything much more dynamic than a movie, as it happens.

I drank a second soft drink, but this time I made it an Uncola, probably because I was brainwashed by Solly telling me Coke would ruin my teeth. It probably would, but the Uncola probably would, too.

Because I was beginning to come to the conclusion that, everything was a con.

Which is a hell of a conclusion to come to, for Pete's

sake, especially when you happen to be descended from a long line of con men. Well, two of them anyway. And when you've decided to become a success along legitimate lines and to work hard and save your money and marry the boss's daughter and do all the other things right, too.

Why go through all that if some smooth-talking little rat could come along and stand on your stoop and twist his cap in his hands and wind up costing you a couple of hundred dollars to kill termites that weren't there to begin with, and that wouldn't hurt your house a whole lot even if they were? (Because this may be something you never thought of, in which case I'm going to be saving you a lot of money over the years, because the first thing we all learned is that maybe ninety-nine houses out of a hundred have some termites, and those houses will go on standing for a couple of hundred years without anybody doing anything about those termites. See, it takes a long time for a termite to eat a house. It even takes a long time for a lot of termites to eat a house. But you take the average idiot and show him a termite eating his house, and he figures that in another week there won't be anything left but the foundation.

(And while I'm on the subject, the second thing we all learned was that you couldn't in a million years sell an extermination job to somebody with a brick house. Flick said you can't sell them fire-proofing, either, and Flick would know; he's sold everything at one time or another, and if that includes his mother and his sister I wouldn't be surprised. But people who have brick houses seem to think the brick is what holds the house together, so—

(You know, I have the feeling that I might be telling you more about termites than you really want to know. Maybe all of this will get cut out before the book gets printed, or maybe the book won't ever *get* printed, which would mean rough sledding for one Chip Harrison, but either way I'm going to cool it at this point with all this inside information about the termite business. That's a firm promise.

(In fact, I'm going to cool it on that forgettable evening, as far as that goes, because it wasn't the kind of evening you would want to read about. I rapped a little with Lester when he came in, and I let Jimmy Joe tell me the plot of the movie he and Keegan saw. And I made up a lie about having a girl in my room and banging her while they were at the movie, and Jimmy Joe made up a lie about picking up a girl after the movie. We were both lying and knew it, but it broke the monotony in a small way. And outside of having a couple more soft drinks and reading an Indianapolis newspaper—which made the *Chicago Tribune* seem like the *Daily Worker*, or close to it—that was all there was to that evening, so there's no point wasting everybody's time with it.

(It was the night after that one that might interest you, when Solly brought the redhead back to the motel and organized a gang bang. I have to admit it was more interesting than Cokes and Uncolas. And it did more damage than any termites I ever saw.)

Chapter Seven

DURING THE DAY I HAD BEEN WORKING the same area where I'd made a sale the day before. Up until then the television weatherman had been saying it was unseasonably cool for mid-July, which meant it was reasonably comfortable. But that day it decided to get seasonable again.

I'm writing this on a cold damp rotten morning. My radiator is some slumlord's idea of decoration, completely nonfunctional. But I can get warm just remembering that day. I didn't make a sale. No one did. No one expected to. I think I worked as long as anyone, and I was back in my air-conditioned room by three-thirty. Flickinger didn't even put in a token gripe. Pointless. We could have sold air conditioners or dry ice or Japanese fans, but that was about the extent of it. It was so hot we didn't even talk about how hot it was, if that makes sense.

I skipped dinner and stretched out on my bed in my shorts and let the air conditioner blow on me. I woke up shivering, figure that one out, when Lester banged on my door. I let him in and he flopped in a chair and waited for his breath to come back. He had gone out for dinner and walked through all that heat, and looking at him made me glad I stayed around the room instead.

We talked about this and that, one thing and the other, and ultimately reached Topic A. I launched into a long story that was kind of loosely based on something that happened with Aileen, except that in this version of the story we didn't worry about being faithful to Gregor, who was a Cuban refugee dentist in the latest version. I don't know if Lester believed it or not. I don't think he cared enough to worry whether it was true or not. When you sit around swapping sex stories to keep from dying of boredom, nobody really gives a shit if they're true or not. Just so they're sufficiently interesting and/or horny to keep you awake.

"You know something?" he demanded, when I had carried Carmelita and myself to the heights of rapture. "When all is said and done, no woman really knows how to give head."

I made a noncommittal noise.

"You agree with me, Chip?"

I said something that sounded like *Rowrbazzle*.

Because it was one of those questions like *Have you stopped beating your meat*? Whatever you said, you came off either more ignorant or more informed than you might want to.

Lester talked for a while, sort of saying but not saying that he was afraid he got more of a kick out of the queers than he wanted to, and hinting that if he did have a woman available on a steady basis he might miss the Greyhound Terminal set, water on the knee and all. I just made grunting sounds, which was all the situation called for. One thing I've noticed is that when you want to talk something out and get it right in your mind, all you really want the other person to do is be there with his mouth shut. It's a way of talking to yourself without feeling a little flaky about it.

He dropped the subject when Jimmy Joe came in unannounced and stuck his head in front of the air conditioner.

"Hey," he wanted to know, "am I interrupting anything?"

"We were talking about sex," Lester said.

"That's the trouble. Everybody talks about it and nobody does anything about it." And he sat down on the carpet and joined the party.

Bit by bit they all filtered in. Keegan first, and then Flickinger himself, standing at the door with a stupid look on his face and a bottle of gin in each hand. He came in and said he felt like company, and why didn't we all join him in a drink? No one could think of a reason not to. We drank gin on the rocks out of water tumblers. Keegan smacked his lips, wrinkled his nose, frowned, and said he wanted a little less vermouth next time around.

111

That reminded Flick of a story. I knew it would, because I had heard the story twice before, the two times I got drunk with him. Every last one of us had heard that goddamned story but nobody wanted to ruin his evening by saying anything about it.

You know, somewhere in this world Flickinger must have a drinking buddy who has the same kind of memory as Flick does. And I can just imagine the two of them sitting up night after night, lapping up the sauce and telling each other the exact same stories every single night. And each time Flick would think he was telling the story for the first time, and each time the other juicehead would think he was hearing it for the first time, and the two of them would go on and on, repeating like a decimal until the world came to an end.

Flick finished his story, finally, and poured everybody another drink whether they needed it or not, and got that look on his face that let you know another story was on its way. Before he could get his mouth in gear, Keegan said, "Why isn't Solly at our little party?"

He wasn't looking for an answer. He just wanted to throw a question in Flickinger's way. But no sooner were the words out than the door flew open, and there, drunker than the five of us put together, was Solly himself.

"Well, it's about time," he said. "Wondered where you all went to. Knocked on this door and that door and thought you were all gone, and you're all here. Goddamn good thing, too. Never forgive yourselves if you missed this."

"Somebody give him a drink," Lester suggested. "Brought you boys a present," Solly said. He stuck out his hand and just left it hanging there, waiting for someone to put a drink in it as Lester had suggested, but that's the trouble with indefinite orders; we all waited for somebody else to give Solly a drink, and Solly's hand just stayed out in the air for a little while before he remembered where he had left it and brought it back.

112

"A present," he repeated, and got his hand back, and stuck it out into the hallway and brought it back in again, only now there was a girl's wrist in it, with a girl attached. A redhead with a see-through sleeveless blouse and a flaring white miniskirt that ended less than an inch short of indecent exposure.

"This is Cherry," he said, and started to laugh.

"Jesus Christ in Marlboro Country, but if this here is Cherry then I'm an unkey's moncle."

He tried to say it straight, and muffed it again, and fell apart laughing. Then he tried again from the beginning.

"This here is Cherry," he said. "Her name. She wants to get checked out for dendivorous insects. No, what she wants is to get laid and relayed and parlayed. Screwed, blewed, and tattooed. She wants to take on everybody who's game, and I thought of my old buddies, and I thought, shit, what else do you do for kicks when it's a hundred and ten in the shade?"

Cherry was just standing there with a simple smile on her face. I guess that was the only kind she was capable of. She did look simple. There was no getting around it. She looked great, with a face that was reasonably pretty even if you didn't fall heart-stoppingly in love with her, and with a body that would have made you willing to have her around even if the face had been horrible.

But there was something in that face, some quality that was part stupidity and part vacancy, in the sense that if you opened up her head you would find a sign saying that part of her mind was on a sabbatical in Europe or something. So she stood there looking dumb and desirable, and that's exactly what she was.

The rest of us were saying encouraging things like *Hey* and *Wow* and *Sounds good* and *No crap.*

And Solly put one of his hands on Cherry's little behind and gave kind of a shove, and she took four or five little running steps into the room. Solly followed her inside and closed the door.

113

"Now show the boys what you got there," he said. "Get your clothes off, Cherry. Hurry it up. Any of you bastards got a deck of cards? High goes first and so on in order, and the same order for seconds and thirds, and after that we'll worry about it."

"Seconds and thirds?"

"Look at her. How often do you get a shot at something like that? You guys, I don't know, you guys get so little ass that when you jerk off you close your eyes and pretend you're jerking off. You think one shot at Cherry here is going to be all you want? Jesus, *look* at her!"

I don't know who he was talking to, because I'm pretty sure we were all looking at her. It seemed to me that she looked awfully young, but that happens with simple people. They don't have the sense to worry about things.

She took everything off, and she stood there with the same smile on her face, and I thought, well, take a good look at this one, Chip, because this is the one you'll never forget, the first girl ever for you, and nothing can stop you now.

"Ace is high. Suits are spades high, then hearts, then diamonds and then clubs. Same as in bridge, but you bastards don't play bridge. Cut the cards, dammit."

Keegan wanted to cut first to determine the cutting order. Jimmy Joe told him to for Christ's sake save the comedy for some other time. Flickinger, for once in his life, wasn't reminded of a story. Lester looked as though they could tear down every Greyhound station and throw all the faggots on the fire and he wouldn't mind for a minute. Solly cut the pack and got the seven of clubs and said something appropriate. Keegan cut the jack of diamonds. Jimmy Joe got the jack of clubs and insisted that put him ahead of Keegan. Keegan told him to piss off. Solly said diamonds were ahead of clubs. Jimmy Joe told Solly to piss off. Flickinger was sitting on a chair next to Cherry.

He had one hand on her behind and was stroking up along the inside of her thigh with the other.

I was going to get an ace. I knew it. I could feel it, the way sometimes you can feel things.

Lester cut a nine, it doesn't matter which suit. Flickinger was so busy with Cherry it was hard to get his attention, but finally he cut the cards and got the queen of hearts.

Solly said, "Son of a bitch, that puts him first. He gets fifteen bucks every time one of us makes a sale, and now he gets first crack at her crack."

"Wait a minute," someone said. "It's the kid's turn."

"Flick might as well start. Queen's gonna be high."

"Aces are higher than queens," I said. I gave the words a Dean Martin drawl because I felt just that cool and confident I reached out for the pack of cards, cut, and got the fucking four of clubs.

They all laughed their heads off, except for old Flick who was too busy getting his pants off.

Lester put a glass of gin in my hand. "No sweat," he said. "Somebody's gotta be last. Just five guys ahead of you. The condition everybody's in, you'll be in the saddle in fifteen minutes. If it takes that long."

"Shit," I said. I drank the gin in one swallow. I don't ever do that, not even with a normal sized drink, and this was a whole glass of gin. I had already swallowed it before I realized what I had done, and even then I didn't give a damn.

"A girl like this, she'll just be warming up when you get her."

"I'll bet."

"Look at her face. Jesus, look at the old bull socking it to her, and she just lies there with that grin on her face. Like she's enjoying herself but it isn't really reaching her. You get a girl like that who wants to pull a train, you'd think of her as basically hot, right? But look at her. Cool as ice. That's the thing. It takes her three or four men just to put her in the mood. God almighty, but will you look at Flickinger. I didn't know he had it in him. Hung like a stud horse, too. If she can't feel what he's throwing her she must have a bun full of novocaine. He's gonna ruin her for the rest of us if he don't hurry up and get it over with."

"He'll ruin her for the entire human race," someone else said. "She won't be fit for anything but donkeys and horses. Take it easy, Flick!"

"And get it over with, Flick, you mother!"

Flickinger got it over with, and almost got himself over with in the process. He finished roaring, and collapsed on the girl, and whether it was the sex or the liquor or what I don't know, but he went out like a light. We had to roll him off of her, and Keegan kept saying that he was probably dead, but he wasn't. We got him into a chair and let him sit there by himself while Keegan took over for him.

Somebody handed me the bottle. I knew what I was doing this time, but all the same I took a drink. Just a short one, though. Not that I was afraid I wouldn't be able to do anything. I knew I would be able to do anything I wanted to do.

But what worried me was that I might be like Flickinger and have a blackout. If I finally got laid after all this time and then couldn't even remember it, for Pete's sake, I might as well kill myself.

I wondered if Flickinger would remember. Maybe he just forgot telling stories to people. I looked around to make sure he was okay. He was conscious now, but his breath was coming along pretty raggedly.

While Keegan gave her a slow rhythmic banging, the rest of us somehow automatically started taking off our own clothes. We didn't say anything but just did this. I suppose the idea was that we were getting ready so that no time would be lost, but it didn't make any real sense for me, for example, to be in such a mad rush to get out of my clothes when there were still four men who were going to have her before my turn came.

What it was, I suppose, was that we were all knocked out enough by the heat and the air conditioning and the sexual excitement of the scene that the usual inhibitions were gone and the raunchier the whole evening got, the better we were going to like it.

When I thought about it later, for example, I couldn't remember anyone actually saying that we would stand around watching while each of us took a turn with Cherry. This was never put into words, and yet once things got into gear, we all more or less took it for granted that that was how it would go. Normally I would have found that idea a little off-putting. I would have gone along with it, maybe, but I would have at least questioned it a little. You would think it would just be more natural for a group of men to want to make it with the girl in private rather than as part of a group thing. Maybe we all wanted to watch each other with Cherry, and maybe we wanted to be watched, but it took the special mood of the evening for all of this to come into the open and to be taken so completely for granted by all six of us.

Keegan suddenly increased the pace, and we were all sort of nodding along in rhythm with him as he hit his stride and finished. He was no sooner out than Jimmy Joe was in his place, all hunched up over Cherry so that he could nibble at her breasts as he humped away at her. I got a look at her face. Her eyes were half lidded and her jaw was slack, and she was drooling a little bit out of the corner of her mouth. That was about the extent of her participation in what was going on. She didn't even move very much, just giving her behind a slight wiggle every once in a while, maybe to prove to us that she hadn't gone and died somewhere along the way.

Jimmy Joe didn't last very long. After just a few seconds he started cursing his head off as he gave a last thrust and came. He was swearing all the way through, and he went on swearing after he withdrew, and he walked all the way across the room still cursing under his breath.

"Hey," Keegan said, pleasantly, "why don't you put a sock in it, huh? Pipe down."

"Goddamn sonofabitching—"

"Happens to everybody," Keegan said.

"What a time to turn into a rabbit."

"You got excited," I said. The world's foremost authority, Chip Harrison, passing out free advice.

"You'll feel easier the second time around."

"Or the third," Keegan said.

Jimmy Joe stopped swearing. Lester was taking his turn, not lying on top of her but standing with his feet on the floor. Maybe all those hours in bus station toilets had him thinking he had to be on his feet to enjoy sex. He had Cherry arranged so that her legs hung over the edge of the bed, and then he picked up her feet and doubled them up with her knees deeply bent, and then he bent over her and got down to brass tacks. It was an interesting position and the rest of us commented on its fine points, like sportsmen checking out a thoroughbred racehorse.

"He's really getting in that way," Solly noted.

"You double 'em up that way, you can just about tickle their tonsils."

Someone else said he preferred to do his work lying down, and the discussion moved along, and Lester turned his head and told us to shut up, managing to do this without missing a beat.

But I noticed something about Cherry. She was starting to get interested in what was happening.

Lester had told me this would happen, but I didn't really believe him. It was true, though. There were loads of sweat on her forehead and upper lip now, and between her breasts. She was breathing hard, and her hips were bucking and twitching, and after all the time she had spent just lying there, she was gradually getting into the mood in a big way.

Which meant I was the lucky one, I thought, reaching for the bottle and knocking back another drink I mean, they were just getting her ready for me. I was the one who was going to have the best time of it.

I guess her excitement had an effect on all of us. The talk gradually died down and stopped completely. The five of us watched in silence, eyes riveted to the two of them on the bed.

Lester finished. He dragged himself off the girl's body and staggered over to the bathroom. Solly took his place and just stood there for a minute, looking down at the girl I wanted to ask him what the hell he was waiting for, but I didn't break the silence.

He sighed, then put a hand down and touched her between her legs.

She moaned. I guess it was the first sound I could remember hearing her make.

He lifted his hand and looked at it. "Soaking wet," he said to himself. "Dripping, the little minx is dripping. And hot."

Come on, I thought. Come on already.

He entered her slowly, very slowly, and she moaned again, a rippling moan that was unlike any sound I'd ever heard. I was a little worried now that Solly was going to be the lucky one to make her come. It was a pretty silly thing to worry about now that I think back on it, but at the time it seemed very important that I be the one to do this. So I stood there with my hands in fists, wishing that Solly would learn Jimmy Joe's impersonation of a rabbit.

He worked slowly at first, in and out, very slowly, and my whole brain was filled up with the picture of the two of them rolling around on my bed, locked together in this slow thoughtful screw. If there's anything that looks more ridiculous than people screwing, I don't know what it is. I mean, if you stopped to think what you look like when you're doing it, the facial expressions and the position and all, you might not feel as much like going through with it. They looked foolish, but they also looked as though what they were doing was a tremendous amount of fun.

Then bit by bit the tempo picked up, with each of them working at the same pace. She spoke for the first time, begging him to do it harder and faster. She talked nonstop, and she didn't use more than five different words all in all, and three of them were obscene, which is a pretty good average if you spread it over a person's whole vocabulary. She begged him to do it, and he did it, and she wrapped her legs around him and dug her nails into him and really let herself go, kicking and screaming her head off.

Solly gave a cross between a growl and a roar. He pitched forward on her the way Flick had done earlier. But Cherry didn't stop kicking and screaming and wiggling her tail, as if she didn't realize that the record was over. For a few seconds Solly just lay there being tossed around by her hips. Then he grunted and heaved himself up and away from her. She tried to hang on. He unhooked her arms from around his neck and dumped her on the bed.

"She don't know when to quit," he said to no one in particular. I started for her, but he was standing in the way, just shaking his head and saying that she was a crazy little broad who didn't know when to quit.

She was writhing on the bed, making noises like cats fighting under a full moon. "Oh, I almost made it," she said. "Oh, I'll make it this time, somebody, help, please, somebody, I'll make it this time."

Keegan started for her. I grabbed him by the shoulder and spun him around.

"My turn," I said.

"Oh," he lied, "I forgot about you."

"Sure you did."

"Easy, now. If you want to stand arguing, someone'll take your turn. That what you want?"

"You know something, Keegan? I never realized it before, but you know what you are?"

"Lad—"

"You're a son of a bitch, Keegan."

"Easy, now," Keegan said.

"Please," Cherry said. "Please please please please—"

"*Open up in there,*" a voice said.

"Please please please—"
"Open that door."

The room went silent again. I had shouldered Keegan aside and was on my way to the girl.

Someone grabbed my arm. I shook the hand off.

They kicked the door in. Four cops the size of the Green Bay Packers. One of them went around waving a badge and a gun at everybody, and the other three pulled me off Cherry.

I bit one of them in the leg and hit one of them in the face and kicked one of them in the family jewels. If there had just been the three of them I think I would have taken them. I really mean it. But the fourth one managed to get behind me and hit me over the head with the butt of his gun.

"Oh, you rats," I heard Cherry howling. "I almost made it. Another minute and I would of made it, you rats. I'll never let you dirty cop rats screw me again. Never, damn you. Oh, I almost made it—"

The gun butt popped me again. The lights went out and so did I.

You know, I can understand how people can become paranoid. It isn't that hard to figure out. When things have been going wrong in one particular way over and over again, it's natural to figure that there's a conspiracy against you.

Take me, for instance. (Take me! I'm yours!) No, seriously. Here I was, for Pete's sake, with just one thing I really wanted to do, and I was being turned at every thwart. I was playing the goddamned Doris Day part in one of those movies where the big question is whether or not Doris can keep her legs together until the end of the film, and the big answer is always yes.

You already know about Francine—remember? To hook your attention? The gun going off—and here I was the last man in line at an orgy and the cops came in just when my number came up.

121

Why shouldn't I be paranoid? Obviously those cops were just waiting in the hallway for it to be my turn. Obviously someone had switched decks of cards, so that I wound up cutting a deck where every card was the fucking four of clubs. Obviously there was a hole in the wall, or a two-way mirror, and good old Gregor was out there taking pictures and old Haskell was watching and beating off in the name of sociological research, and the Head was laughing, and the basketball coach was saying that a winner never quits and a quitter never wins, and Cherry was taking off her red wig and revealing herself as Aileen, being faithful to Gregor in her peculiar way, and Calvin was saying *Rowrbazzle*, which means *Up your ass* in Siamese, and my parents weren't really dead, they were just trying to escape from their boring mess of a kid.

I couldn't have been unconscious for very long, because the first thing I saw when I opened my eyes was a pair of baggy pants. I watched as the pants were pulled up past my face and onto Flickinger, to whom they belonged. I was lying on the floor next to the bed, and Flickinger was sitting on it, and pulling his pants on.

I stayed where I was. There were conversations going on, but my head was buzzing and I was sort of listening *through* the conversations without hearing them, the way you do when you watch an Italian movie. All I knew was that there were four cops in the room, along with the five guys from the crew. I didn't see or hear Cherry.

I guess I must have realized sort of vaguely that nobody was paying attention to me, and that this was Just As Well. So I was very careful to stay where I was, and I closed my eyes again, and I found out that with my eyes shut my ears worked again, and I listened to what they were saying.

A voice I didn't know, a coppish voice, was saying, "Boy, your ass is grass. You're gone be in jail so long you'll be able to homestead your cell. I just hope you like what you got off of that little girl tonight, because you won't get anything else off anybody else for the next twenty years. Indiana don't care about statutory rape, now. Indiana don't care for that at all."

"She did act like a statue at first," Flick said. "But she was no statue toward the end there. Without you jokers were kicking the door in, she was humping like a camel."

"Now I told you about your rights," the cop said. Or maybe it was another cop. If you've heard one cop, you've heard them all. "And about your rights to an attorney, and how statements made voluntarily may be introduced as evidence in criminal prosecutions against you. You recollect I gave you that warning."

"Cut the shit," Flick said.

"Because you're just digging your grave with your tongue, boy, and I want to make sure you know what you're about."

"Something about raping a statue," Keegan said. He sounded as unconcerned as Flickinger, and I couldn't understand it. Neither could the cops. The guys were drunk, but it didn't seem possible that they were drunk enough to be this way.

Solly said, "That was no statue, that was my wife."

"Not funny, boy. That young lady was under the age of consent."

"That was no young lady," Lester put in. "That was my statue."

"What's the age of consent here anyway?"

"Eighteen same as most everywhere else."

"And you mean to say that girl was seventeen?"

"No, sir," the cop said. He sounded very Jack Webbish. "I mean to say she was fifteen."

"Well, I declare," Lester said. "Why, the little liar swore up and down she was thirty-five."

The room rocked with laughter. I didn't laugh, and neither did the cops. They made threatening sounds and talked about going on down to the station house. Jimmy Joe hummed *Dum-Da-Dum-Dum* and got a laugh. Flickinger

stood up, stepped over me, and started rasping away in his
No More Of This Nonsense voice. He saved it for special
occasions, and it was very impressive. He told the cops
that they could cut out this shit about warning us of our
rights, because the same rights meant that they couldn't
kick the door in without a warrant, and since we were in a
private room with a closed and locked door, they had no
case, and—

"We had a warrant," the cop said.

"Huh?"

"Naming you six men." He read our names. "That's you
folks, isn't it?" Flickinger allowed that it was us, all right. I
was relieved, for no particular reason, when he read my
name as Chip Harrison. When he was going down the list
I had the weirdest idea that he was going to read off *Leigh
Harvey Harrison*, and that was all I needed.

"And charging you six men with fraud, attempted fraud,
soliciting without a license, several counts of trespass and
criminal trespass, and miscellaneous violations of the
following civic ordinances—" and he read off a batch of
numbers.

"Now just a minute," Flick said. He still didn't seem at
all worried, and I decided he was crazy.

I didn't know what any of those numbers were supposed
to mean, but it sounded as though they had enough against
us to put us away for hundreds and hundreds of years.
And the worst part of all was that this had happened before
I could get to Cherry. Whatever jail they put me in, the
odds were good that there wouldn't be any women in it,
which meant I'd be a male virgin until I was too old to be
interested.

I shuddered, then tuned Flick in again. "Where you
made your mistake," he was saying, "was that you came
down here without you checked it all out with the Sheriff.
Now if you would of done this we wouldn't have any
trouble. Now what you got to do is get on the phone and
ring the Sheriff and tell him what's happening, and you

can let me have a couple of words with him, and we'll have this whole thing straightened out in a minute."

"You and the Sheriff are close, is that right?"

"The closest. And there's no hard feelings, and to prove it there'll be something in it for you fellows, too. More or less to make it up to you for your time."

"That's attempting to bribe an arresting officer," the cop said. "Write that down, Ken."

"You'll have to spell it for him," Keegan said, and then there was an *oof* sound, as though someone (like Ken) had hit someone (for instance, Keegan) in the stomach.

"Officer," Flick said, coming down hard on the first syllable, "I think I have to spell it out for *you*. The fix is in."

"Is that right?"

"You talk to the Sheriff and—"

"I talked to him an hour ago. That's his signature on the bottom of the warrant there, boy."

"Like hell it is."

A long pause. Then Flickinger said, "It says Harold M. Powers. Now who in the precious hell is Harold M-for-Mother Powers?"

The cops all laughed. They really enjoyed themselves. I guess when you're a cop you don't get all that many opportunities to cut loose and laugh, and they made the most of this one. *"Now who in the precious hell,"* one of them started, and they broke up for a while, and another finished, *"is Harold M-for-Mother Powers?"* and they all fell out all over again.

Until finally one of them said, "Why, I'll tell you, boy, if you're so close with him, how come you don't even recognize the Sheriff's name?"

"What about Barnett Ramsey?"

"Why, we had an election some six or eight months ago, and old Barney got beat."

"He lost the election," Flickinger said. Heavily.

"After all those years. Yeah, it surprised a whole mess of folks."

"Great bleeding shit," Flickinger said. "Jesus frigging Christ with a tambourine. Holy laminated bifurcated ocellated Mother of Pearl."

"I never heard the like," one cop said softly.

"Sweet shit in a bucket," Flickinger said. "I bribed the wrong man."

Everybody started talking at once. I took a deep breath and said a quick prayer and rolled under the bed.

Chapter Eight

I DIDN'T REALLY EXPECT TO GET AWAY with it, but they had been doing such a great job of ignoring me that I figured I ought to give them all the encouragement I could. The easier I made it for them, the better.

So I rolled under the bed, and since I was right next to it already, and on the floor, and more or less face down, it wasn't that hard to do. In a sense I suppose *rolled* is the wrong word for it. I sort of crept on my belly like an earthworm. Sideways, though earthworms, as you probably know, tend to go back and forth. I don't know how you tell an earthworm's back from his forth. It was never very important to me. I don't even like to go fishing, for Pete's sake. I do know, though, that earthworms are male at one end and female at the other, so you know what they can do.

Lying under that bed, I decided that the police force of the fifth largest city in the state of Indiana could do the same thing earthworms can, for all I cared. Because it occurred to me that they were not only going to give me the royal shaft, but they were going to give it to me for something I didn't do. In the first place I was only seventeen myself, so what I did to Cherry wasn't statutory rape, and in the second place I hadn't done anything in the first place.

Which seemed to indicate that as soon as I clued them in, they would let me go.

But I didn't think they would. So I stayed under the bed while Flickinger told everybody who would listen that it would take a while to straighten everything out, but that he knew everything would be straightened out, because one thing you couldn't deny was that he and his men represented Dynamic Termite Extermination, Inc., and that DTE was no fly-by-night outfit but a company that had been a leader in its field for twenty-two-count-em-twenty-two years, and that was by God a lot of goddamn years.

(This was the God's honest truth, as a matter of fact I had trouble believing it myself, but it was. The company didn't ever do a thing that was illegal. If a crew boss ran things on the shady side, they didn't want to know about it. If a crew boss ran things on the up and up, that was fine with DTE. Of course an honest crew boss couldn't possibly clear fifteen cents a month, but that was the way it went. You couldn't call the company crooked just because all its employees were crooked, could you?)

"We'll be out of this in no time," Flick said. "Youse guys just trust me on this without you all lose your heads and get rattled. All right, we gotta go see the Sheriff, that's what we got to do. That's all."

They finished getting dressed, and they talked about things, and they asked the cops if Cherry was really only fifteen, and the cops said she was, and Lester asked one of the cops how often Cherry generally got statutorily raped, and the cop said as often as she possibly could, and Lester asked why anybody would make a fuss over it then, and the cop said it was because it was the sort of thing the city couldn't take lying down, and Lester said that if Cherry could take it lying down, he didn't see why the city couldn't. The cop laughed and said that was sure a good way of putting it. I think this comes under the heading of Fraternizing With The Enemy.

And I kept waiting for somebody to say, "Hey, what happened to the kid we had to hit over the head?"

Or for one of the guys on our side to say, "Say, what the hell happened to Chip?"

Or for somebody, anybody, to sing out, *"Look who's hiding under the bed!"*

But they found other things to say, and the door opened, and they trailed out of it and left it ajar. I don't know to this day where Cherry was during all of this. I didn't see her or hear her, and I didn't hear anybody talk to her, or say anything that gave the impression she was in the room. But I didn't see how she could have been taken anywhere because all of the cops were still in the room, so who would have taken her away? I guess either they sent her home by herself or a matron came for her while I was unconscious. Or else she was what you would call a plant, and the police had sent her over there to begin with so that they could give us all the shaft. (I don't really believe that last one at all. But I'm putting it in to give you an idea of how paranoid a person can get under the right set of circumstances. After all, somewhere out there is my old roommate Haskell, and I want to make sure the book has a certain amount of psychological significance so he won't feel guilty while he reads it and turns the pages with one hand. Hi, Haskell, you hypocritical jerk-off!)

They left the room, as I said before I got off course again. They went out, and I heard them in the hallway, and I got out from under the bed, still waiting for them to wonder what had happened to the kid. I went over to the window and yanked it open. And somebody must have wondered about me, although they were too far away from the room for me to hear them say so, because I heard footsteps racing back up the hall and a voice— Jimmy Joe, God bless him—shout out my name.

I stepped out of the window. It was the first floor, which was the one good thing that had happened that evening. And it was at the back of the motel, away from the parking lot and nowhere near where the other cops had been heading. That was the second good thing that happened that evening. And, because they come in threes, a third good thing happened that evening, which is that I ran like a cat with its tail on fire and got away without being spotted.

Which was very good.

But it could have been better. I mean, even considering the fact that my commissions were all being held for me by the Dynamic Termite Extermination, Inc. office, and that I had been doing my Coke buying and movie going out of my own savings for a couple of months, the fact remained that I had over a hundred dollars in my wallet, along with various cards to prove I was me in case I died and they wanted to make sure the body wasn't Judge Crater or Ambrose Bierce. There was also a picture of Aileen that I kind of liked, and that I would miss.

It would have been good if I had been able to bring my wallet And it would have been even better if I had had something to put my wallet in, because although the night was unseasonably hot, it's never a good idea to run amok in Indiana's fifth-largest city with no clothing whatsoever on your body.

I've read books where the hero suddenly gets struck naked one way or another. Or he breaks out of jail and has to get something to replace his prison uniform. Or he soaks his clothes swimming to safety and can't wait for them to dry. Or there are these telltale bloodstains telling tales all over the place.

When this happens in books, what the guy usually does is swipe clothing from an untended clothesline. The authors don't generally dwell on it too intently. They just throw something like *Dressing himself with clothes purloined from an untended clothesline, Stud Boring relentlessly took up the trail of the three pencil sharpeners.* Then they plunge right into the action without giving you time to think about it.

In the movies, they're even cooler about it. I saw this done just the night before last, as a matter of fact. This guy broke out of prison, out of a chain gang actually, and one moment you saw him running down the road with his prison clothes all shredded from the brambles and wet from the swamp he went through to throw the dogs off his trail, and then there was another shot of him getting off a bus, wearing a shirt and tie and carrying a leather suitcase. They didn't even cheat by giving you the abandoned clothesline bit. They just came right out and admitted that they didn't know how the hell Stud Boring got those clothes, and that they weren't going to try to fake their way out of it. I suppose you have to admire them for it. The thing of it is that if you can find a clothesline in the middle of the night, tended or untended, you are better suited to this sort of thing than I was. I don't even think I'd care to look for one in the daytime, because the checking I did showed that (a) people don't leave their clothes hanging out overnight and (b) most of them don't even have clotheslines nowadays. I went zipping through backyards looking for clothes and the whole thing was a large zero. No lines and certainly no clothes. I wouldn't have thought of looking in the first place except that I remembered all those dumb books. You've got to be very suspicious of everything you read.

I think I know what happened. Years ago nobody had clothes dryers, and everybody who washed clothes had to hang them out to dry, and with that many people washing clothes, there would always be a certain number who would forget to take their clothes in for the night, or who wouldn't get around to it because they were baking bread or beating rugs by hand or putting up preserves or watering the horses or any of those good old-time things that people don't do anymore. So in those days it was perfectly open and aboveboard to have Stud Boring steal clothes from a washline. (Open and aboveboard for the writer, I mean. It was still illegal for Stud Boring.)

But nowadays when a writer is trying to get old Stud out of a tight place, the first thing he thinks of is what he read somewhere else. (That's why so many books are the same. The writers all get ideas from each other.) And because they were never running around naked in the middle of the night, they don't know that they'd be better off looking for an abandoned clothes dryer, for

Pete's sake, in this modern day and age.

After I figured out that I wasn't going to get clothes off a line, I sat in a dark corner of somebody's garage and tried to think what to do next. I thought about going where the clothes were. Clothes in general, I mean. Not my own clothes, which were all in my room, which was a place I knew better than to go back to. But other clothes, that I could sort of find before they were lost. The first ideas I had all involved breaking into some place or other. Somebody's house, or some store that sold clothes.

I figured if I broke in anyplace I would get caught, and if I got caught I would be worse off than ever, because in addition to fraud and statutory rape they could also put me in jail for burglary. And while I thought if worst came to worst I could probably get a suspended sentence for the other charges (assuming Flick remembered who to bribe for a change), I could see myself spending a long time in prison for burglary. I also figured anybody breaking into a house or a store stood a very good chance of getting opened up with a shotgun.

Then I thought, but not for long, about Lying In Ambush and crowning somebody with a brick or something heavy, say a traditional Blunt Instrument for example, like a saxophone. Having just been hit on the head myself, I didn't want to do the same to a stranger. Besides that, you may remember that I'm not even coordinated enough to pace the Upper Valley basketball team to a regional title, and that I get nauseous just thinking about violence for any length of time. I was violent enough with the three cops, but that's something else. I mean, I had something to fight for.

Then I tripped over a muddy shoe.

To give you an idea how brilliant I was, I looked at what I tripped over and said to myself, Oh, it's a shoe, and put it out of the way so I wouldn't trip over it again. And I must have sat around scheming for another five minutes before I remembered that shoes were things you wear on your feet, and that I wasn't wearing any at the moment, and that, therefore, a muddy shoe was better than no shoe at all, and I ought to follow the old proverb that starts out *If the shoe fits.*

Here's another proverb. *If the shoe doesn't exactly fit, wear it anyway, because shoes are almost as hard to come by as clotheslines.*

These shoes were a little loose, and down at the heels, and thin in the soles, and one of the laces had been broken and tied together again. If they'd been in better shape, the owner wouldn't have used them for gardening and I wouldn't have tripped over them, so I didn't really have any right to complain.

I didn't have time to complain, either. Because I figured out that some people had special shoes that they used for gardening or painting or any kind of yard work, and others had special pants and shirts, and that if I looked in enough garages I could probably put together a wardrobe that would get me a lot of curious glances, I'll admit, but that would, all things considered, get me less attention than my present costume of shoes and nothing else.

Some people lock their garages, but most of them don't. Most people don't have anything wearable in their garages, but some of them do. And I wasn't fussy about fit or looks or style, and garages are fairly easy to get in and out of without disturbing anybody, and to make a long story short (or at least as short as possible, at this stage of the game) I wound up wearing the muddy shoes and a pair of paint-blotched dungarees and a red-and-black plaid hunter's jacket and a little peaked gardener's cap.

And in the same garage where I found the hunter's jacket I found something else, and while it didn't take the nose of a bloodhound to ferret it out (or the nose of a ferret to bloodhound it out), I'm going to come right out and say that it was brilliant of me to take it along. Look, I've told you about all of the idiot things, so I might as well take whatever credit I can get.

It was a fishing rod. The way I was dressed, there were only two things on earth I could be—a criminal on the run or a lunatic fisherman. So I took the fishing rod and transformed myself from a Threat To Society to an All-American Boy, and I walked right through the dippy town without a bit of trouble.

If this was a movie, the thing to do now would be to cut straight on through to September. Not for the sake of cheating, the way they do when they refuse to tell you how Stud Boring got dressed again, but just because nothing very interesting happened during the next two months. And if we just cut to two months later and fifteen hundred miles east of there, you wouldn't miss much.

But if you're like me you always want to know about things like that, like what happened during the two months it took me to get from the fifth largest city in Indiana to where I was in September, which is also where I am now. If I like a book and get interested, I want to know everything.

When it comes to novels, I like the old-fashioned approach where they tell you what happened to the characters after the book ended. You know, the plot's all tied up and the story is all used up and done with, and then there's a last chapter where the author explains that Mary and Harold got married and had three children, two boys and a girl, and Harold lived to be sixty-seven when a stroke got him, and Mary survived him by twenty years and never remarried, and George went back together with his wife but they broke up again after three years, and George went to California and has never been heard from since, and his wife died of pleurisy the year after he left. I like to feel that the people are so real that they go on doing things even when the book is done with them, and sometimes I'll make up my own epilogue for a book in my head if the author didn't write one himself. It's called an epilogue when you do this.

Anyway, ever since I started writing this, in fact ever since Mr. Burger said I really ought to write it, I decided I would just act as though the person reading it was more or less like myself. With a similar way of looking at things and so on. So whenever I have to decide whether to put something in or not, I ask myself whether or not I would want to read it. That's why I put in all that crap about the termite racket, for example.

What I did for the rest of July and all of August and the first week of September was farm work, for the most part. I headed east when I left town and didn't stop walking and hitchhiking until I was in Ohio. I didn't think the police would bother sending out an alarm for me, since I wasn't exactly Public Enemy Number One. I mean I wasn't the most sought-after criminal since Arlo Guthrie dumped the garbage in Stockbridge, Mass. I was breathing fairly easy as soon as I got out of the county, but I still thought it would be good to get across the state line without taking any chances.

I kept getting lifts for a couple of miles at a time because this particular highway wasn't one that anybody would take for any great distance. But on a bigger road I would have stood out like acne with my clothes and my fishing rod. On this road people either assumed I was going to a particular fishing spot or when they asked I would just say *Down the road a piece* and they figured I was keeping the spot a secret. Fishermen do crazy things like that all the time. Then I would just sit in the car until they let me out because they were turning off.

Eventually, though, I got sick of having to talk about fishing with people who all knew more about it than I did. And I got sick of carrying the pole. So I left it on a bridge over a little creek that I happened to walk over between rides. I figured whoever found it would be able to get some use out of it right away.

Then, since I didn't have the pole, people assumed I was a drifter, which was what I was, actually. And one man said, "Bet you're looking to get work picking. Cherries is gone but early peaches is coming in, and won't be a week and they be picking summer apples, the weather the way she be."

I hadn't even thought about it. I wasn't in shape to think any further than the Ohio line, to tell the truth. But farm work sounded as good as anything else I could think of, and it turned out to be just right, considering the circumstances.

You didn't need a car or a suit or a degree or any experience whatsoever. You could walk in off the road wearing paint-smeared dungarees and muddy shoes and a hunting jacket and not get looked at twice. If they had berries or melons that needed picking, or peaches or apples or sweetcorn or tomatoes, they didn't care where you went to school or who your father was or if you had a Social Security card. All they cared was if you wanted to get out in the field and pick the stuff.

Of course they didn't pay much, either. They really couldn't. Look, a pint of blueberries, say, will cost you maybe half a dollar at the supermarket, right? Suppose the farmer who grew it got half of that, which he never does, I don't think, unless he sells it himself or something. But anyway, say he gets a quarter a pint. Now if you ever picked blueberries you know that it takes forever to fill a pint container with the stupid little things. You could get the whole quarter for picking those berries and it wouldn't be exactly the highest wages in history, and that would mean the farmer was giving the berries away for nothing.

But even with the pay low, and even with being on your feet all day, and getting up early in the morning and working twelve or fourteen hours at a stretch, even with all of that, there were good things about it. Even with the backache you got from picking stuff that grew on the ground, or the bruises you got from falling off ladders while picking stuff that grows on trees , it was still a good way to cover two months and fifteen hundred miles.

For one thing, you could really eat as though food was free, because it just about was. You were expected to eat all you wanted of whatever you were picking while you picked it. (This was more of a thrill when what you were picking was red raspberries than when it happened to be summer cooking apples.) You also got three meals a day. Breakfast was three or four eggs fresh from the hen and home-baked bread and jam. All the fruits and vegetables were fresh at lunch and dinner, and they kept passing huge oval bowls full of different things around the table.

I had never eaten like that in my life. Not to say anything against my mother, but she wasn't the world's greatest cook. I suppose when you can function as a confidence woman for twenty years without ever getting caught, you can also let other people do the cooking for you. Still, I ate better at home than I did at any of the camps or schools I went to, and from the last school I had gone more or less directly to Aileen's instant coffee and non-dairy creamer and TV dinners, moving on to third-rate restaurant food in Illinois and Indiana towns.

I had gotten so I never cared much about food, probably because I didn't really know what good food tasted like. I always thought I hated vegetables, for instance, because the ones I ate always came out of cans or plastic bags and then sat on the stove for a couple of months.

Besides the food, the life was just generally healthy. They usually let you sleep in the barn, except a couple of times in large apple orchards in New York State, where there were just more pickers than there was floor space. Even then they took care of us, though, with straw

137

mattresses to sleep on and sheets of canvas to tie to the trees and sleep under, not just because it might rain but so that apples wouldn't drop on top of you.

What I mostly picked was apples. Supposedly you could make better money working vegetable farms, but I really hated the stooping, and I never got used to the feel of the sun on the back of my neck. An apple orchard is cool on hot days and had a great smell to it and you work standing up. Of course you have to expect to fall off the ladder once in a while. They say that anybody who doesn't fall now and then isn't picking fast enough. I won't say that you get used to falling off ladders, or that you grow to look forward to it, but in all the time I picked apples, I never got more than a bruise or saw anybody do worse than sprain a wrist. You learn how to fall after the first couple of times, and it sort of struck me, during one of the moments of philosophical reflection that you get plenty of in an apple orchard, that anybody who lived the kind of life I did really ought to learn how to fall.

The average apple knocker is in his twenties and grew up in the country and quit school young and keeps his mouth shut and likes to get in a fight when he's had a couple of drinks. The average apple knocker is a guy, and so is the unaverage apple knocker. There were no girls up in those trees or out in those barns or under those canvas ceilings. There was always the farmer's daughter, but she was a long ways away from what she was like in the jokes. Generally she was home on vacation from college, and she would no sooner go off with a picker than she'd pick her nose in church. Her main object was to get pinned to a fraternity boy and live in the big city where he could get rich sitting at a desk. Now and then I would manage to meet a girl.

Actually a picker could make out pretty well if he happened to be good at it. In any given area there would be certain taverns and bowling alleys that all the pickers would congregate at when they were in the neighborhood. The taverns generally had either a combo or a jukebox primed with country music. The bowling alleys had balls and pins. The pickers would holler and stomp and get drunk and fight, and occasionally someone would get cut up. You wouldn't believe how casual some of these guys would be about this. A guy might have a scar from his neck to his navel, and if you asked about it he would say, "Oh, my buddy over there cut me a touch when we were drinking." And they would still be buddies and joke about it, and eventually they would have another fight and the knives would come out again.

Girls would come to the taverns, and especially to the bowling alleys—I guess it was more respectable for a girl to go to a bowling alley, although you never saw any of them actually go so far as to bowl. And the girls who came to these places were there to get picked up by the pickers, and they knew that pickers were only interested in One Thing, and it wasn't discussions of the Great Books Of The Western World. So any girl who went with a picker was just about putting it in writing that she was willing to put out. That saved a lot of time and wasted effort on both sides, and in a business where you were never in one place very long, it made things simpler all around.

The thing was that you had to be a certain type of person to make out under those conditions. The makeout type, you might say. And it was a type that I obviously wasn't. The guys who were best at it were basically pretty stupid guys who could carry on a conversation all night long without saying anything worth hearing. But they never had to stop and think about anything. Instead they had this loose easy style that I guess made it easy for a girl to relax or something. Whatever it was, I just didn't have it. Whenever I tried to make out at taverns, I would get involved in a conversation with a girl, and she would seem interested, and then she would say she had to go to the ladies room. And I'd see her five minutes later going home with some other picker.

The girls I dated were girls you could talk to and girls you could have a pleasant evening with.

One of them was on vacation from Fredonia State Teachers College, where she was having an awful time with required science courses: she just couldn't seem to get the hang of what they were all about. Another one wanted to talk about liberal religious movements. She didn't believe in God anymore but she was afraid she wouldn't have anything to do on Sunday mornings. She sure won't want to spend them in bed unless she changes a lot, because by the time I got rid of her I needed treatment for frostbite.

There were girls I didn't get to first base with, and there were girls I did get to first base with. And some I got to second base with, and one or two who let me get all the way to third. More than one or two, maybe. But one way or another they all turned in superb clutch pitching, and no matter how many hits I got, the innings would end in a scoreless tie, with my men stranded all over the bases.

I wanted to take my bat and balls and go home.

The last apples I picked were in a small Early Macintosh orchard in Dutchess County, New York. That's about sixty or seventy miles from New York City. When we finished picking those trees, I all of a sudden knew that I didn't want to pick another apple for a very long time, or anything else. The high season was just coming on, and it was the one time of the year when a fruit picker can actually make decent money, but I was sick of it and ready for something else. I was just done and that was all.

I had around thirty dollars and two changes of clothes

including one pair of heavy boots and a pair of regular shoes. I also had a whole load of money coming to me from the termite sales. I was dumb enough to send them a couple of wires asking them to send me the dough. Of course I never heard from them.

One of two things happened: (a) Flickinger managed to bribe his way out of the mess, in which case he certainly wouldn't tell the office what had happened, so they would treat me like any deserter, or (b) they were all rotting in jail, and nobody ever so much as turned those signed orders in, and there was no money coming to me.

Either way, I had thirty dollars. Which means I had made a clear profit of a dollar a month since I left Upper Valley. I had a lot of vocational experience, none of which would get me a job with Opportunity For Advancement. And my cherry, like the winter apples, was still on the tree.

That's how I spent the summer. The more I think of it, the more I figure the movies have the right idea. Start with a long shot of a kid in muddy shoes and a hunter's jacket on a dusty Indiana road, and cut to a shot of the same kid finishing a hard day's work as a wiper in a car wash in Upstate New York. In a town which I won't name, because I'm still here now, writing this, and may be here forever.

It was in this very town that I met Francine.

Remember Francine?

To tell you the absolute truth, I'm having a little trouble remembering her myself. Good old Burger told me it was always a good idea to start off with something dramatic to hook the reader, and then go back and fill in the background and work up to it, but I have a feeling that would have been a better idea if I were someone who knew something about writing a book. If I were starting over again, I would just start at the beginning and go straight through to the end and the hell with hooking your attention and riveting your eye to the page. Either you're with me or you're not. But in case you forgot about Francine, and how things were going when I broke off to start backing and filling, it went like this:

And paused, because it seemed that a herd of elephants was stampeding up the staircase and down the hall, and voices were shouting, and Francine was roaring at me, begging me to do it, to stick it in, and I lay there, paralyzed, and the door to my room exploded inward, and a man the size of a mountain charged inside. He had a hand the size of a leg of lamb, and in that hand he had a gun the size of a cannon.

"You son of a bitch!" he bellowed.

And pointed the gun at me, and pulled the trigger.

Chapter Nine

THE GUN JAMMED.

Chapter Ten

WELL, WHAT DID YOU EXPECT?

Blood?

Look, a guy stuck a gun in my face and pulled the trigger. Now if the gun didn't jam then he would have blown my head off and you would be reading something else because I wouldn't be around to write this.

I mean, I can just hear you ducking like a chicken and saying, "Now how in the hell is he going to get out of this one?" And then on the last page it said *The gun jammed* and you said, "Oh, *shit, the gun jammed*, what a cornball way to save him."

I didn't *plan* it that way, for Pete's sake. If you want to know something, it took me a full day to write the last chapter. One stupid page with three stupid words on it and it took me all day to write it because I couldn't figure out how to tell you that the gun jammed. And finally it came to me that there was only one way. *The gun jammed.* Period, end of chapter.

I'll tell you something. I was going to make something up instead of having the gun jam. You know, to lie to you and figure out something more convincing and satisfying than a jammed gun. (I already put two things in this book that aren't true. They're out-and-out lies, actually. They're both in the second chapter. If you think you know what they are, write to me. I'd be interested to see if you get it right.)

But I couldn't think of a lie. Either I'm dictating this from the grave or the gun jammed. Well, the gun jammed and that's all there is to it, and come to think of it, I don't know why in the hell I'm apologizing, because what it amounts to is I'm apologizing for being *alive*, and that doesn't make any sense.

Chapter Eleven

WHEN HE SAW THAT THE GUN WAS JAMMED, he tried wiggling the trigger with his finger. It wouldn't come back into position. I suppose that was the logical time to pick up a chair and brain him with it, while he was standing there playing with the gun and swearing at it, but I don't have those kind of reflexes. I just sat there on the bed with one hand on my knee and the other on the best part of Francine and waited for him to get the gun fixed and shoot me all over again.

Then he looked at me and said, "You're not Pivnick." His voice was very stern, as if he was *accusing* me of not being Pivnick As though Pivnick was something everybody should be, like clean or loyal or trustworthy.

"No," I said, "I'm not."

"I was sure it was Pivnick. I would have sworn up and down it was Pivnick." He frowned. Then he looked up again and turned his eyes on Francine.

"You," he said. "You're not Marcia."

She didn't say anything. "No," I said, for her. "She's not Marcia. She's Francine."

"No wonder you're not Pivnick." He frowned again, deep in conversation, and then nodded his head emphatically. "Of course," he said. "Of course. I see it all now. That's why you're not Pivnick."

"It's the main reason."

"Then where is my wife?"

"Huh?"

"My wife," he snapped. "Marcia. My wife."

"Oh, Marcia," I said. "Well, it's obvious, isn't it?"

"Tell me."

"She must be with Pivnick."

"Ha," he said, triumphantly. "I thought so! I always thought so. But where?" He lowered his head and paced, then raised it and snapped.

145

"There is another apartment in this building?"

"No. Just the barbershop downstairs."

"This is One-eighteen South Main Street?"

"Yes."

"Damn it to hell," he said. "I was told I would find them at One-eighteen South Main Street. I was told that it was Pivnick. But I was certain. And I was definitely told that it was my wife. They told me I would find her at One-eighteen South Main Street in Rhinebeck."

"This isn't Rhinebeck."

"*What?*"

"This isn't Rhinebeck," I told him. And I told him the name of the town.

"Damn it to hell," he said. "I knew I had made a mistake as soon as I saw it wasn't Pivnick. But what a mistake! What an extraordinary mistake! Marcia will never believe this!"

He was glowing and bubbling. Then his face went suddenly somber, as if he just had a power failure. "But I could have killed you," he said. "An innocent man. I could have shot you down in hot blood. And you were not even Pivnick."

"Not for a moment."

"My God," he said. He looked at the gun in his hand and shuddered. Then he jammed it into his pocket, bowed halfway to the floor, apologized to both of us for the interruption, and headed for what was left of my door. Very little was. He took two steps and the gun went off in his pocket. He lost two toes on his right foot, and it was hell getting the bleeding stopped. I thought sure the cops would come and let him go and arrest me for picking apples out of season. The cops didn't come.

"Bostonians," he said, dully, looking at his feet.

"Marcia and Pivnick?"

"The shoes! One-hundred-and-ten-dollar Bostonians!" He glared at them. "And only seven years old. The salesman swore they would last a lifetime. Bostonians!"

I considered pointing out that one of them was still in perfectly good shape, as were eight of his toes. But I kept this to myself.

Francine ripped up a pillowcase to make bandages. I fixed him up and told him he ought to go to a hospital. He said he had to go to Rhinebeck. I don't know if he ever found Pivnick or not, but if I were Marcia I would be very goddamned careful from now on.

Once we were rid of Marcia's husband, Francine remembered that she didn't have any clothes on. It was really pretty funny. Before the jerk kicked the door in, it was easy enough for her to pretend that she didn't know what was happening, or that we were just necking a little, or whatever she wanted to pretend. And while he was there waving the gun in the air and talking about Pivnick, we both had too much to worry about to think about being naked. But then he went out and closed my broken door behind him, and there we were. I turned to look at Francine, and she pulled a bedsheet over her really sensational body and tried to look everywhere but at me.

I got onto the bed and scurried over next to her.

"My," she said, "I really have to be getting home now, Chip."

"Oh, it's real early, Francine."

"What a strange man! I thought he was going to shoot you or something."

"Well, he tried."

She talked about him, the sort of brainless talk Francine was good at, and meanwhile I got a hand under the sheet and kept putting it on Francine, and she kept moving it off without missing a beat.

Then she said, "I wish you would cover yourself up, Chip."

"Huh?"

"You don't have any clothes on."

"It's a warm night."

"Be nice, Chip."

"Huh?"

She chewed her lip. "I shouldn't even be here. I don't know what got into me." Nothing, I thought. "But I guess I just got carried away because of the things you said and how sweet a boy you are. You're very sweet, Chip."

I went to kiss her, but she got her mouth out of the way very skillfully. "Be nice," she said.

"Nice? I thought we would sort of get back to what we were doing."

"I don't know what you mean by that."

"Before he walked through the door."

"I don't know what—"

"Well, just for the record, Francine, we were about to make love."

"Really, Chip, I don't—"

"I mean I was lying on top of you, for Christ's sake, and you were telling me to shove it in all the way to your neck. I mean let's not pretend we don't know our names, for Pete's sake. I mean that's what we were doing before we were so rudely interrupted, and I don't see why all of a sudden we have to pretend that we just met each other at a church picnic."

She was staring at me.

"I mean it seems pretty silly," I said.

She turned away from me. "You're a very crude boy," she said.

"A minute ago I was very sweet."

"I thought you were, but obviously I was mistaken. I shouldn't even be here."

"Well, give me a minute and I'll cut the ropes."

"What?"

"The ropes that are tying you down so you can't escape my evil clutches. I'll cut you loose and you can hurry home."

"What?"

She sighed a couple of times. Her eyes stole a look at me, moving over my body to the part of me she wanted me to pull a sheet over. She withdrew them, but they came back again of their own accord.

She said, "If you would just be a gentleman, and if you would tell me the things you said before, you know, about thinking I'm really pretty and that you like me as a person and you respect me, then everything could be the way it was before."

I made her say it again. And she said it again in just about the same words.

"That's a great idea," I said. "Say, do you suppose we should put our clothes on first so that we can start over from the beginning?"

"That would be best, Chip."

"That sure is a great idea," I said.

"I'm glad you—Chip, what are you doing?"

"What does it look like I'm doing?"

"Chip, now stop that!"

"It's my thing," I said. "If I want to play with it, I've got every right in the world."

"If you think I'm going to sit here and watch you, you're out of your mind."

"Would you like to do it for me?"

"Chip, I don't know what's the matter with you."

"Go home."

"But I thought—"

"Go home."

"Chip?"

"Go home."

When she went home, I stopped playing with myself. I was only doing it to annoy her. I mean, I wouldn't want you thinking that I got any kick out of it, at least in a sexual sense. But it sure got old Francine's teeth on edge, and that was the general idea.

After she left I sat around for a while. I got dressed again and had a look at the door. If the barber saw it he was going to have a fit and if he didn't see it I didn't want him cutting my hair, because he would be likely to lop off an ear. I mean it was smashed beyond recognition. You couldn't make it look like a door again. The only way to hide it was to hang a picture over it, and I didn't know where to get one at that hour.

What I did was take the door right off its hinges and carry the whole mess downstairs. I put all the pieces back with the garbage from the drugstore two doors down. The next time Mr. Bruno asked for the rent, I asked him when he was going to bring my door back.

"Door? What door? I never tooka your door."

"Then where did it go?"

"Jeez," he said, and added something in Italian.

The next day two of his sons came and hung a new door for me. The next time I saw old Bruno he said he was sorry they had taken the door off without telling me, but it needed painting. I got so I had trouble knowing whether that guy kicked my door in or not.

But all this is off the subject. I guess I'm trying to duck the obvious question, which is was I losing my mind or what?

Because Francine would have let me do it. She just about came right out and said she would let me do it if only I would play up to her the way she wanted. She spelled it out for me, just about, and I wasn't so dumb that I didn't get the message, and what did I do? I sent her home, for Pete's sake. I sat there, pulling my pud like a total dip and told her to take her whatchamacallit and go home, and kept telling her until she went.

I sat around for hours trying to figure it out. And the best I could come up with was that I had just been trying to get laid for so long that finally something snapped inside me and I just wasn't going to go through all that goddamn nonsense again. If you stop to think, ever since I left Upper Valley I had been planning on working hard and applying myself and being straightforward and open and honest and sensible, all in a heroic All-American effort to Get Ahead. And time after time I wound up being dishonest and sneaky and conniving, and floated around aimlessly and didn't save money and wasn't getting ahead, and all because the only thing I really gave a damn about was getting laid. And it might have made sense if I was making out like a maniac, but I wasn't getting anyplace at all, and the whole thing just wasn't worth the trouble.

And Francine wasn't worth the trouble, for Pete's sake. No matter how nice her body was, there was too thick a layer of stupidity and selfishness hovering over it. And no matter what terrific secrets she had hidden between her legs, they just couldn't be worth all the games and crap you had to go through to get to her.

I just wasn't interested.

You may have trouble believing it. I don't blame you for a minute. This is I, Chip Harrison, talking, after all, and to tell you the truth, I didn't believe it all myself. But it was true.

I went outside and walked around until I found a place to have a cup of coffee. I just walked right in and sat down at the counter without giving the place the usual carefully casual are-there-any-girls-here glance. I didn't even care. I sat at the counter, and the waitress who always served me came over and gave me the usual big phony smile and leaned forward to give me the usual cheap thrill, and I talked to her the same way I always did but without even pausing to think for a moment that I would like to bang her. I drank my coffee and ordered another cup. I told myself I might be a virgin for the rest of my life, and if that was the way it was going to be, I would just have to learn to live with it, because no matter how great Doing It felt (and I don't suppose it would really feel a whole hell of a lot different from some of the things I had done with Aileen, as far as that goes), it still couldn't be worth making a horse's ass of yourself or building your whole life around. It just wasn't worth it.

* * *

I was having a third cup of coffee, which I don't usually do, but this wasn't my usual kind of evening, either. A voice said, "Say, is anybody sitting here?"

I turned around. It was a girl about my age, with long brown hair and very wide brown eyes.

She was wearing a pair of those granny glasses and if anything they made her eyes look bigger.

"No one at all," I said.

"What I meant was, do you feel like company or are you involved with your own private thoughts?"

"Company's fine."

"Are you sure? I don't want to come on heavy or anything."

"I'm sure. I ran out of thoughts, anyway."

She parked herself on the stool next to mine. The waitress came over and showed off her breasts. The girl ordered coffee, and I said I didn't want anything, thanks just the same. The waitress gave me one of those tentative dirty looks, as though she didn't know whether to take that the wrong way or not. She brought the girl's coffee and went away.

"I think I've seen you around," the girl said.

"I've been around."

"Are you living in town?"

"For the time being. Just passing through, actually."

"I've been living here for years, but I'm on my way out now. I'm going to college tomorrow morning."

She stirred her coffee. "My first year. I guess I must be a little nervous about it because I couldn't sleep. I had to get out of the house. I didn't think I was nervous but I must be."

"Maybe you're just excited. That can happen."

"I guess so. Do you go to school now or did you finish?"

"I sort of dropped out."

"That's groovy. I guess I'll probably drop out. Most of the kids I know who went already, the more interesting

152

ones, all dropped out after a year or two. But I wanted to see what it was like first."

"That's probably a good idea."

"That's what I figured." She drummed the countertop with her fingers. Her fingernails were chewed ragged and the backs of her hands were brown from the sun. "I'm a Capricorn. Open to new ideas. I believe in that, I think, but I don't know much about it. Astrology, I mean. What are you?"

"Oh. Virgo."

"My name's Hallie."

"Mine's Chip."

"That's very together. I like that." She sipped her coffee and made a face.

"It's pretty bad coffee," I said.

"The worst. But everybody's closed at this hour. Do you work or what?"

"Over at the car wash. They wash and I dry."

"That sounds fair enough."

"I don't love it, but it's a job."

"I think that's where I may have seen you. And you know, walking around."

I looked at her again. "I've seen you, too. I think. With a sort of stocky guy? With shoulders?"

"My brother."

"He's in the Service. The Infantry."

"Oh."

"He enlisted to get it over with and now he's sorry. He hates it."

"I can imagine."

"He thought it would get better after basic training, but he says it's the same shuck all around, and now he thinks they're going to send him overseas."

"Rough."

"You know it."

I looked at her again. She was damned attractive, although it was the kind of good-lookingness that you

153

didn't notice right off. It didn't wave and shout at you, but after you saw it a few times you began to appreciate it. She looked very clean and cool and casual, and she talked with her whole face. I mean, she didn't keep throwing smiles and winks at you and do things with her eyebrows, nothing like that. But the expression on her face always went along with what she was saying. A lot of the time a person's mouth will go off in one direction while their mind is somewhere else.

We didn't talk about anything very important.

I told her about some of the apple knockers I had met, and she talked about spending summers on her uncle's farm when she was a kid. I hadn't really talked to a girl this way in I don't know how long. I used to talk to Aileen in Chicago, but that was all screwed up by the fact that I was all hung up on her sexually. With Hallie, sex didn't have anything to do with it. Not that she wouldn't have appealed to me, but that I had gone through some real changes and I wasn't the same horny kid I had been a couple of hours ago.

She had a second cup of the terrible coffee, and I kept her company and had a fourth. When she finished hers I said I thought I would probably go for a walk, and she said maybe some fresh air would do her good, help her get to sleep. We each paid for our own coffee and went outside together.

We walked two or three blocks without talking. But it was an easy silence, not one of those uncomfortable ones where you try to think of something to say and keep running different sentences through your mind. It was completely relaxed. I didn't even get lost in my own thoughts. I just walked along, hardly thinking of anything.

Then she said, "Chip?" I looked at her and for a second her eyes seemed so deep that I could see for miles into them. Then she lowered them and shifted her weight from one foot to the other.

She said, "I live at home with my folks."

"I know."

"We could go to your place."

"If you're tired of walking, sure."

"I mean if you wanted to ball or anything. Not to come on strong, but like I have to go to college tomorrow so there's no time to let things just happen. I think they would happen because I sort of dig you and everything, and even our signs are compatible, Virgo and Capricorn, or at least I think they are, but I don't really know much about it. Astrology."

"Neither do I."

"So if you don't want to, just say so." Her teeth attacked her lower lip. "Whatever you say."

"I live upstairs of Bruno's Barbershop. On the next block."

"I know where it is."

"There's no door to my room. It got broken and I had to take it off, but there's nobody else in the place at night so it doesn't matter if there's a door or not."

"How did the door get broken?"

"A guy kicked it in. If you don't mind about there not being a door—"

"Well, it wouldn't matter if we're the only ones in the building, would it?"

"No."

"So," she said.

I took hold of her hand. It felt much smaller in mine than you would have expected. We walked to the corner, turned, went to my place, and climbed the stairs. I put a light on and apologized for the mess. She said it didn't matter. She said it looked romantic, with the slanting roof and the exposed rafters. "Like a garret," she said. "You'll be a great but unknown artist dying of tuberculosis and I'll be your mistress and model, and you'll get drunk and cough and spit blood and beat me."

I kissed her. She kissed in the same fresh open way

155

she talked, holding nothing back. We stood there kissing for a long time.

Then she took her sweatshirt off and turned around so that I could unhook her bra for her. She kicked off her sandals and stepped out of her dungarees and threw all her clothes in the corner. She stood watching eagerly as I got my clothes off and tossed them after hers. She put out her hand and touched me, and we floated down onto the bed like falling leaves.

"Oh, wow," she said. She burrowed close to me, her head tucked under my arm. "That was—"

"Uh-huh."

"Like unbelievable."

"Yeah."

"It's never been this good for me before." She rolled over on her back and folded her hands together just below her breasts. I looked at her. She said, "I wish they were bigger."

"They're beautiful."

"Tiny."

"So?"

"So I can never be an actress in Italian movies."

"I can't play basketball."

"Huh?"

"Nothing important."

She sat up, looked down at me. "That's the cutest thing," she said.

"I'm sort of attached to it."

"So am I, but in another way. It's so beautiful. Do you think it would get all embarrassed if I gave it a kiss?"

"There's only one way to find out."

She curled into a ball and nestled her head in my lap. Her hair was clean and silky all over my legs.

"Close your eyes," she said.

I closed them, but then I cheated and opened them again. It was so beautiful to watch her. She had her eyes shut and her face glowed with contentment. She looked like a baby nursing.

She stopped to say, "What a funny taste!"

"That's you."

"It is? I guess it must be. Funny."

She came up for air again to say, "It must like me. Look how big it got."

"Uh-huh."

"I really groove on sucking you. Is that terribly perverted of me?"

"Only of you don't do anything else."

"What else should I do?"

I stretched her out on her back and showed her. Later on she was dozing lightly. I put my hand on her arm and her eyes opened.

"I don't want to scare you or anything, Hallie, but did I hurt you before?"

"I don't think so. Why?"

"Well, look." I pointed to the stain. "That must have come from one of us, and I wouldn't say anything, but if I *did* hurt you or anything—"

"Oh," she said.

"I just thought—"

"I guess I bled a little. I didn't realize."

"Is that common? I mean, oh, do you usually?"

She turned away. "Well, see—"

"What?"

"I should have told you, I guess. But we had such a good thing going and I didn't want anything to get in the way." Her eyes met mine. "I'm a virgin. I mean I was. Until just now. Chip? What's so funny?"

"Nothing."

"Then why are you laughing?"

"It's not important." I put my hands on her. "Look, when do you have to get up in the morning? What I'm getting at is how much longer can you stay?"

"I should have been asleep hours ago."

"Oh."

"But there's time, Chip, if that's what you meant. In

fact, you don't even have to hurry. There's plenty of time, actually."

Epilogue

I ALREADY TOLD YOU THAT I LIKE epilogues, and knowing what happened to the characters after the story ended. Actually there isn't too much I can put in this particular epilogue because not that much time has passed since then. And the only character I know what happened to is me, and I'm still in the same room over the same barbershop. I've got a new door, but otherwise things are about the same.

But I figured this is probably the only book I'll ever write, so when else am I ever going to get a chance to write an epilogue?

Hallie went home, and the next morning she left for college. She said she would drop a card with her address on it, and if I was ever in Wisconsin I could look her up. I haven't gotten the card yet.

Mr. Bruno replaced my door. I guess I already told you about that, though. And he didn't exactly ask about the bullet hole in his ceiling. "You a gooda boy," he said at one point, as if willing himself to believe it. "You donta shoot anybody, and anybody donta shoota you." He seemed vaguely frightened of me after that.

The car wash closed for the winter. This happened almost immediately, and when they told me, I had the crazy feeling that they were closing the car wash because Hallie had gone to college. In a way it was sort of like that. More people get their cars washed in the summer than in the winter anyway, and this is especially true in this particular city, where there are all sorts of people up for the summer from New York City. So when the summer is over and college kids go back to school and summer people go back to the city, there's not enough business to support the car wash. I was out of a job, but since it wasn't one with an Outstanding Opportunity For Advancement, I wasn't what you might call shattered.

Then I happened to get to talking with Mr. Burger. I was lying around my room, reading a book and wondering where I would go next, and what would I do when I got there, when old Bruno came tearing up the stairs to tell me that one of his customers had a flat tire, "You change it, he give-a you money," he said.

I changed it and he gave-a me a dollar. The car was a Lincoln Continental Mark III. Not that it's any more work changing the tire on an expensive car, but if it had been, say, a beat-up '51 Ford, then I might not have been exactly staggered by getting a lousy dollar for changing it. I still don't think I would have been overwhelmed, though.

"Gee," I said, "thanks very much. Now I can go get a hamburger and maybe some french fries. Man, I can hardly wait."

"Sounds as though you haven't eaten in a long time," Mr. Burger said.

He missed the point, but I went along with it.

"I'm out of work," I said, "but through no fault of my own. The position was temporary and the work seasonal."

"The car wash," he said, snapping his fingers. "You were the kid who wiped the windows on the passenger's side."

"I remember your car now. You brought it in every Friday night."

"As soon as I got up from the city. That's right." He offered me a cigarette. I took it even though I don't smoke, and told him that if it was all right with him I would save it and smoke it later, after my meal. He gave me a funny look, then said sure, he didn't care, and lit his own cigarette. "So you're out of work," he said. "Tough break, all right. I wish I could help you out, but I'm afraid I'm not in the car wash business myself."

"What business are you in?"

"Publishing."

"What type?"

"Books," he said warily. "What makes you ask?"

"No reason."

"Because I haven't got anything for a person without experience."

"Oh, I've got experience," I said. "I've got more experience than you would believe, even if it won't do me any good. I've done more things in the past nine or ten months—"

"I can imagine. When I was your age—" He shook his head. "What did I give you, a buck? Why don't you hang on to it and I'll buy you that hamburger you were drooling over and we'll talk."

"About what?"

"I don't know. Maybe we can do each other some good."

So Mr. Burger worked up a contract for my book and gave me money for living expenses and bought me a typewriter and got me a beautiful blond secretary.

Not really.

What he did, really, was listen to me, talk about where I'd been and what I'd done, and nod every now and then, and smoke a lot of cigarettes, and wonder why I wouldn't smoke one but kept saving them for later. And he told me, when I was all done, that I had a hell of a story to tell and that it was the kind of story he'd like to bring to the attention of the reading public.

"You be sure you put all the sex in," he said. "What you have to do is hook the reader's attention and rivet his eyes to the page right from the start, and then you make him laugh and cry by tugging at his heartstrings, but if you want to sell books, you'd better make sure you write something that'll give the son of a bitch a hard-on."

And he said he would take a chance on me.

"I'm a gambling man," he said. "I'm willing to take a risk. Now I'll tell you what I'll do. It won't take you long to write this all up, but you'll need something to live on in the meantime. You got a typewriter?" I didn't. "Well, you got to have a typewriter and money to live on. I figure you ought to be able to get a decent typewriter for twenty dollars. And living expenses—suppose I give you fifty bucks total, and you'll see how it goes."

I finally found a typewriter for thirty-five dollars. Not a very good typewriter, but since I can't type with more than two fingers, I suppose a good typewriter would be wasted on me. That left me with fifteen dollars, plus the dollar for changing the flat tire, plus the few dollars I had set aside.

Now Mr. Burger is supposed to read this, if he remembers who I am. And if he likes it he can publish it, and then I'll get some money, I guess. I don't know exactly how it works but I must get something. I've been killing myself writing all this, though I suppose it doesn't show when you read it. I don't suppose it's very good, either. And I probably put in either too much sex or not enough, and I don't even know which. And I'm sure I told you too many things you didn't want to know and skipped things you would have wanted to hear more about, but I never did this before.

And that's the whole point, actually, now that I think about it. The first time is the hardest. There are probably other morals, too, but as sure as I like epilogues, I hate it when the author steps in at the end of the book and tells you what it was all about. Either you find it out for yourself or it's not worth knowing about. So I'll just say goodbye and thanks for reading this, and I'm sorry it wasn't better than it was.

Chip Harrison Scores Again

Chapter One

AT FIRST I DIDN'T PAY VERY MUCH ATTENTION to the guy. I was washing my hands in the men's room of a movie theater on Forty-second Street, and in a place like that it's not an especially good idea to pay too much attention to anybody or you could wind up getting more involved than you might want to. It's not that everybody is a faggot. But everybody figures everybody *else* is a faggot, so if you let your eyes roam around you could get *(a)* groped by someone who's interested or *(b)* punched in the mouth by someone who's not interested or *(c)* arrested by someone who's a cop.

If any of these things happened I would have had to leave the theater, probably, and I didn't want to. I had already seen both movies, one of them twice, but I still didn't want to leave. It was warm in the theater. Outside it was cold, with day-old snow turning from gray to black, and once I went out there I would have to stay out there, because I had no other place to go.

(Which is not entirely true. There was this apartment on East Fifth Street between Avenues B and C where I could stay if I really had to. Some friends of mine lived there, and while it wasn't exactly a crash pad they would always let me have a section of floor to sleep on and a plate of brown rice to eat. They were into this macrobiotic thing and all they ever ate was brown rice, which is very nourishing and very healthy and very boring after not very long. I could go there and eat and sleep and even talk to people, although most of the people you found there were usually too stoned to say very much, but the thing was that I only had a quarter, which is a nickel less than the subway costs. It was too cold to walk that far, and it was just about as cold inside that place as it was outside, because there was no heat. My friends had been using the stove to heat the place.

That hadn't worked too well in the first place, and it

Lawrence Block

worked less well when Con Ed turned off the gas and
electricity for nonpayment. They burned candles for light
and cooked the rice over little cans of sterno. A couple of
times Robbo had burned old furniture in the bathtub for
heat, but he had more or less given this up, partly because
heating the bathroom didn't do much for the rest of the
apartment, and partly because there was a good chance the
whole building would go up sooner or later.)

The point of this is just that I was washing my hands
and not paying much attention to anything else until I
happened to notice this guy take a wallet out of his pocket
and start going through it. He was sort of hunched toward
me, screening the wallet with his body from the washroom
attendant, who I think existed to make sure that if anybody
did anything dirty, they did it in one of the pay toilets. The
guy with the wallet went through all the compartments of
the thing, taking out money and plastic cards and things,
and jamming everything into his pockets. Then he put the
wallet in another pocket, took out a comb, combed his long
dark hair back into a d.a., and left. I turned and watched
him, and on the way out his hand clipped into a pocket
and came up with the wallet and dropped it into the
wastebasket. There was this huge wastebasket on the
opposite side of the door from the washroom attendant,
and the guy with the d.a. did this whole number in one
graceful motion, and the attendant never saw what
happened. I have to admit that it took me a minute to figure
this out. Why would a guy throw his wallet away? And
why be so slick about it? I mean, if you grow tired of your
wallet, you have a perfect right to throw it away, right?

Oh.

It wasn't his wallet. He was a pickpocket or a mugger or
something, and he had emptied the wallet, and now he
wanted to get rid of it because it was Incriminating
Evidence.

How about that.

My first reaction was just general excitement. Not that I

168

had been an eyewitness to the most spectacular crime since the Brink's robbery. I would guess they get more wallets in those wastebaskets than they get paper towels. In fact, if you ever want a used wallet, that's probably the best place to go looking for one. But my own life hadn't been that thrilling lately, and it didn't take much to make my day.

The next thing that struck me was that I, Chip Harrison, had just been presented with an opportunity. A small one, perhaps, but I was as low on opportunities as I was on excitement. And that wallet was an opportunity.

It might hold important papers, for example. You might argue that people with important papers in their wallets don't spend all that much time in Forty-second Street movie houses, but one never knows for sure. Perhaps the owner would pay a reward for the return of the wallet. (Perhaps he'd call the police and have me arrested as a pickpocket.)

Or perhaps there was some small change in the change compartment, if there was a change compartment. Or a subway token. Or a postage stamp. The Post Office won't redeem unused stamps, but at least I could mail a letter, if there was someone I wanted to write to. Or perhaps—Well, there were endless possibilities.

I mulled them over in my mind while I was drying my hands on a paper towel, and I looked at the attendant and at the wastebasket, and then I went out and combed my hair again. I had just done this before washing my hands in the first place and while my hair tends to need combing frequently it didn't really need it now. But I was about to Take Advantage of Opportunity, and thus I had to Think On My Feet.

I dried my hands again, and I carried the used paper towel over to the wastebasket, keeping the comb in the same hand with it, and I dropped them both into the basket.

Then I took a step or two toward the door, stopped abruptly, made a fist of one hand and hit the palm of the other hand with it.

"Oh, shit," I said. "I dropped my comb in the wastebasket."

169

"I seen you," the attendant said.

"All the stupid things."

"You want another comb, there's a machine over on the side."

"I want *that* comb," I said.

"Prob'ly dirty by now. You wouldn't believe the crap they throw in those baskets."

"I think I can get it." I was leaning into the basket and pawing around through old Kleenex and paper towels. The wallet had plummeted through them to the bottom, and I was having a hell of a time finding it.

"Over there," the clown said helpfully. "You see it?"

I did, damn him. I pawed at some paper towels and made the comb slip away. "Almost had it," I said, and went diving for it again. I had my feet off the ground and was balanced rather precariously, with the edge of the can pushing my belt buckle through my stomach. I had visions of losing my balance and winding up headfirst in the trashcan, which might provide some people with some laughs but which wouldn't provide me with the wallet, the comb, or much in the way of self-respect.

And self-respect, at that point of time, was as hard to come by as excitement, opportunity, and money.

I kept my balance and after another few shots I got the wallet. I can't swear that it's the same wallet I saw go in. For all I know there were a dozen of them somewhere down there. I got a wallet, palmed it off, and slipped it inside my shirt, and then I had to go through the charade of getting the fucking comb. It just didn't seem right to leave it there.

On my way through the lobby I dumped the comb in yet another wastebasket. And did it very surreptitiously, as if I were, well, a pickpocket ditching a wallet. Which is nothing but stupid.

I went outside and walked down to Broadway and watched the news flashing on the Allied Chemical Tower. It was cold, and there was a miserable wind blowing off the Hudson. I stood there shivering. I was out in the cold

170

with no way of getting back into the warm, and I had traded a perfectly adequate pocket comb for a wallet that someone else had already gone through once, and I wasn't entirely certain I had come out ahead on the deal.

The papers in that wallet weren't important enough to wrap fish in. There were a couple of cash register receipts from unidentified stores and a Chinese laundry ticket. There was a head-and-shoulders snapshot of an ugly high school girl signed *Your Pal, Mary Beth Hawkins*. Judging by the hair style, Mary Beth was either *(a)* the squarest teenager in America or *(b)* forty-five-years old by now.

Either way, I would have rather had my comb than her picture.

There were a few other things, but none of them mattered except for the bus ticket. It was in one of the secret compartments, and I guess that had kept it a secret from the pickpocket. A Greyhound bus ticket, good for one-way passage in either direction between Boston, Massachusetts, and Bordentown, South Carolina. It said it was valid anytime within one year from the date stamped on the back. The date was March something, and it was now December something, so the ticket had another three months to go before it became even more worthless than it already was.

I got rid of the rest of the wallet, Mary Beth's picture and all. I dumped it in a trash-can—what else?—and I was as slick as possible about this, because I didn't want any other poor clown to waste his time doing what I had just done. If you're going to steal a wallet, you ought to get it from its original owner.

After that the depreciation is fantastic.

Then I walked around for a while, which kept me warmer than standing still, if just barely. Now and then I would take the ticket out and stare at it. It was that or stare at the quarter. Sensational, I thought. If I happen to be in Boston between now and March, I can catch a bus to Bordentown.

171

Or, should I some fine morning find myself in Bordentown, I can hop on a Greyhound for Boston. Wonderful.

I wound up on Broadway looking at whores.

Not in a particularly acquisitive way. Not that I wasn't tempted. I had been in New York for almost three months, and my sex life during that time could have been inscribed on the head of a pin with plenty of room left for the Lord's Prayer and as many angels as felt like dancing there.

(I had been living with a girl for one of those months, but she had just had a baby and couldn't do anything for six weeks, and by the time the six weeks were up she had gone away. At least she took the baby with her.)

I have always had these ethical objections to patronizing a prostitute, but in this case I might have overcome these objections if I'd had more than twenty-five cents to overcome them with. We'll never know.

So I went window-shopping, and the girls seemed to know it. They would look me up and down, and disapproval would glint in their eyes, and they would turn away, as if there was nothing so obvious as the fact that I couldn't possibly afford them. None of this was very ego-building.

And then one girl, who was either less experienced or a poorer judge of character, gave me a smile. An actual smile. So I stopped dead and smiled back at her, and she asked me if I'd like to go to her apartment.

"Is it warm there?"

"Honey," she said, "where I am, it's always warm."

I told her it sounded great. She asked me if I could spend twenty-five dollars.

"No way."

"Well, see, I like you. Could you spend twenty?"

"I wish I could."

"Well, shit. What can you spend?"

I could spend twenty-five cents, but I was damned if I was going to tell her that. I said, "Where are you from?"

"What do you want to know that for?"

172

"I just wondered."

"Well, I have this place on Fifty-fifth Street. How much can—"

"I mean originally," I said. "You're not from New York, are you?"

"From Memphis," she said. "And never goin' back there again, thanks all the same."

"Oh," I said.

"Why?"

"I thought maybe you were from Bordentown, South Carolina," I said. "Or maybe from Boston."

"You been drinkin', honey?"

"Because I have this bus ticket," I said, and showed it to her. "So if you had any interest in going to Boston or Bordentown—"

"That good?"

I showed her the date. "Perfectly good," I said.

"You want to come home with me?"

"To Memphis?"

"Shit. I told you. Fifty-fifth Street. You want to come?"

I tried on a smile. "All I really have is this ticket," I said. "I don't have any money. Just twenty-five cents and this ticket. I'm sorry for wasting your time—"

But she had my arm tucked under hers.

"You know something? I like you. I really do. What's your name?"

"Chip."

"Yeah? I'm Mary Beth. What's the matter?"

"Nothing. I knew a girl named Mary Beth. I had a picture of her in a wallet that I carried for a while."

"Girl here in New York?"

"No," I said. "I think she lives in Bordentown. Or in Boston. Or she used to."

"You sure you all right?"

"I'm fine," I said. She was still holding onto my arm, and we seemed to be walking uptown, sort of toward Fifty-fifth Street, actually.

173

"I do like you, Chip," she was saying. "You just come home with me and I'll do you like you never been done. You ever had something called the Waterloo? That's a specialty of mine. What I take is a mouthful of warm water, see—"

She told me quite a bit about the Waterloo, and while she talked we walked, and while we walked she held onto my arm and rubbed it against her breast. My pants began getting very cramped.

"You just forget about no money," she said. "Don't make no never mind."

Oh, Jesus, I thought. I can't believe this. Because I couldn't. I mean, it wasn't as though I hadn't had thoughts along this line before. I don't suppose it's the rarest fantasy ever. The ultimate sexual ego trip—that a prostitute, a girl who spends her life getting paid to have sex, will find you so overwhelmingly attractive that she'll want to give it to you for free. And she would know tricks you never dreamed of, and do all these fantastic things, and do them all for love.

Who ever thought it would actually happen?

Her apartment was pleasant in a sort of dull way. I couldn't tell whether or not it was a typical prostitute's apartment, but it seemed to me then that it couldn't be, because it seemed to me then that she was by no means a typical prostitute. By the time we got there I had already decided that she wasn't basically a whore at all. Just because a girl was whoring didn't make her a whore. After all, in the past year I had sold termite extermination service, picked fruit, posed for pornographic pictures and written a book, and I didn't think of myself as a writer or fruitpicker or any of those things. Life deals unpredictable cards, and you have to play each hand as it lays, and little Mary Beth might be walking the streets but that didn't make her a street-walker. It might not make her the Virgin Mary, either, but it didn't make her a whore.

I really had things all figured out. I would Take Her Away From All This. She already loved me, and by the time I got done balling her she would love me to distraction, and at that point the idea of ever having sex with anyone but Chip Harrison would positively turn her stomach. And I would live with her and land a Job With A Future, and we would screw incessantly while I made my way in the world, and we would, uh, Live Happily Ever After.

The thing is, see, that when a fantasy starts coming true before your eyes, it's natural to go on taking the fantasy to its logical (?) conclusion. Did I really expect all of this would happen? Not really, but remember that I never expected it to start happening in the first place. If someone goes and repeals the Law of Gravity and you find yourself flying to the Moon, it's no more unreasonable to plan on flying clear through to Mars.

I stood there working all of this out while she closed the door and turned four or five locks. Doesn't want us to be interrupted, I thought happily. We might be here for days. Weeks. And she wants to make sure we have privacy.

"Well," she said. "Not much, but it's home."

"Mary Beth," I said.

"Hi, Chip."

"Mary Beth." And I put my hands on her shoulders and drew her close. Somewhere along the way her head turned to the side and I was kissing a gold hoop earring.

"Uh-uh," she said.

"Huh?"

She rubbed her breasts against my chest and bounced her groin playfully against mine. I had this tight feeling in my chest.

"I don't kiss on the mouth," she said.

"Huh?"

She gave me another happy bounce, then moved away. "Just something I don't do," she said. "Kiss you anywheres else, kiss you like nobody ever, but not on the mouth."

"But that's silly."

"Shit—"

"But—"

I remembered reading that some prostitutes refused to kiss their clients mouth-to-mouth. They would do anything else, but they reserved that intimacy for the men they loved. It had never made much sense to me at the time, because if you stop and think about it, well, it's pretty ridiculous. Especially since I had spent the past year with a lot of girls who would kiss you mouth-to-mouth until Rome fell but wouldn't do anything more exciting than that. It seemed as though the whores had their value system turned upside down.

But what I couldn't understand was what this had to do with me and Mary Beth. She didn't want money from me. She was doing this for love, so by rights she should be particularly keen on kissing me on the mouth.

And then I got it. The poor kid, I realized, had never really had any sex life to speak of outside of prostitution. So naturally that was her frame of reference. Here she wanted to ball me for the sheer unadulterated pleasure of it, but her mind was so conditioned by the life she led that she had to act with me in much the same way as she acted with her paying customers. It was weird, and sort of disheartening in a way, but there was also something sort of sweet and pathetic about it.

She has never known love, I told myself. But I shall change her. I shall fulfill her.

"Well, now," she said. "And what have we here?"

That must have been a rhetorical question, because what she had there was something she came into contact with quite frequently in her profession, and where we had it was in her hand. She had opened my fly and taken me firmly in hand, and she was stroking me rhythmically. Her wrist did everything; the rest of her arm stayed motionless.

"You come with me," she said. "We'll just wash you up first."

We stood at the bathroom sink and washed me up. The editorial *we* was bugging me a little. Nurses talk like that—"How are we feeling this morning?" —but I never figured whores did, too. Anyway, she soaped me up and rinsed me off, and it was sort of pleasant and unpleasant both at once, pleasant in that it felt good, and unpleasant in that it sort of implied that I was fundamentally too dirty to deal with otherwise. But then I thought of some of the things she had in mind, and some of the things she had done with other people, and I decided I was just as glad that she tended to wash this portion of a person beforehand, and also, to tell the truth, just as pleased that she didn't believe in mouth-to-mouth kissing.

When she was done she filled a glass with hot water and carried it into the bedroom.

"For the Waterloo," she explained. "You're gonna love this."

"Uh."

"Don't you want to take off your clothes, Chip?"

"Uh, sure," I said, and started undressing. I was feeling unbelievably dizzy and stupid, and it wasn't just the excitement. That was a part of it. But another part was the feeling that none of this was really happening. It all seemed so thoroughly unreal. I took off all my clothes and looked up and she was just standing there, with her clothes on.

"Your clothes," I said.

"Huh?"

"Why don't you, uh, get undressed?"

"You want me to?"

"Well, sure."

She shrugged. A very strange girl, I decided. Maybe it wasn't just that she hadn't had any real sex life outside of prostitution. Maybe she was equally inexperienced in prostitution. Maybe she just read about the Waterloo in a book or something.

I stood there watching while she got undressed. She didn't make the process particularly seductive, just shucked off her clothes and draped them over a chair. Her body was skimpy everywhere but the breasts, which were on the large size. I haven't described her too much because I have trouble picturing her now in my mind. She was sort of mousy, really, hair somewhere between blond and brown. I suppose she was around my age, although she seemed older, maybe because she was more at home in this scene than I was.

She left on her stockings and garter belt. I asked her if she didn't want to take them off and get comfortable, and she gave me an impatient look. "Most men like 'em on," she said. "Don't you think they look pretty?"

I thought they looked like something out of those whip-and-chain movies, but I said sure, they were pretty.

"Because it's wasting time, you know, taking 'em off, putting 'em on."

"Then leave them on," I said, and she nodded, and I reached out for her and drew her in close. I went to kiss her again, out of habit, but she turned away automatically and I didn't press the point. I sort of felt like apologizing but couldn't think of an intelligent way to do that, so I kept my mouth shut and let my fingers do the walking. I felt various parts of her, and she did a little deep breathing and such, but nothing that really assured me I was driving her out of her skull.

"Let me," she said, disengaging herself. "You just lay down, Chip, and let me do you up."

I got on the bed. She reached for the glass of water, then stopped with it halfway to her lips. "You tell me if it's too hot," she said.

Then she took a mouthful of water and bent over me.

It was really very nice. She just did it for a second or so, then pulled away and looked at me. I was waiting for her to ask me whatever the hell it was she was going to ask me, and then I realized that she wasn't going to ask me anything because she couldn't because she had her mouth full of hot water.

"It's not too hot," I said. "It's just right."

She nodded and started doing it again. And, as before, it was really very nice indeed. It was strange, too, because I felt totally unconnected with the whole process. I decided that it was a great technique, and it was really great that she knew these great techniques, but that it would be infinitely better when I taught her how to put some love into the whole process. Or at least to make it obvious to me that she was enjoying what she was doing.

Then she stopped again.

"Believe me, it's not too hot," I said, and started to push her head back in place. But her head wouldn't push. She leaned over and spat the water out onto the linoleum.

"The ticket," she said.

"Huh?"

She looked impatient again. "The bus ticket, man. You better give it to me now. I want to make sure it's still good."

"The bus ticket?"

She sat up and stared at me. "Shit, the bus ticket," she said. "What's the matter with you? You got to give it to me and I got to make sure I can cash it before we do anymore. All I need is—"

"Cash the bus ticket?"

"Take it over to Port Authority and cash it," she said. "I told you you didn't need money. Just the ticket is all. If it's good I'll get twenty-thirty dollars out of that ticket."

I suppose you saw it coming all along, but I'm not going to apologize for my stupidity. After all, it was my fantasy that we were acting out.

The Waterloo, I thought. I had already had the hot

water part, and now I was getting the cold water. Buckets of it, all over all my enthusiasm for little old Mary Beth.

"Hey! Where you goin'?"

I was putting on my clothes. Not too quickly, not too slowly. Very mechanically, actually. Tucking the shirt into the pants, getting my socks right-side out and then putting them on, then the shoes—

"You crazy?"

"I have to go," I said.

"Go? Where to?"

"The bus station," I said. "I have to cash the ticket."

"Shit, I said I would cash it. Just hand it on over here."

"Fuck you," I said.

"Are you out of your *mind*?"

I turned toward her, and I guess I must have wanted to kill her, or at least I looked as though I wanted to kill her, because her face drained of color and she backed off fast. I turned away from her again and went to the door.

The whore with the heart of gold. You didn't need money. All you needed was a negotiable bus ticket.

I almost went crazy unlocking all those locks. She never said a word, which was lucky for her. I'm normally about as non-violent as it's possible to get, but I wasn't feeling very normal just then. Nothing makes you hate a person quite so much as being made an absolute asshole out of.

The last lock cleared just as I was about to give up and kick the door down.

It was as cold as ever out there, but I walked three blocks before I even noticed it.

Two thoughts kept me from running around and screaming. One was that, if and when I calmed down, I was certain to see the humor in the situation. I didn't see any humor in it now, but I knew I would sooner or later.

The other comforting thought, and it was the more comforting of the two, was that I had that bus ticket in my pocket. And I could cash it in.

Chapter Two

THIS IS SORT OF A PROBLEM.

See, I was going to open the book by saying who I am and my background and all the rest of it and get that out of the way right at the start. But the thing is that I wrote one book before this. It was called *No Score*, and it just came out last month. Gold Medal published it. *No Score*, by Chip Harrison. That wasn't what I wanted to call it, but forget what I wanted to call it because they changed it. I think *No Score* is a pretty good title, catchy, and probably a lot better than what I had in mind.

The point is that some of you already read *No Score* and some of you didn't, and if you did read it maybe you still remember it and maybe you don't. I remember it very clearly, but that's different.

See, if you read *No Score*, I don't want to bore you by feeding you all that stuff here and there throughout this book. If you didn't read it, I want to tell you as much as you have to know about it, but at the same time I don't want to spoil it for you in case you by some chance enjoy this book and want to read *No Score* later on. Of course the best thing would be if you ran out right now and got a copy of *No Score* and read it first and then came back to this book, but obviously not everybody can do that. If they happen to be reading this on a plane, for instance.

So what I think I'll do is put down some of it right here and now to tell you as much as you have to know about me, and possibly more than you want to know, as far as that goes. If you did read *No Score*, you can skip ahead right now to the next chapter, because none of this will be news to you.

My name is Chip Harrison. I guess you know that. My legal name was originally Leigh Harvey Harrison, but Chip was my nickname from early childhood, and my parents decided in November of 1963 that it might be sensible to forget my legal name and concentrate on Chip, Leigh Harvey being a liability in the name market at that point in time.

Of course, that was so many assassinations ago I don't suppose it matters any more.

No Score opened when I was seventeen and in my last semester at Upper Valley Prep School. I found out then that my parents had been confidence swindlers, and they were about to go to prison, and they committed suicide. I wasn't allowed to finish school, partly because of the scandal and partly because there was no money to pay my bills and I wasn't a good enough basketball player to make a difference, although I was fairly tall for my age.

So I went out to seek my fortune. I went to Chicago and got a job passing out slingers for a sidewalk photographer, and not quite sleeping with his wife, and then I went down through Illinois and Indiana with a termite inspection crew, and almost went to jail for statutory rape, which would have been really weird because *(a)* I was underage myself and *(b)* I didn't get to do anything. Then I wound up picking berries and apples across Ohio and New York, and almost got shot by a jealous husband, which also would have been ironic because *(a)* it wasn't his wife and *(b)* I didn't get to do anything.

In a way, not getting to do anything was what *No Score* was all about. That did work itself out, though, with a surprise touchdown in the final minutes of play. And then I happened to meet Mr. Knox Burger, and he bought me a hamburger because I helped him change a tire on his car, and I got to talking about my experiences and he suggested writing a book. He even gave me fifty dollars so that I could buy a typewriter and live on Maine sardines and day-old bread while I wrote the book. That book turned out to be *No Score*, and when it was done I took it to New York, and in September of 1970 it finally came out. I got some money when I finished the book but not as much as I thought and it didn't last long. It lasted until December, actually, at which time I had twenty-five cents left.

(I don't want to get hung up in time sequences, but let me get the chronology of this down for you. I started writing *No Score* in September of 1969 and finished it about a month later. From October to December of 1969 I was living in New York in the East Village, partly with the girl I mentioned who had just had a baby, and partly here and partly there, and partly at the sort of crash pad where they had all the brown rice and burned chairs in the bathtub. That's when the action in this book starts, in December of 1969. Then in September of 1970 *No Score* was finally published—I don't know why those things take so long, really—and it is now October of 1970 and I am sitting here writing this book, which you are reading. God knows when it will be when you get to read it. 1984, probably. In fact it may be close to then by the time I finish this chapter, because it's really very difficult trying to get all this together.

(Actually it may not come out at all, because Mr. Burger doesn't even work there anymore. He left, probably because of the nervous strain of editing *No Score*. There's a Mr. Walter Fultz there now, and he gave me about the same advice Mr. Burger did. Keep it moving, he said. Keep it warm and sensitive and perceptive and lively, and most of all—make sure there's sex in it.

(I don't know how well it's moving. Not too well in this chapter because of all the boring recapitulation. I really hope most of you already read *No Score* and were able to skip all of this crap. But I promise the pace will pick up in the next chapter. It would almost have to.

(And I also promise that there will be plenty of sex in it. There really can't help being plenty of sex in it. That's why I decided to start this book in December instead of picking up where *No Score* left off. There were those three months when nothing happened, so I decided to skip them and start right when things started to happen.)

So that's who I am. Not the seventeen-year-old virgin

who was there for the start of *No Score*, but an eighteen-year-old virgin-once-removed. A Virgo, with Gemini rising and Moon in Leo, if you pay attention to things like that. Sort of tall and sort of thin and sort of ordinary-looking, and walking full speed through the slush to the Port Authority Bus Terminal.

Chapter Three

THE PORT AUTHORITY BUS TERMINAL IS a well-lighted and spacious modern building, and if you walk through it quickly in the daytime it just looks like a bank or an airport. But at night it's depressing. All bus stations are. It's the people. Half of them are only there because they don't have enough money to fly or take a train, and the other half are there because it's reasonably warm and the benches are reasonably comfortable and you can steal a nap there and other people will think maybe you're waiting for a bus, and will leave you alone. Sooner or later, though, some uniformed old fart will ask you for a ticket, and when you don't have one they tell you to go away.

I didn't have any trouble cashing the ticket. I was in line behind a fat woman whose luggage was a matched set of shopping bags. She wanted to go someplace in Missouri, and she and the clerk had a hell of a job working out the details. This gave me time to figure out various reasons why I was cashing the ticket, but when my turn came I just pushed the ticket through the window and asked for cash. The clerk looked at it as if he suspected I was part of a gang of counterfeiters specializing in old bus tickets. But it passed.

You know, if it hadn't, I really would have been irritated. I mean, the ticket would at least have gotten me Mary Beth.

Instead it got me thirty-seven dollars and eighty-three cents. I went to one of the benches and sat down and counted the money over and over again. Then I put different amounts in different pockets. I was somehow more conscious of pickpockets than ever before. It occurred to me that I could have kept the wallet, and if I had then I'd now have something to put the money in.

Thirty-seven dollars and eighty-three cents. I sat there with different portions of the money in different pockets for a long time, thinking of one thing and another. Then I went to the john. The free stall was in use so I had to use one of the pay toilets, but the attendant wasn't there so I crawled under it. (Under the door. Not under the toilet.)

There should be a law against pay toilets. I did some more thinking, in addition to doing what I had gone there to do, and I bought a comb for a quarter and combed my hair. The comb lost a couple teeth in the process. It was really shoddy compared to the one I'd thrown away.

Then I went back to the ticket window. "Bordentown, South Carolina," I said. "One way."

The clerk started hunting for the Bordentown tickets, then did an elaborate double take. "You were just here a minute ago," he said.

"Well, maybe fifteen minutes."

"You cashed in a ticket. A Bordentown ticket."

"I know."

"And now you want to buy it back?"

"That was a Boston-to-Bordentown ticket," I said. "What I want is a New York-to Bordentown ticket."

"Whyntcha just trade it in the first place and save me the aggravation?"

"I didn't realize that I wanted to go to Bordentown."

"What are you, a wise guy?"

"Can't I just buy a ticket?"

"You people. I don't know. Think everybody's got all the time in the world."

The fare from New York to Bordentown was thirty-three dollars and four cents, and I had to go through various pockets until I got that sum together. While I did this, he talked to himself. He wouldn't tell me when the next bus left. I had to use one of the house phones and call Information. They told me there was a bus leaving in two and a half hours. It made express stops from New York to Raleigh, then made local stops all the way to Miami. It would put me in Bordentown in a little over forty hours.

The only thing I knew about Bordentown was that it was in South Carolina, and that somebody named Mary Beth Hawkins probably lived there once. And that I evidently wanted to go there.

187

I had four dollars and seventy-nine cents left. That was a lot less than thirty-three dollars and four cents, but it was a lot more than a quarter, so I was ahead of the game and playing on the house's money.

I was also starving. I found a lunch counter in the building and had two hamburgers and an order of french fries and three cups of coffee. It certainly wasn't a macrobiotic meal. It wasn't even very good, but that didn't seem to matter. I ate everything but the napkin.

Why Bordentown?

That's a good question. I don't know if I can find an answer that's as good as the question.

See, what happened was that I sat, first on the bench and then on the toilet, and I thought about the money and tried to think of something to do with it. And none of the things that involved staying in New York seemed like very good ideas, and I came to the conclusion that I had bombed out in New York and it was time to go somewhere else. Nothing against the city. Any city or town is as good as or as bad as what you're doing and the people you're doing it with. And for one reason or another I had never quite managed to get it together in New York. There were some good times in among the bad times, and I was glad I had come, but it was time to split.

(I have this tendency to go someplace else whenever I don't like where I am. I never really had a home that I can remember. When I was with my parents we would stay at a different expensive hotel in a different city every couple of months, and when I was at school it was a different boarding school every year, and the pattern hasn't changed since. Sometimes I think it's weakness of character to pick up and run whenever things turn sour. But why stay where you don't want to be? For Pete's sake, there's a whole world out there. I suppose there are things to be said for settling down and sinking roots, but someone else will have to say them.)

The thing is, it's not enough to have some place to go away from. You also need some place to go away *to*. And I didn't have one.

There were places I had already been, but I couldn't see any point in going back to any of them. Chicago was vaguely possible, I had had reasonably good times there, but I thought about that wind coming off Lake Michigan and schussing through the Loop and imagined what that wind would be like in January, and that ruled out Chicago. Besides, it was too big, it would be too much like what I was leaving.

There was a girl named Hallie with whom I had traded virginities on the very best night of my life. She was in college in Wisconsin. I had sent her a postcard before coming to New York, and since then I had written her three or four stupid letters but never mailed any of them, maybe because I wasn't quite sure what I wanted to say to her. I decided that it would be nice to see Hallie again, and then I decided it would be even nicer to see Hallie when I was a little clearer on how I felt about her and what I wanted to do about it. It would also be nicer if I could see her with clean clothes on me and money in my pocket and a little firmer sense of direction.

And then it came to me.

Bordentown.

Maybe you've noticed that when you've gone without sleep and food for a long time, and without really talking to anybody, you start to get messages from God. That's a little less crazy than it sounds. What happens is that a lot of minor things start taking on tremendous significance, and you start reading vital messages into them.

Like the whole bit with the wallet. And what was in the wallet—a picture of Mary Beth Hawkins and a bus ticket. And the first person I met after that was also named Mary Beth, which may be less remarkable in the cold light of dispassionate analysis but which seemed extraordinary at the time. The way all these things seemed to add up was that it was meant for me to get that bus ticket. It was destiny. And for me to cash in the ticket and spend the money was spitting in destiny's face. Obviously the thing to do with that ticket was to use it and go where it went.

Which still gave me two choices, actually.

Boston or Bordentown. But I never seriously considered Boston. It would have been copping out. I mean, the ticket was about eighty-five percent New York-to-Bordentown and fifteen percent New York-to-Boston.

Besides, Boston would be as cold as New York, maybe even colder. And Bordentown was in South Carolina—I knew that much about it; dammit. It would be warm. And it would be a small town, it would have to be fairly small or I probably would have heard of it at one time or another. So if I was looking for a change from New York, I really didn't have to look any farther.

For Pete's sake, I've gone lots of places on less reason than that.

The bus ride started off horrible. Then it became very boring for a while, and then it got wonderful.

The horrible part was brief, from New York to Philadelphia. It was horrible because there were four men two rows back drinking wine and singing, and a third of the way to Philadelphia one of them threw up, and a few miles later so did the rest of them. It was horrible because the woman across the aisle from me was carrying a baby who cried all the way from New York to Philadelphia. The woman didn't seem to mind. Me, I minded. It was horrible because the man in the seat next to me was fat enough to take up all of his seat and a good deal of mine as well. He didn't use Dial, and I don't guess he cared if anybody else did, either.

The four drunks got off in Trenton. The woman with the brat got off in Philadelphia. The smelly fat man was riding clear down to Miami, but when we got to Philadelphia I was able to change my seat. So that ended the horrible part.

The boring part was just boring. Nothing much to be said about it, really. I took crumby naps and woke up and went to the john and came back and sat down and looked out the window and waited for something to happen. Now and then the bus stopped somewhere and we all got off it and went to a terrible lunch counter, and I would have a Coke and a package of those little orange crackers with cheese and peanut butter between them.

(I knew a speed freak in New York who lived on nothing but Cokes and those sandwich crackers. Three packs of the crackers a day and six Cokes. He weighed about eighty-three pounds and the circles under his eyes looked as though they'd been painted on with shoe polish. "Speed doesn't kill," he told me. "That's the lie they feed you. It's the malnutrition that does you in. I figure I've got six months before my liver goes. Once your liver goes you've had it."

("Then why don't you start eating right?"

("Priorities, man. I need to speed to get my head together. Once my head is together I'll kick the speed and stabilize myself with tranks and downs, and then I'll get into eating right. High-protein, fertile eggs, the whole organic foods trip. And I want to get into body building. I've been getting all these catalogues of barbell equipment. But first I have to get my head together. I figure I can get my head together in six months. I figure my liver can make it that long."

(Sure.)

The wonderful part, the part that was not at all horrible or boring, started sometime in the late afternoon and somewhere south of Washington. I don't know the time because I wasn't wearing a watch, and I don't know the name of the town or even the state because I wasn't paying all that much attention to where we were when she joined us. We stopped at some station and I didn't feel like another Coke so I stayed in my seat with my eyes closed. Then just as the bus was starting up a voice said, "Pardon me?" and I looked up and there she was.

She was a little thing, with yellow hair to her shoulders and large round brown eyes and a pointed chin. She was wearing a plaid miniskirt that got halfway to her knee and a cardigan sweater the color of her hair. She had a coat over one arm and was carrying a little suitcase.

At first glance she looked about sixteen. When you looked a little closer at her eyes and the corners of her mouth you could add maybe ten years to that. Say twenty-five.

"Could y'all tell me if this seat is taken?"

It wasn't. Neither were half the seats on the bus, which had emptied out a good deal in Washington. She could have had a whole double seat to herself, actually.

"And could I ask you to help me with this suitcase here?"

It was small and light. I put it in the overhead rack, and then she took a book and a package of cigarettes from her coat pocket and gave me the coat, and I put it alongside the suitcase. I sat down again and she sat down next to me. She didn't have any makeup on except maybe a trace of lipstick, but she was wearing quite a bit of perfume. She smelled very nice, actually. It made me think of Mary Beth, the bus-ticket hooker. Mary Beth had been wearing perfume and hadn't smelled very terrific at all. There's perfume and there's perfume.

"Well, now! I thought we might have rain, but it's turned a nice day after all, hasn't it?"

"Just so there's no snow."

"You from up No'th?"

"I'm not exactly from anywhere," I said. "I was in New York for the past few months."

"And what place do you call home?"

"Wherever I am."

Her face lit up. "Now that's exciting," she said. What she said was *excitin'*, actually, but I hate it when writers spell everything phonetically to get across the fact that somebody has an accent, I'll just say now that she had an accent thicker than spoonbread and you can bear that in mind when you run her dialogue through your head.

192

"When you don't have one home in particular, why, it's like you're never away! Me, I'm an old homebody. My aunt has the pleurisy and I was up doing for her for onto ten days, but except when she has it bad I never get away from home."

"Where's home?"

"Georgia. Mud Kettle, Georgia. Ever been there?"

"No."

"Well, it's not that you missed much." This I believed. The name wasn't Mud Kettle, by the way, but I looked up the town she mentioned in an atlas just now and the population is less than twenty-five hundred, so I changed the name to Mud Kettle because otherwise somebody could probably figure out who she was, and it might shake up the old folks at home. "Not missing much at all. Well, here I am, little old Willie Em Weeks from Mud Kettle, G-A. Lordy!"

"What does the M stand for?" I mean, girls don't usually announce middle initials.

"Emily," she said.

"Emily starts with an *E*," I said.

"Doesn't stand for, it's *short* for! You silly. Willamina Emily Weeks, and isn't that a handle."

Then she waited expectantly, and it occurred to me to tell her my name. She had never met anyone named Chip before, and I had never met any Willie Em, and we got what conversational mileage we could out of that. Which wasn't much.

Then she said, "Chip? Would you mind awfully if I asked you a favor? Would you change seats with me?"

If she wanted to sit by a window, there were windows all over the place she could pick. I didn't tell her this. I changed seats with her, and our bodies bumped a little in passing. Nothing fantastic, just enough to put ideas in my head.

Which was ridiculous, I thought, sitting down again. She would be fun to talk to, someone to break the monotony of the trip, but that was obviously as far as it was going to go. I was getting off in South Carolina and she was riding clear on to Georgia. And anyway she was married, there was a ring on her finger. And besides that we were on a bus, for Pete's sake, in the middle of the afternoon, and all you can do on a bus is sweat and sleep, with sweating considerably more likely than sleeping.

We talked a little more. She asked if I minded if she smoked, and I said I didn't, and she lit a cigarette and opened her book and I settled back in my seat and closed my eyes. I was just as glad she was reading because she wasn't that outstanding to talk to. It was nice watching her and listening to her voice, a very pleasant voice, but it was very hard to concentrate on what she was saying.

So I thought I would doze off again into that sort of half sleep that's possible on a bus, but I couldn't manage it. It was her, the perfume, the presence. I was aware of her. Somehow I was more aware of her now when she wasn't talking and I wasn't looking at her than I had been before.

After a while she said, "Chip? Are you asleep?"

"No."

"Could you do me a favor?"

She was very large on favors. I opened my eyes. "Sure," I said.

She handed me her book, her finger indicating a place on the page. "Starting right here," she said. "Could you just read that scene?"

"Out loud?"

"No, silly."

I took the book and started to read, and the first thing I did was start blinking furiously.

The book was called either *The Swinging Swappers* or *The Swapping Swingers*. It hardly matters which. And the scene she had given me involved six people in a sexual tangle, with everybody doing everything to everybody else, and all in the crudest and most explicit sort of writing. Absolute hard-core pornography. The scene went on for God knows how many pages. I stopped after two and a half of them, and it was just gathering momentum.

And so was I.

I don't know whether I actually blush or not, but if I do, I was doing it then. I closed the book and turned very very slowly to look at her. The expression on her face surprised me. Very serious and matter-of-fact, with a little vertical furrow in the center of her forehead.

"Did you read it?"

"Uh, a couple of pages, yeah."

"You read fast. Could y'all tell me something?"

"What?"

"Was that there an erotic scene? Was it exciting?"

"Yes."

"It was?"

"Uh, yeah. Yes, I would say that you would have to call that an erotic scene. Yes."

Her face relaxed and she gave a little sigh.

"Well, that's good news," she said. "See, I thought maybe it was just the bus that was getting to me. I always get so randy on buses. I swear I get like a mare in heat just from riding on a bus. I don't rightly know what it is that does it. The rhythm of the wheels?"

"Maybe."

"You think that could be it?"

"I suppose."

She nodded thoughtfully. "I can feel it right now," she said. "The rhythm of the wheels on my backside?"

From her tone of voice we could have been discussing the weather. *Think it'll rain? Oh, most likely not. Course we're due for a little rain. Yes, and I always get so randy on buses.* Christ almighty.

She said, "Feel my heart, Chip," and she took my hand and placed it on her left breast.

"Can you feel it?"

I couldn't feel her heartbeat, perhaps because my own had suddenly grown so loud. I could certainly feel her breast, though. I felt it through the thicknesses of sweater and bra, felt the nipple poking against my palm.

I cupped her breast, stroked with my fingers. It was as warm and soft as a little bird. I kept the little bird in my hand and dreamed of giving her two in the bush.

Our mouths found one another. She tasted of cigarettes. I don't like to smoke but I like that taste on a girl's mouth. We slid into an all-out kiss, right off the bat. She was very goddamned good at kissing. We kissed for miles, and I held her breast as if I was afraid it would fly away if I let it go. I wasn't about to take any chances.

When we broke the kiss she sagged back in her seat with her eyes closed and her jaw slack. Her breathing was really ragged. I was a little shook up myself but she was way out ahead of me.

Finally she said, "Get my coat, Chip."

"You can't leave now. I mean, the least you have to do is wait until the bus stops."

"*Leave*? Who's leaving?"

"Not me. I thought you wanted your coat." She sighed and tsssted at me. "Don't you have no sense?" she whispered. "To put over us. To neck under. So nobody sees us."

"Oh."

"Because I'm not about to stop now. Chip, I told you how I get on buses, and then reading that scene with them...and then you messing around with me, I mean I'm not about to stop now."

"Fine by me."

"Now fetch my coat."

I fetched her coat and draped it over us. While I was getting it I checked out the other people in the area. If any of them were checking us out in return they were doing a good job of hiding it. The seats across the aisle were empty, and most of our other neighbors were asleep.

As soon as I was seated beside her she grabbed my hand

and tucked it up under her miniskirt. She was wearing panties. Very moist panties.

I said, "Willie Em—"

"Shhhh!" she whispered. "No more talking, Chip. Oh, Lord have mercy, I'm so hot I could *burn*! But don't talk, don't say anything. Just get me off. God, please get me *off*—"

The thing is, she kept getting off and climbing right back on again. There was only so much we could do. I played with her and that was about the extent of it. She was unbelievably responsive. Each orgasm just seemed to make her that much more anxious for the next one.

This went on for maybe half an hour, and I could see it was destined to go on all the way to Bordentown unless I happened to run out of fingers somewhere along the way.

And I was going to get off the bus in Bordentown with testicles the size of basketballs, and they were going to hurt like hell, and that was just too damned bad because I had already decided it was worth it.

Maybe she wasn't the only one who got horny on buses. Maybe it was the other people around, or maybe it was the build-up and let-down I'd gotten earlier from Mary Beth, or maybe it was just Willamina Emily Weeks herself, but whatever it was, it was worth six Waterloos and an Armageddon. I mean it was very goddamned exciting, believe me.

God knows how many little orgasms she had. I couldn't keep score. But she finally got the big one and collapsed like a tubercular lung.

In less than two minutes we pulled off the highway and stopped for a ten-minute rest break in Erewhon, North Carolina.

I swear she planned it that way.

She said, "Get my suitcase down, Chip. And put your jacket over those two seats across the aisle, and leave my coat here. And when we come back you sit over there and sort

197

of take up both seats until the bus moves. So no one sits across from us, you hear?"

I heard and I did. I didn't know why she wanted her suitcase, or why we had to get off the bus and back on again, or any of those things, really. I would have understood the bit about the coats even if she hadn't explained it to me, although I'll admit I wouldn't have thought of it on my own, not just then.

But I wasn't going to bug her about any of this. I mean, it was pretty obvious this wasn't the first time she ever got randy on a bus, and it wasn't the first time she ever decided to do anything about it. This bus fetish was something she had indulged in before. And probably often. Which was why she sat down next to me to begin with. And why she wanted the window seat—partly so that we could bump bottoms while changing places, and partly because she would be better shielded from observation if she sat away from the aisle.

I didn't really want to get off the bus and back on again. Walking presented certain logistical problems that would be even more obvious to spectators if I had to leave my jacket on the bus. But I got off and I forced myself to drink a Coke and munch a pack of those peanut butter and cheese things. I waited until she emerged from the ladies' room and got on board the bus before I followed her. She put her suitcase on the seat beside her so that no one could sit there, and I sprawled over the two opposite seats and looked as unkempt as possible so that no one would want to sit next to me. She waited until the bus was back on the highway before giving me a nod, and I came over and put her suitcase overhead and sat down next to her.

We huddled together under her coat and kissed briefly. Then I said, "Why the suitcase?"

"Can't you guess?"

The only thing that had occurred to me was that she wanted to put her diaphragm on, but I couldn't believe that. This was a bus, after all, and it wasn't particularly comfortable or roomy even if all you wanted to do was sit in it. I know people screw in the most unlikely places, but only midgets and contortionists could possibly do it on a bus.

I had already decided that the best I could hope for was to shoot in my pants, if you'll forgive me for being crude about it. (I can't really think of any other way to say it.) And I wasn't all that sure I wanted to do that. I don't suppose I really cared about getting off myself. I just wanted to go on thrilling Willie Em.

"No," I said, "I can't guess."

"Did that old suitcase feel heavier this time?"

"No."

"It was, though."

"It was?"

She grinned impishly. "Something in it that wasn't in it before."

What? A roll of toilet paper? A Coke? What?

"What?"

"You have to find out for yourself. But I'll bet you appreciate the change."

"I think you lost me."

"Why, I surely hope not! Now why don't you shut your mouth and start loving me up instead of asking all those questions?"

I had no argument there. I kissed her and put a hand on her breast. It felt softer than ever. I petted it and light dawned.

"Uh-huh. And that's just the half of it."

I could guess the other half, but I sent my hand on an expedition to make sure. I slipped it under her skirt and there were no panties there. The panties, like the bra, were currently in her suitcase.

I hope she wrung them out first.

It certainly did make things easier. We snuggled under her coat and unbuttoned her cardigan and pulled her skirt all

Lawrence Block

the way up, and all of a sudden there was a lot more to do.

She had wonderfully soft skin and nice firm little breasts. The perfume she was wearing mixed nicely with the musk of her.

I was going to put down a whole description of just what we did over the next couple of hours, but I've been thinking about it and I decided the hell with it. Partly because I think that would just be too much sex. And despite what Mr. Fultz said, I think there is such a thing as too much sex.

Because when all you have is a description of what happened, who did what and where and how and all of that, then all you've got is the kind of book Willie Em was reading, *The Swinging Swappers* or *The Swapping Swingers*. And that sort of thing may be exciting in small doses, but it's also pretty disgusting, actually.

What's important, really, is what it was like and where everybody's head was at while it was going on, or otherwise it's just bodies with no people attached to them. And anyway we kept on like this for a couple of hours, and I couldn't honestly remember the whole thing piece by piece. It would be easy enough to fake it and get the tone, right the same way I fake some of the dialogue because I can't actually remember every stupid conversation I ever had word for word. Let's just say that I kept doing things to her and she kept enjoying them and let's let it go at that. I figure that if all you wanted in the way of a book was something to get off with, you would have stopped reading before now and gone on to the swinging switching swapping swill.

Three times in the course of all this I took her hand and put it on me. Twice she gave a little squeeze and murmured "*Later*." The third time she repeated this and added, "When it gets dark, Chip."

You know, I wonder how often she did this.

I mean, she had the whole thing choreographed, for

200

Pete's sake. Sometimes when I think about her I picture her spending her entire life riding north and south on Greyhound buses. Maybe her aunt doesn't even have pleurisy. Maybe she doesn't even have an aunt. Maybe Greyhound gives her a commuter's rate. Maybe they let her ride free because it's such great public relations for them. Maybe—

When it got dark, I didn't even have to reach for her hand. It came over of its own accord and quickly found what it was looking for. She gave a few affectionate squeezes, worked a zipper, reached in, and brought her hand quickly back out again.

She put her lips to my ear and whispered, "Why don't you go to the lavatory and take off your shorts?"

I guess I should have done this at the rest stop. God knows it would have been a lot easier. The lavatory wasn't really spacious enough to change clothes in. It was barely big enough to take a leak in, actually.

I came back with my shorts in my pocket and got under the coat, again. Then she decided we should change places, with me sitting in the window seat and her on the outside, and somehow we managed to do this without getting out from under the coat. Don't ask me how.

"Poor old Chip," she murmured. "Getting me off about a hundred times"—at the very least, I thought—"and you never getting off once your own self. But we'll fix that."

And I sat there with her head in my lap and my hand bunched up in all that yellow hair and she fixed everything in the world. She fixed things that weren't even broken.

Wow.

Afterward, while I waited for the top of my skull to come back down where it belonged, she nestled her sweet and talented little head on my shoulder. After a while she said, "Happy?"

"Mmmmm."

"You like being loved up that way?"

"Mmmmm."

201

"They tell me girls up North don't like to do that. Damned if I know why. First time I did that I wasn't but fourteen years old and at a drive-in movie and too dumb to know about keeping my teeth out of the way, and the good old boy I was with was too dumb to tell me." She giggled. "You like that kind of loving, you're gonna enjoy yourself down South. Southern girls are decent, see. And they know the one thing that's not decent is getting pregnant before you're married, and another thing they know is no girl ever got a big belly from it."

From her tone of voice she could have been talking about crop rotation and soil erosion. It was really weird.

I said, "The purity of Southern womanhood."

"You better believe it. Next Southern girl you meet and get friendly with, you tell her to try it with a mouthful of warm water. Of course you couldn't do that on a bus."

"The Waterloo," I said.

"You know about that?"

"Uh-huh."

"They know about that up North?"

"Not exactly."

"You ever have it done?"

"Not exactly."

"What do you mean, 'Not exactly'?"

"It's hard to explain."

"Well—?"

"I read about it."

"In a *book*?"

"Uh-huh."

"Like the kind of book I was reading before? One of those randy books?"

"More or less."

"Lordy," she said. "I'll usually get a book like that to read if, oh, if I happen to have to take a long trip on a bus." I could believe it. "I've read my share of them, I guess. Never read anything about the Waterloo in any old book."

"Maybe it was written by a Southern girl," I suggested.

"No maybe about it. It must have been."

"Maybe a girl from Tennessee."

"Georgia," she said.

Chapter Four

THE BUS STATION IN BORDENTOWN WAS just an Atlantic gas station that sold bus tickets. They had a Coke machine, but I passed it up. I was down to about two and a half dollars and I didn't know where I was going to get a room, or how much it would cost. I figured the Y was the best bet, and I asked an old guy at the station how to get to it.

He scratched his head and said, "Why?"

"Because I need a place to stay."

"But you asked—"

"The Y," I said. He was still puzzled. "The YMCA," I said.

"Oh, the YMCA. Let me just think. I believe they have one over to Savolia, but I couldn't say for sure."

"How far is that?"

"Oh, I guess I'd put it at twenty-eight miles. Say thirty at the outside."

There was a hotel in Bordentown, he told me. It was called the Bordentown Hotel, which seemed logical enough, and it was on Main Street, which wasn't all that much of a surprise either. Salesmen would stay there, if they had to be in Bordentown overnight, and if they wanted to save money, because those motels over on the highway all ranged from eight to twelve dollars a room, whereas you could stay at the hotel for five dollars, or seven-fifty with a private bath. And then there were some single people who lived there year-round, widowers for the most part, and they paid by the month, which made it considerably cheaper.

"Of course you wouldn't be wanting to spend a month in Bordentown," he said.

I had the feeling he might be right. Anyway, I couldn't afford to pay by the month. I couldn't even afford to pay by the night. I asked if there were any less expensive places.

He said there were some women who took in tourists for two or three dollars a night, but it was too late to go knocking on their doors.

"How would it be if I slept in the back here?" I suggested. "It would just be for tonight."

"Company wouldn't allow that."

I said I wouldn't tell them if he didn't, but he didn't even bother answering that. He didn't get exactly hostile, just sort of turned away. I had the feeling that he didn't see much point in wasting any more time on me, and I could understand his point of view.

I must have spent half an hour walking through the main part of town, and that was enough to cover it pretty thoroughly. There really wasn't a lot there. It was about then that I started wondering if coming to Bordentown might not have been something of a mistake. Of course, it was the middle of the night. You couldn't really expect a small town to be lit up like Times Square.

Until now, though, I had been very much into the idea of going to Bordentown. The weirdness of it, finding the bus ticket and using it, had a special beauty of its own. In the normal course of things I might have spent the last few hours of the bus trip thinking about what I would do after I got off the bus, making plans and working things out in my mind. But you know how I spent the last few hours of the bus trip. I spent the last few hours of the bus trip with Willie Em, and the company of Willie Em tends to make one live very much in the Now.

As a matter of fact, the *memory* of Willie Em tends to make one live very much in the Past, and while I walked around downtown Bordentown, such as it was, I found myself thinking as much about her as about my future. I couldn't really get into anything like long-term planning at all. Just short-term goals, like getting a place to sleep and finding some kind of job, were the only things I could really handle.

The place to sleep was the hard part. At that hour it

seemed impossible. The only place I could go was the hotel, and I couldn't afford it. If I had only had a suitcase it would have been all right, because I could tell them I was staying for a week, and if things went well I would have enough money at the end of the week to pay what I owed. On the other hand, if things went badly I could leave them the suitcase at the end of the week and go someplace else, and all that would mean was that I could never go back to Bordentown again, which didn't sound that terrible anyway.

No suitcase, though. Nothing but the clothes on my back, which had seen cleaner days. So any hotel would be sure to ask for cash in advance. The fact that I was poor but honest wouldn't help. They'd rather have someone who's rich but crooked.

It's funny how problems solve themselves, though, when you just let things happen. I had more or less resigned myself to finding some diner and sitting up drinking coffee until morning, at which time I could get some old lady to rent me a room that I could afford, when I got a place to sleep that didn't cost me a dime.

The Bordentown Jail.

I was walking along when this car pulled up and a voice said, "Git over here, boy." And when I got over there I knew who the guy was without him saying another word. I recognized him right away from all those Dodge commercials.

He never did advise me of my rights, but I don't guess he had to because he never exactly arrested me, either. He just told me to get in the car with him, and he drove over to a little concrete block building a few blocks from where he picked me up, and he asked me a lot of questions and took my fingerprints and put me in a cell. He took my belt and my shoelaces and my comb. I was getting sick of losing combs, and I hadn't been eating much lately and my pants, without the belt, tended to fall down a lot. But I didn't complain.

I didn't complain about any of this, actually. I was at a tremendous psychological disadvantage, especially when he made me empty my pockets and I had to take out that pair of undershorts and put them on the desk. Maybe some people can do that without feeling stupid. Not me.

He said, "No identification, no visible means of support, no clothing. You say you're from New York, boy? What you think you're doing here?"

I don't remember what I said.

"You an' agitator? Come down to make trouble? Or a runaway? You wanted up North? Get your prints and description to Washington and see if there isn't somebody looking for you."

There was something about the way the cell door closed that left me feeling it would never open again. I walked around the cell, which was a lot like walking around Bordentown except that it didn't take quite so long. There was a kind of a toilet, which I'm just as glad I didn't have to use, and a corn husk mattress that was more comfortable than it looked.

During the summer some of my fellow apple-knockers had told me stories about Southern jails. About getting caught in a speed trap and being fined the amount they had on them, and then winding up on the chain gang on a vagrancy charge because they didn't have any money. About trying to hitchhike through Georgia and getting sentenced to three months of chopping weeds with a road crew.

I remembered all this now, and I really didn't think I was going to get much sleep. But I must have been more exhausted than I realized.

I woke up when the sun came through the bars. I just lay there for about an hour before the Sheriff turned up, trying to put together pieces of a story that would keep me off the chain gang.

At first I decided to tell him the truth. I must have read a hundred murder stories where some poor idiot is suspected of a crime, and if he had just played things absolutely straight from the beginning it would have worked out with no trouble, but instead he tells one little lie or holds something back and gets in deeper trouble, until he has to go out and find the real killer himself. Of course, if he played things absolutely straight there wouldn't have been any book, so I can understand why writers do it that way, but the moral always seemed to be that the truth shall make you free.

But it seemed to me that the truth in my case would make me very much unfree. In the first place, nobody was going to believe it. If I said I found a wallet that somebody had already stolen, anyone with half a brain would decide that I had stolen it. And if I said I came to Bordentown because I had a ticket that made it a toss-up between Bordentown and Boston, and Bordentown was warmer, and I didn't want to spit in the face of destiny, and how one Mary Beth could lead to another, well, all that would do was keep me off the chain gang and land me in the insane asylum.

The trouble with the truth was that it just didn't sound true enough. And by the time he unlocked my cell door and came on in, I had thought up a few ways to improve it.

"Well, now," he said. "I guess you ain't precisely Johnny Dillinger after all. Your fingerprints didn't ring any bells and nobody up in Washington got too excited about your description."

I had been a little worried that I might still be wanted in Indiana for statutory rape, but I guess that got straightened out somewhere along the way. I knew my fingerprints had never gotten on file.

(Until now.)

"But that seems to make you what they call an unknown quantity, boy." He clucked his tongue. "Chip Harrison. That some kind of a nickname?"

"It's my real name."

208

"Your folks handed you that, did they? Where are they now?"

"They were killed in an auto crash a little over a year ago."

"Any other kinfolk?"

"None."

"And no way on earth to prove you're who you say you are. No identification at all."

"My wallet was stolen. In New York."

He looked at me.

"They got my wallet and my suitcase. I was on my way to Florida. To Miami, I couldn't stand it in New York with the weather and the kind of people you meet up there. I had my ticket bought and I was on my way to the bus station when they jumped me."

"Jumped you?"

"Three big buck niggers," I said. "One of them held a razor to my throat. I think you can still see the nick. Then one of the others hit me a few times in the stomach. They got my watch and my wallet and my suitcase, they even got the change out of my pocket. I had the ticket in my shoe."

"That was good thinking," he said. "You go to the police?"

"In New York? What good would that do?"

"I hear tell it's another country up there."

"More like another world. If you tell those New York police you've been robbed, they act like you're wasting their time." Which was true enough, incidentally. When I had a place in the East Village, somebody kicked the door in one day and robbed me, which was actually one big reason why I didn't have anything but the clothes on my back. I wasn't there at the time, and there had never been anyone holding a razor to my throat, but you can see that the story had elements of truth to it. It was sort of a matter of arranging the truth so that it made sense.

"So all I had was the ticket," I went on. "I had sixty-two

dollars left after I bought my ticket, but they got it when they got the wallet. I figured it would be plenty to keep me going until I found work in Miami. A fellow was telling me there were plenty of jobs down there. At those hotels."

"That the kind of work you did in New York?"

"No, I was bussing tables in a cafeteria." I actually did that for a day once, in a cafeteria on Second Avenue. That job ended when I dropped a tray. They took it for granted that you would drop a tray now and then, but not on a customer. "But from what I heard you didn't need much experience to hire on as a bellhop or something."

He was nodding. He didn't really look like that Dodge commercial anymore.

"After they robbed me," I said, "I didn't know what to do. I just knew I had to get out of New York."

"No place for a white man."

"That's the truth," I said. "Dope addicts and niggers and long-haired radicals and I don't know what else. And being robbed and all, I just wanted to get away from there. But I didn't want to go to Miami with no money at all. I figured I'd starve before I got settled. So I worked out how much money I would need and traded my ticket so that I could get as close as possible to Miami and still have a few dollars left to live on."

"And that's how you picked Bordentown. I was wondering about that."

"I guess it would have been better to stop further north. In North Carolina, say, because that would have left me with more money. But I wanted to get as far as I could, and anyway my mother was from South Carolina originally—"

"Is that a fact?"

"She was born in Charleston. Her maiden name was Ryder. But there's no family left now."

"I didn't think you seemed like the typical Yankee."

"Well, I've always lived in the North. But I never felt, you know, that it was really home to me."

We went on like this for a while, and he got less and less like that Dodge commercial and I got more and more South Carolina into my voice. I didn't want to get carried away and lay it on too thick, but as long as it was going over well, I figured it was worth staying with. He wanted to know about my plans. I said I would just try to find work in Bordentown. There weren't many jobs, he said. Ever since the space people closed their operations in Savolia, jobs were tight all over the area. Especially in the winter, when there was no farm work to speak of. I said I was willing to do just about anything, and as soon as I had money saved I could go down to Miami.

"Don't want to go anywhere without some identification," he said. "You'd get the same reception anywhere. First police officer who sets eyes on you wouldn't have no choice but to lock you up. I suspect you can write away for certain things. Driver's license, for example."

"I never had one."

"Draft card, for certain. This day and age you don't want to go anywhere without a draft card."

"I'm only seventeen," I said. On my eighteenth birthday I had decided that it wouldn't hurt to stay seventeen as long as possible. It seemed to me that if you didn't get around to registering for the draft you wouldn't have to make any Big Decision as to whether or not you would burn your draft card.

"Need a social security card," he said. "You must of had one, I guess. Recollect the number?"

I didn't.

"Easier to go ahead and get a new one, then. You try writing to them for a replacement and those fellows in Washington, they'll be a year getting back to you. I could tell you stories about those people up there. What else you'll need is a Sheriff's ID Card. I'll fix you up with one of those. At least we can do that without going through a passel of red tape. You just apply for a social security card down to the courthouse, and on the form you put that you never had one before. That's the easiest way to go about it. Not entirely legal, but in police work you learn that there's laws and there's laws. Know what I mean?"

"Laws to help people and laws to get in people's way?"

"I guess you understand my meaning, boy." He looked at me and I looked back at him, deciding that he was a pretty nice guy. He clucked his tongue again. "Reckon you could do with a bath and a change of clothes," he said. "Or with running what clothes you got through the washing machine. The wife can do that while you're in the tub." I almost said I didn't have a wife. Then I realized we were talking about his wife, and his washing machine, and his tub.

"Like to had me wondering when you pulled those drawers out of your pocket last night. I sat up wondering what kind of damned fool pervert carries his underwear in his pocket. Guess they must of been chafing you some on that bus ride. How long were you on that bus?"

"On to forty hours."

He clucked again. "And eating in those greasy diners, were you? Fifty cents for a hamburger sandwich and you have to hunt for the meat, and fifteen cents for coffee that's not but brown water. Never had a real Southern breakfast up there, did you?"

"No."

"Grits and eggs and fries and sausage and coffee that the spoon stands up in? I guess they don't know how to eat up there. What's that Northern food like?"

I didn't mention brown rice. "Like a machine made it," I said.

"You come on now," he said, beaming. He led me out of the cell. "I'll just get you set with a Sheriff's card, and then we'll take a run over to my home and see if you got the kind of appetite that would have made your mother proud. Look at the way those pants are falling off of you. I swear the wife's gone take one look at you and run straight for the kitchen. Nothing brings out her cooking like someone who looks like he could profit from it." He patted his belly, of which there was quite a lot. "She feels guilty, feeding me. But you'll be a real challenge to her."

I said, "This is awfully nice of you," or something like that.

"Oh, just put it down to Southern hospitality," he said, grinning. "We don't cotton to everybody. But we take care of our own kind, boy."

Chapter Five

BY THE END OF THE WEEK I HAD A Sheriff's ID Card, a social security card, and a South Carolina driver's license. I also had two jobs, one of which paid me fifteen dollars a week and my lunches, and the other of which brought in five dollars a week, breakfasts, dinners, and a room of my own. Sheriff Tyles fixed me up with the license and one of the jobs, and his wife Minnie got me the other one.

(I had to take a road test for the license. I had never done much in the way of driving, and I don't know that I had any natural talent for it, but the test was no great problem. When you take the test in the official Sheriff's car, there aren't a hell of a lot of inspectors who are likely to fail you. I didn't hit anybody, so I passed.)

Minnie Tyles took to me right off. I hadn't been that confident she would be thrilled when her husband brought me home. Forty hours on a bus and a night in a jail cell hadn't improved my appearance that much. But when we walked in the door he boomed out, "Minnie, this here boy hasn't had a decent meal in three days and his mother was a Charleston Ryder." I don't know which part of the sentence went over the heaviest. I was a little lost myself, and for a minute there I thought he was saying that my mother was a member of some South Carolina version of the Hell's Angels.

I had about four meals, and I had them all at once. And then I had a bath while my clothes washed and dried, and then I had a big piece of pie and another couple of cups of coffee. The more I ate the happier that woman got. It was really something to watch.

"Of course he'll sleep here until he finds someplace," she told the Sheriff. "Won't be any trouble to fix up the spare room for him." I said something about not wanting to impose, and they both acted as though they hadn't heard me, which was fine with me.

214

* * *

The job situation didn't look very promising. There wasn't much available, and most of the high school kids left town when they graduated, unless their fathers had businesses for them to go into. I spent a couple of days looking for work and couldn't get anywhere. "I couldn't ask you to work for what-all I can afford to pay you," one shopkeeper said. "Easier to hire a nigger for fifty cents an hour, and I wouldn't let you work for that kind of wages even if you said you would. And with business the way it is I couldn't pay you more."

Then Minnie came up with something. "Now I'll tell you right off it isn't so much of a job," she said. "But Reverend Lathrop has been poorly lately that's at the church we go to, and with his wife gone two years in May it's all he can do to look after himself. Lucille, that's his daughter, cooks his meals for him and does the cleaning, what she can keep up with; some of the women from the church do his ironing and all, but if there was someone who would come in a few hours a day, because with it being an old house and all and things always breaking down, and the yard to keep up and the trash to be taken out, and what with one thing or another, and him getting along in years, he was twenty years older than Helen, that was his wife, and her dying first, and Lucille still in school so that she has to run home and cook his dinner for him and then back to school again—"

It wasn't very much work. The main reason that Rev. Lathrop was poorly was that he did in a quart of corn whiskey every day. This tended to limit his movements, and he spent most of his time sitting in the back parlor with a bottle and a glass listening to the radio.

I did things like shoveling ashes out of the coal furnace and taking out the trash (and burying the empty liquor bottles under the rest of the garbage). I would get there around ten in the morning, by which time Lucille was off at school and her father was already at work on the daily bottle. She came home at noon and fixed dinner for us, and then I did things like trimming shrubbery and replacing frayed lamp cords and repainting the upstairs bathroom, sort of doing all the repairs and maintenance work that tends to get neglected when you knock off a quart a day. How late I stayed depended on whether or not Lucille came straight home from school. She was a cheerleader, and if there was a basketball game or a practice session scheduled she wouldn't get home until five or six. No one ever exactly spelled it out, but the idea was that Rev. Lathrop shouldn't be left alone if there was a way to avoid it. I don't know what they were worried about. I never saw him get off that chair. Lucille used to bring his dinner to him, and he ate between drinks. He had a pretty good appetite for someone who drank that much, but he never really paid attention to his food, just ate it because it was there. I had the feeling that if she skipped his dinner he wouldn't notice it.

He didn't bother me, though. He would look at me if I was in the room, and now and then he would quote scripture, but if I spoke he never gave any sign that he had heard, so before long I got out of the habit of talking to him. Once I had an insane urge to polish his bald head along with the furniture, just to see what would happen. Of course I didn't, but I'm not sure he would have noticed.

One Sunday I let Minnie take me to hear him preach a sermon. The Sheriff never went to church, but Minnie went religiously. She introduced me to all her friends, which took in most of the congregation, and told everybody my mother was a Charleston Ryder. (Actually my mother's maiden name was Leigh, which was where my first name came from, but that sounded too Southern to be true. And she was from Lawrence, Kansas, and I think her grandparents ran a way station of the Underground Railway for runaway slaves headed north. I don't think that would have gone over as well with this crowd.)

* * *

The one time I heard him preach, I had trouble believing it was the same vegetable who spent the other six days of the week in the back parlor. He stood straight and tall and had a great deal of presence. The sermon itself wasn't designed to make you think a whole hell of a lot. He came out against sin, creeping socialism, federal intervention, drinking, gambling, and sins of the flesh, without getting too specific on any of these points. I won't say I enjoyed it, but I was really proud of him the way he stayed on top of things. I was sure he would fall over or forget what he was talking about, but he never once dropped the ball. He was pretty impressive.

When I finished up at the Lathrop house, sometimes I would drop over to the station and talk with the Sheriff, and about twice a week I would get invited home for dinner. Or I might see a movie. There was one movie house in town and they changed the bill three times a week, and even so the movie was usually one I had seen four or five years ago. The theater was always close to empty, and whether or not they had an afternoon show depended on how many people showed up.

Mr. Crewe wouldn't run the projector unless he had at least ten people in the audience.

He was one of the people I'd tried to hit for a job. I never heard a man laugh louder. "Why, if I paid *myself* a salary," he said, "I'd go broke tomorrow. I'd have to close."

Then, after the movie, or instead of the movie, I would sometimes stop for a cup of coffee at a diner. The coffee wasn't sensational but one of the waitresses was, and I liked to talk to her. She had told me that she wouldn't go out with me because her boyfriend was in Vietnam, and I was only seventeen and she was nineteen and she didn't go with boys younger than herself. I figured sooner or later she would change her mind, and even if she didn't the coffee wasn't that godawful.

Then I would walk about a mile out of town, or get a lift

if I had had supper with the Sheriff and Minnie. There was a place there on one of the country roads called the Lighthouse, where I had a room and got my morning and evening meals.

"It's not a job with a future," Sheriff Tyles said, "but you could do worse. It puts a roof over your head and a few dollars in your pocket and it's good experience if you ever want to go into law enforcement. Old Geraldine runs a decent place. You won't find water in the liquor and you'll never hear of a customer getting rolled, not even one from out of the state, which you would expect. Now and then a fight will get out of hand and there'll be a certain amount of cutting, but you always have that when you have men and whiskey. Hasn't been anybody killed there in onto four years, and that was Johnny Piersall that everybody was surprised he lasted that long. If there was ever a boy looking to get killed, that was Johnny Piersall.

"And Geraldine has a doctor in once a week, and everything is clean and decent. So for the most part all you have to do is be there. You'll be a deputy in case you have to go so far as to make an arrest, but I doubt that'll happen at all. You might have to stop a fight now and then if it gets too ornery, or you might have to hit some old boy upside the head for abusing one of the girls. But being there is the main thing, and the less you have to do the more Geraldine will like it. It's like a life insurance policy, there's never yet been anybody complaining that he's not getting sufficient use out of it."

So that was my job. From around nine at night until around four in the morning, with time for a nap in the early evening unless something came up and they had to call me. At the Lighthouse, owned and operated by Geraldine Simms.

There are, as Sheriff Tyles and I had agreed, laws and laws. Laws to help people and laws to get in people's way. I guess I had always had more or less that attitude myself, and maybe more of it when you consider my parents' occupation and my own work as a termite salesman. (Not that I actually sold termites.)

Even so, I have to admit that the job came as a surprise to me. I'd already had a lot of unusual jobs, and in fact I had gotten to the point where I took it for granted that I would go on having unusual jobs. I always figured that sooner or later I would find what I had been looking for all along, which is to say a Job With A Future, but that never seemed to be the kind of job I got and I was beginning to see a pattern developing.

But I never expected to be employed as a Deputy Sheriff in a South Carolina whorehouse.

I just never expected it.

Chapter Six

GERALDINE SHOOK HER HEAD. "You're in trouble now, Chip."

"I am?"

"Bad trouble."

"I don't see it."

Her hand, thin with a tracing of blue veins, moved quickly and decisively. She lifted a pawn of mine, set her bishop in its place.

"Check," she said.

"Oh."

"Think it out if you want, but I can speed it up for you. If you play King takes Bishop, I play Queen to King Eight—Checkmate. If you play King to Bishop One, I play Bishop takes Queen."

I looked at the board for a minute, and she was right. She generally was. I nodded slowly.

"You resign?"

"Uh-huh."

"Want another game?"

"Not right now. I have a feeling I'm never going to learn this game."

"You're getting better."

"I can't keep my mind on it the way you can, that's the thing. I used to play in New York and I would win most of the time because I could see a move or so in advance, and that was better than the guys I played against. I even thought I was pretty good, because of generally winning."

"You're not so bad."

"Thanks," I said. I gathered the pieces and put them back in the cigar box. We were in the bar-room, and there were three beer-drinkers in the bar. Geraldine went to see if they wanted refills. They didn't. It was around eleven, the middle of the week, and business couldn't have been much slower. Geraldine came back with a cold Coke for me and her usual glass of banana liqueur.

We talked about this and that, and then Geraldine was starting to say, "That tobacco farmer's been a long time with Claureen," when I looked up and Claureen was standing there in a pink wrapper and house slippers.

She said, "Chip? Could you come on up for a minute?"

"Trouble?"

"Just that he's asleep and I can't wake him and I was afraid if I did wake him and he woke up nasty like they will sometimes—"

"He's not a regular," Geraldine said. "This is his first time." This meant he wasn't a treasured customer, so if it would simplify things to beat his brains in I should just go ahead and do it.

I got to my feet. Geraldine said something about the kind of men who fall asleep the minute they finish. Claureen took my hand and we walked to the stairs.

On the staircase she said, "It's not like she said."

"What isn't?"

"I declare it's too embarrassing to say. He didn't fall asleep after. He fell asleep while."

"While what?"

"What do you think?"

"Oh. Too much to drink, probably."

"No, that's not it. I know when they can't because they been drinking. It's not he can't. Oh, you'll see what I mean."

In her room I saw what she meant. The tobacco farmer was stretched out on his back with his eyes closed and his arms at his sides.

He had his socks and shoes on and nothing else.

"You see how he is, Chip? He's still hard."

"Uh, yeah. So he is."

"He just sprawled out like that and I started doing him, you know, and he got like that right away. Just lying still like that, and hard as a bar of iron. And I did him and did him and did him and nothing happened. And I got to thinking, all right, you silly old son of a bitch, just how long is it gone take before you get where you're going? But I just kept on and then I wasn't even thinking about what I was doing, I thought about getting my hair done and I don't know what-all, and the time just went on by—"

"Geraldine was saying he was taking a long time."

"—and finally I thought maybe he was one of those who couldn't finish that way, and I looked up to ask and he was like you see him, and I talked to him, and nothing; he was dead to the world."

"You tried to wake him?".

"A little. I was scared, you know, to try too much."

I went over and put a hand on the man's shoulder. I gave him a shake.

Nothing happened.

"I even put water on his face," Claureen said.

"No reaction?"

"Nothing."

"I wonder if he's dead."

She grabbed my arm. "Oh, Holy Jesus! Chip, don't you even go and say a thing like that!"

"Did you check?"

"No, but—"

"Because it's possible, you know."

"Would it stay like that after you were dead?"

"I don't know."

"What a horrible thing!"

"I don't know. If you gotta go—"

"Oh, Mother of Pearl," she said. She was trembling. "Imagine me doing that to a dead man. Oh, I'm just shaking fit to die myself!"

I picked up his wrist and looked around for his pulse. It took me a little while, but ultimately I found what I was looking for and told Claureen she wasn't a murderess.

"I thought I Frenched him to death," she said. "Oh, mercy."

"You may have Frenched him into a coma," I told her. "His pulse is there but it's very slow. It's as if he was in some kind of hypnotic trance."

"I hypnotized him? I didn't say anything like, 'Look into my eyes,' or any of that. All I did was—"

"I know what you did," I said, quickly. "Maybe I'd better tell Geraldine to call the doctor."

"At this hour?"

"I don't know what'll happen if we wait until morning. Suppose he comes to in the middle of the night? With nobody around?" I put my ear to his face. "Or suppose he *does* die, for that matter. He's breathing, but it's so faint you wouldn't believe it."

"What'll we do?"

"Maybe an orgasm would wake him."

"That's what I *tried*, Chip. That's what took so long. I did everything I could think of. Even the vibrator."

"And nothing worked?"

"Nothing. If it worked, he wouldn't be here."

"That's a point."

"What'll we do?"

"I'm going to tell Geraldine."

"She'll kill me," Claureen said.

"Don't be ridiculous. It's not your fault."

I went downstairs and told Geraldine what the problem was. Rita was sitting with her at the time. There were just the two girls there during the week, Rita and Claureen. They both had rooms upstairs that they slept in after working hours. On weekends or particularly busy nights another girl would work the busy hours, usually Jo Lee or Marguerite.

Rita just stared while I was talking. "I never heard the like," she said.

"I have," Geraldine said. "Never saw it, but heard of it. Heard of men overdosing with sleeping pills and then going with a girl, and they never wake up afterward, but that's something else because they don't stay hard like that. But I've heard of this, too. What you have to do is get their rocks off and then they wake up."

223

"Claureen hasn't been able to," I said.

"And she tried everything."

"Don't even ask me," Rita said.

"Oh, I won't." Geraldine thought for a moment.

"Claureen's young," she said, and went silent again. Then she said, "God damn it to hell, you just never get to retire in this business. You think you're retired and you find out you're not. God damn it to hell."

She got up and went to the stairs. Rita and I sat and looked at each other.

I said, "I never heard her swear before."

"Neither did I. And I've been here for almost three years. Geraldine wouldn't say shit if she had a mouthful. I can't believe it, Chip."

"What happens now?"

"I don't know."

What happened was that Claureen came downstairs. She was wearing a dress and shoes instead of the wrapper and slippers. We stared at her. She came over and sat down at our table.

"She cursed," she said, hollowly. "Geraldine cursed."

"Did she curse *you*, honey?"

She shook her head. "She just cursed generally, like. She said, 'God damn it to hell.'"

"She said it down here. Twice."

"And then she told me to put a dress on and come downstairs. I didn't want to just go and leave her there with that, uh, with *him*, and I said I don't know what-all, and she just turned and looked at me. And I just put on the dress and the shoes and I came down here."

"You look so pale, girl."

"Look at how I'm shaking—"

Rita said, "Was she doin' anything?"

"What do you mean?"

"With that farmer."

"Oh. She made me leave the room. She wouldn't even look at him until I left the room, and then—"

224

"What?"

"She locked the door. You know what she always said, that you never lock the door unless you-all are alone in the room. Geraldine locked the door."

I started to say something, then stopped.

The girls saw the expression on my face and followed my eyes to the staircase. The tobacco farmer was coming down it, neatly dressed, an absolutely blank look in his eyes. He came down and he walked out and the door closed behind him.

Maybe two minutes later Geraldine came down. She passed our table without a glance and drew a couple of beers for the drinkers at the bar. One of them said something and she joked back with them the way she always did. Then she came back to our table.

For the longest time in the world nobody said anything. It was really weird. We were all waiting for Geraldine to talk up, and she was off in some other world.

Finally she said, "You never really retire. You just can't, want to or not."

Claureen or Rita said, "What happened?"

"He came and went. Or he'd be there still, saluting the ceiling."

Claureen or Rita said, "But what did you—"

There was a pause on the order of the Grand Canyon during which a whole load of expressions flashed over Geraldine's face. You couldn't really read any of them because none of them were there long enough.

Then all at once her whole face smiled. I can't remember ever seeing a smile like that one before or since, and certainly not from Geraldine. A sour grin was more her usual speed. But this smile was the real thing, with lights going on and everything.

And she said, "I'm not going to tell you."

And she never did.

* * *

225

That was a whole lot more excitement than we usually had. Most of the time nothing much happened. You know, if someone had told me I was going to be a Deputy Sheriff in a South Carolina whorehouse I would have thought he was crazy, but if he'd gone on to tell me I'd be generally bored with the job I would have *known* he was crazy. I mean, what could be boring about it?

The thing is, there wasn't much to do. Five days a week there wasn't much for any of us to do, and it was a big night if Claureen and Rita turned half a dozen tricks between them. Fridays and Saturdays were busier, particularly Saturdays, when the workers drew their pay and the farmers came into town to do their trading. I never tried to keep count, but on a decent Saturday the girls would be pretty busy all through the night, with hardly any time at all to sit around and talk. There was also pretty good bar business on Saturday—less on Friday—and there was an average of two fights every Saturday night. One a little before midnight, usually, and the other between one-thirty and two. Geraldine told me at the beginning that that would be the pattern and it usually came out just about that way.

The fights were a pain in the neck but I got so I looked forward to them. I knew they were going to happen sooner or later and I wanted to get them over with. They were the same damned sort of fights the apple pickers used to have in upstate New York. Two guys who were lifelong buddies would try to beat the hell out of each other after a few drinks, and the next week they'd be buddies again.

I had a club to settle fights with but I hardly ever had to use it. See, with most of the guys, they would get drunk enough to start a fight, but not so drunk that they didn't know what they were doing. And one thing they were careful not to forget was that all they had to do was pull a knife or break something and Geraldine would bar them from the Lighthouse forever. Which meant they would be limited in terms of sex to their hands and their sheep and

226

their sisters. They might chance getting killed in a fight, but they sure as hell didn't want to be barred.

So what I learned to do was sort of let it be their idea to take the fight outside. I'd walk through the room calling out, "Awright now, all you boys, let's clear the way for these two. They're trying to take it outside and you better stand back and make a path for them."

Now nine times out of ten there would already be a path for them big enough to drive a tank through, because as soon as one guy yanked a chair back everybody but the guy he was squaring off against would get the hell out of the way. But since the others would be backing off at the same time that I was doing my number, it sort of looked as though they were following my orders and opening a path to the doorway. And the fighters were left with the notion that they were the ones who wanted them to go outside and the crowd had been stopping them.

So out they went.

I never followed them outside. Others would, and would form a ring around them, and the watchers more or less made sure that nobody got too cute with a knife or kept on going after the fight was supposed to be over. There were two reasons why Geraldine didn't want me to do anything more than get them out. For one thing, she was afraid a whole crowd might turn on anybody who did too thorough a job of policing an outside fight. For another, she didn't really give a damn if they killed each other six ways and backwards, as long as they did it outside.

A couple of times I had to hit guys. My club was a steel bar with a thick wrapping of leather, and it scared the hell out of me. If I hit someone too hard I could easily kill him and if I hit too soft I could get a knife in my ribs. Since I am *(a)* basically non-violent and *(b)* a coward, I didn't want either of these things to happen. Sheriff Tyles had given me lessons on just how much force to use and said I had the touch down pat, but I figured there was a difference between the rifle range and the field of battle, and I wasn't all that confident I would do it right.

The first time was when a kid about my age knocked the neck off a beer bottle and started after another kid. I missed his head. He got a broken collarbone out of the deal and I got an extra ten bucks from Geraldine.

Another time one guy pulled a knife and started moving in on his cousin, I think it was. I managed to come up behind him, which helped me keep my cool. I gave him the right kind of tap on the head and it worked just the way it was supposed to.

Now both of those times were exciting enough so that I would just as soon never have them happen again, but that still doesn't change the fact that they were rain on the desert.

I mean, nothing else really happened.

"I'm not really a bouncer," I told Geraldine once. "Not if you figure my occupation by the amount of time I spend on various chores. You know what I am?"

"What?"

"A hired chess player. And you ought to be able to hire somebody who could beat you once in a while."

"I like to win, Chip. And I don't suppose I could hire Sammy Reshevsky for five dollars a week."

"And room and board."

"You don't eat much. And the room is there. I have four more rooms than I have a use for. Would you believe this was a seven-girl house when I opened it? There's not enough weekday trade now to support the two I've got. But if you just have one girl in a house it's a joke, and if a man has to have the same girl every single time he might as well marry her. I used to have seven and I used to collect twenty dollars on Saturdays. Now it's ten every day of the week. Everything costs more at every store in the county and what's the one thing that's dropped in price?"

"The Chamber of Commerce ought to advertise that. As a tourist attraction."

"Tourists? You wouldn't get tourists here if you gave it

away. Bordentown. I never heard of anyone coming to Bordentown by choice."

I could have named one.

"Anyway," she said, "it's worth five dollars a week for a game of chess now and then."

So I played chess, and sent fights outside, and sat around a lot, and talked to Claureen and Rita, and ate eggs and grits and sausages for breakfast and hamburgers for supper, and around two or three or four in the morning Geraldine closed up and I went upstairs to my room and got undressed and hopped into bed and went to sleep.

Alone.

I suppose you find that hard to believe. So do I, now that I think about it. I mean, you may have gotten the idea by now that sex is usually in the forefront of my mind, and if you didn't get that idea you get a low score in reading comprehension. Because it usually is. In fact it just about always is.

But I never once had either Rita or Claureen, and I never once had any of the weekend girls. (I never really got to know the weekend girls, as far as that goes; they were always busy then, and so was I.) And obviously I never had Geraldine. The tobacco farmer was the only one who did all the time I was there. I'm sure she could have given me the equivalent of a college education, and I certainly liked her as a person, but the only game I ever thought of playing with her was chess.

But what stopped me with Claureen and Rita?

Well, I wasn't interested.

It wasn't that they were unattractive. They were pretty enough, but not in any meaningful way. The best way I can think of to explain it is that you could sit and talk with them for an hour or so, and then when you left the room you would have a little trouble remembering what they looked like. I suppose that could be an advantage with a prostitute. I don't know.

But the thing is that the Mary Beth who wanted my bus

ticket had turned me off prostitutes in general, and any of the fantasies I had toyed with about whores with various organs of gold just didn't hold up for me any more. And even if they had, for Pete's sake, I was sitting there every night while these girls went upstairs with men and then came back down and yawned and joked about it. I got to like them a lot in certain ways, especially Claureen. The two of them put together didn't have enough brains to make one reasonably intelligent girl, but I liked them. And they would have come to bed with me if I asked, either of them would have, and they more or less let me know this in a quiet way, but we all knew it would have made it awkward between us afterward. It wouldn't have been so awkward that I wouldn't have been willing to live with it if I had really wanted to ball them, but I didn't, so nothing ever happened.

Besides, after the first week or so I had my hands full with Lucille.

Chapter Seven

THE FIRST TIME I MET LUCILLE WAS THE first day I worked at her house. Minnie took me over that morning after Lucille had already left for school and introduced me to Rev. Lathrop, which was a little like being introduced to a tree or a mountain. I started in on chores and worked up to lunchtime, when Lucille came home to do the honors.

(One thing I'm evidently never going to get right is this business of calling meals by the right name. I grew up with the idea that what you had around noon was lunch, and what you had in the evening was dinner. In Bordentown they called it dinner at lunchtime and what they had at dinnertime was called supper or evening meal. I got this down pat while I was there but it's hard to keep it straight from a distance.)

Anyway, whatever you want to call it, Lucille came home from school and cooked something. And I introduced myself to her and she introduced herself to me (because her father was already too far gone to introduce us, assuming he remembered my name. Or her name, for that matter.) And I looked at Lucille, and Lucille looked at me, and all of a sudden there was enough electricity in the air to cause a power failure.

She was the cleanest, healthiest, prettiest little thing I ever saw in my life. She was really a shock after the East Village. See, for the past three months I had gotten used to girls who would live in a pair of dungarees and a surplus navy jacket. I'm not putting that down, because some of the girls I knew in New York were really beautiful, and with some of them you could sit and talk for hours at a time, really rapping on and on about everything. You could really relate to them as people, which is what it's all about and which makes everything much better.

But Lucille was something completely different. Short blonde hair all neatly cut and combed, and a short navy

blue skirt and a powder blue sweater and blue knee socks
and saddle shoes and a touch of lipstick on her mouth and
a perfect complexion. One look at her and you knew that
(*a*) she took two baths a day, seven days a week, and (*b*) she
never got dirty in between, never even perspired.

When I think about it now, I can't stop thinking that
there was nothing on earth a whole lot squarer than Lucille.
Knee socks and saddle shoes, for Pete's sake. One look at
her and you could hear Bill Haley and the Comets playing
in the background. I mean, she looked like a cheerleader,
which as it turned out she was, and in this day and age the
idea of a girl hopping around like an idiot and doing the
sis-boom-bah number for the basketball team is about as
unhip as you can get.

Even the cleanliness thing, really, is overdoing it. Not
that I'm in favor of being dirty, but there's a point where it
gets ridiculous and you wind up with this feminine ideal
of a girl who's been carefully wrapped in plastic wrap and
never touched by the world. Girls are people, too, and it's
more fun for everybody if you don't lose sight of this.

But I was really ready for Lucille, knee socks and saddle
shoes and sis-boom-bah and all. It occurred to me that she
looked pretty square, but it didn't occur to me that there
was anything wrong with this. All I knew was that she
looked good enough to eat, and it didn't matter much
whether you called it lunch or dinner or coffee break.

Even so, it took me close to a week to do anything about it.
It wasn't that she looked too pure to approach, because I
could tell right away that she was reacting to me the same
way I was reacting to her. But for awhile I had this feeling
that if I so much as touched her hand I would be back in
jail again, and this time it wouldn't be anywhere near as
easy to get out again. I suppose this was partly because she
was a minister's daughter and partly because I still felt like
some sort of fugitive from justice. The trouble with getting
by with a lie is that it's very hard not to go on worrying

that the lie will catch up with you. I hadn't really done anything but change the truth a little in a few unimportant ways. Even so, it took me a while to be comfortable with myself. I felt, oh, as though I was on probation, I guess.

Another thing was that Lucille and I would spend an hour talking while her father was putting his food away in the back parlor. And the conversation was all things like how much trouble she was having with geometry, and how the basketball team was doing, and how her steady boyfriend was taking her to this dance, and how her friend Jeanie saw this really cool sweater in a department store in Charleston, and how Joan Crawford was her favorite actress, and things like that.

It's amazing the conversations didn't bore the hell out of me. I think if I had tapes of them I could use them to put myself asleep on bad nights.

I didn't get bored, though. I probably must have listened with only half of my head. One thing that helped, I think, was that she was younger than I was, and less experienced, and I wasn't used to this. The girls I knew were generally older and brighter and hipper than I was (which it isn't all that hard to be, actually).

I'm sure I would have gotten bored sooner or later. But after about six days of this, with our conversations never getting the least bit personal or intimate and never even beginning to make the transition from talking to rapping, I came up behind her while she was carrying some dishes to the sink, and when she turned around I lowered my mouth to hers and kissed her.

The first time I took her bra off she made so much noise I thought her father was going to come upstairs. It was only the second time we had gone upstairs. She had a small bedroom furnished largely in stuffed animals and pictures of movie stars. The day before we took her sweater off, and today we had her bra off.

Her breasts were large, milk-white, creamy pink at their

tips. I don't know why in hell she thought she had to wear a bra. I can't really understand why any woman would harness herself up that way, and Lucille was so firmly built that she certainly didn't need the support.

Of course I suppose a cheerleader without a bra would really bounce all over the place, but what's wrong with that? It would just increase the crowd at the basketball games.

"Oh, Chip," she said. "We shouldn't be up here."

I was too busy kissing her to answer her.

"You make me feel so funny. I never felt like this before. And you're so *fast!*"

There's a word you don't hear much any more.

"'Cause I been dating Jimmie Butler for three years and steady dating him for two years in April and in all that time he never got as far with me as you did in a week. I'll let him take off my sweater and reach in under the bra but not take it off, that's as much as I'll let him do, and you went and skipped over that step completely, and how long have we known each other? Two weeks?"

The next day she made the old man's dinner in five minutes flat and went upstairs without being asked. I paid a few minutes attention to her breasts and then put a hand under her skirt.

She pushed my hand away, snapped her legs together, sat bolt upright and crossed her arms over her breasts. She looked so frightened that at first I thought her old man had walked into the room or something.

She said, "Chip, I never should have let you kiss me. At first I thought you were never going to get around to trying, and then you did, and right then I should have known what was going to happen."

"Nothing happened, Lucille."

"What you just tried to do."

"I wanted to touch you. That's all."

"You wanted to touch me under my skirt."

"Uh-huh."

"Oh, my *God!*"

"Hey," I said. I put a hand on her bare shoulder and she jumped. "Hey, calm down," I said. "Take it easy."

"Jimmie Butler doesn't even *try* touching me there. He knows if he tries that I just won't let him touch me at all. We'll go out every Friday and Saturday and park in his car for hours and he never so much as tries to do that."

The past Saturday, Jimmie Butler had been a customer at the Lighthouse. He had three quick beers for courage and went upstairs and spent ten dollars with Jo Lee. That worked out to about five dollars a minute. "All the rabbits ain't out in the fields," Jo Lee said afterward.

"Because he knows I won't let him do anything if he tries to touch me there," Lucille was saying.

"Why?"

She looked at me, wide-eyed.

"Why won't you let him?"

"I won't let anybody."

"Why not?"

"Because I want to be *pure*, Chip."

I looked into those wide blue eyes, and then I closed my own, and when I opened them she was still there.

"I want to be pure on my wedding night," she said. "The way you look at me—"

I said, "What does a hand up your skirt have to do with being pure?"

"Chip!"

"Because it doesn't make sense to me, Lucille."

"One thing can lead to another."

"One thing's supposed to lead to another. That's what life is all about. Life is just one damn thing leading to another."

"Chip, nobody *ever* touched me there."

"How about you?"

"Me?"

"Don't you ever touch yourself there, Lucille?"

Her face had gotten gradually whiter during the course

235

of the conversation. Now all the color that had drained out came back in a rush, until most of the blood in her body must have been in her head. She looked like a sunburn ad.

She hugged her breasts. There were tears in her eyes, and I felt awful.

"Hey," I said. "Easy, honey."

"Oh, Chip," she said, and buried her face in my chest. I put my arms around her and rocked her gently. She was sobbing her heart out.

"Easy," I said. "Baby, it's completely normal. Everybody does it."

"It's a sin."

"Lots of things are, if you believe everything they tell you. But the thing is that it feels good."

"I—"

"And makes a person more relaxed."

She drew back, looked at me with pain in her eyes. "I hardly ever used to do it," she said. "Just a little once in a while before I went to bed, if I was feeling dreamy. And I would stop before anything happened. But these past few days—"

"Take it easy, honey."

"—I'm just so *terrible*! And I'm so ashamed of myself. I go back to school and I can't sit in my seat, and I go to the bathroom, and I, I, I, oh, *Chip*!"

"It makes you feel better, doesn't it?" She hesitated, then nodded miserably. "It feels good, doesn't it? And then it relaxes you."

Another nod.

"But you feel bad about it because you think it's a sin."

"Well, it is."

"Then everybody's a sinner," I said. And I told her that everybody did it except for people who were too stupid to figure out how, and that people scratched other parts of their bodies when they itched, and rubbed their muscles when they hurt, and what was the difference? By the time I was finished I sounded like a commercial for self-abuse,

236

but she was sort of nodding along with me towards the end, and the panic scene was over.

So I just held onto her and kissed her a little in a friendly and nonsexual way, and then she remembered that it was time to go back to school, she would be late. She put her clothes back on and brushed her hair and lipsticked her mouth and went on her way, and I went downstairs and did the dinner dishes.

The next day I stayed above the waist and didn't say anything about yesterday's conversation. And out of the blue she said, "I did it again yesterday. Went to the bathroom and touched myself."

"So did I."

"You did?"

"Uh-huh."

"Do you always?"

"Sometimes."

(Actually that was the first time I had followed a session with Lucille with a session with myself. I had never really felt the need—our petting hadn't been all that frustrating, really. But after the conversation we had had and the little speech I gave her, it seemed to me it would be almost a matter of copping out if I didn't.)

"I never thought about that."

"I thought about you," I said. I petted her breast absently. "As a matter of fact, while I was doing it I pictured you in my mind. Doing it."

"Oh, that's just *awful!*"

"Actually it was kind of nice." I propped myself up on an elbow and looked down at her. "You know," I said, "since we're both going to do it, why should we hide out in separate bathrooms? We could just do it here in your room before you go back to school."

She stared.

"It would be fun," I said. "We could watch each other."

"Chip, you are the most terrible boy I ever met."

237

I looked at her and her face went through some interesting changes. "Oh," she said, in a small, desperate voice, and I kissed her. She gave the kiss everything she had.

"I guess I'm terrible, too," she said.

"I'll tell you something that's even nicer, Lucille. Let me do it for you."

"Chip, don't talk that way."

"If you're going to do it anyway," I said reasonably, "it can't be any more of a sin if you use somebody else's hand. All you have to do is lie back and close your eyes and let your mind go anywhere it wants to. It's a lot better when someone else does it for you, you know."

"Is it?"

"And you feel a lot better afterward. You feel together inside instead of feeling all apart by yourself."

"That's how I felt yesterday. I felt tingly and I felt relaxed and I felt I was the only person in the world."

I lifted her skirt and put my hand on her thigh. She was so soft there.

"Chip, I'm afraid."

"Don't be."

"But I am, I am. Look how far we're going already and it's such a short time and, oh, you're not even my boyfriend. Here I'm going steady with a boy I don't do half of this with, and I'm doing all this with you."

"It's what we both want, Lucille."

"I graduate high school a year from June. And after graduation I'll marry Jimmie Butler, and I want to be pure for him. I want to be a virgin, Chip."

"All I'll do is touch you."

"You promise?"

"Yes."

"I don't know if I can trust you."

"You can trust me, Lucille."

"Ohhh," she said.

I raised her skirt all the way and took off her panties. She

238

didn't help and she didn't struggle either. Her face was so unhappy I almost felt like calling the whole thing off, but that would have been even worse for her.

I kissed her mouth, then her breasts, and I put my hand on her belly and let it move down to her. She was all soft and moist and warm.

She didn't get excited right away. I guess part of her was fighting it, but the other part of her won eventually and she panted and squirmed and made beautiful little sounds. She got almost there and hovered on the edge for a long time, trying to make it and trying not to make it, and I was starting to worry that it wouldn't work and she would wind up deciding that bathrooms were better than beds.

But then she got there, got all the way there, and in my mind I was there with her, feeling what she felt. I held her for a long time before I raised myself up and looked at her face.

She was glowing and she looked impossibly beautiful and I felt a lot like God.

Chapter Eight

THE FUNNY THING IS THAT I KEPT getting more and more involved with Lucille without really getting involved with her at all. We spent about fifty minutes out of every lunch hour in her bedroom, but outside of that we didn't see each other at all. I never stayed around after she got home from school, and on Saturdays she would generally manage to spend the day with a girlfriend. We never went to a movie or for a walk or anything.

My job at the Lighthouse had something to do with this. I was working during dating hours, and the one night she could go out on dates was the one night I really had things to do there. But once I asked her if she'd like to catch a movie during the week and she said she couldn't.

"I have to stay with my father," she said. "You know that, Chip."

"He manages well enough Friday and Saturday nights, doesn't he?"

"Well, those are the only nights I can go out. I'm not allowed to date during the week."

"You could ask permission."

"Asking's not getting. Oh, Chip, I can't go out with you anyway. I'm going steady with Jimmie Butler, you know that, I told you a thousand times."

I said something about going steady being a Mickey Mouse institution.

She looked at me. "Do you think I ought to break off with Jimmie?"

"I guess not," I said.

That was the only time I ever asked her for a date, and I was just as glad she turned me down. I guess I wanted to keep this a lunchtime thing and not let it get very intense.

There were a couple of reasons for this. One of them makes me look like Mr. Nice Guy, so I'll throw it in first, and it was just that it wouldn't have been fair of me to take up all that much of Lucille's time. Because what Lucille wanted out of life was to get married as soon as she was done with high school and start having babies and spend the rest of her life there. And while that might not sound like something worth wanting, it was what she wanted, and it was probably what would be best for her. (Especially if Jimmie Butler developed a little control by doing the multiplication tables in his head or something.)

Anyway, Lucille wanted to be Mrs. Somebody. Maybe she would have been just as happy to be Mrs. Harrison as Mrs. Butler, but I really wasn't ready for that. She just wasn't that important to me, so I didn't want to become all that important to her.

The other reason was more selfish.

See, I was just having too much fun the way things were going. It was a fantastic ego trip for me, the whole thing, and even knowing something is an ego trip isn't enough to take the enjoyment out of it. For once in my life I was the teacher and she was the pupil, and I was getting a tremendous charge out of it. Instead of feeling like some utterly hopeless dope of a kid, I was the wise old man and she was the little innocent one. And every time I took her upstairs and let the stuffed animals watch me teach her something new and con her into doing it, well, it made me feel as if I was really somebody sensational.

(Which was another reason, I guess, that I had no desire to get in bed with Claureen or Rita. There was no way on earth I could feel like the wise old man with either of those two, and I guess I knew it would just bring me down in a bad way.)

By only seeing Lucille at lunch hour, I made that part of it be our entire relationship. And because we had so little time together we could just keep on going forward a little at a time instead of rushing straight into all-the-way sex. I didn't realize at the time that this was something I wanted. Instead I told myself it wasn't fair to rush her, that I wanted to let everything come at its own pace so it would be natural and good for her. But that was bullshit, really. Utter bullshit.

"You're like a drug to me, Chip," she said one day. "I just need more and more of you."

"Must be a good kind of drug. You look prettier every day."

"The girls ask me about you."

"What do they ask?"

"What you're like. Everybody knows about that place you work at. Some of them sort of want to go out with you. They want to come home with me and meet you. But they're scared of you at the same time."

"Scared of me?"

She nodded. "They think you must know things other boys don't. The things I could tell them! And sometimes I just could die for wanting to tell someone. I feel I could burst from holding it all inside me."

"I don't think it would be a very good idea to tell anybody."

"I know. I just say we hardly talk at all. That you don't even know I'm alive."

"Oh, I can tell you're alive, all right."

"Ohhhh—"

And a little later she said, "I'm scared of you, too, Chip."

"Oh, come on. You must know by now you can trust me."

"I know. But it used to be I could trust myself, and now I can't. I never knew I was like this."

"Aren't you glad you found out?"

"I don't know."

"Huh?"

"I just, oh, I don't know." Her face clouded, then suddenly brightened and she giggled. I asked her what was so funny.

"I was thinking about Jimmie."

"What about him?"

"If he could see us now."

If he could have seen us right then he would have come on the spot and saved himself ten dollars.

"He asked about you."

"What did you tell him?"

"Same as I told the girls. Not even that much. But I was thinking what would happen if I told him about you and me and all."

"He would probably kill one of us," I said. And if he had to choose, I thought, he would pick her. I had never mentioned to her that I had seen Jimmie now and then at the Lighthouse, so I couldn't tell her that he tended to back down pretty easily from fights. I didn't hold this against him, though. In fact I preferred him that way.

Her hand dropped onto me. "The other night," she said, "he wanted me to touch him."

"Did you?"

"Course not. I asked him what kind of a girl he thought I was."

"What did he say?"

"He apologized," she said, and giggled again. "He's just a baby, I guess. I never used to think so. Not until I met you."

Ego food.

At the beginning I thought I was going to get tired of her, maybe because she was so square. I suppose this would have happened if we had seen each other more, had dates and long conversations, or if I had met her friends or anything like that. But she left the boring part of her personality outside the bedroom, and once she stopped fighting the whole idea of sex she turned out to have quite a natural aptitude for it.

For a long time she spent half her time being passionate and the other half feeling guilty about it. At first she was very uptight every time we did something new, as if we were taking still another step along the road to Hell. This was fun in a way—first I taught her something new, and than I assured her it wasn't awful.

It wasn't long, though, before she wanted to do new things and came to bed looking forward to it. I guess what happened was that her mind finally realized I wasn't going to make her have regular intercourse, so she set that up in her mind as the one absolute sin and decided it was perfectly all right to do absolutely anything else.

So I taught her things I had done before, of which there were not too many, and things I had heard about or read about, of which there were a ton, and some things that I more or less invented. I'm not saying that I thought of things no one had thought of before because I'm not sure there are any of those things left, but they were new to me.

"My God," she would say. "When did you have time to learn all these things, Chip?"

She didn't know we were learning some of them together.

And she liked everything we did. Everything. I did oral things to her and taught her to do them to me, and she lived up to what Willie Em had told me about Southern girls.

And we tried anal things, which I hadn't done before. She didn't like the idea at the beginning, and she thought it would be painful and disgusting, and when we were done she said it was painful and disgusting and cried a little and I told her we wouldn't do it again.

And the next day she wanted to do it again and never said another word about it being painful or disgusting.

One day I brought a vibrator from the Lighthouse. I didn't tell Geraldine I was borrowing it. I didn't tell Lucille where it was from, either, but of course she would have had to know.

And finally one day we got our clothes off and got into bed and she asked me what I wanted to do, and I said we would just see what happened. And after a lot of things had happened she was lying on her back with her eyes closed and I was on top of her and our flesh touched.

She opened her eyes and asked me what I was doing.

I said, "I'm going to fuck you."

"All right," she said, and closed her eyes again.

Afterward she said, "I guess I should have let you do it right off. I knew it would happen the first day you kissed me. I knew it and I never forgot it and I was right, and we might just as well been doing it all along."

"Are you sorry?"

"Yes. No. I don't know."

"Did I hurt you?"

"Not enough to talk about. You hurt me worse other times and I never minded it. Will I get a baby now, Chip?"

"No."

"How come you're sure?"

I showed her the condom.

"It looks so silly," she said. "Did you buy it in a store or what?"

"I took it from—"

"From that place. I guess if Jimmie doesn't marry me I can always work there, can't I?"

"Don't talk like that."

"Knowing all you taught me. Unless you don't think I'm pretty enough."

"You're beautiful."

"I wonder do I look different now."

"No."

"I guess I'll call the school in a few minutes and say I can't come back today because my father needs me. I used to do that before you were working here."

"You don't have to worry, Lucille. No one can tell anything from looking at you."

"That's not why." She stretched and wriggled her toes. "I guess I don't want to get up and go putting on clothes again. I guess I liked what we did. I guess I want to do it again."

"Oh," I said.

"Do you have any more of those little things?"

"Uh, no."

"Can you use them more than once?"

"It's not a very good idea."

"Oh, well," she said. "There's other things we can do, I guess. An old boy named Chip taught me a whole roomful of them."

"You're an angel."

"I'm a devil is what I am. But I just don't care."

That was on a Friday afternoon in early March. I didn't see her at all over the weekend. I was hoping Jimmie Butler would come to the Lighthouse Saturday night and start a fight so that I could brain him with the club. Don't ask me why. Anyway, he didn't show up.

I almost went to church the next morning. Just a nutty impulse.

Monday morning I helped myself to a box of a dozen rubbers on my way out of the Lighthouse. We used one of them that lunch hour, and afterward she told me she almost broke up with Jimmie Saturday night.

"But I didn't. I wanted to, but I thought I'll wait until the proms are over and all, because he'd have to find somebody to take and everything, and it's easier to go along the way it is. And if I stopped going steady with him other boys might want to take me out, and at least I'm used to Jimmie. And I know I can handle him."

"Why did you want to break up?"

"Oh, I don't know. I just don't like being with him is all. And I hate it when he touches me. I just don't feel a thing. Sometimes I'll pretend I like it but I don't and it never does anything to me. He just keeps going with me now because it's a habit. He doesn't like it that I won't let him do any more than he used to do, but if he went out with anybody else he'd have to start all over at the beginning, so I guess he thinks I'm better than nothing."

"I think you're better than anything."

"I wouldn't marry him, anyway. Even if he wanted. I don't love him."

"Did you love him before?"

"No, but I didn't know it. I didn't know anything. Not knowing what I was missing, I guess."

I felt kind of weird. I had more than I had started out wanting in the first place, and I didn't know whether or not I wanted it now, or what I was going to do about it.

She said, "I love you, Chip."

I just wouldn't tell her that I loved her. She never asked for the words, not once, not even by throwing out hopeful pauses which you were supposed to fill with the words. And I just wouldn't say them.

I don't know why I made such a big deal out of it. I mean, *I love you* doesn't mean all that much. Nine times out of ten it's a polite way of saying *I want to ball you*, and you know it and the girl you say it to knows it and just saying the words doesn't send anyone out shopping for engagement rings.

The really dumb thing about it is that I could have said the words and meant them, because I *did* love her, whether or not I knew it at the time. I didn't want to spend the rest of my life with her, but that's not what the words mean anyway. I dug her and I cared about her and I enjoyed being with her and I wanted good things to happen to her and I, well, I loved her.

But instead of saying the words I even managed to keep them out of my own mind. I would ask myself things like, *Well, Chip kid, how will you get yourself out of this one? After all, old man, you've got to be gentle with the kid. You don't want to break her little heart.*

(I'll tell you something, I really hate writing all this down, because until just this minute I never realized what a complete asshole I was. I felt so goddamned adult with Lucille, and when I look back at it all now I can't believe I ever could have acted like such a shitty little snotnose.

And I suppose a year from now I'll be apologizing to myself for being such an immature moron now.)

Of course I loved her, for Pete's sake. I loved her a lot more than she loved me, if you come right down to it, because I at least knew who she was and all, and what she knew about me was more lies than truth. She fell in love with me, or thought she did, because I taught her what her body was for. Maybe I loved her for about the same reason. Oh, the hell with it.

But figure this out. The day she told me she loved me, I sent a postcard to Hallie in Wisconsin.

Chapter Nine

SHERIFF TYLES SAID, "WELL, I HEAR TELL you got a salary increase, boy. I hear you're coming up in the world."

"Oh, I'm getting rich."

"Reckon Geraldine thinks a lot of you."

"It was because I finally won a game of chess," I said. "So she decided I ought to have an extra five dollars a week."

"You wouldn't be getting it if she didn't like the way you were doing the job."

"There's not much job to do. Playing chess with her is about three-quarters of the job." I took a sip of Coke. "Anyway, I don't guess it's enough to retire on."

He clucked. "Well, it's all in how you look at it, isn't it? An extra five dollars a week, look at it that way and I'll admit that it ain't so much. But since you were only getting five dollars to start with, what you got amounts to a hundred percent increase, and I never heard of anybody kicking at a one hundred percent increase that they didn't even have to go and ask for. Even a goddamn nigger labor union ought to be happy about a hundred percent increase."

"I never thought of it that way."

He winked. "You keep doubling up that way, you'll be rich in no time."

"Guess you're right."

"On the subject," he said, "how you making out as far as money is concerned? You able to get by all right?"

"Oh, sure," I said. I had been buying clothes from time to time, and other things, and I was only making twenty a week from the two jobs—well, twenty-five now—but there was really nothing to spend money on. I even got my books free from the local public library, not because I was too cheap to buy a paperback but because the only ones in town were at the Atlantic station, and all they had were four shelves of swinging swapper garbage and one rack of

Brian Garfield westerns. Every once in a while I would go back to see if they got something new, but they never did. I guess they were waiting until they sold the ones they had.

The library had a lot of good books. The only trouble was that they had all come out before the Second World War. This was okay as far as the fiction was concerned, I could get into old stuff well enough, but when I wanted to figure out how to fix the Lathrop television set I ran into a stone wall. There was nothing in the card catalog under *Television*.

"I've even been putting some money aside," I told him.

"Thought you might be. Probably got more than enough for the fare to Miami, I'd say."

"Oh," I said. "Well, probably."

"Be summer in a few months," he went on. "Florida weather's no attraction that time of year. Not that it's a bargain here. Myself, I don't mind the heat one way or the other. I'll sweat on a hot day, but I never minded sweating. Must do a man good. Otherwise you wouldn't do it, the way I see it."

I said something bright, like "Uh-huh."

"Heat bother you much?"

"Not usually."

"Didn't think so. A Yankee, your typical Yankee, the heat'll get him and he won't mind the cold. With folks down here it's the other way around. The way some of us were complaining about the first week in February, and it wasn't all that cold. Of course our heat isn't the kind you'll get in a big city, where the buildings hold it in. Makes somewhat of a difference."

I nodded.

"Minnie was saying you really made a good impression on the Reverend. She'll see him Sundays after the service and as like as not he'll have a good word for you."

"I hardly ever talk to him."

"Well, I wouldn't let on in front of Minnie, but I

wouldn't be all that surprised if that's what the drunken old sonofabitch likes about you. Last thing he wanted was for those old hens to saddle him with a nursemaid. Imagine the kind of person they'd be apt to pick. Some Salvation Army jackass with a ramrod up his ass who'd either be watering the old sonofabitch's whiskey or praying all over the place. Just for the sake of somebody leaving him alone, I don't suppose the Reverend would even mind if you was screwing his daughter six times a week and twice on Sundays."

I came within inches of cardiac arrest. But the Sheriff went sailing right on, and I'm sure to this day he just tried to pick the least likely example he could possibly think of. He gave me a bad moment, though.

"And Geraldine's happy with you, too. Happier than she lets on. She don't let on much, that one, but I got to know her pretty good over the years. Had a place here for the longest time. Set it up herself. There was this woman she was working for who was doing wrong by everyone— girls, customers, law enforcement people. Geraldine, she opened up on her own and got the right backing and the right girls working for her and sent the other old bitch clear out of the state. She knows what she's doing, that one."

"I can believe it."

"In her day, wasn't a better-looking woman in the county. You can believe that one, too."

"I do."

"Wasn't that bad myself, in those days. Before Minnie's cooking." And he patted his paunch and let his eyes drift off to examine old memories. *Before Minnie, too,* I thought, and wondered if Geraldine and the Sheriff still got it together once in a while for Auld Lang Syne. On holidays and birthdays, say. I sort of hoped they did.

"She thinks a lot of you," he was saying. "She thinks you're a good man to have around the place. Me, I think you make a damn fine Deputy Sheriff." He clucked again.

"Well, I'm running off at the mouth again, and you better get on back if you want your supper. Just thought I'd give you a few things to think about."

A couple of days later Geraldine said, "Mate in four, starting with Knight to King Five. See it?"

I studied it for a long time, then nodded and started picking up the pieces.

"Interesting thing happened in the next county over," she said. "Used to be two regular gambling places there. About a year ago Ewell Rodgers had a second coronary, and you generally only get three of them, and he closed up and went and sat on his rocking chair. The other place was run by a man named Morgan from East Tennessee. He was getting all of Ewell's crowd, and success must have gone to his head. He rubbed some people the wrong way that he shouldn't have. He got raided and arrested, and while he was sitting in jail waiting for someone to put up bail money, his place somehow or other caught on fire, and the fire department just happened to take a wrong turn getting there. Not a stick left. Morgan took the insurance money and bought the fastest car he could find and drove all the way back to East Tennessee with the gas pedal on the floor."

She got up and went behind the bar and came back with a Coke for me and her bottle of banana liqueur. I couldn't remember her ever bringing the bottle to the table before. Usually she took her glass back each time and refilled it.

She said, "I used to have gambling in here, you know. I must have told you that."

"I think you mentioned it."

"Did very well with the gambling. Then there was an election and I was let know that there wouldn't be any trouble if the tables and slots and all went, so they went. By the time it was all right to replace them, it just wasn't worth it. Ewell and that Morgan were doing good business and everything was off around here, I was down from seven girls to two, and I couldn't be bothered. When Ewell retired I don't mind telling you it gave me ideas. There was that much business open, and I was sure to get a good portion of it. And then when Morgan's place went up in smoke—"

She picked up her glass, looked at it, and drank it down. This was as surprising as the time I heard her swear. She always took the stuff in little sips, and a drink would last her so long that I doubt she actually drank more than half of it; the rest evaporated.

"I would have six tables for cards," she said. "No more than that. Five tables of poker and one of blackjack. On the poker you let the deal pass and just charge so much an hour to sit in the game. No cutting the pot. Morgan was cutting pots there at the end.

"On the blackjack, you would have to have a dealer. I could deal it myself, as far as that goes. Any fool can. The only problem is if you have a dealer working for you and you can't trust him, because a blackjack dealer can think of fifteen different ways to cheat the house and you'll be forever trying to keep up with him."

She poured herself another drink. And drank it right down.

"And one craps table," she said. "That's all you would need. You let the players run the game, same as the poker. Then what I would do is slap slot machines all over the place. You make a ton on slot machines and all you have to do is take out the money and put a drop of Three-In-One Oil in the works once a month. No one ever lost money on a slot machine. Except the damned fools who play them."

"Where would you put all of this?"

"Right here in this room. It's big enough so there'd be space left over, no one would be crowded."

"What about the drinkers?"

She filled her glass but left it on the table. "Over on the right. Nobody ever goes in that room and you wouldn't know it's there, but it wouldn't be anything to put a bar in there."

"I don't know," I said. "You'd never fit our Saturday crowd in there unless you packed them like sardines."

"Chip, you wouldn't want that kind of crowd if you had gambling. I don't even want them now, but there's not enough money just in the girls and I have to have every drink sale I can get. Put in tables and the idea would be to cut that crowd to a third of what it is. Maybe less than that, maybe a fifth, say, on Saturdays."

"Some of those drinkers wind up going upstairs."

"And most of them don't. Instead they make noise and start fights, and that's the last thing you can tolerate when you have gambling tables."

"How would you cut the drinking crowd?"

"Easiest thing in the world. Leave out the beer taps. Sell imported beer by the bottle at seventy or eighty cents. Push the hard liquor price up to a dollar a drink, nothing cheaper. The way it is now, we're selling girls to men who come here to drink. The other way, we'd be selling whiskey to men who come here for girls and gambling. And when a man's gambling he doesn't mind paying high prices for whiskey, and when he wins he likes to celebrate with a girl."

"You've got it all figured out," I said.

She drained her glass. "It's not something that just came to me in a flash. I've been thinking about it."

"Without the drinking crowd, I guess you wouldn't have much need for a bouncer."

She didn't seem to hear me. "There won't be anybody opening up over the county line. And there won't be anybody else opening up here as long as Claude Tyles is Sheriff, and they won't get him out without burying him. Nobody even bothered running against Claude in the last election. He's well liked, Claude is. Not that he likes that many people himself. It's a rare person that Claude Tyles takes a shine to.

"Nobody else opening up, and all the gambling trade in this county and the next one. The drink business would go down but the profits would go up, and less aggravation involved. Be a five-girl house in no time at all, maybe go all the way up to seven girls if it worked that way. And with gambling, business spreads out more. It doesn't all concentrate on Saturday night. Might even raise the price on the girls to fifteen dollars. And they'd be making tips on top of that with the right kind of crowd."

She poured herself another drink. If it was affecting her, I couldn't see how.

"Make more money on drinks and more money on girls, and that's not counting what the gambling brings in. I haven't made that kind of money in so long I have trouble recollecting what it feels like."

She drank her drink.

"Only one thing wrong," she said.

"What's that?"

Her eyes locked with mine. "I'm too old to be bothered with it. It means all that work and concentration, and I ask myself what's the point? Would you like a drink instead of that Coke, Chip?"

"No, thanks."

"What I should be doing is cutting down, not building up. I'm not ready to pack it all in yet. Not this year. If I closed up now I'd die of boredom. But you feel yourself slowing down, you know. You feel yourself getting sick of people. The customers. You don't have the patience to put up with them. Little signs like that. Another couple of years, next year or the year after that, and it won't be a bad idea to get out of here and live in a big hotel in Puerto Rico and let people fetch me things. I have money saved. Not enough to do it in style, but more than a little."

She gave her head a shake. "But if I expanded I'd have all I need and then some. Thing is, I'd have things just about ideal by the time I wanted to retire. And who in the world would take it over? Rita and Claureen between them couldn't run a pool hall. They couldn't run a race. Two days of operating this place and the whole thing would fall apart.

"In fact, they couldn't even help me out enough in getting things organized. I'd need a man, and he would have to be somebody smart and sure of himself, somebody who could get on good with Claude Tyles, somebody who wouldn't rub the girls the wrong way or be after them all the time. And assuming I had the luck to turn up someone like that in this part of the country, which is as likely as mucking out a stable and finding an emerald, why, what chance in the world would there be that he'd be someone I can trust?"

"I see what you mean," I said.

Her eyes challenged me. "Do you?"

"Well, uh, sure."

"I wonder if you do. You think about it, Chip. You think about it, and one of these days I'll bring up the subject and then we'll talk about it some more. Meanwhile you just give my problem some thought, will you?"

The thing is, subtlety generally sails right on past me. When Geraldine first started opening up that night I wondered why she was telling me all this, and I decided she just wanted somebody to use for a sounding board, bouncing words off me when she was actually talking to herself. And I figured she picked me for the same reason that she played chess with me—I was working for her, and I didn't have anything better to do.

She closed for the night as soon as we finished talking, and I went upstairs and got undressed for bed. And I stretched out and put my head on the pillow and closed my eyes, and then I immediately opened them and sat up and switched the light on.

She hadn't just been talking to me. She had been talking *about* me.

(Of course when you read this it's probably pretty obvious all along, especially because I put her conversation right after the one with the Sheriff. But that other conversation wasn't even in my mind when I sat listening to Geraldine, so maybe it should have been obvious to me anyway, but not as obvious as it seems.)

Anyway, I sat up in bed and figured out what it was all about. Sheriff Tyles thought I should stay in Bordentown, and said that Geraldine thought the world of me. And Geraldine wanted to expand the business but couldn't do it without the help of some man who was capable and honest and had an in with the Sheriff, someone she liked and trusted, someone who could take over the whole operation when she was ready for complete retirement.

Which meant that I had found the one thing I never even thought to look for in Bordentown.

A Job With A Future.

I got up and walked around the room a little. I had that sensation in my mind and body of having had too much coffee and all I had was one cup with supper. I just kept pacing, and then I went down the hall to the bathroom only to find out that I didn't really have to go after all. Just nerves, I told myself nervously, and went back to my room and paced the floor again.

A Job With A Future. A Position With Real Opportunities For Advancement.

I couldn't believe it.

Because, after all, that was the one thing I had been looking for ever since they booted me out of Upper Valley Preparatory Academy. I left that stupid school determined to make my way in the world and do all the good old Horatio Alger type things and work my way up in the world. And I never got anywhere. In fact I never got close to getting anywhere, because I kept getting idiotic jobs and drifting into idiotic situations.

Until finally the most idiotic situation of all brought me to Bordentown, a town that barely offered opportunities for stagnation, let alone advancement. And instead of one idiotic job I got two of them, and instead of trying to make my mark in the world I just tried to stay alive and let time pass, figuring that sooner or later I would get up and get out of Bordentown, but not even being in any rush to do that because the whole idea of getting ahead in the world seemed like something I was never going to get around to.

(If you really knock yourself out trying not to end sentences with prepositions, that last sentence would wind up *seemed like something around to which I was never going to get*. I mean, it's an awkward sentence anyway, just sprawling all over the place, but I think it would be even worse if it didn't end with a preposition. Or two prepositions, actually.)

Some of the kids I knew in New York were very much into Zen, and one girl made me read a description of Zen Archery, in which you don't exactly aim the arrow at the target and don't exactly ever let go of it. You just become part of the bow and arrow and let yourself happen along with the bow and the arrow, and somewhere along the line the arrow goes from your fingertips to the target. It read very nicely, but I wasn't sure if it made any sense. The girl said it was easier to understand if you were stoned. I tried to get stoned a couple of times but nothing happened. Now, though, I was beginning to understand.

Because this seemed to me like a case of Zen Advancement, of Zen Making-One's Way-In-The-World. I hadn't tried to do anything, just sort of becoming part of Bordentown and letting the rest happen, not even pointing myself at the target, not even letting go of the string.

Bull's-eye!

Chapter Ten

"YOU SEEM DIFFERENT," LUCILLE SAID.

"I do?"

"Maybe not," she said. She yawned and stretched. She was lying on her back with one arm at her side and her other hand tucked palm-up under her head. I touched her armpit. (It's a shame there isn't a better word for it. When you hear the word *armpit* you think of deodorant. When I touched Lucille's, all secretly smooth and hairless, I didn't think of deodorant. I thought of other warm private places, and of better things to do with an armpit than rub deodorant on it.) I touched hers now, rubbing a little with the tip of my finger.

"Maybe it's me," she said.

"Maybe what is?"

"I don't know."

It was the middle of the week and the lunch hour was only twenty minutes over with. We had another half hour to ourselves and had already done what we did during lunch hours. Usually we would take our time, but this afternoon she didn't want to pause along the way and admire the view. She just wanted to get there full speed ahead, and she did and I did, and it was very nice.

But now she was in a mood, and it was something I wasn't used to with her. I asked her what was the matter.

"Oh, nothing," she said. "Just that you seem all wrapped up in thoughts lately, and you might as well be a hundred miles away."

"I'm right here," I said, and touched her to prove it.

She moved my hand away. "Have you been thinking things, Chip?"

"Nothing in particular."

"Oh."

"I always think things," I said. "I mean, I'm alone a lot, so I'll let my mind just wander off on its own some of the time."

"You like doing that?"

"It beats talking to yourself."

"I do that sometimes. Talk to myself. I don't think much, though."

"Uh."

"I guess you must think I'm awful simple."

"What makes you say that, Lucille?"

"I don't know. Maybe on account of it's true."

"I don't think so."

"Just an old preacher's daughter. Never been anywhere and never done anything."

"You've done a few things."

She sat up suddenly and put her legs over the side of the bed. Without looking at me she said, "Do you know what it's like when you start thinking things and you can't stop? You don't want to think them but there they all are in your head and you can't make them stop?"

"I know."

"Does it sometimes happen to you?"

"A lot of the time."

"It never happened to me before. I would just, oh, you know, I would just go along. Hardly thinking about anything, and if I ever had a thought that bothered me I would just whisk it off out of my head and not think about it anymore. Like a program on the television that you don't want to watch so you turn it off. But now I can't do that."

"What's bothering you?"

"You know what it's like? Like having that bad television program going on in a set that's inside of your head, and there's no way you can turn it off or pull the plug or change the channel, so what do you do?"

"Pray for a commercial," I suggested.

"Oh, you don't see what I mean."

"Yes, I do. I'm sorry, Lucille. It was just a dumb joke."

"No commercials and the program's never through, it just goes on. I reckon that's why Daddy drinks. You know he told me about it once. He said one day he looked into his soul and saw something there that he couldn't bear the sight of, and drink kept him from seeing it. And I always thought, well, why didn't he think on something else. I knew what he was saying but I thought if something like that ever happened to me I would just make the thought go away, but you can't, can you?"

"You want to talk about it, Lucille?"

"I guess not."

I put my arms around her and turned her face toward me. There were tears in the corners of her eyes.

I said, "Hey."

"Lemme be, Chip."

"If something's bothering you——"

"Oh, I'm making something out of nothing is all. Never had a thought in my head before and I'm just not used to it. Just a mood I'm in that I'll get over."

"Maybe it's your period coming on."

"You think so?"

"I don't know."

"Maybe that's what it is," she said. What it probably was, I felt, was that she had gotten a contact high from my own moods. Because I couldn't stop thinking about what Geraldine and I had not quite discussed and what Sheriff Tyles and I had not quite talked over. Which was that I would stay in Bordentown and share the management of the Lighthouse with Geraldine, and together we would expand the operation and hire more girls and put in gambling tables, and in a year or two when she was ready to spend the rest of her days sipping banana liqueur in Puerto Rico, the Lighthouse would be mine.

And I could see it all happening just that way.

I got a paper and pencil and did a little rough figuring, and then I threw the paper away because the numbers I was using were just ones I was picking out of the blue. And the numbers didn't matter, anyway, because you didn't need them to realize that the Lighthouse, run the way Geraldine was talking about running it, couldn't help but make a fortune.

I mean, it wasn't just a matter of being secure and established and successful.

I'd get rich.

It wouldn't be hard, either. At first I thought that Geraldine only thought I was right for it for the same reason that she thought I was fit to play chess with. There just weren't that many people around to choose from. But I had to admit it went further than that. I *was* honest, and I *did* get along well with the girls, and I seemed to have a feeling for handling the customers, and Sheriff Tyles, who she said didn't take to many people, had done everything on earth short of adopting me. On top of all that, I kind of liked the business itself. I had always thought that the only reason anyone would want to go and live in a whorehouse was so he could have his pick of the whores, but I hadn't picked one of them yet and I really liked living there. I mean, I felt at home there.

And as far as the gambling part of it was concerned, I suppose I was suited for that, too. I had played cards a few times without getting caught up in it, and I couldn't imagine ever risking anything important on whether two pair was the best hand at the table or what number would come up on the next roll of dice. And why anyone would drop a perfectly good quarter in a slot machine was beyond me.

Now it seems to me that the one thing you wouldn't want to be if you ran a gambling operation is a gambler. It was like a blackout alcoholic owning a liquor store, or a sex maniac running a whorehouse. You would just eat up all the profits. And at the time I was kind of interested in gambling in a spectator-type way. I mean, as long as it's not my money, the excitement's fine.

I would be rich, and I would be comfortable with what I was doing, and I would be good at it. The whole thing would be officially illegal, but there are laws and laws. And even if Sheriff Tyles stopped being Sheriff sooner or later, by then I would be one of the important men in Bordentown. It doesn't take all that much to be one of the important men in Bordentown, it's not like being President of the United States. I would be important.

I kept just playing all of this through my mind. It was like Lucille had said, a television set in your head that you can't turn off.

The thing was, I liked the program.

Of course thinking about all this made me think about Lucille, too, because she was part of it. Until I talked with Geraldine (or listened to her, because she was the one who did all the talking) I took it for granted that I was going to leave Bordentown sooner or later. I was in no rush, and I had more or less forgotten all that business about Miami, until the Sheriff reminded me, but I would be leaving sooner or later.

And, although I didn't like to dwell on it, when I left Bordentown I would also be leaving Lucille.

Oh, once in a while I would play around with the thought of taking her with me. But I don't think I ever gave that any serious consideration. In Bordentown, for an hour a day five days a week, she was perfect. In the rest of the world, and on a full-time basis, she just wouldn't work out. (Maybe that line makes me sound like a shit, but it's honest. She wouldn't work out for me and I wouldn't work out for her and it's silly to pretend otherwise.)

But if I stayed in Bordentown, that meant I would eventually marry Lucille.

In that kind of situation, she would be perfect, actually. It was her home town and she belonged there. The idea of the preacher's daughter marrying the keeper of the cathouse sounds pretty ridiculous, but I can't think of anybody who would have gotten really uptight about it. Except maybe her father, but who was going to tell him? And why should he pay attention?

It would be perfect for Lucille, and in that situation she would be the perfect wife for me. And what I always wanted was a job with a future and a girl who loved to have me make love to her. Which meant I would be getting everything I always wanted.

That was the whole trouble.

I once read a book by Fredric Brown called *The Screaming Mimi*. (I also read about twenty other books by Fredric Brown, and there wasn't one I didn't like. I like lots of books, but I don't always finish one feeling that I'd really like to meet the author sometime. I always feel that way about Fredric Brown.)

Anyway, this book starts with two drunks sitting on a bench, and one of them says that you can always have what you want as long as you want it badly enough. (The catch is that, when you don't get it, that just goes to show that you didn't want it badly enough.) The other guy sees a beautiful girl pass by and says that what *he* really wants is to spend a night with her, and for her to be stark naked.

Well, this happens at the end, only it isn't quite the way he hoped. (I don't want to spoil the book for you.) But the ultimate point, the philosophical point, is that if you want something badly enough you *will* get it, sooner or later, and then you'll find out that you don't want it anymore, and maybe you never really wanted it in the first place.

So this is what kept going through my mind, not steadily but off and on. It was all there, and all I had to do was reach out and take it.

But did I still want it?

I liked Bordentown, but I wasn't sure I wanted to live there permanently. I mean, I like swimming, but I'd hate to spend the next fifty years in the middle of the ocean. And more important, there was this major question of identity that was suddenly bothering me. I liked the idea of running the Lighthouse and putting down roots there and all, but I wasn't convinced that it was me.

Oh, even the way I was talking, the South Carolina accent. I wasn't consciously putting it on. I talked that way without thinking because everybody else talked that way and I tend to fall into the patterns of wherever I am. But if you woke me up in the middle of the night I wouldn't sound that way. So it felt natural when I did it but it really wasn't, not inside.

And the attitudes I had. Like being against long-haired hippies and black people and Yankees and everything else. It didn't particularly bother me to act that way, or to use the word nigger, for example, because as far as I was concerned it was just part of doing the Bordentown thing for as long as I happened to be there.

But if I was there forever I would be doing all of that business forever, and when you do something long enough either it becomes real for you, which might be bad, or else you spend your whole life living a lie, which might be worse.

If I stayed in Bordentown, it meant I would probably never in my life rap with anybody the way I had rapped with some friends in the East Village, the way I rapped with Hallie the one night I spent with her. I might make a lot of friends, and I might get to know them very well, but they would never really get to know me.

Even Lucille. I could marry her and live with her for the rest of my life, and she would never really know who I was. Even if I didn't try to keep anything from her, even if I opened up completely. There was no way for me to get through to her that completely.

And sooner or later that part of me that no one knew about wouldn't even be there any more. Because I would be the only one who knew about it, and I would tend to forget.

This scared the hell out of me.

The trouble with writing all this down is that there's no real way to get across exactly how I felt from day to day. See, it was never a constant thing. It was a seesaw, really. I would feel very strongly one way on one day, and the next day I would feel very strongly the other way. And after a little while of this I would be aware of the pattern myself. I would know while I was feeling like staying in Bordentown that the next day I would feel like running for my life. When you get like that it's really terrible because you're afraid to trust yourself. You don't dare make a decision because you know that whatever you decide will seem like the wrong choice in a day or two.

If I left, that was the end of it. I could never come back, and I would probably never have a chance like this for the rest of my life. And if I stayed I would gradually get in deeper and deeper, and we would expand the Lighthouse, and I would marry Lucille, and by the time I realized I should have left, I would be too tied down and it would be too late, and I would spend the rest of my life regretting that I didn't get out while I had the chance. What I wanted to do was keep my options open as long as possible, but you can't, really, not for very long.

Lucille helped keep me sane, or as close to sane as I was. My moods kept switching and she was vaguely aware of this but she had her own moods to contend with. And no matter what mood either of us was in, those lunch hours in her bedroom helped. I always wanted to make love to her, and she always wanted me to, and it always worked. Sex isn't the only thing in the world, despite what you might read in *The Swinging Swappers*. But when it's good it can do a lot to take your mind off the other things.

Until finally one afternoon I got so groovily lost in her warm body, so completely out of myself and away from myself, that when the world settled together again all I could think of was how much I owed her. Not what I felt for her, or what future I wanted with her or without her, but how much I owed her.

I wanted to give her something, and it seemed to me that I wasn't giving her enough. I wasn't even sharing thoughts with her, and I couldn't do that, not yet, but there was one thing I could give her, one phrase I had been holding back all along for no good reason at all. There were words I could say that she had been waiting to hear, and I could say them whether they were true or not.

I turned and looked into her eyes, and she looked back into mine. And I said the three words she had been waiting so long to hear:

"I love you."

And she looked back at me, drinking the words, her eyes widening as she heard them. And she opened her mouth hesitantly, and I heard the echo of my own words in my head and waited for her to speak.

And she said three words back to me:

Chapter Eleven

"CHIP, I'M PREGNANT."

Chapter Twelve

"GERALDINE? THERE WAS THIS THING I was sort of wondering about."

"What we talked about awhile ago? I thought you might have been thinking about it."

"Well, I was sort of doing some heavy thinking about the business. And then this one little point got stuck in my head, and I thought I would just ask."

"Be my guest."

"Well, I was sort of wondering what you would do if one of the girls, if Rita or Claureen, if one of them got pregnant."

"I'd be powerfully surprised," she said. "Rita's step-aunt did a knitting needle abortion on her when she was fourteen, and they had to take out some of the parts you need if you want to have a baby. And Claureen had to go to the hospital for a scraping a year and a half ago and while he was in there the doc tied off her tubes."

"Well, Jo Lee or Marguerite, then. I mean, you know, any girl who happened to work here."

"Just any girl."

"That's right."

"Any girl at all."

"Uh-huh."

"Like Lucille Lathrop, even."

"_____"

"Chip, I'm an old woman. I've been years in the same business and seen every kind of man there is to see, and I can tell whether a man's getting it or not, or if he's the kind of man who wants it or not. And I know you're getting it, and getting it regular, and I know you like what you're getting. And you're not getting it here where it's all over the place for the taking, and you're not out catting around, so where else *would* you be getting it?"

"You've known all along?"

"Took it for granted."

"Does anyone else—"

"Claude Tyles asked what you were doing for love, and I imagine I led him to think you were alternating between Rita and Claureen. When did you find out she was pregnant?"

"This afternoon."

"How long gone is she?"

"Almost two months."

"She's sure about it?"

"She seems to be."

"Instead of stealing rubbers from around here, you should have told me and I would have gotten pills for her. You can't count on rubbers, don't you know that? Well, that's under the bridge. What do you want to do?"

"I don't know."

"Marry the girl? Have an abortion? What?"

"I don't know."

She did something odd. She put her hand on top of mine for a minute, then gave a squeeze and took her own hand back.

She said, "Chip, if she just told you today then you're in a bad way. You sure she didn't tell you a week ago?"

"No. Why?"

"You didn't suspect until today?"

"Never."

"Because you've been walking round in grand confusion for better than a week, and if it's not that it's something else, and now with this on top of it you must be in a bad way."

"I guess I am."

"Chip, I'm too old to get shocked or disappointed or anything but older, and I can't even get that too much. I'm not much for questions. But you got something that you got to tell to somebody, and I guess I can do a better job of listening than most. You can just put it straight out and not stop first to think how it'll sound."

I didn't say anything.

"Or you can tell me to forget it and I will. I'm good at forgetting. I can forget just about anything."

"No," I said. "I was just trying to figure out where to start."

The words were all there waiting, and once I opened the valve they poured out. A couple of times she filled in with a question but she didn't have to do that very often. I just went ahead and talked until there were no words left. I probably said the same thing half a dozen times in different ways. If I repeated myself, she pretended not to notice. She sat there and took it all in until I was done.

Then she went to the bar and came back with a water glass full of something. She handed it to me and I looked at it.

"Just plain corn," she said. For a minute I thought she was referring to what I had said. "Corn whiskey," she said. "Drink it."

"The whole thing? It'll kill me."

"The state you're in, it would take a quart before you'd feel a thing. All this'll do is settle you some. Go ahead and drink it."

I finished it in three gulps. It went down like fire. I guess it settled me some.

"Now I'll tell you a story, Chip. Story about a girl like Rita or Claureen, just a down-home girl who wasn't much and wound up going with men for money. Her pa ran off when she wasn't more than a bit of a girl and all she ever had from him was a postcard once in a while. Maybe she built him up a little in her mind but not all that much. Then one day after she's been hustling for a time she hears from one of her aunts that got a telegram from Norfolk. My...this girl's father was in a fight in a waterfront bar and some sailor broke a bottle over his head and he's in the hospital with his skull fractured.

"So this girl goes to Norfolk to see her pa, and he's in a

271

hospital there. She visits him but he's in a coma, and after a week he dies without ever coming out of it. And she makes arrangements to ship the body back here to be buried next to my mother.

"Now while this girl was in Norfolk...that's two slips so far, I suspect you could put a name to this girl if you were pressed, couldn't you? Doesn't matter. This girl, while she's in Norfolk, she meets this man and one thing leads to another. This man is in naval stores in Baltimore. A good family. He wants her to marry him and come on back to Baltimore.

"And it's like a dream to her. This man, he's rich, and he's a good man, and he wants her to marry him. But she thinks, Now, how can I marry up with him when I've got all this in my past? And what if he finds out?

"So she decides to tell him, and she tells him. And he says what does he care, because that's something that happened in South Carolina and what does it have to do with Baltimore, and as far as he's concerned it never happened at all, and it doesn't bother him one bit, and if it bothers her then she's a fool, and he knows she's not a fool.

"And she thinks, well, it'll bother him in the years to come. But if it ever does she never knows about it, he never once throws it back to her, as it turns out.

"So she goes to Baltimore, and they're married, and there were all these things she was afraid of, how his family would take to her and what his friends would think, and none of the things she worries about ever come to pass. She thinks maybe she'll meet someone from her past and it'll ruin everything, but none of this ever happens. There are all of these things she worries about and it turns out she needn't have worried about any of them, because none of them ever come to pass.

"And she's an intelligent girl, Chip. She has a good mind. She always educated herself and paid some mind to how people talked, and she goes on doing this in Baltimore, and his family and friends like her. They accept her completely. Completely. They never even think he married beneath him because they get to thinking that she comes from quality people down in South Carolina.

"She's there for three years, and in that space of time she sees that the things that worried her are nothing at all. And she has a child. A little boy."

She stopped talking and her eyes were focused into the distance at a point somewhere over my shoulder. Whatever she was looking at was in some other room.

"And one day she said *I'm not me no more*. And she put a few weeks into thinking on that, and one morning she left the baby with the maid and took a taxi downtown to the railroad station. She wouldn't look out that train window for fear she might get off at the next stop. She just sat there, this fine lady in these expensive clothes, and she stared straight ahead and didn't see a thing...

"She never looked back, ever.

"Whether they looked for her or not she never knew. She left him a note saying she was running off with another man. She figured if you want to hurt somebody you do it quick and clean, and if you want to do one thing decent it's to have the guts to make people hate you if it'll be easier for them that way. Because the hate won't reach you because you'll be out of it, and if it'll sear another person's wounds..."

She was silent for a long time, but I didn't say anything because I knew she hadn't finished.

Then she said, "Of course, she wasn't the same girl who went off to Norfolk three years earlier. She saw things in a way she never would have seen them before. She knew how to talk like a lady. She knew manners. But she could let them slide off and nobody knew the difference. Except for what she knew of herself.

"She was lonely, but she would have been that anywhere. She was where she deepdown belonged, whether it was better or worse for her to belong there. She never regretted it. She would be sad sometimes, and she would wonder what happened to that man in Baltimore, and to that baby..."

In another voice she said, "Somewhere along the way it gets determined just what a person is, and for the rest of his life he's stuck with it. Whoever else he may try to be is just play-acting. I guess you know you'll have to go, Chip."

"I know."

"I guess you knew it all along."

"I guess I did."

"Once you got to do something, there's nothing but to do it. Tonight is better than tomorrow. You'll take my car."

"I can't—"

"It's no use to me. I haven't driven it myself in ten years. It's almost as old as you are. I don't guess it has as many miles on it, though. You can drive, can't you?"

"I have a license. I've used the Reverend's car a couple of times on errands."

"This has a stick shift. You know how to work it?"

"In a sort of academic way."

"You'll get the hang of it. I'll make the registration over to you. Oh, now, it's not so much. A 1954 Cadillac, what would I get selling it? Not even an antique yet. That star of yours will guarantee against a ticket anywhere in the state, and by then you'll be comfortable driving it. I let the girls use it. It runs all right. It's still a Cadillac. Always will be, old as it gets."

I said, "Lucille."

"You want to take her along?"

"I don't know."

"She would go."

"I know. I keep feeling I ought to take her."

"You could take her with you. But she'd never really *be* with you. No more than you could stay here. Listen to me. You can hurt her now quickly or spend fifty years killing her by halves. Because whether you stay here or take her with you one thing is sure, and that's that she will never complete you. And you would never tell her that but she

274

would always know, and never know why."

I swallowed.

"The Sheriff will get a report and he'll tell her about it. You had an accident on a road out of town. You were driving my car, and you were in a wreck and were killed, and the body was shipped north for burial with your parents."

"The Sheriff—"

"Claude will tell her that. He'll get that report."

"How?"

"From me."

"Oh."

"Claude Tyles knows all a man has to know about who you have to be whether you want to or not. Sometimes what you have to do is stay. Not in a place, necessarily, but with a person. He had to, and he did, and he knows. For my part, I'll see she gets the baby taken care of. Whichever she wants, having it and then getting shut of it or just getting shut of it. If she's even pregnant in the first place, which we're none of us sure of. Chip?"

"What?"

"You can feel as guilty as you want to, but all it is is foolishness. What the two of you had was good for the two of you. Nobody can ask more than that. It's no kindness to take something good and keep it going when it's no good no more. She had a beautiful young romance and her lover died. Why, you'll be more in her memory than you ever could have been in her life."

She gave me a couple old suitcases of hers. I packed everything and put the suitcases in the trunk. I went back to say goodbye to her and she looked as though she wished I hadn't.

"You send me a card from time to time. Just so I'll have an idea of where you're at. No need to sign it or the snoops at the Post Office'll have something to talk about. I don't get that much mail," she said. "I guess I'll know who it's from."

Chapter Thirteen

THERE WAS A STRETCH OF TIME THEN when nothing happened you would want to read about. I didn't do much but drive, and I didn't work too hard at that, either. I would push the old Cadillac until I came to a town that looked decent enough and pick out one of the large Victorian houses with a sign in front that said TOURISTS or ROOMS or something of the sort. They would generally be run by a widow living alone, or two old maids, or a widow and her old maid sister, and the rooms were clean and comfortable and only cost two or three dollars a night, which was less than half what the cheapest motel would charge. Sometimes they included breakfast, or sold it to you for something ridiculous like fifty cents.

I stayed in so many of those places I have trouble remembering which was which. They were all the same in so many ways. There would always be a small portable television set, and it would be the only piece of furniture in the house that was less than thirty years old. There was usually a spinet piano in the parlor that no one had played in almost that long, and if I stayed more than a night the woman would ask wistfully if I played the piano, and would be sad to hear that I didn't.

"No one ever does," she would say. "I suppose I ought to sell it for all the use it is, but I cannot bear to, Mr. Harrison. I just cannot bear to sell that piano."

If they all sell them all at once, the market for second-hand pianos is going to collapse overnight.

There were always framed photographs on the piano, and on the carved sideboard in the hallway. You could tell the frames were silver because they were usually slightly tarnished. And there was generally a vase of cut flowers on the sideboard next to the photographs, and there were potted plants all over the place. The plants were usually green and healthy.

276

Sometimes there would be a cat or a dog. More cats than dogs, all in all. The cats tended to keep to themselves. The dogs tended to be very small, and bark a lot, primarily at me.

I couldn't tell you just how many houses like this I stayed in, or how much time I spent this way. I wasn't very much involved in time, for some reason. I would be very conscious of the time of day because as soon as it was nine or ten at night I could go to bed and not think about anything until it was time to get up the next morning. But I didn't bother with days of the week, or what month it was, or that sort of thing. I didn't read newspapers or look at television. I knew there was a whole world out there but I didn't want to think about it. I had a bath every night and put on clean clothes every morning and when my clean clothes began to run short I did a load of wash in my current landlady's washing machine. Some of them didn't have washing machines of their own but knew a neighbor who would let me use theirs.

Sometimes I stayed one night and then left, particularly if there was a yipping dog in the house, or if there were other boarders. If I felt like staying, I would have a look around the house for something that needed fixing. Usually I didn't have to look very hard because the woman would apologize for whatever it is.

"You'll have to forgive the appearance of that room because it needs repapering, Mr. Harrison"…"The boy who used to do my yard work was drafted into the Army last month, Mr. Harrison, and I just can't keep up with my rose beds"…"I don't know how this house can go another year without painting, Mr. Harrison, but I had a man out to give me an estimate and, land, the price he asked!"

I changed a lot of faucet washers and replaced a lot of broken panes of glass. I cleaned out some basements and mowed and reseeded lawns and trimmed shrubbery and hauled trash. I patched plaster, which wasn't as hard as I thought it would be, and I put up wallpaper, which was.

In Columbia, Missouri, I painted a whole house without falling off the ladder once. I guess that summer of apple-picking was valuable.

That was for the woman who hadn't known how the house could go another year without painting. She told me this at breakfast, and it was a breakfast that came free with my three-dollar room rent, and it was such a good breakfast and such a clean comfortable house that I figured I wouldn't mind spending another week or two there.

So I said, "Well, I could paint it for you."

"But I couldn't afford it. The size of this house, and he wanted nine hundred dollars."

"If you'll pay for the paint and brushes, and find out where I can borrow a ladder, I'll do it for five dollars a day and my keep."

"Why, I just can't believe that, Mr. Harrison! How can you afford to do that?"

"Well," I said, "I don't have all that much else to do, actually."

It was really very satisfying doing things like that. With that house, I saw that she bought the best paint, and I took my time and did a good job. At the beginning I'm sure she was scared to death I would fall off the ladder and kill myself. The same thing had occurred to me. But I didn't, and the house got painted, and I slept ten hours a night in my room and ate three good meals a day, and when I washed out my brush for the last time she paid me fifty dollars and couldn't believe that was all it was going to cost her.

"It looks so fine now," she said, walking around the house and admiring it from every angle. "It hasn't looked so fine since he was alive. You don't know what it's been like, Mr. Harrison, thinking I would never live to see it looking right again."

It made me feel good to leave a place in better shape than I found it. Sometimes I felt like Johnny Appleseed and other times like the Lone Ranger.

And I needed that kind of feeling, because if I let myself

think about other things, about Bordentown things, I didn't feel like Johnny or Lone. I just felt like a son of a bitch.

That first night, driving the Cadillac generally north and generally east, I was too numb to feel much of anything at all. It was a good thing Geraldine sent me away right off. If I had had a night to sleep on it God only knows what I would have done, but I was on the road before I knew exactly what was happening and there was never a point where I could turn back.

I kept wanting to for the longest time. But that was the one thing I knew I couldn't do. I just couldn't go back there again.

The car was a good one, old as it was, and plain driving was a good way to get away from yourself while getting away from Bordentown. I hadn't realized they made Cadillacs with stick shifts, even back in 1954. I don't suppose they made very many of them. The ones they made, they did a good job with. I got the hang of shifting pretty quickly, and after that there was nothing to do but drive.

What I would think about while I was driving, well, the hell with all that. Nothing very brilliant, I don't guess.

I stayed at a motel the first night, and didn't sleep much. It wasn't exactly the Hilton. It was what I think they call a hot-pillow joint, and the room next door to mine was one of the ones they would rent out by the hour. If the walls had been any thinner they would have been transparent. All night long the bed-springs squeaked and groaned, and all night long different men and women told each other they loved each other, and they were all of them lying in their teeth. I don't suppose I would have slept much anyway, but this didn't help.

After that, though, it got easier. One thing the widows' houses didn't have was bed-springs wailing all night long. And I also learned that sleep was a great way to get through time without going crazy. I got so I could fall asleep right away, pulling the sleep over my head like a blanket, and

I'd be good for ten hours, sometimes more. I never used to sleep that way before and never have since, just burrowing into sleep and sort of using it. Every day Bordentown was a few miles further south and east and one day deeper in the past. You just let the past slip away from you and one day you turn around and it's out of sight.

It's that simple, and that hard.

I wrote three letters, one to Sheriff Tyles, one to Geraldine, one to Lucille. This was just a game I was playing with myself because I knew I didn't intend to mail the letters. What was interesting was that the one to Geraldine was the hardest to write. I would have thought it would be the other way around. I tore them all up when I was done, and tore the pieces into smaller pieces, as if the FBI might come around and try to put the stupid letters back together again like jigsaw puzzles.

I also wrote a letter to Hallie telling her about the whole business in Bordentown. I actually expected to mail that letter when I was done with it, and I took a lot of time trying to get it just right, and of course when it was through I tore it up, too.

I did send Geraldine a postcard. I sent her a couple of them at different times. I could never once think of anything to write, so I would leave the message part blank or else just run the address across the whole length of the card. Miss Geraldine Simms, The Lighthouse, Bordentown, South Carolina. And the zip code, which I don't remember, but I knew it at the time.

A lot of the time when I was driving there would be hitchhikers on the road, guys alone or two of them together or sometimes a guy and a girl. Back when I did a lot of hitching I would always promise myself that if I ever had a car I would never pass up a hitchhiker. And the people who gave me rides generally mentioned that they had thumbed their way around when they were younger, and that was why they felt they had to stop for me in return, even though they knew that it was supposed to be a dangerous thing to do.

Now I had a car, a big car with nothing but room in it, and there were all these people on the road, I never went a day without seeing a dozen of them, and I never once stopped. There were soldiers in uniform and hippies and straight-looking kids and older people, everything, and I passed them all up. Not because it was dangerous to stop, although I guess it is, but because I just didn't want to talk to anybody.

It was a funny stretch of time. I guess I wouldn't want to go through it again.

Chapter Fourteen

I HAD TO WRITE THE LAST CHAPTER twice. The first time I did it, I put in a six-page scene that never happened. It was the first night after I left Bordentown, when I stayed in the motel with cardboard walls. The way I wrote it the first time, there was this long scene where I listened to a couple through the wall, and the guy finished before the girl was satisfied, and he just left her there, and she was storming around the room throwing things and crying. So then I went next door and brought her back to my own room and took her to bed, and afterward she was sleeping and I heard the same thing happen again in the room next door, except this time the guy was drunk and passed out before he could do anything. Whereupon the heroic Chip Harrison went next door and found the second girl, and she was also ready to walk up the wall and across the ceiling, and good old Chipperoo brought her back, too, and balled her in the bed while the first girl was still sleeping, and then the first girl woke up, and the three of us had this wild orgy with everybody doing everything to everybody else all at once.

I filled up six pages with that crap. It was a pretty good scene, actually, and I think it would have been pretty erotic.

But I thought about it and tore it all up and did it over the way it really happened.

So I wrote that scene, and it didn't bother me while I was writing it. In fact while I was typing it all out I could actually believe it really happened. Sometimes it's a little frightening the way your imagination will take a lie and make it almost true.

Then why did I tear it up? I could say it was because I didn't want to put any lies in this book, but that's not it because there are already a couple of lies in it that I'm leaving in. Just small lies, but that doesn't make them true. The real reason, I think, is that putting in a scene like that would just make a lie out of everything that happened in Bordentown and a lot of what went on afterward. Because that scene I wrote could never have happened. If the beginning of it happened, and if a guy did leave a girl there all unsatisfied, I never would have gone next door. Not the way I felt. If anything I would have just left the motel and gotten back in the car and kept on driving. And if I *tried* to do anything with a girl just then, if somehow I really did make an effort, I'm sure I couldn't have managed to accomplish it.

I didn't leave my heart in San Francisco, but for a while there I guess I left my balls in Bordentown.

Chapter Fifteen

I GUESS I KNEW ALL ALONG I WAS ON my way to Wisconsin. In fact the first night out I tried to figure out just how long it would take me to drive there if I drove sixteen hours a day and slept eight. (If I had tried it, I think I would have killed that Cadillac in a matter of days. It was good for another fifteen years if you didn't push it more than fifty or a hundred miles at a stretch, but it tended to burn oil when it overheated and I would have thrown a rod or burned out a bearing sooner or later.)

But the thing is that I wanted to be going to Wisconsin but I didn't want to get there. I wanted to see Hallie. I always wanted to see Hallie, ever since that one night in September when she came to my room over the barber shop. The next morning she went to Madison to start college, and ever since then I had been not quite going there to see her.

Because if I went there, and if it turned out that there was nothing there for me, then what would I do? I wouldn't have Hallie to send postcards to, or to write letters to and not mail. Or to think about the way knights used to think about the Holy Grail.

Once I was out of Bordentown I really didn't want to see anybody right away, Hallie included. I knew that there had to be some time in between Bordentown and whatever was going to come after it. I don't mean that I spelled all of this out in my mind, but when I think back on it I can see it was something I must have known.

So I took my time, and took down a lot of storm windows and put up a lot of screens, and touched up woodwork and repaired furniture. And before long it was June and the colleges were out for the summer, so there was no point in rushing up there because she would be away on summer vacation.

Of course I knew where she lived, in the same town

where I originally met her, a little town on the Hudson between New York and Albany. It stood to reason that she would go home for the summer, and I suppose I could have gone to see her there, but the way I looked at it was that I was already out in the Midwest and it would make more sense to stay there and see her in Wisconsin when the fall term started.

Which meant that all I had to do was kill a couple of months. I didn't even have to pretend I was on the way to Wisconsin. All I had to do was kill time, and I was getting pretty good at that.

I think some of the pressure came off about the time that the school year ended in Wisconsin. I don't know that one thing had much to do with the other. Maybe it did and maybe it didn't, but within a week after the end of the semester, I did something I hadn't done since I left Bordentown.

By this time I was starting to worry about it. Not that I wasn't doing it—because let's face it, I had gone almost eighteen years without doing it, so a couple of months off wasn't anything remarkable. But I didn't even want to do it. I didn't even particularly think about it, for Pete's sake, and it's usually all I do think about.

In fact, I wasn't even doing what I had told Lucille it was perfectly normal to do.

I would see a pretty girl on the street, say, and I would tell myself, *There's a pretty girl.* I still had the brains to realize this. But what I wouldn't tell myself was, *Man, would I ever like to ball that chick until her eyes fall out of her head.* And that sort of thing had always been my normal response to a pretty girl, and now it didn't happen, and I was beginning to worry.

For months I had been with Lucille five days a week. The same girl, lunch hour after lunch hour, and I never once got tired of it. I was always ready and willing and able, and it was always good, and I always enjoyed it. And now it began to seem possible to me that *(a)* I was never going to want it again with anybody or *(b)* I was only going to want it with Lucille. And both of these things amounted to the same thing, because I was never going to be able to see Lucille again.

And if *(b)* was true (and it might have been, I couldn't tell, because I wasn't sure I still wanted to make love to Lucille but I couldn't prove that I didn't, either) then it stood to reason that leaving Bordentown had been a mistake. But not one of those mistakes you can do anything about, except maybe cut your throat, which still seemed a little too extreme. So it reassured me when it finally happened. And it's reassuring me right now, because I can write about it, and if I didn't have some sex in this book pretty soon I suppose Mr. Fultz would give it back to me and tell me to use it to line a birdcage or something. He may anyway.

I hope not.

It was in Iowa. I don't remember the name of the town. (There's another lie for you. I remember it perfectly well, but I'm not putting it in.) The house I was staying at this time was like most of the others, a sprawling old place in the middle of town with bay windows and gables and extra rooms that were nicely furnished and everything, but nothing happened in them and nobody ever went in there. This house had two widows instead of one. One of them was about sixty, a plump little old lady with cataracts and hardly any chin, so that her face just curved back from her mouth to her neck. This took a little getting used to.

The other widow was her daughter. Her name was Mrs. Cooper, and her mother's name was Mrs. Wollsacket. Mrs. Cooper was about thirty-five and she had a perfectly good chin and no cataracts. She also had a son, who was about seven years old and retarded. Very retarded. They had to feed him with a spoon and he would drool most of it out, and his eyes never seemed to focus on anything.

Between the kid and his grandmother's non-chin, I had more or less decided not to look for anything that needed fixing. After breakfast Mrs. Cooper left for work and I got ready to go, and when I went to pay Mrs. Wollsacket she started talking about all the things that needed doing, and how difficult it was to make do without a man around the place, and how here it was June and the second-floor storms were still on the windows. (Incidentally, somebody is missing a good bet; if someone would only sell combination aluminum storm windows to all those lonely old ladies, half their worries would be over.)

Well, I couldn't just leave. It wouldn't fit the Lone Ranger image at all to run off yelling "Hi-yo, Silver!" without changing those storm windows for her. I offered to do the job for her in exchange for the two-fifty I owed her and another day's room and board. She said, "Oh, I wasn't asking *you* to do it, Mr. Harrison," and I started to say, well, then, I guessed I'd be on my way, and she said, "but I'm surely glad to take you up on your generous offer," and I was locked in.

It didn't take long. I took care of the storm windows and took apart a lamp with a broken switch and put it back together again so that it worked, which completely amazed her. Then I ate a sandwich for lunch and walked around town until I found the library.

The librarian looked vaguely familiar, and when she gave me a tentative smile I realized it was Mrs. Cooper. We had a dumb conversation, and then I looked around until I found a couple of early Nero Wolfe mysteries that I couldn't remember if I had read or not. Mrs. Cooper told me I could take them back to the house even though I didn't have a card. I read them in my room. One of them, anyway; it turned out I had read the other one.

They fed the kid early, thank God. Then the three of us had dinner and I talked about how I was a student at the University of Wisconsin on summer vacation, and trying to see something of the country and possibly earn a little money toward next year's tuition. (I had been saying this since the term ended. Before that I was the same student at Wisconsin but had dropped out in January for lack of funds and hoped to go back in the fall.) I couldn't tell you very much about the dinner conversation because it was basically the same as all my dinner conversations, and I had learned to handle my end of it without paying much attention to anything but the food.

Afterward I took a loose leg off one of the dining room chairs and glued it back on. This went over well. Then I went up to my room and read the other Nero Wolfe, the one I had already read once before. I had forgotten how it came out and was willing to find out all over again.

Around ten there was a timid knock on the door. I opened it, and it was Mrs. Cooper. She was a little bird of a woman, as thin as her mother was fat, with a slightly pinched look around her eyes and nose. She was prettier than that sentence makes her sound, and would have looked very nice, I think, if she had done something intelligent with her hair. It was the color of a field mouse and she had it pulled back into a bun.

"I couldn't sleep," she said, "and I thought you might like a nice cup of tea, Mr. Harrison."

We had tea in one of the living rooms. Mrs. Cooper talked about how nice it was to work at the library, except that so few people actually read books anymore, with so many of them wasting their time in front of television sets. And she talked about how lonely it was in that town, and how she had wanted to leave, but she couldn't leave her mother all alone and besides there was the boy to consider, and she guessed she would just stay there while life passed her by.

"This must be a lonely summer for you, Mr. Harrison," she said.

"It is," I said. "But I do meet a lot of people."

"I'm sure you must."

"Yes, I do." Brilliant, Chip. If you're supposed to be the Lone Ranger, why do you talk like Tonto?

"I suppose you meet a great many lonely women."

"Uh," Tonto said.

She folded her little hands under her little breasts. "You must bring them a great deal of excitement, Mr. Harrison. Excitement that is sorely missing in their wretched and cloistered lives."

Her eyes were shining weirdly, and she moistened her thin lips with her tongue.

I said, "Well, I guess I change a lot of storm windows, if you can call that excitement."

She leaned forward and put her teacup on the coffee table. She did this very deliberately, as if it would slide off the table unless she placed it in just the right spot. I realized suddenly that she was not wearing the same dress she had had on at dinner. And she was wearing lipstick, and hadn't been wearing any at dinner.

She stood up and crossed the room and sat on the couch beside me. She folded her hands and rested them in her lap.

"My husband died eight years ago," she said.

"I'm very sorry."

"But there is still a fire in me," she said. "My fire has never been quenched."

She put her hand on the front of my pants. I tried out a lot of lines in my head, like asking her how her husband died, or how long she had been working at the library, or if she thought it would rain tomorrow. Somehow none of them seemed like the right thing to say. I considered telling her that I was a fairy or had been wounded in a campus riot or that I had syphilis. It was like having absolutely no appetite and then having somebody put a plate of boiled turnips in front of you.

"My fire burns for you, Mr. Harrison," she said. She really said that. "Oh, Chip, darling!"

And her hand did things, and of course nothing happened, and I thought, well, maybe I can sort of move the turnips around on my plate. Because while I was sure

I would never be able to rise to the occasion, so to speak, I also figured there was more than one way to skin a cat, or quench a fire, and if she had gone eight years without it she could probably get off without too much trouble if I just went through the motions.

So I kissed her.

The way it started out, I was like a Boy Scout helping her across the street. But somewhere along the way everything changed. It really surprised me. I opened her dress and touched her and kissed her, and in the course of it all I began to groove on her body.

It was a much better body than you would have expected. It didn't look that great—she was much too thin and didn't have much of a waist, so that she was almost a straight line from her shoulders to her feet. Her skin was very soft and smooth, though, and there was no fat on her, and, well, her body just *felt* nice. Some do and some don't, and hers did.

Maybe what I got was a contact arousal from her, because she was certainly excited and she certainly made it obvious. Anyway, I was on the couch with her, just going through the motions, when all of a sudden I realized that I had an erection.

And I thought, Hey, where did that come from?

God knows where it came from. But even I knew where it was supposed to go, and it suddenly seemed absolutely essential that I put it there as soon as I possibly could. It didn't seem to matter if she was ready or not, although I guess she must have been ready for the past eight years. All that mattered to me was to get into her, and I shucked my pants and rolled on top of her and jabbed at her with all the subtlety of a tomcat.

It went straight in on the first shot as if she had a magnet in her cervix. She wrapped her arms and legs around me as if she was scared I would take it away. She had nothing to worry about. I kept taking it a little ways away and then putting it back, as fast and as hard and as deep as I could.

Throughout all of this, there was something slightly schizophrenic about the whole thing. Because it was as though there were two Chip Harrisons. One of them was banging away at the poor woman as if he was trying to splinter her pelvic bone, and the other was sitting in a chair on the other side of the room, watching the whole thing and not quite believing what he was seeing.

It went on for a long time, this totally unsubtle relentless sledgehammer screwing, and she came about half a dozen times, and then so did I.

"We'll go to your room now," she said. There was a little puddle on the couch. She put a doily over it, put her dress and my pants over her arm, and took my arm with her free hand. "We'll go to your room," she said, "and do it some more."

"We'll fuck," she said. "We can try different positions. I would like to try it with me on top, if that's all right with you. That way you can pinch my breasts while we do it. You may pinch them as hard as you like. I won't mind."

"You may even bite them if you like."

"Your mother," I said.

"She sleeps very soundly."

"Well, uh, I'm not sure I can do it again. It took a lot out of me."

"I know. Most of it is running down my leg."

"Uh."

"You'll be able to," she said confidently, giving my arm a happy-like squeeze. "I just know you will."

She was right.

Afterward, it seemed as if there ought to be something to say. I asked her about her husband, and if he died before the kid was born. Seven months before the kid was born, she told me.

And how long had her mother been a widow?

"Eight years also."

"That's really terrible," I said. "You must have lost them both about the same time."

"Exactly the same time."

"Gee," I said. "An automobile accident, I suppose."

"They committed suicide." She was lying on her back. She had taken her hair down and it looked much better. The pinched-in expression was gone from her face. Sex certainly does wonders for a woman's appearance.

"You probably don't want to talk about it."

"Oh, I don't mind," she assured me. "It happened the very day I told them that I was pregnant. That very day, I told them, my husband and my father, and they went downstairs to the basement and into the tool room, and they got the shotgun, and they put the barrel in their mouths and pulled the trigger and blew off the top of their heads."

"Oh."

"I was never married," she said.

"Oh."

"It started when I was twelve. He came to my room and told me I was a big girl and it was time I learned how to fuck. I hope you don't mind my using that word."

"Not at all."

"And then he fucked me. I didn't like it, but my mother said it was my duty because he was my father. She read from the Bible. About Lot and his daughters. I didn't like it at all for the first few years, but then I got to enjoy it pretty well."

"Oh."

"What I didn't like was he would always pull it out just before the end. And when he couldn't in time I was always lucky, until one time when I was twenty-six years old and I found out I was pregnant and he shot himself." She thought for a moment. "I don't see why he shot himself," she said reasonably. "There was no need."

"Oh."

"I went to Kansas City, and then mother told everyone that I was married, and I had the baby, and then mother told everyone that Mr. Cooper was killed in an airplane crash and I would be coming back to live with her. But I think everybody knows. Wouldn't you think so?"

"Maybe."

"I think they must. Especially with the baby being an idiot and all. I wish they had told me right away he was an idiot. I would have drowned him. But by the time I knew about it I was attached to him and I couldn't do it. That happens, you know. You get attached to them, even if they are."

She went silent then. Thank God. After a while I said, "Uh, I'm kind of exhausted. I have to get to sleep, and you probably ought to go to your own room. I mean, you wouldn't want your mother to find out about this."

"Why not?"

"Well," I said, "I would be embarrassed."

"Oh," she said. She thought about it, then nodded. "All right," she said, and off she went, her dress over her arm.

I was just falling asleep when the door opened again. There she was, carrying a cup and saucer. No dress this time. She was still naked.

"I brought you a surprise," she said gaily.

"If that's my tea, I don't really want it."

"It's not," she said.

"I still don't want it."

"Well, it's not for you."

"Huh?"

"Lie down and shut up," she said. "It's for the surprise."

"What surprise?"

"You'll see. You'll like it."

"Look, all I really want is to go to sleep."

"You can go to sleep in a minute. Lie down."

"What's in the cup?"

"Just warm water," she said, and filled her mouth with it, and leaned over me.

Oh, the hell with it. I wasn't going to mention it but it's too perfect, and if it ruins her reputation that's just the way it goes. I don't think she'll mind, anyway.

It was Waterloo, Iowa. I swear to God.

Chapter Sixteen

THERE WERE SOME OTHER GIRLS DURING the rest of the summer. Some I got to and some I struck out with. None of them were very important.

Chapter Seventeen

I DROVE INTO MADISON A COUPLE OF weeks after the fall term started. I would have gotten there earlier but I kept putting it off until finally I knew it was time. The old Cadillac got me there in good shape. I started looking around for a tourist home like the ones I had been staying in for the past half a year, and I drove around for a long time without seeing any of the usual signs. Then I remembered that Madison was a university town, and that people with rooms to rent would take in college students by the year.

And I also remembered, just about the same time, that if Hallie was here and stuck in some dormitory it might be pretty stupid to room with some widow. So I got a room at a motel. Sixteen bucks, and payable in advance, and it wasn't even all that much of a room.

I didn't care. I was in pretty good shape financially, with almost two hundred and fifty dollars, which was more than I had had when I left Bordentown. Even with all the gas that the old car burned, I had been earning money faster than I spent it.

I unpacked in my motel room and put my clothes away. I took a shower and shaved, although I had already shaved and showered in the morning. Then I got dressed and noticed I was sweating, and I took another shower and put on a clean shirt and made myself stretch out on the bed and calm down so I would stop sweating.

The campus was huge. It sprawled all over the place. There were a lot of kids sitting in groups under trees and other groups of kids hurrying here and there. I couldn't understand how they could possibly find their way around. It was immense.

I asked a lot of people various dumb questions until someone told me where you could find out where a student was staying, and somebody there told me what dorm she was in, and various other people pointed me toward it.

I went and stood in front of it. I didn't know whether it was all right for me to go in or not. I thought of stopping some girl on the way out and asking her to find Hallie for me, but instead I just waited.

And then two girls came out, and one of them was Hallie.

She looked exactly the way she had looked a year ago. Exactly. She was wearing dungarees and a sweatshirt and sandals, and her granny glasses made her brown eyes look even bigger than they were. Her hair, straight and glossy brown, was a year longer than it had been.

I said, "Hallie?"

She looked at me, and stared, and said, "Chip?"

I nodded, waiting for her to run up and throw herself into my arms. (I had rehearsed this scene a lot.) She didn't exactly do this. What she did was say something to the other girl about seeing her in class, and then she walked slowly toward me, a smile spreading on her lips, and reached out her hands for mine.

Her hands felt small and very soft.

"I can't believe it," she said. "When did you get here?"

"About an hour ago."

"Are you going to be studying here?"

"No."

"Oh."

"I was in the area," I said, "and I thought I would drop in and see you."

"Wow, that's really great. Oh, wow. Like I can't really believe all this."

"Yeah."

"I got your cards. I was going to write to you, but there was never a return address."

"Well, I never stayed in one place very long."

"Oh."

"I wrote you a couple of letters, too."

"I never got them."

"I never mailed them."

"Oh."

"You look fantastic."

"So do you. You filled out a lot, didn't you? You were thinner. You didn't used to be so big in the shoulders, did you?"

"I guess not. Hallie—"

"Could we sort of walk this way, Chip? I have this class."

"Oh, sure."

"I suppose I could cut it."

"You don't have to do that."

"Well, I really shouldn't. They keep a record of cuts. It's pretty idiotic but they do."

"I don't want you to get in trouble."

"It wouldn't be trouble, exactly—"

"I mean, it's not as if I have to be on the road in an hour or anything. I mean, I could meet you after class."

"That would be great."

"What is it, an hour?"

"Uh-huh. If you could meet me out in front? By the step over there?"

"In an hour. Sure."

"Great."

You want to know something? I wasn't going to write all this shit. I had it planned differently. The last chapter, Chapter Sixteen, only has twenty-seven words in it. (In case you forgot: *There were some other girls during the rest of the summer. Some I got to and some I struck out with.* Paragraph. *None of them were very important.*)

Well, it wouldn't have been a hell of a lot of trouble to take those twenty-seven words and make twenty-seven pages out of them. Or even more. Because whether what happened for the rest of the summer was important or not, it might have been mildly interesting. One time I double-dated with this farmhand. We took out two sisters and each screwed one of them and then traded girls and screwed them again. I had never done anything like that before, and it would have been interesting enough to make a scene out of it. It would have made a damned good scene, as a matter of fact.

So there would have been plenty to write about, and the book would have been long enough to stop with me just getting to Wisconsin, or just getting ready to drive to Wisconsin. That was the way I originally planned to do it.

Hell.

That would have been cheating. Because the way this book ends, the way I'm ending it now, is sort of the point of it. Or part of the point of it.

But it's a fucking pain in the ass to write it. (They may take that line out. I hope not.)

I went someplace and had a hamburger and a cup of coffee. On one side of me some students were talking about the draft lottery, and on the other side some students were talking about Gay Liberation. They already seemed liberated enough to me.

I was back in front of the building ten minutes before the hour was up. Those ten minutes took another hour. Then some clown rang a bell and a few seconds later people started coming out of the building. Eventually one of them was Hallie, and she came over to me and held out her hands again, and I took them again. I asked her how the class was, and she told me, and we wasted a few words on that kind of garbage.

Then I said, "Is there some place we can talk?"

"My room?"

"I don't know. Am I allowed there?"

"I'll allow you."

"I mean—"

"We have twenty-four hour open halls," she said.

"I thought maybe we could go for a ride."

"Oh, you've got a car?"

"Uh-huh."

"Okay."

When we got to it she said, "Wow, a Cadillac! Look who turned out to be rich."

"It's a '54. I mean it's worth maybe fifty dollars."

"It looks great. When did you buy it?"

"I got it in the spring. Somebody gave it to me."

"Oh."

"It runs pretty good, though."

"I didn't know they made them with standard shift."

"I think this may have been the only one."

"Maybe it's an antique or something."

"I suppose if I keep it long enough."

"Yeah."

There was a lot more brilliant conversation like that. I just drove around forever without paying much attention to where we were, and we kept trying to get conversations going, and they kept being like what I quoted. She told me what courses she was taking and I told her some of the places I had been, and I kept getting more uptight about the whole thing, and I guess she did, too.

At one point I said, "Listen, I have this room. You know, a motel room. I mean we could talk there."

"Oh."

Eventually there was a red light and I stopped for it. I turned to her and said, "I don't mean to ball or I would have said it, but I want to open up and rap with you because we have to, and I don't want to do it sitting under a tree or in your dormitory or in this fucking car."

"Okay."

"You don't mind?"

"No, of course not. It's weird, isn't it? A whole year, and we never really knew each other."

"It'll be all right."

It was still a little awkward at first, partly because the bed took up about eighty percent of the room, and there was only one chair. No matter how much you say that you just want to talk, in a situation like that it's hard to pretend there isn't a bed in the room. I had her sit on the chair and I sat on the edge of the bed.

It wasn't really rapping at first, but it got there. I told her some of the things I had done. I especially told her about Geraldine and the Sheriff, and how I had sort of become the child the two of them had never had together.

She told me about her brother, who had been in the service when we met, just on his way overseas at the time. They sent him to Vietnam and he was on a patrol and stepped on a landmine.

"It happened in the middle of December. But they waited until I came home for Christmas vacation before they told me about it. We were just starting to get close that summer. Before then, you know, an older brother and a younger sister, we never had that much to say to each other. And now I'll never get to talk to him again. Sometimes I think I'm beginning to get used to it, and then I find out that I'm not."

And later she said, "I never knew you were a writer. *No Score.*"

"Huh?"

"*No Score.*"

"You lost me."

"Your book," she said. "*No Score*, by Chip Harrison. I read it about a week ago."

"It's published?"

"You didn't know? It's all over the stands. All over Madison, anyway."

"That's really weird. I even forgot about it. I mean, I kept looking for it and it never turned up, and I guess I thought they decided not to bother. They didn't pay me very much money and I thought they decided to write it off. What was the title?"

"*No Score.* Don't you even remember the title?"

"I had a different title for it. I guess they decided to change it. It's been about a year since I wrote it." Then something occurred to me. "Oh," I said. "I guess you read it, huh?"

301

She nodded.

"It wasn't very good, huh?"

"I thought it was good." She had a funny look on her face. "I never expected to be in it, though."

"Oh."

"You didn't even change my name. I thought you could get in trouble that way, not changing names."

"I changed everybody else's name."

"What made me so lucky?"

"I just couldn't think of another name for you," I said. "It was just *Hallie Hallie Hallie* in my mind and I couldn't think of you any other way."

"You put down the things we did and everything. The words we said to each other."

"I didn't think anybody would know who it was."

"Oh, of course not. How could they? Hallie from the Hudson Valley who goes to school in Wisconsin. How could anybody possibly figure out it was me?"

"Oh, wow."

"It's okay, Chip."

"Yeah, it's sensational. I never even thought. I didn't think about anybody reading it that I would actually know. Or that was in it."

"It doesn't matter."

"It doesn't?"

"No. Honest." I looked at her, and she was smiling shyly. "I never guessed it was your first time. With me, I mean."

"Oh. Well, it didn't seem like something I wanted to announce."

"When I first read it I was furious."

"I can imagine."

"What really got me was that I couldn't even write to you and tell you how mad I was. I wrote a letter to your publisher just the other day. If they send it to you, you've got to promise not to read it."

"They wouldn't know where to send it."

"I guess they'll send it back to me then. I'll tear it up."

302

Her face opened. "But after I stopped being mad, I guess it made me proud. Do you know what I mean?"

"I hardly remember what I wrote, Hallie."

"Maybe I can refresh your memory," she said. She stood up and took off her sweatshirt.

I said, "Last time you were wearing a bra."

"I got into Women's Lib a little last spring. I decided they were generally full of shit, but they're right about bras. Do you think I need one?"

"No."

She kicked off her sandals, unfastened her dungarees. "You've still got all your clothes on," she pointed out.

"Hallie, we don't have to. Honestly."

"Don't you want to?"

"Yeah, but I don't think you do."

"Would I do it if I didn't want to?"

I looked into those big eyes. "You might," I said. "You might just because you thought you should."

"I really want to, Chip."

"Come here."

I kissed her and felt her breasts against my chest. For some reason or other I felt like crying. I kissed her again and let her go, and she took her dungarees off and I started to get out of my clothes.

We made love.

She had her eyes closed. I put my hand on her stomach. She was shiny with sweat.

After a while I said, "Tell me about it."

"Huh?"

"What went wrong?"

"Huh?" Her eyes opened. "Nothing went wrong. I had an orgasm."

"I know."

"So?"

"So you weren't really there. You were somewhere else

303

and it wasn't right."

"Oh, wow."

"Or else I'm a little flaky, which is possible."

"No."

"I'm right, then."

"Yeah. Shit."

"What's the matter?"

She turned away. "I didn't think you would be able to tell. I guess that was pretty stupid, thinking that. I'm sorry, Chip."

"There's nothing to be sorry about."

"Yes there is. The thing is, oh, I don't know—"

I waited.

"The only way is to say it. I have an old man."

For a minute I thought she meant her father. I had spent the past nine months with people who were several years behind on their slang. Then I realized what she meant and I said, "Oh. A guy."

"Uh-huh."

"Well, I figured you would be seeing guys. And the rest of it, as far as that goes."

(This was a lie. Not that I had ever expected that Hallie would be sitting up in Wisconsin saving herself for me. But I just managed never to think about her with anybody else. I don't much like to think about it now, if you want to know.)

"I'm sort of involved with him."

"In a heavy way?"

"Kind of heavy, yeah."

"Oh."

"Like we're living together."

"Oh." Why did I suddenly feel as though I was dying? "For very long?"

"Well, we were sort of together starting in April, but not actually living together. And he was in New York for the summer, he lives out on the Island, and we saw each other a few times during the summer, and when we came back to campus we started, uh, living together."

"In your room?"

"No. He has this apartment off campus. I keep some of my clothes and things at my room because there isn't much space at his place. But I sleep there, and cook meals and like that."

"Oh."

"I don't think it's a forever thing or anything, but, oh, I dig him, you know, and it's very much what I'm into right now."

"Sure."

She turned to me. There were tears running out of her eyes but she wasn't really crying, and the tears never got anywhere near her voice.

She said, "I'm really a bitch. I should have told you out in front and we never should have balled. Maybe all I really am is a cunt."

"Don't talk like that."

"I just don't want you to hate me and you've got every right in the world."

"Why should I hate you? I love you, why the hell should I hate you?"

"Oh, *shit*," she said, and this time she let go and cried.

Epilogue

October 17, 1970
Miss Geraldine Simms
c/o The Lighthouse
Bordentown, South Carolina

Dear Geraldine:

Awhile ago I sent you a copy of a book I wrote called *No Score*. I hope you got it, because otherwise this won't make too much sense. Or maybe it will—it seems to me I told you most of what happened in *No Score* at one time or another.

Anyway, along with this letter I'm sending you the carbon copy of another book I wrote. I just finished it. In fact I haven't finished it yet, I'm finishing it right now.

If you read *No Score*, you may remember that there was an Epilogue at the end that told what happened to me after the actual story of the book ended. I decided the other day that this book ought to have an Epilogue also and I couldn't decide exactly how to do it. While I was trying to work it out in my head I also decided I wanted to write you a letter, and I thought about it some more and decided that, in a sense, this whole book was a letter to you. So I'm killing two stones with one bird.

What I hope you'll do now, Geraldine, is read the carbon of the book all the way through and then come back to the letter.

Did you go back and read the carbon copy? Thanks. And if you didn't, I forgive you. I never heard of a letter with an intermission before.

After Hallie said *Oh, shit* and started crying, that was about it. Of course in books it can just end like that (which is why I ended it like that) and in life it can't, because the two people are stuck there in the room and, unless the boiler blows up and kills them all, they still have certain dumb unimportant things they have to say to each other, like while they're putting on their clothes.

Just as an example:

"You know, Chip, you would really like him. I mean it, you ought to meet him sometime."

"No way."

"No way you could like him or no way you could meet him?"

"Right both times."

"Yeah."

That kind of dialogue, Geraldine. It was tons of fun, believe me. I had a wonderful time.

Then I drove her back to her dormitory, and then she insisted that I wait while she got the copy of my book so I could autograph it for her. I wanted to drive away but I also wanted to see her again.

I won't tell you what I wrote in the book. I wrote something, and closed the book, and told her not to read it until later. She nodded.

"Well," I said.

"Chip."

"What?"

"Write to me."

"Should I?"

"And this time put a return address."

"Really? All right, sure."

"Chip? It was the timing, I think. I mean, oh, you know what I mean."

"Sure."

"I mean, people like us, we'll probably run into each other again."

"We probably will."

There was more but that's enough. I went back to the motel and packed because all I wanted to do was drive away from there, though I was afraid to trust myself on the road. But I couldn't sleep either.

I thought about getting drunk but if you were between eighteen and twenty-one all they would serve you was beer. I was a couple of days short of nineteen but my ID said I was a couple of days short of eighteen. Maybe they would have served me beer anyway. I didn't really care because I didn't think I could get drunk enough on beer, not the way I felt.

Do you remember the glass of corn whiskey you gave me that last night? That's what I really wanted.

I sat around there for a while feeling numb and empty and lost and alone. I had never felt this alone before because there had always been Hallie somewhere in the distance, and now there wasn't. It didn't feel good.

Then I remembered my book, *No Score*. I had hardly looked at the copy I signed for Hallie. I left the motel and went to drugstores and bookstores looking for it. It was really weird seeing it on the stands. My name all over the place, on the spine and the cover and at the top of every even-numbered page.

I wanted to buy all the copies they had, but who was I going to give them to? I bought one copy and took it back to my room and read it.

What a strange feeling. Here was this kid talking, and he was me, except he wasn't, because when I talk to myself it's something that happens inside of my head, and this kid was talking on a page. Well, quite a few pages, actually. And he sounded so young. It was just impossible to believe that this punk was me. And just a year ago.

Poor Hallie. It must have been really traumatic to read all that, especially when she had no idea it was coming. I guess on all those postcards I never mentioned anything about writing a book, or that somebody was going to publish it.

I guess the book settled me the way liquor might have. I read it all the way through and then I got undressed again and went right to sleep.

I left Madison early the next morning. I drove east and almost stopped in Chicago but changed my mind at the last moment and took the Belt around the city. I burned a lot of oil but kept stopping for more so that I didn't do any damage to the car. It still runs perfectly, by the way.

I drove all the way to Cleveland. I guess I was ready for a big city again. I put the car in a parking garage and took a hotel room and paid a week in advance. I was in no hurry to go anywhere.

It was easy to find things to do. I would go to a movie and when it ended I would go to another one. I bought paperbacks and read them. Sometimes they seemed to be sending me special messages. I would find great personal meaning in very ordinary things. But I recognized this as just a temporary mild madness and let it pass.

That's the thing. You don't outgrow that kind of garbage, but you learn to see it coming. Maybe growing up is largely a matter of being surprised by fewer things.

Everywhere I went I would see copies of my book. I wanted to tell people I wrote it, but who was I going to tell? I sent you a copy (which I really hope you got) and I sent a copy to the Headmaster of Upper Valley, the asshole who threw me out. I told what a fink he was in the book and I wanted him to read about it.

I couldn't think of anyone else.

Then one day I was looking at ads for jobs, and I could find some things that I probably could do, but I didn't want to do any of them. And I said, Wait a minute, I'm a published author.

I think that's the first time it occurred to me to write another book. I spent a day or two trying to work out a novel but every idea I came up with was corny, and then I thought maybe I could do the same thing I did in *No Score* and just continue that story. I didn't know if the material would be as good, though. It seemed to me when I read it that *No Score* was pretty funny, and my memories of the past year weren't.

I guess that brings it all up to date. I bought a typewriter in a pawn shop and got some paper and started writing. At least this time I knew about keeping a carbon.

The book got written faster than I thought it would.

Well, that's about it. Now I'll drive to New York and let Mr. Fultz look at this. I could sell the car and fly there, I suppose, but I don't like the idea of selling the car. Because you gave it to me.

Geraldine, I read through all of this and it feels very funny. All those changes. There are things I wonder about and can't know, like what happened with Lucille, whether she was really pregnant, whether she had an abortion or had the baby, whether she put it up for adoption or decided to keep it. I have this persistent fantasy in which she keeps the baby as a memento of her dead lover. That would probably be the worst thing for everybody, but evidently my ego gets a boost out of it.

One thing that's bad is that I still can't get away from the idea that sooner or later Hallie and I are going to wind up together. I suppose I'm fooling myself but I can't get it out of my head.

I don't know what comes next, but you never do, do you? Just one damned thing after another. Thanks for suffering through this. It's a pretty funny letter, but then the whole thing adds up to a pretty funny book.

I was just looking at *No Score* to see how I ended it, and it went like this:

I hate it when the author steps in at the end of the book and tells you what it was all about. Either you find it out for yourself or it's not worth knowing about. So I'll just say goodbye and thanks for reading this, and I'm sorry it wasn't better than it was.

That makes a good ending for the book. And for the letter, too.

Love,
Chip

Make Out With Murder

Chapter One

THE MAN WAS ABOUT FORTY OR FORTY-FIVE. I guessed his height at five-seven, which made him about four inches too short for his weight. He was wearing a brown suit, one of those double-knit deals that are not supposed to wrinkle. His was sort of rumpled. He was wearing gleaming brown wing-tip shoes and chocolate-brown socks. He wore a ring on his left pinky with what looked like a sapphire in it. Anyway, it was a blue stone, and I figure any blue stone is either a sapphire or trying to look like one.

I don't know all this because I have some kind of terrific memory or anything. I know it because I wrote it all down. Leo Haig says that ultimately I won't have to write things down in my notebook. He says I can train my memory to report all conversations verbatim and remember photographically what people are wearing and things like that. He says if Archie Goodwin can do it, so can I. It's a matter of training, he says.

Maybe he's right. I don't know. If so, I need all the training I can get. I figure it's going to be a good day if I remember in the morning where I put my wristwatch the night before.

Anyway, there's something we'd better get straight right in front. In the course of writing all this up for you, some of the facts will be as I've jotted them down in my notebook, and some will be as I happen to remember them, and things like conversations are as close as my memory can make them to how they happened originally. I don't have a tape recorder in my head, but I do tend to listen to people and remember not only what they said but how they said it. I suppose that's as close to the truth as you can generally come.

The guy in the brown suit was very boring to follow. I picked him up outside of the Gaily Gaily Theater on Eighth

Avenue between 45th and 46th. That was 1:37 in the afternoon, and the particular afternoon was the third Wednesday in August. He emerged from the theater (All-Male Cast! XXX-rated! Adults Only Positively!) making those hesitant eye movements that you would expect anybody to make under those circumstances, as if he wanted to make sure that nobody he knew was watching him, but without making it obvious that he was looking around.

I picked him up because I liked the idea that he was already behaving with suspicion. It seemed likely that he would be more of a challenge.

See, I had no real reason to follow this man in particular. This was what Leo Haig calls a training exercise. We didn't have a case at the time, and while he enjoyed having me hang around and listen to him talk while he played with his tropical fish, we both eventually felt guilty if I wasn't doing something to earn the salary he paid me. So he sent me out to follow people. I would do this for as many hours as I could stand, and then I would go back and type up a report on my activities as a shadow. He would then read the report very critically. (I'm surprised he managed to read these reports at all, to tell you the truth. When all you do is follow a woman from her apartment building to Gristede's and back again, there is not a hell of a lot of excitement in a detailed report of what you have seen.)

But all of this would develop my powers of observation, he said, plus my skills in following people, in case we got a case that demanded that sort of thing. And it would also point up my journalistic talents. Leo Haig is very firm on this last subject, incidentally. It's not enough to be a great detective, he says, unless somebody writes about it well enough to let the world know about you.

Well, the guy in the brown suit certainly moved around enough. From the theater he went to a cafeteria on Broadway and had a cup of coffee and a prune Danish. I sat half a dozen tables away and pretended to drink my iced tea. He left the cafeteria and walked around the corner onto 42nd

Street, where he entered First Amendment Books, a hole-in-the-wall that specializes in reading matter that abuses the amendment it's named after. I don't know what he bought there because I didn't want to go in there after him. I loitered outside, trying not to look like a male hustler. By concentrating on Melanie Trelawney, I figured it might be easier to project a determinedly heterosexual image.

Thinking about Melanie Trelawney may not have made me *look* more heterosexual, but it certainly made me *feel* heterosexual as all hell. And thinking about Melanie came fairly easily to me because I had been thinking of very little else for the past month. In a sense, thinking about Melanie was more rewarding than spending time with her, because I allowed myself to play a more active role in thought than I did in life itself.

In the little plays I acted out in my head, for example, Melanie did not deliver lines like, "I think we should wait until we know each other better, Chip." Or, "I'm just not sure I'm stable enough for an active sexual relationship." Or, "Stop!"

My mental Melanie, my liberated, receptive Melanie was purring like a kitten while I stroked the soft skin of her upper thigh, when the man in the brown suit picked that moment to emerge from First Amendment with a parcel under his arm. Magazines, by the size and shape of the parcel. I had a fair idea what kind of magazines they were.

He headed west and walked briskly to Eighth Avenue. Just before he reached the corner he stopped in a doorway and talked to a tall slender young man wearing faded jeans and brand-new cowboy boots. They talked for a few moments and evidently failed to come to an agreement. My target heaved his shoulders and lurched away, and the kid with the boots gave him the finger.

On the other side of Eighth he had better luck. He stopped again in a doorway, and I loitered as unobtrusively as possible while they got it together.

Then they walked side by side over to Ninth Avenue

and two blocks north to something that was supposed to be a hotel. That's what the sign said, anyhow. From the looks of it I got the feeling that if you ever needed a cockroach in a hurry, that was the place to look for one.

There was a liquor store next to the hotel, and they stopped there first, with the hustler waiting outside while Brown Suit bought a bottle. He came out with a pint of something and they went into the hotel together.

I was going to leave him there and say the hell with it, and either follow somebody else or call it a day, but Haig had told me just a couple of days ago that the attribute of a successful surveillance man most difficult to develop was patience. "You must cultivate *sitzfleisch*, Chip. Sitting flesh. A mark of professionalism is the ability to do absolutely nothing when to do otherwise would be an improper course of action."

I went into a coffee shop across the street and settled my *sitzfleisch* on a wobbly counter stool. The special of the day was meat loaf, which suggested that the activity of the night before had been sweeping the floor. I had a glazed doughnut and a lot of weak coffee, and concentrated on developing the ability to do absolutely nothing.

While I worked on this I did a little more thinking about Melanie Trelawney.

I had met her about a month ago. I was in Tompkins Square Park trying to decide whether or not I wanted a Good Humor. The Special Flavor of the Month was Chocolate Pastrami and I wasn't sure I could handle it, but it did sound off the beaten track. Somebody came by that I knew, and then someone else materialized with a guitar, and eventually a batch of us were sitting around singing songs of social significance. After a while somebody started passing out home-made cigarettes with an organic and non-carcinogenic tobacco substitute in them, but I just passed them up, because by this time I had seen Melanie and I was high already.

We got to talking. Nine times out of ten when I meet a really sensational girl it takes an exchange of perhaps fourteen sentences before one or both of us realizes we could easily bore each other to death. Sometimes, say one time in ten, it doesn't happen that way. In which case I tend to flip out a little.

I'll tell you something. Sometimes when two people meet each other, the best thing that can happen is that they go directly to the nearest bed. Other times the best thing can happen is that they take their time and really get to know each other first. Either way is cool. The problem comes when the two people perceive the situation differently.

Not that she was precisely driving me up a wall. There were times when it felt that way, I'll admit, but basically it was a question of Melanie's feeling it was very necessary for us to take our time, while I felt that all the time we had to take was whatever time it took to get out of our clothes. Since Melanie always wore jeans and a tie-dyed top and sandals, and nothing under any of those three articles of clothing but her own sweet self, and since I was sufficiently motivated to take off my shirt without unbuttoning it, this process would not have taken much time.

It probably wasn't as bad as I'm making it sound. I mean, I'm not Stanley Stud who has to have a woman every night or his thing will turn green. I *want* a woman every night, but I've learned to live with failure. We were getting to know each other, Melanie and I, and we were getting to know each other slightly in a physical way, and eventually things were going to work out. Until then I wasn't sleeping very well, but I had decided I could put up with that.

I sat at the counter and stirred my coffee, trying to convince myself that I wanted to drink it. Every few seconds I would glance out through the window to see if the man in the brown suit was finished and ready to lead me off to still more exciting places. Every once in a while someone with the same general orientation as Brown Suit would give me a sidelong glance. Which made me think defensively again of Melanie.

One thing had been bothering me lately. I couldn't escape the feeling that Melanie might be a little bit out of touch with reality.

For maybe the past ten days she had been behaving strangely. She would laugh suddenly at nothing at all, and then a few minutes later she would start crying and not say what it was about. And then a couple of days earlier she explained what it was. She was convinced she was going to die.

"Two of my sisters are already gone," she said. "First Robin was killed in a car accident. Then Jessica threw herself out the window. There's just three of us left, Caitlin and Kim and me, and then we'll all be gone."

"In seventy years, maybe. But not like tomorrow, Melanie."

"Maybe tomorrow, Chip."

"I think maybe you do drugs a little too much."

"It's not drugs. Anyway, I'm straight now."

"Then I don't get it."

Her eyes, which range from blue to green and back again, were a very vivid blue now. "I am going to be killed," she said. "I can sense it."

"What do you mean?"

"Just what I said. Robin and Jessica were killed—"

"Well, Jessica killed herself, didn't she?"

"Did she?"

"Jesus, Melanie, that's what you just said, isn't it? You said she threw herself out a window."

"Maybe she did. Maybe she…she was pushed."

"Oh, wow!"

She lowered her head, closed her eyes. "Oh, I don't know what I'm talking about. I don't know anything, Chip. All I know is the feelings I've had lately. That all of the Trelawney girls are going to die and that I'm going to be next. Maybe Robin's accident really was an accident. Maybe Jessica did kill herself. She wasn't terribly stable, she had a weird lifestyle. And maybe Robin's accident really was an accident. I know it must have been. But—I'm *afraid*, Chip."

I saw her a couple of times after that, and she was never that hysterical again. She did mention the subject, though. She tried to be cool about it.

"Well, like it's a good thing you're working for a private detective, Chip. That way you can investigate the case when I'm murdered."

I would tell her to cut the shit, that she was not going to be murdered, and she would say she was just making a joke out of it. Except it was only partly a joke.

I guess that coffee shop wasn't the best place to pick for a stake-out. Not just because the coffee was rotten, but because the clientele was largely gay.

Which is all right as far as I'm concerned. I don't get uncomfortable in homosexual company. I have a couple of gay friends, as far as that goes. But the thing is this: if you sit in a place like that, just killing time over a cup of coffee, and if you're young and tallish and thinnish, which is to say the general physical type which is likely to hang out in such a place for a particular purpose, well, people come to an obvious conclusion.

It was getting a little heavy, so I paid for my coffee and went out to wait outside. I guess that turned out to be worse. I wasn't outside for five minutes before a heavy-set man with a slim attaché case and a neatly trimmed white moustache asked me if he could buy me a drink.

I took my wallet out and flipped it open briefly.

"Police," I said. "Surveillance," I said. "Scram," I said.

"Oh, dear," the man said.

"Just go away," I said.

"I didn't actually do anything," the man said. "Just an offer of a drink, all in good faith—"

"Jesus, go away," I said.

"I'm not under arrest?"

Across the street, the man in the brown suit emerged

323

from the hotel. He still had his package of magazines with him. I told the idiot with the moustache that he was not under arrest, but that he would be if he didn't piss off.

"You're not Vice Squad?"

"Narcotics," I said, trying to get past him.

"But you should be on the Vice Squad," he insisted. "You'd fool anyone."

I've decided since that he must have intended this as a compliment. At the time I couldn't pay that much attention to what he was saying because Brown Suit was on his way into a subway kiosk and I had to hurry if I didn't want to lose him. It occurred to me that perhaps I did want to lose him, but I wanted to get away from the creep with the moustache in any case, so I charged down to the subway entrance and caught sight of the man in brown just as I dropped my own token into the turnstile. Actually, it was his turn to follow me for the next little bit, because he had to buy a token. I always have a pocket full of them. Leo Haig believes his right-hand man should be prepared for any contingency.

I bought a paper to give myself something to hide behind and to kill time so that he could let me know which train we were going to ride. It turned out to be the downtown A train and we rode it to Washington Square. Then we went up and around and caught the E train as far as Long Island City. This puzzled me a little because he could have caught that same E train at 42nd Street and saved going out of the way a couple of miles, but I figured maybe he changed his mind and had some particular last-minute reason to go out to Queens.

At Long Island City he got out of the train just as the doors were closing, and if I hadn't been standing right next to the door at the time I would have gone on riding to Flushing or someplace weird like that. But I got out, and I immediately began walking off in the opposite direction from him. After I had gone about twenty yards I turned and looked over my shoulder and there he was. I started to turn again, but he was making motions with his hands.

I just stood there. I didn't really know what else to do.

"Look," he said. "This is beginning to get on my nerves."

"Huh?"

"You've been following me all afternoon, son. Would you like to tell me why?"

Leo Haig always tells me to use my instinct, guided by my experience. He stole this bit of advice from Nero Wolfe. My problem is, I haven't had too much experience and my instincts aren't always that razor-sharp.

But what I said was, "I have to say something to you."

"Well, you could have said it back on Ninth Avenue, son. You didn't have to wait until we both rode back and forth underneath Manhattan Island."

"The thing is, I don't know if you're the right man."

"What right man?"

"The married man who's been running around with my sister, and if you are—"

Well, he damned well wasn't, and that was a load off both our minds. He laughed a lot, and he did everything but explain to me precisely why he was extremely unlikely to be running around with anybody's sister, or to be married, and we went our separate ways to our mutual relief. I got another E train heading back in the direction I'd come from and he went somewhere else.

At least he hadn't made me until I'd tailed him to Ninth Avenue. I suppose that was something.

There's probably a good way to connect from the E train to something that goes somewhere near the Lower East Side, but I'm still not brilliant about the subway system and the maps they have there are impossible to figure out, especially when the train is (a) moving and (b) crowded, which this one certainly was. So I rode down to Washington Square again, feeling a little foolish about the whole thing, and then I got out and walked cross-town. I called Melanie a couple of times en route, but the line was busy.

Melanie's place was on Fifth Street between Avenue C and Avenue D. I could never figure out why. I mean, I could figure out why the building was there. It had no choice. Buildings tend to stay where you put them, and nobody would have allowed this building in a decent neighborhood anyway. But Melanie did have a choice. She wasn't wildly rich, and I don't suppose she could have stayed at the Sherry Netherland, but she could have had a better apartment in a safer neighborhood with the income she got from her father's estate. Instead she lived on one of the most squalid and unsafe blocks in the city.

"You know," I'd told her a day or two ago, "if you really insist on having this irrational fear of being murdered, you ought to move out of this rathole. Because when you live here, being murdered isn't an irrational fear. It's a damned rational one."

"I feel secure here," she said.

"The streets are wall-to-wall junkies and perverts," I said. "The muggers have their own assigned territories so they don't mug each other by mistake. What makes you feel secure?"

"It's a settled neighborhood, Chip."

I walked through it now. It was at its very worst in the afternoon because the light was bright enough to see how grungy it was. It was also bright in the morning, but there was no one around. Starting a little after noon, the rats would begin to peep out of their holes.

I got to her building. They still hadn't replaced the front door. No one knew who had taken it, or why.

I walked up four very steep flights of stairs and knocked on her door.

There was no answer.

I knocked a couple more times, called her name a lot, and then tried the door. It was locked, and that worried me.

See, Melanie would only lock her door when she was home. I know most people do it the other way around, or

326

else lock it all the time, but she had a theory on the subject. If a junkie burglar knew she wasn't home, and found the door locked, he would simply kick it in. This would mean she would have to pay for a new lock. If, however, she left it unlocked, he would come in, discover there was nothing around to take, and finally settle for ripping off her radio. Since the radio had cost fifteen dollars and the big cylinder lock had cost forty, it was clear where the priorities lay.

I knocked again, a lot louder. She would not be asleep at this hour. And her telephone had been busy just a few minutes ago. Of course telephones in New York are capable of being busy just for the hell of it, but—I got this sudden flash and didn't like it at all. So I did something I've wanted to do for years. I think it's something everybody secretly wants to do.

I kicked the door in.

You'd be surprised how easy that is. Or maybe you wouldn't when you stop to think that some of the most decrepit drug addicts in the world do it a couple of times a day. I hauled back and kicked with my heel, hitting the door right on the lock. On the third try the door flew open and the forty-dollar lock went flying, and I lost my balance and sat down without having planned to. I suppose a few tenants heard me do all these things, but they evidently knew better than to get involved.

The apartment was a rabbit warren, a big living room and a long hallway that kept leading to other rooms, some of them containing Salvation Army reject furniture, some of them papered with posters of Che and stuff like that. Actually I think Melanie paid as much rent for the place as I paid for a room in a decent neighborhood. She said she liked having plenty of space. Personally, considering the condition of the rooms, I would think that a person would pay more for less space. One room in that building would have been bad enough. Five rooms was ridiculous.

The telephone was in the living room. It was off the hook. I worked my way through the apartment, calling out her name, picking up more and more negative vibrations and getting less and less happy about the whole thing.

I found her in the back room. She was spread out stark naked on her air mattress, which is just how I had always hoped to find her.

But she was also absolutely dead, and that was not what I had had in mind at all.

Chapter Two

SHE WASN'T THE FIRST CORPSE I HAD EVER SEEN. One summer I picked apples for a while in upstate New York, a job which consisted largely of falling off ladders. The other pickers would go out drinking when they were done, and sometimes I would tag along. There was usually at least one fight an evening. Sometimes somebody would pull a knife, and one time when this happened it wound up that one guy, a wiry man with a harelip, caught a knife-blade in his heart and died. I saw him when they carried him out.

The first book I wrote, I covered my experiences apple-picking, but never put that part in. God knows why.

So she wasn't the first corpse I ever looked at, but she might as well have been. I kept thinking how horrible it was that she looked so beautiful, even in death. Her pale white skin had a blue tint to it, especially in her face. Her eyes were wide open and I could swear they were staring at me.

I knew she was dead. No living eyes ever looked like that. But I had to reach down and touch her. I put one hand on her shoulder. She'd been dead long enough to grow cool, however long that takes. I don't know much about things like that. I'd never had to.

I almost didn't see the hypodermic needle. She was on her back, legs stretched out in front of her, one arm at her side, the other placed so that her hand was on her little bowl of a stomach. That hand almost covered the hypodermic needle. After I saw it, I picked up her other arm and found a needle mark. Just one, and it looked fresh.

I put her arm back the way I had found it. I went to the bathroom and threw up and came back and looked at her some more. I must have stood there staring at her for five minutes. Then I paced around the whole apartment for another five minutes and came back and stared at her some more.

This wasn't shock. I was in shock, of course, but I was being very methodical about this. I wanted to notice everything and I wanted to make sure I remembered whatever I noticed.

I left her apartment, closed the door, walked down the stairs and out. I walked all the way over to First Avenue before I caught a cab. The cab dropped me at 14th Street and Seventh. I walked quickly from there to my rooming house on 18th Street, a few doors west of Eighth.

When I was in my own room on the third floor, the first thing I did was lock the door. The second thing was to go into the bathroom and remove the towel bar from the wall. It's a hollow stainless steel bar, and there was a little plastic vial in it that contained several dollars' worth of reasonably good grass. I poured the grass in the toilet and flushed, rinsed out the vial, and tossed it out the window. Then I went through the medicine cabinet. I couldn't find anything to worry about except for a few codeine pills that my doctor had prescribed for a sinus headache. I thought about it and decided to hell with them, and I flushed them away, too. That left nothing but aspirin and Dristan, and I didn't think the cops would hassle me much for either of those. I put the towel bar back and washed my hands.

I looked in the mirror and decided I didn't like the way I was dressed. I put on a fresh shirt and a pair of slacks that didn't need pressing too badly. I traded in my loafers for my black dress shoes.

Then I went downstairs to the payphone in the hall. I dropped a dime in the slot and dialed the number I know best.

Haig answered the telephone himself for a change. We talked for a few minutes. Mostly I talked and he listened, and then he made a couple of suggestions, and I hung up the phone and went off to discover the body.

I guess I'll have to tell you something about Leo Haig.

The place to start, I suppose, is how I happen to be working for him. I had been looking for a job for a while, and things had not been going particularly well. I got work from time to time, washing dishes or bussing tables or delivering messages and parcels, but none of these positions amounted to what you might call A Job With A Future, which is what I have always been seeking, though in a sort of inept way.

My problem, really, was that I wasn't qualified for anything too dynamic. My education stopped a couple of months before graduation from Upper Valley Preparatory Academy, which is to say that I haven't even got a high school diploma, for Pete's sake. And my previous work experience—well, when you tell a prospective employer that you have been an assistant to Gregor the Pavement Photographer, a termite salesman, a fruit picker, and a deputy Sheriff in a whorehouse in South Carolina, well, what usually happens is his eyes glaze and he points at the door a lot.

(I don't want to go into all this ancient history now, really, but if you're interested you could read about it. My first two books, *No Score* and *Chip Harrison Scores Again*, pretty well cover the territory. I don't know that they're much good, but you could read them for background information or something. Assuming you care.)

Anyway, I was living in New York and doing the hand-to-mouth number and reading the want ads in *The Times*, and there were loads of opportunities to earn $40 a week if you had a doctorate in chemical engineering or something like that, but not much if you didn't. Then I ran into an ad that went something like this:

> RESOURCEFUL YOUTH wanted to
> assist detective. Low pay, long hours,
> hard work, demanding employer.
> Journalistic experience will be given
> special consideration. Familiarity with

tropical fish helpful but not absolutely
necessary. An excellent opportunity for
one man in a million....

I didn't know if I was one man in a million, but it was
certainly one advertisement in a million, and nothing could
have kept me from answering it. I called the number listed
in the ad and answered a few questions over the phone.
He gave me an address and I went to it, and at first I thought
the whole thing was someone's idea of a joke, because the
building was obviously a whorehouse. But it turned out
that only the lower two floors were a whorehouse. The
upper two floors were the office and living quarters of Leo
Haig.

He wasn't what I expected. I don't know exactly what I
expected, but whatever it might have been, he wasn't it.
He's about five-two and very round. It's not that he's terribly
heavy, just that the combination of his height and girth
makes him look something like a beachball. He has a head
of wiry black hair and a pointed black goatee with a few
gray hairs in it. That beard is very important to him. I've
never seen it when it was not trimmed and groomed to
perfection. He touches it a lot, smoothing and shaping it.
He says it's an aid to thought.

I spent three hours with him that first day, and at the
end of the three hours I had a job. He spent the first hour
pumping me, the second showing off his tropical fish, and
the final hour talking about everything in the world,
himself included. I went out of there with a lot more
knowledge than I had brought with me, A Job With A
Future, and a whole lot of uncertainty about the man I was
working for. He was either a genius or a lunatic and I
couldn't make up my mind which.

I still haven't got it all worked out. I mean, maybe the
two are not mutually exclusive. Maybe he's a genius *and* a
lunatic.

The thing is, the main reason I got the job was that I had

had two books published. You may wonder what this has to do with being the assistant of a private detective. It's very simple, really. Leo Haig isn't content with being the world's greatest detective. He wants the world to know it.

"There are a handful of detectives whose names are household words," he told me. "Sherlock Holmes. Nero Wolfe. Their brilliance alone would not have guaranteed them fame. It took the efforts of other men to bring their deeds to public attention. Holmes had his Watson. Wolfe has his Archie Goodwin. If a detective is to make the big time, a trustworthy associate with literary talent is as much a prerequisite as a personality quirk and an eccentric hobby."

Here's something I have to explain to you if you are going to understand Leo Haig at all.

He believes Nero Wolfe exists.

He really believes this. He believes Wolfe exists in the brownstone, with the orchids and Theodore and Fritz and all the rest of it, and Archie Goodwin assists him and writes up the cases and publishes them under the pen name of Rex Stout.

"The most telling piece of evidence, Chip. Consider that *nom de plume*, if you will. And of course it's just that; no one was ever born with so contrived a name as Rex Stout. But let us examine it. Rex is the Latin for king, of course. As in *Oedipus Rex*. And Stout means, well, fat. Thus we have what? A fat king—and could one ask for a more perfect appellation to hang upon such an extraordinary example of corpulence and majesty as Nero Wolfe?"

Haig hasn't always been a detective. Actually he's only been a detective about a year longer than I've been an assistant detective. Until that time he lived in a two-room apartment in the Bronx and raised tropical fish to sell to local pet shops. This may strike you as a hard way to make a living. You'd be right. Most tropical fish are pretty inexpensive when you buy them from the pet shop, and even that price has to be three or four times what the shopkeeper pays for them, because he has to worry about a certain percentage of them dying before he can get them sold. Haig had developed a particularly good strain of velvet swordtails—the color was deeper than usual, or something—and he had a ready market for most of the other fish he raised as well, but he was not getting rich this way.

The way he got rich took relatively little effort on his part. His uncle died and left him $128,000.

As you can probably imagine, that made quite a difference in his life. Because all of a sudden he didn't have to run around New York with plastic bags full of little fishes for sale. He could do what he had always dreamed of doing. He could become the World's Greatest Detective.

Raising fish had been Leo Haig's only way to make a living, but it had not been his only interest. He has what is probably the largest library of mystery and detective fiction in the world. I think he has just about everything ever written on the subject. The Nero Wolfe novels, from *Fer-De-Lance* to the latest one, are all in hardcover; after he received his inheritance he had them all rebound in hand-tooled leather. He's been reading all of these things since he was a kid, and he remembers what he reads. I mean, he can tell you not only the plot, but the names of all the characters in some Ngaio Marsh mystery that he read fifteen years ago. It's pretty impressive, let me tell you.

The house is pretty impressive, too, and he has emphasized that he wants me to write about the house, but I'll wait until I come to the part about going there and then I'll describe it for you. I'll just say now that he picked it when he had collected his inheritance and started to set up shop as a detective. He moved in with his books and fish tanks, he managed to get a license as a private investigator, he listed himself in the Yellow Pages, and he sat back and waited for the world to discover him.

The trouble is that he's too rich and he's not rich enough.

If he had more money, like a couple of million, it wouldn't matter if he ever worked or not. If he had less money, like nothing substantial in the checking account, it would mean that he'd have to take the few cases that come his way. But he's got just enough money to let him maintain high standards. He won't touch divorce work, for example. He won't do any sort of snooping that requires electronic gear, which he regards as the handtools of the devil. And he won't accept anything routine. What he wants, really, is to handle nothing but baffling murder cases that he can solve through the exercise of his incredible brain, with the faithful Chip Harrison doing the legwork and writing up everything afterwards.

I know his secret hope. Someday, if he makes enough of a name for himself, if he keeps his standards high, develops just the right sort of eccentricities and idiosyncrasies, possibly someday Nero Wolfe will invite him over to the house on 35th Street for dinner.

That's really what he lives for.

I suppose my civic duty called upon me to phone the police as soon as I discovered Melanie's body. I'm glad I didn't let my civic duty interfere with my instinct for self-preservation, because it turned out that Detective Gregorio took my towel bar off the wall and checked it out to see if I had drugs stashed in it. That was just about the first place he looked. I'm never keeping anything incriminating in there again, believe me. Pick a place that you figure is the last place the police would think of looking, and that's the *first* place they think of looking. It's the damnedest thing.

But I'm getting ahead of myself. What happened was, I went back to Melanie's place, figuring it was possible that the police had already found her without my help, but they hadn't. I had left a book on the floor so that it would be moved if anybody pushed the door more than a third of the way open, and it was still in its original position, so it seemed unlikely anybody had been in the apartment since I'd left it.

I went on inside, and I had an irrational hope that I had been somehow mistaken and Melanie would turn out to be alive after all, which is pretty stupid to write down and all, but impossible to avoid wishing at the time. Of course she was still there, and of course she was dead, and of course I felt sick all over again, but instead of throwing up any more I went into the living room and called 911.

The person who picked up the phone put me on HOLD before I had a chance to say anything, which would have been aggravating if I'd been bleeding to death or something, but then a couple of seconds later a cop came on the line and I gave him the story. They were fast enough after that. It was 5:18 when I placed the call and the first two patrolmen arrived at 5:31. You would have thought it would take them almost that long to climb the stairs. They spent most of their time walking around and opening drawers and telling me not to touch anything. They were basically waiting for the detectives but they didn't want it to look as though they were waiting for the detectives, so they asked me a lot of boring questions and sneaked a lot of peeks at Melanie's body. This seemed very disrespectful to me, but I didn't think they would care to hear my feelings on the matter so I kept them to myself.

The detectives got there before very long and took over. There was Detective Gregorio, whom I mentioned before, and his partner Detective Seidenwall. Gregorio is tall and dark and handsome, and he has one of those twenty-dollar haircuts, and he didn't like me much. Seidenwall is older, say fifty, and his name is easy to remember because he looks like the side of a wall, and he didn't like me at all.

They both seemed to despise me, to tell you the truth.

The trouble started with my name. They said they wanted a full name, not a nickname, and I explained that Chip was my legal first name, and eventually I had to show identification to prove it. They wanted to know what I was doing in Melanie's apartment and I said she was a friend and had invited me to stop in after work.

"Oh, you work, huh?" said Seidenwall.

"I work for Leo Haig. The detective."

"You mean some kind of a private cop? You on some kind of a case?"

"No. Melanie was my friend."

"Uh-huh. You a junkie too?"

"Of course not."

"Roll up your sleeves, punk."

This struck me as silly, since I was wearing a short-sleeved shirt, but I rolled up what little sleeves I had. Gregorio got a little suspicious over a mosquito bite, but turned his attention to other things. He and Seidenwall asked me approximately seven million questions, many of them consisting of the same ones over again. How long had Melanie been a junkie? How long had I been sleeping with her? Had she died right away, or was it gradual?

This last question was a trap, of course. There were a lot of questions like this, designed to trick me into admitting I had been with her when she died. There were other trick questions, geared to establish that I had sold the heroin to her. They seemed to take it for granted that it was heroin, and she had died of an overdose of it.

The questions went on for a while. They probably would have asked me fewer questions if they hadn't hated me on sight, and they would have gone on hassling me longer except they were bored with the whole thing. It was all pretty obvious to them. Melanie had overdosed herself with heroin and that was why she was dead. When I pointed out that she had never to my knowledge been a drug addict, had never used a needle, they nodded without much enthusiasm and said that made an OD that much more likely. She wouldn't know about the proper dose, for one thing. And she would have had no time to build up a gradual tolerance to the drug. Finally, some people go into something called anaphylactic shock the first time they try certain substances. Penicillin, for some people. Or a bee sting, or heroin.

Anyway, she was dead, and as far as they were concerned it was an accidental drug-related homicide, and they got too many of them to be terribly interested in each new one that came along. So they asked me all their questions and took a short statement from me, and then they asked me for permission to accompany me to my own residence and search the premises, and of course I could have refused because they didn't have a warrant. But they already hated me enough for one day, I figured, and besides I had thrown away not only the illegal marijuana but the legal codeine tablets, so in a way I was almost glad they wanted to search my room. I mean, I'd have felt a little foolish if I had gone through all of that for nothing.

Gregorio and Seidenwall seemed unhappy when they didn't find anything. They held a whispered conversation by the bathroom door, and I caught enough of it to get an idea what it was about. Seidenwall wanted to plant some drugs so they would have an excuse to arrest me. Gregorio talked him out of it, not out of fondness for me, but because he felt I wasn't worth the trouble.

"I'll tell you, Harrison," he said on his way out. "You're the only thing in this that doesn't make sense. Everything else is pretty open and shut. But you don't figure."

"Why?"

"You swear it's not a business thing with the girl. That she's a friend. And then you tell us you've known her for a month and you weren't balling her."

"I wasn't."

"You a faggot?"

"No."

"Everybody knows those hippie chicks go like rabbits. It's what you call common knowledge. But you knew her for a month without getting in her pants. It don't add up."

I didn't say anything.

"Number two. You go to her apartment and find her

dead with a needle in her arm." The needle was not in her arm, but I let it pass. "And what do you do? You call the cops."

"Isn't that what a person is supposed to do?"

"Of course it's what a person is supposed to do. Nobody in this fucking city does what he's supposed to do. Nobody wants to get involved. Nobody wants to call himself to the attention of the police, especially in a drug-related homicide, especially when the person in question is a hippie punk that probably uses drugs himself."

"I don't."

"Yeah, you don't. And you're not a hippie punk either, are you? You're some kind of a cop."

"I work—"

"Yeah, I know. You work for this Haig, who's some kind of a private cop that I never heard of. You're his assistant. What do you assist him with?"

"Cases."

"Uh-huh. I'll tell you one thing, Harrison. I hope this Haig character looks more like a cop than you do. Because you just don't fit the image of a cop, Harrison. Private or otherwise, you're not my idea of a cop."

I pictured Leo Haig and tried to decide which of the two of us looked more like a cop. I gave up thinking about it because it made me feel like giggling and I didn't want to giggle. I had the feeling that one giggle from me was all Seidenwall would need.

I wasn't sleeping with Melanie, I had done my civic duty and called the police, and I didn't look like any kind of a cop. Those were the three things about me that made Gregorio and Seidenwall suspicious. I couldn't quite follow their reasoning on this, but then again I didn't have to.

Suspicious or not, they walked out my door and down the stairs without even telling me not to leave town. So their suspicion was evidently just on general principles, coupled with instinctive dislike.

I suppose they would have given me a much worse time if they'd had the brains to realize Melanie had been murdered.

Chapter Three

"IT WAS DEFINITELY MURDER," I said. "First of all, Melanie would never give herself a shot of heroin. She told me she tried heroin once, she snorted it, and it made her nauseous without giving her any kind of a high at all."

"She might try it a second time."

"She might, but there were too many other things she liked better. And if she did try it again, it wouldn't be with a needle. She's terrified of needles. Some nurse had to give her an injection once and botched it, kept stabbing around trying to find the vein, and she still has nightmares about it. Still *had* nightmares about it. Oh, shit."

"Settle yourself, Chip."

I nodded across the desk at him. It's what they call a partners' desk, with drawers and stuff on both sides so two people can use it. I was on my side of the desk. I was very flattered to have a whole side of a desk to myself, but I really didn't have much of anything to keep in the drawers.

Haig took a pipe out of a little wooden rack on his side of the desk. This was during his pipe period. He had trouble keeping them lit, and they kept burning his mouth. He was convinced that he would sooner or later break a pipe in, and sooner or later find a mild enough tobacco, but in the meantime he was doing his best. He thought pipe-smoking might be good for the image. He took the pipe apart and cleaned it while I settled myself. He never did get around to smoking it that night.

I said, "Another thing. Melanie was extremely careful about that air mattress. You had to take your shoes off before you sat on it, and she would make me check to see if I had anything sharp in my pockets. She was very nervous about puncturing the thing."

Haig nodded. "The syringe."

"Right. Even assuming she decides to take heroin, and even assuming she's going to shoot it, the last place in that apartment she'd pick to use a hypodermic needle is the air mattress."

"You didn't point this out to the police."

"No. I didn't point out anything to them, like telling them how she was afraid she was going to die."

"Perfectly within your rights." He touched his beard, stroked it with love and affection. "A citizen is under no compulsion to volunteer unrequested information to the police. He is merely obliged to answer their questions honestly and completely, and make no false statements."

"Well, I fell down there."

"The lock."

"Right. They asked how I got in and I told them the lock was wrecked a couple of weeks ago in a burglary and she hadn't got around to replacing it yet."

"And of course you didn't tell them you had been there once before."

"No. I, uh, more or less gave them the impression I spent the past four hours with you."

"I think that was wise," he said. "They should have noticed the syringe and the air mattress. That should have been as obvious as a third nostril." He closed his eyes for a moment and his hand worked on his beard. "You should have told me of Miss Trelawney's fear of death."

"What could you have done?"

"Probably nothing. Hmmm. There were five girls altogether, I understand. Five Misses Trelawney."

"That's right. And now three of them are dead."

"And two alive. Are the survivors living here in New York?"

"I don't know. I don't really know anything about them."

"Hmmmm. Perhaps you know more than you think. Melanie must have talked about them."

"Actually, she didn't talk too much about anything. She wasn't very verbal."

He nodded approvingly. "I've never felt loquacity is a

mark of excellence in a woman. Nevertheless, she no doubt mentioned something about the girls who died. Their names, if nothing else."

"Robin and Jessica."

"One died in an auto wreck and the other fell from a window?"

"Yes. Let me think. Jessica went out the window and Robin died in the car accident."

He pursed his lips. At least he did something weird with his lips, and I have never quite known what it is that you do when you purse your lips, but this was probably it. "Let's not call it an accident, Chip," he said. "Let's merely call it a wreck, just as we'll say that Jessica fell from a window, not that she threw herself out."

"You think they were both murdered?"

"I think we ought to take it as a postulate for the time being. And we have to assume that whoever had a motive for murdering three of five sisters is not going to discontinue his activities before he has done for the remaining two into the bargain. Which of the sisters was the first to die?"

I had to think. "Robin first, then Jessica. I don't know about the timing, though. All of this happened before I met Melanie. I have the impression that Jessica died two or three months ago, but I really don't know how long before then Robin died."

He closed his eyes. "That's very interesting," he said.

"What is?"

"First an auto wreck," he said. "Then a fall, then an overdose of heroin. Assuming that an autopsy reveals that was indeed the cause of death. Which would seem a logical assumption at this stage of things. There were no signs of struggle?"

"None that I could see. Uh, in Melanie's apartment, you might say there were always signs of struggle. I mean, she wasn't the world's most fanatical housekeeper."

"But nothing out of the ordinary? And no sign of another

person's presence?"

"No. Except the phone off the hook, of course. I hung up myself after I called the police."

"And neglected to mention to the police that it had been off the hook when you arrived?"

"I felt they would wonder why I happened to notice it."

He nodded. "And they'd resent you for it. It's infinitely simpler for them to process this as an accidental overdose than as a murder, and a loose end like a telephone off the hook would only impress them as a complication. They'd file the case the same way, but they would be annoyed with you for bringing up irrelevancies and inconsistencies. They would have been happiest if you could have told them Melanie had been planning on trying heroin. It's as well you didn't, but that's how any bureaucratic mind works."

He spun around in his swivel chair and gazed into the fish tank at eye level. The entire room, and it is a large one, is paneled in English oak and lined from floor to ceiling with shelves. Most of the shelf space is devoted to books, the overwhelming majority of them detective stories, but fish tanks are spotted here and there on the shelves. There are a dozen of them.

They are all what Haig calls recreational aquariums, as opposed to the breeding tanks and rearing tanks on the top floor. Actually, to tell you the truth, they're what Haig calls recreational *aquaria*. I call them aquariums because I'm not entirely literate yet.

This particular tank was very restful to look at. It was a fifteen-gallon tank, which means it was one foot deep by one foot wide by two feet long, and its sole occupants were eleven *Rasbora heteramorpha*. I have a feeling that you either know what they are or you don't, and a description won't help much, but Haig wants me to make an effort on matters like this. Rasboras are fish about an inch long, a delicate rose pink with a blackish wedge on their sides. They're pretty, and they swim in schools, and in this particular tank they swam in and around a dwarf amazon sword plant and a piece of crystalline quartz. The tank was top-lighted, and if you watched the fish for a while you got a happy feeling.

At least I did. Haig watched the fish for a while and stroked his beard a lot and turned around in the swivel chair with a thoughtful expression on his face.

"How old was Melanie?"

"I don't know. A little older than me. I guess about twenty-one."

"And Jessica?"

"Older, but I don't know by how much. Wait a minute. Melanie was the second youngest. And Robin was older than she was, so one of the girls still alive is younger than Melanie."

"Were any of them married?"

"Yes, but I don't know which ones. Obviously Melanie wasn't married." And never would be, I thought, and something vaguely resembling a lump formed in my throat, but I swallowed and it went away.

Haig said, "Hmmmmmm." He turned and looked at the rasboras some more. I watched him do this for a while and saw that it was going to be an extensive thing, so I got up and went over to the wall and looked at some fish myself. A pair of African gouramis, two very beautiful fish, rendered in shades of chocolate. I'm not putting down the Latin name, because there's no agreement on it yet; the species was just discovered a couple years ago and has never been bred in captivity, a state of affairs which Leo Haig regards as a personal challenge. I stared into the tank and decided that I had never seen two living creatures display less interest in each other. We will breed the damned things sooner or later, but we were not going to accomplish it that particular evening.

Nor were we going to accomplish much else. Haig swung around and said as much. "*Sitzfleisch*," was how he put it. "We have to let the newspapers do some of our work

345

for us, and then you can go to the public library and do some of the rest. At the moment the library is closed and the newspaper has not yet materialized, so we exercise our sitting flesh. Get the chessboard."

I got the chessboard. I didn't much want to get the chessboard, but I could see no way out of it. Leo Haig was about as effective at chess as he was at smoking a pipe. Whenever there was nothing to do he was apt to want to play. I'm not very good myself. When I worked in the whorehouse in South Carolina, most of my job consisted of playing chess with Geraldine. She almost always beat me, and I in turn almost always beat Leo Haig.

We played three quick games, and they went as they usually did. I exchanged a knight for a rook in the first game and wore him down, and in the second I put a strong queen-side attack together and more or less lucked into a mating combination. In the last game he left his queen *en prise*, and when I pointed it out to him he tipped his king over and resigned gracefully.

"I've a feeling," he said, "that I shall never be a satisfactory chess player."

I didn't want to argue and knew better than to agree.

"I don't think the character tag of being a hopeless chess player will endear me to the reading public," he continued.

I still didn't say anything.

"We shall pursue this a bit further," he went on. "But I think we must ultimately find another sport. In your spare moments, Chip, you might compile a list of sedentary sports requiring a certain degree of mental dexterity."

We had coffee together, and then he went upstairs to discuss chess openings with the upstairs fish. I wandered into the front room and played a quick game of backgammon with Wong. He said, "Ah, so," a lot, which I think is why Haig hired him, and he beat the hell out of me. Then I went downstairs and around the corner for a beer.

Leo Haig's house is on West 20th Street between Eighth

and Ninth Avenues, which puts it just two blocks away from my rooming house. (Which is why I selected the rooming house in the first place; before I went to work for Haig I was living on the Upper West Side, near Columbia University.) I promised I would tell you about Haig's house, and I guess now is as good a time as any.

The address is 311½ West 20th, and the ½ is because it does not front on the street. There's a house out in front, and there's an alley next to it, and if you buzz the buzzer a door opens and you can walk down the alley to the house in back, which is half Leo Haig's and half a whorehouse. It started off life as a carriage house. Many years ago, rich people lived in the house on the street and had the one in back for their horses and servants. The horses lived on the bottom and the servants on top. Now the horses have been replaced by Puerto Rican prostitutes and the servants have been replaced by Leo Haig and Wong Fat.

My rooming house is a compromise. Haig wants me to live in the carriage house. There's an extra room on the lower floor that's at least as spacious as the one I pay twenty dollars a week for, two blocks to the south. It's furnished nicely and it's reassuringly devoid of cockroaches, which are fairly abundant in my place on 18th Street. He keeps trying to move me in there and I keep resisting.

"The thing is," I told him finally, "I'm sort of, uh, interested in girls. I mean, sometimes something comes along that looks like the foundation of a meaningful relationship, uh, and, uh—"

Haig's spine stiffened, which doesn't happen often.

"Your friends would always be welcome in my house," he said.

"It's not that, exactly."

"Your relations with women are your own business. It's been my observation that the great detectives are inclined to be celibate. Not through inadequacy, but because they have passed through the stage of sexual activity before developing their highest powers. Wolfe, of course, fathered

a daughter before embracing misogyny wholeheartedly.
Holmes was devoted to The Woman but lived alone. Perry
Mason never so much as took hold of Della Street's hand.
Poirot always had an eye for a pretty figure, but no more
than his eye was ever engaged. Their assistants, however,
were apt to go to the opposite extreme. I don't want to put
too fine a point on this, but I would have no objection to
your leading an active sexual life. You could bring women
here, Chip. They could attend the breakfast table with no
embarrassment."

But of course the embarrassment would come long before
they got to the breakfast table. Because you cannot make an
initial pitch to a girl and lead her up an alleyway and into
what is unmistakably a Puerto Rican whorehouse without
creating an atmosphere which is not precisely perfect. So I
keep my room on 18th Street, and consistently fail to lure
girls to it anyway, and Haig and I maintain this running
argument.

I drank two beers at Dominick's and hung around there
until the late news came and went. There was nothing
about Melanie, which wasn't all that surprising. If every
drug overdose made the eleven o'clock news, they wouldn't
have time for wars or assassinations. I threw darts at
Dominick's dartboard without distinguishing myself. I
thought a lot about Melanie, and I remembered what she'd
been like alive and how she had looked in death, and all of
a sudden I was very damned glad I was working for Leo
Haig, because we were going to get the son of a bitch who
killed her and nail his hide to the wall.

Chapter Four

IN THE MORNING the man next door had a coughing fit, and I woke up before the alarm clock went off. I picked up a *Times* on the way over to Haig's house. In the courtyard, Carmelita was hanging out underwear on a clothesline running between two ailanthus trees. I have a lot of respect for those trees; anything that can come up out of a crack in a New York sidewalk deserves a lot of credit.

"You up early," she said.

"So are you."

"I am not go to bed yet. Busy night."

"Business is good, huh?"

"All time sailors. Want to fock like crazy. Drink and fock, drink and fock."

"Well," I said.

"Margarita, she so sore. Fockin' sailors. Mos' tricks, all they want is the blow job. Get the other from their wife. Fockin' sailors, they get blow job alla time on the boat, alla they wanna do is fock. So everybody gets sore."

"Oh," I said.

I went upstairs and into the office. Haig was busy playing with his fish tanks. I opened the paper and found the article about Melanie and started reading it. Wong came in on tiptoe with a couple of cups of strong coffee. He and I smiled at each other and he went away. Haig went on feeding the fish and I went on reading. A couple of paragraphs from the bottom I must have voiced a thought without realizing it, because Haig turned to face me and said, "Why?"

"Huh?"

"You said you'll be a son of a bitch. I was wondering why."

"I knew she had some income," I said. "But I never thought it amounted to that much. I mean, she never even offered to pay for her own brown rice, for Pete's sake."

349

"Make sense, Chip."

I blinked at him. "I was right about her age," I said. "She turned twenty-one in May and came into the principal of her inheritance. According to *The Times* her share came to a little over two million dollars."

"Interesting," he said.

"But then why did she live like that? Suppose she didn't want to touch the principal, what would the interest be on two million dollars?"

"Well over a hundred thousand dollars a year."

"I'll be a son of a bitch."

"So you've said."

"I used to buy subway tokens for her. She could have gone home in a limousine. It's unreal."

He seated himself on his side of the desk and held out his hand for the paper. I gave it to him and he read the article through several times, pausing to stroke his beard between paragraphs. Now and then he made a sort of clicking sound with his tongue or teeth. I don't know how he makes that sound exactly or just what it's supposed to indicate. When he had read most of the print off the page he set the paper down and closed his eyes for a moment.

Then he said, "You have your notebook? Good. There are several things you have to do. The funeral is at two tomorrow afternoon. Had you planned to go?"

"I hadn't even thought about it. Of course I'll go."

"I think you should, for reasons in addition to your feelings for Miss Trelawney. In the meantime, there are places you should go and people you might profitably meet."

He talked for a while, and I wrote things down in my notebook.

I got to the library at 42nd and Fifth a little before the lunch crowd took over the steps. I went through the *New York Times* Index for the past three years and made a lot of notes, then headed over to the microfilm room and filled out a request slip. A girl with Dick Tracy's chin brought me little boxes of film and showed me how to use the viewer.

At first it was slow going because I tended to get side-tracked. I would be scanning my way through back issues and happen to hit an article that looked interesting, so I would stop and read it. After this happened a couple of times I realized what was going on and kept my mind on what I was there for.

Cyrus Trelawney had died three years ago. A combination of heart trouble, cirrhosis of the liver and general cussedness had taken him out five days after his eighty-first birthday. He was a widower at the time, and he left five daughters. The eldest, Caitlin, was then thirty-three. The others were Robin (twenty-seven), Jessica (twenty-one), Melanie (eighteen) and Kim (fifteen). It seemed to me that there ought to have been a thirty-year-old between Caitlin and Robin, just to preserve the symmetry. Maybe he'd had financial reverses around that time.

Although he didn't seem to have had many financial reverses generally. The *Times* obit must have been an easy one to write, because Trelawney seems to have been a properly crusty old pirate. He had come to the States from Cornwall at the age of sixteen with a couple of silver shillings in his shoe, and I guess he was better at finding A Job With A Future than I'll ever be, because in the next sixty-five years he parlayed those shillings into almost eleven million dollars, after taxes. He did most of this in ways that I'm not equipped to understand, financial transactions and mergers and takeovers and all those words you find in the business pages of the newspaper.

Trelawney used to claim he was descended from Cornish pirates, and the *Times* writer sort of implied that no one had any reason to doubt his claim on the basis of his performance in the world of finance. He was past forty before he married, and shortly thereafter he sat about producing daughters at three-year intervals, except for the one gap of six years. He was twenty years older than his wife and he outlived her by eight years.

I got a lot of information from the obituary notice and more information from various social page articles and the stories about the deaths of Robin and Jessica, but there's no particular point in saying just what I learned where. I had to report it that way to Leo Haig, but I'll just sketch in the general facts here.

Caitlin, the firstborn, was thirty-six now. She had been married at sixteen, but old Cyrus had it annulled. She was married again six years later, divorced two years after that, married again the following year and divorced again within a year. Now she was married for the fourth time—unless there had been a divorce since then that hadn't made the papers. A couple of months before her father's death, she'd exchanged gold bands with Gregory Depew Vandiver, of the Sands Point Vandivers, whoever the hell they are. The wedding announcement told all the schools he had attended and all the clubs he belonged to and described him as connected with a Wall Street firm with half a dozen very Protestant names in its title. After a honeymoon in Gstaad, *The Times* said, the Vandivers would make their home on the North Shore of Long Island.

Robin had been married twice. When she was twenty-three she married Phillip Flanner, a man twice her age who had been her psych professor at Sarah Lawrence. Two years after the wedding, Flanner fell in front of a subway train. If your wife's that rich, what are you doing in the subway? Robin remarried three years after that. Her second husband was Ferdinand Bell. (I kept writing this down as Ferdinand Bull, by the way.) The article described Bell as a professional numismatist, which is what a coin dealer becomes when he marries an heiress.

Robin's auto wreck—Haig said not to call it an accident—took place in Cobleskill, New York, in January. She and her husband were returning from a three-day convention of the Empire State Numismatic Association held in Utica. There was a patch of ice on the road and Bell lost control of the car. He was wearing his seat belt and sustained superficial injuries. Robin was in the back taking a nap and was not wearing a seat belt. She broke her neck, among quite a few other things, and died instantly.

Jessica went out the window three months after Robin's death. The window she went out of was in the penthouse of the Correggio, one of the more desirable high-rise apartment buildings in the Village. She had lived in the penthouse with a girl named Andrea Sugar, who had been working at the time of the fall at Indulgence, which was described as an East Side massage parlor and recreation center. Jessica also worked at Indulgence as a recreational therapist, but had taken the afternoon off.

Jessica had never been married, and by reading between the lines I developed a fair idea why.

Melanie you know about.

I couldn't learn very much about Kim. She had been only fifteen when her father died and was only eighteen now. I could tell you what high school she attended but I don't think you'd care any more than I did. The items I turned up through the *Times* index were not much help by the time I found them on microfilm. They just mentioned her as "also appearing" in a variety of off-off-Broadway shows. The shows in which she also appeared got uniformly rotten reviews. In one review, a brief pan of something called *America, You Suck!* the critic wrote: "Young Kim Trelawney constitutes the one bright spot in this otherwise unmitigated disaster. Although not called upon to act, Miss Trelawney is unquestionably an ornament to the stage."

By the time I left the library I had sore eyes from the viewer and a sore right hand from scribbling in my notebook. I also had the name of the lawyer who had handled Cyrus Trelawney's affairs. I called him from a phone booth and learned that he was out to lunch, which reminded me that

I ought to be out to lunch myself. I went to the Alamo and had a plate of chili with beans. They charge an extra fifteen cents for any dish without beans. Don't ask me why.

The payphone at the Alamo was out of order. So were the first two booths I tried, and before I found a third one I decided not to call him anyway. It wasn't likely he'd be desperately anxious to see me, and it's always easier to get rid of a pest over the phone than in person.

His name was Addison Shivers, and if I was making this up I wouldn't dream of fastening a name like that onto him, because it didn't fit him at all. I expected someone tall and cadaverous and permanently constipated. I can't tell you anything about the state of his bowels, actually, but he was nothing like what I had anticipated. To begin with, it wasn't hard to get to see him at all.

His office was on Chambers Street, near City Hall. I took the subway there and found the building and was elevated to the sixth floor, where a frosted glass window said *Addison Shivers/Attorney-at-Law*. Then there were half a dozen other names in much smaller print underneath. I don't happen to remember a single one of them.

I told the witch at the desk that my name was Harrison and I worked for Leo Haig. (If you give that the right inflection, people think they've heard of Haig even though they haven't.) I said I wanted to see Mr. Shivers. She went through a door and came back to ask what my visit was in reference to.

"Melanie Trelawney," I said. She relayed this and came back with the news that Mr. Shivers would see me. She seemed even more surprised than I was.

His office was very simple, very sparsely furnished. I guess you have to be richer than God to have the confidence to get away with that. All the furniture was oak, and you could tell right away that he hadn't bought it in an antique shop; he had bought it brand-new and kept it for fifty years. The only decorative things were a couple of sailing prints in inexpensive frames and some brass fixtures from ships. I think one of them was what is called a sextant, but I honestly don't know enough about that sort of thing to tell you what the rest of them were. Or even to swear that the one was a sextant, for that matter.

He looked old enough to be Cyrus Trelawney's father. He had a little white hair left around the rim of his head. His face was sort of red, and his nose was more than sort of red. He was well padded, although you couldn't call him fat. The strongest impression I got from him was one of genuine benevolence. He just plain looked like a nice man. Sometimes you can't tell, but then again, sometimes you can.

"You'll excuse me if I don't stand," he said. His voice was dry but gentle. "I read about Melanie, of course. When that sort of thing happens I merely wish they could hold off until I either die or become senile. I've given up asking that tragedy be averted entirely. I merely wish to be spared the knowledge of it." He looked off into space for a moment, then returned his eyes to mine. "I didn't see Melanie often after her father's death. But I always liked her. She was a good person."

"Yes, she was."

"Your name is Harrison, I believe. And you work for a man named Haig, but I don't believe I know him."

"Leo Haig," I said. "The detective."

"No, I don't know him. I don't know any detectives, I don't believe. Any living detectives. What's your connection with Melanie Trelawney?"

I'd had a whole approach planned, but it didn't seem to fit the person Addison Shivers turned out to be. "It's not much of a connection," I said. "I knew her for the past month; she was my friend."

"And?"

"She was murdered," I said. "Leo Haig and I are trying

355

to find out who killed her."

This, let me tell you, was not part of the original game plan. Haig had emphasized that there was no need to pass on our suspicions and convictions to anyone else for the time being. But he had also always told me about instinct guided by experience, or intuition guided by experience, or intelligence guided by experience, and that's what I was using.

Mr. Shivers sat there and listened while I told him all the reasons why Leo Haig and I knew Melanie had been murdered. He knew how to listen, and his eyes showed that he was following what he was hearing. He heard me all the way through and then asked a few questions, such as why I had not mentioned any of this to the police, and when I answered his questions he nodded and sat forward in his chair and folded his hands on the top of his old oak desk.

After a moment he said, "You'll want information, of course. About the will, about the disposition of funds. I can tell you all that." He got a remote look in his eyes again. "Poor Cyrus," he said. "He was my client for fifty years, you know. Needless to say he employed a great many other attorneys, but I was his lawyer in all personal matters. And he was my friend for as long as he was my client. He was a very great man, you know."

"He must have been."

"A great man. I'm not sure that he was a good man, mind you. Goodness and greatness rarely keep house together. But I can say that he was a good friend. And now three of his daughters are dead. And his only son."

"His son?"

"Cyrus, Junior. He was the second born, he died in infancy. Cyrus never ceased to mourn him, especially when it became evident that he would not be fathering any more children. He wanted the name continued, you see. He was resigned to the fact that it would not be, ultimately, and felt it would be sufficient that his seed would endure through his daughters." He cleared his throat. "And now three of his daughters are dead in less than a year."

Cyrus, Jr. That explained the six-year gap between Caitlin and Robin.

"I respect your logic concerning Melanie's death," he said. "I agree that she must almost certainly have been murdered. You realize, of course, that this does not call for the conclusion that Robin and Jessica were murdered as well."

"I know."

"Though one cannot deny the possibility. Or the danger to the two remaining Trelawney girls."

I nodded.

"What do you and Mr. Haig intend to do?"

"Try to warn Mrs. Vandiver and Kim. And try to figure out who killed Melanie and how to prove it."

"You ought to have a client," he said. He opened his desk drawer and took out a large checkbook, the kind with three checks on a page. He wrote out a check, noted it on the stub, and handed it across the desk to me. It was made out to Leo Haig and the amount was a thousand dollars.

"I don't know what your rates are," he said. Neither, to tell you the truth, did I. "This will serve as a retainer. Note that I am engaging you to look out for the interests of Cyrus Trelawney, deceased. That leaves you a considerable degree of leeway."

"I think I understand."

He had one of his junior clerks find various papers about the Trelawney estate. He went over them with me and explained the parts I couldn't understand, and I filled the rest of my notebook. He poured himself a large brandy in the course of this, and asked me if I wanted anything myself. I told him I didn't.

When I had everything he could give me, he excused himself again for not getting to his feet. He leaned across the desk and we shook hands.

I asked if I would be seeing him the following day at Melanie's funeral.

"No, I don't go to funerals any more," he said. "If I did, I shouldn't have time for anything else."

Chapter Five

I HAD NEVER BEEN TO A FUNERAL BEFORE. When my parents committed suicide, I was away at school. I suppose the funeral took place before I could have gotten to it, but I have to admit I never even thought about it. I just packed a bag and started hitchhiking.

If Melanie's funeral was typical, I'm surprised the custom hasn't died out. I mean, I can sort of understand the way the Irish do it. Everybody stays drunk for three or four days. That makes a certain amount of sense. But here we were all gathered in this stark, modernistic, nondenominational cesspool on Lexington and 54th in the middle of the afternoon, listening to a man who had never met her say dumb things about a dead girl. One of the worst parts was that the jerk was sort of glossing over the fact that Melanie was either a junkie or a suicide, or both. He didn't come right out and say anything about casting first stones, but you could see it was running through his mind. I wanted to jump up and tell the world Melanie was murdered. I managed to control myself.

I wouldn't have been telling the world, anyway. Just a tiny portion of it. There were none of Melanie's friends there except me. Her relationships with the people in her neighborhood had been deliberately casual, and even if some of them had decided to come to the funeral, they would have been too stoned to get it all together. *"Hey, man, like we got to go see them plant old Melanie." "No, baby, that was last week." "Far out!"*

I recognized Caitlin and Kim with no trouble. I would have figured out who they were anyway since they were seated in the front pew, but the family resemblance was unmistakable. They didn't exactly look alike, and they didn't look like Melanie exactly, but all of them looked like old Cyrus Trelawney. Except on them it looked becoming. They had what I guess we can call the Trelawney nose, strong and assertive, and the deep-set eyes. Caitlin was blond and fair-skinned, a tall woman, expensively dressed. The man beside her wore a tweed suit that didn't have leather elbow patches yet. His nose and lips were thin and his expression was pained. I didn't have much trouble figuring out that he was Gregory Vandiver. Of the Sands Point Vandivers.

Kim was very short and slender, also fair-skinned, but with hair as dark as Melanie's. She seemed to be crying a lot, which set her apart from the rest of the company. Crying or not, I could see what the theater critic meant; she would have been an ornament to any stage. The guy next to her, on the other hand, had no decorative effect whatsoever. He kept reaching over and patting her hand. He looked familiar, and I finally figured out where I had seen him before. He played the title role in *King Kong.*

Kim was wearing a simple black dress, and she managed simultaneously to look good in it and to give the impression that she didn't generally wear dresses. The ape was wearing a suit for the first time in his life.

There was a handful of other people I hadn't seen before and couldn't identify. I guessed that the plump, boyish man in the gray sharkskin suit might be Ferdinand Bell, Robin's husband. If there was a professional numismatist in the room, he was likely to be it. And a girl off to one side was probably Andrea Sugar, if Andrea Sugar was there at all, because nobody else around could possibly have been a recreational therapist at something called Indulgence. The rest of the crowd was mostly old, and you sensed somehow that they were there because they liked funerals better than daytime television. I understand there are a lot of people like that. Every couple of days they trot down to the local mortuary to see who's playing.

The casket was open. I guess they do this so that the more skeptical mourners can assure themselves that the person they're mourning is genuinely dead. And so that the undertaker can show off his cosmetic skill.

I wasn't going to look. But then I decided that was silly, and I went up and looked, and it wasn't Melanie at all. There was rouge on her cheeks and lipstick on her mouth and eyebrow pencil on her eyebrows and some tasteless shit had cut her pretty hair and styled it, if you could call it that. Melanie never wore makeup in her life. This wasn't Melanie. This was a reject from the waxworks.

I really felt like hitting somebody.

Haig had told me to approach one of the sisters after the funeral. It was up to me which one I chose. "The older girl is probably better equipped to make a decision," he said, "while the younger one would probably be more receptive to overtures from someone your age. Use your judgment."

I used my judgment, and decided Kim might well be more receptive to overtures from someone my age, especially in view of the fact that I was more receptive to the idea of making them to her than to Caitlin. But I used a little more of my judgment and came to the conclusion that I would rather talk to Kim without that Neanderthal of hers hulking nearby. The idea of trying to Broach A Serious Subject to her while she was intermittently dissolving in tears also left something to be desired. So it was Caitlin by default.

If you don't mind, I won't go into detail about the trip to the cemetery or the burial. I rode out in a car full of old ladies talking about convertible debentures. There was a machine at the graveside to lower the casket, untouched by human hands, and off in the distance a couple of old men stood leaning on their shovels. They reminded me of the vultures in cartoons about people lost in the desert.

Anyway, the same limousines drove everybody back from Long Island and deposited us in front of the mortuary, and I managed to walk over to Caitlin Vandiver and her husband. I introduced myself and asked if I could talk with her about Melanie.

I got a smile from her and a blank look from him, and I

also got the impression that she smiled a lot and he looked blank a lot. "So you were a friend of Melanie's," she said. "Well, I don't know that I can tell you very much about her. I don't even know what you would want to hear. We were never terribly close, you know. I'm several years older than she was."

She paused there, as if waiting for me to express doubt. She didn't look old by any means. I'm a terrible judge of age, but I probably would have guessed her at thirty and I knew she was six years older than that.

"There are a couple of things," I said. "I think it would be worthwhile for us to talk."

Her smile froze up a little, and at the same time her eyes showed a little more than the polite interest they had held earlier. "I see," she said.

I don't know what she saw.

"Well," she said, the smile in full force again, "actually I could use some company. I hate to eat alone and funerals always make me ravenous. Is that shameful, do you think?"

I mumbled some dumb thing or other. Caitlin turned to her husband and put her cheek out for a kiss. He picked up his cue and kissed her.

"Greg always plays squash on Fridays," she said. "Neither rain nor snow nor heat nor gloom of night, you understand." The two of them said pleasant things to one another and Vandiver strode athletically down the street, arms swinging at his sides. I decided that he probably jogged every morning.

"He jogs every morning before breakfast," Caitlin said. It unsettles me when people do this. I feel as though I must have a window in the middle of my forehead. "He's keeping himself in marvelous physical condition."

"That's very good," I said.

"Oh, it's simply great. I wonder what he thinks he's saving himself for. I haven't had a really decent orgasm with him since the first time I saw him in his jogging suit. Romance tiptoed out the window. Shall we eat? I know a charming little French place near here. Never crowded, quite intimate, and they make a decent martini; and if I don't have one soon—fellow-me-lad—I shall positively *die.*"

And, after we had walked about a block, she said, "I pick the wrong words sometimes, damn it. I shouldn't have said that about positively dying. Too many people are doing it lately. Robin, Jessica, now Melanie. It's scary, isn't it?"

She took my hand as she said this and gave it a squeeze. I gave a squeeze back, and I think she smiled when I did.

We went to a restaurant on 48th Street. It was empty, except for a couple of serious drinkers at the bar and a couple at a side table trying to stretch out lunch so that it reached all the way to quitting time. We walked through to the garden in the rear and took a table.

"Tanqueray martini, straight up, bone dry, twist," she told the waiter. It sounded as though she'd had practice with the line. To me she said, "Do you drink? I know so many people your age don't these days."

I'd been trying to decide between a Coke and a beer, but that did it. "Double Irish whiskey," I said. "With water back."

Her eyebrows went up, but just a little. She told me I was to call her Caitlin. I was not certain that I was going to do this, and supposed I would sidestep the issue by not calling her anything at all. She seemed to think Harrison was my first name and wanted to know what my last name was, and I told her, and she got a little rattled and said that Harrison Harrison was unusual, to say the least, and ultimately we got that straightened out. She didn't ask me what Chip was short for, which was one strong point in her favor.

There were other points in her favor. Maybe her husband jogged every morning before breakfast because he was trying to catch up with her. The money she spent on her clothes and her hair didn't hurt, but it didn't account for her figure or the general youthfulness of her appearance. She was tall for a woman, and quite slender, and her breasts were not especially easy to ignore.

There was more to it than all that, though. She was damned attractive and damned well knew it, and she knew how to play off this attractiveness and, oh, hell, there's only one way to say it. She was very good at getting people horny.

She ordered mussels and a glass of white wine and another martini. I didn't want anything to eat, which surprised her but didn't seem to annoy her. She made a lot of small talk during her meal, and when I would start to turn the conversation around to Melanie she managed to sidetrack it. After this happened a few times I stopped thinking that she was more shook up than she was showing and Got The Message.

What I remembered, actually, was one time when I was taken out to lunch by Joe Elder, who is my editor. We went to a place around the corner from his office where they have a working antique telephone on each table. The food is better than you'd expect. The only thing wrong with Mr. Elder is that he can actually drink a Daiquiri without making a face. God knows how. But all through lunch I kept trying to talk about an idea I had for a book, and he kept changing the subject, and later they brought the coffee and he started talking about the book, and it was the same way now with Caitlin Vandiver. She had decided that we were having a business lunch and she knew that meant not saying a word about business until we were done with the lunch.

She finished her mussels about the same time I ran out of Irish to sip at. When the coffee came she settled herself in her chair and came in right on cue.

"You were a friend of Melanie's," she said. Which was my cue, so I picked it up.

"I was the one who discovered the body," I said.

"Oh, dear. That must have been awful for you."

It had been, but that wasn't what I wanted to talk about. I told her I was concerned professionally, which, brought that tension into her expression, which I later realized was because she thought I might be working up to some sort of blackmail pitch.

But I went on to say that I worked for Leo Haig. "The prominent detective," I said.

"Oh, yes."

Sure, lady. "I have to tell you this in confidence. We have grounds to believe that Melanie was murdered."

"But I thought it was an overdose of heroin."

"It was." The autopsy had confirmed this. "That doesn't mean she gave it to herself."

"I see." She thought for a minute. Then she said, "Oh."

"I'm afraid so. It puts things in sort of a different light. Jessica's suicide and Robin's accident—"

"Might not be a suicide and an accident. Well, Robin's certainly was, although I suppose someone could have tampered with Ferdie's car. Do those things happen? I know they do in books, but my God, if I were going to kill someone I would take my trusty little gun and shoot him in the back of the head." She was silent for a moment, and I wondered who she was killing in fantasy. (Whom, I mean.) Then she said, "I never thought Jessica was the type to commit suicide. She was always a tougher and bitchier broad than I am, and that's going some. And she was a dyke, too."

I had sort of assumed this, but I still didn't have a reply worked out. "Of course she might have grown out of that," Caitlin went on. "I did, you know. Although I never embraced lesbianism as wholeheartedly as Jessica did, I never stopped liking men, you see."

"Uh," I said.

"Do you want to know something interesting? When I was a girl, oh, way back before Noah built his ark, I always had a special preference for older men."

"Er."

"But now that I've slithered onto the dark side of thirty, I find I've done an about-face. I have a thing for young men these days."

"Uh."

"I've noticed, Chip, that some young men have a thing for older women."

I don't have a thing for older women, but I certainly haven't got anything against them. Actually, I don't suppose chronological age means very much. There are women of thirty-six who are too old. There are other women the same age who are not. Caitlin was in the second category, and I was becoming more aware of this every minute. Her perfume may have had something to do with this. Her leg, which had somehow moved against mine under the table, may also have had something to do with it.

"Well," I said. "About Melanie—"

"Were you sleeping with her, Chip?" Everybody wanted to know if I was sleeping with Melanie. First those cops, now Caitlin. I said, "We hadn't known each other very long."

"Sometimes it doesn't take very long."

"Er. The thing is, you know, that someone killed Melanie. And if someone also killed Jessica, and if it's the same someone—"

"Then Kim and I might be on somebody's Christmas list."

"Uh-huh. Something like that."

She lit a cigarette. She had been lighting cigarettes all along, but I don't think it's absolutely essential to call it to your attention every time somebody lights a cigarette. This time, though, she made a production number out of it, winding up taking a big drag and sighing out a cloud of smoke.

She said, "You know, Chip, I do have a little trouble taking this seriously."

"There may not be anything to it."

"But there also *may* be something to it, is that what you

mean? Assuming there is, what do I do about it? Put myself in a convent? Hire around-the-clock bodyguards? Quickly marry the president so I qualify for Secret Service protection?"

"The most important thing is to find Melanie's killer."

"'Catch him before he kills more?' That makes a certain amount of sense." She studied me for a moment. "The man you work for," she said.

"Leo Haig."

"He's really good?"

"He's brilliant."

"Hmmm. And what do you do for him exactly? You're a little young to be a detective, aren't you?"

"I'm his assistant. That doesn't mean my job is taking out the garbage." Actually, I do take the garbage out of the fish tanks some of the time. "I work with him on cases."

"So you'd be working on this, too."

"That's right. I do the leg work." I regretted saying that because she sort of winked and did some leg work of her own.

"I'll just bet you do, Chip."

"Uh."

"I'd like to see you devote all your energies to my case," she said. As I guess you've noticed, she tended to say things with double meanings. "I'd like you working hard on my behalf. You don't have a client, do you? You're just investigating because of your friendship for my sister?"

We had a client but he didn't want his name mentioned, so I didn't mention it. I agreed that we were involved in this out of friendship for Melanie. Which was true—I would have been working every bit as hard without Addison Shivers as a client.

She opened her bag and found a checkbook. She wrote for a minute, tore out a check, folded it in half and slipped it to me. "That's an advance," she said.

I took the check.

"An advance," she repeated. "Actually this is no day to

be making advances, is it?"

"Uh."

"It's about that time, isn't it? I have to pick up my darling husband at his club. On the way home I can hear how good it is to work up a sweat. That depends how you work it up, don't you think?"

"I guess."

"Do you? I suspect you do. I have that feeling about you, Chip. And I'm sure we'll see a lot of each other in the course of your investigation of the case."

"I'm sure we will, Mrs. Vandiver."

"Caitlin."

"Caitlin," I agreed.

"It's a difficult name to remember, isn't it?"

"No, but—"

"Some of my best friends call me Cat. Just plain Cat. You know, as in pussy."

The waiter brought the check. She put money on the table and we left. I was really in no condition to walk, to tell you the truth, and I think she noticed this, and I think she was pleased.

On the street she offered me her cheek as she had offered it to her husband, but when I went to kiss her, she turned her head quickly and my mouth landed on hers. She did something very nice with her tongue, then drew quickly away, an amused light in her eyes.

"Oh, we'll get along," she said.

I felt like springing for a cab, so of course there weren't any around. I took the subway. It was hot and crowded and smelly and I wound up pressed up against a homebound secretary. I was in the wrong condition to be pressed up against anyone and the secretary noticed it. She gave me the look people give when they find a cockroach in their oatmeal.

When I got off the train I finally looked at Caitlin's check. It was for five hundred dollars and it was made out to me rather than to Haig. She'd spelled my first name Chipp, which explained why she hadn't asked me what my real name was. She was probably used to people with first names like that.

Actually, it would simplify my life in a lot of ways if I spelled it with two p's. I should have thought of that years ago.

Haig didn't see anything wrong with accepting retainers from both Addison Shivers and Caitlin Vandiver. "Our work will be in both their interests," he said. "I see no likely conflict. And there's certainly precedent for it. Nero Wolfe frequently represents more than one person in the same matter, and does so without either party being aware of his association with the other. In the case that was reported under the title *Too Many Clients*, for example—"

I had just read *Too Many Clients* a month or so ago, but there was no point in telling him that. You might as well try telling Billy Graham you read the Bible once, for all the good it would do you.

Chapter Six

I WAS UPSTAIRS UNTIL SIX-THIRTY, helping Haig with the fish. He had a strain of sailfin mollies he was trying to fix. The object was to develop the dorsal fin to the greatest possible size through selective breeding and inbreeding and by giving the young the best possible nutritional start on life. One of the molly mothers had dropped young earlier in the day and we had to net her and remove her from the breeding tank. Mollies are less likely to eat their young than most livebearers, but every once in a while you get a female who hasn't read the book, and she can polish off an entire generation in a couple of hungry hours.

We gave the babies a heavy feeding of live brine shrimp. Haig buys enormous quantities of frozen brine shrimp for general use, but hatches his own for feeding young fishes. He tends to be a fanatic about things like this, and while he fed live brine shrimp to a few dozen tanks of young fish, I hosed out one of the tubs and prepared a brine mixture and sprinkled the little dry eggs on it.

Then we went downstairs and Wong announced that dinner was ready, and it was a Szechuan shrimp dish with scallions and those little black peppers that it is a terrible idea to bite into. Wong's shrimps had very little in common with the ones I had been feeding to our fish. He's a fairly sensational cook, and never seems to make the same thing twice.

I stayed around long enough to win a few games of chess. Then I went downstairs and said polite things to Consuela and Carmelita and Maria and some other girls whose names I didn't know, and let Juana the Madame pinch my cheek, which I wish she would stop doing, and then I started walking downtown.

The Cornelia Street Theater was located in a basement. You can probably guess what street it was on. There was a banner outside at street level announcing that they were doing *Uncle Vanya*, by Chekhov.

Maybe you know what the play is about. If not, I'm not going to be much help to you. I paid two dollars for a ticket and sat fairly close to the stage.

(Actually, there were only about fifty seats in the house, so it wouldn't have been possible to sit very far from the stage.) Maybe thirty of the fifty seats were empty. I sat and watched the play without paying any attention to it. I don't know whether it was good or not. I just couldn't concentrate. I would drift off into thought chains and just let my mind wander all over the place, and once in a while Kim Trelawney would appear on stage and I would take some time out to look at her, but she didn't have many lines and never hung around long, and as soon as she went off I went off myself.

I guess the show must go on, although with this show I couldn't quite see it. I mean, anybody could have played Kim's part that night, for all she had to do up there. And it wasn't as though an audience of thousands would have killed themselves if they didn't see *Uncle Vanya* that night. The way she had acted at the funeral, obviously taking it all hard, I hadn't really expected her to show up for the play.

There were two intermissions, and each of them drained a little of the audience away, so by the time the final curtain went down there were only about a dozen of us there to applaud, and not all of us did it very enthusiastically. The cast tried to take two bows, but by the time the curtain came up a second time everybody had already stopped applauding and people were on their way out of the theater. It was sort of sad.

I managed to get backstage and meet Kim. She blinked a little while I introduced myself, and when I said I was a friend of Melanie's, she nodded in recognition. "I saw you at the funeral," she said.

"I'd like to talk to you, if I could."

371

"About Melanie?"

"Sort of."

"I'll meet you out front," she said. "Just give me a few minutes."

She took about four of them, and came out wearing jeans and a peasant blouse and carrying a canvas shoulder bag in red, white and blue. She suggested we have coffee at O'John's, a little place on the corner of West 4th.

"Gordie's going to meet me there in a few minutes," she said. "He doesn't like me walking home alone."

We got a window table and ordered two cups of coffee. "Gordie's a little overprotective," she said. "Sometimes it bothers me. But sometimes I like it."

"Was Gordie the fellow you were with this afternoon?"

"Yes." She smiled suddenly, and instantly reminded me very much of Melanie, the way her entire face was so immediately transformed by her smile. "I haven't known him very long," she said, "and I don't really know him very well. In certain ways, that is. He's very different from the type of boy I usually go out with."

"How?"

"Well, you know. He's not educated; he dropped out of high school and went right to work on the docks. Sometimes I have the feeling that we don't really have very much to talk about. And his ideas about women, I mean they're very old-fashioned. He believes a woman's place is in the home and everything, and he doesn't really think very much of my being an actress. He's proud when I get a part and like that, but he thinks it's just something for me to amuse myself with until we get married and start making babies."

"And you don't feel that way?"

She gnawed the tip of her index finger. "I don't know exactly *how* I feel, Chip. From the time I was a little girl I wanted to be an actress. It was what I always wanted. After one semester of college I knew I had to get away from classrooms and spend all my time around theaters. But it's so hard. You can't imagine."

"I guess it's very hard to get started."

"It's almost impossible. You saw how many people we had in the theater tonight. Maybe thirty."

"If that."

"I know. It was closer to twenty, and most of them were friends who didn't pay for their tickets. And the actors didn't get paid anything, we're all working for free in the hope that somebody important will see us on stage and have something else for us, and—"

She told me a lot more about what was wrong with trying to act for a living. And then she said, "Sometimes I think I should just forget the whole thing and marry Gordie. That's what he wants me to do. It's a temptation, you know. Just give it all up and have babies and enjoy life. Except I worry that I would wake up some day years from now and wonder what I had done with my life. It's very confusing."

She looked straight into my eyes during this last speech and I felt as though I could see clear through to the back of her head. I found it easy to understand why Gordie was overprotective. There was something about Kim that made you want to put your arms around her and tell her everything was going to be all right. Even if it wasn't.

I was just about to reach across the table and take her hand when something changed on her face. She raised her eyes over my shoulder, then waved a hand. I turned, and of course it was good old Gordie.

He pulled a chair up and sat down. He did not seem overjoyed to see me there. (Which made it mutual, actually.) Kim introduced us, and I found out that he had a last name, McLeod. Then he found out that I was a friend of Melanie's and some of the suspicion left his face. Not all of it, but some.

"You see the play?" I admitted that I had. "Saw it myself a couple of times. Rather catch a movie myself. All these people just talking back and forth. What did you think of Kim?"

"I thought she was very good," I said.

"Yeah, only good thing about the play, far as I'm concerned. She's very talented."

I said she certainly was, or something equally significant.

"But I don't like the people she has to hang around with. It's a well-known fact they're all fairies in that business. A well-known fact. Still in all, as a way for her to pass the time until she settles herself down—"

He went off on a speech that Gloria Steinem would not have enjoyed. I have to admit that I didn't follow it too closely. It was already becoming clear to me that Gordie McLeod and I were never going to become best buddies. I was noting Kim's reactions to what he was saying and trying to figure out just what it was about this ape that attracted her. I had no trouble figuring out what it was about her that appealed to him.

"Well," he said, "it's gettin' to be about that time. Nice meetin' you, guy."

"There was something I wanted to discuss with Kim," I said.

"Oh, yeah?"

"About Melanie," Kim said.

He settled back in his chair. "Well, sure," he said.

"It's a little public here," I said. "Could we go somewhere more private?"

"What for?"

"So that we could talk in private."

"What's this all about, anyway?"

I wasn't making much headway. Kim came to the rescue and suggested we all go back to the apartment. She didn't say *her* apartment or *their* apartment, just *the* apartment. He didn't seem wild about the idea, but we went anyway. He insisted on paying for my coffee. I have to admit I didn't put up a fight.

The apartment, which did turn out to be their apartment, was on Bethune Street a few doors west of Hudson, which made it about equidistant from Kim's theater and the

Hudson docks where Gordie did something muscular. It was on the second floor of a good old four-story building. There were three high-ceilinged rooms and a little balcony with a view of nothing spectacular.

There was a good feeling to the apartment, and it was hard to believe Kim had rented it less than a year ago. There were some nice Oriental rugs, a couple of floor-to-ceiling bookshelves, and furniture that was both attractive and comfortable. It was not hard to guess which of the two of them had done the decorating.

Gordie got himself a beer and asked me as an afterthought if I wanted one. I didn't disappoint him by accepting. He sprawled on the couch, took a gurgling swig of beer, and put his feet up. "Let's have it," he said.

I started my pitch. That I worked for Leo-Haig-the-Famous-Detective. That Haig and I had uncovered evidence that indicated a strong possibility that Melanie had been murdered. That there were grounds for speculation that Jessica, and perhaps Robin as well, had been similarly done in. That a client who I was not at liberty to name had hired Haig to nail the killer. That it was important to recognize that Caitlin and Kim might be in a certain amount of danger.

And so on.

I didn't get to deliver this entire rap all at once because Gordie kept interrupting. He seemed to find it extremely difficult to follow a simple English sentence and even more difficult to put together one of his own, and he kept turning the conversation onto weird tangents. Earlier, I had found it disturbing that a girl like Kim was thinking about marrying an idiot like Gordie. Now I found it disturbing that she was living with him. What in hell did they talk about?

When I had been able to get it all out, and when Kim had a chance to ask a few questions of her own, Gordie took a last long drink of beer, crumpled the can impressively in one hand, and tossed it unsuccessfully at the wastebasket. "I'll tell you what I think," he said.

I was sure he would.

"What I think, I think it's a load of crap."

"I see," I lied.

"You know what your trouble is, Harrison? You're one of these college boys. You read all these books and listened to all these egghead professors and it scrambled your brains."

I didn't say anything.

"Me, I'm an ordinary Joe, you know what I mean? An ordinary man, your average human being. What I mean, I didn't have your advantages. I never even finished high school. I did my learning on the streets."

"So?"

"So I don't look for a complicated answer when there's a simple one staring me in the face. The whole trouble with this country is too many guys like you who went to Harvard and they couldn't recognize crap if they stepped in it."

"I didn't go to Harvard."

"Manner of speaking. Where'd you go? Yale? Princeton?"

"I didn't go to college. I didn't finish high school; I got thrown out in my last year."

"What are you trying to hand me?"

"Nothing in particular, I just—"

"Jesus Christ," he said. "I got no use for college boys, I'll tell you that straight out, but one thing I got less use for is a college boy pretends he's not a college boy. Who do you think you're kidding?"

Enough. "The point is," I said, "that if Kim is in any danger—"

"Kim's not in no danger. And if she is, that's what I'm here for. What are you saying, you're gonna protect her? I mean, I can't see you protecting a pigeon from a cat. No offense, but you get my meaning."

I got his meaning.

"Look," he said, "I'll be protecting Kim no matter what.

This city's a fuckin' jungle; nothing but junkies and spades and fairies and weirdos. But all this murder shit, you're making a mountain out of a mole's hill. Robin, she's in a car and it cracks up. That sound like a murder? How many people go out like that every weekend?"

"Yes, but—"

"Then there's Jessica. She's a dyke and a whore and they're all crazy, so maybe she wasn't getting it regular enough or who knows why, but she goes out the window. Happens all the time. Then there's Melanie, who's some kind of a crazy hippie with drugs and shit and who knows what, and junkies are all the time shoving needles in their arm and winding up dead, you see it every night on television. I mean, let's face it, Kim's the only one in the goddamned family that has anything much on the ball. The older one, Caitlin, she's just a nymphomaniac and a lush. Old man Trelawney must have been pretty sharp to make the score he made, I'll give him that, but he wasn't too good at having kids. Kim's okay but the other four were a batch of sickies."

"They had problems," Kim said. "Don't talk about them like that."

"Look, everybody has problems, kid, but those nuts—"

Kim's eyes flared. "I *loved* Melanie," she said. "And I love Caitlin. I loved all my sisters, and I don't want to hear you *talk* like that about them!"

She stormed out of the room. Gordie's face darkened briefly, then relaxed. "Women," he said. "I'll tell you something, they're all of them a little nuts. They don't have thoughts the way men do. They have feelings. You got to know how to handle them."

After they were married, I knew how he would handle her. He would beat her up whenever he felt she needed it.

"Look," he said, "I want you to stay out of Kim's life. You get me?"

"Huh?"

"I know you got to work your angle like everybody else.

377

You already got a client, you don't need to hang around Kim. I don't want her getting upset."

"I didn't know that I did anything to upset her."

"Seeing you upsets me. And when I get upset Kim gets upset, and I don't want that. You got an angle to work and I can respect that, but I don't want you getting in my way."

"I really want it to be him," I told Haig. "I want it to be him and I want them to bring back capital punishment. Someone has to throw the switch. I volunteer."

"Surely the fact he's living with Kim has nothing to do with your motivation."

"You mean am I interested myself? I don't honestly know. She reminds me of Melanie, and I can't make up my mind whether that turns me on or off. The thing is I *like* her, and I can't see her spending a lifetime with a clown like him. Hell, I can't see her spending a social evening with him."

"But he seems an unlikely suspect."

"I know. I can see him committing murder. I don't think he'd draw the line at something like that. But he wouldn't be so clever in choosing different murder methods. He'd probably just hit each of them over the head."

"I gather he's not enormously intelligent," Haig said dryly.

"He's about as dumb as you can get and still function."

"Is he crafty, though?"

I thought about that. I said, "Yes, I think he is. Animal cunning, that kind of thing."

"He assumed you were 'working an angle.' I submit he so assumed because he's working an angle of his own."

I nodded. "He was more or less telling me to stay off his turf. And he knows about the money. In fact he seems to know a lot about all the sisters. He hasn't been with Kim that long, and they weren't that close."

"That struck me," Haig said. His fingers went to his beard and his eyelids dropped shut. "He knows about the Trelawney money. He wants to marry Kim, to the point

378

where she apparently feels pressured. She hasn't come into the principal of her inheritance yet, of course. And won't for three years." He remained silent for a few minutes. I knew his mind was working, but I had no idea what it was working on. Mine was just sort of treading water.

I got up and went over to watch the African gouramis. There were three half-grown guppies still swimming around. While I watched, the female gourami swam over to one of the guppies but didn't bother devouring it. I guess she wasn't hungry at the moment.

Haig raises several strains of fancy guppies. The species is a fascinating one, and the males of *Lebistes reticulata* are as individual as thumbprints. When they're about half-grown, you can tell (if you're Leo Haig) which ones are going to amount to something. Those you keep.

The others serve as food for other fish. Haig is fond of remarking that the best food for fish is fish, and some of ours require a certain proportion of live food in their diet. We have a pair of leaf fish, for example, who go through a dozen young guppies apiece every day. It used to bother me, the whole idea of purposely raising fish so that you can feed them to other fish, but that's the way Nature does it in the ocean. I used to know a guy who had a pet king snake and used to buy mice and feed them to it. That would bother me a lot more, I think.

"Chip." I turned. "There is a motive lurking here. I keep getting teasing glimpses of it but I don't have enough hard information to see it. We need to know more about wills and such. Tomorrow—"

But he didn't get to finish the sentence, because just then we heard glass shatter somewhere in the front of the house. We looked at each other, and I started to say something, and then the bomb went off and the whole house shook.

I stood there for a minute. Waiting for the next explosion, probably, but there wasn't one. I went into the front room and saw a crack in one of the front windows.

Then the girls downstairs started shrieking.

Chapter Seven

IT WAS A PIPE BOMB consisting of a length of pipe filled with various goodies, but I'm not going to go into detail. I mean, who knows what lunatic out there might get inspired and follow my directions and bomb a whorehouse on his own? Haig says that Alfred Hitchcock once had a scene in which an assassin used a gun built into a camera, and then a few months after the picture was released someone assassinated somebody just that way, in Portugal I think, and Hitchcock felt very ginchy about it. I can understand that.

What happened was this: someone threw a pipe bomb into the second floor front of our building. That was the broken glass, the sound of the bomb going through the window, which had not been open at the time. Then the bomb went off, shaking the whole house and, more to the point, giving Maria Tijerino and Able-Bodied Seaman Elmer J. Seaton a greater thrill than they could possibly have anticipated.

Shit. I don't want to be cute about this because it was not at all nice. Maria and the sailor were in bed in the front room at the time and the damned bomb blew them to hell and gone. I went in there and looked, God knows why, and then I went into the john and threw up. I mean, I could make a few dozen jokes along the lines of If-you-gotta-go-etc. But the hell with it. I saw it, and it was ugly.

The explosion didn't hurt anybody but Maria and the sailor. It put some cracks in the plaster throughout the house without doing any real structural damage.

It also made some of our fish tanks leak.

Haig and Wong Fat and I missed a lot of the action because we were running around trying to make sure the fish were all right. That probably sounds very callous, but you have to realize that there was nothing we could possibly do for

Maria or the sailor. And a leaking fish tank is something that requires attention. If a fish tank absolutely cracks to hell and gone, you can just go to church and light candles for the fish, but we didn't have any that got cracked. The thing is, shock waves will interfere with the structural soundness of an aquarium, which is basically a metal frame with a slate bottom and four glass sides, and quite a few of ours sprung slow leaks, and that meant we had to transfer the fish to sound tanks and empty the leakers before they leaked all over the place. Eventually we would have to repair all the leakers, a process which involves coating all the edges with rubber cement and cursing a lot when the tank leaks anyway.

So while we were scurrying around examining tanks on the third and fourth floor, I gather half the police in Manhattan were stumbling around on the first two floors. There were a couple of ambulances out front and a Fire Department rescue vehicle. There were beat patrolmen and Bomb Squad detectives and God knows who else, and, because it was established that Maria and her sailor were dead, which could not have been too difficult to establish, there were two cops from Homicide.

Yeah.

I suppose you already figured out that it would be the same two cops, Gregorio and Seidenwall. You must have. Because you're reading this, and if I were reading it I would certainly expect to keep encountering the same two cops. (I gather this never happens in real life, but just the other day I read a mystery by Justin Scott called *Many Happy Returns* and the lead character kept cracking up oil trucks, of all things, and each time he turned a truck over the same two humorous cops turned up to glare at him. It didn't seem to matter what part of the city he was in, he always ran into the same goddam cops.)

The thing is, you're reading this in a book, so you know it's Gregorio and Seidenwall again. I wasn't reading it, I was living gamely through it, and they were the last thing I expected.

But there they were.

"...check on the possibility of..." Gregorio said. I don't know how the sentence had started or how he was planning to end it. He had evidently begun it in the hallway, undeterred by the lack of anyone to hear it, and he didn't end it, because he caught sight of me. "I'll be a ring-tailed son of a bitch," he said.

"Er," I said.

"You again," he said.

You again, I thought.

"I don't like this at all," he said. "A hippie girl OD's in a toilet on the Lower East Side and you're the one who discovers the body. A sailor and a spic hooker fuck themselves into an explosion and you're living upstairs. You know something, Harrison? I'm not crazy about any of this."

"We oughta take him in," Seidenwall said.

"I never believed in coincidence," Gregorio said. "It makes me nervous. I hate to be nervous. I got a stomach that when I get nervous my stomach gets nervous, and I can live without a nervous stomach. I can live better and longer without a nervous stomach."

"We oughta take him in," Seidenwall said.

"I don't like the sense of things fitting together like this," Gregorio said. "How long have you lived in New York, Harrison?"

"A couple of years," I said. "Off and on."

"We oughta take him in," Seidenwall said.

"Off and on," Gregorio said. "A couple of years off and on."

"We oughta take him in."

"A couple of years you were here, and a lot of years I was here, and all that time I never heard of you, Harrison. I never knew you existed. Now I see you twice in two days."

"Three days," I said.

"Shut up," Gregorio said.

"We oughta take him in," Seidenwall said.

Leo Haig said, "Sir!"

And everybody else shut up.

He said, "Sir. You are on my property without my invitation or enthusiastic approval. You have come, as well I can appreciate, to investigate a bombing. You wish to ascertain whether or not the bombing is impinging in any way upon myself and my associates. It is not. We are not involved. The building has been bombed. Living in a building which is sooner or later bombed is evidently a natural consequence of living in the city of New York. It is perhaps an even more natural consequence of living above a house of ill repute. I am not happy about this, sir, as no doubt neither are you. I am distressed, especially as this bombing causes me considerable inconvenience. I am increasingly displeased at your attitude toward my associate, and, by extension, toward myself."

Gregorio and Seidenwall looked down. Leo Haig looked up. Hard. Gregorio and Seidenwall looked away.

Haig said, "Sir. I assume you have no warrant. I further assume your contingency privileges obviate the necessity for a warrant to intrude upon my property. But, sir, I now ask you to leave. You cannot seriously entertain the notion that I or my associate did in fact bomb our own building. We are not witlings. Each of us can vouch for the other's presence at the time of the bombing, as can my associate Mr. Wong Fat." Wong was at that moment cowering under his bed saying the rosary. "You can, sir, as your estimable colleague suggests, take Mr. Harrison into custody. It would be an unutterably stupid act. You could, on the other hand, quit these premises. It appears to me that these are your alternatives. You have only to choose."

I never heard the like. Neither, I guess, did Gregorio. They scooted.

* * *

"I always wanted to call someone a witling," Haig said

later. "Wolfe does it all the time. I always wanted to do that."

"You did it very well," I said.

"I have my uncle to thank for that," Leo Haig said. "I have my uncle to thank for many things, but one fact sums it all up. But for him, I would have gone through life without ever being able to call a policeman a witling."

We had a beer on the strength of that.

Chapter Eight

I SPENT THE NIGHT IN HAIG'S HOUSE. It was late by the time we were done with the fish, even later before we finished talking about the bombing. We agreed that it was possible someone had bombed the whorehouse on purpose, and we also agreed that we didn't believe it had happened that way. That bomb had gone through the wrong window. It had been meant for us, and whoever threw it had his signals crossed.

Which was one of the reasons I spent the night on the couch. Somebody was trying to kill us, and I really didn't want to give him any encouragement.

"You ought to move in here," Haig said over breakfast. "It would expedite matters."

"Not if I have to spend any time on that couch."

"It was uncomfortable?"

"It was horrible," I said. "I kept waking up and wanting to stretch out on the floor, but moving was too painful."

"Of course you'd have a proper bed," Haig said stiffly. "And a proper room of your own, and the implicit right to entertain friends of your own choosing. In addition—"

He paraded the usual arguments. I paid a little attention to them and a lot of attention to breakfast. Corned beef hash, fried eggs, and the world's best coffee. I don't always like coffee all that much, but Wong Fat makes the best I've ever tasted. It's a Louisiana blend with chickory in it and he uses this special porcelain drip pot and it really makes a difference.

After breakfast Haig gave me a list of things to do regarding the fish. While I was upstairs attending to them he was on the phone in his office. I finished up and was sitting on my side of the partners' desk at a quarter after eleven. Haig was reading one of Richard Stark's Parker novels. I forget which one. He said, "Formidable," once or twice. I spent ten minutes watching him read. Then he closed the book and leaned back in his chair and played with his beard. After a few minutes of that he took one of his pipes apart. He put it back together again and started to take it apart a second time, but stopped himself.

"Chip," he said.

I tried to look bright-eyed.

"I've made some calls. I spoke with Mr. Shivers and Mrs. Vandiver. Also with several other lawyers. Also with Mr. Bell and a man named LiCastro. Also—no matter. There are several courses of inquiry you might pursue today. You have your notebook?"

I had my notebook.

Indulgence was on the second floor of a renovated brownstone on 53rd Street, between Lexington and Third. The shop on the first floor sold gourmet cookware. I walked up a flight of stairs and paused for a moment in front of a Chinese red door with a brass nameplate on it. There was a bell, and another brass plate instructed me to ring it before opening the door. I followed orders.

The man behind the reception desk was small and precise and black. He had his hair in a tight Afro and wore thick horn-rimmed glasses. His suit was black mohair and he was wearing a red paisley vest with it. His tie was a narrow black knit.

It was air-conditioned in there, but I couldn't imagine how he could have come to work through all that heat in those clothes. And he looked as though he had never perspired in his life.

He asked if he could help me. I said that I wanted to see a girl named Andrea Sugar.

"Of course," he said, and smiled briefly. "Miss Sugar is one of our recreational therapists. Do you require a massage?"

"Uh, yeah."

"Very good. Are you a member?"

I wasn't, but it turned out that I could purchase a trial

membership for ten dollars. This would entitle me to the services of a recreational therapist for thirty minutes. I handed over ten of Leo Haig's dollars and he filled out a little membership card for me. When he asked me my name I said "Norman Conquest." Don't ask me why.

"Miss Sugar is engaged at the moment," he said, after my ten dollar bill had disappeared. "She'll be available in approximately ten minutes. Or you may put yourself in the hands of one of our other therapists. Here are photographs of several of them."

He gave me a little leatherette photo album and I looked through it. There were a dozen photographs of recreational therapists, all of them naked and smiling. In the interests of therapy, I guess. I said I would prefer to wait for Miss Sugar and he nodded me to a couch and went back to his book. It was a collection of essays by Noam Chomsky, if you care.

I sat around for ten minutes during which the phone rang twice. The desk man answered, but didn't say much. I leafed through *Sports Illustrated* and read something very boring about sailboat racing. He went into another room and came back to report that Miss Sugar was waiting for me in the third cubicle on the right. I walked down a short hallway and into a room a little larger than a throw rug. The walls were painted the same Chinese red as the door. The floor was cork tile. The only piece of furniture in the room was a massage table with a fresh white sheet on it.

Andrea Sugar was standing beside the table. She wasn't the girl I had seen at the funeral. She was wearing a white nurse's smock. (I think that's the right word for it.) She was tall, almost my height, and she looked a little like pictures of Susan Sontag. She said hello and wasn't it hot out and other conventional things, and I said hello and agreed that it was hot out there, all right, and she suggested I take off all my clothes and get on the table.

"I'm not really here for a massage," I said.

"You're not supposed to say that, honey."

"But the thing is—"

"You're here for a massage, sweetie. Your back hurts and you want a nice massage, you just paid ten dollars and for that you'll get a very nice massage, and if something else should happen to develop, that's between you and me, but I'm a recreational therapist and you're a young man who needs a massage, and that's how the rulebook reads. Okay?"

The thing is, I did sort of need a massage. My back still had kinks in it from Leo Haig's corrugated couch. I just felt a little weird about taking all my clothes off in front of a stranger. I don't think I have any particular hangups in that direction, actually, but the whole scene was somehow unreal. Anyway, I took off my clothes and hung them over a wooden thing designed for the purpose and got up on the table and onto my stomach.

"Now," she said. "What seems to be the trouble?" I guess the question didn't need an answer, because she was already beginning to work on my back. She really knew how to give a back rub. Her hands were very strong and she had a nice sense of touch and knew what muscles to concentrate on. When she got to the small of my back I could feel all the pain of a bad night's sleep being sucked out of the base of my spine, like poison out of a snakebite.

"It's about Jessica Trelawney," I said.

The hands stopped abruptly. "Christ Almighty," she said softly. "Who *are* you?"

"Chip Harrison," I said. "I work for Leo Haig, the detective."

"You're not a cop."

"No. Haig is a private investigator. I was also a friend of Melanie Trelawney's."

"She OD'd the other day."

"That's right."

By now she had gone back to the massage. Her hands moved here and there as we talked, and when they strayed below the belt they began to have an effect that was interesting. I felt an urge to wriggle my toes a little.

"You really didn't come for a massage."

"No, but that doesn't mean you should stop. I came to ask you some questions. If you want me to get dressed—"

"No, that's no good. They look in from time to time and I should be doing what I'm supposed to be doing. You're a friend of Melanie's and you want to ask about Jess?"

"Yes."

"I hope you're trying to find out who murdered her. I just surprised you, didn't I? I never bought that suicide story. Not for a minute. I've never known anyone less suicidal than Jess. She was one of the strongest women I've ever known. How does this feel?"

"Great."

"You've got nice skin. And you're clean. You wouldn't believe some of the men who come in here. Have you ever had a massage before?"

"No."

"What were we talking about? Jess. No, I never believed she killed herself and I always believed she was murdered. It was a waste of time telling the police this. I was very close to Jess. As a matter of fact we were lovers. I met her in a Women's Lib group. Consciousness-raising. We responded to each other right away. She had made love with women before, but she had never had a real relationship. We lived together; I moved into her apartment. We bought each other silly little presents. Roll over."

"Pardon?"

"You're done on this side. Roll over onto your back."

I did.

"I got her a job here," she went on. "She didn't have to work, of course. She was rich. But she wanted to work, she didn't like the idea of living off her inheritance and not establishing herself as a person responsible for her own existence. She was extremely tough-minded, Chip."

Her hands were working on my arms and shoulders and chest and stomach. She used a firm touch at first, but as she got further south she switched to a feathery stroking.

My mind was not at all interested in sex, for a change, but my body was beginning to display a mind of its own.

I forced myself to talk about Melanie, and how Haig and I were convinced she had been murdered. I didn't go into details and I didn't mention the bombing the night before. I asked her if she had any ideas who might have wanted to kill Jessica.

"Some man," she said.

"I meant specifically."

She shook her head and ran her fingers over my thighs. "You meet strange people in this business," she said. "Some very unreal men. The names they'll call a woman when they get off. I don't think they're even conscious of it most of the time. It's automatic, some deep built-in hatred of the entire female sex, and their own sexuality is all mixed up with a desire to dominate and hurt. I had a theory about Jess."

"Tell me."

"Well, it doesn't point anywhere in particular. But I figured she had a client for a massage and he managed to get her home address. He went up there and fucked her and hurt her and then he killed her and threw her out the window. He could have beaten her up, you know. It wouldn't have showed because the fall would have hidden any injuries."

Haig and I had already discussed this. Anything less than a bullet hole would have been consistent with injuries suffered in that great a fall.

"But if Melanie was murdered, then probably it was the same person both times."

"Right," I said.

"Which makes my theory fall down. It's not just a man who hates women. It's a man with a particular hatred for women named Trelawney."

"Right."

"I can't think who it could be."

"Possibly someone who stands to gain by killing the five sisters."

390

"Who stands to gain?"

"It's hard to tell. The money wasn't entailed, it passed over completely to the girls under Cyrus Trelawney's will. Leo Haig is working on it."

"I wish I could help."

We chatted a little more, and then she drew her hands away and I thought the massage was over. I sort of hoped it was. I couldn't take very much more of this.

She said, "It's very warm in here, Chip. Would you mind if I removed my uniform?"

She had a fine body, long and lean and supple. Her breasts were very firm and her stomach perfectly flat. Her skin smelled spicy.

She put her hands right where I hoped she would put them. She pressed gently, then moved her fingers in that feathery stroke.

"There's one muscle group I haven't been able to relax," she said.

"Yeah. It's sort of embarrassing, if you want to know."

"I'd be embarrassed if you didn't react that way. Would you like me to do something about it?"

"I'd like that."

"You have to tell me what you want me to do." "Uh."

She was not touching me now. "This isn't part of the standard massage," she explained. "You've had the standard treatment already." I had had the treatment, all right. "If there's anything else you would like, you have to tell me specifically what it is. And then you give me a present because you like me, and I do something very nice for you because I like you, and that's how it's done."

"I see."

"What would you like?"

"Uh. I don't know what the choices are."

"For a small present I could do something manual. For a large present I could do something oral."

"I see."

"You already know I have nice hands. I also have a very

nice mouth."

"I'm sure you do."

"I've received lots of compliments on it."

"I'm sure you have."

"So if you'd like to ask me to do something—"

"How much is a small present?"

"Ten dollars would be a small present. Twenty dollars would be a large present. A lot of people give me larger presents than that, but I sort of like you. You're clean and you're not an unpleasant person."

I had about twenty-five dollars with me after paying my trial membership fee. But I was going to have to take cabs and be ready to spend money if the need arose. The twenty dollar present was out of the question and the ten dollar present seemed like a lot of money for a very second-best experience. And I really didn't like the idea of paying for sex. I could almost rationalize this on the grounds that it wouldn't be sex, exactly. I mean, there was nothing really sexual about it, for Pete's sake. It would just be a release from tension. Recreational therapy, you could call it.

What it comes to, really, is that if I had had a hundred dollars in my pocket I would probably have given twenty of them to Andrea. Since I had twenty-five, I told her I was afraid I would have to pass.

"That's cool," she said, slipping back into her uniform. "Maybe you'll drop around again sometime."

"Maybe I will."

"And if there's any way I can help you find out who killed Jess—"

"Maybe there is," I said.

"How?"

"It might help if we knew the names of her customers for the week before she was killed. I don't suppose there would be any connection, but something might turn up."

She gave a low whistle. "That's a tough one. There's no record kept of what guy goes with what girl. They keep track of the number of massages everybody does because you get a percentage of that on top of the presents clients give you. And they keep the names from the membership forms, but you'd be surprised how many men are ashamed to give their right name."

"Not all that surprised, actually."

"I suppose I could find those records, though. For the week before Jessica died? I'll have to be sneaky. You're not supposed to have access to the records. I think they're afraid some of the girls might try a little blackmail. But I'm good at schemes and I shouldn't have much trouble getting around Rastus out there."

My face must have showed something. She laughed. "No, I'm not a racist," she said. "No more than the next bigot, anyway. That's his name."

"You're kidding."

"I don't think he was born with it. But it's his name now and he likes to watch people when he introduces himself. Don't forget your watch, Chip."

The watch I almost forgot told me that it was ten minutes after two when I left Indulgence. I went around the corner and had a cheeseburger and some iced tea. Walking was not a very pleasurable experience at the moment. Andrea Sugar had drained all the pain out of my backbone and rolled it up into a ball and stuffed it into my groin.

I'd given her Leo Haig's number and told her to call as soon as she had the records of clients for the week in question. I couldn't see how it would help, especially since anyone planning to kill Jessica would have likely used a name about as legitimate as old Norm Conquest himself, but it was something to do.

She had always been convinced that Jessica had been murdered. That was the sort of fact Leo Haig usually found interesting and suggestive, so I spent a dime telling him about it. By the time I left the restaurant I could almost walk without limping.

Almost.

Chapter Nine

FERDINAND BELL'S OFFICE was within limping distance on the ninth floor of a tall narrow building on 48th Street, just east of Fifth. The building directory in the lobby showed that most of the tenants dealt in stamps or coins. Or both.

In the elevator a man with a European accent said, "I can never recommend for appreciation any surcharges or overprints priced significantly higher than their regular issue counterparts. It is not merely that they may be counterfeited, but that the mere prospect of counterfeiting prevents their reaching their logical levels." I still do not have the slightest idea what he was talking about. I repeated the conversation to Haig, who understands everything, and of course he nodded wisely. He wouldn't tell me what it meant, though.

"If you want to learn about anything under the sun," he said, "you have only to read the right detective story. *The Nine Tailors* will tell you as much as you need to know about bell-ringing in English country churches, for example." (It told me more than I needed to know, to tell you the truth.) "For philately, MacDonald's *The Scarlet Ruse* is excellent. There are others that are less likely to be to your taste—"

"Philately? They were talking about stamps?"

"Of course."

"Well, I didn't know," I said. "How was I supposed to know?"

I haven't read *The Scarlet Ruse* yet. I suppose I'll get to it eventually. The thing is, Haig keeps giving me books to read, and it's impossible to keep up. I did read a couple of books with a coin-collecting background recently, one by Raymond Chandler and another by Michael Innes, so I now know a little more about numismatics than I did when I walked into Ferdinand Bell's office.

He was the man I'd picked out at the funeral as the most likely candidate for the Ferdinand Bell lookalike contest. Today he was wearing a short-sleeved white shirt, open at the throat, and a pair of gray pants that might have been from the suit he'd worn a day ago. They certainly looked as though he had been wearing them for a while.

I had established earlier that he was around forty-seven. He looked both older and younger, depending on how you looked at him. He was plump, with chipmunk cheeks and happy little eyes, and that made him appear younger than he was, but his hair (short and snow white, with a slightly receding hairline) added a few years to his appearance. He sat on a stool behind a row of glass showcases in which coins rested on top of two-by-two brown envelopes. There was a bookcase to his right, filled to capacity, and a desk to his left with a great many books and magazines piled sloppily on it.

He looked up when I entered, which I guess is not too surprising, and he blinked rapidly when I told him who I was.

"Yes, Mr. Haig called me. So I've been awaiting you. But somehow I expected an older man. Aren't you a little young to be a detective? And didn't I see you at the funeral?"

I gave him a qualified yes. Since I wasn't officially a detective the first question was hard to answer. And the second was impossible; I had been at the funeral, and I saw him there, but how did I know whether he saw me?

"Have a seat," he said. "Or should we go somewhere and have a cup of coffee? But I don't think we'll be disturbed here today. My Saturdays are usually quiet. I tend to mail orders and such matters. That's if I'm not out of town working a convention. The A.N.A. is coming up in two weeks. It's in Boston this year, you know."

I didn't. I also didn't know what the A.N.A. was, but I've since learned. It's the American Numismatic Association, and it's the most important coin convention of the year. He went on to tell me that he had a bourse table reserved and expected to be bidding on some choice lots in the auction. Large cents, I think he said.

"I understand you believe Melanie was murdered," he said. "I'm reading between the lines there. Your Mr. Haig was deliberately vague. Dear me, I've made an unintentional rhyme, haven't I? *Your Mr. Haig/ Was deliberately vague.* And I gather you have a client in this matter?"

"Yes."

"I don't suppose you could tell me who it is?"

Haig had said I could, and so I did. I told him one of them, anyway.

"Caitlin! Extraordinary."

I wanted to ask him why it was extraordinary. Instead I started asking him some questions about his wife, Robin. Had she seemed at all nervous in the weeks immediately preceding her death? Had her behavior changed in any remarkable way?

He squinted in concentration and I swear his nose twitched like a bunny's. "As if she had some precognitive feelings about her fate? I never thought of that."

"Or as if she were afraid someone would murder her."

"Dear me. Now *that's* a speculation I've never entertained. Just let me think now. Do you know, I can't even concentrate on her attitude then because the whole idea of her having been murdered is so startling to me."

I nodded.

"Naturally I blamed myself for her death. After all, I was driving. I have a tendency to let my mind wander when I drive. Especially when tired, and I *was* tired that day; it had been a grueling weekend." He leaned forward and pressed his forehead with the fingertips of one hand. "I had never had an accident before. My woolgathering never seemed to interfere with my driving. Although I could never help thinking that if I had been paying a bit more attention to what I was doing I might have seen that patch of ice." He moved his hand to shade his eyes. "And Robin might be alive today."

I didn't say anything for a minute or two. He wiped his eyes with the back of his hand and straightened up on his stool. He forced his smile back in place.

A wistful look came into his eyes. "There's something I've always wondered about, Chip. May I call you that?"

"Sure."

"Something I've always wondered about. That skid I took. I grew up in an area where winter was long and severe. I learned to drive on snow and ice, how to react to sudden skids. Not to fight the wheel, to turn with the skid, all of those actions that are contrary to instinct and must consequently be learned and reinforced. And on the day of the accident I reacted as I had been trained to react."

"But it didn't work."

"No, it did not. And I've wondered if there couldn't have been a possibility of mechanical failure involved. I had the car looked at. It wasn't damaged all that severely, and if Robin had been sitting beside me and wearing a belt—" His face darkened. He bit his lip and went on. "They found that the steering column was damaged. I had never thought before that it might have been tampered with. Now I find myself wanting to seize on the possibility to white wash my own role in the affair. If the car had been sabotaged, if some fiend intentionally caused that accident—"

He got to his feet. "You must excuse me," he said. "I have a nervous stomach. I'll be a few moments. You might like to have a look at the coins in that case. There are some nice Colonials."

I had a look at the Colonials. I couldn't really tell you if they were nice or not. I also had a look at the books on his desk and in the glass-fronted bookcase. They all seemed to be about coins, which probably stood to reason. Some of them looked very old.

I was thumbing through a book called *The United States Trade Dollar*, by John Willem, when Bell came back. "An illuminating book," he said over my shoulder. "The Trade dollar was coined purely to facilitate commerce in the Orient. The Chinese traders would put their personal chop marks on them to attest to their silver value. I've a few pieces in stock if you'd care for a look at the genuine article."

He showed me three or four coins, returned them to their little brown envelopes and put them away. "My library is my most important asset," he said. "There's a motto in professional numismatics—Buy the book before the coin. The wisest sort of advice and all too few people follow it. Numismatics is a science, not just a matter of sorting change and filling holes in a Whitman folder. Take those Trade dollars. The whole history of the China trade is waiting to be read there."

He went on like that for a while. I tend to look interested even when I'm not, which Haig tells me is an asset; people reveal more of themselves to people who appear interested. So I listened, and it really was pretty interesting, but it wasn't getting me any closer to the man who killed Melanie and tried to bomb Leo Haig's house.

I found an opportunity to get the conversation back on the rails and brought up the question of motive. "Suppose someone did sabotage your car. He couldn't have been certain of killing just Robin. He would have had a shot at killing you, too."

"That had occurred to me."

"Well, anyone who's busy killing off five sisters probably wouldn't draw the line at including someone else here and there. Who benefited by Robin's death?"

"Financially?" He shrugged his shoulders. "That's no secret, surely. Except for a few minor bequests, I inherited Robin's entire estate."

"But suppose you had both been killed in the accident."

"Dear me. I hadn't thought of that. I'd have to check that, but it seems to me that I recall a provision to cover my dying before Robin. It would also cover simultaneous death, I presume. It's my recollection that the estate would be divided among her surviving sisters."

"I see."

"I'd have to check, but that would present no difficulty. My lawyer has a copy of Robin's will. I could call him first thing Monday morning. Just let me make a note of that."

He made a note of it, then looked up suddenly. "I say, Chip. You don't think I ought to consider myself in danger now, do you?" He laughed nervously. "It's hard to take seriously, isn't it? But if it *ought* to be taken seriously—"

"Do you have a will?"

"Yes, of course. I drew up a new will shortly after Robin's death. A few thousand dollars to a couple of numismatic research foundations, some smaller charitable bequests, and the balance to my sister in Lyons Falls."

"And you inherited Robin's estate free and clear?"

"Yes. Shortly after we were married we drew wills leaving everything to one another absolutely without encumbrance." His eyes clouded. "I expected it would be my will which would be put to the test first. I was seventeen years Robin's senior. She preferred older men, you know. Her first husband was as old as I am now when she married him. There's a history of heart trouble in my family. I naturally expected to predecease Robin, and although I hadn't all that much to leave her I wanted my affairs to be in order."

I told him I didn't think he was in any danger. No one could now expect to profit from his death. The news didn't cheer him much. He was too caught up in thoughts of his dead wife.

I asked if he knew anything about Jessica's will. "I barely knew Jessica," he said. "The Trelawney sisters were not close, and Robin and I kept pretty much to ourselves. Most of our close friends were business associates of mine. Coin dealers are gregarious folk, you know. We hardly regard one another as competitors. Often we do more business buying from each other, and selling to each other than we do with actual collectors. No, I don't know anything about

Jessica's will. I did go to her funeral, just as I went to Melanie's. I don't honestly know why I attended either of them. I had little enough to say to anyone there. I suppose it was a way of preserving my ties to Robin." He lowered his eyes. "We had so little time together."

"How did you meet her? Was she interested in coins?"

"Oh, not at all. Although she did come to share some of my interest during our life together. She was growing interested in love money, those little pins and brooches made of three-cent pieces, a very popular jewelry form of the mid-nineteenth century. I would always pick up pieces for her when I saw them. No real value, of course, but she liked them." He smiled at some private memory. "How did I meet her? I was a friend of her first husband, Phil Flanner. I suppose I fell in love with Robin while she was married to him, although I honestly didn't realize it at the time. Phil died tragically; a stupid accident. I began seeing her not too long after the funeral. I was drawn to her and enjoyed her company, still not recognizing what I felt as love. Gradually we both came to realize that we were in love with one another. I wish we had realized this sooner, so that we might have been married sooner. We had so very little time."

Chapter Ten

WHEN I GOT BACK TO THE HOUSE on 20th Street, Haig was on the top floor playing with his fish, repairing the leakers with rubber cement. When I asked if he wanted me to help, he grunted. I stopped in the kitchen where Wong was hacking a steak into bite-sized pieces with a cleaver. I left without a word. When he's chopping things he looks positively dangerous and I try to stay out of his way. I went downstairs and talked a little with some of the girls.

"Why they wanna blow up Maria?" Carmelita wanted to know. "She don' never hurt nobody. One guy, he say she give him a clop, but Maria never give nobody no clop. He get his clop somewhere else. Maria tell him, you get your clop from your mother, she say."

That was even more of a down than watching Haig swearing at his fish tanks, so I went over to Dominick's and had a beer and watched the Mets find a new way to lose. Matlack had a one-run lead going into the bottom of the ninth, struck out the first man, hit the second man on the arm, and got the third man to hit a double-play ball to short.

That was his mistake. They had Garrett playing short and he made the play without the ball. The ball went to left field and the runners went to second and third, and somebody walked and Bobby Bonds hit a 2-2 pitch off the fence and Dominick turned the set off.

"Shit," he said.

So I went back and read a couple chapters of an old Fredric Brown mystery until Haig came down, and then I gave him a full report. He made me go over everything a few hundred times. Then he closed his eyes and fiddled with his beard and put his head back and said "Indeed" fifteen times and "Curious" eighteen times. He wouldn't tell me what was curious.

I spent most of the night walking around the Village looking for somebody to sleep with. It was hotter than hell and there wasn't much air in the air. I didn't have any luck. I have a feeling I wasn't trying very hard. I had a couple of beers and a few cups of coffee and called Kim a couple of times, but no one answered.

I went back to my room and played a Dylan record over and over. I remember thinking that a little grass would be nice and regretting having flushed it to oblivion. It was a rotten night. I had run all over town and hadn't accomplished anything much. I was sorry I hadn't spent twenty of Haig's dollars on a massage and realized I would have been just as sorry if I had.

I thought about going downstairs to give Kim one more call, and I decided the hell with it, and eventually I went to sleep.

Nothing much happened Sunday. I slept late and had breakfast around noon and walked over to Haig's house because I couldn't think of anything else to do. I got there in time to watch Wong devastate him at backgammon. Wong beats hell out of me, but that was nothing compared to the way he routed Haig. It was pathetic to watch.

"There's nothing for you to do," he said.

Which would have been all right except that I felt like doing something. I hung around for a while and did some routine maintenance on the fish, although Sunday was supposed to be a free day for me. Just before dinner I called Andrea Sugar at home to find out if she had managed to get the records. She wasn't in. I called her a couple of hours later and reached her and learned that she hadn't had a chance to do anything yet.

I read a couple of books at Haig's. After dinner I caught a movie. I don't remember which one.

On the way home I stopped at a payphone and called Kim. I was a little worried about her, if you want to know. I also just found myself thinking about her a lot. I asked her if she had thought of anything significant, or if anybody had been following her or anything. She had nothing to report.

"The thing is," I said, "I'd like to go over things with you sometime. When Gordie's working or something, if you follow me."

"I think I follow you."

"Because he's not exactly crazy about me, and it's hard to get anyplace with him around. I mean as far as a conversation is concerned."

"He's here right now. He's in the other room. I don't think I'll tell him it's you on the phone."

"That sounds like a good idea."

"He'll be working tomorrow from noon to eight. I have a couple of classes during the afternoon, but the evening's clear."

"Don't you have a performance?"

"Monday's the dark night off-Broadway. Anyway, the play closed today."

"I'm sorry to hear that."

"Well, it wasn't very good. The critics hated it. Would you want to come over around six tomorrow?"

I said I would.

I went home and decided Gordie was the killer and that meant Kim was safe. He wouldn't kill her now. First he would kill Caitlin, and possibly her husband as well, and then he would marry Kim, and then he would kill her.

Monday there were things for me to do and places for me to go, so of course it rained. Haig had made appointments for me all over the place. I had to see a couple of lawyers, one on Fifth Avenue and one near City Hall just a block from Addison Shivers. I decided to drop in on him and let him know how we were doing, but he was in conference with a client when I got there. I went out and had fish and chips for lunch and dropped in on him again, but this time he was out having lunch, so I said the hell with it and took the subway uptown as far as Canal Street, which is not all that far. I walked up Mulberry to the address Haig had given me.

It didn't look like a place where I was going to feel tremendously welcome. It was the Palermo Social and Recreation Club, and there were a couple of old men playing bocce over to the right, and two other men sitting over a lackadaisical game of dominoes, and a fifth man watching the curl of lemon peel swim around in his cup of espresso. They all looked at me when I walked in. There was no discernible gleam of welcome in their eyes.

I went to the man sitting alone and asked him if he was John LiCastro. He asked who wanted to know, and I told him who I was and who I worked for and he smiled with the lower half of his face and pointed to a chair. I sat down and he told me I was privileged to work for a great man.

I agreed with him, but I wasn't too sure of this at the moment, because it was beginning to seem to me that the great man was not accomplishing a whole hell of a lot. The great man had not left the house yet, which certainly gave him a lot in common with Nero Wolfe, but neither had the great man called any suspects together, or even established that there *were* any suspects, for Pete's sake. The great man was spending a lot of time on his fish while I was keeping the New York Subway System out of the red, or trying to.

I didn't say any of this to Mr. LiCastro. I had a pretty good feeling that it was extremely unintelligent to say anything to Mr. LiCastro that Mr. LiCastro didn't want to hear. I told him what I had been instructed to tell him, and asked him what I had been instructed to ask him, and he took in my words with little darting affirmative movements of his head. At one point his eyes narrowed as he fixed on some private thought, and I realized that I was sitting across the table from a man who could kill a man at five o'clock and sit down to a huge dinner at five-thirty and not even worry about indigestion.

Then he ordered espresso for both of us and leaned back in his chair and asked some questions of his own, and there was a warm glow in his eyes and a look of complete relaxation on his face.

It was really something to see.

"So LiCastro is crazy about tropical fish," I said later. "I was wondering how on earth you would know somebody like him. His discus spawned, but a fungus got the eggs."

"That usually happens."

"He was tickled enough that he got them to spawn in the first place. He's trying a new fungicide and he wants your opinion of it. He didn't remember the name. He's going to call you later."

"And he'll make some inquiries about Gordon McLeod?"

"That's what he said. I had a very eerie feeling about that. I wanted to make sure he just made inquiries. I thought he might think I was asking for something more serious than inquiries. Like he might have thought I was being subtle and indicating you wanted McLeod killed if I didn't spell things out."

"I doubt it."

"Well, I wasn't sure. Also I had the feeling that if you did want McLeod killed, and you said as much to LiCastro, then that would be the end of McLeod."

"That I do not doubt," Haig said. "Continue."

I continued. "Jessica Trelawney drew a will a couple of weeks after Robin died. I have the date written down if it matters."

"It may."

"Her lawyer says that's a common response to the death of someone close. He also says she left everything to a feminist group called Radicalesbians. I'm not making this up. He is sure the will is going to be challenged by attorneys for Caitlin Vandiver, and he told me off the record that he's just as sure it won't stand up. He more or less implied that he drew it in such a way as to make it easy to challenge. I'm pretty sure he's not a big fan of Radicalesbians."

"Indeed."

"So no one stood to gain a penny by Jessica's death, except for Radicalesbians, but that doesn't prove anything because no one necessarily knew about her will. Before that she had never drawn a will, and if she had died intestate, everything would have been divided among the surviving sisters. Which is what would have happened to Robin's money if she and Bell had died together in the car accident."

"Car wreck," Haig said.

"Indeed," I said.

"Precision is important. Language is a tool, its edge must be kept sharp."

"Indeed. Melanie did die intestate, which is a word I have now used twice in two minutes and can't remember ever using before. I suppose it's a part of keeping the edge of my tool sharp. So her money will be divided among Caitlin and Kim, and—"

"Between."

"Huh?"

"One divides among three persons and between two. I don't like to keep correcting you, Chip."

"I can tell you don't. I found out who Caitlin's lawyer is, but couldn't reach him."

"He wouldn't divulge information about her will anyway."

"He probably will, because it's Addison Shivers, but I couldn't get to see him. Anyway, I figured he would tell us or not tell us over the phone. I would guess that her money is scheduled to go to her husband, but you can't be sure, can you? I mean, she changes husbands pretty quickly, and if she's not morbid she might not want to have to change her will that frequently. The problem is that I keep going out after information and I keep getting it and it doesn't seem to get me anywhere."

"Sooner or later everything will fit into place."

"By that time everyone could be dead."

"In the long run everyone always is, Chip." He began filling a pipe, tamping down each pinch of tobacco very carefully. "We have to make haste slowly," he went on, while making haste slowly with the pipe. "We are making progress. We are in the possession of data we previously lacked. That is progress."

"I suppose."

"There are cases that lend themselves to Sherlockian methodology. Cases which are solved by the substance in a man's trouser turnups. Cases which hinge on a dog's silence in the night or the chemical analysis of coffee grounds." He closed his eyes and put the deliberately filled pipe back in the pipe rack. His hand went to his beard and he leaned back in his chair. "This, I think, is another sort of case entirely. There is someone somewhere with a logical reason to kill the five daughters of Cyrus Trelawney. He had a reason to sabotage Ferdinand Bell's car, a reason to pitch Jessica Trelawney out a window, a reason to inject Melanie Trelawney with a fatal overdose of heroin. If we determine the reason, we will have determined the killer."

He sat forward suddenly, and his eyes opened like those dolls that go sleepy-bye when you lay them down on their backs. "Do you know something, Chip? I think there's an element of Ross MacDonald in this. I can't avoid the feeling that the underlying motive is buried somewhere deep in the past. As though it all has its roots forty years ago, in Canada."

"Canada?"

"A figure of speech. So often Lew Archer uncovers something that started forty years ago in Canada, you know." He spun around in his chair and gazed at the rasboras. They didn't seem at all self-conscious. While he let them provide inspiration, I took out my nail file and cleaned out the dirt from under my fingernails. I only tell you this so you won't think I was just sitting there doing nothing.

He turned around again, eventually, and folded his hands on his round belly. He looked elfin but determined. "I shall call Addison Shivers," he said. "I have some questions to ask him."

He reached for the telephone, and it rang. So he picked it up, naturally enough. It doesn't seem to surprise him much when things like this happen. In fact he made it look as though he had been waiting for it to ring.

He talked briefly, mostly saying things like "Yes," and "Indeed." Then he hung up and raised his eyebrows at me.

"Our client," he said.

"Mr. Shivers?"

"Mrs. Vandiver. She's at her house on Long Island. She wants to see you immediately. She says it's rather urgent."

Chapter Eleven

YOU GET TO SANDS POINT by taking the Long Island Rail Road to the Port Washington stop. I understand that there are people who do this every day. What I don't understand is why.

I got on the train at Penn Station, and got off it at Port Washington. I stood there on the platform for a minute, and a very tall and very thin man came up to me. "You would be Mr. Harrison," he said.

"I would," I said. "I mean, uh, I am. Yes."

"I am Seamus," he said. "I've brought the car."

The car was a Mercedes, about the size of Chicago. I started to get in the front next to Seamus, but stopped when he gave me a very disappointed glance. I closed the door and got in back instead. He seemed happier about this.

There was a partition between the front and rear seats, which kept Seamus and me from having to make small talk to each other. I sat back and looked out the window at one expensive home after another. Finally, we turned onto what I thought was a side road but turned out to be the Vandiver driveway. It wandered through a stand of old trees and finally led to a house.

The house gave you an idea of what God could have done if he'd had the money. That's not my line; I read it somewhere, but I can't think of a way to improve on it. There were these Grecian columns in front which you would think no house could live up to, and then the house went on to overpower the columns, and it was all about as impressive as anything I've ever seen. Caitlin and Melanie had each inherited the same amount of money, and Caitlin lived here, while Melanie had lived in Cockroach Heaven, and it wasn't hard to feel that Caitlin had a better appreciation of creature comfort.

She was waiting for me in a room carpeted in white shag and decorated in what I think they call French provincial. The furniture did not come from the Salvation Army. There were oil paintings on the walls, including one that I recognized as a portrait of Cyrus Trelawney.

"I'm so glad you're here," she said. "It's been such a bore of a day. Your drink is Irish whiskey, if I remember correctly. Straight, with a soda chaser?"

It was the last thing I wanted, but I evidently had an image to maintain. She made the drinks, fixing herself a massive Martini, and her eyes sparkled as we touched our glasses together. "To crime," she said.

I took a sip and avoided coughing. I'm sure it was excellent whiskey, but at that point it tasted a lot like shellac.

"I hope you didn't mind my sending Seamus for you," she said. "He's not really a chauffeur. He's more of a general houseman. I usually prefer to do my own driving, actually, but I hate waiting for anything. Especially trains, and the Long Island is hardly ever in on time. Did you have a dreadful ride?"

"It wasn't too bad."

"You were sweet to come. And your Mr. Haig does inspire confidence, doesn't he? It put my mind at rest just to talk to him for a few minutes."

"He's quite a man," I said.

She moved closer to me and put her hand on my arm. She was wearing the same perfume she had worn at the funeral. Her blouse was a black and white print and it was cut low in front. She was not wearing a bra.

"Let's step outside," she said. "Did it rain in the city? We had quite a storm out here this morning and it's actually cooled things off a bit. It's rather pleasant outside."

We took our drinks and walked through some paths in back of the house to a little garden walled in by oaks and beeches. Caitlin sat down on the grass and kicked her shoes off. I stood there for a moment, then sat down next to her.

"I gather there was something you wanted to tell me," I said.

"Oh?"

410

"Mr. Haig said you told him it was urgent."

She nodded solemnly. "I said it was rather urgent that I see you."

"That's what he said."

"Because I felt an urgent need to see you, Chip." She finished her drink and set the glass down on the lawn. She sat back, her arms out behind her to support her weight, and her breasts strained against the black and white blouse. "I felt quite bored," she said. "And quite lonely."

"I see."

"Do you? And of course I wanted a first-hand report on the case. Do you really think someone wants to murder me?"

"It looks that way."

"But why?"

"That's what we're trying to find out." It occurred to me that this would be a good time to find out about her will. "Haig says motive is the big question. He wants to know who would benefit from your death."

"Practically everyone, I imagine. I'm a very wicked woman, Chip."

"Uh."

"You have no idea just how wicked I can be. But of course, you're talking about my will. It's very straightforward, actually. Gregory and I made wills in each other's favor at the time of our marriage. Whichever of us goes first, the other picks up all the marbles."

"I see."

"But I really don't think Greg would murder me, do you? Or if he did, it wouldn't be for money or anything so vulgar. He might kill me out of justifiable rage. I do behave rather badly, you know." She ran her tongue over her lips. This is a very trite gesture, but she made it work anyway. "I suppose I could change my will and leave everything to Radicalesbians like my brilliant sister Jessica. Did you hear about that?"

"I just saw her lawyer today."

"What a dimwitted dyke she was. Not that I have anything against lesbians myself. I think they limit themselves, that's all. Like vegetarians."

"Vegetarians?"

"Vegetables are nice, but so is meat."

"Oh."

"And girls are nice, but so are men." She smiled softly. "I went through a gay period myself in my girlhood. I think I may have mentioned it to you the other day."

"Uh, sort of."

"I was in school at the time. There was this girl who was absolutely mad for me. She was a pretty thing, very small and dark, not like me physically at all. Her breasts just filled my hands. I liked that. She, on the other hand, was partial to large breasts. Do you like large breasts, Chip?"

"Uh, sure."

"I thought you probably did. She told me one day what she wanted to do to me. She wanted to lick me here." She indicated with her hand where the other girl had wanted to lick her. "So I let her. It was such heaven. She didn't insist that I do anything in return, but do you know something, Chip? I discovered that I wanted to. I suppose it was curiosity at first, but I found I enjoyed it very much. Going down on her, that is."

"Er."

"I liked the taste. I'll tell you something fascinating. At the time I only thought girls did it to each other. I didn't imagine that a man would want to do it. But I've since learned that some men enjoy it very much. Have you ever done it?"

"Yes."

"Do you enjoy doing it?"

"Yes."

"I rather thought you might." She opened the top buttons of her blouse. Her skin was creamy and flawless. "But to get back to what I was saying," she said. "About lesbians and how limited they are. Now I adored eating my little friend, you understand, but then I went to bed with an older man and he taught me ever so many things, and while I still found girls amusing, I certainly wasn't about to go without men for the rest of my life. Do you know what I particularly enjoyed?"

"What?"

"Fellatio."

"Oh."

"It's such a technical term for such an intimate act, isn't it?"

"I never thought about it."

"You never thought about fellatio?"

"I never thought about the, uh, term, uh."

"Such an intimate act," she said. Her hand was on my thigh now. "I'm mad for penises. Isn't that terrible of me? I like to feel them grow in my mouth. Oh, but yours has already grown, hasn't it? Oh, lovely. Lovely."

I took her by the shoulders and kissed her. Her mouth tasted of gin and tobacco and honey, and her perfume wrapped me up like a blanket. Her hand kept doing great things while we kissed.

She said, "This is a very private place, Chip. No one can see us here. We can take off all our clothes and roll around in the grass all we want."

We took off all our clothes and rolled around in the grass a lot. Her body was delicious, taut and sleek and smooth, and if there was any age worn into it, I couldn't tell you about it. We did a whole host of things I somehow don't feel compelled to tell you about, and then she decided that she wanted to conclude with the thing she particularly enjoyed.

"I can taste myself on you," she said. "I like that." Then she didn't say anything any more, and neither did I, and it was a lot like going to heaven without the aggravation of dying first.

I'll tell you something. It was pretty embarrassing to write

413

that last scene. According to Haig, the less sexual detail in these books, the better. "Archie Goodwin very obviously leads an active sex life," he says, "but he does no more than allude to it. He doesn't throw it in your face, doesn't drag you into various bedchambers with him."

But Mr. Elder says times have changed, and that if we expect him to publish these books, there better be a lot of screwing in them. "You've got to arouse the reader," he said. "The reports on the murders and what an interesting character Haig is, that's all fine, but you've got to turn the reader on in this day and age. And of course you've got to do it in good taste."

I don't know if I turned you on, and I don't know if it was in good taste or not. I have to admit I turned myself on just now, though. Just remembering how terrific it was.

A while later we were back in our clothes. We were also back in the room with the white shag carpet, and Caitlin was drinking another jumbo Martini. I had turned down the Irish whiskey in favor of a Dr Pepper with a lot of ice.

"Oh, my," she said. "That was quite wonderful, wasn't it? I have a confession to make, Chip. I lured you out here for no other reason than to seduce you. Do you think you can possibly forgive me?"

I said I thought I probably could.

"You're such a charming boy, you know. And terribly attractive, and I've been wanting to take you to bed ever since our lunch together." She stretched like a waking cat. "And it's so deadly dull out here. There's Seamus, of course, but when one has sex with one's servants one is limited to the more conventional approaches. It is considered terribly déclassé to perform fellatio upon the domestic help. Now if only I were Jewish, I could blow my chauffeur all I wanted."

That's a pun. Maybe you already knew that. I didn't, and so I didn't laugh, which must have annoyed Caitlin a little. The idea is that Jews have a trumpet made out of a ram's horn which they blow in synagogue on certain holy days, and it's called a *shofar*.

We talked about various things, most of them at least slightly sexual, and I had another Dr Pepper while she had another Martini, and then I remembered that I had an appointment to see Kim around six. I mentioned this and Caitlin glanced at her watch.

"Hell," she said. "I'd planned on driving you back to the city myself."

"I can take a train."

"No, you wouldn't want to do that. One trip on the Long Island is as much as should be required of anyone. I wanted to drive you, but Gregory's due home soon and he likes me to be here when he arrives. I can't imagine why. I'll have Seamus drive you."

"You really don't have to bother."

"It's no bother," she said. "I've no use for him around here at the moment." She picked up the telephone and made a bell ring in another part of the house. When Seamus answered, she told him to bring the car around in a few minutes.

I kissed her a few times and told her not to worry about the murderer, which was silly in view of the fact that she could not have been worrying less about the murderer. Then we went out and stood on the porch and watched Seamus drive the car almost fifteen feet before it exploded.

I was going to write that it was like nothing I had ever seen before, but of course I'd seen it a hundred times in a hundred movies. That's just what it looked like. All of a sudden the car went up into the air and came down in pieces. Most of the pieces were metal, but some of them were Seamus, and they were raining down all over the lawn. One hunk of metal actually landed within a few yards of us, and we were standing half a football field away from the car when it blew up.

"Oh Christ," Caitlin kept saying. "Oh Christ."

I didn't know what to do first. The police would have to be called, obviously, but the most immediate problem was

Caitlin. She was shaking and all the color was gone from her face and she looked ready to pass out. I got her inside and tried to make her sit down, but her body went rigid.

"You have to fuck me," she said.

I stared at her, but she was already getting out of her clothes. "I have to have it right now, right now. I have to, you have to do it for me, that could have been me in that car, somebody planted a bomb to kill me, somebody wants to murder me. It's true, it's really true. Christ, you have to fuck me, you just have to."

I was positive I wouldn't be able to. I mean, watching a car blow up isn't normally my idea of a turn on. But they say that a close escape from death makes you want to reaffirm the fact that you're alive in a sexual way, and it had crossed my mind that it could have been me in the car when it blew up, too, and I guess that made the difference. I got out of my clothes in a hurry, got down on the white shag rug with her, and we began screwing like minks, which is a vulgar way to put it, I guess, but that's what we were doing.

I never heard the door open. I may have left it open, as far as that goes. I don't think I would have heard an earthquake at that point. It was very basic and intense and without frills, and I don't suppose much time elapsed from start to finish, but the finish was a good one and I lay there on top of her wondering if my heart would ever go back to beating at its usual rate, and a man's voice said, "Caitlin, I believe I'm entitled to an explanation."

"He has always had an instinct for disastrous timing," she said in my ear. "Always."

"Caitlin—"

"At least he refrained from speaking until we finished," she went on. "Breeding tells, after all. That's something."

"I come home from work," Gregory Vandiver said reasonably. "I return to my house at my usual hour. I find my car blown to bits all over my lawn; I find my manservant dead in the wreckage and I find my wife copulating with

416

some strange young man on the middle of the drawing room floor. Now *wait* a minute. I've seen you before, haven't I? Yes, I daresay I have. Don't tell me, it'll come to me in a minute."

Chapter Twelve

BETWEEN THE SANDS POINT POLICE and the Long Island Rail Road, it was almost ten o'clock before I got back to the city. I did manage to call Kim before that, from the station in Port Washington, but it probably would have been better if I hadn't called her at all. I didn't manage to say three sentences to her before Gordie took the phone away from her.

"You take a lot of telling," he said. "I don't want you coming here, I don't want you calling here, I don't want you sticking your nose in where it ain't wanted." Then he told me to do something I wouldn't have been able to do if I had wanted to, which I didn't in the first place, and then he slammed the phone down.

I walked from Penn Station to Haig's house. I had given him a little of it earlier over the phone and now I gave him the whole thing in detail. (I left out the sex part, at least as far as going into details was concerned. I mean, I had to let him know that Gregory Vandiver walked in and found me screwing his wife. That was the kind of thing that might turn out to be pertinent. So I told him what I had done, you might say, without telling him how much I had enjoyed it.)

"The timing," he said, "is very critical here."

"Right. The killer had about an hour and a half to plant the bomb. The car was all right when Seamus picked me up at the station."

"Indeed."

"She usually did her own driving. Anybody who knew her well would probably know that."

"Do the police know that?"

"No. The police think that the killer did what he was trying to do. It seems that Seamus was involved with some faction of the I.R.A. The police had a sheet on him because he was suspected of playing a role in a gun-running

418

operation. So they think Seamus was the intended victim, and they also think they have several leads."

"I take it you and the Vandivers permitted them to continue thinking this."

"Yes."

"I'm not sure that was wise."

"Neither am I, but it seemed like a good idea at the time. I was passed off as a friend of Mrs. Vandiver's who happened to be visiting at the time. Her husband could have confirmed that we were friendly."

"Indeed."

"Gordie McLeod was back in the Village by eight-fifteen. Because I talked to him on the phone, and no, it wasn't my idea. I wanted to talk to Kim, but he included himself in. Of course he didn't have to stick around while a batch of Long Island public employees asked dumb questions and took pictures of everything, but I'm sure he was at work all day."

"He was not."

"Oh?"

"Mr. LiCastro called. The fungicide he wants to use will render the discus spawn infertile. I so informed him and gave him some suggestions. Gordon McLeod did not show up today for what I believe is called a shape-up. Mr. McLeod has been betting on quite a few horses lately. With little success."

"That's interesting."

"It is. Nor is he in debt to his bookmaker. His losses, however, have of late exceeded his wages, and yet he has been consistently able to settle his debts promptly, and in cash."

"He must be sponging off Kim."

"Perhaps. It would be useful to determine this."

I nodded. Haig put his feet up on the desk. He tries this every once in a while, but he's always uncomfortable because his legs are too short and his abdomen too large. He gave it up after a few seconds.

He said, "I had a visitor during your absence. Mr. Ferdinand Bell."

"What did he want?"

"To be helpful. A noble ambition, but I'm not sure he achieved its realization. He described the swerving of his automobile with an excess of detail. Listening to him, I very nearly felt that I was in it at the time. It was not a feeling I particularly enjoyed."

"Did he have anything else to say?"

"He had some things to say about Miss Andrea Sugar. He brought to my attention the possibility that a lesbian relationship might have existed between her and Jessica Trelawney."

"No kidding."

"He seemed shocked by this. I find his shock more interesting than the relationship itself, certainly. He also said that Mr. Vandiver is in serious financial difficulties."

"You couldn't prove it by the house."

"So I gather. Mr. Vandiver has apparently suffered some financial reverses."

"How would Bell know that?"

"I'm not sure he knew that he knew it. He was letting his mind wander in my presence, talking generally about the flightiness of the sisters Trelawney. Jessica's homosexuality, Melanie's hippie lifestyle, Kim's hour upon the stage—"

"Kim seems pretty straight-ahead to me."

"Your bias on the subject has already been noted. He also alluded to Caitlin's liberated sexuality, which he cloaked with the euphemism of nymphomania."

"I'm not positive it's a euphemism."

"Be that as it may. And that led him to Gregory Vandiver's infirmity of purpose. Vandiver made some substantial investments in rare coins about a year ago. He consulted Bell, and purchased the pieces through Bell and on Bell's recommendation. He specifically sought out items for long-term growth, the blue chips of the coin market.

420

Barber proofs, Charlotte and Dahlonega gold, that sort of thing. Then a matter of months ago, Vandiver insisted that Bell unload everything and get him cash overnight. It seems Vandiver did realize a profit on his investment, if a tiny one, but that Bell would have advised him to hold indefinitely, and certainly to hold for several months, as an upturn could be expected in the market. But Vandiver insisted on selling immediately, even if he had to take a loss."

"Meaning that he needed cash, I guess."

"So it would seem. The money involved was considerable. I had to pry this from Bell, who evidently believes that matters communicated to a professional numismatist come under the category of privileged information. Gregory Vandiver liquidated his numismatic holdings for a net sum of $110,000."

"He had that much invested in coins?"

"I find that remarkable. I find it more remarkable that he had a sudden need for that much cash."

I nodded. "I wonder," I said.

"If he could have placed the bomb in the car?"

"Yeah. I suppose it's possible. Say he gets a train earlier than his usual one. He comes straight home and goes straight to the garage and wires the bomb to the Mercedes. He knows he's safe because he's not going to drive the car. He doesn't even think about Seamus because Caitlin usually drives herself." I stopped for a moment. "No, it doesn't add up. He wouldn't know she was going to use the car then. He didn't know I was there, so there was no way to know she would drive me home."

"He could assume she would use the car eventually, however."

"But why bother getting home earlier than usual? He could have planted the bomb some other time."

Haig leaned back and played with his beard. I asked a few more questions that he didn't respond to. I went over and watched the African gouramis while he did his genius-in-residence number. While I was watching them, I saw the female knock off a guppy. It didn't bother me a bit.

Haig said, "I would like to know at what time Gregory Vandiver left his office."

"So would I."

"I would also like to know where Gordon McLeod spent the afternoon. And his source of income."

"So would I."

"There are other things, too. Several extremely curious things. I am going to have to know considerably more about Cyrus Trelawney."

"I don't get it."

"Hmmmm," he said.

Wong brought us some beer and we sat opposite each other drinking it and arguing about where I was going to spend the night. "There is a pattern to all of this, Chip," he told me. "There are going to be more deaths. One develops the ability to sense this sort of thing. There have been four deaths already since the case engaged our interest. Melanie's was the first. The other three have been gratuitous. The prostitute, the sailor, the chauffeur."

"Manservant," I said.

"When a manservant dies at the wheel of his employer's car I have difficulty in not regarding him as a chauffeur. Three gratuitous deaths. There will be more deaths, and they will be more to the point. I sense this."

I went through my usual mental hassle as to whether he was a genius or a nutcase.

"I would prefer that these deaths not occur. I will, in fact, endeavor to prevent them to the best of my ability. It is for this, after all, that I am employed. But, failing that, I would at least prefer that one of these deaths not be suffered by you."

"I'd prefer it, too," I said. "To tell you the truth."

"You expose yourself unnecessarily by returning to your rooming house."

"I expose myself to worse than that on the couch. I could

422

die of a backache."

"You could have my bed," Haig said.

"Oh, don't be ridiculous."

"I would not mind the couch."

"Oh, come on. I'll walk a couple of blocks and I'll be home, for Pete's sake. It's nothing to worry about."

So I headed back to my rooming house.

That was my first mistake.

My second mistake happened as I was on my way up the steps to the front door. A guy came out of the doorway to the left of my building, and two other guys came out of the doorway to the right of my building, and one of them asked me if I was Harrison, and I made my second mistake. I said I was.

Chapter Thirteen

They kicked the shit out of me.

Chapter Fourteen

I'M GOING TO LEAVE IT AT THAT.

Haig doesn't think I ought to. He wants me to handle it like Dick Francis and describe the beating they gave me, a blow at a time. With the proper discipline, he maintains, I can run the scene to ten or twelve pages instead of getting it over and done with in seven words. The thing is, I don't want to spend that much time remembering it. They kicked the shit out of me, very coldly and systematically, doing everything to assure me that there was nothing personal in what they were doing. Then they walked off in different directions, and I crawled into my rooming house and upstairs and got into bed.

Everything was worse in the morning. Things really ached. I dragged myself over to Haig's office and he took one look at me and threw a fit. What infuriated him the most was that I hadn't called him immediately so that he could have had his doctor look at me. I said I was pretty sure nothing was broken. He called his doctor, who made a housecall, which I felt was completely unnecessary. I think he came over for an excuse to look at the fish. But while he was there he also looked at me and pronounced me physically fit. I had a lot of bruises, and they were going to look increasingly ugly for the next week to ten days, but I had no broken bones and there was no evidence of internal injuries.

"You should have stayed here last night," Haig said.

I suppose he couldn't resist saying that. I didn't bother replying to it.

I had things to do, but they started with Kim and I couldn't see her until afternoon when the hulk would either go to the docks or pretend to. I called Andrea Sugar, but failed to reach her. So I helped Haig with the fish until Wong brought us some lunch. I can't remember what it was, only that it had slivers of almonds in it and it was

425

delicious. Afterward Haig picked up the phone and called Addison Shivers' office. The old lawyer was in conference, but would return his call.

When Haig hung up I got through to Kim. "Gordie left a few minutes ago," she said. "Chip, maybe you shouldn't come over here. Gordie scares me a little."

He scared me more than a little, but I kept this fact to myself. "There was another murder attempt yesterday," I told her. "I'm on my way over."

This peeved Haig. "Mr. Shivers will be calling me shortly," he said. "You ought to be here when he does."

"I thought you wanted to talk to him yourself."

He leaned back in his chair and folded his hands on his stomach. "I do," he said. "But you should be present. I have a strong feeling that he is going to provide me with the solution to the case."

"Just like that?"

"Let us say he is going to give me evidence to support the conclusion I have drawn already."

"Conclusion?"

"On the basis of evidence already available to us."

"Evidence?"

"You're beginning to sound like an echo, Chip. Try to curb that tendency."

"I'll do my best. What evidence do we have already available to us? We have to find where Gordie spent yesterday afternoon and where he's been getting his money; we have to find out when Gregory Vandiver left his office and how deep a financial hole he's in, we have to—"

He waved a small hand at me. The right one, probably. "Superficial," he said.

"But we don't know anything. Unless you've found out something and haven't told me."

"You have all the information I have."

"Do you want to tell me what I missed?"

"That would be premature," he said. He was

disgustingly pleased with himself. "If you'll wait for Mr. Shivers' call—"

I decided he was grandstanding and I also decided I had better things to do than sit around waiting for the phone to ring. I sprung for a cab and rode down to Kim's place on Bethune Street. When she opened the door, the first thing I did was give her hell for not making sure it was me before unlocking the door.

"Then I'm in real danger," she said.

"You'd have to call it that. I was out on Long Island yesterday. To see Caitlin. Somebody wired a bomb to her car."

"Oh, God! She's not—"

"She's all right. But her chauffeur isn't. He was killed. It's pretty unmistakable, Kim. Somebody wants to kill every last one of you."

I got her to sit down and made her a cup of coffee. I sat on the couch next to her and patted her hand a lot and tried to be reassuring, which was tough because I had started off trying to scare her silly. I went on patting her hand, though, because I was beginning to enjoy it.

"I don't know what to do," she said.

Her eyes were wide with fear and innocence, and she was just so damned beautiful I wanted to kiss her. Instead I said, "Look, there are a lot of possibilities. One possibility is that you're not in any real danger at all. For the time being."

"I don't understand."

"Depending on who the killer is."

She thought that over, and then her face tightened. "You mean if I'm the one. I suppose you have to suspect everyone—"

"That's not what I meant at all, for Pete's sake. Look, I have to ask you this. Where was Gordie yesterday afternoon?"

"He was at work."

"The hell he was. Mr. Haig knows somebody who can

427

ask questions on the docks and get the right answers. Gordie didn't show up for the shape-up yesterday. He didn't work at all."

She looked at me.

"He told you he worked from noon to eight?"

"Yes. Where was he if he wasn't at work?"

"That's what I'd like to find out. It also seems he's been losing big sums of money betting on slow horses. He's been losing more than he's been earning and I'd like to know where he's been getting his money. Have you been giving him any?" I took her hand. "I know it's an embarrassing question, but I have to ask it."

"I don't mind. Because I've never given him anything. He's even tried to pay a share of the rent, but I haven't let him. He always takes the check when we go out together. He always seems to have plenty of money. A longshoreman can make a decent living and I thought—" She stopped suddenly.

"What's the matter?"

"I'm a slow study today, aren't I? You think he's been murdering my sisters."

"I think it's possible, yes. It's not the only possibility, but it's reasonably strong."

"It's so hard to believe."

"Could he have killed Melanie? That was Wednesday, sometime during the afternoon."

"He was working then. At least he told me so."

"And yesterday he had plenty of time to get out to Long Island and back. We'll have to find out if he has an alibi for Jessica's murder. I don't think he tracked Robin upstate and sabotaged her car. That sounds a little tricky. I think her death was accidental after all, but maybe it gave him the idea for the whole thing."

"How do you mean?"

"He must have figured that you would benefit financially by Robin's death. You don't, the money all goes to her husband, but he wouldn't necessarily know that. So he could have decided that if he killed off Jessica and Melanie and Caitlin you would have that much more money for him to marry."

She nodded with understanding. "So that's why I'm safe for the time being."

"Until you marry him and make out a will in his favor. That's if he's the killer. There are other possibilities."

"Who else do you suspect?"

"I don't want to mention any names yet. I wouldn't have said I suspected Gordie if there had been any other way to ask the questions I had to ask."

She went to make herself another cup of coffee and asked me if I wanted one. I said I wouldn't mind a beer. She brought one and poured it into a glass for me. She didn't crumple the can when it was empty.

"I don't know how I'm going to behave in front of him," she said thoughtfully. "Just being aware that he might be a murderer is going to make it difficult for me."

"You can't let him know that you suspect. He wouldn't want to murder you ahead of schedule, but if it's a choice of doing that or being caught for the murders he's already committed—"

"It's going to be hard not to let anything show."

"Well, you'll get a chance to find out how good an actress you are."

"I will, won't I?" She set her coffee cup down and folded her hands on her knee. "I could believe that he might become violent. He's that type of person, there's a real potential for violence there. But I can't see him doing it in a calculated manner, if you know what I mean."

"That's bothered me from the start."

"Well, I'll be very careful."

"You'd better. That means two things, you know. Being careful not to let Gordie know you suspect him, and being careful not to be alone with anybody else. Don't open your door when you're here alone."

"For strangers, you mean."

429

"Or for people you know."

"God," she said. "You mean I have to suspect everybody, is that it?"

"Just about."

"It's been hard enough living with Gordie lately. And now to have this on my mind—"

I said, "Look, it's not my place to say this, but I'll say it anyway. I agree it's hard to imagine Gordie involved in such a complicated series of murders. It's also hard to imagine him involved with you. I mean, I really can't figure out what you see in a baboon like him."

She picked up her coffee cup and looked into it for a long time. Then without raising her eyes she said, "Oh, I don't know exactly. I haven't had much experience with men. Before I met Gordie I fell in love with one of the boys in my acting class. He was a completely different type from Gordie. Very gentle and sensitive."

"I have a feeling I know how this ends."

"Of course. He turned out to be gay, which was something I probably should have recognized in the first place. The signs were all there. And it wasn't as though he did anything to encourage me to fall in love with him. He thought I knew what he was and just wanted to be friends." She looked up. "I took all of this terribly hard. And I decided that my next man was going to be as heterosexual as possible. Gordie was such a change, he had all this macho strength, and at the time I thought it was what I wanted."

"I gather you've changed your mind since."

"I know I couldn't marry him. Or even live with him much longer. Last night after your phone call I was furious with him. He had no right to act that way. I wanted to tell him to leave."

"What stopped you?"

"I think maybe I'm a little afraid of him. That he would take a punch at me or something." She managed a lopsided grin. "I'm a lot more afraid of him now than I was last night. After what you told me."

"Well, don't act any differently for the time being."

"I'll try not to. I can be a pretty good little actress when I have to."

"And an ornament to the stage. I think we'll crack the case in the next couple of days. And when all this is over—"

I left the sentence unfinished. I also left Kim's apartment after a few minutes because otherwise I might have found myself talking about what would happen when all this was over. I couldn't keep from having thoughts on the subject, but it was pretty silly to voice them at that stage. Premature, Haig would have called it.

I tried Andrea again. "I feel like a secret agent," she said. "I hoff zee documents."

"That's the worst Peter Lorre impression I ever heard, but it's good news. Can I come over?"

She gave me the address.

Chapter Fifteen

SHE LIVED IN THE SAME BUILDING she had occupied as Jessica's roommate. Not in the penthouse, however, but in a studio apartment on the third floor. She opened the door for me and motioned me inside. "Excuse the place," she said. "I haven't had time to buy any furniture that I like. That chair's not too bad."

As I was on my way to the chair that wasn't too bad she asked me if my leg was bothering me.

"Everything's bothering me," I said.

"I mean the way you walk. Did you hurt yourself?"

"I didn't have to. Someone did it for me."

"Huh?"

"I was beaten up last night. By professionals, I think. They didn't break any bones or anything like that. They just beat me to a pulp."

"Oh, God. Take your shirt off."

"Huh?"

"Take your shirt off and let me see. Christ, they really did a job on you. You're going to be stiff. Get undressed, Chip."

"Huh?"

"Take your clothes off and lie down on my bed. I'm serious, dumbbell. The only thing that's going to do you any good at this point is a massage. You should get a daily massage for the next week, as a matter of fact. Well, you came to the right place. I happen to be a damned good masseuse."

"I remember."

"Most of the girls don't know anything about muscle groups. I took the trouble to take a decent course. Come on, lie down on your stomach. Oh, you poor baby. They really worked you over, didn't they?"

"Ouch."

"Your flesh is very tender and I'll have to hurt you a

432

little, but you'll feel a lot better afterward. Just trust me and try to relax."

"Okay."

She really knew what she was doing. She hurt me a little from time to time, but I could feel a lot of soreness and tension draining away. I began to feel very drowsy, and she had stopped touching me for a while before I realized the absence of her hands.

I asked if we were finished.

"Nope," she said cheerfully. "I'm taking my clothes off. I work better in the nude. Okay, tiger. Roll over."

I rolled over and opened my eyes. That long lean body was even nicer than I remembered it.

I said, "I don't know about this."

"You don't have to," she said. "Just shut up and relax. Does this hurt?"

"Yes."

"Those rotten bastards. There, that's better, isn't it?"

I was beginning to feel a little stirring. You probably don't find that hard to believe. Her hands were very firm and very gentle, and her body was very beautiful, and she had that nice spicy smell to her skin. When she started touching my thighs with that feathery way she had, I started to sit up. She made me lie down again.

"Hey," I said.

"Feels nice, doesn't it?"

"Yeah, but I really don't want to wind up frustrated."

"That must have been awful the other day. I hated to see you leave like that."

"I didn't like it much myself, but I don't have any money now and I—"

"Who said anything about money, Chip?"

"Huh?"

She grinned wickedly. "Dumbbell. I'm not working now, you jerk. I'm on my own time, and I'm giving you a massage because you can use one. This is just therapy for you, baby. I'm not going to leave you tied up in knots. I'm

433

going to untie knots you never knew you had."

"Oh."

"Now you lie still and just enjoy this. I'm going to take my time, and it may seem as though I'm teasing you, but it'll just make it that much better at the end. You're going to love this, baby."

She used her hands and her breasts and her lips and tongue. She found erogenous zones I hadn't known I had, and at times it did seem as though she was teasing me, and at times I thought I would die if it didn't end soon, and at times I wanted it to go on forever, and at the very end she turned her sweet mouth into a vacuum cleaner and turned me inside out.

"Jesus," I said.

"I told you you were gonna love it."

"You're absolutely fantastic."

"Well, I do this for a living, honey. There's a lot to be said for professionalism."

"I guess there is."

"If I weren't reasonably competent by now, I'd go into some other line of work. But I don't get many complaints."

"You won't get one from me."

"Come on," she said, slapping me lightly on the thigh. "Put some clothes on and I'll show you what I stole for you. And where do you get off saying I do a lousy impression of Peter Lorre? That wasn't Peter Lorre. That was Akim Tamiroff, and I do a great Akim Tamiroff."

There was quite a stack of membership application forms from the two-week period preceding Jessica's death. Indulgence evidently did a hell of a business, and if all its recreational therapists were like Andrea, I could understand why.

What I couldn't understand at first was why I was bothering to go through this pile of paper, since every third person seemed to be named John Smith. And most of the others were pretty obvious aliases.

I read in one of Haig's books that amateurs almost always use a first name, or a form of one, as the last name of their alias. So I ran into a high percentage of names like John Richards, Joe Andrews, Sam Joseph, and so on.

Then I hit a name I knew, and then I hit it again, and then I hit it a third time, and I cabbed to Haig's house with three pieces of paper in my pocket that would wrap up a murderer.

Chapter Sixteen

HE WAS AT HIS DESK. "You left just before Mr. Shivers called me," he said. He looked intolerably smug. "You'll perhaps be pleased to know that my instincts were quite on the mark. I thought I knew who the killer was, and now all doubt has been removed."

"So has mine."

"Oh? That's interesting. I'd enjoy hearing the line of reasoning you followed."

"I didn't follow any line of reasoning," I said. "My legwork evidently got to the same place as your brainwork, and at about the same time. I reached Andrea Sugar and checked the records of men who had been to Indulgence shortly before Jessica was killed. I didn't expect anything to come of it because I didn't figure he would use his right name, but he probably had to because Jessica would recognize him."

"That's logical."

"Thank you. He didn't just go there once. He went there three times within the week preceding her death. I was thinking that you could call that a lot of nerve, but one thing the guy has not lacked is nerve. He's about the nerviest bastard I've ever heard of."

"That's well put."

"Thank you."

"You are welcome." His hand went to his beard. "I find it fascinating the way your legwork and my mental work found the same goal by opposite routes. Do you remember something I told you the other day? That there was a definite Ross MacDonald cast to this entire affair?"

"Something about forty years ago in Canada."

"That's correct. But it's closer to fifty years than forty, and the locale is somewhat south of the Canadian border." He closed his eyes and stroked his beard some more, "What an extraordinary amount of planning he devoted to all of this. The man has elements of genius. He's also quite mad, of course. The combination is by no means unheard of."

"Well, we've got him now. And these three slips of paper nail him to the wall."

And I passed them across to Haig.

"Gregory Vandiver," he read aloud.

"May he rot in hell."

"But this is very curious," he said.

"What's curious about it? I already explained why he must have figured he had to use his right name. Because Jessica would have known him already. You told me I was logical."

"I never said you were logical. I said that particular statement was logical."

"Well, what's the problem? Vandiver has had cash problems. Of all the people in the case, he's the only one with a real money motive. For most people the difference between two million dollars and ten million dollars doesn't matter much, but he got into investments over his head and needed the prospect of really big money. So he—"

"Be quiet, Chip."

"Oh, for Pete's sake—"

"Chip. Be quiet."

I became quiet. He turned around and watched the rasboras for awhile. They ignored him and I tried to. He turned to face me, but his eyes were closed and he was playing with his beard. Sometime I'm going to shave him in his sleep, and he'll never be able to think straight again.

He had been wearing his beard away for maybe five minutes when the doorbell rang. I stayed where I was and let Wong get it. A few seconds later he brought in a man who looked familiar. It took me a second or two to place him as one of the Sands Point police officers.

He said, "Mr. Harrison? I'm Luther Polk, we met yesterday afternoon."

"Yes," I said. I introduced him to Haig, who had by now opened his eyes. "I suppose you want a further statement, but I don't think—"

"No, it's not that," he said. "I will need a further statement from you eventually, but there's something else. Do you want to sit down?"

"No, but if you'd be more comfortable—"

He shook his head. "I have some bad news for you," he said slowly. "I felt I ought to bring it in person. Late last night or early this morning Mrs. Vandiver shot and killed her husband. She then took her own life. The bodies were discovered by servants at approximately ten this morning. Mrs. Vandiver left a sealed envelope addressed to you beside her typewriter. Under the circumstances it was necessary to open and read the letter. It's a suicide note, and explains the reasons for her actions. I thought you would like to have it. I'll need to retain it as evidence, but you may examine it now if you wish."

This is the note:

Dear Chip,

By the time you read this I will probably be dead by my own hand. Unless I lose my nerve, and I might. But I don't think so.

It was Gregory who tried to kill me by planting a bomb in my car. It was also Gregory who killed Melanie and Jessica and Robin, and he would have killed Kim too in due time. I found this out an hour ago when he tried a second time to kill me. He was attempting to strangle me in my sleep. I woke up in time to get loose. I've always kept a small pistol in my bedside table. I managed to get it in time. I shot him and killed him. In a few minutes I think I'll shoot myself.

I'm just so tired, Chip. Tired of everything. It's astonishing that I could have been married to this man for so long without sensing his

evil nature. I merely took it for granted that
he was a bore. I never had an inkling that he
was a homicidal maniac into the bargain.

Maybe I'm in shock. Maybe suicide is an
irrational act for me to perform. I certainly
don't feel guilty for having killed Gregory. It
was self-defense, certainly, and I would be let
off for that reason. So maybe I'm just using
this as an excuse for something I've wanted to
do for a long time.

I don't know if you can understand this,
since I scarcely understand it myself. But I
somehow think you might be able to, Chip.

Please don't think too badly of me.

I read it through a couple of times. Then I gave it to
Haig. "She was my client," he said, "and I failed to protect
her."

Luther Polk said, "Sir, if she was determined to take her
own life—"

"If I had had one more day," Haig said. "One more day."

"It was definitely self-defense, just as she wrote it," Polk
went on. "There were abrasions on her throat from where
her husband had tried to strangle her, and—"

"Pfui!" Haig said. "Caitlin Vandiver did not write this
bit of fiction. Gregory Vandiver did not attempt to strangle
her. She did not shoot him. She did not shoot herself."

Polk just stared down at him.

"A little over forty years ago," Haig said. "And a bit to the
south of Canada."

I probably should have picked up on it by then, but I
was only half hearing the words. I picked up one of the
membership forms from the desk and looked at the
signature, and then I got it.

"Oh," I said.

Haig looked at me.

"I just recognized the handwriting," I told him. "But

439

what I can't figure out is why. I know, forty years ago in Canada. But why?"

"In a quick phrase?" He touched his beard. "Because he didn't have the guts to kill his father," he said.

I tried to make some sense out of that one while Haig began listing names on a memorandum slip. Polk was saying something in the background. He must have felt as though he had walked into a Pinter play after having missed the first act. We both ignored him. Haig finished making his list and handed it to me.

"I want these people in this room in an hour's time. Do what you have to do to arrange it."

I read half the list and looked at him. "Oh, for Pete's sake," I said. "You're not really going to do a whole production number, are you? Everybody in one room together while you show them what a genius you are. I mean, all you have to do is call the police."

"Chip." He folded his hands on his desk. "This is the most extraordinary case I have ever had. The criminal is an archfiend of terrifying proportions. I am going to play this one strictly according to the book."

Chapter Seventeen

YOU WOULDN'T BELIEVE what I went through, getting them all there. And I couldn't possibly bring it off in an hour, even with Luther Polk on hand to expedite matters. Polk was helpful, especially once he came to the conclusion that he was not going to know anything about what was going on until Leo Haig was ready to tell him.

"He's a genius," I explained. "He was telling me just a few hours ago that there's a very thin line between genius and insanity. You can think of him as walking along that line, doing a high-wire act on it."

"But you say he's about to come up with a killer."

"He's going to come down on one," I said. "With both feet. And he's got enough weight to land hard."

"Not all that much weight," Polk said. "He'd be right trim if you was to stretch him out to a suitable length."

I pushed the image of Leo Haig being lengthened on a medieval rack as far out of mind as possible, and settled down to the serious business of setting the stage and assembling the audience. It took two hours and twelve minutes, and I think that was pretty good.

They arrived in stages, of course, but I won't burden you with the order of their coming, or the way I fielded their questions and settled them down. I'll just tell you what the room looked like when Haig condescended to enter it.

Wong Fat and I had set up a double row of chairs on my side of the partners' desk, facing Haig. My own chair was off to the side, between the audience and the door.

In the front row, farthest from me, sat Detective Vincent Gregorio. He was wearing a black silk suit with a subtle dark blue stripe and a pair of wing-tip loafers you could see your face in if you were in a house where they covered the mirrors. I don't know where he bought his clothes, but between them and his twenty-dollar haircut he looked like a walking advertisement for police corruption. I was surprised that he had agreed to come so readily. Maybe he got a charge out of it when Haig called him a witling.

Andrea Sugar sat on Gregorio's right, which was an obvious source of pleasure to Kid Handsome, because he was doing a courtship dance that a male *Betta splendens* would have been proud of, preening and posing and not knowing how little good it was going to do him. Andrea was wearing a maroon dress with bright red cherries all over it, and if you can't think of the thoughts it inspired, that's too damned bad, because I am not going to spell them out for you.

I had put Addison Shivers, our sole surviving client, alongside Andrea. That also put him directly across the desk from Haig, which seemed only proper. He was the angel for this theatrical production. His suit was probably as old as detective Gregorio, but it still looked good. He sat quite stiff in his chair, and when Haig came into the room he took off his glasses and cleaned them with his necktie.

Kim was seated next to Mr. Shivers, with Gordie McLeod on the other side of her, which put him in the chair closest to mine. This had not been my idea. I would have preferred to be able to look directly at Kim without having him around to play the role of an automobile graveyard at the foot of a beautiful mountain. That's a bad choice of words, actually, because Kim could not have looked less mountainous. She seemed to have grown smaller and more petite in the short time since I had seen her. She was wearing what she had worn earlier. I had seen nothing to object to then and I saw nothing to object to now, except for the hulking moron who was holding her hand in his paw.

McLeod was wearing something loutish. I think he'd put on a clean bowling shirt in honor of the occasion. His shoes needed a shine and probably weren't going to get one. They had thick soles, for stepping on people.

Detective Wallace Seidenwall was directly behind McLeod, which put him closer to me than I might have wanted him. He had not grown discernibly fonder of me since our last meeting. "This better be good," was a phrase which came trippingly to his lips during the waiting period. He didn't say it as though he thought it was going to, either. He was wearing a gray glen plaid suit that Robert Hall had marked down for good reason. Either his partner got all the graft, or Seidenwall was running a yacht, or something, because he was due for a bitter disappointment again this fall when the Best Dressed list came out.

Ferdinand Bell was next to Seidenwall, and he was the only one in the crowd who looked genuinely happy to be present. "This will be a treat," he said upon entering, and he enjoyed himself immensely making small talk with the others and asking the names of all of the fish. He had on the same suit he'd worn to Melanie's funeral. His short white hair set off his pink scalp, or maybe it was the other way around, and his plump cheeks reminded you more than ever of a chipmunk when he smiled, which was most of the time.

I had stuck Luther Polk next to Bell, which put him directly behind Addison Shivers. (I know I'm taking forever giving you the geography of all this, and I know you could probably care less about the whole thing, but Haig spent so much time charting it out that it is conceivably important. I know I'd catch hell if I didn't go through it all.) I don't think I described Polk before, but if you've seen Dennis Weaver in that television series where he plays an Arizona marshal attached to the New York Police Department, then I won't have to describe him for you. He had had relatively little to say to the two Homicide detectives, or they to him, and he sat there keeping his hand comfortingly close to the revolver on his hip.

Madam Juana was sitting on the far side of Polk. She was wearing her basic black dress and a string of pearls, and she looked like the stern-lipped administrator of a parochial school for girls. (I can't help it, that's what she looked like.)

Well, it wasn't what you would call perfect. I mean, there should have been three or four more obvious suspects present. John LiCastro would have been a nice addition to the group, but Haig had pointed out that it would have been an insensitive act to place him in the same room with policemen for no compelling reason. And it would have been even nicer if our other client had been present; if Haig had had just a few more hours to work with, Caitlin would have been alive.

So it wasn't perfect, but it was still a pretty decent showing, and I have to admit I got a kick out of it when Leo Haig marched into the room and every eye turned to take in the sight of him.

He seated himself very carefully behind his desk. I had a bad moment when I thought he was going to put his feet up, but he got control of himself. He took his time meeting the eyes of each person in the room, including me, and then he closed his eyes and touched his beard and went into a tiny huddle with himself. It didn't last as long as it might have.

He opened his eyes and said, "I want to thank you for coming here. I am going to unmask a killer this afternoon, a killer who has in one way or another affected all our lives. Each of us has been thus affected, but not all of you are aware of the extent of this killer's activities. So you must permit me to rehash some recent events. Not all of them will be news to any of you, and one of you will know all of what I am about to say, and more. Because the murderer is in this room."

He was grandstanding, but of course it went over well. Everybody turned and looked at everybody else.

"This past Wednesday," Haig said, "my associate Mr. Harrison discovered the body of Miss Melanie Trelawney. She had died of an overdose of heroin. Previously she had told Mr. Harrison that she feared for her life. His observations of the scene at Miss Trelawney's apartment led Mr. Harrison to the certain conclusion that she had been murdered. When he confided his observations to me—"

"Wait a minute," Gregorio cut in. "Where do you get off concealing evidence from the police?"

"I concealed no evidence," Haig said. "Nor did Mr. Harrison. Nothing was suppressed, nothing distorted. It is not incumbent upon a citizen to apprise the police of his suspicions. Indeed, it is often unwise.

"To continue. When Mr. Harrison confided his observations to me, I concurred in his conclusion. Miss Trelawney's fears were predicated, it appeared, upon the fact that two of her sisters had recently suffered violent deaths, one the apparent victim of suicide, the other the apparent victim of an automobile accident. I determined at once to ferret out the killer and prevent him from doing further damage. I have at least succeeded in the first attempt, if not in the second."

Gregorio broke in again. "I'd like to know what made you think that OD was murder," he said. "If we missed something, I'd like to know what it was."

"In due time, sir. In due time. Permit me, if you will, to explore events chronologically. The day after Miss Trelawney's death, Mr. Harrison and I began a series of inquiries. In the course of so doing, we were engaged by Mr. Addison Shivers to look after the best interests of Cyrus Trelawney, deceased. It is perhaps unusual for an attorney to engage detectives for the benefit of a client who is no longer living. In my eyes, Mr. Shivers' act stands greatly to his credit."

The hand went to the beard again. I looked around the room and watched everybody watching Haig. Gordie McLeod looked as though he was trying to understand the big words. Juana looked as though she was trying to understand the English words. Kim looked as though she was trying to figure out how Haig could hold an audience in the palm of his hand, just by sitting there with his eyes closed while he played with his facial hair.

"On the following day Mr. Harrison attended Miss Trelawney's funeral, both to pay his respects to the deceased and to press our investigation. There he met Mrs. Gregory Vandiver, the former Caitlin Trelawney, who also engaged us to look into the matter of her sister's death. I accepted a retainer from her, feeling no conflict of interest was likely to be involved."

He paused to glance directly at Addison Shivers, who gave a barely perceptible nod.

"Mr. Harrison returned to this office. We were seated in this very room when a pipe bomb was thrown into the front room a floor below. Several of my *aquaria* suffered minor damage. This was galling, but of little actual importance. Of major importance was the fact that the bombing caused two deaths. Maria Tijerino, an associate of Miss Juana Dominguez, and Elmer J. Seaton, a seaman on shore leave, were in the room into which the bomb was hurled. Both were killed instantly."

A couple of heads turned to look at Madame Juana, who crossed herself several times.

"Detectives Gregorio and Seidenwall, who investigated the bombing, assumed that the premises below were the bomber's target. The nature of the business carried on downstairs would tend to further such a suspicion. The world overflows with maniacs who feel they are doing the Creator's work by blowing brothels to smithereens. Mr. Harrison and I interpreted the bombing in a different fashion."

"I told you we oughta take him in," Seidenwall said. "What did I tell you? I told you we oughta take him in."

Haig ignored this. "My immediate thought was that the bomber had chosen the wrong window. It did not take me long to realize that I was in error. A person anxious to kill me would do a better job of it, especially in view of his skill in arranging other murders. No, the bombing had been meant either to discourage me from further investigations, or to pique my interest in the case. I could not, at that stage, determine which.

"But the bombing did tell me certain things about the killer. It told me, first of all, that he knew I was on his trail. This did little to narrow the field of suspects. It told me, too, that the man I was dealing with was quite ruthless, willing to liquidate innocent strangers in order to advance his machinations. I was on the trail of a dangerous, desperate and wholly immoral human being."

Haig picked up a pipe, took it deliberately apart, ran a pipe cleaner unnecessarily through it and put it back together again.

"My investigations continued. Yesterday my associate visited Mrs. Vandiver at her home on Long Island. While he was there, a bomb wired to the automobile of Mrs. Vandiver was detonated, killing her chauffeur, one Seamus Fogarty. The local police officers assumed Mr. Fogarty was the intended victim because of his political activities. I assumed otherwise. An attempt had been made on my client's life.

"Last night my associate, Mr. Harrison, left this house against my advice—" He had to rub it in, damn it. "—and returned to his own lodgings. He was set upon and badly beaten by three strangers, evidently professionals at that sort of thing." Eyes swung around to look at me. There was concern in Kim's, surprise in Ferdinand Bell's, and what looked annoyingly like satisfaction in Seidenwall's.

"And later last night," Haig went on, "or perhaps early this morning, the killer struck again. He murdered Mr. and Mrs. Gregory Vandiver and arranged things to suggest that Mrs. Vandiver shot her husband and then took her own life."

Kim let out a shriek, and the whole room began mumbling to itself. McLeod reached for her. She drew away. Haig tapped on the desktop with a pipe.

"I learned of this last act just a few hours ago. My first reaction was to feel personally responsible for the deaths of Mr. and Mrs. Vandiver. By the time I learned of their fate, I already knew the identity of their killer. I did not know,

447

however, at the time they were killed. Perhaps I could still have done something, taken some action, to prevent what happened to them. I had held strong suspicions of the murderer's identity for some time."

He closed his eyes for a moment. I took a good long look at the killer, and did not obtain the slightest idea of what was going through his mind.

"Officer Polk brought me the news of what happened to my client and her husband. He also brought a typed and unsigned suicide note which the murderer had had the temerity to write. The note was designed to wrap up all of the crimes to date and pin them upon Gregory Vandiver, who was supposed to have attempted to kill his wife, was then killed by her, after which my client is supposed to have suffered an uncharacteristic fit of remorse at the conclusion of which she killed herself.

"There was no reason for Officer Polk to doubt this charade. I suspect his department might have doubted it ultimately. But Mr. Harrison and myself immediately recognized it as illusion, and read in the purported suicide note additional confirmation of the identity of the actual killer."

Polk said, "How did you know so quickly the note was a fake?"

I fielded that one. "I knew it on the first line," I said. "The murderer spelled my first name right. C-h-i-p. Caitlin thought I spelled it with two p's; she made out a check that way. I never corrected her." I didn't add that I had suspected Greg Vandiver all along and it just about took the note to change my mind. Let them think I was as brilliant as Leo Haig.

"The concept of leaving a typewritten suicide note was a bad one," Haig added. "But the murderer had developed an extraordinary degree of gall. Success engenders confidence. Mr. Harrison has described the killer as the nerviest bastard he ever heard of. I told him that was exceedingly well put, as you will come to realize."

I watched the killer's face on that line. I think it got to him a little bit.

"The killer wanted to round things off neatly," Haig went on. "He knew better than to leave a note when he pushed Jessica Trelawney out of her window. Now, though, he wanted to establish Gregory Vandiver as the villain of the piece, and award him a posthumous citation for multiple homicide. At this very moment he may be cursing himself for his stupidity. He might better save himself the effort. I already knew him as the killer. This was by no means his first witless act. But it is to be his last."

Haig closed his eyes again. I can't speak for the rest of the company, but for me the tension was getting unbearable. I knew something the rest of them didn't know, and I wished he would hurry up and get to the end.

"This morning I called Mr. Shivers. In addition to being my client, he was for a great many years both attorney and friend to the late Cyrus Trelawney. He was able to supply me with the last piece of my jigsaw puzzle, the question of motive.

"I had realized almost from the beginning that motive was the key element of these murders. The most immediately obvious motive was money. The case is awash with money. Cyrus Trelawney left a fortune in excess of ten million dollars. But the more I examined the facts, the less likely it seemed that money could constitute a motive.

"Why, then, would someone want to murder five women who had virtually nothing in common but their kinship? Several possibilities presented themselves. The first was that, having determined to murder one of them for a logical reason, he might have wished to disguise his act by making it one link in a chain of homicides. Gregory Vandiver, for example, could have had reason to do away with his wife. If he first killed some of her sisters, he would be a less obvious suspect for the single murder for which he had a visible motive.

"The fault in this line of reasoning is not difficult to pinpoint. If a person wished to create the appearance of a chain of murders, he would make the facade an unmistakable one. He would not disguise his handiwork as accidental death or suicide. He would make each act an obvious murder, and would probably use the same murder method in each instance. So this was not a *faked* chain of murders, but a very *real* chain of murders.

"And then I saw that the answer had to lie in the past. These girls were being killed because they were the daughters of Cyrus Trelawney. The man had died three years ago, and after his death his daughters began dying. First Robin, then Jessica, then Melanie. And now Caitlin."

He did start to put his feet up then, I'm positive of it, but he caught himself in time.

"I've told Mr. Harrison that this case reminded me of the work of a certain author of detective stories. Our New York has little of the texture of Lew Archer's California, but in much the same way the sins of the past work upon those of us trapped in the present. If I were to find the killer, I had to consider Cyrus Trelawney.

"Cyrus Trelawney." He folded his hands on the desktop. "An interesting man, I should say. Fathered his first child at the age of forty-eight, having beforehand amassed a fortune. Continued fathering them every three years, spawning as regularly as a guppy. Brought five girls into the world. And one son who died in his cradle. I began to wonder about Cyrus Trelawney's life before he married. I speculated, and I constructed an hypothesis."

He paused and looked across his desk at Addison Shivers. "This morning I asked Mr. Shivers a question. Do you recall the question, sir?"

"I do."

"Indeed. Would you repeat it?"

"You asked if Cyrus Trelawney had been a man of celibate habits before his marriage."

"And your reply?"

"That he had not."

(This was paraphrase. What Mr. Shivers had actually said, Haig told me later, was that Cyrus Trelawney would fuck a coral snake if somebody would hold its head.)

"I then asked Mr. Shivers several other questions which elicited responses I had expected to elicit. I learned, in brief, that Mr. Trelawney's business interests forty-five to fifty years ago included substantial holdings in timberlands and paper mills in upstate New York. That he spent considerable time in that area during those years. That one of those mills was located in the town of Lyons Falls, New York."

"That's very interesting," the killer said.

"Indeed. But the others do not understand what makes it interesting, Mr. Bell. Would you care to tell them?"

"I was born in Lyons Falls," Bell said.

"Indeed. You were born in Lyons Falls, New York, forty-seven years ago last April 18th. Your mother was a woman named Barbara Hohlbein who was the wife of a man named James Bell. James Bell was not your father. Cyrus Trelawney was your father. Cyrus Trelawney's daughters were your half-sisters and you have killed four of the five, Mr. Bell, and you will not kill any more of them. You will not, Mr. Bell. No, sir. You will not."

Chapter Eighteen

OF COURSE EVERYBODY STARED at the son of a bitch. He didn't seem to notice. His eyes were on Leo Haig and he was as cool as a gherkin. His forehead looked a little pinker, but that may have been my imagination. I couldn't really tell you.

"This is quite fascinating," Bell said. "I asked around when I heard you were investigating Melanie's death. I was told that you were quite insane. I wondered what this elaborate charade would lead to."

"I would prefer that it lead to the gas chamber, sir. I fear it will lead only to permanent incarceration in a hospital for the criminally insane."

"Fascinating."

"Indeed. I shouldn't attempt to leave if I were you, Mr. Bell. There are police officers seated on either side of you. They would take umbrage."

"Oh, I wouldn't miss this for the world," Bell said. His cheeks puffed out as he grinned. "Why, if this were a movie I'd *pay* to see it. It's *far* more thrilling in real life."

Haig closed his eyes. Without opening them he said, "I have no way of knowing whether or not Cyrus Trelawney was your father. You do not resemble him, nor do I perceive any resemblance between yourself and his legitimate offspring. Very strong men tend to be prepotent, which is to say that their genes are dominant. Much the same is true of fishes, you might be interested to know. I would guess that you resemble your mother. I suspect you inherited your madness from her."

A muscle worked in Bell's temple. He didn't say anything.

"I don't doubt that she told you Trelawney was your father. I don't doubt that you believe it, that you grew up hearing little from her than that a rich man had fathered you. It certainly made an impression upon you. You grew up loving and hating this man you had never met. You were obsessed by the idea that he had sired you. Had he acknowledged you, you would have been rich. Money became an obsession.

"One learns much about a man from his hobbies. You collect money, Mr. Bell. Not in an attempt to amass wealth, but as a way of playing with the symbols of wealth. Little pieces of stamped metal moving from hand to hand at exorbitant prices. Pfui!"

"Numismatics is a science."

"Anything may be taken for a science when enough of its devotees attempt to codify their madness. There is a young man in this city, I understand, who spends his spare time, of which I trust he has an abundance, analyzing the garbage of persons understandably more prominent than himself. For the time being he is acknowledged to be a lunatic. If, heaven forfend, his pastime amasses a following, garbage analysis will be esteemed a science. Learned books will be published on the subject. Fools will write them. Greater fools will purchase and read them. Pfui!"

"You know nothing about numismatics," Bell said.

Haig grunted. "I could dispute that. I shall not take the trouble. I am not concerned with numismatics, sir. I am concerned with murder."

"And you're calling me a murderer."

"I have done so already." He stroked his beard briefly. "I've no idea just when you planned to become a murderer. At your mother's knee, I would suppose. You came to New York. You established yourself in your profession. You kept tabs on your father. And, because of your infirmity of purpose, you bided your time.

"Because you could not kill this man, nor could you think of relinquishing the dream of killing him. You waited until time achieved what you could not: the death of Cyrus Trelawney."

"And then I married Robin."

"Then you married Robin Trelawney," Haig agreed with him.

"And then I crashed up the car and killed her, I suppose. The only person I ever loved and I crashed up my car on the chance that I would live through the wreck and she would not."

"No, sir. No in every respect. But I'll back up a bit. Before you married Robin, indeed before Cyrus Trelawney died, you had all of your plan worked out. The first step called for you to murder Philip Flanner."

"Now I *know* you're insane," Bell said.

"You told Mr. Harrison that you were a friend of Flanner's, that he was a fellow numismatist. He was not. You did become a friend of his, but not until after he and Robin were married. You ingratiated yourself with him because he had recently taken her as a wife."

"He fell in front of a subway car."

"You threw him in front of a subway car."

"You couldn't prove that in a million years."

"I haven't the slightest need to prove it. You are a very curious man, Mr. Bell. You took your time ingratiating yourself with Robin. You waited until her father was at last in his grave before you persuaded her to marry you. Then you waited a couple of years before you killed her. You must have thought about the murder method for all of that time and more."

"I loved Robin."

"No, sir. You have never loved anyone, except insofar as you loved Cyrus Trelawney. I leave that to the psychiatrists, who will have ample opportunity to inquire. You drove with Robin to a coin convention. At some time in the course of the ride back, you broke her neck. That would not have been terribly difficult to manage. Then you put her in the back of the car and found a place where an icy road surface could explain an accident. You then effected that accident, sir, which no doubt took a certain amount of insane courage on your part."

"No one will believe this."

"I suspect everyone in the room already believes it, sir.

But they will not have to, nor will anyone else." Haig turned around and looked at the rasboras. I was astonished, and I was used to him, so you can imagine what it did to everybody else. But I'll be damned if anyone said a word. I was wondering how long he was going to milk it, when he turned around again and got to his feet.

"The order of the murders," he said. "Robin, Jessica, Melanie, Caitlin. I was shocked when I learned that Caitlin was dead. Doubly shocked, because I thought you would save her for last. You were trying so hard to throw suspicion upon Gregory Vandiver. Inventing some nonsense about financial insolvency, some prattle about his having invested large sums in rare coins and being forced to liquidate them. One would have thought you would wait until Kim was safely dead before disposing of him. He, surely, would have done so before killing his wife, had he the financial motive you suggested.

"But that becomes clear when one devotes some thought to it. You did not merely want to murder your half-sisters. You wanted to have sexual relations with them as well.

First Robin. You married her in order to have sex with her. Then Jessica. You went at least three times to her place of employment in the week preceding her death. You signed Gregory Vandiver's name to the membership application, having already planned to use him as a scapegoat should there be need for one. Through this contact with Jessica, you were able to arrange to see her privately at her apartment. You did so, sir, and you pitched her out of her window."

"You can't prove that," Bell said.

"But I can. Miss Sugar no doubt recognizes you. If not, her colleagues very possibly will. In any event, I have here three pieces of paper confirming the dates of your visit. They identify you as Gregory Vandiver, sir, but they are in your handwriting."

Which is how I had tipped to the whole thing. I remembered where I had seen that precise penmanship. It was on a 2 x 2 coin envelope.

"You had an affair with Caitlin. I have had it established that this was not terribly difficult for one to achieve. I knew at an early date that you were probably in touch with her. I learned that when Mr. Harrison reported on his conversation with you Saturday."

I said, "How?"

Haig glared at me.

"I'm serious. How did you know that?"

"Because you've learned to report conversations verbatim. I spoke to Mr. Bell over the telephone to prepare him for your visit. I identified you as my associate, Mr. Harrison. I did not mention your first name. Nor did you mention it when introducing yourself. Mr. Bell asked if it was all right for him to call you Chip. The only person likely to have told him your name was Caitlin, yet he gave the impression that everything you were saying to him was coming as a great surprise. This made me instantly suspicious of Mr. Bell, a suspicion I never had cause to relinquish."

"I was not having an affair with Caitlin," Bell said stiffly. "As a matter of fact, she did ask my advice after Harrison talked to her. She had second thoughts about hiring him, and wanted my opinion."

"Indeed."

"I never had sexual relations with her. Or with Jessica. Perhaps it's true that I visited her at that massage parlor. If I signed Gregory's name, it was on a whim. I only visited her to have a half hour of her time, so that we could talk about Robin. It was a way of bringing Robin back to life for me."

Haig closed his eyes. He opened them and sighed and sat down behind his desk again. "I won't comment on that," he said. "Nor shall I attempt to determine what sexual act you performed with Melanie Trelawney. I suspect it might have been you who put the thought in her mind that her two sisters had been killed. Or you might have become aware of her suspicions by virtue of

456

her having called you to inquire if there was any possibility that Robin's death was not wholly accidental. At any rate, it should have posed no problem for you to gain access to her apartment. Once there, you could have had little difficulty in rendering her unconscious. She was completely nude when Mr. Harrison discovered the body. It has not been my observation that people habitually disrobe before injecting themselves with heroin."

"Happens some of the time," Gregorio said.

"Sometimes yes, sometimes no. You wouldn't get suspicious either way," Seidenwall said.

Haig nodded. "So you would not have disrobed her to make her the more obvious victim of death from a drug overdose. I'm sure you did something with her. I do not care to know what it was, nor do I care to know whether it took place before or after you injected a fatal overdose of the drug into her bloodstream."

I don't care to know that either, to tell you the truth.

"You can't prove any of this," Bell said. Not for the first time.

Haig stared at him. He was on his feet again. "I can prove almost all of it," he said. "Once the facts are known and established, the proof is rarely hard to come by. Had you taken your time, you might have managed to bring it off. You did come very close at that. You killed four out of five. Had sex with four of your sisters, killed four of your sisters.

"And you were very patient at the onset. You waited to kill Philip Flanner, waited to marry his widow, waited to kill her. But then you got a taste of it and you liked it, didn't you? *You loved it.*"

Bell didn't say anything. The muscle was really having a workout in his temple, and he didn't look his usual happy self.

"You incestuous murdering bastard," Haig said. "You never did what you wanted to do. You never killed your father and you never slept with your mother, and you used your sisters as surrogates for both, one after another. But you'll never get the last one, Bell, you'll never put a hand on her!"

The son of a bitch moved fast. He had the knife out of his pocket and the blade open before I could even blink.

A fat lot of good it did him. He wasn't even out of his chair before Seidenwall had an arm wrapped around his throat and Luther Polk's long-barreled automatic was jabbed into the side of his head.

They took turns advising him of his rights. He went limp, but that didn't make Seidenwall let go of his throat or Polk stop jabbing him in the head with the gun barrel.

On the way out, his hands cuffed behind his back, he turned and smiled at me. It was a smile I will never forget as long as I live. I can close my eyes and see it now. I wish I couldn't.

"You know," he said, "I had absolutely nothing to do with having you beaten up. I hope you can believe that."

Chapter Nineteen

AFTER THE THREE COPS had escorted Ferdinand Bell out of there, I figured everybody would start talking at once. I guess nobody wanted to make the first move. They all just sat there staring at each other.

Finally Addison Shivers said, "The vagaries and inconsistencies of human nature. How many persons did that man kill?"

"I know of nine," Haig said. "The four sisters; Philip Flanner; Maria Tijerina; Elmer Seaton, the sailor; Seamus Fogarty; Gregory Vandiver. Nine. There may have been others, but I doubt it."

"And yet the one crime he was anxious to deny was the administration of a beating to young Chip."

"Indeed," Haig said. "He was not responsible for it, as it happens."

Kim said to me, "You never told me you were beaten up."

I agreed that I never did.

"If he didn't do it, then who did?"

I got to my feet. It was doomed to be anticlimactic, but it was my part of the show. "That's easy to answer," I said. "Gordie McLeod set me up. Didn't you, old buddy?"

Everybody stared at him. He didn't return the favor. He stared at his hands, mostly. Kim got up and drew away from him as if he was a leper. Which, come to think of it, he more or less was.

I said, "Well?"

He stood up. "I made a mistake," he said.

I just looked at him.

"Well, I'll tell you, man. All I could see is you're nosin' around my girl. And then I find out you've got some people down to the docks askin' questions about me. What do I need with people askin' questions, and I don't know about any murders, and I figure maybe you're doin' a number, and if you're doin' a number

I figure maybe I can cool things out is all. I told 'em to take it easy with you."

The look on Kim's face was worth the price of admission.

"So I made a mistake," he went on. "You know, the way I feel about Kim and all, and so I got carried away. I never had your advantages, I never went to college, never joined a fraternity, I'm just your ordinary guy, works hard all his life and tries to make a go of it."

"You were also born stupid. Don't forget that."

"Well, I never said I was the brightest guy in the world. Just your average Joe." He gave his shoulders a shrug. He had a lot of shoulders and they moved impressively. "Look," he said, "I'm the kind of guy gives credit where credit's due. I had you wrong. You're okay. I made a mistake." He extended a paw like an overtrained retriever. "No hard feelings, huh?"

"None at all," I said, and I extended my hand and moved toward him, and for some odd reason or other my hand kept going right on past his hand, fingers bunched and rigid, and the fingers jabbed him almost exactly three inches north of his navel, assuming he was born once and had one, and that's where the solar plexus is supposed to be, and that's where his was, and I'll be damned if it didn't work like a charm.

He doubled up and turned sort of orange, and he started folding inward like a dying accordion, and I interlaced my fingers and cupped the back of his head with both hands and helped him fold up, and at the same time I raised my right knee as high as it would go, and it couldn't go all the way up because it met his face coming down.

You wouldn't believe the sound it made.

After Wong sponged the blood off him, we put him in a chair, and I stood in front of him trying not to look at his nose. It was a pleasure not to look at it.

"No hard feelings," I said, "but I've had a yen to do that since I first saw you. It was the sort of yen that kept getting stronger until there was just no restraining myself. Do you understand what I'm saying, or should I use smaller words?"

He tried to glare at me.

"Here's the point," I said. "I have a feeling I'm going to get that yen over and over. It's not the sort of thing you do once and get bored with. So it would probably be a good idea if you arranged your life so that you and I were not in the same place at the same time, because kicking the shit out of you could get to be a habit with me.

"I'll tell you something else. You don't give a shit about Kim, beyond the fact that she's easy to look at and worth a couple of million dollars. She's far too good for you, and even you must be bright enough to realize that. She would have written you off a long time ago, but she was afraid of you. I think she can see that you're nothing much to be afraid of. You're not going to see Kim anymore."

He tried a little harder to glare at me.

"You didn't beat me up to keep me away from Kim. You had your buddies work me over to keep me off your back, because you've got a nice little hustle going and you figured I might turn it up. I did. We got a call just before you got here today. It was from—never mind who it was from. You take days off from the docks now and then. You have one talent on God's earth: you can start a car without the key, and that's what you've been doing for a living. I could tell you just where you drive them, and just how much you get for them, but you already know. Or maybe you write the address on your shirt cuff so you won't forget it."

"Who told you?"

"Mr. Haig has some very good friends. Mr. Haig's friend asked that his name not be mentioned so I'm not going to mention it. Mr. Haig's friend asked if he could take care of this for us. He said a good friend of his has a paving contract up in Rockland County. He wanted to know if we wanted him to arrange to tuck you under a section of four-lane divided highway."

His face got very white. Except for around the nose, where it was still doing a little low-grade bleeding.

"We told him you weren't worth the trouble. If you start being worth the trouble, meaning if you turn up on Kim's doorstep again, Mr. Haig will call him and say he changed his mind. A lot of this man's friends are in the highway construction business. I guess it's profitable."

"You son of a bitch," he said.

"I'm not finished. I'm also supposed to tell you that the auto theft people don't want to work with you anymore. And that you may have a certain amount of trouble getting picked in the dock shape-up. People may tend to overlook you. You think I'm bluffing, don't you? Mr. Haig's friend didn't want his name mentioned, but there was another name he told me to mention to you."

I did so, and I never thought four syllables could have such an effect. He did everything but die on the spot.

I said, "I think you should go away now."

He went away.

So did the rest of them, ultimately. They had questions, most of them, and Haig answered them. He got into a long psychoanalytical rap with Andrea Sugar, who turned out to be very knowledgeable on Jungian psychology.

Madam Juana took him aside and told him something, and kissed his cheek, and Haig went beet-red. He had never done this before in my presence. I can't swear to what she said to him, but I can make a guess based on my instincts and my experience, because before his blush had a chance to fade she came over to me and gave me a kiss on the cheek and whispered in my ear, and what she whispered was, "You a wonnerful boy and you get the bom who kill my Maria, and anytime you wanna girl you come down and I give you best inna house, no charge, anytime you wanna fock."

Eventually Kim was the only one left. I took her upstairs and showed her the fish. She was very interested. She was also still a little nervous, so I waved at Haig and took her back to her apartment.

"I never thought you were violent, Chip. I thought of you as, you know, gentle and sensitive and aware."

Like the actor who turned out to be a faggot, I thought.

"And Gordie is so big and strong—"

"Well, Wong Fat showed me how to do a few things. I'm basically a very non-violent person. The only time I ever had to hit anybody was when I was a deputy Sheriff in South Carolina."

"A what?"

"It was an honorary position, basically. What it came down to was that I was a bouncer in a, well, in a whorehouse, if you want to know. Sometimes guys would get drunk and pull knives, and I would have to hit 'em upside the head with this club they gave me."

"Upside the head?"

"The local expression."

"You really didn't go to college, did you?"

"I told you. I had to drop out of high school. My parents were sort of high-class con men, although I didn't know it at the time, and they got caught, and they killed themselves, and Upper Valley threw me out a few months before graduation. They were all heart."

She looked at me with those wide eyes. "You've really lived," she said.

"Well, I tend to keep moving."

"I've never met anyone like you before, Chip."

So that's about it. Ferdinand Bell is wearing a straitjacket, and will spend what's left of his life in a cell with spongy walls. This infuriates Haig, who would like to see the return of public hanging. We still haven't spawned the African gouramis, but John LiCastro finally got the results he wanted, and has a whole twenty-nine-gallon tank full of baby discus fish. Haig went over to see them the other day and says they're doing fine, and that you would have thought LiCastro had fathered them himself, the way he was carrying on.

Gordie McLeod hasn't been heard from. He never turned up to take his stuff out of Kim's apartment, and a couple of days ago I got all his things together and tucked them neatly into the incinerator. Kim said that wasn't very nice, and I said it was too bad.

I ran into Andrea Sugar at the funeral for the Vandivers. She volunteered to teach Kim the art of massage. I sort of sidestepped that one. It was probably just a nice gesture on her part, but she may have had an ulterior motive. I have nothing against lesbians, but I wouldn't want my girl to marry one.

What else? Addison Shivers called the other day. He sent a check around, and Haig returned it, and the old gentleman was displeased.

"I have not earned it, sir," Haig told him. "You hired me to look out for the interests of the late Cyrus Trelawney. I exerted myself enough to justify retaining the advances I received from yourself and Mrs. Vandiver, but I cannot say that I did much for Cyrus Trelawney, certainly not enough to warrant my accepting additional payment."

They talked some more, and an hour later the check arrived again. A messenger brought it and he tried to deliver it downstairs, which confused the girls. No one had ever tried to pay by check before. This particular check was for five thousand dollars, and it was no longer payment for work performed. Instead it was an advance against work to be performed. Because Haig had been rehired to look out for the interests of Cyrus Trelawney. Specifically, he's going to prove that Ferdinand Bell's mother was nutty as a Mars bar, and the killer wasn't Trelawney's son in the first place.

Which means I'll be making a trip to Lyons Falls before very long. I can't say I'm looking forward to it, if you want to know. The heatwave just broke and New York is not a bad place to be.

Haig has been driving me crazy lately. He keeps handing me furniture catalogues and asking me to pick out the kind of bed I like best. He won't give up, he's as single-minded as Cato on the subject of Carthage. So far I've been stubborn and have gone on paying the rent on my furnished room.

Which is probably silly. I've been spending most of my nights on Bethune Street lately, anyway.

The Topless Tulip Caper

Chapter One

AS I STARTED THROUGH THE DOOR a man stepped in front of me and stood there like the front four of the Miami Dolphins. I was about six inches taller than him, and he was about forty pounds heavier than I was, and I figured that gave him quite an edge. He was wearing plaid pants and a striped jacket over a sky-blue silk shirt. He had the face of an ex-boxer who had put on a lot of weight without going to fat. His nose had been broken more than once, and his eyes said he was just waiting for someone to try breaking it again. Someone very well might, sooner or later, because people usually get what they want, but I wasn't going to oblige him.

He said, "Read the sign, kid."

There were a lot of signs, so I started reading them aloud. "'Treasure Chest,'" I said. "'Girls! Girls! Girls!' 'Topless Stopless Dancing!' 'Come in and see what Fun City is all about!'"

"You read nice," he said.

"Thanks."

"What you call reading with expression," he said. He took a step closer to me. "That particular sign," he said, pointing. "Let's see you read that one."

"'You must be twenty-one and prove it,'" I intoned.

"Beautiful," he said. "Nice phrasing," he said. "Now get the fuck out of here," he said.

"I'm twenty-one," I lied.

"Sure you are, kid."

"Twenty-two, actually," I embroidered.

"Sure. You wanna try proving it?"

I took my wallet from the inside breast pocket of the sport jacket it was too damned hot to be wearing, and from the wallet I took a green rectangle with Alexander Hamilton's picture on it. I folded the piece of paper in half and put it carefully into his paw.

"My I.D.," I said.

His eyes grew very thoughtful. Actually, you don't have to be twenty-one to drink in New York. You have to be eighteen, which is something I can be with no problem whatsoever. But you have to be twenty-one to go into a place where ladies flash various portions of their anatomy at you. This is rarely a problem for me since I don't generally bother with that kind of place. Not because it does nothing for me to look at ladies with no clothes on, but because it does. I mean, I also don't go browsing in French restaurants when I don't have the price of a meal in my pocket Why torture yourself, for Pete's sake?

But this was business. Leo Haig had a case and a client, and his client was performing at the Treasure Chest, and since Leo Haig was no more likely to hie himself off to a topless club than I was to enter a monastery, I, Chip Harrison, was elected to serve as Haig's eyes, ears, nose, and throat.

Which explains why I had just tucked a ten-dollar bill into a very large and callused hand.

"Ten bucks?" said the owner of the hand. "For ten bucks you could go to a massage parlor and get a fancy hand job."

"I'm allergic to hand lotion."

"Huh?"

"I get this horrible rash."

He frowned at me, evidently suspecting I was joking with him. He had a ready wit, all right, "Yeah," he said. "Well, I guess you just proved your age to the satisfaction of the management. One-drink minimum at the bar. Enjoy yourself, tell your friends what a good time you had."

He stepped aside and I moved past him. At least it was cooler inside. The Treasure Chest was located on Seventh Avenue between Forty-Eight and Forty-Ninth, a block which is basically devoted to porno movies and dirty bookstores and peep shows, but they didn't account for the temperature outside all by themselves. What accounted

for it was that it was August and it hadn't rained in weeks
and some perverse deity had taken a huge vacuum cleaner
and sucked all the air out of Manhattan, leaving nothing
behind but soot and sulphur dioxide and carbon monoxide
and all the other goodies that only rats and pigeons and
cockroaches can breathe with impunity. The sun was out
there every day, having a fine old time, and when night
finally came it didn't do much good because the buildings
just grabbed onto the heat and held it in place until the
sun could come up again and start the whole process over.
It had been a sensational couple of weeks, let me tell you.
Haig's place was air-conditioned, which was nice during
the day, but my furnished room two blocks away was not.
This made the nights terrible, and it also made it
increasingly difficult for me to resist Haig's suggestion that
I give up my room and move into his quarters.

"Archie Goodwin lives with Nero Wolfe," Haig said,
more than once. "He is a ladies' man in every sense of the
word. His cohabitation with Wolfe does not seem to inhibit
his pursuit of the fair sex."

There were a lot of answers to this one. Such as
mentioning that Wolfe had a brownstone to himself, while
Haig had the top two floors of a carriage house in Chelsea,
and you can't very well bring home an innocent young
thing to the top two floors of a place the bottom two floors
of which are occupied by Madam Juana's Puerto Rican
cathouse. But what it came down to was that I liked having
my own room in my own building, and that I could be
very stubborn on the subject, almost as stubborn as Leo
Haig himself.

But this is all beside the point, the point being that it
was cooler inside the Treasure Chest. There wasn't much
more to be said for the place, however. It was dimly lit,
which worked to its advantage; what I could see of the
furnishings suggested that they were better off the less you
could make them out. There was a long bar on the left side
as you entered, and behind the bar there was a stage, and

on the stage, dancing in the glare of a baby spotlight, was our client, the one and probably only Tulip Willing.

She didn't have any clothes on.

I wasn't prepared for this. I mean, I should have been, and everything, but I somehow wasn't. I had seen Tulip that afternoon and what she'd been wearing then had made her figure overwhelmingly obvious to me. Tight jeans and a tight tee-shirt, both worn over nothing but skin, don't leave you very much up in the air as to what's going on underneath them. And also when you go into a topless-bottomless place you ought to be prepared to be confronted by some skin. That's what people go there for, for Pete's sake. Not because the drinks are terrific.

If it had been somebody else up there I think I could have handled it better. But I'd spent a few hours with Tulip, first at Haig's place and then at her apartment, and I had gotten to know her as a human being, and at the same time I had become enormously turned on by her personally, and there she was up there, twisting her unbelievable body around to a barrage of loud recorded hard rock, swinging her breasts and bumping her behind and strutting around on those long legs that seemed to go all the way up to her neck, and—

Well, you get the picture.

I took a deep breath of air that was probably just as polluted as all the other air but seemed better because it was several degrees cooler. I held the breath for a while, looking at Tulip, surveying the club, then looking at Tulip again. She looked a lot better than the club. I let the breath out and walked over to the bar. There were two empty stools and I took the closest one. I had the other empty stool on my right, and on my left I had a man wearing a dark three-button suit and an expression of rapt adoration. I wouldn't say that his eyes were on stems exactly, but they weren't as far back in his head as most people's are, either. He looked as though he'd leaped out of a fairy tale, trapped forever halfway between prince and frog.

472

"Jesus Christ," he said. He may or may not have been talking to me. He wasn't looking at me, but I don't think he'd have bothered looking at me if I had had a live chicken perched on my shoulder. Nothing was going to make him take his eyes off Tulip.

"Jesus," he said again, reverently. "Never saw anything like that. Longest legs I ever seen in my life. Biggest tits I ever seen in my life. Jesus Christ on wheels."

The barmaid came over. A record ended and another began without interruption and Tulip went on doing creative things with her body. The barmaid wasn't a beast herself, a slim redhead wearing black fishnet tights and a black body stocking. She had a heart-shaped face and almond eyes, and I got the feeling that she'd spent her last incarnation as a cat. I started to think of all the different ways I could rub her to make her purr, but she was shifting her feet impatiently, and I decided that my heart (among other parts of me) already belonged to Tulip. I didn't want to spread myself too thin.

"Bottle of beer," I said.

I probably would have preferred something like whiskey and water but Tulip had warned me against it. "They make all the whiskey in New Jersey," she had said, "and it all comes out tasting like something you use to take the old finish off furniture, and then they water it, and then they serve it in shot glasses with false bottoms, and then they charge two dollars a drink for it." So I ordered beer, which came straight from the brewery in a nice hygienic bottle. It also cost two dollars a copy, which is a little high for beer, but it was a business expense if there ever was one so I didn't mind.

"Just look at that bush," my companion said. "Soft and blond and gorgeous. I wonder is she gonna do a spread."

I was rather hoping she wasn't. I was feeling rather weird, if you want to know. On the one hand Tulip was turning me on with her dancing and all, and on the other hand I was a little upset about the fact that this was someone whom

473

I knew personally and professionally, and whom I sort of wanted to know a lot better in the future, and here she was not only turning me on but also turning on a whole roomful of creeps, including this particular creep next to me.

"Some clubs they come right up on the bar," the creep said. He must have been about forty-five, and he had a pencil-line moustache that was really pretty offensive. I noticed he was wearing a wedding ring. "Right up on the bar," he went on, and I still didn't know if he was talking to himself or to me or to the man on the other side of him. "Right up on the bar," he said again, "and you give 'em a tip, you slip 'em a buck, and they squat down so you can eat 'em. Go right down the line and everybody who wants to slip 'em a buck and goes ahead and has theirselves a taste."

I thought seriously about hitting him. Half-seriously, anyway I'm not particularly good at hitting people, and also he couldn't possibly know that he was talking about the girl I fully intended to be in love with.

"Love to eat this one," he said. "Start at her toes and go clear to her nose. Then go back down again."

He went on like this. He got into some rather clinical anatomical detail and I gave some further thought to hitting him. Or I could do something less extreme. I could tip my beer into his lap, for example.

It was about that time that Tulip noticed I was there. You might have thought she would have spotted me right off, but you have to remember that she was up on an elevated platform with a bright spotlight in her eyes, and that the rest of the room was dark. Also she was off to the side so that I was not standing directly in front of her. But she did notice me now, and for a second I thought she was going to blush a little, but I guess when you do this sort of thing five nights out of seven you lose the capacity to blush, because instead she just flashed me a little half-smile and tipped me a wink and went on dancing.

This time the creep did turn to me. "See that?" he said.

"I'll be a son of a bitch. The cunt is crazy about me."

"Huh?"

"She winked at me," he said. "She smiled at me. Some of these broads, they wink at everybody, but that's the first since she came on and she was smiling straight at me. What do you bet she comes over here after her number's done? Man, I'm gonna get lucky tonight. I can feel it."

The thing is, I happened to know that she *would* come over after her number. This wasn't standard; one of the good things about the Treasure Chest, from the dancers' point of view, was that you didn't have to work the bar hustling drinks between numbers. A lot of the clubs worked that way but not Treasure Chest, which was one of the reasons Tulip and her roommate Cherry were willing to work there. But Tulip would come over to meet me because we had arranged it that way, and the last thing I wanted was for her to be confronted by this idiot who was convinced she was crazy about him.

I said, "It was me she smiled at."

His mouth spread in an unpleasant grin. "You? You gotta be kidding."

"She was smiling at me."

"A young punk like you? Don't make me laugh."

"She's my sister," I said.

The grin went away, reversing itself in slow motion. "My sister," I said again, "and I don't much care for the way you were talking about her."

"Listen," he said, "don't get me wrong. A person, you know, a person'll make remarks—"

"What I was thinking," I said, "is this. I was thinking about taking my knife out of my pocket and cutting you a little. Just a little bit."

"Listen," he said. He got off his stool and edged away from the bar. "Listen," he said, "the last thing I want is trouble."

"Maybe you ought to go home," I said.

"Jesus," he said. He headed for the door but he went

475

most of the way walking backward so that he could keep his eyes on me and make sure my hand didn't come out of my pocket. It's awkward walking like that, and he kept stumbling but not quite falling down, and at the door he turned and fled.

I let out my breath and took my hand out of my pocket. I *had* been holding a knife in it, as a matter of fact. The knife is attached to my key chain. It's an inch long, and it has a half-inch blade. It takes about a minute to get the thing open, and I usually break my fingernails in the attempt. Haig gave it to me once. I've never figured out a use for it, but you never know when something will come in handy. I doubt that it would be the greatest thing in the world for cutting someone open with. You'd be better stabbing him with one of the keys on the chain.

A few seconds later the barmaid turned up. She pointed to the creep's half-finished drink and the pile of bills next to it. There was a ten in the pile and five or six singles.

"He coming back?"

"Not without a gun."

"Pardon me?"

"He had to leave in a hurry," I said. "He remembered a previous engagement."

"He forgot his change."

"It's for you," I said.

"It is now," she said, scooping up the bills and change. "What do you know."

"No, he meant it for you," I said.

"Oh, yeah?"

"That's what he said."

"What do you know," she said. "I pegged him for El Cheapo. You never know, do you?"

"I guess not," I said.

I sipped at my beer and turned my eyes to Tulip again. Or they turned that way of their own accord, without my having much to do with it. The music was moving toward a climax, and so was half the audience. There was a little rumble of encouragement from my fellow patrons at the bar. You could make out little encouraging showbiz phrases like "Show me that pretty pussy, baby," and other tasteful bons mots. Tulip had her head back, her long blond hair swaying from side to side behind her, her large breasts pointing at the ceiling in a way that would have forced Newton to reappraise the Law of Gravity. Her whole body shuddered, and the record hit its final grooves, and she put her hands on her thighs and opened herself to the band of dirty old men, and I told myself to close my eyes, and didn't, and I'm sure it was my imagination but I thought I could see all the way to her throat.

Then the lights went out.

There was quite a bit of applause. Not a roar or anything, but more than a polite ovation. A few of my fellow voyeurs scooped change from the bar and headed for the exit. Most of us stayed where we were. The lights had only stayed off for a second, and another record had already been cued and started up, more of the same monotonous rock. If that's the music of my generation, then I guess I'm a throwback or something.

There was no emcee. I had been sort of afraid of some Neanderthal in a checkered sport coat coming up and telling dirty jokes, but Treasure Chest stuck with the basics; when one girl went off, another one came on. A male voice came over the loudspeaker and said, "That was Miss Tulip Willing, ladies and gentlemen. Let's have a big hand for her now. Tulip Willing." I looked around the club for the ladies he'd been talking about and didn't see a one. I suppose there might have been some at the tables but there certainly weren't any at the bar. Nor, for that matter, did I see anybody I would be inclined to label a gentleman. The audience gave Tulip another weaker round of applause in response to his request, and as it died out he said, "And now, ladies and gentlemen, for your viewing pleasure here at the one and only Treasure Chest, a girl with a chestful of pleasure, a pint-sized lady with queen-sized attributes, the one and only Cherry Bounce."

A pair of curtains parted and Tulip's roommate stepped into the spotlight. I knew she was Tulip's roommate because Tulip had told me so. I was seeing her for the first time and my immediate reaction was to wish that she was *my* roommate.

She was a tremendous contrast to Tulip. Tulip was about six feet tall, give or take an inch, and Cherry was maybe five-two in platform shoes. Tulip's hair was long and blond, Cherry's short and jet black. Tulip was built on a grand scale, reminding you that you can't have too much of a good thing, and Cherry was slim, pointing out that good things come in small packages. The one thing that both of them made you dramatically aware of was that human beings are mammals.

She started to dance. She was naked, incidentally. I guess I didn't mention that. I understand that some of the topless-bottomless clubs start out with the girls wearing something, but Treasure Chest kept it simple. She was naked, and she started dancing, and as grubby as the club was and as much as I disliked the music and atmosphere, I decided there were places I would be less happy to be.

The thing is, she was a pretty good dancer. Tulip had moved around nicely and all, but what she was there for was to show you her body and the dancing was more or less incidental. With Cherry, the whole performance was enhanced by the fact that she could really dance. I don't know if this made any difference to the rest of the crowd but I noticed it and I suppose in some way it heightened my reaction to her.

"That's my roommate," a voice said.

A hand touched my arm. I turned to see Tulip standing beside me. She was wearing clothes, but not the jeans and Beethoven tee-shirt I had seen her in earlier.

Now she wore a loose-fitting navy dress. You still got a fair idea of what was lurking beneath the dress, but it was a good deal less obvious.

"Oh, hi," I said.

"Hi yourself. I gather you like my roommate."

"Uh."

"She's pretty, isn't she?"

"Uh, yeah. She's, uh, pretty."

I had been wondering what it would be like when Tulip joined me at the bar. I more or less expected some aggravation from the other males, which was why I had been moved to do the number on the creep with the thin moustache. But evidently men who get off on staring at naked girls are unsettled to be in the company of those very girls, naked or otherwise, and nobody tried to sit in on our conversation. As a matter of fact, the fat man on Tulip's right actually moved a stool away.

"Cherry dances better than I do," she said.

"I thought you danced very well."

"Oh, come on, Chip. You're sweet, but I'm not a dancer. I'm just up there to wiggle my tits and ass at the customers. That's really all it is."

"Well, uh—"

"Cherry's a real dancer. Look how graceful she is." I looked. "The trouble with Cherry is she thinks this is going to lead her to a career in dance. At least I have a realistic attitude. This is an easy way to make a dollar and not much more. Cherry thinks she can make the easy dollar and still use the place as a stepping stone. But she's generally naïve, you know. I take a harder line on reality."

I didn't take any kind of line on reality at that point. What I took was a sip of beer. I did this carefully. I don't know if I'm Mr. Ultra Cool generally, but we had established earlier that whatever cool I normally possessed tended to get lost when Tulip was in the immediate vicinity. So I sipped the beer carefully to avoid gagging on it if she said something disarming.

"Did you like my act, Chip?"

"Yes. Very much."

"Did it turn you on?"

When I didn't answer she said, "I'm not asking because

I'm trying to embarrass you. It's just that I'm trying to understand the particular head of the men who come here. You know, like I don't think I would get off watching a man dance around naked. I can't say for certain because I never watched that, although I was reading where a bar at one of the big mid-western colleges has one night a week with male nude dancers, and the college girls go there and really get off on the whole thing. So maybe it would get me excited, but I don't think so. In fact I don't think those college girls would get off after the first few times. Like they would be getting off on the idea of it, you know, but after it became a frequent thing it would be boring for them."

"I see what you mean."

"But men really get off looking at naked women, don't they?"

I glanced briefly at the absorbed men on either side of us. "Evidently," I said.

"So I wasn't asking to put you on the spot. But you seem like a sane, healthy guy, and I was wondering how you reacted, because sometimes I'm inclined to think of the general audience here as a batch of perverts, which may or may not be fair of me, and I was wondering how someone like you would react."

I didn't know exactly what to say, because I didn't know what my reaction was, exactly. It had been a turn-on watching her on stage, but then it had been at least as exciting in many ways being with her that afternoon, and it was hard to decide whether I would have reacted to her the same way on stage if she had been a total stranger instead of someone who had already Put Ideas In My Head. In some ways it might have been more of a turn-on if I hadn't known her, especially at the end when she did the spread number. That might have been a turn-off in any context—it was sort of humiliating and demeaning and like that—but how could I tell? If it was a total stranger up there I might have gone ape like all the other card-carrying sex maniacs in the audience.

I tried to judge some of this on the basis of my reaction to Cherry, but that didn't really work either. Because even though I hadn't met her she was already someone I knew by proxy. I had stood in her messy bedroom, I had pictured her in my mind, so it wasn't the same thing.

I was trying to decide how all this worked, and how much of it I wanted to mention to Tulip, when the barmaid turned up and asked if I was ready for another beer. I still had a half-filled glass and there was some left in the bottle, so what she meant was that I was drinking too slowly and the joint wasn't in business for its health.

"Chip's with me," Tulip said. "You can let up on the salesmanship number, Jan."

"Sorry about that," Jan said, and winked. "Didn't know."

I smiled back, and we sort of carried on a conversation without getting back to the subject Tulip had raised. She said that Cherry would join us after the show. It was her last number, and we could all get the hell out and go someplace quiet for coffee, and I could ask Cherry various questions and we could see if we learned anything.

"It should be fascinating," she said. "I've always wanted to see how a detective works."

"Well, you know the questions Haig and I asked you this afternoon."

"Oh, this is different. I mean, I was the one you were asking questions. I'll be watching you ask questions of somebody else and that should make a big difference."

"Maybe."

"Do you know what questions you're going to ask her?"

I was looking for an answer to that one when Cherry's first number ended. There was a round of applause approximately equal in volume to what Tulip got, and then another record was cued and Cherry went into her second and last number.

"Do you know what questions you're going to ask her, Chip?"

I knew what questions I wanted to ask her. I wanted to

ask her where she'd been all my life. She was putting a little more sex into her routine on this number, letting her hands glide upward from the sides of her thighs to her genuinely impressive breasts, and giving little ooohs and ahhhs to indicate that she was turning herself on. I don't know if she was really turning herself on, but I can swear to you that she was turning me on, and I don't think I was the only person in the audience who was having that reaction.

"Chip?"

"Er," I said. "Uh, with questions and all that. You sort of have to play it by ear."

"I see."

"It's best not to have everything all scheduled in advance like a presidential press conference or something. You sort of see how one question leads to another."

"It sounds fascinating."

I was glad she thought it was fascinating, because what I thought it was was bullshit. The fact of the matter was that I didn't have the foggiest idea what I was going to ask Cherry, or even why. The more I thought about this case of ours, the more I found myself leaning toward the conclusion that Leo Haig had finally done it. He'd finally slipped over that thin line between genius and insanity, because we never should have taken this absurd case in the first place, because—no matter who Tulip Willing happened to be in her spare time—there was absolutely no excuse for investigating a case involving—

"Chip?"

I broke off my reverie and looked at her. "What?"

"Is Cherry a suspect?"

"Everybody's a suspect."

"Because it's hard to believe she could commit murder."

I looked at her, and I decided it wasn't at all hard to believe that she could commit murder. Not directly, but I could see where she could hand out coronaries to half her audience every night just by doing what she was doing.

I said, "There's one thing you have to realize. Everybody's a suspect until proven otherwise."

"I thought everyone's innocent until proved guilty."

"Absolutely. And everybody's suspicious until proved innocent. That's how it works. Cherry's a suspect, Glenn Flatt's a suspect. Haskell Henderson's a suspect. So's his wife. That Danzig is a suspect. Simon What's-his-name—"

"Barckover."

"Barckover, right," I was supposed to remember things like Barckover's last name, Haig had told me, just as I was supposed to be able to repeat all conversations verbatim. If Archie Goodwin can do something, I'm supposed to train myself to do it, too. (Sometimes, let me tell you, Archie Goodwin gives me a stiff pain.) "Barckover," I said again, carefully training my memory. "And Andrew Merganser—"

"You mean Mallard."

"Well, I knew it was some kind of a duck. The hell with Archie Goodwin."

"Pardon me?"

"Forget it," I said, a little more savagely than I'd intended. "Mallard and Helen Tattersall and Gus Leemy and whoever the hell else you mentioned. Everybody—"

"Don't say Gus's name so loud. He's probably in the club tonight."

"Well, they're all suspects," I said, not so loud this time around. "And so are other people we haven't even thought of yet, and one of them's a killer."

"It's still hard to believe."

I let the conversation die there. If she thought that was hard to believe, she didn't know the half of it. What I found hard to believe was that Haig and I were involved. True, Haig was only really happy when he had a murder case to bother his brain with. And true, this case involved murder, and not just one murder, not just another murder, but—

Tulip's fingers closed on my elbow. "Watch now, Chip. She's coming to the end and she really makes a production

483

out of it. She shows a lot more than I do. Watch!"

So I watched. I mean, maybe you would have looked up at the ceiling or something. Anything's possible. But what I did, see, is I watched.

Watched as she lowered herself first to her knees, then lay almost full-length, her perfect breasts suspended over the apron of the stage. Watched her straighten up and swing that body around, shaking those breasts from side to side, always perfectly in time to that awful music. Watched as she displayed herself, giving everybody a much longer look than everybody needed. Watched as she put one little hand to her mouth, miming shock at what she had done, straightening up now, drawing herself primly together, her shoulders held back to bring her breasts into the sharpest possible relief.

And heard her sudden gasp.

And saw the bead of blood on her left breast just an inch above the nipple. And watched her hands, moving in awful slow motion, struggling to touch the bead of blood.

And watched her fall, still in slow motion, falling backwards and to her left, falling as only dead things fall, landing at last on the floorboards of the stage with the impact of a gunshot.

I guess my reaction time was pretty good. It didn't seem to be at the time, but the fact remains that I was the first person to vault the bar and leap onto the stage and have a look at Cherry Bounce.

On the other hand, fast or slow, my reaction was wrong. What I should have done was forget the stage entirely and go straight to the door to keep anybody else from going through it. Because I had seen the way Cherry tried to reach her breast and couldn't, and I had seen her fall, and I really didn't have to go up onto the stage to examine her in order to know there was nothing I could do for her.

Haig has always said it's nothing to berate myself for. He says anybody's natural and proper reaction is to establish first of all that the victim is beyond assistance. Well, that was my reaction, all right, and that was what I established.

Our murderer had just claimed his one hundred twenty-fourth victim, and he had done it right in front of my eyes.

Chapter Two

WHEN THE DOORBELL RANG that afternoon I was spooning brine shrimp into a tank of *Labeo chrysophekadion*. They were cute little rascals, about half an inch long, and most people who keep tropical fish call them black sharks. Which is sort of weird, because they are not sharks at all and in no sense sharklike, being peaceful types who function as scavengers in an aquarium, picking up on food that other fish have missed. Ours weren't black, either, but white and pink-eyed like Easter bunnies. Leo Haig had come up with a couple of albinos in an earlier spawning, and now he had bred them to each other, and the two hundred or so fish I was presently feeding were the result.

Haig couldn't have been prouder if he had sired them himself. I was kind of pleased with them too, but I couldn't see what they had to do with Being a Resourceful Private Detective, which was what I was supposed to be. When I would bring up the subject Haig would tell me that the aquarium was the universe in microcosm, and the lessons it taught me would ultimately find application in life itself. He says things like that a lot.

Anyway, the doorbell rang. I gave the unblack unsharks a last spoonful of brine shrimp and went to the door and opened it, and it was good I had left the spoon and the saucer of shrimp in the other room, because otherwise I would have dropped them.

Instead I dropped my jaw. I stood there with my mouth open and stared at her.

There was a whole lot of her to stare at. I'm reasonably tall, although no one would mistake me for a professional basketball player, and she was just about my height. There the resemblance ended. She had long golden hair framing a face with absolutely nothing wrong with it. High cheekbones, wide-set blue eyes the color of a New York sky at sunset, a complexion out of an advertisement for

486

sun-tan lotion, a mouth out of an advertisement for fellatio.

The part below the face was no disappointment, either. She was wearing jeans and a Beethoven-for-President tee-shirt, and she wasn't wearing anything under the tee-shirt, and I really couldn't find anything about her body to object to. I suppose a purist might argue that her legs were a little too long and her breasts were a little too large. Somehow this didn't bother me a bit.

For a while she watched me stare at her. She gave a sort of half-smile, which suggested that she was used to this reaction but liked it all the same, and then she said, "Mr. Haig?"

"No."

"Pardon me?"

"I'm not him. I mean, I'm me. Uh."

"Perhaps I came at a bad time."

"Oh, no," I said. "You came at a wonderful time. I mean you can come anytime you want to. I mean. Uh."

"Is this Leo Haig's residence?"

"Yes."

"Leo Haig the detective?"

He's Leo Haig the detective all right, but that's not a phrase that rolls off most people's tongues. As a matter of fact he's pretty close to being an unknown, which is not the way he wants it, and one of the main reasons he hired me as his assistant. A chief function of mine is to write up his cases—at least the ones that turn out triumphant—so that the world will know about him. If it weren't for Dr. Watson, he says, who would have heard of Sherlock Holmes? If Archie Goodwin never sat down at a typewriter, who would be aware of Nero Wolfe? Anyway, that's why he hired me, to make Leo Haig The Detective a household phrase, and that's how come you get to read all this.

"Leo Haig the detective," I agreed.

"Then I came to the right place," she said.

"Oh, definitely. No question about it. You came to the right place."

487

"Are you all right?"

"Oh, sure. I'm terrific."

"May I come in?"

"Oh, sure. Right. Great idea."

She gave me an odd look, which I certainly deserved, and I stood aside and she came in and I closed the door. I led her into the office which Haig and I share. There's a huge old partners' desk, which we also share, although I don't really have much use for my side of it. I pointed to a chair for her, and when she sat down I swiveled my desk chair around and sat in it and looked at her some more. She was a little less intimidating when she was sitting down. There was still just as much of her but the overall effect was not quite so awesome.

"Is Mr. Haig in?"

"He's upstairs," I said. "He's playing with his fish."

"Playing with them?"

"Sort of. I'm his assistant. My name is Harrison. Chip Harrison."

"Mine is Tulip."

"Oh."

"Tulip Willing."

"It certainly is," I said.

"Pardon me?"

I was really having a difficult time getting my brain in gear. I took a deep breath and tried again. I said, "You wanted to see Mr. Haig?"

"That's right. I want to hire him."

"I see."

"There's a matter that I want him to investigate."

"I see," I said again. "Could you tell me something about the matter?"

"Well—"

"I'm his assistant," I said. "His confidential assistant."

"Aren't you young to be a detective?"

I'm not exactly a detective. I mean I don't have a license or anything. But I didn't see any point in telling her that.

What I wanted to say was that you don't have to be all that old to spoon brine shrimp into a fish tank, but I didn't say that either. I said, "If you could give me some idea—"

"Of course." She leaned forward and I took another quick look at Beethoven's eyebrows. Her breasts had fantastic stage presence. It was hard not to stare at them, and you sort of got the feeling they were staring back.

"It's a murder case," she said.

I don't know if my heartbeat actually quickened, because it had been operating faster than normal ever since I opened the door and took my first look at her. But I certainly did get excited. I mean, people don't generally turn up on our doorstep wanting us to investigate a murder. But it happens all the time in books, and that's the kind of detective Haig wants to be, the kind you read about in mystery novels.

I said, "A homicide."

"Not exactly."

"I thought you said a murder."

She nodded. "But homicide means that a person has been killed, doesn't it?"

"I think so."

"Well, this is murder. But it's not homicide."

"I don't think I understand."

She put her hand to her mouth and nibbled thoughtfully at a cuticle. If she ever ran out of cuticles to nibble I decided I'd gladly lend her one of mine. Or any other part of me that interested her. "It's hard to say this," she said.

I waited her out.

"I had to come to Leo Haig," she said eventually. "I couldn't go to the police. I never even considered going to the police. Even if they didn't actually laugh at me there's no way they would bother investigating. So I had to go to a private detective, and I couldn't go to an ordinary private detective. It has to be Leo Haig."

That's the kind of thing you want every client to say, but Tulip Willing was the first one ever to say it.

"I guess the only way to say it is to come right out with it," she said. "Someone murdered my tropical fish. I want Leo Haig to catch the killer."

I climbed a flight of stairs to the fourth floor, where Haig was playing with his fish. There are tanks in all the rooms on the third floor, but on the fourth floor there are nothing but tanks, rows and rows of them. I found Haig glowering at a school of cichlids from Lake Tanganyika. They had set him back about fifty bucks a fish, which is a lot, and no one had yet induced them to spawn in captivity. Haig intended to be the first, and thus far the fish had shown no sign of preparing to cooperate.

"There's an element missing," he said. "Maybe the rockwork should be extended. Maybe they're accustomed to spawning in caves. Maybe they want less light."

"Maybe they're all boys," I suggested.

"Phooey. There are eight of them. With six fish one is mathematically certain of having a pair. That is to say that the certainty is in excess of ninety-five percent. With eight the certainty is that much greater."

"Unless the cunning Africans only ship one sex."

He looked at me. "You have a devious mind," he said. "It will be an asset professionally."

"I have a devious mind," I agreed. "You have a client."

"Oh?"

"A beautiful young woman," I said.

"Trust you to notice that."

"I wouldn't trust anyone who didn't notice. Her name is Tulip Willing."

"Indeed."

"She wants you to investigate a murder and trap a killer."

He bounced to his feet, and the African cichlids no longer meant a thing to him. He's about five feet tall and built like a beachball, with a neatly trimmed little black goatee and head of wiry black hair. He likes to touch the beard, and he started doing it now.

490

"A homicide," he said.

I didn't make the distinction between murder and homicide. "She says only Leo Haig can help her," I went on. "She hasn't been to the police. She needs a private detective, and you're the only man on earth who can possibly do the job for her."

"She honestly said that?"

"Her very words."

"Remarkable."

"She's in the office. I told her I was sure you would want to talk to her yourself."

"Of course I want to talk to her." He was on his way to the stairs and even though his legs are about half the length of mine I had to hustle to catch up with him.

"One thing you ought to know before you talk to her," I said.

"Oh?"

"About the victims."

He was positively beaming. "Victims? Plural? More than one victim?"

"Over a hundred of them."

He stared, and his face showed a struggle between delight and disbelief. He really wanted it to be a murder case with a hundred victims, and at the same time he was beginning to read the whole number as a put-on.

"One thing you ought to know," I said. "The victims aren't people. They're fish."

He said, "Miss Willing? I'm Leo Haig. I believe you've already met my assistant, Mr. Harrison."

"Yes, I have."

"I understand some fishes of yours were murdered. Could you give me some specific information on the crime?"

I had to hand it to him. I don't know what kind of reaction I'd been hoping for but it wasn't what I got. I had sent him up in a pretty rotten way, when you stop to think of it, and he

491

was returning the favor by treating Tulip Willing and her massacred fish like the crime of the century. Instead of telling me to get rid of her, either by showing her the door or calling the men in the white coats, he was going to take his time getting her whole story, and I was going to have to write it all down in my notebook. I made it game, set and match to him.

So I sat there with my notebook on my side of the desk, and Haig sat on his side of the desk and played with a pipe, and Tulip Willing sat in the chair I'd put her in originally. I sensed that the three of us were going to waste an hour or so of each other's time. I didn't really mind. I hadn't been doing anything that sensational with my time in the first place, and I couldn't think of anyone I'd rather waste it with. (Than Tulip, I mean. Wasting time with Haig is something I do almost every day of my life. It's enjoyable, but there's nothing all that exotic about it.)

"There are many ways an entire tank of fishes can be destroyed at once," he was saying. He has this professorial air that he likes to use. "Certain diseases strike with the rapidity and force of the Black Death, wiping out a whole fish population overnight. Air pollution, paint fumes, these can cause annihilation on an extraordinary scale."

"Mr. Haig—"

"Occasionally equipment malfunctions. A thermostat may go haywire, boiling the inhabitants of an aquarium. On the other hand, a heater may burn out and the resulting drop in temperature may prove fatal, although this is more likely to be a gradual matter. In other situations—"

"Mr. Haig, I'm not an idiot."

"I didn't mean to imply that you were."

"I'm familiar with the ways fishes can die. Naturally you would assume that the death was accidental. I made the same assumption myself. I ruled out the possibilities of natural and accidental death."

"Indeed."

"The fish were poisoned."

He took his pipe apart. He's given up smoking them

because they burn his tongue, but he likes to fiddle with them. He bought the pipes originally because he thought they might be a good character tag and he knows that great detectives have to have charming idiosyncrasies. He keeps trying on idiosyncrasies looking for one that will fit. I've wanted to tell him that he's odd enough all by himself, but I can't think of an acceptable way to phrase it.

I waited for him to ask how she knew the fish were poisoned. Instead he said, "What sort of fish? A community tank, I suppose? Mollies and swordtails and the like?"

"No. I don't have a community tank. These were Scats."

"Ah. *Scatophagus argus.*"

"These were *Scatophagus tetracanthus,* actually."

"Indeed." He seemed impressed. He thinks everybody should know the Latin name of everything, and I get a lecture to that effect on the average of once every three days. "The *tetracanthus* are imported less often. And most retailers sell them as *argus* because few hobbyists know the difference. These were definitely *tetracanthus,* you say?"

"Yes."

"How many did you have?"

"One hundred twenty-three."

"Indeed. You must be rather fond of the species. You must also have had an extremely large tank."

"It's a twenty-nine gallon tank."

He frowned. "Good heavens," he said. "You must have stacked them like cordwood."

"All but two were fry. They had plenty of room."

"Fry?" His eyebrows went up, first at the word she used, then at the implications. Most people who keep fish, and certainly most people who look anything like Tulip Willing, call baby fish baby fish. She called them fry. Then, when the whole idea sank in, he leaned forward and waggled a finger at her. "Impossible," he said.

"What's impossible?"

"Neither of the *Scatophagus* species has ever spawned in captivity."

493

"I spawned them. And it's been done before."

"By Rachow, yes. But he had an accident and lost the lot, and he was never able to repeat the procedure. Nor has anyone else had any success."

"I had success," she said.

"Impossible," he said again. "No one but Rachow ever induced the little devils to spawn. And he was working with *argus*, not *tetracanthus*." He paused abruptly and his eyes crawled upward and examined the ceiling. "Wait just one moment," he said. "Just one moment."

I looked at Tulip and watched her wait one moment. There was the hint of a private smile on her lips.

"There was a spawning," he said finally. "Not of *argus*. Of *tetracanthus*. It was reported in *Copeia* a year ago. The fish spawned but a fungus destroyed the spawn before they hatched. The author was—let me think. Wolinski. T. J. Wolinski. He's done other articles for aquarist publications."

"Not he," Tulip said.

"Pardon me?"

She was really smiling now. "Not *he*," she repeated. "She. Me, actually. They spawned a second time and I used a fungicide and it worked. I got a seventy percent hatch. One hundred twenty-one fry, and they were doing beautifully. I left the parent fish with them."

"Your name is Willing. Tulip Willing."

"That's a stage name."

"And your real name is—"

"Thelma Wolinski."

Haig was on his feet, his jaw set firmly beneath the neat little beard. "T. J. Wolinski," he said, with something verging on reverence. "T. J. Wolinski. Extraordinary. And some creature poisoned your scats? Good heavens. You'll pardon me, I hope, for treating you like a witling. I never would have guessed—well, that's by the way. Some villain poisoned your fishes, did he? Well, we shall get to the bottom of this. And I

494

shall have his head, madam. Rest assured of that. I shall have his head."

So the whole thing was out of control. It was my fault, and although there was a certain amount of thrill in the idea of being on a case, I can't say I was anywhere near as thrilled as Haig was.

Well, I'd asked for it. I'd been baiting him, never figuring he'd bite, and now he was hooked right through the gills.

Chapter Three

IT MUST HAVE been around three in the afternoon when Tulip Willing rang the doorbell. It was close to five when Haig was finished asking questions. He went over everything and enabled me to fill a great many pages in my notebook with facts that would probably turn out to be unimportant. It's his theory that there is no such thing as an absolutely inconsequential fact. (The first time he told me this I replied that in 1938 the state of Wyoming produced one-third of a pound of dry edible beans for every man, woman, and child in the nation. He agreed that it was certainly hard to see how that could turn out to be consequential, but he wasn't going to rule out the possibility entirely.)

I'm taking matters into my own hands and leaving out some items that never did seem to have any more bearing on the case than the fascinating fact about dry edible beans. That still leaves plenty of bits and pieces to report from Haig's questioning of Tulip.

Item: The fish had died four days ago, on a Saturday. Tulip had come home at four Saturday morning after a long night at the Treasure Chest, where she had been working for five months, having been previously employed in a similar capacity at similar nightspots, among them Tippler's Cove and Shake It Or Leave It. (I am not making any of this up.) She came home, exhausted and ready for bed, and she went over to say goodnight to the fish, and they were all floating on the top, which is never a sign of radiant good health. When she was done being hysterical she did something intelligent. She removed the two parent fish and preserved them in jars of rubbing alcohol in case an autopsy should ultimately be indicated, and she took a sample of the water in the tank and another sample of water from another aquarium as a control. These she took to a chemical laboratory on Varick Street for

496

scientific analysis, and Monday the laboratory called her and informed her that the sample from the tank of scats contained strychnine, which is no better for fish than it is for people. There was enough strychnine present to kill any human being who drank a glass of the water, but then not that many people go around drinking out of aquariums, and I'd venture to say that those who do are asking for it.

Item: She assumed that the murder of the scats was motivated not by a specific hatred of the fish themselves but by hatred of their owner. Someone was trying to upset her or punish her or terrify her by killing her pets. This was, as far as she could determine, the first instance of hostile behavior to be directed at her, aside from the usual obscene telephone calls she received intermittently. The phone calls had not increased in frequency lately, and in fact she hadn't heard from one of the callers in a long time and was a little concerned that something might have happened to him. She said that he had a very unusual approach, but she didn't go into detail.

Item: The scats had been in fine fettle when she left the apartment Friday afternoon at two o'clock. The strychnine would presumably have worked instantly upon its introduction into the aquarium, but she had been unable to determine just how long the fish had been dead. So somewhere between two Friday afternoon and four Saturday morning the villain had entered her apartment and had done the dirty deed.

Item: While I don't guess there was anybody who could properly be labeled a suspect at this stage of the game, the following people were sufficiently a part of Tulip's life to find their way into my notebook:

Cherry Bounce. I know, I know, but if you can accept a name like Tulip Willing, why be put off by Cherry Bounce? Cherry and Tulip had been roommates for just about five months. They met when Tulip went to work at Treasure Chest, where Cherry had already been employed. Tulip had recently broken up with her boyfriend and needed a place to live, and Cherry had recently broken up with a boyfriend of her own and needed someone to share her rent. The two of them had been getting along well enough, although they didn't have much in common outside of their profession. Tulip characterized her as flighty, flitting from one pursuit to another, health foods to astrology to bio-feedback. As far as the fish were concerned, Cherry thought they were cute. Cherry's name off-stage was Mabel Abramowicz, so I guess she would have had to change it to something.

Glenn Flatt. Tulip's ex-husband, whom she had met and married four years ago when she was picking up a doctorate in marine biology at the University of Miami, and whom she had divorced two years later. I could understand why she had divorced him—she wanted her own name back. No one built like Tulip could be happy with Flatt for a surname. (According to her, she left her husband because he was a compulsive gambler. If you said *Good Morning* to him he'd lay odds that it wasn't. This would have been all right if he won, but he evidently didn't.) Flatt lived on Long Island where he was employed as a research bio-chemist by a pharmaceutical manufacturer. This fact prompted Haig and me to glance meaningfully at each other—Flatt's job would undoubtedly give him access to strychnine. On the other hand, it would probably give him just as good access to any number of non-detectable vehicles for ichthyicide. Flatt and Tulip were "very good friends now," she said, and they occasionally had dinner or drinks together, and now and then he turned up at the club to catch her act. Flatt had never remarried.

Haskell Henderson. Tulip's current boyfriend and the owner of a half-dozen local health food stores. They had been seeing each other for almost three months. Henderson would spend two or three afternoons a week at Tulip's apartment. I don't guess he devoted much of this time to staring at the fish. When he wasn't keeping company with Tulip or minding the stores he was in Closter, New Jersey, where he shared a cozy little house with...

Mrs. Haskell Henderson. Tulip had never met Mrs. H.H., and had no way of knowing whether or not the woman even knew of her existence, but anyone with that sound a reason for wanting unpleasant things to happen to Tulip certainly deserved an entry in my notebook. The entry was pretty much limited to her name because Henderson evidently didn't talk about his wife very much.

Simon Barckover. Tulip's agent, and Cherry's agent too, for that matter. His relationship with both clients was strictly professional, but he got in the notebook because he was the only person around who might have a specific grudge against the fish. He thought Tulip was genuinely talented and that she had a future in show business if she applied herself. Tulip admitted that he might be right but she wasn't interested. The topless dancing paid well and was generally undemanding, leaving her free to concentrate on her chief interest, which was ichthyology. Barckover had told her on several occasions that the damn fish were standing in the way of her career and that he would like to flush the lot of them down the toilet. She couldn't believe he would actually do it, but then she couldn't believe anybody would want to poison the scats, so he got in the notebook.

Leonard Danzig. Cherry's boyfriend. She had been dating him for a month or so, although she continued to see other men as well. He got on the list because Tulip couldn't stand him, describing him charitably as "a kind of a slimy character." I gather she disliked him because he kept trying to get her into bed, either just with him or with Cherry along for threesies. Tulip was spectacularly uninterested in either prospect. No one seemed to know what Danzig did for a living, but Tulip guessed it was at least somewhat criminal. Cherry had met him at the club. He always seemed to have a lot of money, and if he worked at all he didn't seem to have any set hours. His feelings toward the fish were unknown, except that he had once remarked that it would "take a hell of a lot of the bastards to make a decent meal."

Helen Tattersall. All that Tulip knew about Mrs. Tattersall was that she lived in the apartment immediately below hers and was a pain in the ass, constantly complaining about noise, even when no noise whatsoever was emanating from the apartment. She had on one occasion reported Tulip and Cherry to the police, alleging that the two were running a bordello in their apartment. Tulip wasn't sure whether the woman actually believed this or was just making a nuisance of herself. "She's the sort of frustrated old bitch who might poison somebody's pets just out of meanness," Tulip said.

Andrew Mallard. Tulip's former boyfriend, the one she was living with before she got together with Cherry. He was an advertising account executive, recently divorced, and evidently rather strange. He had moved in with Tulip; then, when they broke up, she had moved out and let him keep the apartment because the idea of actually going out and finding a place of his own gave him anxiety attacks. He still called her occasionally when he was drunk, generally at an hour when he should have known she was sleeping. Now and then he caught her act at Treasure Chest, always tipping heavily in order to get a ringside table, always attending by himself, always staring at her breasts as if hypnotized, and never speaking a word to her. Every once in a while she got flowers delivered backstage with no note enclosed—though never on nights when he was in the audience—and she sort of assumed he was the source. He had liked the fish very much while they lived together, but she figured he was a possible suspect because murdering fish was clearly an insane act, and Andrew Mallard was hardly playing with a full deck himself.

Gus Leemy. He owned the Treasure Chest. At least he was the owner of record, but Tulip had the impression that the club was a Mafia joint of one sort or another and that Leemy was fronting for the real owners. She wasn't even sure he

knew she had fish and couldn't imagine why he would
have anything against her or them. I think she brought his
name up because she didn't like him.

So I had those nine names in my notebook, and there
was a fourteen-hour period of time during which any of
them could have gone to Tulip's apartment and done
something fishy to her fish. Possibly any or all of them
could account for their time, but Tulip didn't know about
it. And possibly one of the fourteen million other residents
of the New York metropolitan area was the killer. I mean, if
you're going to do something as fundamentally insane as
feeding strychnine to tropical fish, they wouldn't have to
be the fish of someone you know, would they? If you're
going to be a lunatic about it, one fish tank is as good as
another.

A little before five Haig leaned back in his chair and put
his feet on top of his desk. I've tried to break him of this
habit but it's impossible. Tulip and I sat there respectfully
and studied the soles of his shoes while the great man
searched for meaning in the ceiling.

Without opening his eyes he said, "Chip."

"Sir."

"I need your eyes and ears and legs. The scene of the
crime must be examined. You will go with Miss Wolinski
to her apartment. Miss Wolinski? I assume that will be
convenient?"

Tulip agreed that it would be. She had a dinner date at
eight-thirty and a performance at ten o'clock but she was
free until then.

"Satisfactory," Haig said. He swung his feet down from
the desk. "You will visit Miss Wolinski's apartment. You
will be guided by your intelligence and intuition and
experience. You will then return here to report."

"If that's all—" Tulip said.

Haig had turned to look at the Rasboras. They're little
pinkish fish with dark triangles on their sides, and Haig
has a ten-gallon tank of them directly behind his desk chair

at eye level. He's apt to turn around and study them in the middle of a conversation. This time, though, his attention to the Rasboras was a sign that the conversation was over.

The hell it was. I said, "I'll make out a receipt for Miss Wolinski for her retainer."

Haig said, "Retainer?"

Tulip said, "Oh, of course. You'll be wanting a retainer, won't you?"

I don't know what he'd do without me. I swear I don't. The trouble is, Haig keeps forgetting that if you're going to be a detective for a living you ought to do your best to make a living out of it. For most of his life he lived in two ratty rooms in the Bronx, breeding tropical fish and trucking plastic bags around to pet shops, peddling his little babies for a nickel here and a dime there. All the while he read every mystery and detective story ever published, and then his uncle died and left him a fortune, and he bought this house and let Madam Juana keep the lower two floors and set up shop as a detective, which is terrific, no question about it. But his capital isn't really enough to keep us together, so when we get a case it's a good idea for us to get money out of it, and here he was going to let Tulip hire us without paying anything.

"Of course," Tulip said again, digging in her bag for a checkbook. When she came up with it I uncapped a pen and handed it to her. She started to make out the check, then looked up to ask the amount.

"Five hundred is standard," I said.

Haig almost fainted. I think he would have asked her for fifty bucks and let her talk him down. But the five hundred didn't phase our client for a second. I guess all she had to be told was that it was standard. She finished making out the check and passed it to me, and I wrote out a receipt on a sheet from my notebook and gave it to Haig for him to sign. He wrote his name with a flourish, as usual. Imagine what he could do if he had more than seven letters to work with.

"I intend to earn this," he said, holding the check in his pudgy little hand. "You'll receive full value for your money, Miss Wolinski. In a sense, you might say your troubles are over."

And ours are just beginning, I thought. But then Tulip got to her feet, sort of uncoiling from her chair like a trained cobra responding to a flute, and I decided that any case that forced me to go to her apartment with her couldn't possibly be all bad.

"He's quite a man," Tulip said. "It must be very inspiring to work for someone like Leo Haig."

"It's all of that," I agreed. "And do I call you Miss Wolinski or Miss Willing?"

"Call me Tulip. And may I call you Chip?"

Call me darling, I thought. "Sure," I said. "Call me Chip."

"What's that a nickname for?"

"It's the only name I've got," I said, which is certainly true now. I had started life as Leigh Harvey Harrison, both Leigh and Harvey being proper names in my less-than-proper family, but in the fall of '63 my parents decided that wouldn't do at all, and I've been Chip ever since. I understand there are a lot of Jews named Arthur who were known to the world as Adolph until sometime in the '30s.

We talked a little more about Haig, and then the cab dropped us at her building, a high-rise on the corner of 54th and Eighth. The lobby reminded you a little of an airline terminal. "It's not exactly overflowing with warmth and charm," Tulip said. "It's sort of sterile, isn't it? Before I moved here I lived in a brownstone in the Village. I really liked that apartment and I would have kept it except it would have meant keeping Andrew, too. This place has all the character of an office building, but on the other hand the elevators are fast and there's plenty of closet space and there aren't any cockroaches. My other place was crawling with them, and of course I couldn't spray because of the fish."

"Couldn't you try trapping them and feeding them to the fish?"

"Is that what Leo Haig does?"

"No, it just occurred to me. What we do, Wong Fat puts some kind of crystals in the corners of the kitchen, and the roaches eat it and die. They come from miles around to do themselves in. I don't know what Wong does with them. I suppose he throws them out." I thought for a moment. "I *hope* he throws them out."

On the elevator she told me another bad feature of the building. "There are prostitutes living here," she said. "I wouldn't mind if they just lived here. They also work here, and you can't imagine what that's like."

I could imagine.

"There are these men coming and going all the time," she said, which was probably true in more ways than she meant. "And they see a girl in the building, any girl, and they take it for granted that you're in the business yourself. It's very unpleasant."

"I'm sure it is."

"As if I didn't get enough of that aggravation at the club. Just because a girl displays her body men tend to assume that it's for sale. I mean, I don't kid myself, Chip. Cherry thinks she's an artist, she takes singing lessons and dancing lessons, the whole bit. She's waiting to be discovered. I think she's a little bit whacky. Men don't come to watch me because I'm such a sensational dancer. I'm a pretty rotten dancer, as a matter of fact. They come to see me and they pay two dollars a drink for watered rotgut because they enjoy looking at my tits."

"Oh."

"That's all it is, really. Tits."

"Uh."

"If it weren't for my tits," she said, "I'd be teaching high school biology."

I couldn't think of anything to say to that one, but as it turned out I didn't have to because we had reached her door and she was fishing in her purse for the key. She got it out, then rang the bell. "In case Cherry's home," she explained. We stood around for a while, long enough for her to conclude that Cherry wasn't home, and then she opened the door and walked inside. I didn't follow her, and she asked me what I was waiting out in the hall for.

"Just a minute," I said. I dropped to one knee and examined the lock. There were two cylinders but one was just a blind to confuse burglars. The other was a Rabson, a good one, and I couldn't find any scratches on the cylinder or on the bolt. That didn't necessarily mean the killer had had a key; if he had a good set of picks and knew how to use them he could open the lock without leaving evidence behind. "Of the nine people you mentioned before," I said, "how many have keys?"

"Oh. He got in with a key?"

"It's possible."

"So you want to know who has keys?"

I got out my notebook and went through the nine of them. Cherry had a key, of course, it being her apartment. Glenn Flatt, the ex-husband, had been to the apartment a few times but had never been given a key. Haskell Henderson, the current boyfriend, had a key. Mrs. Haskell Henderson hadn't been given one, but she could have swiped or duplicated her husband's, assuming she knew anything about it. Leonard Danzig had a key, as did any number of past and present boyfriends of Cherry's. Helen Tattersall, the neighbor, didn't, but there was always the possibility that she had access to the building's master key. There was a chainbolt on the inside of the door, but when nobody was home it wasn't locked and the master key would open the other lock.

Andrew Mallard did not have a key and had never been to the apartment. Maybe Tulip was afraid that if she ever let him in she would have to move again. Simon Barckover might well have a key, since Cherry gave them out rather indiscriminately, but Tulip wasn't sure one way or the other. And Gus Leemy probably didn't have a key.

"But anybody *could* have one easily enough," Tulip said.

"The thing about Cherry, she tends to misplace things. Especially keys. I think she's borrowed my key four times in the past five months to have duplicates made, and she always has several made at a time. Anyone could have borrowed her key to have a duplicate made, and if he didn't put it back when he was done she would just assume she lost it again. It's sort of a nuisance."

"It must be."

"And then sometimes she sets the latch and doesn't bother taking a key, and it's even possible that she came back here Friday night to change or something and left the door unlocked, and then came back again and locked it. So anybody at all could have walked in. Just some ordinary prowler, trying doors and finding this one unlocked."

"Just some ordinary prowler looking to find an open apartment with a fish tank he could pour strychnine into?"

"Oh."

"I think we can rule out the Ordinary Prowler theory!"

"I guess you're right. I'm not thinking very clearly."

She dropped into a chair, then bounced back up again. And *bounced* is precisely the word to fit the act. She bounced, and her breasts bounced, and I'd just about reached the point where I was able to look at her without being very close to drooling, and that little bounce she did put me right back at square one again.

"I'm a terrible hostess," she said. "I didn't offer you a drink. You'll have a drink, won't you?"

"If you're having one."

"I am, but what does that have to do with it? What would you like?"

I tried not to look at the front of her tee-shirt. "I'll have a glass of milk," I said.

"Gee, I don't think we've got any."

"That's all right," I said. "I don't even like milk."

"Then why did you ask for it?"

"I don't know," I said. "The words just came out that way. I'll have whatever you're having."

"Great. I'm having bourbon and yogurt. Do you want yours on the rocks or straight up?"

"I guess on the rocks. What's so funny?"

But she didn't answer. She was too busy laughing. Most women tend to giggle, which can be pleasant enough, but Tulip put her head back and gave out with a full-scale belly laugh, and it really sounded great. While she stood there laughing her head off I rewound some mental recording tape and played back the conversation, and I said, "Oh."

"Bourbon and yogurt!"

"Very funny," I said.

"On the *rocks*!"

She actually slapped her thigh. You hear about people doing that but I didn't think anybody really did. She laughed her head off and slapped her thigh.

"I guess I got distracted," I said.

"A glass of *milk*!"

"Look, Miss Wolinski—"

"Oh, Chip, I'm sorry," She came to me and put her hand on my arm. I didn't want to react because I wasn't feeling sexy, I was feeling mad, but what I wanted didn't have very much to do with it. She put her hand on my arm, and it was as if I'd stuck my big toe into an electrical outlet.

"I was just teasing you a little," she said.

"I hope you never tease me a lot. I don't think I could handle it."

"How about a beer?"

"Great."

I told her I'd like to look around the apartment while she poured the beer. She said that was fine. There was the living room, fairly good sized, and there were two small bedrooms, each furnished with a platform bed and a night table and a chest of drawers. The first bedroom I entered looked like an ad for disaster insurance. The bed was unmade, assuming it had ever been made to begin with, and there was so much underwear scattered around that it was hard to find the floor. I sort of hoped that was Cherry's bedroom because I didn't want to learn that our client was that much of a slob. When I looked in the other bedroom I established that it was Tulip's. It was immaculate, and there was a fish tank in it.

I sat on the edge of the bed and looked in the tank. There was a glass divider in the middle and an African Gourami on each side of it.

"Here's your beer," she said from the doorway. "Hey, did anything happen to those guys?"

There was real alarm in her voice. "They're fine," I said. "What species are they? I mean I know they're *Ctenapoma* but I don't recognize the species."

"*Ctenapoma fasciolatum.* I don't suppose he's started building a bubble nest, has he?" She came over and looked over my shoulder. "He hasn't, darn it. That's the third female I've had in there with him. He killed the other two. I used the divider when I put the second female in, and I waited until he had a nest built, and I figured that was a clear signal that he was madly and passionately in love, so I lifted out the divider and the little bastard charged right at her and killed her." She sat down on the bed next to me and gave me a glass of beer. I took a long drink of it. "So I don't really know what to do," she went on. "This time he's not even building a nest. He just ignores the poor old girl completely. And you can see she's ready to spawn. She's positively bursting with eggs, the little angel. I must be doing something wrong."

"Mr. Haig might be able to tell you."

"Has he bred *fasciolatum*?"

"No, but he's had results with some of the other *Ctenapoma* species. He has some secrets."

"Do you think he'd tell me?"

"If you told him how you managed the scats."

She grinned, then suddenly lost the grin when she remembered what had happened to the scats. "I didn't even show you that tank," she said. "Or did you find it yourself? It's in the living room."

I hadn't noticed it on my way through, so the two of us went back to look at it. There wasn't really a hell of a lot to look at. When you've seen one aquarium you've seen them all, when all they contain is water. This particular water may have had enough strychnine in it to kill a lot of people, but it certainly looked innocuous enough.

"I siphoned out the dead fry," she said. "Then I was going to get rid of the rest of the water, but is it safe to pour it down the sink? There's poison in it, after all, and I don't want to wipe out half of Manhattan."

"It would just go in the sewers," I said. "It would probably get completely diluted. But if you don't want to risk it I guess you can let the water evaporate and then throw out the tank."

"Throw out the tank?"

"Well, I don't know much about strychnine. Would it evaporate along with the water? And meanwhile there's the chance someone would drink out of the aquarium. I admit it's not much of a chance, but why take it?"

"Maybe we'd better flush it down the toilet," she said. "I can find out later how to clean the tank so that it's usable again. It won't be destroying the evidence, will it? I have the lab report and everything."

I assured her that it wouldn't be destroying evidence, and the two of us lugged the tank into the bathroom and emptied it down the toilet. And yet, it did take two of us, and if she hadn't been a big strong lady it would have taken three of us, because water is a lot heavier than you might think. After it was empty Tulip sloshed water into it from a bucket and rinsed it out a few times, and then she put it in the closet where it could rest until she found out how to cleanse it thoroughly.

I couldn't see how we had destroyed any evidence, but what I didn't bother to tell her was that evidence didn't make much difference. Granted that she wanted to know who had killed her fish, but with all the evidence in the world we weren't going to take whoever it was to court and prosecute him. I didn't mention this because it might lead her to wonder why she was spending good money to track the villain down, and I didn't want this thought to cross her mind until her check cleared.

When the tank was tucked away in the closet, Tulip heaved a sigh. "That's a lot of exercise," she said. "Not like dancing all night, but all that lifting and toting. I used muscles I don't normally have any call for. Look, I'm all sweated up."

She didn't have to tell me to look. I was already looking. Her tee-shirt was damp now and Beethoven was plastered all over her. I've been apt to envy a lot of people in the course of my young life, but this was the first time I had ever been jealous of a dead composer.

"Just look at me," she said, lifting her arms to show the circles of perspiration beneath them, and then she saw that I was indeed looking at her, and she managed to read the expression on my face, which I guess you didn't have to be a genius to read anyhow, and then she laughed again. "Bourbon and yogurt! On the *rocks!*"

I told her to stop it.

And that was about that. She had a dinner date, and she was going to have to shower and change, but we had time to sit around and talk for a while. She told me a little about some of the names in my notebook but nothing worth recording, or even worth training my memory to retain. She also told me a great deal about herself—how someone had given her a couple of baby guppies when she was eleven years old, and how she had really gotten into fish in a big way until her parents' house was hip-deep in fish tanks, and how in high school she had grown profoundly interested in biology and genetics, and how someday she hoped to make an important contribution to ichthyological knowledge. In the meantime she was dancing naked, making decent money, saving as much of it as she could, and not at all certain where her career should go from here.

"I suppose I could get some sort of institutional job," she

said. "At a public aquarium, or preparing specimens for museum collections. I have good qualifications. But I haven't found an opening that turns me on at all, and I'd rather prefer to live in New York, and I can't see myself clerking in some place like Aquarium Stock Company for two-fifty an hour."

There was a lot of conversation which I didn't bother reporting to Haig and won't bother reporting to you because it was trivial. But trivial or not, it was also pleasant, and I was sorry when it got to be time to go.

"Come to the club tonight," she said. "Come around one and you can catch my last set, and you'll get to see Cherry too. You'll want to talk to her, won't you?"

"Sure," I said. "But she might have plans, and—"

"So at least you'll get to see my number, Chip." She grinned hugely. "You wouldn't mind watching me do my dance, would you?"

I took the subway to 23rd and Eighth and walked the few blocks to Leo Haig's house. Wong had waited dinner until my return. He doesn't say much, but he cooks really fantastic Chinese things, and he never seems to dish up the same thing twice. Which is a shame, because there are plenty of dishes I'd like to return to.

I hope he throws out the roaches—We talked business throughout our dinner. Haig has this tendency to imitate Nero Wolfe, and he attempts to avoid it by not making Wolfean rules for himself, like no business at meals and set hours with the orchids—which is to say fish in his case. So we talked, or rather I talked and he gave the appearance of listening, pausing periodically in his eating to ask a question or wipe some hoi-sin sauce from his beard. When the meal was finished we went back into the office and Wong brought the coffee. There was no dessert. There never is at Haig's house. He thinks if he never has dessert he will get thin. So we skipped dessert, as usual, and he opened his desk drawer, the second from the top on the left, and took out a Mars bar and two Mallo Cups. I passed, and he

511

ate all three of them. If he keeps up like this he'll be nothing but skin and bones before you know it. "Five hundred dollars," he said at one point, between bites, "is a rather large retainer for a case involving the murder of fish."

"It's standard," I said.

"Phooey."

"All right, it's large. It works out to almost five dollars a fish, which is about the going rate for scats, although I don't suppose fry would bring that much, would they? On the other hand she lost a breeding pair, and since they're the only known breeding pair of *Scatophagus tetracanthus* they might be worth the full five hundred all by themselves. On the other hand—"

"You already said that."

"On the third hand, if you prefer, we're not going to bring the fish back to life even if you *are* a genius, so maybe that's the wrong way to approach it. Look at it this way—"

"Chip."

"Yes, sir."

"I assume you had a reason for setting so high a price."

"Yes. A few of them. First of all, the rent Madam Juana pays you isn't enough to cover our overhead, and I have a vested interest in that overhead since I'm part of it. We can use the money. That's one. Two is I wanted to see if she could write a check for five hundred dollars without batting an eyelash. I watched her closely and she didn't bat a single one of them."

"You were not looking at her eyelashes."

"I'll let that go. The third reason is I thought that a high retainer might shame you into telling her to go swim upstream and spawn. How the hell are we going to find out who wiped out her scats? And where's the glory in it for you if we do? I know you didn't take the case for the money or you would have remembered to ask for the money, so you've got to be doing it for the glory, and if you think this is going to make your name a household word like stove and refrigerator and carpet—"

"Chip."

I stopped in mid-sentence. When he uses that particular tone of voice I stop. I stopped, and he spun around and regarded the Rasboras, and I waited for something to happen.

He spoke without turning from his fish. "I suppose it must be as it is," he said. "The Watson character is expected to lack subtlety. Thus the detective sparkles in comparison to his less nimble-witted assistant."

"You always pick the nicest ways to tell me how stupid I am."

"Indeed. You're quite useful to me, you know, and yet it's remarkable how you can simultaneously ignore subtleties while overlooking the obvious."

"I can also walk down the street while chewing gum."

"I'll accept your word on that." He turned around again and put his feet up, dammit. "Of course you'll go see our client perform tonight."

"All right. If you're determined that she's still our client—"

"I am."

"Then I'll go."

"And you'll interview Miss Bounce after the performance."

"If you say so."

"I do. With whom is Miss Wolinski dining tonight?"

"I don't know. Someone who's luckier than I am. Why?"

"You didn't ask?"

"Sure I asked. She said it wasn't one of the names in the notebook, so I—"

"But she didn't give the name."

"No."

He closed his eyes. I was still there when he opened them, and I don't think the fact delighted him. "You may leave," he said. "I want to read. Could you get me that new Bill Pronzini mystery?" He pointed and I fetched. I asked politely if the book was part of Pronzini's series in which the detective does not have a name.

"He has a name," Haig said. "The name is not revealed to the reader, but clearly the man has a name."

"Well, you know what I mean."

"What Pronzini's detective does not have," he said, "is an assistant." He glared at me, then lowered his eyes to the book. I thought about wishing him goodnight and decided against it.

I went out and killed time. I had a beer at Dominick's and watched the Mets. They were playing the Padres and they lost anyhow. It took some doing. They went into the ninth two runs ahead. Then Sadecki struck out the first two batters and it looked hard to lose. He hit the next batter, and this rattled him so that he walked the next two, at which point Berra yanked him and sent in Harry Parker, who got the batter to hit a slow grounder to Garrett. Garrett fielded it cleanly but didn't throw to first because he couldn't find the ball. It was lost somewhere in his glove. That loaded the bases and upset Parker, who threw the next pitch six feet over Grote's head, cutting the lead to one. That was it for Parker. Berra brought in somebody just up from Tidewater, who made his major league debut by promptly hanging a curve for Nate Colbert. I think the ball's still in the air somewhere over Queens. That made it 5 to 3, and we went down in order in our half of the ninth, and that, to coin a phrase, was the ballgame.

"Jeez, they stink," Dominick said.

I couldn't argue with that. I walked around for a while, and then I went to Treasure Chest, and I guess that brings you up to date, because there I was on the stage and there was a beautiful girl named Cherry Bounce on the stage next to me and she was a hundred percent dead and this was something my ingenuity and intelligence and experience had not prepared.

Chapter Four

I JUMPED DOWN from the stage, and then I vaulted up onto the bar and slid on the residue of someone's drink. I landed somewhat imperfectly on the customers' side of the bar. A lot of people were moving toward the stage, curious to know what was happening, and a lot of other people were moving toward the door, and the second group were the ones I was concerned with. I did some fancy broken-field running and got to the door ahead of most of them. I planted myself in the doorway with my arms and legs wide and tried to look as substantial as possible.

"Nobody leaves," I said. "A girl has been killed. Nobody leaves until the cops get here."

A couple of men took my word and turned away. I was on the point of congratulating myself on my menacing snarl when a few other guys headed toward me and looked prepared to walk right through me.

"Nobody leaves," I said again, terrified that my voice would crack. They kept right on walking.

Then someone moved up against me from my right, and I turned my head, and it was my friend the door-tender, plaid pants and striped jacket and sky-blue shirt and all. He moved into the doorway and I moved over to give him room, and he planted himself there in the identical stance I had taken, but he looked as though he meant it.

"Everybody stay where you are," he said. He didn't speak as loudly as I had. Then again, he didn't have to. The people milled a little, but then they turned back and resigned themselves to the fact that they weren't going anywhere.

"I gotta hand it to you, kid," the doorstop grunted. "You got moxie."

I beamed idiotically for a moment, then ducked back into the club myself. A lot of people were behaving pretty hysterically at this point and I can't say I blamed them much. I hadn't noticed any women in the club—except for Tulip and Cherry and the barmaid, obviously—but evidently there had been women at some of the back tables, or else someone had hired a batch of women to run into the club and scream when Cherry's body hit the stage. There was plenty of screaming, that's for sure.

I managed to find Tulip, who was not contributing to the screaming one bit. At first she looked oddly calm, but then I took a second look and recognized her expression as the kind of calm you get when someone has recently hit you over the head with a mallet.

She said, "She's—"

I was going to let her finish the sentence herself but she just plain stopped. So I finished it for her. "Dead," I said.

"What was it? A heart attack?"

"It was murder."

"But—"

"There's no time," I said. "This must be tied in with the scats and it proves Leo Haig is a lot smarter than I'll ever be but I already knew that. Listen to me. Are you listening?"

She nodded.

"All right. You and I don't know each other. No, the barmaid knows we do. Shit. All right."

"Chip?"

"You don't know anything about Haig. You don't mention anything about fish. You don't even know Cherry was murdered except that's what people have been saying. Are you a good liar?"

"I don't know. I guess so."

"Well, do the best you can. Now all I have to do is figure out a way to get the hell out of here." I looked at the door, and my friend the gorilla was still in place; now that I had taught him not to let anybody out, it was a cinch he wasn't going to let *me* out. I tried to figure out something, and while I was standing there like an idiot a man in a tuxedo came along and supplied the one powerful argument that would have whisked me past the gorilla in nothing flat.

516

"You!"

He was looking at me, and he was pointing at me, but the expression of absolute fury and indignation on the face of a man I had never seen before in my life convinced me that he had someone else in mind. I figured maybe he was a little cockeyed, and I looked over my shoulder to see who it was that he was furious with, but there was nobody there. Then he was standing right in front of me and his finger would have been touching my nose if either the finger or the nose had been half an inch longer.

"You!"

Tulip said, "Mr. Leemy—"

"Shut up," Leemy said, and my trained memory remembered that one Gus Leemy was the owner of record of Treasure Chest, and it stood to reason, Leemy being in another class entirely from Smith and Jones, that the Leemy with his finger in my face was Gus himself. Tulip said his name again, and he told her brusquely to shut up again, and that inspired exchange gave me a couple of seconds to look him over.

I decided that what he looked like was a bald penguin. The tuxedo, of course, and an absolutely hairless dome atop a long narrow head. He moved like a penguin, too; little jerky motions like old silent movies before they learned how to get the timing right.

"You're not twenty-one," Leemy said.

I opened my mouth and closed it again. Somehow I didn't think another portrait of Alexander Hamilton was going to cut much ice with the man.

"My fucking dancer drops dead on the fucking stage and the place is going to crawl with fucking cops and I need you like a fucking hole in my head. Out!"

"But—"

"Out!" He grabbed me by the arm, tugged me toward the door. He wasn't all that big or strong and at first I stood my ground, and then I remembered that he and I agreed that I should get out of there. At which point I stopped resisting.

517

He said, "Joint crawling with cops and all I need is trouble with the fucking S.L.A. about my fucking liquor license, all I fucking need, out, you little prick, and don't come back, and—"

I couldn't have agreed with him more, and I could have walked faster if he'd just let go of my arm. But he didn't, and I couldn't have walked fast enough anyway, because we were still maybe a dozen steps from the door when three of four gentlemen in blue uniforms filled the doorway.

"Oh, shit," Gus Leemy said.

The patrolmen mostly stood around and made sure that nobody entered or left the premises. One of them went up on the stage to confirm that Cherry was dead. When he came back down somebody asked if the girl was dead and he refused to commit himself. "We'll let the medical examiner settle that question," he said. I guess Dylan was wrong; some people really do need a weatherman to know which way the wind is blowing. I did manage one feat while the patrolmen stood around waiting for the heavyweights to reach the scene. I found the phone booth and looked in my pocket for a dime. I only had a quarter, and my ingenuity and experience told me not to waste time getting change. I dropped the quarter and dialed my favorite telephone number, and when Wong Fat answered I told him to wake Haig, and he said he couldn't because Haig hadn't gone to sleep yet. He put the great man on the phone and I talked a little and listened a little and was off the phone by the time the detectives from Homicide, flanked by a couple of other detectives from Midtown West, came plainclothesing their way through the door.

The phone booth was not far from the door they entered. I saw them before they saw me, but not very much before. Just long enough for my heart to sink a little. I recognized them right away, but they needed two looks at me to make the connection. They worked in perfect unison, those two homicide cops in the middle, looking simultaneously at me, looking away, then doing a beautifully synchronized double-take.

"You!" they said. Much as Gus Leemy had said it. And I figured if we were going to stand their trading Gus Leemy lines, I had mine all picked out.

"Oh, shit," I said.

The one on the left was Detective Vincent Gregorio, a tall and dark and handsome number with one of those twenty-dollar haircuts and a suit you'd never find at Robert Hall. The one on the right was Detective Wallace Seidenwall, and I'd decided some time ago that Gregorio liked having him for a partner for the same reason pretty girls like having ugly girlfriends. Seidenwall's suits always looked as though someone else had bought them at Robert Hall, then wore them day and night for a year before passing them on to Seidenwall. I never had trouble remembering his name because he was built like the side of a wall.

The first time I met the two of them was when I discovered the body of a girl named Melanie Trelawney. The second time I met them was when somebody bombed Madam Juana's whorehouse. That was the memorable day when Haig called them witlings, which was accurate if not diplomatic. The third meeting was in Haig's office, when he unmasked a murderer and presented him to them on a Sheffield platter. You'd think they might be grateful, but you'd be wrong.

If there were two things Seidenwall and Gregorio hated, I was one of them. Haig was the other.

"IT WAS A Mexican standoff," I told Leo Haig. "Gregorio wanted to arrest me and Seidenwall wanted to arrest your client. I was hoping they would arrest us both and lock us up in the same cell, but then I figured you'd have Addison Shivers down there with a writ just when Tulip began to realize that it's hip to be involved with younger men."

Haig grunted. "There are other things in life beside sex," he said.

"I know," I said. "That's the whole trouble. One of the things there is beside sex is coffee. At the moment I'll settle for second best. Is there any?"

Haig picked up a little bell and rang it, and before the vibrations quit Wong entered with a couple of mugs full of hot black coffee. He's extraordinary that way. You hardly ever have to tell him what it is you want.

In this case maybe it wasn't all that extraordinary. It was six-thirty in the morning and I had been up all night, and while Haig had dozed on the couch waiting for me to turn up he hadn't had anything you'd be likely to call real sleep. Of course we wanted coffee.

By the time I had finished my cup and rung for a refill, I had brought Haig up to date to the point where the cops walked in. I gave him everything reasonably verbatim and he took me back over various points until he was satisfied.

Then I went through my own interrogation. I had gotten off some good lines and I was careful to repeat them all, but since then I've re-evaluated them, and while they were nice enough at the time, I don't think I'm going to inflict them on you. I'm not really all that inclined to play smartass with New York's Finest, but those two bring out the wiseacre in me and I have trouble controlling myself. To give you an example of the level of repartee, at one point Gregorio tried a trap question, asking me why I'd been jealous of the girl in the first place, and I said Haig had selected her to crossbreed with one of his fish in the hope that half the offspring would be mermaids and the other half would be Esther Williams. And that was one of my better lines, so now you know why you'll never hear the others.

Haig perked up at that particular line, as a matter of fact. "Then they know about Miss Wolinski's fish?"

"Yes, sir. They were going to find out she had fish, and even the police can add two and two. I told them I was at the club because I was friendly with Tulip, and I said the friendship had happened because Tulip had consulted you as a fellow aquarist about a problem connected with her hobby."

"Which is not untrue," Haig murmured.

"I know that. I don't lie to the police unless I have to. Tulip overheard me say this, and she picked up the ball neatly enough. She said she doesn't know how good a liar she is. If they grill her I guess she'll find out."

"And will they grill her?"

"Over and over again. She was Cherry's roommate, she was a few yards away from her when she was murdered. They'd have to be crazy not to grill her."

"There's no doubt that Miss Bounce was poisoned?"

"None. I saw the blood on her breast. So did someone else, so the M.E. knew where to look for a wound. Just a pinpoint puncture."

"And the cause of the puncture was not found."

"No. I looked. The first thing that I thought of was poison. I thought of it before she hit the ground. God damn it, I was looking right at her and I never saw anything hit her. I just saw the blood and then she reached for herself and started to fall. Christ."

"Chip?"

"I'm all right. When I got up on the stage I was looking for the weapon at the same time that I was determining that she was dead. Not that it was hard to determine. She was all blue in the face. I forget what that's called. Cyanitis?"

"Cyanosis. And you weren't looking for the weapon. You were looking for the projectile. A gun is a weapon and a bullet is a projectile."

"Well, you knew what I meant."

"My cryptographic ability does not justify your abandoning the English language. You found nothing?"

"Nothing. I didn't know what I was looking for. Something sharp, but that was as far as I got. A dart or a needle or, hell, anything at all. I didn't have much time and of course the lighting was terrible, and if it was something like a needle it could have rolled between the floorboards and disappeared."

"If it's there, the police will find it. Whatever it may be."

"Maybe."

"Absolutely." He took a pipe from the rack and began twisting it apart. The end of the stem broke off inside the shank and he stared at it, sighed, and dropped both pieces into his wastebasket. He looked at me to see if I was going to smirk, and when I didn't he went on. "That is their strength. Scientific methodology, exhaustive investigation. If pressed they could find a needle in a haystack. Certainly they can locate one in a nightclub. Unless the murderer has already removed it."

I thought about that. "He could have," I said. "It must have hit her and bounced off after puncturing her skin, and if he saw it land he'd have had plenty of time to pick it up. I didn't make the world's greatest search for it. I felt it was important to keep as many people inside the place as possible until the police got there."

"You were probably right," he said. He cupped his beard, making sure that all the hairs were the right length. "I gather the murderer could have left before you barred the door."

"Easily. He could have been out the door before Cherry hit the stage, and then he would have had another minute or two while I was checking out the body. A lot of people did leave, I know that much."

"Hardly an admission of guilt on their part. One can readily appreciate the concern of any number of innocent citizens not to have their presence in such an establishment a matter of public record. All those gentlemen who habitually assure their wives that they are working late at the office."

"There were enough of those who didn't get out. When the cops went around taking names, you wouldn't believe the number of John Smiths who turned up. Of course the cops insisted on seeing identification and took down everybody's name and address."

"And you recognized some of the names."

I stared at him, which of course pleased him no end. "How did you know that?"

He waggled a finger at me. "You're still a boy who eats the cake and then the frosting, Chip. You save the best for last. If none of our suspects had been present you would have said so earlier. Who was there?"

I got out my notebook and flipped it open. "I can't say who might have left beforehand. And I can't be sure that I got the names of all the suspects who were there, because Seidenwall and Gregorio didn't take me into their confidence. I overheard a few names and I got together with Tulip and she pointed out a couple of people. She didn't know any of them were there until she happened to see them. Incidentally, her dinner date tonight was with a cousin from Chillicothe, Ohio. He came into town on business yesterday morning and flew home after they had dinner at the Autopub. I didn't find out what they had for dinner but I could probably check it out for you."

"Chip."

"Yes, sir. Gus Leemy was there, obviously. I told you how he did his impression of a bald penguin. That's not suspicious because he's always there. Andrew Mallard was there. That's the ex-boyfriend, the one who kept Tulip's apartment so she had to find another one."

"Indeed. And Tulip did not know of his presence beforehand?"

"No. He never talks to her. He usually gets a good table, but what I found out is that there's no such thing as a good table as far as being up close is concerned. The bar is between the tables and the stage. He came alone, of course. Tulip said he always does."

"Did you speak to him?"

"I didn't have a chance. I got a good look at him, though, and I got the impression of a man who goes through life in a fog. He's tall and thin and he'd be taller if he straightened out his spine a little. He walks with a stoop. Oh, and he wears very thick glasses. From where he was sitting, if he shot a dart or something into Cherry, he was probably aiming at Tulip."

"Continue."

"Simon Barckover was there. Tulip didn't know about this, either, but that wasn't unusual either. He drops in occasionally with someone he's trying to convince to book one of his clients. And he usually doesn't give advance warning that he's coming to keep his clients from getting uptight. He was there with a man who books acts for a nightclub in West Orange. I didn't get the name."

"I doubt that it matters."

"Well, I tried, all the same. Barckover's a forty-five-year-old hippie. Embroidered pre-faded jeans, the kind of counterculture clothing you can buy for about two hundred dollars a pair in the East Sixties. A buckskin jacket with fringe that probably cost him double that. Aviator glasses, wears his hair in a Hebro."

"I beg your pardon?"

"It's Tulip's word but I think I like it and I'm going to make it mine. A Hebro. Sort of a Jewish Afro."

"Indeed."

I closed the notebook. "That's it. Just those three, and it wasn't unusual for any of them to be there. Leemy owns the place, or pretends to. Mallard comes in a lot because he likes to look at Tulip's breasts while he drinks. Barckover had a professional reason for being there. It's possible that there were other suspects there. I don't mean of the ones who ducked out when they had the chance, but besides that. For instance, Mrs. Haskell Henderson might have been there and how would we know it? Tulip's never met her."

Haig sighed. Then he folded his hands, and then he extended his index fingers and played here's-the-church-here's-the-steeple. I got up and looked at some fish.

He said, "The poison. Strychnine?"

"I don't know. They'll have to do an autopsy. What do people look like when they die of strychnine poisoning? Besides dead, I mean."

"The symptoms you described are not incompatible with a diagnosis of strychnine poisoning. It works on the nervous system, the effects are rapid, there's spasmodic paralysis. But it's almost invariably given orally. I suppose it could be used to tip a dart or arrow or whatever projectile was employed." He furrowed his eyebrows. "If it was a poison other than strychnine—"

"Then what?"

He grunted, shook off the question.

"If it was strychnine, then it ties in with the fish. Is that what you mean?"

"No," he said.

"Well—"

"It's tied to the fish in any case," Haig said impatiently. "A young woman comes to see us. Her fish have been deliberately poisoned. Less than twelve hours after she sets foot in this office, her roommate and co-worker is also deliberately poisoned, and under our eyes. Your eyes, at any rate, and you in turn function as my eyes. The connection is undeniable. Anyone who would raise the gray banner of coincidence would—how did that congressman put it? If a mouse walked into the room, he would say that one could not be certain that it was a mouse, that it might well be an elephant with a glandular condition."

It was the other way around; if an elephant walks into

the room one says it might be a mouse with a glandular condition. But as much as I like to nitpick with Haig, if only to give him some of his own back, this didn't seem to be the time to pick that particular nit.

Instead I said, "Well, I took it for granted the two things were connected. Obviously. But what difference does it make if it was strychnine both times?"

"Perhaps none. Who else was in the club?"

"The names of all the people whose names didn't ring a bell? God, I don't know. I couldn't run around writing everything down, for Pete's sake. I think most of the men I overheard were from out of town. There could have been a boyfriend or two of Cherry's there. She evidently had a lot of them, former and current. Tulip wouldn't recognize them either by name or face, so I couldn't say. I know Leonard Danzig wasn't there because Tulip would have spotted him."

"You mentioned a short heavy man who tended the door. A bouncer, I presume."

"Well, he tried to bounce me. And if I hadn't slipped him a ten he would have done it with no trouble. His name is Buddy Lippa. I assume he has an official first name, but all I heard was Buddy."

"Waitresses? Or waiters?"

"Definitely waitresses. Two of them working the tables, and I didn't bother to get their names, but not because I was being stupid. I figured I could get them later from Tulip. Or from Leemy or anywhere else."

"And behind the bar?"

"Her name is Jan and I could probably fall in love with her if I wasn't already committed to Tulip. I understand Tulip doesn't like to play threesies. Leonard Danzig tried to arrange that once and she didn't go for it. But maybe she was just saying that because she was shy, meeting me for the first time and all. After this is over Tulip and Jan and I can get together and work it all out. As a matter of fact—"

"Chip."

I finished my coffee. It was cold, but that was all right. We sat around for a while, and then Haig turned on the news and we had the story, and there wasn't much to it that we didn't already know. They gave Cherry's real name but they got it wrong, and they said that the police expected to make an arrest very shortly.

Haig grunted and shut off the radio.

"Well, we're out of it," I said. "The police expect to make an arrest at any moment. Of course whoever killed Cherry also killed the fish, so they'll be solving your case for you. Do we give Tulip her check back or not? I'm not sure of the ethics involved."

Haig didn't answer me. After a moment he said, "You'll want to sleep, I suppose. There's a convertible sofa in your room. I've had Wong—"

"There's nothing but a bed and chest of drawers in my room and you know it. If you mean the guest room, that is not my room, and we've been through this enough so that you should have figured it out by now."

He held up a hand. "Please," he said. "The police are not going to apprehend the murderer. Either they will not make an arrest at all or they will arrest the wrong person. That was the seven o'clock news. Sometime between now and noon the police will come here. I want you here when they arrive."

"You're sure they'll come?"

"It's beyond doubt. Wong has made up the bed for you. This does not commit you to living here. You know as much. Get what sleep you can."

"All right."

I got to my feet. He said, "Chip? I'd like to amend a comment I made earlier. Your talents are a very important part of this operation of ours. You performed satisfactorily tonight."

"I was slow getting onto the stage and slow getting to the door."

"Immaterial. You think well on your feet while I think

527

well seated. We work well together. Don't doubt that you're appreciated."

"For Pete's sake," I said. "I'm not used to that kind of talk." He averted his eyes. "I mean, I'll be up for hours wondering what you meant by that. How am I going to get any sleep now?"

As a matter of fact, I did have a tough time getting to sleep. I went so far as to take off my clothes and get under the covers. Then I closed my eyes.

And that was all it took. The next thing I knew Wong Fat was shaking me awake. I made a few horrible noises and buried my face in the pillow but this didn't seem to faze him.

"Police gentlemen here," he said. "Mistuh Haig want you downstairs chop-chop."

I sat up and rubbed my eyes. "What time is it?"

"Is ten-thirty. He want you velly soon, chop-chop."

"Oh, come off it, Wong," I said. "Nobody talks like that. Not even you."

"Is to make innasting character for book you lite," Wong insisted. "Mistuh Haig, he want it just so."

I got out of bed. "Tell him I'll be down in a minute, will you?"

"Ah, so."

"And Wong?"

"Mistuh Chip?"

"Tell him he's a plick."

Chapter Six

AS I APPROACHED the door I heard Haig telling them that it was no use, that he wasn't going to tell them anything until I was present. Seidenwall sputtered a little at that, and I was tempted to wait out in the hall and let him sputter, but instead I went in and nodded at them and sat down in my chair at the desk. Haig was in his chair across the desk from me and Seidenwall was slumped in the floral wing chair and Gregorio was on his feet. He had changed his suit since I saw him. His partner hadn't.

Haig said good morning, which it clearly wasn't, and I backed him up and wished him a good morning right back. He said he hoped I slept well, and I said it was long on quality if short on quantity, and Seidenwall mentioned a popular organic fertilizer often to be found in stables.

"Now then," Haig said. "What seems to be the matter, gentlemen?"

Seidenwall went purple in the face and squeezed the arms of his chair. Gregorio said, "Look, you silly little butterball, I want some cooperation from you. When I saw this punk who works for you last night I figured you were all wrapped up in this one. I never yet ran into Harrison here without somebody being dead. And what do I get from him? I get a fish story."

"Precisely," Haig said.

"A whole load of crap about how this Tulip broad is just a good friend of his, and he's friends with her because she raises fish and you raise fish and you had a cute little conference about your goddamned fish, and on the strength of that he went to see her dance."

"But that's quite true," Haig said. "Miss Wolinski lost a valuable batch of fish. She wanted me to determine how the fish had perished."

"Yeah, fish." Gregorio looked disgusted. "She even gave me their goddamned names. *Scatophagus tetracanthus.* For the hell of it I looked it up. You know what *Scatophagus* means?"

"Certainly."

"It means eater of excrement. In other words they eat shit, and so does your story."

"It's a misappellation," Haig said dreamily. "The species lives in foul water and subsists on detritus, but I don't believe they actually consume excrement."

"Well, your story does. The fish didn't just die. They were poisoned."

"So it would appear."

"Strychnine," Seidenwall said.

"Strychnine," Gregorio said. "Now who in the hell would dump strychnine into a tankful of fish?"

"An excellent question, Mr. Gregorio. And it was precisely Miss Wolinski's question, which prompted her to consult me. I have as yet been unable to hit on the answer."

Gregorio stared at him. Staring at Leo Haig does you no good whatsoever, but I didn't point this out to Gregorio. There's no point in volunteering information to the police. They never really know what to do with it, anyway.

"Awright," Seidenwall said. "Where does your little pal Harrison get off keeping this all to himself last night?"

"I'm sure I don't know," Haig said. "Chip? Did the police ask you if Miss Wolinski's fish were poisoned?"

"The subject never came up," I said.

"Now wait a minute—"

"Did they mention strychnine? Did they inquire as to whether any professional relationship existed between ourselves and Miss Wolinski?"

"Nope."

"Well then," Haig said. "Gentlemen, I don't understand. You accuse my associate of failing to cooperate. Of prevaricating. Yet he has neither lied nor withheld information. Why should he assume that the death of a group of fish bore any relationship to the death of a topless

530

dancer? Had he even suggested this line of inquiry, no doubt you would have accused him of wasting your time."

They both started calling Haig names. Seidenwall called him a lump of shit while Gregorio called him a fat dwarf. Haig did not seemed ruffled. He took a pipe apart and put it back together again. This time he didn't break it.

Seidenwall said, "The hell, Vinnie. Let's get to the point."

"Right." Gregorio walked over to the desk. He planted himself next to me so that he could glower down at Haig. I was tempted to check out the material of his suit but I restrained myself. "All right," he said. "We could go round and round with this but it's a waste of time. You're too damn cute. You sit on your fat ass and play with your pipes and your fish and talk your way out of everything. But you're covering for a client, dammit, and you're withholding evidence and I want it."

Haig looked at him.

"You know what I'm talking about. Or didn't your little chum tell you? He was sitting right next to the Wolinski broad when she put the dart in her roommate. I'd make it twenty-to-one he saw her do it, but I don't suppose we could ever prove it."

"Indeed."

"Then he was on the stage before the body stopped twitching. That's when he picked up the murder weapon." Haig didn't tell him he meant projectile. "And you can't deny he was on the stage, damn it. A dozen people saw him hop over the bar and onto the stage."

"Why deny it?" I put in. "I told you all that last night. I might have looked around for a murder weapon if I knew she'd been murdered, but how was I supposed to know that? I didn't even know she was dead. That's what I went up onto the stage to find out, and she was. What does that prove?"

"It proves you're a fucking liar," Seidenwall said.

"Harrison has the murder weapon," Gregorio went on. "He's got it and I know he's got it and, damn it, you know he's got it. Some dumb broad raises tropical fish and that makes her okay in your book and you're covering for her. Well, I've got her locked up and I'm going to nail her on Murder One, and if you don't come up with the dart or whatever it was I'll have you and Harrison in the dock on an accessory charge."

"Indeed," Haig said. He heaved a sigh. "Your thesis seems to be that Miss Wolinski murdered Miss Abramowicz."

"You know damned well she did."

"It's curious. First Miss Wolinski poisoned her own fish with strychnine for reasons we cannot begin to explain. Then, no doubt wracked by guilt over what she had done, she hired me to find her out. And, unbalanced at the thought of discovery, she pumped more strychnine into her roommate while my associate sat beside her. Ingenious reasoning, Mr. Gregorio. I applaud you."

"It wasn't strychnine."

"Pardon me?"

"It was curare. The stuff South American Indians put on their arrows."

"I know what curare is," Haig said.

"So she didn't poison her own fish. The two girls hated each other. One of them took a boyfriend away from the other one, so the Abramowicz one got hold of some strychnine—"

"How?" Haig demanded. "Where?"

Gregorio ignored the demands. "—and poisoned Wolinski's fish. Wolinski hired you and you found out Abramowicz did the job. So Wolinski got ahold of some curare and gave Abramowicz the needle, and now you're trying to cover for her."

Haig stood up. This didn't increase his height all that much, but he has a way of getting to his feet that is pretty theatrical. Maybe it's because he stands as infrequently as possible, so that when he finally gets around to it you're really ready for something spectacular.

"Mr. Gregorio. Mr. Seidenwall. I have intimated in the

past that I regard you as witlings. I cannot imagine that you are sufficiently mindless to believe the story you have just propounded. It is enough of a mark of your lack of intellect to recognize that you expect me to believe you believe it."

(I don't think they got the gist of that. If you have to read it over a few times yourself, don't feel like an idiot. It's a complicated paragraph. Haig might think you're a witling if you don't get it first time out of the box, but I won't hold it against you.)

"I will not dignify your conjecture with rebuttal," he went on. "Why refute something you already know to be absurd? We have already wasted enough time. Have you taken my client into custody?"

"You're damn right."

"Have you indeed. Mr. Gregorio, there is a blind man who operates a news-stand at the corner of Sixth Avenue and 42nd Street. Perhaps you know him."

"So?"

"Simply this. Were that blind man my client of the moment instead of Miss Wolinski, and had Mr. Harrison been present last night when Miss Abramowicz was murdered, you would have arrested the news-dealer and let Miss Wolinski go. You are trying to put pressure upon me, sir. You are trying to coax me to solve a case which baffles you, and you are trying to force me to do so on your own terms instead of my own. Have you formally charged my client?"

"Not yet."

"Not yet and not ever, as you well know. You have put her through a profound indignity in order to obtain from me information which I do not have and would not be obliged to give you if I did. You do not know by whom Miss Abramowicz was killed. You do not know the motive. Do you at least know what weapon was employed?"

"Something small and sharp with curare on the tip."

"So you do not know that either. You do not know anything except, I am sorry to say, my address. My

533

inclination is to close up like a clam. First I will volunteer certain information to you. Negative information. Neither I nor Mr. Harrison knows who poisoned Miss Wolinski's fish. Neither of us knows who murdered Miss Abramowicz. Neither of us possesses any factual knowledge not in your own possession. And, finally, neither of us intends to respond further to accusations, charges, questions, or such other irritation as you might be inclined to visit upon us. I have previously merely intimated that you are witlings. I now state it categorically. You are witlings, gentlemen. Your behavior defines the term to perfection. I would urge you to leave my house."

"Now wait a minute—"

"I will wait for eternity if I must. Having admitted you, I cannot legally order you to leave. In the future you shall not be admitted without a warrant. Since you are inside, you may wait here until hell freezes. Such a course of action would be futile for you, but not inconsistent with your character and mental agility. You will excuse me if I do not offer you refreshment."

He rang the bell. Wong came in with his tray. There were two cups of coffee on it. Not four. Just two. Wong gave one to Haig and one to me. He always knows.

They didn't wait for hell to freeze. They tried a couple of questions and bright lines, concentrating on me. "I don't like it," Seidenwall said. "Whenever there's drugs in the picture, this punk turns up."

Gregorio told me to roll up my sleeves.

"Oh, for Pete's sake," I said. "Drugs? Because somebody put strychnine in a fish tank? And what do you mean I turn up when there's drugs involved? What drugs?"

"That hippie chick who took an overdose a while back."

I stared at him, and I started to say something, and Haig said, "Chip. I don't think it's incumbent upon you to play a role in this farce. You need not reply to questions."

"I think you're right," I said. "Do I have to roll up my sleeves?"

"Yes," Seidenwall said.

"No,", Leo Haig said.

I took Haig's word for it and sat there sipping coffee. They asked some more questions and got no replies from either of us, so they made some threats and left. I bolted the door after them, and when I got back into the office Haig was already on the phone to Addison Shivers, making arrangements for Tulip's release from custody. Since Addison Shivers is around a hundred-and-ten-years-old, I didn't figure he would run around from precinct to precinct himself. But he would make sure someone did it and did it right.

When the phone was cradled again Haig leaned back in his chair. I said, "They're terrific, those two."

"Mmmmm," he said. "I wonder what they meant about drugs."

"Oh, it's just their way of being playful. The first time I met them they asked me to roll up my sleeves and I was wearing a short-sleeved shirt, for Pete's sake."

"I wonder."

"It doesn't mean anything."

"Everything means something," Haig said sleepily. He leaned back and put his feet up and closed his eyes. I didn't object to the gesture now because he was thinking, and a genius is fully entitled to think in whatever position suits him best. He thought for a long time, and when it was questionable whether he was thinking or sleeping I gave up and got some brine shrimp and wheatgerm and Tetramin and went around feeding the downstairs fish. I did the other rooms first, then came back to the office. Haig was still leaning back with his feet up and his eyes closed, but at my approach he opened his eyes and fixed them on me.

"The unadulterated nerve," he said. "As if we would willingly shield a murderer. Chip."

"Sir?"

"Could she have done it?"

"Yes, sir. Easily. She made a point of urging me to watch

535

Cherry go into the finale of her act. She could have had a little blowpipe palmed out of sight, and she could have plinked Cherry's tit while I wasn't looking, and Bob's your uncle. There's not a chance in hell that that's what happened, but she could have done it. It would have been a cinch."

"But then why would she have come here?" He sighed. "No. Impossible. Our client is innocent. Someone else committed the murder."

"The same person who dosed the fish with strychnine."

"No. I believe I *know* who killed the fish. And someone else killed Miss Abramowicz."

"What? You know who killed the fish?"

"I believe so. It would be premature to offer conjecture at this point in time. Chip."

"Sir?"

"I never said 'At this point in time' before Watergate. It is a cumbersome cliché. I don't like it. Should I use it in the future, please call it to my attention."

"Sure thing. All part of my job. Feed the fish, clean out the filter traps, change the glass wool and charcoal, chase the murderers, and correct your English. Who killed the fish and how does it tie in with everything?"

He shook his head. "Not now. It would be premature. And we have more pressing concerns. You are going to have to see a great many people and learn as much as you possibly can. Your notebook, please."

Chapter Seven

HASKELL HENDERSON OWNED SIX health food stores, all of them in Manhattan, all located between 72nd Street and Eighth Street. I called one of them and established that he wasn't there, but that he was most likely at the store on Lexington and 38th. I called that one, and they said he was there, and I hung up before he could come to the phone and went out and got a cab.

The store was called Doctor Ecology, and it was a lot larger than the usual watering holes for health nuts. It was the size of a small supermarket, with about half a dozen aisles and shopping carts that you could wheel up and down them while stocking up on gluten bread and soy flour and raw sugar and Jerusalem artichokes and tiger's milk and other gourmet treats. At the back there was a lunch counter for people who probably weren't all that hungry in the first place. I hadn't really eaten anything yet that day, and it was close to noon, so I took a stool at the counter and looked at a menu. If only I'd been a rabbit I could have had a hell of a time. I decided that I didn't want anything they had, so I settled for a cup of coffee. Only it wasn't coffee. It was a coffee substitute made by grinding up dandelion roots. The idea was that it wouldn't keep you awake, and it's always seemed to me that the only thing coffee really has going for it is that it *will* keep you awake.

You probably think you can imagine what that dandelion coffee tasted like. Don't bet on it.

I sipped enough of it to know that it was never going to be one of my all-time favorites. I paid for it and left the waiter a large tip because I felt sorry for him. Then I looked around to see if I could pick Haskell Henderson out of the crowd. When that didn't work I asked a cashier if he was around, and she told me he was in his office and pointed out the door that led to it. I knocked on the door and a voice told me to come in.

I walked into a tiny office. Haskell Henderson was standing behind a desk piled so full of invoices and pamphlets and correspondence that the desktop didn't show through anywhere. He was talking on the phone, and the conversation seemed to involve just which brand of brown rice was the most yang, which has something important to do with the macrobiotic diet. I was sort of familiar with the macrobiotic diet because there was a time when I lived with some people in the East Village who were very into it. They ate nothing but brown rice. They also did a lot of speed, which I don't believe is a standard part of the macrobiotic diet, and they talked about all the sensational things they were going to accomplish once they got their heads together. Sure.

While he talked I looked at him. I didn't see anything marvelous, but the fact that he was Tulip's current boyfriend probably prejudiced me against him. He was maybe thirty-five, and he had his hair combed to hide the fact that his hairline was ebbing, and he had a scraggly little goatee to hide the fact that he didn't have much of a chin. He was wearing white jeans and a tee-shirt with "Doctor Ecology" in white letters on a blue background. All the employees wore tee-shirts like that.

He finished his conversation, told the person at the other end of the line to stay healthy, and scuttled out from behind the desk. He thrust out his hand, which I shook, and he gave me a smile designed to show me what great shape his teeth were in.

"Well now," he said. "Haskell Henderson. What can I do for you?"

"My name is Harrison," I said, "and I work for Leo Haig."

"Leo Haig. Leo Haig. Let me see. Dew-Bright Farms? Over in Jersey? I've heard good things about your vegetables."

"Leo Haig the detective," I said.

"Detective?"

I nodded. "Mr. Haig is working for Tulip Willing. Or Thelma Wolinski."

He looked at me suspiciously. "Why would Tulip need a detective? She's not jealous. Wait a minute. Just *wait* a minute now. You're not working for Tulip."

"Mr. Henderson—"

"You're working for my wife," he said, pointing his finger at me. At least it didn't come as close to my nose as Gus Leemy's finger. "You're working for my wife," he said again. "Well, get this straight, fella. I don't know any Tulip Willing, or whatever you said her name was, whoever she may be, and—"

"Shut up."

I don't know why I said that. As far as that goes, I don't know why it worked. Maybe nobody had ever told Haskell Henderson to shut up before, and maybe he didn't know how to relate to it. He opened his mouth, and he closed it, and he stared at me.

I said, "Cherry Bounce was murdered last night."

"Oh, Christ. Yeah, I heard about that. Somebody killed her in the middle of her act. They get the guy yet?"

"They made an arrest. But they didn't get the killer, and the person they got isn't a guy. It's Tulip."

"They arrested Tulip? Jesus, that's ridiculous. I don't get it."

"Well, that's why Tulip hired a detective," I said. "She doesn't get it either, and she's not crazy about it. I want to ask you some questions."

"Why me?"

"Because you're Tulip's boyfriend, and because—"

"Whoa!" He displayed his teeth again and the light glinted on them. "Tulip's boyfriend? You gotta be kidding, fella. I'm a happily married man. Oh, I see Tulip from time to time, no question about that. When a man keeps himself in good physical shape he's got all this energy, he has to find an outlet for it. But Tulip's just one of the girls I see from time to time. It's nothing heavy, you understand? Just a friend, that's all. A casual friend with whom I have an enjoyable physical relationship. You don't want to make a whole big deal out of it."

What I wanted to do was play a tape of this speech for Tulip. Why was she wasting her time on this playboy when I was available? I said, "Look, your wife didn't send me. Honest."

"So?"

"So don't make speeches about how you relate to Tulip like a sister. That's not the point. You're her friend, and you were at the Treasure Chest last night, and—"

"The hell I was!"

I did my best to look confused. I even scratched my head, mainly because I've seen so many people do it when they're confused, especially in movies. The only time I normally scratch my head is when it itches. "That's funny," I said. "According to the information we have, you were at Treasure Chest until just before the time of the murder."

"Well, that's bullshit," he said. He reached into a jar on his desk and stuffed a handful of things into his mouth. They looked like newly hatched fish, little spherical bodies and long stringy tails. (I found out later that they were alfalfa sprouts.) He munched them and said, "I don't know where the hell you heard that. Where did you hear it, anyway?"

"You got me. Mr. Haig said that was his information, but I don't know who told him. Where were you last night, then? Because when I tell Mr. Haig his information was wrong, he'll want to know where you were."

He told me what I could tell Haig to do. It was something I've often wanted to tell Haig to do, as a matter of fact. "I don't have to account for my movements to Leo Haig," he said. "That's for damn sure."

"You don't have to," I agreed. "But, see, the police don't really know anything about you, and if Mr. Haig doesn't have any other way of finding out where you were, he'll let them know about you and let them ask you the same question. If Haig is satisfied, he wouldn't have any reason to mention your name to the police. After all, they're not his clients. Tulip is his client."

I watched his eyes while I delivered this little set piece. There was a moment when he contemplated a show of righteous indignation, but then his eyes shifted and I could tell he knew it wouldn't wash. "Oh, the hell with it," he said. "I have nothing to hide. As a matter of fact, I was home last night. I was watching television. Do you want to know what programs I saw?"

"Not particularly, but maybe the Neilson people would be interested. Well, that's no problem, then. You were home watching television so that lets you off the hook."

"What hook? You don't suspect me of killing Cherry, do you?"

"Of course not," I said. "How could you? You were home watching television."

"Right."

I started toward the door, then turned around. "While I'm here," I said, "could you tell me a little about Tulip and Cherry? There's a lot I don't know, and since I know you're not a suspect I would be able to rely on what you tell me. It won't take too much of your time."

He wasn't tickled with the idea but he liked the notion of not being a suspect. I asked him a lot of questions and he answered them and I made some notes in my notebook. His chief slant on both of the girls was nutritional. Tulip ate a lot of garbage, he said. Nature had given her a spectacular physique and she was taking a chance of ruining it because she actually ate meat and fruit that had been sprayed and a lot of other no nos. He had tried to interest her in nutrition but so far it hadn't taken. Cherry, on the other hand, was far more open to new ideas. The impression I got was that he liked Cherry more than he liked Tulip, probably because she was dumb enough to pay attention to him, but he didn't like having Cherry around that much because when he stole over there for an afternoon all he really wanted to do was crawl into the feathers with Tulip, who turned him on something wonderful.

541

No, he didn't know anyone who would want to kill Cherry. No, he didn't know anyone who had anything against Tulip, either. I slipped in an oblique reference to Tulip's fish and he didn't seem to have strong feelings about them one way or the other. Instead he turned them into nutritional propaganda.

"She knows nutrition is the secret of conditioning," he said. "That's how she gets the breeding results she does. Plenty of live foods. Everything raw. Nothing cooked. She even knows to mix kelp and wheatgerm into their formula. My God, they eat a better diet than she does! If she ate what she gives the fish, she'd be in fantastic shape."

If she were in any better shape, I thought, she'd be capable of turning on statues. I was beginning to understand why Tulip had offered me a bourbon and yogurt. It was probably Haskell Henderson's favorite cocktail.

"I guess that's it," I said finally. "Thanks very much for your cooperation, and I'm glad to know you were home watching television last night. That's one name off the list."

"Well, it's not the kind of list I'd want to be on."

"I don't blame you." I gave him my no. 3 warm smile. "Mr. Haig will just ring up your wife and confirm your story, and then we'll be all set."

I would probably respect myself a lot more if I didn't get such a kick out of doing things like that. I mean, I couldn't feature old Haskell as the killer. If he wanted to do somebody in he'd probably poison them with refined sugar and synthetic vitamins, not strychnine or curare. But we still had to know what he was doing last night, and anybody who'd believe the television story has probably already bought the Brooklyn Bridge several times over.

It was fun to watch him. He made the kind of noise in his throat that you make when you get a shirt back from the laundry and button the collar and find out it wasn't Sanforized. Then he took six deep breaths and said, very very quietly, "You can't call my wife."

542

"Why not?" I grinned. "Oh, sure. You don't want her to know anything about Tulip, right?"

"That's right. She probably suspects I...uh...see other women. But to have it thrown in her face, and the fact that a girl I know is peripherally involved in a murder case—"

"You don't have a thing to worry about."

"I don't?"

"Not a thing. Mr. Haig is very discreet. The way we'll do it, see, is we'll call up and pretend we're a television survey. Ask her what programs she was watching last night. Then we'll ask if anyone else in her family was also watching television, and she'll say you were, and—"

"She won't say that."

"Oh?"

"I wasn't actually *watching* television. I was in the other room, you see, so she'll say she was the only one *watching* the set, and—"

"We'll ask if other family members were home but weren't watching. Mr. Haig knows all the angles, Mr. Henderson."

"Uh."

I put a little steel into my voice. Or maybe it was brass. "*All* the angles," I said.

"Uh—"

"Where does your wife think you were last night?"

He went for the alfalfa sprouts like a drunk for a drink. He munched and shuddered. "Meeting with the owner of a rival store to discuss a possible merger."

"That's a pretty good line. I don't suppose you can use it too often but it has a nice ring to it. What time did you get to Treasure Chest and what time did you leave?"

"I wasn't there!"

"Where were you? And don't tell me you were with one of the other girls with whom you have a warm physical relationship and you can't drag her name into it because she's respectable. Don't even try that one on."

He met my eyes. "Jesus," he said. "You're just a kid."

"I've had a hard life. What did you do last night?"

543

"I went to a movie."

"All by yourself, of course."

"As a matter of fact, yes."

I had the notebook open. "What movie?"

"I don't know."

"Oh, come on."

"I don't know the name of it. It was a pornographic movie, one of those, you know, one of those X-rated pictures. I don't remember the title and I can't tell you the plot because it didn't have one. They never have a plot. And of course I went to it alone because who goes to those things *with* somebody? Shit. I thought you believed me about watching television." He got another hit from the jar of sprouts. "I guess I don't have much of an alibi," he said miserably. "Do I?"

Now the next thing that happened is something I never bothered to recount to Haig. I hadn't planned to recount it to you, either, and if you want to skip right on ahead to the beginning of the next chapter, I wouldn't blame you a bit. The following sequence has nothing whatsoever to do with the annihilation of Tulip's fish or the murder of Tulip's roommate, not so far as I can see. Of course if you're into cosmic tides and karmic things and like that, and if you can grok the concept that all things are intimately bound up in one another, then maybe you can justify including the following in this book. I can't, but I don't have much choice in the matter.

What happened was this: I left Haskell Henderson at Doctor Ecology at Lexington and 38th, and I decided to head over to Simon Barckover's office in the Brill Building. But in the meantime I remembered that a friend of mine lived on 37th Street between Third and Second, which wasn't all that far out of my way, and I remembered that I hadn't seen her in a long time, and I remembered what it had been like the last time I had seen her.

So I went over there.

On the way I stopped at a florist's and bought a dollar's worth of flowers. I don't know what kind of flowers they were. (I don't think it matters.) I carried them for a block and remembered that I was going to see Ruthellen, and there was just no way I could walk in there carrying flowers. I didn't really know what to do with them. I mean, you have to be pretty much of a callous clod to stuff a fresh bouquet of flowers into a trash can. I stood there feeling slightly stupid, and then I saw one of the oldest ladies in the world walking one of the oldest dachshunds in the world, and I gave her the flowers. (The lady, not the dachshund.) I walked quickly on while she was still instructing God to bless me.

I couldn't take flowers to Ruthellen because that wasn't the kind of relationship we had. Her problem, which she had laid out for me early on, is that she can't respond at all to people who are nice to her. She's not into whips and chains or anything, but she suffers from what her shrink calls "low estimate of self," and thus she's only turned on by people who despise her. I don't despise her, but I'm willing to pretend to, and it's not hard for me to be aloof and never call her and just drop in on her now and then because, to tell you the truth, she doesn't do all that terribly much for me and I really don't want to get very heavily involved with anybody quite as sick as she is. So maybe I do despise her, come to think of it, and maybe that's why she enjoys seeing me.

(Not that it matters. None of this matters at all. That's the whole point.)

I rang her bell. Her voice over the intercom asked who it was. "Chip," I snapped. She asked again. "Chip Harrison," I snarled. She buzzed and I opened the door and climbed two flights of stairs.

She was waiting in the doorway of her apartment. She's about twenty-five, maybe a little older, with a surprisingly good complexion considering that she hardly ever leaves her apartment during daylight hours except for her weekly visit to the shrink. She keeps her shades drawn day and night. She has this thing about daylight. She and the shrink are working on it, she's told me. I don't think they're making much progress, either of them.

"Haven't seen you in ages," she said.

I shrugged. "Been busy."

"Come on in. Can I get you something? A drink?"

"Haven't got time," I said. I sort of swaggered into her apartment and sat down in the comfortable chair. (There's only one.) Ruthellen sat on the couch in a nest of pillows and lit a cigarette.

"Put it out," I said.

"The cigarette?"

"I don't like the smell."

"All right," she said, and put it out. One of the reasons I see her as infrequently as I do is that I don't really like to be a total bastard with a woman. And what I especially don't like is that I can occasionally get into it, and that's a little scary, if you stop to think about it.

(Not that any of this has anything to do with Tulip and her fish and her roommate.)

"Well," she said. "So what's new?"

"Nothing much."

"You don't feel like talking?"

"No."

"That's cool. We'll just sort of sit around and relax. Sure I can't get you anything?"

I grunted. It was a grunt Haig would have been proud of. I sat back and looked at Ruthellen, who, while not the best-looking woman in the world, was by no means the worst. She's tall, about five-eight or so, and very thin, but not so much so that you'd mistake her for Twiggy. Her hair is a dirty blond. Literally, I'm afraid; she doesn't wash it too often. She doesn't do much of anything, really, which is another of the things she and the shrink are supposed to be working on. What she does is sit in her apartment, live on things like Rice Krispies and candy bars—you wouldn't believe how little she and Haskell Henderson would have in common—and cash the monthly check from her father in Grosse Pointe. The check pays for the rent and the Rice Krispies and the candy bars and the shrink, and since that's about all she has to do in life, that's about all she does.

"Chip?"

I looked at her.

"Would you like me to do anything?"

"Take your clothes off."

"Okay," she said.

I could have said *Take your robe off* because a robe was all she was wearing. She took it off and put it on the couch. Then she turned to face me, her hands at her sides, and stood still as if offering her body to me for inspection. Her small breasts were flushed, the nipples erect. She was excited already. So was I, in an undemanding sort of a way, but I didn't let it show. I had to go on being Mr. Casual because that was what was turning her on.

"Chip—"

"You could go down on me," I suggested.

"Okay. Do you want to come to bed?"

"Right here's good. You could like kneel on the floor."

"Okay."

And she did. I sat there, Mr. Cool, while she knelt in front of me and unzipped my zipper and, like Jack Homer, put in her hand and pulled out a gland. "Oh, he's so strong and beautiful," she said, talking to it. "Oh, I love him so. Oh, I want to eat him up."

And she did.

It's all we ever do. And it's all according to the same ritual—she always invites me to bed and I always tell her to kneel in front of me like a servant girl, and she always does, and I'll tell you something. Maybe the repertoire is limited, but she certainly plays that one piece perfectly. She doesn't do all that much, Ruthellen, but what she does she does just fine.

Afterward she sat back on her haunches, grinned, wiped one elusive drop from the tip of her chin with the tip of her forefinger, and told me she was glad I had come. She wasn't the only one. "I like it when you drop by," she said. "It gets lonely here."

"You should get out more."

"I guess. The shrink says we're making progress."

"Well, that's good, I guess."

"I guess."

"Well, I'll, uh, see you."

"Take care, Chip."

"Yeah, you too."

Okay.

I feel I owe you an explanation. You're probably wondering why the hell that episode was dragged in out of the blue and thrust in front of your eyes. Of course it took place during the time we were working on this case, but lots of things take place that I don't plague you with. I don't mention every time I go to the toilet for instance. Which is not to say that seeing Ruthellen is like going to the toilet. Except, come to think of it, it is, sort of.

Okay.

When I wrote this book, the Ruthellen bit wasn't in it. And then I got a call from Joe Elder, who is my editor at Gold Medal.

"Like the book," he said. "But there's a problem."

"Oh."

"Not enough sex."

"Oh."

"I'm sure you can think of something."

I argued a lot, but I didn't get anyplace. "We're not in business to sell books," he said. "We're selling hard-ons. Hard-ons sell books. You need a sex scene fairly early on in the book to hook the reader's attention and rivet his eye to the page."

Well, that's why the Ruthellen bit is in. I mean, it did happen, so I suppose it's legitimate. But I'm not really happy with it, and I'd be much happier if Mr. Elder would change his mind and cut it out after all, and—Oh, the hell with it. Let's get back to the story.

Chapter Eight

SIMON BARCKOVER'S OFFICE was in the Brill Building at 1619 Broadway.

I went into the lobby and found his name on the board while half the musicians and performers in America walked past me. I rode up to the seventh floor in an elevator I shared with two men carrying saxophones and one swarthy woman toting a caged parrot. I got off and found a door with a frosted glass window labeled *Simon Barckover—Artists' Representative.* There was a buzzer. I pressed it, and a female voice told me to come in.

A girl with red hair and freckles smiled at me from behind a green metal desk that almost matched her eyes. She asked if she could help me. "My name is Harrison," I said, "and I work for Leo Haig. I believe Mr. Barckover is expecting me."

"Oh, yes. You called earlier."

"That's right."

She glanced at the phone on her desk. One of its four buttons was glowing. "He's on a call right now. Won't you have a seat?"

"Thanks but I'll stand."

She took a cigarette from a pack on her desk. "I guess you want to see him about Cherry," she said. "That was a shock. It was really terrible."

"Did you know her? I guess you must have, working in this office."

"I've only been here a couple months."

I looked at her for a moment. "I've seen you before," I said. "You were there last night."

"I was working there. Sometimes if I have a free night I do substitute waitress work in some of the clubs that book a lot of acts through Mr. Barckover. Mostly as a favor, but the extra money helps. Some places you get really decent tips."

"Do they tip well at Treasure Chest?"

"They didn't last night. I've only worked there a couple times and actually they never tip well there. They figure they're being taken, you know, paying such high prices for such rotten drinks, and then there's a cover charge at the tables, so they take it out on the poor waitress by leaving her next to nothing. Last night most of the people didn't even pay their checks in the confusion and everything. But I don't like clubs like Treasure Chest. I just did it last night as a favor to Mr. Barckover."

"Is he a good man to work for?"

Her hesitation answered the question for me. "Well, the pay isn't great," she said. "He's a nice man. He loses his temper a lot but that's because he's in such a high-pressure business. And he's very tolerant. He doesn't get uptight if I smoke dope or like that, and we have an agreement that I can take off whenever there's an audition I want to check out."

"You're in show business?"

"Let's say I'm going to be in show business. I'm a singer. So far nobody's in a rush to pay me money to sing, but I'll make it. Someday you can hear me at the Persian Room of the Plaza."

"I'll take a ringside table."

"You'd better make your reservations now. My opening's going to be sold out months in advance." The green eyes twinkled. "That's why I'm working for Mr. Barckover. He may not be the best agent in the business, but you get a real inside view of things working in an office like this. It's not just making contacts, although that doesn't hurt. It's learning how the business works and how to make your own openings."

I considered telling her that if her voice was as pretty as the rest of her she had nothing to worry about. But in a job like that she'd probably heard every line in the world, and mine was neither all that original nor all that terrific. While I hunted for a way to revise it, the little light on the phone went off.

"I'll tell him you're here," she said, and did. "He'll see you now," she said. "Right through that door."

I went right through that door. Barckover took a bite out of a sandwich and motioned me toward a seat, chewing furiously. He washed it down with a swig of coffee from a styrofoam container, bit a chunk out of a jelly doughnut, swallowed some more coffee, then lit a half-smoked cigar and leaned back in his chair. It was one hell of a change from Haskell Henderson and the alfalfa sprouts.

So was the conversation. Barckover didn't have to try hiding his presence at Treasure Chest from me because the police already knew about it, and he had a bonafide business reason for being there. The police had already pumped him dry. He'd agreed to see me because he couldn't very well refuse to, since Tulip was his client, but this didn't make him enthusiastic about it. He figured it was a waste of time. Actually more of my time than his got wasted, because he went ahead taking calls during the course of our interview, telling clients that he didn't have anything for them, telling club owners how sensational his clients were. The interruptions were a nuisance but there wasn't much I could do about it.

"I been over this with the police five or six times already," he said. "I was off in the back with this spastic prick from New Jersey. Like I only looked at the stage every ten minutes or so to make sure somebody was on it. You don't know what this business is like, man. After a few years you get so sick of tits and asses that the only way you can get a hard-on is if your woman wears clothes to bed. I never even saw Cherry take her fall. I heard the commotion and I looked up and I couldn't see anything by then because she was lying down and out of sight. I didn't see anybody do anything suspicious. I didn't even think to look for anything suspicious I figure she fainted from popping too many pills or else she had a bad heart or something. What was it, something pygmies put on darts?"

"Something like that," I said. "Did Cherry take a lot of drugs?"

"For all I know she never even dropped an aspirin. Just going on generalities. Most of the go-go dancers and the topless-bottomless chicks do uppers. All that moving around and all those geeks gaping at them and it gets to them, and a little dexie straightens everything out and they can prevail, they can maintain, if you dig it. Like Lennie Bruce, baby, you got to be on top of it in order to get it out."

I had already been thinking of Lennie Bruce. One line of his in particular. He said there's nothing sadder than an old hipster.

I asked what Cherry was like.

"A comer," he said. "That kid started with nothing. She showed me some pictures of herself taken four, five years ago. Nothing. Big nose, flat in the chest. Not a pig but you'd never look at her twice."

"Cherry?"

He flicked the ash from his cigar. "Plastic surgery," he said. "Her old lady died and left her a couple of K's, no fortune, just of couple of K's, and she went and spent the whole bundle putting herself together. New nose, a trim job for the ears, silicone for the tits, a little of this, a little of that. Changed her name from something nobody can pronounce to Cherry Bounce. Great little name. Usually I pick names for them because most of these girls, they aren't too long in the imagination line. Cherry already had her name picked out when I got ahold of her."

"Did you pick out Tulip's name?"

He shook his head. "Nobody picks out anything for that one. She's smart, you got to hand it to her. Smart, well-educated, the whole bit. I'll tell you something, I think she's too fucking smart for her own good. With the face and body she's got she could have a future in this business. But she won't put out."

"I thought you didn't really have to do that anymore."

"Huh?"

"Put out."

He waved the cigar impatiently. "I don't mean sexual. I mean give out with everything you've got. Take the singing lessons, take the dancing lessons, make all the auditions, cultivate the right people. Cherry took the trouble. She put out. Tulip, she's got so much going for her, and all she wants to do is coast on what she's got. Pick up the easy bread showing her tits to the visiting firemen and waste all her time with those fucking fish."

"Well, that's her career."

"Career?" He looked at me as though I was an ambulatory psychotic. "You call that a career? Siphoning shit out of fish tanks? What's she gonna make, fifteen K a year running some fucking museum? You call that a career? There's chicks clearing that much a week in Vegas that haven't got half the equipment that girl has."

"But that's not what she wants."

"This year it's not what she wants. Five years from now she'll be Assistant Fish Librarian in East Jesus, Kansas, and that's when she'll realize what she wanted all along was a career in show business. And by then it'll be too late."

I turned the conversation back to Cherry and tried to learn more about her personal life. Barckover turned out to be a less than perfect source. At one point he said that an agent was always in the middle, he was the one with the shoulders that everybody cried on, but Cherry evidently either didn't cry or found other shoulders. He didn't know much of anything about the men in her life, and in his opinion she had been murdered by some sort of weird pervert who got a thrill out of killing strange girls. "You watch it," he said. "There's gonna be a string of hits like this, a Jack the Ripper type killing topless dancers. Probably a religious fanatic." Evidently he didn't know that Tulip's fish had been poisoned, which poked a few holes in the Ripper theory.

An admirable thing about Cherry, according to Barckover, was that she never got seriously involved with any individual male. "Her career always came first," he said. "You get chicks who get hung up on one guy, and I get 'em a week in the mountains and they don't want to leave the guy, so either they pass up a gig or they take it and then they're lousy because they spend all their time pissing and moaning about being lonely. Not Cherry. She knows the priorities. If she's playing house and I get her two weeks in Monticello she goes without a second thought. There's always some dude around to go to bed with, but there aren't always jobs growing on trees."

(He would have been proud of a girl I know named Kim Trelawney. For a while we were almost living together, and she got signed for the ingenue part in a road company version of *The Estimable Sailor*, and although she may have shed a tear or two, off she went. That had been three months ago, and she was still treading the boards in places like Memphis, and we didn't bother writing to each other, and by the time she came back I had the feeling we wouldn't have much to say to each other. It had been a long three months, let me tell you, and maybe that was a contributing factor to the way I reacted to Tulip, but I have to say I'd have probably gone just as bananas over her anyway, to be perfectly honest.)

I asked him about some of the people on our suspects list, and others who had been around Treasure Chest when Cherry was murdered. He had never heard of Haskell Henderson. He'd met Andrew Mallard while Mallard and Tulip were living together, and he said that in his book Mallard was a total feeb. His word, not mine. He'd been delighted when Tulip and Mallard split up.

He knew Leonard Danzig by sight and reputation and could not recall having seen him at the club. And he was surprised to know that Danzig had been keeping company with Cherry. "He's no good," he said. "He's trouble."

"What does he do for a living?"

"You hear lots of things," he said.

"Would you happen to remember any of them?"

"A little of this, a little of that. He plays angles, he hangs with some heavies. I don't know what he does but if it's honest I'll spread it on toast and eat it." He hesitated for a moment. "If he had a beef with a chick, he wouldn't get fancy with poison darts. I don't even think he'd kill her. Maybe he'd beat her up. Or with a beautiful girl like Cherry he'd do something like throw acid on her or cut her so it would leave a scar. That's more his style."

I didn't get a whole lot more than that. If Cherry was having trouble with Helen Tattersall, the downstairs neighbor, Barckover didn't know about it. He had never met Glenn Flatt, Tulip's ex-husband, and didn't know anything about him. He was on nodding terms with Buddy Lippa, Leemy's bouncer and gate-tender, and said only that Lippa was a former boxer, a good club fighter who did a decent job of keeping order in the joint. He got evasive when I asked about Leemy, and when I probed to find out who really owned the nightclub he made it obvious that he didn't want to carry that particular ball any further. I asked if either Leemy or Lippa made a practice of making passes at the hired help. He assured me they were both happily married men, which didn't strike me as an answer to the question I had asked, but I let it go.

He didn't know the other waitress or the barmaid, and I didn't ask him about his own secretary because I figured it would be more fun to ask her myself. I wound up the session with Barckover and went into the outer office and perched on the corner of her desk, notebook in hand. "I'm playing detective," I said. "Mind if I ask a couple of questions?"

She grinned. "You mean you're going to grill me? I already told you everything I know."

I told her we'd just go over a couple of things, and we did. I didn't learn much. I found out that the other waitress was named Rita and that was all she knew about her. Jan the barmaid was a regular at Treasure Chest, but my green-eyed friend hadn't had much contact with her except to order drinks and get change. She hadn't seen anything suspicious, hadn't recognized anybody except for Barckover and the people who worked at the club, and she knew nothing about Cherry's private life.

"There's something else," I said. "How am I going to catch you at the Persian Room if I don't know your name?"

She smiled. She didn't show me as many teeth as Haskell Henderson, but they looked better on her. "It's Maeve O'Connor," she said. I made her spell her first name and she did. She also told me it was Irish, but I could have figured that part out by myself. Then she pointed out that she didn't know my first name, so I supplied it, and then I told her I'd better take down her phone number.

"Is that what detectives always do?"

"Not always," I said.

"You could reach me through the office."

"But what if a case starts to break in the middle of the night and I need to check something with you? Mr. Haig would give me hell if I didn't have your number."

She gave it to me and I wrote it down. Then we looked at each other for a minute or two, and I could feel myself beginning to fall in love, which is something I probably do more readily than I should. I would have enjoyed perching on her desk for the rest of the afternoon, but Haig had given me a million things to do and there wasn't all that much time to do them in. I said I guessed I'd better be going, and she said, "Goodbye, Chip," and I said, "I'll see you, Maeve," and that was that.

I called the advertising agency where Andrew Mallard worked and got a secretary who said that he was away from his desk. I asked when he would be likely to return to his desk and she said she didn't know. I pressed a little, and it turned out that he hadn't been at his desk all day, that he in fact had evidently taken the day off. I don't know why she couldn't come right out and tell me this straight out, but I guess when you work in advertising you get in the habit of doing things obliquely.

I tried Mallard at his home number and the line was busy. I looked at my watch and saw that it was almost three and remembered that I hadn't had anything to eat all day except for a sip of dandelion coffee substitute. I realized that I had to be hungry. I don't know if this would have occurred to me if I hadn't happened to look at my watch, but once I did I was starving. I found a luncheonette down the block and had a hamburger and three glasses of milk and a cup of coffee. I decided not to look at my watch again because it might remind me how little sleep I had had and I wanted to be awake when I talked to Mallard. Except that I wasn't destined to talk to Mallard. I called him after I'd finished my meal and the line was busy again, and I decided it wasn't the usual sort of busy signal, and I called the operator and asked her to check the line for me. She went into a huddle and came back with the news that the phone was off the hook. (What she actually said was that the instrument's receiver was disengaged, and it took me a second or two to translate it.) That had been my guess, and I decided Mallard had been up half the night with the police and the other half brooding, and now he was taking the day off and having himself a nap.

There's a way the operator can make the phone ring even when it's off the hook, and I considered telling her something about it being a matter of life and death, but they probably hear that line all the time and I didn't think I was likely to get the right note of conviction into my voice. Then too, if Mallard was sleeping it off he probably wouldn't welcome my making the bell ring in his apartment.

The next name on my list was Glenn Flatt, Tulip's ex-husband and current friend. He worked at Barger and Wright Pharmaceuticals in Huntington, Long Island. I got the number from Information and placed the call. The switchboard at Barger and Wright put me through to a man who told me that Flatt was in some laboratory

557

or other and couldn't be disturbed. He asked me if I wanted to leave a number, so I left Haig's.

I didn't have a number for Leonard Danzig, and from what I'd heard about him I decided I wanted to take my time approaching him. Mrs. Haskell Henderson—I still didn't know her first name—lived on the other side of the Hudson. I would eventually want to see her in person, and I'd have to do that during the day when there would be no chance of running into Mr. Wheatgerm himself.

Helen Tattersall was on my list. I had no idea what questions to ask her, but sooner or later I would have to get a look at her, if only to see whether I had spotted her at the club. Tulip's building was in the neighborhood; I could just walk over there and invent a story.

Except that I didn't really want to. Treasure Chest was also in the neighborhood, and Tulip had said that they were open afternoons so that businessmen could stop and goggle at some breasts before heading home to their wives. I wasn't sure that I wanted to look at breasts, but I had to talk to Gus Leemy and he could give me a line on the other waitress and supply Jan's last name and address. He could also pin my arms behind my back while Buddy Lippa beat me to a pulp.

I decided to chance it.

Chapter Nine

"THEY DIDN'T BEAT me up," I said. "What they basically did was ignore me. I had a lot of trouble making them believe I was a detective. They thought I wanted the girls' names because I was trying to make out with them, for Pete's sake."

"They seem good judges of character," Haig murmured.

I ignored that. "The barmaid is Jan Remo. She's been working there for almost a year. She's divorced and has a two-year-old kid. The other waitress—not Maeve—is named Rita Cubbage . She just started there about a week ago. I can see them both late tonight if I'm awake because they'll be working their usual shifts."

"The club will be open, then? In spite of the tragedy?"

"Leemy doesn't think it's a tragedy. He thinks it's a bonanza. He's got a sign in the window that you'd love. *'See the stage where Cherry Bounce was murdered! See the show so hot it might kill you!'*"

"You're making this up."

"I am not."

"Heavens," Haig said.

We were in his office. It was almost five-thirty and I had just finished summing up my day in my inimitable fashion. I had wanted to rush my report so that I could see Tulip, who had finally been sprung from jail by one of Addison Shiver's underlings and had been conveyed directly to Haig's house after a quick stop at her apartment to shower and change her clothes and feed her fish. Haig had spent about an hour grilling her, and then when I got back I hardly had time to say hello before he'd banished her to the fourth floor so that he could hear my report privately.

She hadn't seemed to mind the banishment—she'd been itching to study Haig's operation up there—but I minded. So I tried to hurry my report but Haig wasn't having any. He made me go over everything in detail and then he sat there with his feet up and I wanted to yell at him.

I said, "So far I'm putting my money on Haskell Henderson. His motives aren't entirely rational, but no one who eats like that is going to behave rationally. You wind up with alfalfa on the brain. Here's what happened. He resented the fact that Tulip's fish ate a better diet than she did. He kept giving her wheatgerm and she kept feeding it to the fish and this infuriated him. He figured if he poisoned her fish she'd have to eat the wheatgerm herself because there wouldn't be any fish to feed it to and she wouldn't want to let it go to waste. So he made himself some strychnine. I looked up poisons in the encyclopedia, incidentally. Strychnine and curare are both neurotics, which would give them something in common with old Haskell."

"That means they act on the nervous system."

"I know what it means. I was making a funny. I learned that strychnine is extracted from the seeds and bark of various plants. Henderson's got seeds and bark of everything else at Doctor Ecology, so why not *Strychnos nux-vomica*? I've been training my memory, that's how come I remember the name of the plant. I hope you're proud of me. He extracted the strychnine and poisoned the fish."

"Phooey."

"Is that all you're going to say? I thought it was a brilliant theory."

He raised his eyebrows. "And Miss Abramowicz? Why did he murder her, pray tell?"

"Give me a minute. I'll come up with something."

"Bah. This is childish. Call Miss Wolinski and—"

"Wait, I just figured it out. Tulip was his girl because he was crazy about her and enjoyed having a warm physical relationship with her, but Cherry was more experimental about nutrition. So he kept bringing health food to Tulip and what the fish didn't eat Cherry ate. So he killed Cherry for the same reason he killed the fish. All in the interest of getting Tulip to stop eating cooked meat and other poisonous things. What's the matter? I think it's neat the way I tied it all together. Why don't you call Gregorio and tell him to pick up Henderson? I won't let on that it was all my idea. When I write up the case I'll give you all the credit."

"Fetch Miss Wolinski," he said. "Perhaps she'd like a cocktail before dinner."

"Maybe some carrot juice," I suggested. "Alcohol's bad for the vital bodily fluids."

He gave me a look and I went upstairs to fetch Tulip.

I don't know exactly what dinner consisted of but I'm sure Haskell Henderson would have turned green at the thought of it. Wong had marinated squares of beef in something or other, then sprinkled them with toasted sesame seeds and mixed in some stir-fried vegetables, and the whole thing came together beautifully as always. During the meal Haig talked with Tulip about the problems of breeding the *Ctenapoma* species. I didn't get the hang of more than a third of their conversation, and I won't plague you with any of it.

Afterward the three of us sat in the office. Tulip and I had coffee. So did Haig, who also had two Mounds bars in lieu of dessert. I picked up the phone and dialed Andrew Mallard's number again, and I got the same odd busy signal as before.

"Sometimes he just leaves it off the hook for long stretches of time," Tulip said. "He gets into these depressed states where he decides that there's no one on earth he could possibly want to talk to. It was really aggravating when I was living with him. I'd get calls for jobs and I would never know about it."

"What does he do if somebody rings his doorbell when he's in a state like that?"

"He generally answers it. But not always."

"That's great."

Haig said, "Miss Wolinski, you formerly shared that

apartment. Do you still possess a key?"

"I think so. Yes, I'm sure I do. I think it's still on my key ring." She fumbled in her purse and detached a key from the ring. "This is it," she said.

"Might he have changed the locks? You moved out some time ago, I believe."

"It was five months ago." She thought for a moment. "No, he wouldn't change the locks. He'd think of it but he would never get around to it."

I wondered why she had ever set up housekeeping with Mallard in the first place. He wasn't all that much to look at, and the more I heard about him the less enthusiastic I got about seeing him.

"You had better take that key," Haig said. "You needn't see Miss Remo or Miss Cubbage until late tonight. Mrs. Henderson can keep until tomorrow. Miss Tattersall can probably keep throughout eternity as far as we are concerned. A cranky old woman might be capable of harassment. Such persons frequently poison other people's dogs and cats. It's a form of paranoia, I believe. I cannot imagine her flipping curare-tipped darts at a topless dancer."

"She wouldn't even walk into Treasure Chest," Tulip said. "Not a chance."

I felt like a character in a comic strip with a little light bulb forming over my head. "Just a minute," I said. "Earlier today you said the person who poisoned the fish was someone different from the person who poisoned Cherry." Tulip gaped and started to say something but I pressed on. "Does that mean the Tattersall woman poisoned the fish? And how do you know that, and why don't I talk to her and find out why? Because we already decided the two things tied in, they had to tie in, and—"

Haig showed me the palm of his right hand. "Stop," he said. "Helen Tattersall did not poison the fish. Let us for the moment forget Helen Tattersall entirely."

"Then who did poison the fish? And how—"

"In due course," Haig said. "There is a distinction between a surmise and conclusion. There is no need to air one's surmises. It's odd that Mr. Flatt hasn't called. When did you see him last, Miss Wolinski?"

She thought it over, trying to frown her memory into supplying the answer, and the phone picked that minute to ring. I reached for it but Haig waved me off and snatched it himself.

He said, "Hello? Ah, Mr. Flatt. I was expecting your call. Yes. Let me make this short and to the point. I am representing your ex-wife, Miss Thelma Wolinski, in an investigation of the murder of her roommate.... If you'll permit me to continue, Mr. Flatt. Thank you. I have only one question to ask you. Why did you quit the premises of Treasure Chest so abruptly last night when Miss Bounce was murdered? No, sir, the identification was positive. No, I have not informed them. The police and I do not pool our information, sir. Indeed." There was a pause, and Tulip and I spent it looking at each other. "I want you in my office tomorrow afternoon, Mr. Flatt. At three o'clock. No, make that three-thirty. I don't care what you tell your employers. Three thirty. 311½ West 20th Street, third floor. I look forward to it."

He hung up the phone and tried not to look smug. It was a nice try but he didn't quite make it.

Tulip said, "How did you know he was there? I didn't see him. Who told you?"

"Mr. Flatt told me. Just now."

"But you said—"

He shrugged. "Chip left a message for Mr. Flatt almost five hours ago. He might have called back immediately, routinely returning a call. He did not. He took time to establish that I am a detective and to stew a bit in his own juices. Then, knowing that I am a detective and guessing what I wanted of him, he ultimately returned my call. If he had called back immediately or not at all he might well have had nothing to hide. By taking the middle course, so to speak, he established to my satisfaction that he was at Treasure Chest last night."

This absolutely impressed the daylights out of Tulip. She couldn't get over how brilliant he was, and he was so delighted with her admiration that he celebrated with a Clark bar and rang Wong for more coffee.

Wong brought two cups. He must have sensed that I wasn't having any. I would have liked another cup but I would have had to stay in that room to drink it and that was out of the question. And he'd had the nerve to say phooey to my theory about Haskell Henderson and the health food conspiracy! I'd been babbling, for Pete's sake, but I'd come as close to reality as that load of crap about he-didn't-call-early-and-he-didn't not-call.

It had been a bluff, pure and simple. If Flatt just told him he was crazy he could roll with the punch, and if Flatt bought the whole pitch then he was home free. It was a bluff, and a fairly standard bluff, and not too far removed from what I'd pulled on Henderson. I had to give him credit, he'd read his lines beautifully, but all it was was a bluff and the explanation he thought up later was just that, something he thought up afterward to fit the facts and make him look like the genius he wanted to be.

Of all the goddamned cheap grandstand plays, and of course Tulip bought it all across the board. And I'd had to sit there and watch. Well, I didn't have to put up with any more of it. I dialed Mallard's number once more, just as a matter of form, and then I scooped the key off the desk and got away from Miss Willing and Mr. Wonderful.

Andrew Mallard's apartment—by virtue of squatter's rights it was his, anyway—was on Arbor Street near the corner of Bank. I had more time than I needed to get his story before I was due at Treasure Chest, and I wanted to walk off some of the irritation I felt toward Haig, so I hiked down Eighth until it turned into Hudson Street, and then I groped around until I found Bank, made a lucky guess, and located

Arbor Street. I usually get lost in the West Village, and the
farther west I go the loster I get. I can find almost any place,
but only if I start out in the right place. (I'm not the only
one who has that trouble. When you've got a geometrically
sensible city with streets running east and west and avenues
running north and south, and then you rig up a
neighborhood in which everything goes in curves and
diagonals and Fourth Street intersects with Eleventh Street,
you're just begging for trouble.)

I looked for a bell with Mallard on it and couldn't find
one. Then I went through the listings carefully and found
one that said Wolinski. He really was an inert type, no
question about it. I mean, he'd been there five months by
himself, and for a certain amount of time before that he'd
shared the place with her, and her name was still on the
bell and his wasn't.

I rang his bell and nothing happened. I rang it again
and some more nothing happened, and I tried Tulip's key
in the downstairs door and of course it didn't fit, it was the
key to the apartment. I wondered why she hadn't given
me both keys and then I wondered why this hadn't
occurred to me earlier. I said a twelve-letter word that I
don't usually say aloud, and then I rang a couple of other
bells, and somebody pushed a buzzer and I opened the
door.

Mallard's apartment was on the third floor. I knocked
on his door for a while and nothing happened. I decided
he was either out or asleep or catatonic and there was no
point in persisting, but it had been a long walk and I had
the damned key in my hand so I persisted.

At 8:37 I let myself into his apartment.

Chapter Ten

AT 8:51 I let myself out.

Chapter Eleven

I WALKED INTO the first bar I saw, went straight up to the bar and ordered a double Irish whiskey. The bar tender poured it and I drank it right down. Then I paid for it, and I scooped up a dime from my change and headed for the phone booth in the rear. I invested the dime and dialed seven numbers and Leo Haig answered on the fourth ring.

I said, "How clean is our phone? Do you suppose we're all alone or do we have company?"

"Let us act as though we have company."

"Probably a good idea. I'm at a payphone and I understand they're all tapped. But who has the time to monitor all of them? Of course if somebody was listening in I'd be a dead duck and that would make two tonight."

"I see."

"I was hoping you would."

"You're certain of the fact?"

"Positive."

"Do you know how the condition was induced?"

I shook my head, then realized that wouldn't work over the telephone. "No," I said. "He could have done it himself, he could have had help, or it might be God's will. No way I could tell."

"Hmmmm." I waited, and turned to glance through the fly-specked glass door of the phone booth. Several heads were turned in my direction. I turned away from them and Haig said, "I trust you have covered your traces."

"No. I took my lipstick and wrote *Catch me before I kill more* on the bathroom mirror."

"There is no need for sarcasm."

"I'm sorry," I said. "It shook me, I'll admit it. Do I report this?"

"Yes, and right away. Use a different phone."

"I know that."

"You said you were shaken."

567

"Not *that* shaken," I said. "Hell."

"Report the discovery and return here directly."

"Is our friend still with you? Because she's—"

"Yes," he cut in. "Don't waste time." And he hung up on me, which was probably all to the good because I really *was* a little rattled and I might have found ways to prolong the conversation indefinitely.

I went back to the bar and ordered another shot, a single this time, and a man came over to me and said, "Oh, let me buy you this one, why don't you. You seem terribly agitated. Nothing too alarming, I hope?"

I looked at him, and at some of the other customers, and I realized I was in a gay bar. "Oh," I said.

"I beg your pardon?"

I couldn't really resent it. You go drinking in a gay bar and people have the right to jump to conclusions. "Never mind," I said. "I don't want the drink anyway." I pocketed my change and left, feeling very foolish.

Two blocks over I found a booth on the street. I dialed 911 and changed my voice and told whoever it was that answered that there was a dead man at 134 Arbor Street and gave the apartment number and hung up before any questions could be asked of me. I walked another block and got in a cab.

I had found Andrew Mallard in the bedroom. The whole apartment had reeked of whiskey and vomit, and I figured he'd passed out. He was lying on his bed with his shoes off but the rest of his clothes on, laying on his back, a trickle of puke running from the corner of his mouth down his cheek.

I very nearly turned around and left at that point, and if I'd done that I'd have been in trouble, because I wouldn't have bothered wiping my fingerprints off the doorknob and a few other surfaces I'd touched. But something made me put my hand to his forehead. Maybe I sensed unconsciously that he wasn't breathing. Maybe I was toying with the idea of shaking him awake, though why would I have wanted a wide-awake drunk on my hands? For whatever reason, I did touch him, and he was cold, the kind of cold that you're not if you're alive. Then I reached for his hand and it was also cold, and his fingers were stiff, and at that point there was no getting around the fact that Andrew Mallard was a dead duck.

"But I can't tell you what killed him," I told Haig. "I counted five empty scotch bottles around the apartment, and that was without a particularly intensive search. If he emptied them all since the police let him go this morning then I know what killed him. Alcohol poisoning."

"He tended to leave garbage around," Tulip said. "I went back once for some stuff and there were mewspapers three weeks old, and lots of empty bottles."

"Well, he emptied one of them today. The whole place smelled of booze and he reeked of it. I don't know if he drank enough to kill him."

Haig frowned. "You said he had been sick."

"You mean he threw up? Yes. Not a lot, though. Just a trickle."

"Hmmmm."

"He could have been poisoned. He could have had a heart attack or a stroke. I couldn't tell anything from what I saw, but then I'm not a medical examiner, I don't know what to look for. If his throat had been cut or if there was a bullet hole in his head I probably would have noticed. Then again, somebody could have strangled him or shot him in the chest and I probably *wouldn't* have noticed. I didn't want to disturb the body or anything."

"That was wise," Haig said. "The police will determine cause of death and time of death. They are sound enough in that area. Any efforts you might have made would only have served to render their work more difficult."

"That's what I figured."

"Did anyone see you enter the building?"

"I don't know. I wasn't trying to avoid being seen. I made sure nobody saw me leave. Anyway it doesn't really matter if they can prove I was there around 8:30. I don't know how long he was dead, I don't know how long it takes a body to lose body heat, but it was awhile."

Haig nodded absently, then leaned back in his chair. This time he kept his feet on the floor. His hand went to his beard and petted it affectionately.

I turned to Tulip. The expression on her face was like the one I had seen last night when Cherry was killed, a sort of numb look.

"It's so hard to believe," she said. "I slept with him, I lived with him. I was in love with him." She stopped to consider, then amended this. "At least I *thought* I was in love with him. For a while. And then he got to be a kind of a habit, you know. He was there and he needed me, and it took awhile to break the habit. But it's horrible that he's dead. He was a very nice man. He was a loser, you know, but he was a decent sort of a guy. If he could ever have gotten ahold of himself he would have been all right, but he never quite managed to, and now he never will, will he?"

I moved my chair away from the desk and closer to hers. She reached out a hand and I took it. Her hands were large—everything about her was large, for Pete's sake—but her fingers were very long and thin, and the touch of her hand was cool. She got her hand around mine and squeezed. There was a sad half-smile on her face and her eyes looked to be backed up with tears she had no intention of shedding.

"We shall have to play something of a waiting game," Haig said thoughtfully. "Three possibilities exist. No, four. Mallard could have been murdered. He could have committed suicide. He could have had a heart attack or something of the sort. Finally, he could have committed a sort of involuntary suicide due to overindulgence in alcohol. I don't suppose there was an empty bottle of sleeping tablets beside the bed?"

"It's the sort of thing I probably would have mentioned."

"Quite." Haig heaved a sigh. I'd say he heaved it just

about halfway across the room. "We'll act on the supposition that the man was murdered. All deaths in the course of a homicide investigation ought to be regarded as homicides themselves until proven otherwise. It's by far the best working hypothesis. Miss Wolinski."

"Yes?"

"You will remain here this evening. There is a reasonably comfortable bed in the guest room. Wong Fat will change the linen for you. There is a murderer on the loose and he has already demonstrated that he can gain access to your apartment. I would be remiss in my duties if I permitted you to spend the night alone. I will brook no argument."

"I wasn't going to argue," Tulip said.

"Oh? Then you are a rational woman, and I am delighted. Mr. Harrison always resists my urgings to spend the night. But he too will stay here."

"No argument," I said.

"Oh? Extraordinary."

I didn't see what was so extraordinary about it. Anybody who wouldn't welcome the chance to spend the night under the same roof as Tulip needed hormone shots.

"Wong will make up the couch for you," he went on. "But first you have some places to go and some people to see."

Buddy Lippa was wearing a sport jacket that would have kept him safe in the hunting season. It had inch-square checks of bright orange and black, and I had the feeling that it glowed in the dark. He was also wearing blue-and-white striped slacks, a canary silk shirt, and a troubled frown. "You're gettin' to be a regular," he said. "I don't know if it's such a good idea. Bein' as you're underage and all."

"I showed proof of age last night," I reminded him. "I can't afford another ten."

"Oh, I wasn't lookin' for that. All it is, the boss might get tired of seein' you. Say, you happen to know when Tulip's gonna be workin' again? The two bimbos we got on tonight are strictly from Doggie Heaven."

I told him Tulip wasn't sure when she'd be returning to work. He let me through and I went up to the bar and ordered a bottle of beer. Jan uncapped it and poured it into a glass for me. "How's Tulip?" she wanted to know. "Is it true she was arrested? Are you really a detective? Do they know who murdered Cherry?"

I said, "She's fine. Yes, I am. No, they don't, but Leo Haig is working on it."

She squinted for a moment and assigned the three answers to the three questions. She started to say something else but some clown from Iowa was tapping his glass impatiently on the bar to indicate that it was empty. She moved off to take care of him. I looked up at the stage and watched a rather skinny blonde move around. She had a vacant expression on her face and whatever music she was dancing to was not the music they were playing. I guessed that she was tripping on something, either mescaline or speed. Whichever it was she probably did a lot of it, which would help to explain why she looked like she was suffering from terminal starvation. Her ribcage was more prominent than her breasts.

"Jesus, you again." I turned around and it was Gus Leemy and he still looked like a bald penguin, except now he looked like a constipated bald penguin. "Finish the beer and move on," he said. "Guys like you could cost me my license. No hard feelings, but I want to stay in business." He accompanied this last sentence with the most unconvincing smile anyone has ever flashed at me.

"I could cost you your license anyway," I said. "How long do you think you'd stay open if Leo Haig decided to go after you? There's a racket going on in your own club and you don't even know about it. You should be more worried about that than about me drinking a beer."

His eyes widened. "I don't know what you're talking about," he said.

"Of course you don't. That's the whole point. I think you'd better show up at Leo Haig's office tomorrow at three-thirty in the afternoon."

"What's it all about?"

"Three-thirty tomorrow," I said. "That's when you'll find out."

He started to say something else but changed his mind. He gave me a long look. I held his eyes for a few seconds, then turned back to my beer. If he'd kept up a barrage of questions I don't know exactly where I would have gone with them. It's easy to say no comment to a reporter, but reporters don't have Buddy Lippa around to hit you if you give them a hard time. I think this may have been running through his mind. Anyway, he decided against it and left me to drink my beer in peace.

I moved down the bar to where the waitresses came to pick up their drinks. I sat there nursing my beer. Maeve O'Connor came over after a few minutes to order three whiskey sours and a pousse-café. Jan said she didn't know how to make a pousse-café and it was no time for her to experiment. Maeve said she'd see what else they'd settle for and went away. She hadn't noticed me, which was sad. She came back and said to change the pousse-café to a stinger, and I said hello, and she smiled as if genuinely pleased to see me. Which was nice.

I asked if her boss was around. She said he'd dropped in earlier but had left about an hour and a half ago.

"The other waitress," I said. "Is that Rita Cubbage? The girl who was working last night?" Maeve nodded. "I'd like to talk with her," I said. "Ask her to stop by for a minute."

Rita Cubbage turned out to be a black girl wearing a blond wig. I hoped she took it off when she left the club; most of the Times Square hookers wear wigs like that, and if Rita walked down the street with it on she probably got a lot of offers.

I said, "Hello. My name's Chip Harrison and I work for Leo Haig."

"The detective," she said. "Maeve told me. You were here last night, weren't you?"

"Yes, but were you? Not with that wig."

"No, I left it off last night. Do you like it?"

"It's striking," I said.

"You don't like it." She grinned. "That's all right. Neither do I. But it boosts the tips, if you can dig it. My hair's normally in an Afro and it puts the dudes up tight because they figure I must be terribly militant. This way they figure I put out."

I asked her about what she had seen last night, and what she knew about Cherry and Tulip and the other people involved in the case. She didn't seem to know very much. There wasn't much point to it, as far as I could see, but I invited her to come to Haig's house at three-thirty. If he wanted a party, the least I could do was provide a full list of guests. She copied down the street address and put the tip of the pencil between her lips, a sudden frown of concentration on her face.

"Something," she said.

"You can't make it?"

"Oh, I guess I can. Something just on the tip of my tongue and now I can't get hold of it. You know how that'll happen?"

"Something about last night?"

"No, goes back a few days. Damn."

"Maybe it'll come to you."

"I just know it will," she said. "What I'll do, I'll sleep on it. Then in the middle of the night it'll come to me."

"Keep paper and pencil on the table next to your bed so you can write it down."

"Oh, that's what I always do. I'll be sleeping, and all of a sudden something'll pop into my head, and I'll write it down. Only thing is half the time the next morning I won't know what it means. Like one time I woke up and there was the pad of paper on the bedside table, and what it said on it was, 'Every silver lining has a cloud.'"

574

"That's really far out."

"Yeah, but what did I have in mind? Never did figure that one out." She winked. "See you tomorrow, Chip."

I went back to my beer. When Maeve came to pick up an order of drinks I gave her the same invitation. "And tell your boss it would be a good idea for him to show up, too. Three-thirty at Haig's place."

A few minutes later I got to extend the invitation to Jan Remo. I waited until she was pouring me a second beer and then I told her the time and place. If her hand shook any, I didn't notice it.

"Three-thirty," she said. "I suppose I can make it. I'm having my hair done earlier but I should be through in plenty of time. But what's it all about?"

"Mr. Haig doesn't tell me everything," I said. "If I had to guess, I'd say he intends to trap a murderer."

"I thought the police solve murders."

"They do, occasionally. So does Leo Haig."

"And you're his assistant."

"That's right."

"Does Mr. Haig know who killed Cherry?"

"I told you he doesn't tell me everything. That's one of the things he hasn't told me."

She broke off the conversation to fill a drink order, then got Maeve's attention and asked her to handle the bar while she took a break. "You won't have to do much," she said. "If you don't push drinks at them they don't order much. Just cover for me while I go to the head."

I chatted with Maeve for a few minutes. Not about murder or other nasty things but about her career in show business and how she had a driving need to make a success of herself. I was pleased to hear this. It's a theory of mine that women with one driving need have other driving needs as well, which tends to make them more interesting company than other women. I don't know how valid this is, but I guess it'll do until a better theory comes along.

We didn't have all that much time to talk before Jan was

back. They stood side by side for a moment, both of them rather spectacular to look at and both of them redheads, and a part of my mind started thinking idly in troilistic terms, which I gather is a fairly standard male fantasy. I suppose it's something I'll have to try sooner or later, but I have the feeling it wouldn't be as terrific in actuality as it is in fantasy, because it would be hard to concentrate and you wouldn't know which way to turn. At any rate, I was fairly certain I wouldn't get to try it with Maeve and Jan. I had the feeling they were less than crazy about one another.

Then Maeve went back to her tables and Jan said, "I guess I'll be there tomorrow, Chip. But there's really nothing I know. Nothing that would help."

"You were right here when she got killed," I said. "Didn't you see anything at all?"

"The police asked me all that."

"Well, maybe you saw something and didn't know you saw it. I mean, you know, it didn't seem important at the time."

"I didn't even see it," she said. "I was pouring a drink. The first I knew something was wrong was when everybody took a deep breath all at once. Then I turned around and Cherry was lying on the stage and that was the first I saw of it."

"Well, I think you should come tomorrow anyway."

"I will."

I finished most of my beer and decided I could live without the rest of it. I left some change on the bar for Jan, decided it was a puny tip and added a dollar bill. I nodded a sort of collective goodnight on the chance that someone was looking my way and I walked to the door and out onto Seventh Avenue.

I thought about a cab and decided I would take the subway instead. The AA train stops at Eighth Avenue and Fiftieth, so I started uptown, and I walked about ten steps and felt a pair of hands take hold of my right arm. I was just getting ready to find out who owned them when two more hands took hold of my left arm and a voice said, "Easy does it, kid."

I said, "Oh, come on. It's the middle of Times Square and there are cops all over the place."

"Oh, yeah? I don't see no cops around, kid. Where are all the cops?"

Collecting graft, I decided. Sleeping in their cars. Because I couldn't see a single cop anywhere. I heard a calypso verse once that maintained that policemen, women, and taxi cabs are never there when you want them. It's the God's honest truth.

"We're just gonna take a nice ride," the voice said. They were walking me along and they had my arms in a disturbingly effective grip.

"Suppose I don't want to go?"

"That would be silly."

"Getting in a car would be sillier."

"Now what you got to do is use your head," said another voice, the one on my left. "A man wants to talk to you. That's all there is to it. He says not to hurt you long as you cooperate. What the hell, you're cooperating, aren't you? There's the car, right around the corner, and you're walking to it like a nice reasonable kid. So what's the problem?"

"Who's the boss?"

"The guy we're going to see."

"Yeah, right," I said. We walked up to the car, a long low Lincoln with a black man behind the wheel. He was wearing sunglasses, his head was shaved, there was a gold earring in his ear, and he had a little gold spoon on a gold chain around his neck. That's either a sign that you use cocaine or that you want people to think you do.

I said, "Look, tell me who the boss is or I don't get in the car."

"If we want you to get in the car, kid, there's not a hell of a lot you can do about it."

"I can make it easier," I said. "Just tell me who we're going to see."

One of them let go of my arms and stepped around to where I could see him. He wasn't much to look at, but he didn't have to be to do his job. He looked like a hood, which stood to reason, because that was evidently what he was.

He said, "What the hell, you'll know in ten minutes anyway. The boss is Mr. Danzig. You gonna get in the car now?"

"Oh, sure," I said. "I mean, why not? I was supposed to see him anyway."

Chapter Twelve

I DON'T KNOW what I expected exactly. He had already surprised me. I'd had the impression that he was very small-time, not important enough to have a couple of musclemen and a driver working for him. Of course he could have hired them for the occasion from Hertz Rent-a-Hood, but somehow I doubted this.

But whatever I had expected, he wasn't it. He was waiting for me in a penthouse apartment on top of a high-rise on York Avenue in the Eighties. One whole wall of the living room was glass, and you could look out across the East River and gaze at more of the Borough of Queens than anyone in his right mind would want to see. He was doing just that when we walked in, all dolled up in a black mohair suit and holding a glass of something-on-the-rocks in his hand. When he turned to look at me I got the feeling he was disappointed that it was only me and not the photographer from *Playgirl* magazine.

But he wasn't disappointed at all. He flashed me a smile that showed almost as many teeth as Haskell Henderson's without looking half as phony. "You must be Mr. Harrison," he said. "I'm so glad to see you."

He crossed the room. This wasn't as easy as it sounds because there was a lot of room to cross and all of it was covered by a light blue carpet deep enough to make walking a tricky proposition. He transferred his drink to his left hand and held out his right hand. I took it, and we shook hands briskly, and he let me have the smile again.

"I hope these gentlemen behaved properly," he said, indicating the two muscle types. The driver had stayed with the car. "And let me apologize for the manner in which I had you brought here. In my field, the direct approach is often the only possible approach. You weren't abused, I hope?"

"No."

"That's good to know," he said. He smiled past me at the two heavies. "That's all for tonight," he said. "And thanks very much."

There was something about the way he talked that made his sentences go on ringing in my head after he was done saying them. You just knew that he hadn't talked like this years ago, and that he wouldn't speak the same words or use the same accent if, say, you woke him up suddenly in the middle of the night. He was all dressed up in a suit as good as one of Gregorio's, and he had at least as good a barber, and his teeth were capped by the world's greatest dentist, and underneath it all you had a hard tough monkey who could beat a man to death with a baseball bat and then go home and tuck himself in for a good eight hours' sleep.

I had met the type before. Haig has a good friend named John LiCastro who spends a lot of his time sipping espresso in a neighborhood social club on Mulberry Street, making little executive decisions, such as who lives and who dies. LiCastro raises tropical fish, mostly cichlids, and when his fish die he practically puts on a black armband. Leonard Danzig was an up-to-date version of the same type.

"You'll want something to drink," he said to me now. "I believe you generally drink beer. I have Heineken's and Lowenbrau."

There's nothing wrong with either, but I'd had enough beer. I asked if he happened to have Irish whiskey. He didn't, and he seemed genuinely apologetic. He gave me my choice of three different brands of expensive scotch. I took Dewar's Ancestor, which turned out to be what he was drinking, too. He made a drink for me and freshened his own and motioned me to a pair of chairs near the wall of glass. He took one and I took the other and we both sipped whiskey.

He said, "I have a problem. It started last night when Cherry was murdered. It's not getting simpler. It's getting more difficult."

I didn't say anything.

"You're with Leo Haig. He's a private detective. I also understand he's something of an oddball."

I admitted that some people probably thought so. I didn't bother to add that I was one of them.

"But I also understand he gets results."

"Well, he's a genius," I said. "And the only way to prove he's a genius is by solving impossible crimes, so that's what he does. He gets results."

"So I've heard." Danzig leaned forward, set his glass down on top of a small marble-topped table. He didn't use a coaster. Either glasses don't leave rings on marble or he didn't care. He could always throw the table away. I kept my drink in my hand. He said, "Cherry was a friend of mine, you know."

"I know."

"I had been seeing her for about a month, maybe a little longer than that. I probably would have gone on seeing her for another month. No more than that." He smiled disarmingly. "I don't seem to be very good at sticking to a woman. I find that any reasonably good-looking woman can be exciting company for perhaps two months. Then they become boring."

I didn't have an answer for that one.

"Unfortunately," he went on, "Cherry was murdered. I'm sorry about that if only because I genuinely liked her. She was a warm, sweet person." The smile went away. "I'm particularly sorry that she happened to be killed while I was involved with her. It's awkward for me. As long as the case remains unsolved, the police have an excuse to intrude in my affairs. They might even keep the case open on purpose in order to provide themselves with an excuse to harass me. In my business, that's a liability."

I didn't ask him what his business was.

"It's unfortunate that I have to be exposed to this simply because of my friendship for Cherry. I've been friendly with quite a few of the young ladies who've worked at Treasure Chest. I go there frequently, I get acquainted with the people who work there. The dancers, the barmaids, the waitresses. I'm in a position to be of assistance to them in their careers, you understand. And they like a taste of the high life. They work hard, they don't earn all that much money, they appreciate a decent dinner and civilized company."

"I see," I said. I didn't, if you want to know, but it was something to say.

"You familiar with a fellow named Andrew Mallard?"

"I never met him."

"Neither did I," Danzig said. He smiled again. "That's not what I asked."

"I know who he is." (I'm very proud of that sentence, let me tell you. Is. Not was. That's thinking on your feet, if I say so myself.)

"Was," Danzig said. "Not is. He died tonight."

"Oh?" (I'm less proud of that sentence, but they can't all be zingers.)

He nodded. "It was just on the radio. They identified him as a former close associate of Tulip Willing, roommate of murdered dancer Cherry Bounce. Somebody tipped the police and they found him dead in bed. His bed."

"How did he die?"

"Choked to death on his own vomit," Danzig said. He picked up his scotch and took a dainty sip. "Got drunk, passed out, then threw up in his sleep and sucked it into his lungs or something. You all right?"

"Just a little nauseous."

"Yeah, well, it's only dangerous if you happen to be unconscious at the time. Freshen that drink for you?"

"No thanks."

He crossed to the bar and put another ounce or so of scotch in his own glass. "Now here's my line of thought," he went on, returning to his chair. "I think it would be very convenient if it happened to turn out that Andrew Mallard murdered Cherry. He was there. He could have done it. Any list of suspects would have to have him on it, wouldn't you say?"

"I suppose so."

"There it is," he said. "All Leo Haig has to do is prove Mallard killed Cherry. Then he got full of remorse over what he'd done and did some heavy drinking. And so on. How do you like it?"

"Well, it's certainly possible."

"That's the ticket." He drew an alligator wallet from his jacket pocket and pulled out a sheaf of bills. They were hundreds, and he counted out ten of them, paused, studied me for a moment, and counted out ten more. I don't know what he saw in my face that doubled the ante. Maybe the whole thing was just theatrics. "Two thousand dollars," he said.

Then he did something incredible. He took the twenty bills and tore them in half. I guess I wasn't perfect at keeping a straight face, because he grinned at my expression.

"For Haig," he said, offering me what managed to be half of two thousand dollars without being one thousand dollars. "Here, take it. He gets the other half when he proves that Andrew Mallard murdered Cherry Bounce. That's if he brings it off within three days. Take it."

I took it because it was impossible not to, but instead of holding onto it I set it down on the table next to Leonard Danzig's glass of scotch. "There's one problem," I said.

"Let's hear it. I'm usually fairly good at straightening out problems."

I could believe it. I said, "The thing is, you don't know Mr. Haig. I'm not saying he wouldn't work for you, but suppose Andrew Mallard didn't murder Cherry Bounce? Suppose someone else did?"

Danzig thought this over. I'd hate to play poker with him. Nothing at all showed in his face. At length he shrugged and said, "All right, I just thought it was easier that way. No loose ends. What I'm concerned with is the time element. If Haig gets the murderer in three days he gets the other half of the two thousand. How's that?"

"Whoever the murderer is?"

"Whoever."

I asked if I could use the phone. He pointed at one halfway across the room. I don't suppose it was more than forty yards from me. "It might be tapped," he said. "I pay a guy to check them out periodically, but he hasn't been around for a few days."

I told him it didn't matter. I didn't dial Haig's number because the phone had buttons instead of a dial. I *pushed* Haig's number and got him. I said, "I'm at Mr. Leonard Danzig's apartment. I just learned that Andrew Mallard died earlier today. It was on the radio." I went on to tell him the cause of death, then brought him up to date on Danzig's proposal and my counter proposal. He said "Satisfactory" a couple of times, which made me very proud of myself, and then he talked some more and I listened. Finally he said, "I am going to sleep now, Chip. Don't disturb me when you return. Your report can wait until morning. You made all the necessary arrangements?"

"Yes."

"Goodnight, then. And come directly home when you leave Mr. Danzig's apartment."

I said I would and hung up. To Danzig I said, "Mr. Haig says I should take your money."

Danzig smiled and pointed to the little pile of bills.

"There are a couple of qualifiers first. You mentioned a three-day limit."

"If it went a few hours over—"

"That's not the point. Would it be worth a bonus if Haig wrapped it up within twenty-four hours. Say tomorrow afternoon?"

"It wouldn't hurt any. What kind of a bonus?"

I was supposed to use my judgment on this one, so I judged quickly. "Double," I said. "Four thousand if it's wrapped up tomorrow. Two thousand if we make the three-day limit. Beyond that you don't owe us anything and you get the stack of homemade fifties back."

"Done."

"All right. The second point is that I'm supposed to ask you some questions now. Mr. Haig said he's assuming that you did not kill Cherry and don't know who did. He says only a rank fool would hire him under those circumstances, and I've used my intelligence guided by my experience to decide that you're not a fool."

"I'm honored."

"Were you at Treasure Chest the night Cherry was murdered?"

"Yes."

The admission was so direct that it stopped me momentarily. I got back into gear and said, "Were you there when it happened?"

"I was on the premises."

"You missed the police dragnet."

"I went out the back. I didn't know it was murder but I gathered she was dead and I didn't want to be found on the premises in an official investigation."

"Are you the owner of Treasure Chest?"

"Let's say I'm a good friend of Gus Leemy's. Will that do for the moment?"

"Sure. Do you have any idea who might want to kill Cherry?"

"No one now. She's already dead."

"I mean—"

He crossed one leg over the other. "Just a small joke," he said. "No, frankly, I have no suspects. I rather like the idea of Andrew Mallard, but that's simply because it would be so convenient that way. And he seemed to be a disturbed person. Would a sane man choose that way to kill a woman?"

I wanted to say that a sane man wouldn't kill anybody for any reason but I didn't know how well this would go down, because I had the feeling that Danzig had killed people now and then, or had had them killed, and this would mean calling him a lunatic by implication.

"And you saw nothing suspicious?"

"Nothing. I was in no position to see anything at the time the incident occurred. I was in the office in the rear with Gus."

"Was anyone else with you at the time? I don't mean that you and Gus can't alibi each other, that's all right. But if other people were with you we could also rule them out."

"I'm afraid we were alone together."

I drank the last of my scotch. It was really great scotch. I said I guessed that was about it. "Mr. Haig wants you at his office at three-thirty tomorrow afternoon," I said. "You might as well bring the other half of the two thousand. Plus another two thousand."

He got to his feet and we began the long walk to the door. "Three-thirty," he said. "I'll be there. I wouldn't want to miss it. He really thinks he can come through in that short a time?"

"Evidently. He wants to earn the bonus."

But the bonus wasn't the big consideration, I knew. What Haig really wanted was the applause.

Chapter Thirteen

THE CAB DROPPED me at West 20th Street around two-thirty. I used one key to let myself into the courtyard, climbed two flights of stairs, and used another key to let me into Haig's half of the house. There was a light on in the office and I guessed that he hadn't been to sleep after all, but when I went in ready to hit him with some smartass remark or other his chair was empty and Tulip was sitting on the couch reading a Fredric Brown novel. *Mrs. Murphy's Underpants*, one of the late ones.

"This is pretty good," she said. "Have you read it?"

"Sure. Mr. Haig made me read everything of Fredric Brown's. That's not supposed to be one of his best."

"I'm enjoying it anyway. I like the way the two detectives play against each other. An uncle and a nephew."

"Ed and Am Hunter, right."

"Do you and Mr. Haig interact the same way?"

"Not exactly. Of course we're not related, which helps. Or hinders. I'm never entirely sure which. Also Ambrose Hunter is supposed to be reasonably sane."

"Well, Mr. Haig—"

"Is crazy," I said.

"But—"

"That doesn't mean he isn't a genius. Maybe all geniuses are crazy. I couldn't honestly say. For instance, thirteen hours from now he's going to trap a murderer. Don't ask me how because I don't know. Don't ask him, either, because I'm not convinced he knows, and even if he does he's not telling. But he's going to have the whole crowd here, all sitting on chairs with their hands folded, and if he doesn't deliver he's going to look like Babe Ruth would have looked if he pointed to the fence and then struck out. The one thing he doesn't want is to look ridiculous, and with his shape and mannerisms he has a good head start in that direction, so he really has to deliver. And he probably will, but don't ask me how."

"It's kind of exciting," she said.

I agreed that it was. I said I thought I'd have a beer and asked her if she wanted anything. She didn't. I uncapped the beer in the kitchen and brought the bottle into the office with me. I asked her when Haig had gone to sleep.

"Right after he got your call. He said he was very tired. I guess he didn't get much sleep last night."

"Nobody did," I said, and yawned. "I'm completely shot myself. As soon as I finish this beer and unwind a little I'm going to stretch out on the couch and make Z's."

"Oh! I'm sorry, this is where you're going to be sleeping, isn't it? I'll go upstairs now."

I waved her back to the couch. "I have to unwind first," I said. "And you're the one who ought to be exhausted. Did you get any sleep last night?"

"Not really. They kept moving me around from one stationhouse to another."

"Yeah, the old cop shuffle. The hell of it is that they knew damned well you didn't kill Cherry. They just wanted to give you a hard time because you were Haig's client." I yawned. "Ed and Am Hunter. That's funny. Am Hunter was in a carnival for years. Can you see Leo Haig as a pitchman? I can't."

"Oh, I don't know." She considered, then giggled. I liked her wide-open laugh better.

"What's so funny?"

"Well, Ed Hunter certainly goes over well with the girls in this book."

"Thanks," I said.

"No, I meant it as a compliment."

"You did?"

"Well, yeah. You probably do pretty well yourself. And the two of you do play off each other the same way, even if you're not related."

"We were almost related," I said. "A couple of months ago the cops picked me up and held me for seventy-two hours. They were just making a nuisance of themselves. As usual."

(It was an interesting case, incidentally. I never wrote it up because there wasn't enough to it to make a book out of it, and there was no sex in it, and Joe Elder at Gold Medal insists it's impossible to sell a book without sex in it. Maybe I'll try to write it up as a magazine story one of these days.)

Tulip frowned. "I don't get it," she said. "I mean, it's terrible that they locked you up and all, but how does that make you and Haig almost related?"

"It doesn't *make* us almost related. What it did was *almost* make us related. See, they wouldn't let him visit me in jail because he was neither a relative nor an attorney. He decided this might come up in the future so what he wanted to do was adopt me. He said it made perfect sense considering that my parents are dead. I told him it was ridiculous because I might someday become a partner in the firm."

"So?"

"So Haig & Harrison is possible," I said. "But Haig & Haig is ridiculous, unless you happen to be producing scotch whiskey. That wasn't the reason I wanted to avoid being adopted but it was a reason that made perfect sense to him, and—"

She began to laugh, and I joined in, and we really did quite a bit of hard-core laughing. Then we stopped as suddenly as we started and Tulip looked at me with her upper lip trembling slightly and I thought she was going to cry. I sat on the couch next to her and took hold of her hand.

"Everything's so funny," she said, "and then I remember that Cherry's dead and Andy's dead and I don't know how I can laugh at anything. And the murderer must be someone I know. That's the most frightening thing in the world. Somebody I know committed murder."

I put an arm around her and she sort of settled in against my shoulder. I gave her shoulder a squeeze and took her hand with my other hand.

"Who do you think did it, Chip?"

"I don't know."

"Could it have been Andy?"

"I suppose it could have been anybody. How did he get on with Cherry?"

"I'm not even sure they ever met. Where would he get hold of poison? Where would he get a key to my apartment? I don't understand."

"Neither do I."

"I'm just so confused."

She snuggled closer and I got a healthy lungful of her perfume. It was all I needed. I mean, the whole scene was beginning to get a little strange. I was playing a kind of comforting Big Brother role, which was weird in that she was not only older than me but bigger. And at the same time she was turning me on something terrible, and it shouldn't have been that way because the scene itself wasn't fundamentally sexual, but go tell yourself that when you're turned on. I looked down at her body and remembered what it looked like with no clothes on it, dancing merrily away on the stage at Treasure Chest, and then I closed my eyes because the sight of her was doing things to me, and having my eyes shut didn't really help at all because I could see her just as well with them shut.

"It's all so rotten," she said.

I took a breath. "Look," I said, "I think you'd better go to sleep, Tulip. It's late and you're exhausted, we're both exhausted. Things will look better in the morning."

"That's what people always say, isn't it?"

"Well, I didn't claim to originate the line."

"Maybe things *will* look better in the morning. But will they *be* any better?"

"Uh."

"I guess you're right," she said. She got to her feet. "Could you show me where my room is?"

I walked her to her room. "Come in for a minute," she said. "You don't mind, do you?"

We went into the room. She flicked on a light. The bed had been opened and Wong had changed the sheets. I hadn't really had enough time to dirty them.

"It looks comfortable," she said.

"I'm not sure whether it is or not. I spent a couple hours on it this morning, but I was too tired to notice whether the bed was any good. It probably beats the couch. I slept on that one night before Haig bought the bed and it was like spending a night on the rack. I woke up with my spine in the shape of the letter S."

"Oh, and now you have to sleep on it again because of me! I'm sorry, Chip."

I used both hands to get my foot out of my mouth. It was a struggle. "Oh, I was exaggerating," I said, not too convincingly, I think. "It's not really all that bad. Anyway as tired as I am it won't make any difference." I made myself yawn. "See? Can't keep my eyes open. Well, goodnight, Tulip. Guess I'll see you in the morning, and in the meantime—"

"Chip?"

"What?"

"Look, we don't really know each other, and maybe this is silly, and of course I'm probably too old for you and you couldn't possibly be interested, but—"

"Tulip?"

"Don't go, Chip."

It started off being basically closeness and warmth and comfort, and we were both deliciously exhausted, and we drifted gradually into a beautiful lazy kind of lovemaking. Then it stopped being lazy and we stopped being aware that we were all that exhausted, and then we stopped being aware of much of anything, actually, and then, well, it became too good to talk about.

And a while later she said, "I thought it might turn you off. Me being older than you."

"Oh, sure. You really turned me off, Tulip. That's what you did, all right. Like a bucket of cold water."

She giggled. It was a pretty sexy giggle, actually. "Well, I thought it might turn *me* off, then. I was attracted to you, you know, but I'm used to older men. And we were both so tired but I wanted to do it anyway." She put her hand on my stomach and moved it gradually lower. "You must be really exhausted now," she said, holding on to me. "Oh."

"Uh-huh."

"How did you get so wide awake so fast?"

"It's one of the advantages of younger men," I said. "We have these incredible recuperative powers. Especially when we're in bed with somebody like you."

"How nice," she said. "But you must be tired."

"I'm not *that* tired," I said.

The last conscious thought I had was that I'd damn well better get from her bed to the couch before I fell asleep. Because Haig would either say something or maintain a diplomatic silence, and one would be as infuriating as the other. I had that thought, all right, but that was as far as it went. The next morning I knew it was morning.

Chapter Fourteen

I WAS THE last one awake. I yawned and stretched and reached for Tulip and encountered nothing but air and linen. I yawned some more and got up and put clothes on. They were having breakfast. I slipped out without saying hello, walked the few blocks to my own rooming house, showered and changed clothes and went back to Haig's. By then they were in the office and the great man was on the telephone. I couldn't tell who was on the other end of the line or what they were talking about, because all Haig said was "Yes" and "No" and "Indeed" and, at last, "Satisfactory." For all I could tell he had called the weather bureau and was talking back to the recording.

"There you are," he said to me. "I thought you'd gone off without instructions. You'll want to see Mrs. Henderson without further delay. And there are other errands for you as well."

I got out my notebook.

"I also want your report. Last night, from the time you left for Treasure Chest until your return. Verbatim, please."

I came as close to verbatim as possible and he listened to it with his feet on the desk. When I'd brought it to the point where I left Danzig at his apartment and hopped a cab home, he took his feet off the desk and leaned forward and frowned at me. "How did Mr. Danzig know where to find you?" he demanded.

"I thought about that. Jan Remo."

"The barmaid."

I nodded. "She excused herself to go to the bathroom. I don't think she went to the bathroom. I think she went to the telephone."

"And called Mr. Danzig."

"Right. I think she fingered me. That's the right term, isn't it?"

"I believe so."

"Well, I believe she fingered me." I pictured Jan, the red hair, the feline face, the fishnet stockings, the body stocking filled with just what I'd always wanted for Christmas. "She fingered me," I said. "I'd like to return the favor."

"I beg your pardon?"

"Just thinking out loud," I said.

Haig grunted—his way of thinking out loud—and spun around to consider the Rasboras. I looked over at Tulip and she gave me the world's most solemn wink. I don't know if I blushed or not. I probably did.

Haig turned around again. "There's another variable. Rather surprising. You had a telephone call this morning during your absence."

"Oh?"

"From another topless dancer, I assume. One of those inane stage names." He turned to Tulip. "Your pardon, Miss Wolinski. No criticism is intended."

She assured him none was inferred.

"I don't recall that you've mentioned this one," he went on. "You know your reports must be as comprehensive as possible. The slightest detail—"

"There was no other dancer. Oh, there were a couple new ones last night, but I didn't talk to them. I didn't even get their names, and if that was an oversight I'm sorry. Who was it that called?"

He consulted a slip of paper. "She gave her name as Clover Swann," he said. "I've no idea what her real name might chance to be. She left a number."

"Oh, for Pete's sake," I said. "She's not a topless dancer."

"Indeed?"

"She's an editor," I said. "At Gold Medal." The image of Clover Swann, Gold Medal's resident hippie, dancing nude on the stage of Treasure Chest, suddenly flashed somewhere in my mind. It was by no means an unappealing image, but I had the feeling she was happier editing books.

594

"It was not an illogical assumption," Haig said. "Clover Swann indeed."

"Well, she's an editor. She probably wants to know when I'm going to do another book for them. I'll call her tomorrow or the next day."

"You'll call her now."

I just looked at him.

"Now," he repeated. "Bear in mind, Chip, that I hired you as much for your journalistic ability as anything else. It is not enough to be a brilliant detective. The world must know that one is a brilliant detective. Call Miss Swann. I have the number right here."

"I know the number," I said. I picked up the phone and dialed it, and after I'd given the operator everything but my Social Security number I got through to Clover.

"I've been reading the papers," she said. "It sounds as though you're right in the middle of an exciting case. Topless dancers and everything."

"And everything," I agreed.

"It ought to be perfect for your next book. Are you going to write it up?"

"That depends," I said. "A few hours from now Mr. Haig is going to reach into a hat. If he pulls out a rabbit I'll have something to write about. If he comes up empty it's not going to make much of a book."

Haig scribbled furiously, passed me a note. I read it quickly. It said: *Show more enthusiasm.*

Clover must have read the note because she showed plenty of enthusiasm. She went on telling me what a great book it would make, that it had all the ingredients. "And it should be a cinch to have a lot of sex in this one," she said. "You know what Joe always says."

I knew what he said, all right. *People like to read about what a character Haig is and all that, Chip, but if you want to sell books to them you have to give them a hard-on.* That's what he always said.

"I'm not sure there's too much sex in it," I said. "Oh, who

do you think you're kidding?" She laughed heartily. "Topless dancers? Chip Harrison cavorting with a batch of topless dancers? If I know you, you're bouncing around like a satyr in a harem."

"Er," I said.

"Just let me know how it goes today, Chip, and we'll draw up a contract. You could even start thinking about a title."

"Uh," I said.

I wrapped up the conversation and then I had to give Haig a *Reader's Digest* version of it. Then he told me what I had to do next, and I made some notes in my notebook and headed for the door.

Tulip walked me to the door. When we were out of Haig's hearing range she slipped an arm around my waist. She turned her body so that her breasts rubbed companionably against my chest.

"Not enough sex," she purred. "Ho, boy! How about a fast bourbon and yogurt?"

I'm sure I blushed that time. Damn it.

I got the Cadillac from the garage. It's my car, but if it weren't for Haig I wouldn't be able to go on owning it. He pays fifty dollars a month so that it can live in a garage on Tenth Avenue. Maybe twice a year I have occasion to use it, and yes, it would be a lot cheaper to rent a car, but I like this one and Haig doesn't seem to mind the expense. The car was given to me by Geraldine, who runs a whorehouse in Bordentown, South Carolina, where I worked for a while as a deputy Sheriff.

(You could read about it if you want. It's in a book called *Chip Harrison Scores Again*. I want you to know that the title was not my idea.)

Anyway, the car's a Cadillac, which sounds impressive, but it's also more than twenty years old, and I guess it's the last stick-shift automobile that Cadillac ever made. It's in beautiful shape, though. Geraldine only drove it on

Sundays. To church and back.

I picked it up at the garage, crossed over to Jersey and managed to find the Palisades Parkway. I got off at the Alpine exit and found the town of Closter, and I only had to ask directions four times before I found Haskell Henderson's house. It was a colonial, painted yellow with forest green trim, set fairly far back on a lot shaded by a great many large trees. A huge dog in a fenced yard next door barked at me. I waved at him and walked up a flagstone path to the front door and poked the bell. An elaborate series of chimes sounded within the house. I waited for a while and was about to hit the bell again when the door opened. A woman stood in the doorway with a cigarette in one hand and a glass of colorless liquid in the other. She said, "If you're from the Boy Scouts, the newspapers are stacked in the garage. If you're from the ecology drive the bottles and cans are in a bin next to the newspapers. If you're selling something I've probably already got it and it doesn't work and the last thing I want is to buy another one."

I was standing close enough during her little speech to identify the colorless liquid in her glass. It was gin. Mrs. Haskell Henderson was in her early thirties, built like the Maginot Line, and already sloshed to the gills at ten twenty-five in the morning.

"I'm not," I said.

"You're not which?"

"Any of them," I said. "My name is Chip Harrison and I work for Leo Haig."

"I don't."

"I beg your pardon?"

"I don't work for Leo Haig. I don't work for anybody. My name is Althea Henderson and I drink a lot. And why shouldn't I, huh? That's what I want to know."

"Well. May I come in?"

"What the hell, why not." She stood aside and I entered the house. "Why shouldn't I drink?" she demanded. "Kids are at camp, husband's at the office, why shouldn't I drink?"

597

She gestured vaguely and some of the gin moved abruptly from the glass to the oriental rug. She didn't appear to notice. "Bad for the liver," she said. "Well, what the hell do I care, huh? Who wants to drop dead and leave a perfectly good liver behind? What you got to do in this world is wear out all at once. It's a question of timing."

"Oh."

"Wanna drink?"

"It's a little early for me, thanks."

"Then how 'bout some carrot juice? Carrot juice, papaya juice, dandelion coffee—that's the kind of crap my husband drinks. How 'bout a nice bowlful of sprouted alfalfa, huh? Just the thing to set you up for a hard day's work, right?"

"Speaking of your husband, Mrs. Henderson—"

"Call me Althea."

"Speaking of your husband, Althea—"

"What about him?" Her eyes narrowed, and I got the impression she wasn't quite as drunk as she made out. She'd been drinking, certainly, and it was getting to her, but she had been riding it a little, either for my benefit or because it felt good. "What about him? Is he in some kind of trouble?"

"It's possible."

"It's that girl who was murdered, isn't it? The one with the big tits."

"Cherry Bounce, yes."

"Cherry Bounce my ass," she said. "That little bitch must have given her cherry the bounce when she was eleven years old. Was he fucking her?"

"No."

"That's a surprise. Maybe her tits weren't big enough. Were they big ones?"

"Well. Uh. Yes, uh, they were."

"Then I'm surprised he could keep his hands off them," she said. She took another swig of gin and asked if I was sure I didn't want to drink. I was sure, and said so. "He's a tit man, Haskell is. Always has been. A health freak and a tit freak. That's why he runs around the way he does. Oh, hell, if you were thinking about keeping his secret, he hasn't got any secret to keep. The two of us play a game. He pretends I don't know he runs around and I pretend the same, but all it is is a game."

She flopped into a chair. "He can't fool me. All the health crap he eats, all the vitamins he takes, the man's got more energy than Con Edison. He used to make it with me twice a night and once every morning. Rain or shine, three times a day. He was wearing me out. And now he hasn't made it with me in almost three years."

I didn't say anything.

"Because of these," she said, cupping her enormous breasts in her hands.

"I don't get it."

"Neither do I," she said. "Used to get it three times a day and now I don't get it at all. Because of these. They used to be the reason he married me, and now—"

"Uh—"

"The hell of it is that I love the bastard. And he loves me. But I don't turn him on anymore. Because he's a tit man and that's all there is to it."

"You lost me," I said.

She stood up. "C'mere," she said. I stepped closer to her. She put the index finger of her right hand to the tip of her left breast. "Feel," she said. "Christ sake, don't just stand there. Grab yourself a handful. Go on, dammit!"

I cupped her breast with my hand.

"Don't be shy. Give it a little squeeze." I gave it a little squeeze.

"Feel good?"

"Uh, yes."

"Now the other one."

"Look, Mrs. Henderson—"

"Althea, dammit."

"Look, Althea—"

"Shut up. Feel the other one, will you?" I followed orders.

599

"Well?"

"Well what?"

"Uh."

"Both feel the same?"

"Sure."

"Not from this end they don't. Wait right here. Don't go away." I waited right there and didn't go away and she came back with a hatpin about four inches long. "Stick it in my tit," she said. "The left one."

"Don't be ridiculous. Look, Mrs. Henderson, Althea, maybe I should come back some other time. I—"

"Oh, hell," she said, and plunged the hatpin into her left breast. My stomach flipped a little but she didn't seem to feel a thing. She drew out the pin. There was no blood on it. Her eyes challenged me and I began to get the picture.

"Foam rubber," she said. "The other one's real. Until a couple of years ago they were both real and Haskell was crazy about them. Then I had to have a mastectomy because some knife-happy surgeon decided I had the big C. Turned out it was benign but by that time he'd already done his cutting. Only half a woman now. Used to turn Haskell on. Now all I turn him is off. Still loves me, I still love him, but he takes all his vitamins and drinks his carrot juice and eats his alfalfa and walks around horny as a toad and I don't do him any good. That's why he needs his topless dancers."

I stood there wondering why floors never open up and swallow you when you want them to. She went out to the kitchen for more gin. I thought she was lucky she wasn't too drunk when she did her trick with the hatpin or she might get the wrong breast by mistake and it would probably hurt. When she came back I managed to steer the conversation back in its original direction. I asked her what she had been doing the night before last, and what her husband had been doing.

"He was working late at the store," she said. "Do you believe that?"

"Well—"

"And I was drinking carrot juice and counting my nipples. Do you believe that?"

"Althea—"

"He was chasing women in New York. And I was here, sitting in front of the television set and drinking scotch. Not gin. I never drink gin after four in the afternoon. Only a pansy would drink gin after four in the afternoon."

"I see. Can you prove it?"

"Prove it? Hell, everybody knows only a pansy would drink gin in the night-time. What's there to prove?"

"Can you prove you were home watching television?"

"Oh," she said. She thought it over. "You think I went into New York and stuck a pin in that girl's tit. What was her name again?"

"Cherry Bounce."

"Why the hell would I do a thing like that? I don't go around sticking pins in tits all the time like some kind of a nut. I just did it now to prove a point. Lessee. Kids are at camp so they can't gimme an alibi. Oh, sure. My neighbor from down the street was over here. Got here about nine o'clock, left when Johnny Carson went off the air. Marge Whitman lives just down the street. She's in the same boat as me. Well, not exactly. She's got two tits but she's got a pansy for a husband. Leaves her out here and spends his night picking up sailors on Times Square, the fucking pansy. Drinks gin all night long, the goddamn fruit."

I got the Whitman woman's address and started backing toward the door. She asked me where I was going. "I have some other calls to make," I said.

"I turn you off too, don't I?"

"No, not at all, but—"

"You're a tit man like my husband."

"Not exactly."

"You don't like tits?"

"I like them fine, but—"

"You're not a pansy, are you?" I shook my head. "What do you drink in the evening?"

"Whiskey, usually. Sometimes a beer. Why?"

"Not a pansy," she said. And then she took her blouse off, and then she took her bra off, and I just stood there. She had one absolutely perfect breast, and where the other had been there was smooth skin with an almost imperceptible scar from the incision.

"Sickening, isn't it?"

"No, not at all."

"Deformed."

"No."

The weird thing is that it was turning me on. I don't know how to account for it and I'd rather not stop and figure it out. It probably just proves I'm kinkier than I realized, but why go into it too closely?

"C'mere," she said. I did, and she opened my zipper and groped around. "I'll be a sonofabitch," she said. "Well, you're not a faggot, are you?"

"No, and—"

"And I don't turn you off, do I? Maybe you're a sensible fit man, that's what it must be. You figure half a loaf is better than none. Right?"

"Uh."

Her hand clutched me possessively. She turned and began leading me toward the staircase. I had the choice of following her or leaving part of my anatomy behind, and I've always been attached to it. I followed.

If Althea had had her way she would have kept me there for hours. And I'll tell you something. If we weren't in the middle of a case I would have stayed. She evidently had an enormous complex about her absent breast, which old Haskell must have done a good job of reinforcing, and as a result she did everything she could to compensate for what she regarded as a terrible deficiency. As far as I was concerned, passing her up because she only had one breast was like refusing to listen to Schubert's Eighth Symphony because he never got around to finishing it.

I finally managed to get out of there after promising to return when I got the chance. Then I stopped at the Whitman house to confirm Althea's alibi, although I didn't really need confirmation. But Haig would be sure to ask and I would have to have the answers.

Mrs. Whitman was quick to recall watching television with Althea on the night in question. She was also quick to offer me a cup of coffee, which I declined because I was really in a hurry. And I got the impression that she would have gladly offered me a lot more than coffee. She was a good-looking woman, a little older than Althea, but certainly nothing to complain about.

Back in the car, I wondered if Mr. Whitman was really homosexual. The fact that he drank gin in the evening didn't strike me as sufficient evidence in and of itself. I know a lot of perfectly straight people who drink gin in the evening. I think they're crazy, but it doesn't make them gay.

Then I began thinking about the conversation with Clover, and how I'd told her there probably wouldn't be much sex in the book. I wondered if our talk had had anything to do with the fact that Althea and I wound up in bed. I suppose it could have operated on a sort of subliminal level. Maybe it was my aspirations as an author that goaded me to respond to Althea's advances.

Somehow I doubt it.

I drove back over the George Washington Bridge and down the West Side Drive. I got off at 72nd Street and drove down to Tulip's building. Of course there was no place to park. I circled a few blocks a few times and then stuck it in a lot. The attendant was very impressed by the car and flipped completely when he saw he was going to have to shift it. "A Cad with a stick shift," he said. "Where'd you ever find it?"

"South Carolina."

"There a lot of 'em down there?"

"Thousands," I said.

On the way to Tulip's building I spent a dime on a

telephone and made my report. It took some time and I had
to feed the phone extra change. I left out the part about
going to bed with Althea. Verbatim only goes so far is the
way I figure it.

Haig told me it was satisfactory. I was glad to hear it. He
said, "After you see Miss Tattersall, you'll go to Tulip's
apartment and feed her fish. You have the key?"

"Yes, sir. She gave it to me a couple of hours ago. You
told her to, remember?"

"The *Ctenapoma* receive brine shrimp. There's some in
the freezer compartment of the refrigerator. I believe that's
all they receive. One moment."

He asked Tulip if this was so, and she said there were
also some bloodworms and mealworms in jars in the
refrigerator, and I should give them that if it was no trouble.
"They're strictly carnivores," I heard her say. "Unless—I
wonder if that's what's keeping them from spawning! I
used to give the scats a lot of wheatgerm and it put them in
great breeding condition."

Haig said, "Chip."

"Yes."

He covered the mouthpiece with his hand and I couldn't
make out what he and Tulip were saying to each other.
Then he said, "There is a jar of Kretchmer wheatgerm in
the cupboard to the right of the sink. On the second or
third shelf, Miss Wolinski doesn't recall precisely where."

"I'll manage to find it. You want me to give some to the
Ctenapoma?"

"No! Absolutely not."

"Fine. Hold your horses. Then what difference does it
make what shelf it's on?"

"Bring the wheatgerm back here with you. Do not open
the jar. Be very careful of the jar. Wrap it so that it won't
break should you happen to drop it. Do you understand?"

"Oh."

"Do you understand, Chip?"

"I think so," I said. "I think I do."

Chapter Fifteen

HAIG MAKES ME read a lot of mysteries. Since we don't get all that many cases, and since you can only spend so much time feeding fish and cleaning out filters, that leaves me with plenty of time to humor him. It's his theory that you can learn anything and solve any puzzle if you just read enough mystery novels. Maybe he's right. It certainly seems to work for him, but he's a genius and I feel that constitutes special circumstances.

Well, if you've read as many of them as I have—not even as many as Haig has, because nobody has read that many—then you know what happened when I finally got around to seeing Helen Tattersall. I mean, her name came up early on, and I kept ducking opportunities to see her, so naturally one of two things had to happen. Either she turned out to be the killer or she supplied the one missing piece of information that tied the whole mess together. Right?

Wrong. Absolutely wrong.

I got in to see her by posing as someone investigating her complaint about her neighbors. Even then I had a hard time because she really didn't like the idea of opening her door, but I explained that I couldn't act on the complaint unless I interviewed her face-to-face. Much as she didn't want to open her door, she decided to risk it if it would facilitate her making trouble for somebody.

When she opened the door I decided on my own that she hadn't gone to Treasure Chest and planted a poisoned dart in Cherry Bounce's breast. Because Helen Tattersall was in a wheelchair with her leg in a cast, and the first thing she did was inform me that she'd been in the cast for two months and expected to be in it for another four months, and she didn't sound very happy about it.

The next thing she said was, "Now which complaint have you come about? The upstairs neighbors? Those prostitutes? Or the man next door who plays the flute all day and all night? Or the married couple on the other side of me with that dreadful squalling baby? Or the man across the hall who gives me dirty looks? Or the evil man down by the elevator who puts poison gas in everybody's air-conditioners? Or could it be my complaints about the building employees? The superintendent is a Soviet agent, you know—"

So she didn't even have a personal vendetta against Tulip and Cherry. Instead she had just one enemy: mankind. And she complained about and tried to make trouble for every member of the human race who called himself to her attention.

Well, I couldn't get out of there fast enough. I began wishing I were Richard Widmark in *Kiss of Death* so that I could push the old bitch down a staircase, wheelchair and all. I'm not saying I would have done it, but I might have given it serious consideration.

I suppose there should have been one little thing she said that got my mind working in the right direction, one little thread she might unwittingly supply, but I'm sorry, there just wasn't anything like that. It was a waste of time. I had sort of thought it would be a waste of time, and that's why I'd postponed seeing Helen Tattersall as long as I did, in addition to having suspected that meeting her wouldn't be one of my all-time favorite experiences. I was right on all counts, and it was a pleasure to get out of her apartment, believe me.

I found a staircase and climbed a flight to Tulip's apartment and used her key to open her door. I got a rush when I walked in, remembering how I had let myself into Andrew Mallard's apartment the previous evening, and half-expecting to find another corpse or two now. I don't guess I really thought that would happen, but I have to admit I went around touching things with the heel of my hand to avoid leaving fingerprints.

No corpses, thank God. Not in the fish tank, either. The

two *Ctenapoma fasciolatum* swam around on either side of their glass divider. They were doing a great job of ignoring each other, and the male had done absolutely nothing about building a bubble nest.

I sat on the edge of the bed and watched them for a while. "C'mon," I said at one point. "Clover Swann wants plenty of sex in this book, gang. You can't expect me to supply all of it myself, can you?"

I don't think they cared.

So I gave up on them and went into the kitchen. I found brine shrimp in the freezer and broke off a chunk, and I found containers of bloodworms and mealworms in the fridge. I went back to the bedroom and fed them until they wouldn't eat any more, then returned the food to the kitchen. I opened a couple of cupboards until I spotted the jar of wheatgerm. I reached for it, and then I stopped with my hand halfway to it, and I told myself not to be silly, fingerprints never solved anything anyway and all that, and then I got a paper towel and used it to take the jar from the shelf and set it on the counter top. There wouldn't be any useful prints and I knew it, but if Haig did check the jar for prints and found mine all over it I would never hear the end of it.

I wrapped the jar in several thicknesses of paper towels and found a paper bag in another cupboard and put the jar in that. Then I left it in the kitchen and took a careful look around the apartment without knowing what I was looking for.

I suppose the police must have tossed the place fairly thoroughly the night of the murder, but I had to credit them with doing a neat job of it. As far as I could tell nothing was out of place.

I went into Cherry's room, and of course it was impossible to tell whether anything was out of place there or not, because nothing had been in place to begin with. I remember standing there just two days ago when the only victims had been scats, remembered thinking that Cherry was evidently something of a slob, and now I found myself muttering an apology to her. I guess a girl can throw her underwear around the room if she wants to. I guess it's her own business.

We'll get him, I promised her. I don't know who he is, and I don't know if Haig knows who he is, but we'll get the bastard.

I tucked the jar of wheatgerm under my arm and got out of there. The guy at the parking lot ground the Caddy's gears a little but it didn't sound as though he'd done any permanent damage. I gave him a quarter and drove back to our garage and turned the car over to Emilio, who never grinds the gears, and who occasionally polishes it when he has nothing else to do. We don't pay him to polish the Cadillac. He does it because he likes to.

Then I tucked the jar of wheatgerm under my arm again and walked back to Haig's house.

Chapter Sixteen

I WANTED TO get up a pool on who would be the first to arrive. But Haig wouldn't play. At a quarter to three he sent Tulip to the guest room and ordered her to stay there until he called for her. After she was tucked away he and I discussed the seating arrangements. I hate having to tell people where to sit, although I have to admit it usually works out fairly well. You can take a person into a room with twenty chairs in it, tell him he's expected to sit in one specific one, and it's a rare case when he gives you an argument. I suppose that proves we're a nation of sheep just looking to be led, but I'm not sure about that. I figure people are just relieved to be saved the aggravation of making an unimportant decision.

At twenty minutes to three Haig went upstairs to ask the fish who killed Cherry Bounce. I hoped they would tell him because it was going to be awfully embarrassing if he ran the whole number and nothing happened. I don't know whether he had it all worked out at that point or not. I figured the reason he went upstairs was so that he would be able to make a grand entrance after they were all seated and waiting for him.

Anyway, I would have been glad to get up a pool, and I would have lost. My pick was Haskell Henderson, and I had a reason for picking him, but since I was wrong there's no point in going into the reason. The first person to show rang the doorbell at four minutes to three. I passed the kitchen on my way to the door and exchanged glances with Wong. "Here we go," I said, and he said something in his native tongue, and I opened the door. There was a man standing on the welcome mat whom I had never seen before in my life.

He had a very youthful face if you didn't spot the pouches under the eyes or the lines at their corners. His hair was the color of sand, neither long nor short, and his eyes were as clear a blue as I have ever seen. He had an open friendly Van Johnson kind of face. He was wearing a gray plaid suit and his tie, loose around his neck, was a striped job.

He said, "I have an appointment with a Mr. Haig."

"You're in luck," I said. "We have a Mr. Haig who will probably fit the bill very nicely. Your name is Glenn Flatt and you're early."

He stared at me. He looked as though he had had his next line of dialogue prepared days in advance and I had blown his timing with an ad lib. I told him to come in, closed the door, and led him to the office. Wong and I had set up a double row of chairs on my side of the partner's desk, facing Haig's chair. I showed Flatt which chair was his and he sat, then popped up again as if there had been a tack on the seat.

"Just a minute," he said. "I don't understand any of this. I came here because I wanted to help Mr. Haig. He said he was working on my ex-wife's behalf and I wanted to help him. Where is he?"

"He's busy," I said. "He'll be along in a while. That's your chair but you don't have to sit in it if you don't want to. You can look at the fish if you'd rather."

"Fish," he said.

I was waiting for him to ask me who I was, but he didn't. I guess he didn't care. Nor did he look at the fish. He sat down again, opened his briefcase, and took out a copy of the Post. He opened it to Jack Anderson's column and checked out the current entry in the corruption sweepstakes. I sat in my chair for a minute or two but it got to be sort of heavy, just the two of us in a roomful of empty chairs, so I went into the kitchen and watched Wong sharpen his cleaver.

The next two customers showed up together, and neither of them was Haskell Henderson, so I lost the place and show money too. They were Simon Barckover and Maeve O'Connor. Maeve looked bubbly and radiant and beautiful and Barckover looked pissed off.

"What's this all about?" he demanded. "I'm a busy man. I've got things to do. Who does this Leo Haig think he is? Where does he get off ordering me to come here?"

There were just too many questions so I didn't answer any of them. I told him he was absolutely right, which gave him pause, and I led the two of them into the office and showed them to their seats. They looked at Glenn Flatt and he looked at them, and then he went back to his newspaper and Barckover sat staring straight ahead while Maeve went and looked at some fish.

After that they all started to show up, and I kept scurrying back and forth from the door to the office, ignoring questions and mumbling inane replies and getting everybody in the right seats. First Haskell Henderson showed up, looking about the same as yesterday but twice as nervous. He'd changed from white jeans to dove-gray jeans, but the goatee was still scraggly and he was wearing either the same Doctor Ecology tee-shirt or one just like it. I no sooner got him parked than Gus Leemy came along with Buddy Lippa in tow. Neither of them said a word, and when I brought them into the office they acted as if they were entering an empty room. They took their seats without acknowledging the presence of any of the others in any way whatsoever.

As far as that goes, there was a lot of mutual ignoring going on in the office. A lot of these people had met before, but evidently they had managed to piece out the fact that Haig intended to expose a murderer, which meant that one of them was due to be the exposee, and I guess they didn't quite know how to relate to that. It was fine with me, just so they stayed in their chairs and didn't make waves.

Jan Remo came next, asking if she was late. I told her she was right on time, and as I was leading her to the office the bell rang again. I hurried her in and came back to admit Rita Cubbage. She wasn't wearing the wig this time and her tight Afro cap was a significant improvement. "Much better," I told her, taking a long look. "You ought to give that wig to the boss. Your boss, not mine. He's bald as an egg and it might be an improvement. Did you remember what it was that you couldn't quite remember last night?"

"I dreamed something," she said. She opened her purse and took out a slip of paper. "And when I woke up this was on the bedside table, but I don't recall writing it down."

I took the slip of paper from her. On it, in a very precise handwriting that no one would be capable of managing in the middle of the night, she had written:

"Some white boys can be fun to sleep with."

"I do wish I recalled that dream," she said. "It must have been a good one."

"I wish I'd been there."

"Just might be that you were," she said.

I opened my mouth, and then I closed my mouth, and then I seated her and came back in time to open the door for Leonard Danzig. There was a man on either side of him, and they were the very same men who had taken hold of my arms the night before. I was trying to decide how to tell them they couldn't come in when he turned to them and told them to wait outside, which made things a whole lot simpler for me.

"Well," he said. "Everything proceeding on schedule?"

"So far."

"And your boss is going to make it all come together, is that right?"

"That's the plan."

"Well, if he makes it work, I'll pay off on the spot." He tapped the breast pocket of his suit, indicating that he'd brought the money along. "If I owe somebody something, I see to it that the debt is paid."

A sort of chill grabbed me when he said that. He was talking about money, about paying money if he owed it, but I had the feeling that I never wanted him to owe me something else. Like a bullet in the head, for example. Because I was sure he'd pay that debt just as promptly, and with the same kind of satisfaction.

I took him into the office and parked him, and there were two seats left, one on either side of the second row. I went into the kitchen, picked up the phone and buzzed the fourth floor.

"All but two," I said.

"Who hasn't arrived?"

"The twins. New York's Finest."

"They'll be here within five minutes. Buzz me when they arrive."

They were on hand within three minutes, and they were not happy to see me. "I don't like any of this," Gregorio informed me. "If Haig has something he should tell us. If he's got nothing he should stop wasting our time. If he wants to put on a performance let him hire a hall."

"Sure," I said. "That's his plan, actually. He's going to play the title role in *Tiny Alice*. Let's face it, you're here because this case has you up a tree and you figure Haig's going to hold the ladder for you. Either he'll get your murderer or he won't, and either way is fine with you. You wind up with a case solved or you get to see Haig fall on his face."

"I'd like that," Seidenwall said.

"You probably would but I don't think he's going to oblige you. Now you know the rules. You take your seats and you let Leo Haig run the show. This is his house and you're here by invitation. Understood?"

I swear the best part of my job is getting to talk to cops that way now and then. It makes it all worth while. They didn't like to put up with it, but they knew they didn't have any choice. I showed them their chairs, putting Gregorio on the far side of the room and Seidenwall nearest to the door. That way anyone who tried to leave in a hurry would have to go through Seidenwall, and I wouldn't want to try that myself unless I was driving a tank.

Let me go over the seating for you, in case you care. *I* don't, but it's one of the things Haig insists on.

The desk was where it always was, with Haig's chair behind it and mine in front of it and an armchair alongside of it, presently empty.

Then two rows of chairs facing the desk. In the first row, from the far side, were Leonard Danzig, Rita Cubbage, Glenn Flatt, Maeve O'Connor, and Simon Barckover. In the back row we had Detective Vincent Gregorio, Haskell Henderson, Gus Leemy, Buddy Lippa, Jan Remo, and Detective Wallace Seidenwall. I looked at them and decided they were a reasonably attractive group, well-mannered and neatly groomed. Leemy was wearing a business suit instead of a tuxedo so he didn't look like a penguin today, and Buddy wasn't wearing a sport jacket at all so he had nothing to clash with his slacks and shirt, but otherwise they looked about the same as always. I wished they would fold their hands on the tops of their desks and wait for the teacher to come and write something adorable on the blackboard.

I buzzed Haig from the kitchen. Then I went back to the office and sat down in my chair, and a minute or so later our client entered the room. Our original client, that is. Tulip. She took the armchair alongside the desk without being told.

Then Haig walked in and sat behind his desk and every eye in the room was drawn to him.

Including mine.

Chapter Seventeen

FOR A LONG moment he just sat there looking at them. His eyes scanned the room carefully. I thought I saw the hint of a smile for a second, but then it was gone and his round face maintained a properly stern and serious look. He put his hands on top of the desk, selected a pipe, put it back in the rack, and drew a breath.

"Good afternoon," he said. "I want to thank you all for coming. All but one of you are welcome in this house. That one is not welcome, but his presence is essential. One of you is a murderer. One of you is responsible for one hundred twenty-five deaths."

There was a collective gasp at that figure but he went on without appearing to notice. "All but two of those deaths were the deaths of fish. The penalty which society attaches to ichthyicide is minimal. Malicious mischief, perhaps. Certainly a misdemeanor. The other two victims were human, however. One would be difficult to substantiate as homicide. While I am mortally certain that Andrew Mallard was murdered—"

"Hey, wait a minute," Gregorio cut in. "If you've got any information on that you've been holding it out, and—"

"Mr. Gregorio." Gregorio stopped in midsentence. "I have withheld nothing, sir. I remind you again that you are here by invitation." He scanned the room again, then went on. "To continue. While I may be certain that Mr. Mallard was murdered, and while I could explain how the murder was committed, no jury would convict anyone for that murder. Indeed, no district attorney in his right mind would presume to bring charges. But the other murder, that of Miss Abramowicz, was unquestionably a case of premeditated homicide. The killer is in this room, and I intend to see him hang for it."

He'd have a long wait. While Haig longs for a return of capital punishment, and thinks public hanging was a hell of a fine way to run a society, the bulk of contemporary opinion seems to be flowing in the other direction.

"The day before yesterday," he said, "Miss Thelma Wolinski sought my assistance. An entire tank of young *Scatophagus tetracanthus* plus her breeder fish had died suddenly and of no apparent cause. Miss Wolinski is possessed of a scientific temperament. She had a chemical analysis of the aquarium water performed, and the laboratory certified that the water had been poisoned with strychnine. Miss Wolinski could not imagine why anyone would want to kill her generally inoffensive fish. She concluded that the crime was the work of a madman, that an attack upon her fish represented hostility toward her own person, and that she herself might consequently be in danger."

"She should have called the police," Seidenwall said. Haig glared at him. "Indeed," he said. "No doubt you would have rushed to investigate the poisoning of a tankful of fish. Miss Wolinski is no witling." Seidenwall winced at the word. "She came to me. She could scarcely have made a wiser decision."

That sounded a little pompous to me, but nobody's hackles rose as far as I could tell. I looked at Tulip. I couldn't tell what she was thinking. She looked beautiful, and quite spectacular, but then she always did.

"Of course I agreed to investigate. That was quite proper on my part, but it also precipitated a murder. That very evening Miss Mabel Abramowicz was murdered. Some of you may know her as Cherry Bounce. She was killed while performing at a nightclub. Your nightclub, Mr. Leemy."

"Not my fault. I run a decent place."

"That is moot, and a non sequitur in the bargain. Miss Abramowicz was also poisoned, but not with strychnine. She was killed with curare, a lethal paralytic poison with which certain South American savages tip their arrows."

Haig picked up his pipe again and took it apart. He looked at the two pieces, and for a moment I thought that was all he had and he was waiting for a miracle. We'd be out four grand and I wouldn't get to write a book.

"It was instantly evident that the deaths of the fish and the death of Miss Abramowicz were related. It was furthermore a working hypothesis that the same person was responsible for both outrages. Finally, it seemed more than coincidence that Miss Abramowicz's death followed so speedily upon Miss Wolinski's engaging me to represent her interests. Once I was working on the case, Miss Abramowicz had to be disposed of as rapidly as possible. Had the time element not been of paramount importance, the murderer would not have had to take the great risk of committing his crime in full view of perhaps a hundred people.

"And it was an enormous risk, to be sure. But our murderer was very fortunate. While I have never met her, my associate Mr. Harrison assures me that Miss Abramowicz's endowments were such as to make her the center of attention during her performance. Everyone watched her as her act neared its climax. No one saw—or, more accurately, no one paid attention to—her murderer.

"With one exception, I would submit. Andrew Mallard saw something. He may not have known what he saw. He was clearly not certain enough or self-assured enough to make any mention of his observations to the police. Whether this testifies to Mr. Mallard's lethargy and reticence or to the inefficiency of police interrogation is beside the point. In any event—"

"I'll pretend I didn't hear that," Gregorio said.

"An excellent policy," Haig murmured. "In any event, the murderer struck, the murder weapon was not recovered, and the murderer seemed to be in the clear."

The projectile, I thought. Not the weapon.

"A surface examination would suggest that the murderer was irrational. Item: He poisons Miss Wolinski's fish with strychnine. Item: He poisons Miss Abramowicz with curare. The two incidents cannot fail to be related, yet how are

617

they linked in the mind of the murderer? I must admit
that, after I learned of Mr. Mallard's death, there was a
moment when I entertained the hypothesis that the
murderer was attempting to strike at Miss Wolinski by
destroying everything associated with her—first her pets,
then her roommate, finally a former lover. I dismissed this
possibility almost at once. I returned to the fish. I decided
to assume the killer was rational, and I asked myself why a
rational killer would poison fish with strychnine.

"The answer was that he would not. If he wished to kill
the fish and make it obvious that he had done so, he might
have tipped over their aquarium and let them perish
gasping upon the floor. If he wished to make the death
look accidental he could have caused their demise in any
of a dozen ways which would not have aroused any
suspicion. Instead he chose a readily detectable poison
without having any grounds for assuming that Miss
Wolinski would bother to detect it via chemical analysis.

"The conclusion was obvious. The fish had been killed
by mistake. The murderer did not put the strychnine into
the aquarium."

Tulip frowned. "Then who did?"

"Ah," Haig said. He turned to her, a gentle smile on his
round face. "I'm afraid you did, Miss Wolinski.
Unwittingly, you poisoned your own fish."

Tulip gaped at him. I looked around the room to check
out the reactions of the audience. They ran the gamut from
puzzlement to disinterest. Seidenwall looked as though
he might drop off to sleep any minute now. Gregorio seemed
to be enduring all of this, waiting for Haig either to make
his point or wind up with egg on his face. I tried to find a
suspect who indicated that he or she already knew how
the strychnine got in the tank. I didn't have a clue.

Haig opened a desk drawer and took out a paper bag
that looked familiar. Gingerly he extracted the jar of
wheatgerm from it and peeled away the protective layers
of paper toweling. He wrapped a towel around his hand

618

and pushed the jar toward my side of the desk.

"This is a jar of wheatgerm," he said. "I have found it to be an excellent dietary supplement for fishes. I am told it is similarly useful for human beings. I have no grounds for confirming or disputing the latter. Mr. Henderson, do you recognize this jar? You may examine it closely, but I urge you not to touch it."

Henderson shrugged. "I don't need a close look," he said. "It's Kretchmer, one of the standard brands. They sell it all over the place, supermarkets, everywhere. What about it?"

"Do they also sell it in health food emporia?"

"Sometimes."

"I understand you run a chain of such establishments. Do your stores carry Kretchmer wheatgerm?"

"I think so."

"You don't know for certain, Mr. Henderson?"

"As a matter of fact we do carry it. Why not? It's a good brand, we move a lot of cases of it."

"Do you recognize this particular jar, Mr. Henderson?"

"They're all the same. If you're asking did it come from my place, I couldn't tell you one way or the other."

"I could," Haig said. "On the reverse of this jar there is a label. It says 'Doctor Ecology' and there is an address beneath the store name. That label would tend to suggest that this jar of wheatgerm came from one of your stores."

"Well, then it must have. What's the point?"

Haig ignored the question. He picked up the bell and rang it, and Wong Fat came in carrying a two-quart goldfish bowl. There were a pair of inch-and-a-half common goldfish in the bowl. Haig buys them from Aquarium Stock Company for $4.75 a hundred and feeds them to larger fish that have to have live fish as food. Wong put the bowl on the desk. I wondered if it was going to leave a ring.

His hand covered with a paper towel, Haig screwed the top off the jar. He reached into the jar with a little spoon he used to use to clean the crud out of his pipes back in the days when he was trying to smoke them. He spooned up a few grains of wheatgerm and sprinkled them into the goldfish bowl.

The fish swam around for a few seconds, not knowing they'd been fed. They weren't enormously bright. Then they surfaced and began scoffing down the wheatgerm.

"Now watch," Haig said.

We all watched, and we didn't have to watch for very long before both fish were floating belly-up on the surface. They did not look to be in perfect health.

"They are dead," Haig said. "As dead as the *Scatophagus tetracanthus*. As dead as Miss Mabel Abramowicz. I have not had a chemical analysis run on the contents of this jar of wheatgerm. It does seem reasonable to assume that the wheatgerm is laced with strychnine. Miss Wolinski."

"Yes?"

"How did this jar of wheatgerm come into your possession?"

"Haskell gave it to me."

Henderson's eyes were halfway out of his head. Alfalfa sprouts or no, he looked as though a coronary occlusion was just around the corner. "Now wait a minute," he said. "You just wait a goddamned minute now."

"You deny having given this jar to Miss Wolinski?"

"I sure as hell deny putting strychnine in it. Maybe that's the jar I gave her and maybe it isn't. How the hell do I know?"

"You did give her a jar, however?"

"I gave her lots of things."

"Indeed. You gave her a jar of wheatgerm?"

"Yeah, I guess so."

"Have you any reason to assume this is other than the jar you gave her?"

"How the hell do I know?" Haig glared at him. "Okay," he said. "It's probably the same jar."

Haig nodded, satisfied. "Miss Wolinski. Was Mr. Henderson in the habit of gifting you with health foods?"

"Yes."

"And what did you do with them?"

Tulip lowered her eyes. "I didn't do anything with them," she said.

"You didn't eat them?"

"No." She shrugged, and when you're built like Tulip a shrug is a hell of a gesture. "I know that kind of food is supposed to be good for you," she said, "but I just don't *like* it. I like things like hamburgers and french fries and beer, things like that."

"If you would just *try* them—" Henderson began.

"Mr. Henderson. Had Miss Wolinski tried the wheatgerm she would be dead." Henderson shut up. "Miss Wolinski," Haig went on pleasantly. "You did nothing with the health foods? You merely put them aside?"

"Well, I used to feed the wheatgerm to the fish some of the time. It's a good conditioner for breeding."

"It is indeed. I employ it myself. What else became of the health foods Mr. Henderson was considerate enough to give to you?"

"Sometimes Cherry ate them."

"Indeed," Haig said. He got to his feet. "At this point things begin to clarify themselves. The strychnine was introduced into the aquarium not by the murderer but by Miss Wolinski herself. And it was added to the wheatgerm not in an attempt to kill fish but in an attempt to kill Miss Abramowicz. Oh, sit down, Mr. Henderson. Do sit down. I am not accusing you of presenting Miss Wolinski with poisoned wheatgerm. You are neither that stupid nor that clever. The strychnine was added to the wheatgerm after it had come into Miss Wolinski's possession, added by someone who knew that Miss Abramowicz rather than Miss Wolinski was likely to ingest it. Sit *down!*"

Haskell Henderson sat down. I decided Haig was wrong on one point. Old Haskell was stupid enough to do almost anything. Anybody who would discontinue making love to Althea simply because she had less than the usual number of breasts didn't have all that much going for him in the brains department.

Haig turned to Tulip once more. "Miss Wolinski," he said. "I first made your acquaintance approximately forty-eight hours ago. They have been eventful hours, to be sure. When did you decide to consult me?"

"Tuesday. The day after I got the lab report. That was when I decided, and then I thought it over for a while, and then I came here."

"Who knew of your decision?"

"Nobody."

"No one at all?"

"I didn't tell anyone after I saw you. You told me not to. Oh, wait a minute. I said something to Cherry that morning, that I was going to see you and you would find out how it happened."

"So you told Miss Abramowicz. And she might have told anyone."

"Cherry wasn't very good at keeping things to herself."

"She may have told anyone at all," Haig went on. "What we do know for certain is that she told her murderer. He realized that I would rapidly determine that the poisoning of the scats constituted a misdirected attempt at Miss Abramowicz's life. He had to act quickly."

Haig cleared his throat and let his eyes take a tour of the audience. I don't know what he was looking for so I don't know whether or not he found it. What I saw was Rita Cubbage picking at a cuticle, Buddy Lippa scratching his head, Gus Leemy frowning, Vincent Gregorio picking lint off his lapel, Simon Barckover glancing at his watch, Maeve O'Connor licking her lower lip, Glenn Flatt cracking his knuckles, Jan Remo rubbing her temples with her fingertips, Wallace Seidenwall yawning, and Leonard Danzig sitting in perfect repose, giving Leo Haig every bit of his attention.

Whatever Haig was looking for and whether he found it or not, he evidently decided that the Rasboras were more interesting to look at than the eleven of them. He swung his chair around and stared into the fish tank, presenting his audience with a great view of the back of his head.

That's it, I thought. That's all he's got. I decided it was still pretty good, better than the police had managed to come up with, but why blow it by putting the show together prematurely? Unless he expected one of them to crack, but could you count on that happening? I decided you couldn't.

Haig swiveled his chair around again. "Mr. Flatt," he said. "Mr. Glenn Flatt."

There was a lot of head-turning as our customers tried to figure out which of them was Glenn Flatt. They finally took a cue from Haig and looked where he was looking, and the boyish Ivy Leaguer frowned back at Haig.

"Yes, I was hoping you'd get around to me," Flatt said. "I came here to help Tulip. I used to be married to her and we're still good friends and you said you were working for her. I didn't know I was going to be part of a carnival." He stood up. "I told you I had work to do. I came here as a favor to Tulip but this is ridiculous. I'm leaving."

"You are not. You will stay where you are. If you attempt to leave Mr. Harrison will knock you down and return you to your chair. Sit down, Mr. Flatt."

Flatt sat down, which took a load off my mind, believe me. If you think I was all that confident of my ability to knock him down you don't know me very well.

"Mr. Flatt. You came here because last evening I told you that I knew you were at Treasure Chest on the evening when Miss Abramowicz was murdered. That is why you are present this afternoon. When I told you I had a witness placing you at the scene you elected to cooperate."

"Where'd you get a witness?" Gregorio wanted to know. "And why did you hold that out?"

Haig made a face. "I had no witness," he said. "I merely said I had one."

"You were lying," Flatt said. It was a pretty dumb thing

to say, and he sounded pretty dumb saying it.

"You might put it that way," Haig allowed. "Or you might say that I was bluffing. I trust you're conversant with the term, Mr. Flatt. You gamble quite a great deal, do you not?"

"Sometimes I'll make a bet on a horse."

"Indeed. Or on an athletic event, or on an election, or on the turn of a card. Would you say you are a compulsive gambler, Mr. Flatt?"

"Not in a million years," Flatt said. He looked somewhat less boyish now. "I like a little action, that's all. So I gamble. There's no law against it."

"Tommyrot. There are innumerable laws against various forms of gambling. The fact that such statutes are absurd does not wipe them from the criminal code. But we are not assembled here to convict you of gambling, Mr. Flatt. Rest assured of that."

"Look, I don't—"

Haig put his pipe back together again and tapped the bowl on the top of the desk. "I would be inclined to label you a compulsive gambler," he said. "The evidence seems clear enough. Your marriage to my client dissolved largely because you kept going into debt as a result of your gambling. Your debts have increased considerably over the years. A friend of mine was in a position to make inquiries among various bookmakers on Long Island. You are well known to several of them. You gamble heavily. You almost invariably lose."

"I don't do so badly."

"You do pay your debts," Haig said. "According to my information, in the past four months you paid an amount to bookmakers slightly in excess of your salary during the same period."

"That's ridiculous. And you couldn't possibly prove it."

"I don't have to. I told you I don't intend to convict you of gambling. And your gambling doesn't interfere with your ability to earn a livelihood, does it? You continue to be gainfully employed in a responsible position."

Flatt eyed him warily. "So?"

"As a pharmaceutical chemist, I understand."

"That's right."

"A position which would give you ready access to any number of interesting compounds. Such as strychnine and curare, to cite two examples."

"Now wait a goddamned minute—"

"Mr. Flatt, you're much better off if you keep your mouth shut. Take my word for it. You have access to such compounds and it would be puerile of you to deny it. That crossed my mind when first I learned of your occupation. Various poisons are readily obtainable. Strychnine is not. Neither is curare. You and I have not met before, Mr. Flatt, and we did not speak to one another until last evening, but you have been an important suspect since I first learned how the fish had died." He said all this in a calm conversational tone. Then abruptly he raised his voice to as close as he could come to a bellow. *"Why were you at Treasure Chest the night before last?"*

"You can't prove I was there."

"Phooey. You've already admitted you were there. Have the courage of your errors, Mr. Flatt. Why were you there?"

Flatt bought himself a couple of seconds by glancing to either side of himself. If he was looking for support he picked the wrong place to look for it. Everybody seemed to want to hear the answer to the question.

"I wasn't there when Cherry was killed," he said. "I left before her act started, I was miles away when she was killed. And I can prove it."

"That won't be necessary," Haig said. "You did not kill Miss Abramowicz."

"But—"

"Nor have you answered the question. Why did you go to that night club that evening?"

He shrugged. "No particular reason. I'm sorry if I was out of line but I thought you were accusing me of murder." He managed a boyish grin. "It certainly sounded that way

625

for a while. For a little guy, you certainly know how to boss people around."

"You still haven't answered my question, Mr. Flatt."

"Oh, hell. Look, I wanted a couple of drinks. Why did I pick a topless club? Jesus, you know the answer to that one. Or maybe you don't, who knows with you? I like to look at girls. That's all there is to it. I used to be married to Tulip and we're still friends so I picked that club rather than one of the others. My luck I had to be there on that particular night. But, you know, I go there a lot. Maybe not a lot but I'll drop in now and then."

"Interesting," Haig said. "Mr. Lippa? Can you confirm that?"

Buddy Lippa nodded. "I seen him before," he said. "I dint make him at first but I seen him. Comes in once, twice a week, sits at the bar. Never stays any length of time. And he's right about leaving before Cherry got the needle. I can't swear to the time but I'd guess he came in like nine-thirty and left by ten o'clock. That's not on the dot but it's close."

"Absolutely right," Flatt said. "I was out of there by ten. And I was in a bar on Long Island by midnight, and I can prove that with no trouble whatsoever."

"You needn't," Haig said. "So you've been in the habit of patronizing Treasure Chest once or twice a week. That's interesting."

Flatt didn't say anything.

"There are topless clubs on Long Island, are there not? And are they not more conveniently located, since you both live and work there?"

"Sometimes I'm in New York on business."

"Precisely my point. I submit that your visits to Treasure Chest are a business matter."

"I don't know what you're talking about."

"Nonsense," Haig said. "You know precisely what I am talking about. Five months ago Miss Wolinski went to work at Treasure Chest. You have kept in contact with her and visited the club, perhaps out of curiosity. You needed money, you have always needed money, your gambling habit is such that you shall always need money. And you met someone at Treasure Chest who showed you a way to make all the money that you needed."

"You're out of your mind."

"That's not inconceivable. It is, however, irrelevant to the present discussion. You met someone at Treasure Chest, someone who was regularly present there during the ensuing months. You got into conversation. You mentioned your occupation, and your new acquaintance saw possibilities for profit. You had access, I have mentioned earlier, to poisonous compounds. There is, thanks be to God, no enormous profit at present in such compounds. But you also had access to quantities of a subtler, slower form of poison. As a pharmaceutical chemist, Mr. Flatt, you had access to drugs."

I looked at Flatt. He was keeping a stiff upper lip but the effort was showing. I glanced at Gregorio and saw him nodding thoughtfully. Leonard Danzig had a wary look in his eyes. Gus Leemy was frowning.

"You stole drugs from your employers," Haig was saying. "Perhaps you produced others. I understand lysergic acid can be readily synthesized by anyone with a middling knowledge of chemistry. With your background and your laboratory facilities it would be child's play. You brought consignments of drugs to New York, once or twice a week, and you delivered them to your associate at Treasure Chest—"

"That's horseshit." Gus Leemy was leaning forward, the light glinting off the top of his head. "I run that place clean. It's not a front for nothing at all. It's a decent operation."

Gregorio said, "There's drugs coming out of there, Gus. Been going on for months, the rumbles we get."

"You're crazy." He glanced at Danzig, then averted his eyes quickly as if remembering that he and Danzig were supposed to be pretending they didn't know each other.

Since the two of them gave each other an alibi for Cherry's murder I didn't quite grasp the logic of this, but they could play it whatever way they wanted. "I run that place clean," Leemy said. "I don't fuck with drugs, I never did and I never will."

"I never accused you, sir." Haig tapped his pipe on the desk again, then frowned suddenly at the bowl with the two dead goldfish in it. He rang the bell. I thought that would probably throw Wong, who wouldn't know what to come in with, but instead Wong came in empty-handed. Haig nodded at the bowl and Wong removed it. "I never accused you, Mr. Leemy," Haig went on. "If you stand accused of anything it is incompetence. Your nightclub served as a focal point for the dissemination of drugs, but this occurred without your knowledge. While that does not make you a particularly efficient manager, neither does it make you a criminal. It certainly does not make you a murderer." Haig stroked his beard. "Or you, Mr. Danzig. You or Mr. Leemy might well have killed the person selling drugs out of the Treasure Chest, or issued an order that the person be killed, but neither of you would have had any reason to do away with Miss Abramowicz."

Danzig didn't exactly glower but his face hardened a little. "Your reasoning is interesting," he said. "But I'm not sure how my name got in that last sentence. I was going out with Cherry, that's all. That's the only reason I'm here."

"Oh, come off it, Danzig," Gregorio said. He leaned forward and put a hand on Danzig's shoulder. "Everybody knows Leemy just fronts for you. And nobody much gives a shit. The boys from the State Liquor Authority might be unhappy but they can't prove anything, and as far as we're concerned we don't care."

Danzig smiled. "I have no connection with Treasure Chest. Mr. Leemy is a friend."

"Sure, if that's the way you want it."

"That's what the record should show," Danzig said. All of this was fascinating, but none of it had much to do with who killed Cherry and I was getting impatient. The suspense was fairly thick in the room. I looked at all of them, and the most agitated one was Glenn Flatt, although he wasn't approaching hysteria yet. He should have been the coolest; I mean, he presumably knew who his contact was, and thus he knew who committed the murder.

"I could sue you," Flatt said.

"Oh, come now," Haig said. "You're going to go to jail at the very least for selling illegal drugs and as accessory to the fact of murder in the first degree. Do you really think you could find a lawyer to represent you in a libel action? I somehow doubt it."

"You can't prove any of this."

Haig grunted. "I will tell you something," he said. "There is nothing much simpler than proving something one already knows to be true. The proof generally makes itself available in relatively short order. No, Mr. Flatt, your position is hopeless. You have been selling drugs through a confederate. And what do we know about this accomplice of yours?" He ticked off the points on his fingers. "Your accomplice is regularly to be found at Treasure Chest, either as an employee or an habitual hanger-on. There are several here in this room who fit that description. Miss Wolinski, for one. Mr. Danzig. Mr. Leemy. Mr. Barckover. Miss Remo. Miss Cubbage. Mr. Henderson frequents Treasure Chest often, but if he were selling drugs he would no doubt do so through the medium of one or another of his stores, and—"

"Drugs!" Haskell was outraged. "Me sell drugs? You have to be out of your mind. Drugs are a death trip."

"Indeed. We have already excluded you, Mr. Henderson, so you've no need to offer comments. To continue. Miss O'Connor has not been regularly employed at Treasure Chest, so she too may be ruled out. Mr. Leemy and Mr. Danzig may also be excused; they quite clearly did not know what was going on in the establishment. I would further exclude Mr. Lippa because I find the whole nature of this operation incompatible with my impressions of the man."

"Does that mean I'm in or out?" Buddy wanted to know, and Haig nodded and said that was exactly his point, and that Buddy was in the clear.

"Now let us reconstruct the day of the crime. Mr. Flatt's accomplice in the drug operation—let us call him X, as a sop to tradition—has learned directly or indirectly from Miss Abramowicz that I have been hired to investigate the death of the fish. X realizes that my participation will quickly establish that an attempt has been made on Miss Abramowicz's life and that the fish were unintentional victims. When this became known, Miss Abramowicz would realize that she possesses some information which makes her dangerous to X, and this information would at once be brought to my attention. That, to be sure, was the original motive for disposing of Miss Abramowicz. She somehow learned enough about the drug operation to make her dangerous, especially in view of the fact that she seems to have been rather scatterbrained and loose-tongued. One hesitates to speak thus of the dead, but the fact appears to be beyond dispute.

"Thus X must act, and act quickly. So X contacts Mr. Flatt— yes, sir, it happened just that way, and you needn't attempt to deny it by shaking your head. X contacted you, Mr. Flatt, and demanded a contact poison. Whether curare was specified or not I have no idea. It hardly matters. You had already supplied strychnine to X, although I cannot state with certainty that you knew how it was to be employed. It is often used as an adulterant in drugs to boost their potency and you might well have furnished it without knowing you were to be the instrument in a homicide. But if there is any other use for curare I am unaware of it. You knew Miss Abramowicz was to be killed, sir. You brought the curare that night with that specific purpose in mind. That was why you took pains to leave the club early, why you established an alibi in Long Island. You are a knowing accessory to murder, sir."

Flatt stared at him, and Haig stared back, and Flatt couldn't take it. He looked down at his hands.

"You brought the curare," Haig went on. "You delivered it to X. You left. And X waited, because the last thing X wanted was to murder Miss Abramowicz on the premises of the nightclub. Ideally X would have waited until the evening had come to a close. X and Miss Abramowicz would have left together, and X would have managed to perform the deed in private. This plan was spiked when Mr. Harrison made an appearance at the club. X learned his identity, realized he was my associate, and recognized that there would be no opportunity to go off with Miss Abramowicz and deal with her as planned. Mr. Harrison would instead be interrogating Miss Abramowicz immediately after she finished her performance, at which time her knowledge might well be passed on to him. And this was something X was wholly unprepared to leave to chance.

"And so X waited, waited until the last minute. Waited until Miss Abramowicz was at the very conclusion of her act, and then injected curare into her bloodstream and killed her."

I saw it all again in slow motion. The finale of the act, Cherry shaking her breasts over the edge of the stage, straightening up, doing her spread, going coyly prim, then trying so desperately to reach her breast—"When we think of curare," Haig said, "we think of savages in the jungle. We think of blow darts, we think of arrows tipped with the deadly elixir. And when we consider this crime, we assume that X must have employed such a device, that some projectile served to carry curare from X's hand to Miss Abramowicz's breast. No projectile remained stuck in the breast in question; hence we assume that the dart or arrow or whatever struck the breast, pierced the skin, and then fell away. Mr. Harrison was the first person to leap onto the stage after Miss Abramowicz fell. He had the presence of mind, after determining there was no office he could

631

perform for the victim, to make a quick search for the projectile. And he—"

"And he put it in his pocket." This from my old friend Wallace Seidenwall. "I knew Harrison had it. I been saying so all along, and I been saying—"

"You have been saying far too much, sir. Mr. Harrison did not find the projectile. Neither did the police, who may be presumed to have subjected the premises to an exhaustive search. Dismissing such preposterous theories as an arrow with an elastic band tied to it—and I trust we can dismiss such rot out of hand—it is quite inconceivable that X could have retrieved the projectile. Sherlock Holmes established the principle beyond doubt, and I reiterate it here and now: When all impossibilities have been eliminated, that which remains is all that is possible. There was no projectile."

I suppose everybody was supposed to gasp when he said this. That's not what happened. Instead everybody just sat there staring. Maybe they had trouble following what he'd just said. Maybe they were confused about the difference between a weapon and a projectile. I'd already had a lesson in that department so I managed to stay on top of things, and at that moment I finally figured out who X was. Instead of feeling brilliant I sat there wondering how it had taken me so long.

"There was no projectile," Haig said again. "Miss Abramowicz was stabbed with some sort of pin. A hairpin, a hatpin, it scarcely matters. The pin was pressed into her breast and withdrawn. Then—"

"Wait." It was Gregorio. "Unless I'm off-base, she was all alone on that stage. How did someone stick a pin in her breast without anyone seeing it?"

"Because she was bending over the edge of the stage. She did this at the conclusion of every performance, leaning forward almost parallel to the floor with her breasts suspended over the stage apron. This was X's genius—it would have been simpler by far to inflict a wound in her foot, for example, but by waiting for the one perfect moment X could guarantee that everyone would assume that a non-existent projectile had been employed."

I said, "How come she didn't feel anything? She went right ahead and got up and danced around for a minute, and then there was suddenly blood on her breast and she started to crumble."

"Curare is not instantaneous. Poisons borne by the bloodstream need time to reach the heart. And small puncture wounds rarely begin bleeding immediately. Indeed they often fail to bleed at all. As for her failure to react, she was caught up in an intense dance routine. She might have been too involved to feel a pin prick. She might have assumed it was an insect bite and ignored it. For that matter, she might not have felt it at all. She had had silicone implants. The skin of her breasts was thus stretched to accommodate their enlargement, the nerve endings consequently far apart. Some nerves may even have been severed when the silicone was implanted."

Haig shrugged. "But it hardly matters. Once one knows how the murder was committed, the identity of X is instantly obvious. Indeed it has been obvious to me for some time that only one person was ideally situated to commit the murder. That same person was also ideally situated to receive consignments of drugs from Mr. Flatt and dispense them in the normal course of occupational routine.

"Miss Remo. I suggest you keep your hands in plain sight and avoid sudden movements. Mr. Wong Fat has you within line of sight. He could plant his cleaver in your head before you could get your purse open. Yes, keep your hands right where they are, Miss Remo. Mr. Seidenwall, I trust you thought to bring a pair of handcuffs? I suggest you put them on Miss Remo. She is rather more dangerous than she looks."

Chapter Eighteen

SEIDENWALL PUT THE cuffs on her. He may have been a witling but he knew how to follow orders. I didn't take my eyes off her until the bracelets snapped shut. Then I let out a breath I hadn't remembered taking and glanced at the doorway. Wong was standing there and he still had the cleaver raised. He wasn't taking any chances.

Gregorio lit a cigarette and blew out a lot of smoke. He said, "You don't really have anything, do you? Just a theory. I'm not arguing with your theory I have to hand it to you, you tied all the ends together and made it work. And if we put the jury in this room and let you put on a show for them they might bring in a conviction, but that's not how the system works. Maybe it should be but it isn't."

"You need proof."

"Right."

"And I told you earlier that proof is the world's cheapest commodity. The contents of Miss Remo's purse might prove interesting. Even if she has been bright enough to avoid bringing anything incriminating with her, you should have little trouble tying her to Flatt and to the drug operation. Once you know what to look for it's a simple matter to find it. You might start by establishing a link between Mr. Flatt and the strychnine in this jar." He tapped the jar of wheatgerm. "Odd that this would be left accessible, but perhaps neither of them had an opportunity to retrieve it."

That was all Glenn Flatt needed. He whirled around and glared at Jan Remo. "You stupid ass-faced little bitch! You said you switched jars yesterday afternoon. What in the hell is the matter with you?"

Jan Remo didn't turn a hair. She just closed her eyes for a moment, and when she opened them she spoke in a calm and level voice.

She said, "Now I know why you're such a terrible gambler, Glenn. How many times do you let the same man bluff you out of a pot? There was nothing in that jar of wheatgerm. He doctored it with something that would kill the fish." She sighed. "I think it's about time somebody advised me of my rights. I have the right to remain silent. I intend to remain silent. Glenn, I think you should remain silent, too. I really do."

Gregorio advised them both of their rights and put cuffs on Flatt, and he and Seidenwall led the two of them away. Wong closed the door after them and returned to the kitchen to hang up his cleaver. In the office everybody seemed to be waiting for somebody else to say something. When the silence got unbearable I broke it by asking how he knew Mallard had been killed.

"I don't," he said. "I *believe* he was killed. A police investigation might establish that either Mr. Flatt or Miss Remo was at his apartment yesterday."

"And made him choke on his own vomit?"

Haig nodded slowly. "A simple murder method," he said, "and quite undetectable. It requires a victim who has had a lot to drink. When he has passed out or fallen asleep, one puts one's hand over his mouth and drives one's knee into the pit of his stomach. The victim regurgitates, cannot open his mouth, and the vomit is drawn into the lungs. One might find that Mr. Mallard's abdomen is bruised. This would still prove nothing. It's my guess that Miss Remo killed him, and it's virtually certain that she will never be charged with the crime."

"Nobody could make it stick," Leonard Danzig said.

"Quite so. But both she and Mr. Flatt will serve long sentences for the murder of Miss Abramowicz. Perhaps that is sufficient."

There was some more conversation, and then they left, a few at a time. Leonard Danzig took me aside on his way out and handed me two envelopes. "The other half of what I gave you last night," he said, "plus the bonus we agreed on. All in cash. If Haig wants to pay taxes on it that's his business, but it won't show up on my books so it's strictly up to him. Your boss is everything you said he was. It was worth four grand to watch him operate. It was worth more than that to find out that Gus Leemy hasn't been running as tight a ship as he should. No wonder the police were leaning on me. They thought I had a hand in a drug operation. I don't touch drugs." He smiled. "You're okay yourself. Anytime you drop by the club, there won't be any check."

Within half an hour they were all gone. Maeve O'Connor told me to hang onto her phone number even though the case was solved, and Rita Cubbage gave me her number, too. "In case you want to call me in the middle of the night," she said, "if something should suddenly come up." Simon Barckover asked Haig if he had ever thought of working up a nightclub routine. He started to sketch out what he had in mind but Haig glowered at him and he let it lie. Gus Leemy walked out looking very unhappy and Buddy Lippa trailed after him, looking very stupid. That left our client and her boyfriend, and I got rid of him myself.

I took old Haskell aside and told him he ought to divorce his wife, and he got into a riff about how he couldn't leave her because she would never be able to get another man, so I figured the hell with it and told him how nicely she had done in that department just that morning. This rattled him, and then I told him that I didn't think he should hang around Tulip anymore, and this rattled him a little too, and he went away.

So Tulip was the only one left, and she went home after Haig gave back her check for five hundred dollars. When she refused to take it he tore it up and threw it in the wastebasket.

"But that's not fair," she said. "I hired you to do a job and you did more than I hired you to do and now you won't let me pay you for it."

"I have been amply paid by someone else," he said. "And I am not refusing your payment. I am buying something in

636

return. Use some of that five hundred to buy some good equipment and a group of breeder scats. Select a pair. Breed them. Then tell me exactly how you did it."

Chapter Nineteen

WE SPENT PART of the evening Scotch-taping hundred-dollar bills together. This would have been easier if we'd kept them in order but I dropped the second batch and they got all jumbled up. We had to match serial numbers. It didn't really take all that long, but the process kept getting interrupted by people calling from the newspapers and things like that.

Then Haig made me play a few games of chess with him, which I won, and then I played a game with Wong and lost in ten moves. And finally I stood up and said, "I'm going home."

"Very well."

"Oh, hell. You were beautiful today and I can't ruin things by not playing my part. I give up. How did you know to doctor the wheatgerm?"

"I gave some of it to some fish while you were seating our guests. They lived to tell the tale." He examined a fingernail. "It was showmanship. I'll admit that. Without it, the police could still turn up enough evidence to convict handily. Addicts who have bought drugs from Miss Remo. Witnesses who could place her and Mr. Flatt in various places at various times." He straightened in his chair. "But I wanted to break them in public. The police dig harder when they know they're digging for something that exists."

"And you got a kick out of the performance."

He grunted.

"So how did you do it? I didn't know we had any strychnine in the house."

"We don't."

"What did you use?"

"Those roach crystals Wong sprinkles around. I dissolved a handful in water and soaked the wheatgerm with it."

"How did you know it would kill fish?"

"I didn't. I fed some to some fish and they died."

"I probably should have figured that part out myself. I guess I'm a little punchy. But that's not the main point. How did you know they switched jars? How did you know the strychnine was in the wheatgerm in the first place?"

He just smiled.

"Oh, hell," I said. "Actually I'm taking some of the credit for this one. Do you remember the pipe dream I was spinning about Haskell Henderson? How he poisoned the fish because Tulip wouldn't eat the health foods but gave them to the fish instead? And how he killed Cherry because she was eating the crap instead of passing it on to Tulip? Remember?"

"That piffle," he said. "How could I possibly forget it?"

"Well, that's what put the idea in your head. And the notion of Jan Remo stabbing Cherry with a pin, you even said hatpin, and you got that idea because I told you how Althea Henderson stuck a hatpin in her tit. For Pete's sake, I'm the one who does all the work around here. Why is it that you get all the credit?"

He petted his beard. "Surely you can make yourself look somewhat more intelligent when you write up this case, Chip. It's only fair that you should have the opportunity."

"Thanks a lot."

"And don't forget what Miss Swann advised you this morning," he went on. "The book needs sex. Not nearly so much as you seem to need it, but it does need sex." He gazed past my shoulder and got a very innocent look on his face. "I see no reason why you couldn't embroider the truth somewhat in that department. In the interest of increasing the book's marketability you might, oh, fabricate an incident in which you had sexual relations with our client, for example."

I glared at him.

"But that might not be enough in and of itself." He played with his beard some more. "Perhaps you could

639

enlarge this morning's interview with Mrs. Henderson. Suggest that, after she bared her breast to you, you took her to bed. A bit far-fetched, to be sure, but perhaps the circumstances warrant it."

Hell.

Was he just guessing? Did he know? Or was he really sincerely suggesting I make up something that he didn't know actually happened?

You tell me. I *still* can't make up my mind.